Jack Rabinovitch founded The Giller Prize fifteen years ago as a tribute to his late wife, the noted literary journalist and editor Doris Giller. Since then, it's become the country's richest and most prestigious literary award for fiction.

This book commemorates fifteen years' worth of stellar Canadian talent—the best writers this magnificent country has to offer—as recognized by The Scotiabank Giller Prize.

Scotiabank's sponsorship began in 2005. Our bank has a long history of supporting the communities where we live and work, and that includes support for the arts and culture—of which literature is a cornerstone. We believe in the power of the arts to enrich the lives of Canadians, and we are delighted that our support for The Scotiabank Giller Prize has helped introduce our country's finest writers to a wider audience, at home in Canada and abroad—and also boost sales of their books dramatically.

Congratulations to all the winners whose award-winning work is featured in this fine anniversary collection. We hope that once you've had a taste of their talents through this anthology, you'll be motivated to look for their books the next time you're craving a great literary experience.

Happy reading!

Rick Waugh
President and Chief Executive Officer, Scotiabank

The Scotiabank
GILLER PRIZE
15 years

AN ANTHOLOGY OF
PRIZE-WINNING
CANADIAN FICTION

Introduction by Jack Rabinovitch

PENGUIN
CANADA

PENGUIN CANADA
Published by the Penguin Group

Penguin Group (Canada), 90 Eglinton Avenue East, Suite 700, Toronto, Ontario, Canada M4P 2Y3 (a division of Pearson Canada Inc.)

Penguin Group (USA) Inc., 375 Hudson Street, New York, New York 10014, U.S.A.
Penguin Books Ltd, 80 Strand, London WC2R 0RL, England
Penguin Ireland, 25 St Stephen's Green, Dublin 2, Ireland (a division of Penguin Books Ltd)
Penguin Group (Australia), 250 Camberwell Road, Camberwell, Victoria 3124, Australia (a division of Pearson Australia Group Pty Ltd)
Penguin Books India Pvt Ltd, 11 Community Centre, Panchsheel Park, New Delhi – 110 017, India
Penguin Group (NZ), 67 Apollo Drive, Rosedale, North Shore 0745, Auckland, New Zealand (a division of Pearson New Zealand Ltd)
Penguin Books (South Africa) (Pty) Ltd, 24 Sturdee Avenue, Rosebank, Johannesburg 2196, South Africa

Penguin Books Ltd, Registered Offices: 80 Strand, London WC2R 0RL, England

First published 2008

1 2 3 4 5 6 7 8 9 10 (RRD)

Introduction copyright © The Doris Giller Rabinovitch Foundation, 2008

The copyright acknowledgments on pages 535–536 constitute an extension of this copyright page.

Manufactured in the U.S.A.

Scotiabank edition ISBN: 978-0-670-06801-2
Leatherbound Scotiabank edition ISBN: 978-0-670-06980-4

Library and Archives Canada Cataloguing in Publication data available upon request to the publisher.

Visit the Penguin Group (Canada) website at **www.penguin.ca**

Special and corporate bulk purchase rates available; please see **www.penguin.ca/corporatesales** or call 1-800-810-3104, ext. 477 or 474

This book is dedicated to Canadian writers everywhere:
the new, the established, those no longer with us,
and those yet to come.

The Giller Prize, now The Scotiabank Giller Prize, was founded in 1994 by Jack Rabinovitch in honour of his late wife, literary journalist Doris Giller, who passed away from cancer the year before. The award recognizes excellence in Canadian fiction and, thanks to the partnership with Scotiabank, endows the largest cash prize for literature in the country.

This anthology celebrates the fifteenth anniversary of The Scotiabank Giller Prize by showcasing the outstanding fiction of the past winners and the 2008 finalists.

Contents

Introduction

BY JACK RABINOVITCH

This year we celebrate the fifteenth anniversary of The Scotiabank Giller Prize. To commemorate this important literary event, Penguin Group (Canada), with the co-operation of the authors' publishers, has compiled this anthology, which includes selections or short stories from all the winning books, as well as the 2008 shortlist. Sincere thanks to Doubleday Canada, Freehand Books/Broadview Press, HarperCollins Canada, Henry Holt/H.B. Fenn, House of Anansi Press, Knopf Canada, McClelland & Stewart, Penguin Group (Canada)/Viking Canada, Random House Canada, and Thomas Allen Publishers for their efforts and contributions.

Sincere thanks as well to the contributing authors for their co-operation in making this anthology possible. The excerpts from their respective books represent an outstanding array of the best in Canadian literary fiction during the last fifteen years. Additionally, these authors and their books have achieved international recognition and enhanced Canada's literary reputation on the world stage.

Every year people ask me about the origin and outstanding success of The Scotiabank Giller Prize. The answer to the first part of the question is simple. The prize was launched on January 20, 1994, at a Toronto press conference, and the first Giller Gala was held at the Four Seasons Hotel Toronto in the first week of November 1994. The prize value then was $25,000. Within a few years, "the Giller" became the most pre-eminent and prestigious fiction prize in Canada.

In 2005, following a partnership agreement with Scotiabank, the prize was renamed The Scotiabank Giller Prize. The award is now $50,000 for the winner and $5,000 for each of the remaining shortlisted authors, highlighting the fact that they, too, are winners. Thanks to Scotiabank's passionate interest in Canadian literature and letters, the longevity of the prize is now well-assured.

To understand the warm reception and outstanding success of the prize (the second part of the question), one has to know a little about Doris Giller; about this humble author, her husband, and his collaborators; and about Montreal in the dirty thirties and turbulent forties. Talking about Doris and our life together is not as simple as one might imagine. Doris and I were raised in a time when intimate details were not shared easily. What counted most, especially to her, was what one did, not what one said.

Doris's parents came to Canada from Western Ukraine in the mid-twenties. So did mine. Her parents settled in Montreal because there was a large group of Ukrainian Jews already established in that city. My parents came to Montreal for the same reason. Her father became a cab driver, even back then an entry-level job for new immigrants. My father became a newsy, another entry-level job in those days. Her father became the head of a newly formed cab driver union. My father became the head of the Ukrainian Free Loan Society. Her father died before he was sixty. So did mine.

Even though our backgrounds were similar in many ways, Doris and I grew up in different areas. She lived on Clark Street, just one street east of St. Urbain Street, which our late friend Mordecai Richler immortalized. I grew up on Henri Julien Avenue, which is near St. Denis Street, then considered the east end. Boulevard Saint-Laurent, better known as "The Main," divided this part of the city. On both sides of "The Main," during the thirties and forties, immigrant families and their overachieving progeny populated the area. "The Main" was an old-time version of the modern food court. You could walk from Pine Avenue to Mount Royal Street, roughly six blocks, saying, "Deli, fruit store, bakery" and never miss a beat or a store.

Doris went to Commercial High, which specialized in stenographic and bookkeeping courses, because in those days Jewish girls were supposed to become secretaries or bookkeepers until they got married. I went to Baron Byng, the school that Mordecai made famous. It was then that he and I became friends.

As teenagers, Doris and I knew each other. Tall, graceful, and striking, she cut a wide swath, first in our neighbourhood community, later in her chosen journalistic field. She dated mostly older boys; I, being just six months older, became the exception.

A major point of contention, then and throughout our entire life together, was that her parents thought their family was better than mine, and, naturally, my parents were convinced that our family was much superior. The matter was never resolved.

Another lifelong point of contention was establishing who was the better dancer. That, too, was never resolved. There was many a tussle when Doris would demand that she lead only to be rebuffed by her adamant husband. "Rivalry is the enemy of intimacy" goes the old adage. But our rivalry was only on the dance floor and in our parents' minds.

Although we went our separate ways for a while, we never lost contact. In 1972, after my divorce, we got married. She had never married but now had my three daughters, Noni, Daphna, and Elana, to contend with. The role of stepmother to three young girls was a challenge she met with honesty, candour, and rare insight, and she soon gained their trust, affection, and love.

After high school, she had worked as a secretary for several years and then was hired as the editor of a house organ called *Parade,* put out by Steinberg's, a large supermarket company headquartered in Montreal. Doris was a natural autodidact, and she read prodigiously. In 1963, she joined the *Montreal Star* and after several years became its first female Entertainment Editor. After that newspaper folded in 1979, she joined *The Gazette* as Book Editor. When we moved to Toronto in late 1985, she joined the *Toronto Star* as Assistant Book Editor and launched her outstanding column, "Reading Habits."

Throughout her career, Doris brought honesty, integrity, and a fierce love of books and journalism to each and every assignment—but especially humour. Her best friend and co-worker Beverly Mitchell recalls when Doris went on one of her verbal rampages about WASPs. Finally, Beverly complained, "You know, Doris, I'm a WASP, and I don't think it's right that you should carry on this way. You've been doing it for years."

"And this is the first time you thought to complain?" Doris replied.

"Yes, it is," said Beverly.

"Isn't that just like a WASP," Doris, nonplussed, replied with a smile.

Joey Slinger, a former *Toronto Star* humour columnist and a wonderful friend, spoke at the initial Giller Prize press conference and also hosted the first Giller Gala. He laughingly referred to his favourite Gillerism: Whenever he tried to challenge her, Doris, hands on hips, would brazenly stare him down with "Am I right or am I goddamned right?"

Although her public persona emphasized her feistiness and confrontational style (she certainly could not be accused of being scatologically challenged), she was sensitive and insecure in private. It can be challenging and tiring to always project supreme self-confidence when you come from humble circumstances. It was this background that made her an easy mark for any panhandler. But her honest, self-deprecating humour never deserted her.

At the 1986 Winter Olympics in Calgary, we were invited to visit the American Olympic broadcaster, ABC. As we wandered through the studio, Doris spotted an electrician with an ABC cap with an ABC pin on it. Coquettishly fluttering her eyelids, she asked if she could have his ABC pin.

"Sorry, lady, it's the only one I have," he replied.

Looking glum and disappointed as we walked away, Doris nudged me and said wistfully, "You know, Jackson, ten years ago I would have got both the hat and the pin."

Doris died of lung cancer on April 25, 1993, at the age of sixty-two. She died at home, and her death came as a surprise to all but family and a few close friends. She hadn't told people of her illness because she didn't want pity or condescension. Her radiation treatments were scheduled so as not to interfere with her work, and she continued to work at the *Star* until about six weeks before she died. Even toward the end, she never lost her sense of humour. One day, as I muttered whispered complaints about running up and down the stairs to satisfy her every whim, she chastised me, saying, "Jackson, I'm the one who's dying. You have to do anything I say."

A few months after Doris died, I woke up one morning with the germ of an idea. Doris represented a unique life force that should be cherished and remembered. At least, that was what I told myself. Part of it was that I was still trying to impress her, just as I'd always tried to impress her, from the day we first met.

That August, I flew to Montreal to meet with Mordecai and tell him about my idea. Doris and Mordecai, together with Terry Mosher, Nicky Auf der Maur, and several other journalists, had singlehandedly kept the Montreal Press Club solvent, so Mordecai knew her well.

We met at Woody's on Bishop Street, which was then his favourite watering hole. It is one of those pubs for which Montreal is famous: four steps down to a door that opens into a semi-lit room with tight booths and hard wooden seats tended to by friendly and engaging staff. When I arrived, Stevie Cameron was telling Mordecai about her new book. After they had finished talking, Mordecai and I repaired to one of those tight booths.

"So what do you want to drink?" he asked.

"Fine, thank you," I replied. "How are you? And, yes, I'll have a Macallan, neat, with water on the side."

"Good choice," he said, motioning to the waitress. "I'll have the same but a double."

Once the drinks arrived, I started. "Mordecai, you and Florence knew Doris so well. I want to do something special in her memory. I thought of setting up a literary prize for fiction patterned after the Booker. I spoke to one of Doris's friends, Susan Walker, and she sent me to Greg Gatenby, who is the artistic director of the Harbourfront Reading Series in Toronto. He liked the idea, but he wants to run it himself and integrate it into the reading series. To me, that doesn't feel right. It should have its own identity and its own venue. Doris will come back and kill me if it isn't done right. What do you think?"

"First, how much is the prize?"

"Twenty-five thousand."

"What's the name?"

"What kind of question is that?"

"What's the name?" he insisted.

"The Giller Prize," I replied. "What did you think it would be?"

"Relax. Tell me what you want me to do."

"Mordecai, you knew Doris. She hated bullshit and could detect it a mile away."

"Yes, she did have an ear for the fraudulent."

"That's what I said. Anyway, she would want this prize to be credible and fun, like a celebration. I need your help to get it started in the right way."

We decided that the prize did indeed merit its own venue, that whatever we did should be open and transparent, and, most important, that we should have fun with it. Grudgingly, but with good humour, Mordecai agreed to be a judge for the first two or three years. As we left, he muttered, "The nationalists will never believe that I'm involved in this prize."

Mordecai recommended that we ask Alice Munro and David Staines, a well-known academic who had edited McClelland & Stewart's New Canadian Library series, to join our group. Since David was going to be visiting Mordecai and Florence the following week, it was agreed that we would meet that Saturday afternoon at Moishes, a steakhouse on The Main a few steps north of Schwartz's Delicatessen.

Although Mordecai and Doris and I grew up wanting to be unhyphenated Canadians free from any ethnic stereotypes, when it came to food, ethnicity won the day. I remember them discussing which deli had the best kishka (otherwise known as stuffed Derma) and revelling over its many fine features. You don't have to be Jewish to like Jewish delicatessens, but it surely helps. Over drinks and Moishes' chopped liver smothered with fried onions—with David Staines looking at us like we were from another planet—we began to round out the details of the new prize. David had written book reviews for Doris for many years, and she had been very fond of him, but he and I had never met. David agreed to be a juror for the first two or three years. Later, Alice Munro agreed to be a juror for the first year. She said she loved the idea of being part of a new award that was not influenced by anything other than merit.

It was difficult emotionally for me to chair the launch press conference. Therefore, I enlisted the aid of Joey Slinger and Mordecai. I did make some opening comments, highlighting that of Doris's many role models, the most important ones were Lauren Bacall and Dorothy Parker. Bacall for voice and Parker for wit. I briefly outlined the prize and mentioned that the winner would also receive a statuette by Chaki, a Greek-born artist living in Montreal, who was one of our best friends.

Joey highlighted Doris's penchant for honest, frank, and ribald dialogue, as well as her love of books and journalism.

Then Mordecai took over and in his own inimitable way described the Giller in a fashion that has characterized the prize from that day to the present. "Doris, Jack, and I come off the same Montreal streets and endured the same schools. Doris was for many years the cherished friend of both my wife and me.

"I should have thought that the literary community would have welcomed Jack's tribute to the memory of his wife. But this, after all, being Canada, a grudging country, there have been some complaints. Given an apple in this country you would immediately suspect there is a razor blade inside. I've heard complaints from some sectors of the community. Announcing the Giller award in November, they say, will conflict with the Governor General's Awards.

"No it won't. Instead, it will make for even more seasonal jollies. In England, there are many literary awards presented in November—not only the Booker, but also the Sunday Express Award, the Guardian Fiction Prize, the Whitbread Award, and others.

"The truth is, I would be happy if there were even more awards here. It would be gratifying if Maclean Hunter, Torstar, Southam, and *The Globe and Mail*—all of whom have profited from peddling basic English for years—offered, if only out of a sense of aesthetic guilt, prizes to those who could actually make sentences.

"Another complaint I've heard about the Giller—also typically Canadian—is that not only would there be a winner each year but, oh dear, oh dear, losers as well. Bruised feelings.

"So let me say it once. Nobody ever suggested that competitions are fair. From the Booker through the Prix Goncourt and Pulitzer, it's a crap shoot. Eventually, I hope the Giller, like the Booker in England, will do a great deal for writers' sales and that, most of all, everybody involved will have fun.

"I should point out that all three of us [the judges] are politically incorrect. Looking for the first winner of this substantial prize, we will not favour young writers over old or vice versa. We don't give a damn whether a book has been written by a man or a woman, a black, gay, or native writer, or somebody whose family has been here for two hundred years. What we are looking for is the best work of fiction published by a Canadian in 1994, and we will expect you to correct us if you think we are wrong."

Ironically, the prize was introduced at a time when Canadian fiction writers were achieving international acclaim but Canadian publishers were having a rough time. At the press conference, Margaret Atwood pulled me aside and said that she was concerned that in the near future publishers might no longer bring out hardcover books of Canadian fiction.

Although we were neophytes in the field of literary awards, we were guided by certain convictions. The first was that each author who made the shortlist was a winner and should be treated as such—because choosing the winner was, as Mordecai put it, "a crap shoot." The celebration that came to be known as the Giller Gala would therefore highlight the five nominees, and each one would get his or her time in the spotlight. We took a leaf from the Oscars and developed a video bio about each of the nominees and their respective books.

The approach had the desired effect. At the first Giller Gala, M.G. Vassanji told David Staines: "I was very nervous before the evening started, but once I got into the lobby and saw all the nominees being equally celebrated, I really felt good. The way it was arranged, everyone seemed a winner."

Our second conviction was that there should be some drama to the occasion. The winner would be named at the end of the evening, and until that point, nobody but the jury would know the name of the winner. I would have a signed cheque for each contender in my jacket pocket and then hand over the one made out to the author who won. This worked well, until in

2000, the judges selected two winners, Michael Ondaatje and David Adams Richards. I swallowed hard and handed over two cheques.

Needless to say, the next year we made the rules more explicit: only one winner allowed. But although we changed the rules, we could not eliminate the problem that the selection of the final winner is extremely difficult. In 1997, the jury panel had a tough time choosing between Mordecai's *Barney's Version* and Carol Shields's *Larry's Party*. Mavis Gallant was a judge that year. She told me that choosing one over the other was one of the most difficult decisions she had ever had to make.

That is why we celebrate, and now reward, each contender. And it's also why, each and every year, we devote a great deal of time and effort to selecting a diverse jury panel. We have selected people outside of CanLit, such as Rosie Abella, now a Supreme Court judge; as well as booksellers, such as Judy Mappin; and well-known people of letters, such as the Right Honourable Adrienne Clarkson. This year we invited an international writer, Colm Tóibín, who joins Margaret Atwood and the Honourable Bob Rae on the 2008 jury panel.

Our third conviction was that the Giller Gala should be a celebration, a fun evening. Make it like a house party for a special event, just like Doris herself would have done. Doris was great at arranging special events. Position and prestige were of little consequence to her; what mattered most was that the invitees were entertaining and fun to be with. She had a knack for taking the mickey out of pompous people. It was as if she had a gene that forced her to tell the unwelcome truth to self-satisfied people of position.

But Doris could also be compassionate and helpful when friends felt too sorry for themselves and were going through a period of self-pity. She would listen carefully and then bluntly remind them that "nobody promised you a rose garden."

My daughter Noni delivered the eulogy at Doris's funeral. Speaking for herself and her two sisters, she said, "What stands out most in our minds is her sense of humour and joy in living ... a sense of finding the extraordinary in the ordinary, the ability to find the waiter or waitress more interesting than her dinner companions. No matter what colour, gender, or sexual bias, Doris only saw the person, the real person in front of her. And if you were telling the truth and not trying to pull the wool over her eyes, you and she would get along famously."

At the first Giller Gala, we took another leaf from Doris's modus operandi and included a red rose with each invitation. She loved flowers; her headstone is adorned with them. The red rose has now become a standard Giller feature—it announces the forthcoming celebration as a special event.

To handle the administration, I hired Kelly Duffin, then an assistant literary agent. Although she had many qualifications, including imagination and integrity, the main reason I hired her was that she had known Doris and that Doris had been very fond of her. Kelly proved to be an outstanding asset, and it was her invaluable advice and guidance that helped make the Giller great. Today the administration is under the control of my daughter Elana, who has also proved to be exceptionally talented. Her sisters Noni and Daphna each contribute and assist as required.

The invitation list to the first Gala included the shortlisted authors, the contenders, their publishers, their agents, and all of Doris's and my friends. That these friends were primarily journalists or members of the chattering class helped to create a buzz. The fact that there was an open bar helped as well.

Being aware that, as Mordecai had pointed out, authors are interested in the sales of their books, we invited booksellers from across the country. Many came, as this was a wonderful opportunity to share a social occasion with authors and publishers.

We also invited people interested in language and literature, such as Robert Weaver. He had helped find assignments and grubstakes for many young and aspiring authors during the lean fifties and sixties. Mordecai and Alice were but two of the many he had helped.

A special guest in that first year was the premier of Ontario, Bob Rae. He was invited because he was a friend and an avid reader, and because his wife, Arlene, had been a friend to Doris, who had been Arlene's editor at the *Toronto Star*. The premier's attendance gave a special imprimatur to that first Gala. Since then, he has authored three books and many articles, adding to his qualifications as a man of letters and language. As one of the 2008 judges, he has committed a great deal of time and effort to the evaluation and promotion of Canadian fiction.

Before the first Giller Gala, the late Val Ross, then an influential arts and entertainment reporter for *The Globe and Mail* and a friend of both Doris and mine, wrote about the Giller on the front page of the *Globe*'s entertainment section, highlighting the odds of winning for each shortlisted author. This stimulated the betting instinct in all the invitees, and at each table somebody won a modest bundle when the winner finally was revealed. I subsequently attempted to introduce across-the-board betting on the Giller, similar to what happens in England for the Booker. Alas, I came a cropper because the Ontario Gaming and Lottery Commission suggested that saliva tests might be needed for the judges.

We have tried hard not to stray from the original Giller Gala concept, although about ten years ago, we did introduce television into the evening's proceedings—primarily to reach a wider audience and to help sell more books. For the past three years, CTV has produced the telecast. Viewer numbers have been phenomenal and sales of the shortlisted books have gone through the roof. Special credit is due CTV for promoting and high-lighting the Giller shortlist and the final winner.

I should highlight at this point that selecting the shortlist and the final winner is a reflection of the jury panel, and often the results are unpredictable. As columnist Richard Gwyn of the *Toronto Star* said of the first year's shortlist:

> Rather than reaching for applause, the three [Giller] judges were reaching for excellence—for those writers who had "the truest voices ... and who gave me as a reader the most lively and constant pleasure," as Alice Munro put it.
>
> The five short listed books encompass two women, two writers of color, three who were born outside Canada and one self-declared gay.
>
> A more politically correct list would be impossible to imagine. Yet a less politically correct trio of judges than the novelists Alice Munro and Mordecai Richler [any way an old grouch] and the English Literature professor David Staines, would [also] be impossible to imagine.
>
> The judges' choice this year confirms that Canada has become the kind of country in which the best writers now come in all colors, in all sexes, and from all parts of the world.
>
> We've already entered our own future, that is to say.
>
> We'll call it a post-multiculturalism future. It's the formation—still far from complete—of a society unlike any other in the world today. It may turn out to be a society in which citizens have so little in common that the space they happen to share is no longer a country. But it may turn out to be a society that is uniquely creative because it has, somehow, found a way for every one to be whatever they choose to be and to be full citizens.

If Doris were alive today, she'd be elated with the explosion of international success Canadian authors have achieved in the last fifteen years. A decade ago, George Will famously remarked in *Newsweek* that the United States would have to produce ten world-class writers to be on par with just one of Canada's—Robertson Davies, whom he considered the finest writer ever.

Canadians continue to get recognized on this continent and beyond. And not just with the Giller. Michael Ondaatje, Margaret Atwood, and Yann Martel have all won The Booker Prize—Ondaatje for *The English Patient* in 1992, Atwood for *The Blind Assassin* in 2000, Martel for *Life of Pi* in 2002. Carol Shields earned a Pulitzer Prize in 1995 for *The Stone Diaries* as well as the National Book Critics Circle Award. Both she and Anne Michaels have taken home the Orange Broadband Prize for Fiction—for *Larry's Party* and *Fugitive Pieces*, respectively. Alistair MacLeod won the International Dublin IMPAC Literary Award for *No Great Mischief* in 2001; Rawi Hage won in 2008 for *De Niro's Game*. I'm proud that The Scotiabank Giller Prize has played some part in helping Canadian literature come of age.

Every year at the Gala evening, I repeat the same suggestion: "For the price of a meal in this town, you can buy all the shortlisted books. Therefore, eat at home and buy the books." In the case of this anthology, I would say, "Read and enjoy. If any of these chapters whets your appetite, please go out and buy the book."

The Scotiabank
GILLER PRIZE
15 years

M. G. Vassanji

M.G. Vassanji was born in Kenya and raised in Tanzania. He went to university at MIT and took a doctorate in theoretical nuclear physics at the University of Pennsylvania before coming to Canada in 1978. While working as a research associate and lecturer at the University of Toronto in the 1980s he began to dedicate himself seriously to a long-standing passion: writing.

His first novel, *The Gunny Sack,* won a regional Commonwealth Writers' Prize in 1990, and he was invited to be writer-in-residence at the International Writing Program of the University of Iowa. In 1989 he quit his job and began researching *The Book of Secrets,* which won the inaugural Giller Prize in 1994. That same year Vassanji was awarded the Harbourfront Festival Prize in recognition of his achievement in and contribution to the world of letters and was chosen as one of twelve Canadians on the *Maclean's* Honour Roll.

Vassanji's other books include the acclaimed novels *No New Land* (1991) and *Amriika* (1999) and the short story collections *Uhuru Street* (1991) and *When She Was Queen* (2005). Vassanji became the first writer to win The Giller Prize twice, in 2003, when his bestselling novel *The In-Between World of Vikram Lall* garnered the award.

The Assassin's Song, Vassanji's most recent bestselling novel, was shortlisted for the 2007 Scotiabank Giller Prize and the Governor General's Literary Awards and was a finalist for the 2007 Rogers Writers' Trust Fiction Prize and a *Globe and Mail* Best Book of 2007. It was also shortlisted for the Crossword Prize in India. Vassanji lives in Toronto with his wife and two sons.

The Book of Secrets

BY M.G. VASSANJI

Winner 1994

⊷

1

"We seem to have sighted Mombasa at last," wrote Alfred Corbin in his diary on 1 March, 1913, aboard the German vessel *Prinzregent*. He concluded his brief entry with a reminder to himself to order more pipe tobacco the next time he wrote home. After that he strolled out on deck. Passengers had crowded on the starboard side to gather in the new vista which presented itself to eyes long weary of the sea and the ghostly distant shapes of land.

How fitting, he thought then of this sight of Africa, that it should greet you so gently; how melodramatic and unaffecting if it were to show you straight away its power and wildness, its strong colours, the pulling force. It was in order to be impressed, to confirm his schoolboy expectations fed on tales of famous adventurers and explorers, that he had strained his eyes seaward ever since they'd left Marseilles with a fresh load of passengers from the British Isles. He himself had boarded the *Prinzregent* at Hamburg. It was the sixteenth day at sea, the ship had turned southwestwards to round the island town and bring into view the town's full glory in the sun. A sight that even then he knew he would never forget. The coast of Africa, the harbour of Mombasa. Its modesty, the composed exoticism of its orientalness, stayed with you like the strong lines of a deceptively simple masterwork. White houses shimmered on a hill rendered lush green with vegetation. A fringe of palm trees decorated the shoreline, a white road came up to the beach where a restless waving crowd awaited. The waters were dark blue but choppy, the sky spotless that day. Even before they entered the southern harbour, dhows and bagalas hailed them, smaller craft hustled cheerfully alongside with expectations of business.

On the ship, his fellow passengers would have noticed a man of medium build and average height; he had fair hair and a thick moustache, droopy eyes. He would have been observed as being somewhat shy.

ALFRED CORBIN HAD SPENT HIS CHILDHOOD DAYS with governesses and in schools in Stockholm and Prague and Hamburg, speaking more of the languages of these foreign lands—at least in his youth—than he did his mother tongue. His father, Charles, after a stint at cattle farming in Argentina, had settled on a career in the Consular Service. The family had a house in Devon, and the only claim to distinction it could make was through relation to Sir George Corbin-Brown of the Punjab, and through a vague connection on his mother's Scottish side to William Pitt's war minister, Dundas. Of his two brothers, Robert was an officer in the Indian army and Kenneth was an Area Commissioner in Nyasaland. To start off his youngest son in a different direction, Charles Corbin found for Alfred a post at the Hamburg agents of the Union Mail Shipping Lines. This job was not without interest for Alfred—it was in Hamburg harbour that he first laid eyes upon natives of Africa, ship hands conscripted from the west coast of the continent—but Alfred was soon eyeing other opportunities. A chance came when he was returning from London to Hamburg via Paris.

Years later, in his published memoirs, he would describe how he was conscripted into the Colonial Service. In Paris he'd been told the undersecretary for the colonies, Mr. Winston Churchill, was resting in a local hotel, having returned from a trip to East Africa. On an impulse he went and presented his card at the hotel, noting his relation to Sir George. "If he is related to Kenneth Corbin, send him up," came the reply. Mr. Churchill, it seemed, had met his brother in British East Africa (as Kenya was then called). In a room strewn with paper and filled with cigarette smoke, the undersecretary, in the midst of a late breakfast, accepted Alfred Corbin's application for a job, which would require from him, as he put it, "his whole life and soul."

Even though it would be a few years later that he took up the offer (having become involved with a woman in the meantime), Alfred Corbin would always consider it propitious to have been initiated into the Colonial Service with these credentials, whose value would grow with the years. And he never left the Service until he retired.

We were taken into dugout boats, called "ngalawas," and were rowed to the shore by boisterous boatmen who sang in clear voices to each other. As soon as we stepped on solid ground we were completely taken over by a surge of porters wearing that white Swahili cotton smock so popular here and called "kanzu." Cranstone the surveyor, who had been chattering so tiresomely since Port Said about Mombasa, the eye in a socket, the leafy hiding place where Sinbad must surely have wandered through and perhaps seen the roc's egg, began muttering now about the den of forty thieves, saying "apana-apana, enda-enda" and more. Two Indian policemen in enormous beards and red turbans watched the scene calmly; a group of scantily dressed Indian men searched nervously among their arriving compatriots whom we had picked up in Aden. Many of the Europeans on the boat were met or knew their way about. It was unbearably hot and noisy, the clamour contagious and unsettling. As I looked around me uncertainly, the focus of a cacophony of solicitations, an Indian man pushed through the throng and introduced himself with a restrained smile.

"Sir, please allow me," he said in a soft voice.

Gratefully I relinquished my holdall to this short dark man who was wrapped in a black tunic with a shawl around his neck. He said his name was Thomas and would I follow him. He had a rather musical voice and the curious habit of moving his head from side to side as he spoke. He turned around and I followed, keeping my eye fixed on the back of his glistening black head. It took me the rest of the day to realize that the man was perhaps attempting to muffle his cold with the silly-looking woolly shawl, for there was a faint whiff of camphor in the air ...

THOMAS LED HIM to a corrugated-iron shed, a blazing furnace of a place. This was the Customs House, where a long line of Europeans and a few American hunters awaited inspection. An Indian clerk sat at a table, filling out forms in quadruplicate, periodically releasing an angry or fuming passenger with a hoarse "Next!" and a stamp on a passport. He saw and acknowledged Thomas. Beads of sweat fell visibly from his brow onto the papers he wrote on. From time to time he would move an index finger across his forehead and sweep a rain of sweat onto the earthen floor.

"You have a gun, sir?" asked Thomas.

"A rifle ..."

"Not to worry."

Thomas looked away with the air of someone ready to wait indefinitely, and Corbin looked outside through the barred window at the sunny courtyard, ready to do the same but with less composure.

"Please point out your baggage, sir," said Thomas suddenly.

Corbin did so. Then by some unseen magic all his belongings appeared at the head of the queue and he was summoned with a deference the other Europeans could not challenge. His gun and ammunition registered, he was whisked with style out of Customs and his baggage loaded by a porter onto a cart bound for the Mombasa Club up the road.

Only then did it occur to Corbin to enquire about the man into whose hands he had put himself, now walking solidly beside him. "Don't worry sir," said the man, but the special treatment at Customs had cost five rupees.

They walked through the exclusive English settlement called The Point, strewn without regard for economy or geometry with picturesque villas in lush gardens connected to each other by roads barely better than tracks. The sun-hat was heavy on his head; without it, he understood, he would collapse. The temperature was ninety, he felt clammy, and the slight breeze from the ocean lacked the spirit to revive. Not too soon, it seemed, the large white building of the Club appeared in sight. With a relief that overwhelmed him, Corbin almost ran into its spacious shade.

The manager, Hanning, greeted him with a lemonade. He was a big red-faced man with thin yellow hair and a handlebar moustache, and wearing a rather sparkling white shirt and tie for the time of day. He'd had a swim and a bath, it appeared. Thomas left, promising to return. Corbin took a small table inside the bar, next to the doorway, through which he could look out at the verandah and the garden. There were two other entrances to the bar, one leading from the dining room where lunch was being served by black waiters in kanzus and red fezzes. There were African hunting and war trophies on the walls, a niche held an Arab copper-work jar under a pair of daggers. Behind the bar, at which stood a barman looking busy, were three group photographs of men with hunting or fishing spoils. A corridor past the snooker room led to a small number of guest rooms, to one of which Corbin was presently shown. The window faced the back, and he could see part of the road leading down to the old town.

3 March

The room is large and airy. It has two beds, two chairs, a chest of drawers and a mirror, otherwise it is absolutely bare. There is no carpet. Several passengers on board ship called this club the best in Africa!...

4 March

"Venice has its gondola, London its cab, and Mombasa has its gharry, as I always say," says Hanning. He is a drifter, who answered the Club's notice, which was placed in the Cape Town *Times*, and came over to see the place, he says. The gharry is a train running on rails and pulled by one or two natives. It is the only way to travel on the island, I am told. The PC is away and I might as well enjoy the metropolis while I can, before I get posted somewhere where I'll be lucky to have a roof over my head. He has given me a list of the sites to visit. The Club has a small guide book, which he has lent me to browse through. The old Portuguese fort is a must. The old name of Mombasa was Mvita, for war.... Then the ancient mosque, the northern harbour where the dhows anchor, the water gate. And, no visitor to Mombasa misses the boat ride around the Island ...

THE CLUB VERANDAH LOOKED UPON a dense garden of brilliant colours running all the way to the cliff edge, which was demarcated by a wire fence and white stones. Beyond lay the ocean, its shimmering, misty horizon a fitting sight for an expatriate or tourist or colonial servant to contemplate over a cocktail.

He began his sightseeing the same day. A tram had been called, and it emerged now from under the shade of a bougainvillaea bush. It was rolled noisily to the rail and lifted upon it, after which he sat on the wooden seat under its canopy and was pushed and free-wheeled all the way down the tree-lined shady Kilindini Road.

If The Point presented meditative vistas—dreamy groves, brightly coloured gardens, vast ocean, coral cliffs—Mombasa town assailed all the senses at once. The smells of overripe pineapples and mangoes, the open drains, animal droppings; costumes of a dozen cultures and the babble of as many languages.

He played tennis every evening at the Sports Club while he waited for the Provincial Commissioner, the PC. At the new and already potholed cricket pitch he watched a friendly game on the first Sunday he was there: Indians versus the English, one tribe on either side of the pitch. It was a clear rout of the ragged Indians, most of whom had never held a bat before and had merely been assembled for the Englishmen's pleasure. Dinner parties at the Club degenerated into drunken orgies, after which members had to be assisted into their trains. On the second Sunday of his stay, he participated first in an oyster picnic on the shore, followed by a "cocktail parade," in which the object was to mix enough drinks to knock oneself out.

THERE WAS ONE LION TROPHY on the wall beside the bar. A fierce, huge head, its mouth stretched wide open, the contemplation of which could make your stomach turn, your hair rise. As you turned away uneasily from this meeting you might be told by the barman that this lion had carried off twenty-seven victims in Tsavo: a coolie from an open railway carriage; an unknowing porter from a campfire away over a four-foot fence before his companions discovered him missing, the following day finding his bloodied clothes, some bones, and a severed head; a sleeping labourer dragged out from between two oblivious companions inside a tent ... and so the bloody toll went. If it was late in the afternoon, your attention would invariably drift, from that vanquished terror on the wall to the oversized human head below it, belonging to its hunter, Frank Maynard, who was sitting at a small table holding a whisky. There were stories about him, too, but they were told in his absence.

He was a big man in army khaki, who came every day for his sundowner. From where he sat he quietly watched all the goings-on in the room—the bluster and chit-chat, the deals and complaints, the dart and card games, of the merchants, the officials, and the engineers. His presence, once he arrived, like the man-eater's above him, became part of the character of the room. The hair on his large head was brown and sparse, he wore a small moustache, and the cold green eyes revoked any trace of warmth betrayed by the faint toothy smile at his lips. Nevertheless, he was liked and much respected for what he was, the more so for the predicament in which he had (unfairly, it was said) been put.

Frank Maynard was a captain in the King's African Rifles who would pursue a recalcitrant animal or tribesman with like ferocity and ruthlessness. Currently he was on suspension pending an inquiry regarding his conduct on a punitive expedition against a tribe and was biding his time on the coast.

On several occasions Corbin's eyes had met and acknowledged that searching look from the trophy wall. Then one day, after he had been deposited at the Club door by a tram after a sightseeing tour, as he sat in the bar wiping sweat from his brow and contemplating his second bath, despairing over yet another change of clothes, Alfred Corbin's eyes fell briefly on the soldier. That momentary look seemed to spark a resolve, for Maynard got up, and with slow deliberate steps came straight towards his table.

"Frank Maynard," he said, shaking hands and sitting down.

"Corbin, Alfred Corbin."

"So I've heard, old chap."

Corbin tried not to feel like a mouse under that overbearing smile, that brilliant predatory gaze, not to become too conscious of the heads turned to stare at them from the bar. He was waiting for his first posting in Africa, and this was a man who had trampled the land from corner to corner, slept in the forests and killed its wildlife and natives.

"I knew your brother in India. Robert. Good man."

"In the Punjab?"

Maynard nodded. The same amused look.

"And I met Kenneth in Voi. Didn't get to know him well though, he was on his way out—home leave, it was, and Nyasa land after that, I believe."

They had a drink together. The lion on the wall, Maynard told him, catching his gaze, had measured nine-foot-eleven, tip to tip, nose to tail; it took eight men to carry it.

The following evening Corbin was invited for supper.

MAYNARD KEPT ROOMS on the second storey of an Arab house on the Kilindini Road, not far from the Club. He greeted Corbin at the door in a yellow kanzu and a tasselled red fez. The reception room was furnished simply in the Arab style and they sat on pillows. Maynard produced a hookah and Corbin a cheroot. By this time the younger man was more composed, the other relaxed and less intimidating. A woman suddenly entered the room with a sharp rustle of clothing which made Corbin start. She was strikingly beautiful, a half-caste of partly Arab or Indian blood, partly African. The short length of buibui, worn around her shoulder over a colourful dress, was what had rustled; she hovered around them for a while before finally taking a stool some distance away.

"Stop gaping, man!"

Corbin raised an eyebrow. Maynard chuckled.

"A few years ago practically every man in Nairobi kept a native girl—or two or three. Now they are more civilized and busy with each other's wives."

The night was cool, a light breeze blew in through the open window; there was a mosque not far off, from which the muezzin's "Allahu Akber" presently came through clearly. Below, from the courtyard of the building came the sounds of boys playing, men chatting on stone benches by the little garden, probably over their coffee. Over whiskies Corbin and Maynard talked of their schools, their families. Maynard's was a banking family; his refusal to join his father caused him much guilt and brooding. He was now estranged from his family.

The woman got up and left the room again with the distinct rustle of her buibui. She returned with a pitcher of water for washing hands. Then she brought their food: meat curry, and rice and bread. They drank more whisky and had plum pudding from home for dessert.

"I don't always eat this much, but in company I tend to indulge. Africa teaches you how little food you really need, and how much we in civilized England tend to overeat."

They sat up late into the evening. Maynard did most of the talking, mostly about Africa. He loved it and he hated it, above all he feared it for what it could do to him. "This is a savage country, and it could turn you into a savage. It is so easy to be overcome by its savagery, to lose one's veneer of Western civilization. This is what I have learned, what I dread most. So in a way I look forward to leaving it. But I have nowhere to go. India, perhaps. Egypt …"

He respected the African, yet would call him nigger. He loved animals. He had killed scores of both. He believed in Empire, but had no patience with settling the country with whites. "I," said the soldier, "respect the African—as a redoubtable enemy or as a friend. I would kill him with as little compunction as he would me. But the settler, and the low class of official we have in East Africa—excuse me, Corbin, but there are not enough of you here—despises the black and would use me to kill him."

They sat in silence for a long time. The courtyard below was quiet now. The moon had risen and passed the window and was somewhere above the house. From outside came the sound of frogs and night insects, with the richness of a symphony, it seemed, when he paid attention to it, and from the kitchen came the occasional clatter of utensils. One more time Corbin glanced around the room, preparing mentally to leave. There was one question he had about this man, based on what he had heard at the parties and picnics. But it was not his place to ask.

As if sensing this unease, Maynard began explanations.

"Imagine," he said, "the centre of the village where they hold the baraza. Cleared hard ground. A white man—an Englishman—pegged to the ground. Lying on his back, mouth wedged open. Savage men and women come and urinate in his mouth. Men standing and laughing, women crouching, all drunk on pombé. The man drowns in nigger urine. He is disembowelled, used as a latrine.... Imagine the insects feeding on him ... the stench ... the scavengers ... hyenas who would not leave a scrap of meat on a bone, vultures, crows. It had to be avenged, Corbin. For the white man, for authority, for order—they are the same thing here.

"We went in at dawn. Spies had given us the layout. No man or woman to be spared, I ordered. We set fire to the huts, waited outside for the niggers to emerge. I myself bayoneted them, men and women they came running out.... No mercy, I said ...

"You'd be surprised at the ease with which a bayonet enters a human chest.... How cheap human life is really ...

"You disapprove—obviously. Tell me, what would you do? I myself am not sure I did the right thing—I am haunted at times—and I believed then I was doing the right thing. To show strength, fury. This is a savage country, it makes a savage out of you. What would you do?"

"I'm not sure I can say ... not being a military man. I do think the Colonial Office holds vastly different views of the natives."

"Yes, I wonder which will prevail. Yours, obviously, when I've cleaned up and subdued the land for you to administer."

But they departed on cordial terms. "I disapprove of his actions, not of the man," Corbin went back and wrote. In fact he was strangely drawn to the soldier, and joined him several times for drinks, until his posting came.

17 March, 1913

"Send the poor devil in," I heard the Provincial Commissioner say, and the secretary looked rather apologetically at me. "Poor devil" because I had been posted to a place called Kikono near the border with German East. It is a substation that has been sporadically manned depending on the availability of junior staff. There are a few mission stations in the area that lies to the east and next to the foothills of Kilimanjaro. The town is populated by a community of Indians and some Swahilis from the Coast. Henley, the PC, is something of a student of African tribes, hence his sympathy for me. He had just returned from a field safari in Giriyama. I must say I was not a little disappointed. In Africa one does not expect to be saddled with overseeing Indians. These, I am told, already have a conflict under way with local missionaries. Nevertheless I was eager to get away. And so, after yet another dinner party and dancing at the Grand Hotel (grand in name only, as everyone here hastily explains—but the Club is no good for such events, as it is out of bounds to women after 7 P.M.) and a picnic lunch the following morning with a charming couple called the Unsworths, I set off on the Uganda Railway for Voi.

I had resolved to catch up on duty to write letters to Mother and Robert, but as soon as I sat down with paper and pen I realized how futile it was to attempt that mundane chore, to conjure up England out of a night in Africa. The darkest, blackest night that simply shut out the world of European Mombasa. From where I sat contemplating my epistolary failure, the window of the Uganda Railway coach sent back an eerie reflection of myself. I pressed my face to the pane and watched the darkness fly past ... shadows in the moonlight swiftly rushing by, shadows that could be trees or some species of wildlife.... It was impossible to surrender to sleep with the knowledge that finally I was entering the interior of Africa ... the huge and dark continent that had defied the rest of the world for millennia, now opening up to European civilization, to a great Empire of which I was a minor but privileged functionary. "Life and soul," Mr. Churchill had said. My body had blistered in the heat and swelled to the bites of insects, and as I lay on the most uncomfortable bunk the Uganda Railway possessed, my soul was stirring.

19 March

Thirty porters were engaged for me at Voi, from where I set off this morning after spending two nights at the Dak bungalow. There has been much singing and merriment. The porters are of the Wataita tribe and speak a little Swahili. They wear a strip of cloth around their waist. Their front teeth are sharpened to a point, and some carry objects such as tin boxes or small animal horns in the slits in their ears. With me is Thomas, who was the first person to welcome me in Africa and has doggedly stayed with me, willing to serve me for anything I can pay him. He has told me an interesting story of how a woman from his people was once Queen of Mombasa for a very short period during Portuguese times. Thus the vanquished clutch at straws of glory.... He has a rather irritating habit of equating his status with mine, and never tires of pointing out the shortcomings of the poor Wataita. He doesn't realize that they all have fun at his expense.

Part of our way is thick, thorny bramble, which we have to cut through. I am utterly in the hands of the porters and guides. What do they think of me? I feel strange and nervous, helpless with the smattering of Swahili I picked up in Mombasa. Sometimes I am the subject of their song, but whether they ply me with compliment or abuse I cannot say. Baboons chatter in the trees above us, rhino spoor has been pointed out to me, I have seen a snake cross my path. At one time we were followed by lion grunts, and even now in the dark night perhaps I hear them growl. I am reminded of the lion head at the Mombasa Club and the red-fezzed Captain Maynard sitting under it. I cannot help thinking that if the blacks in my caravan decide to butcher me and my Indian, it would be Maynard or someone like him who would be sent to avenge us.

2

Kikona, "The Little Hand," lay some thirty miles from the border with German East Africa, a convenient stop on the east-west trail from Voi to Moshi that connected the two colonies. The mighty snow-capped Kilimanjaro attended by fluffs of cloud loomed in the near distance: a presence at once enigmatic, benign, and mystical, a symbol of the eternal. But the heart of this town in the thorny desert country was the little mbuyu—baobab—tree, a short thick deformity struggling out from the side of a hill, from which twisted, mangled branches grappled uselessly against the sky. In somewhat light-hearted fashion, and in keeping with legends surrounding mbuyu trees, this one was sometimes called "the little hand of the devil"; but at night, and especially at sudden encounter, it would appear quite ghostly, not to say satanic, and was avoided. During the day it was a shady meeting place. Facing it in two rows perpendicular to each other were the shops and houses and two mosques of the small town.

Early one afternoon the townsfolk began to prepare to welcome the new Assistant District Commissioner. The rest time had passed unnoticed. At last, amidst much anticipation and after a few false alarms, a boy was seen to go up to the little mbuyu tree, from under whose branches he began to beat on his drum, at which signal the shopkeepers stepped out from their shops to join the gathered crowd. The men in the police band, twelve-strong, set themselves up under the tree, and the drummer boy sat with them. The Indians stood in a row, somewhat solemn-looking in white drill suits and red or black fezzes, or in dhoties and turbans. Next to them formed a shorter line of Swahilis, in kanzus and embroidered caps, some in waistcoats. There was a third, large group of vendors, servants, and occasional labourers, and, with them, tribesmen and women from the neighbouring area. Thus they stood waiting, occasionally looking up, turning or craning their necks towards the road that entered town and would bring the new representative of the King.

WHAT MANNER OF TOWN WAS KIKONO, an Indian haven improbably placed miles away from the railway at the western edge of Taita country? It was said, with some truth, that open one Indian duka, or shop, in the middle of nowhere and soon you'd have a row of dukas, in the same way as a potato or yam proliferates. The first duka appears when a wind-riding seed falls on the ground and decides to make its home there. So the first duka appeared, so the town grew.

A young English naturalist and sportsman had one day taken off from the ancient port of Lamu on the Indian Ocean, where he had been a guest of the British Consul. He had borrowed a large sum of money from his unofficial banker, an Indian shopkeeper of the Shamsi sect called Jamal Dewji. The shopkeeper sent one of his sons along with the explorer-naturalist, ostensibly to assist him and even cook for him, but actually to keep an eye on him. "In his country he may be king," he bragged in mosque, "but here I trust nobody." "Stick to the hat-wearer's heels and don't come back without him or the money," he told his son. Indeed, it was known that the Englishman, who had done much prying around town, had slipped into his bag an antique China bowl from an old tomb, and the news of his departure was received with some relief. He first went off to Zanzibar, from whence he sailed to Bagamoyo and marched with a caravan to Moshi and Taveta and finally to the station of the Mission of Christ in Africa, in the Taita country. At the mission he stayed two weeks, spending his time hunting and exploring. During this time Jamal Dewji's boy, Abdul, fell in love with one of the converts, a Swahili girl called Hannah, and convinced the explorer to release to him some of his father's money so he could set himself up in the area. The eminence was only too happy to rid himself of the watchdog at a discount. The boy and girl married, the girl reconverted to Islam and reverted to her original name, Khanoum.

Abdul Jamal Dewji, known thenceforth as Jamali, started his shop some miles down from the Mission at the little mbuyu tree which was long known as a resting place for caravans. The Shamsi community to which he belonged was well-organized, and news of this single-family settlement spread to Mombasa and beyond. There is a railway to the north and a railway to the south—how can a town fail to grow between them? the young man's father boasted in Lamu. All that is needed is a line to join the two and pass through the village for it to become a town, a city. A few months later two men arrived from India, and later their families. Grocers, dispensers, sellers of cloth, jewellery and hardware: a line of dukas sprang up. Where there are two Shamsis, as the adage says, let one be the headman, father and priest—the mukhi—and let the other form the congregation. That is, let them without further ado start a mosque.

The mukhi of the Shamsis here was currently Jamali himself. Like mukhis everywhere, he was paid not financially but with honour and respect, and promises of rewards in the hereafter. He was a shopkeeper, tall and lanky for his kind, with a face a little short of humble and the doggedness of a hyena when he had to help a community member. His Swahili wife spoke Cutchi to add to her mission English and had borne him three children.

Thus setting themselves up, loyal British subjects—and vociferously so—with visions of growth and prosperity for the town, they had applied to the government for official township status. While it made up its mind, the government responded by sending an Assistant District Commissioner of the Mombasa Province when it could spare one. The current ADC was Fred Axworthy, now on a march out of town to welcome and initiate his successor, Alfred Corbin. Word had reached town earlier in the day that ten of his thirty porters had deserted the new ADC the night before. Four of the ten were apprehended on the road outside Kikono, and now languished in the lockup.

Apparently heralding the arrival, a bevy of little boys in kanzus, loin cloths, or nothing at all, came running down the road, followed by a man rolling on his heels. They all joined the more irregular sections of the waiting crowd. The Indians formed a straighter line, the Swahilis stirred.

All eyes were on the road now. There was a sudden silence, then everybody clapped hands as the two Europeans in white suits and sun-hats came striding into town at the head of a trail of porters. The police band broke into "For He's a Jolly Good Fellow," and the Englishmen stopped to hear it out.

AND THIS WAS WHAT APPEARED to the new ADC as he approached the town: fleeting glimpses caught between bush and tree and anthill—a figure draped in white, dashing from left to right, cutting across his path in the distance. It could have been a man in kanzu but for the black hair flying, the lithe movement, the nimble step ... then a red head-cover over the hair to complete the female figure. So amazed was he by the sight that he had stopped to watch. She disappeared behind an incline, where he was told lay the settlement ...

25 March

... a mound really, of red earth, covered sparsely with the predominant vegetation of the area, namely thorn. Soon after that apparition disappeared, into one side of it, as it were, there emerged from the other side and directly in front of us a party lead by a white man in sun helmet.

"Dr. Livingstone, I presume, what? I dare say you must be the new ADC, the replacement I've been begging for on my knees, for months. Axworthy's the name."

Red-faced and stocky, perspiring freely, he was jovial, if anything. I introduced myself.

"We've caught some of your porters who absconded, so we've been expecting you rather. I dare say you'll have to prescribe some strokes of the kiboko as deterrent. I don't believe in the whip myself; too damn humiliating, but it's what works best."

I don't remember what else he said, but it was a lot. I glanced briefly behind to see poor Thomas trudging along, bringing up the rear.

The entire town came into view almost instantly. To our left ran a row of shops and houses, meeting another row at a right angle at its far end. We were at the head of the only street and the town square, its centerpiece a baobab, or mbuyu, tree that led to the administrative centre and the ADC's house.

This was Kikono, its inhabitants gathered under the mbuyu tree waiting patiently to greet me. As we approached, the police band struck up a tune. I was introduced to the local dignitaries, Indian and Swahili, the chiefs and dignitaries of nearby villages, and the local police force. After a supper of chicken stew and fried plantain, served by a young African girl who was rather scantily dressed, followed by pudding, brandy, and tobacco which I contributed, we retired.

The following day a rather unpleasant task awaited me. Those porters who had deserted on the way from Voi and had been caught were lined up to receive their dues. One fellow was brought in that morning with fervent protestations of having lost his way, so his case had to be heard. It was decided against him. Each received 10 strokes of the whip. "6 is too little, 20 too much," said Axworthy.

It seems to me there has to be a better way of making the native willing to carry burden for a wage, some attractive inducement at journey's end perhaps ...

It's been 5 days since I arrived, and Axworthy left this morning. The girl who cooked and waited at table for him has also disappeared, having joined the departing entourage, so Thomas swears. I am now lord under this mbuyu tree.

26 March

... My powers are modest.... In criminal cases I can inflict only one month's imprisonment and a fine of Rs 50, whilst in civil cases my jurisdiction amounts to fines of up to Rs 250.... Bothered by boils, saw dispenser.
Ask for—
½ doz whisky
6 tablespoons
biscuits, any kind
... already Mombasa seems far away—and Europe?

HE ADMINISTERED with a quiet, forceful diligence, a monastic rigour, in the unquestioned belief that what he did in his small way was part of a bigger enterprise in which he had some stake. His method—for he was a methodical man and thought carefully about what he did—was to understand the motives behind his people's reluctance, recalcitrance, or hostility and to make them understand his own position. He was there to administer in the name of his king and nation, to bring the land into the twentieth century in as painless a way as possible, in the belief that the British Empire with its experience of ruling other lands and with its humane system was the best nurturing ground for an emerging nation, for backward Africans and Orientals to enter the society of civilized peoples.

Governor's Memoranda for PCs and DCs (1910)
(Native Policy, pages 5-6)

... The Fundamental principle and the only humane policy to be followed in dealing with peoples who have not reached a high stage of civilisation is to develop them on their own lines and in accordance with their own ideas and customs, purified in so far as is necessary. Whilst retaining all the good in their government, which makes for manliness, self-respect, and honest dealing, only that which is repugnant to higher ideals of morality and justice should be rejected; and the introduction of so-called civilisation, when it has a denationalising and demoralising tendency should be avoided. It is not from the present generation that we may look for much; the succeeding generations are in the hands of the Provincial Commissioners with their district staffs.... It must certainly be their endeavour to lift the natives to a higher plane of civilisation; but this can only be achieved by gradual methods and by observing existing conditions.

HE WAS POLICE CHIEF, magistrate, doctor, tax collector and, when his superiors demanded, surveyor. It was a job that required infinite patience, a certain amount but not an excess of good humour, an ability to turn cold, a knack for improvisation, an ability to forget the day's concerns. Only by the most abstract idealism could you try to convince tribes to send their sons to work with the Indians, or of the benefits of paying taxes. How to convince them to abandon their own laws, their universes, for a European view of being? How to explain that an ugly girl was not an evil omen, when if the people really believed in the portent they could will bad luck and prove their prophecy right?

Much of his work involved arbitration and administering British justice. The former took cajoling, reasoning, using threats or the lockup, always with native custom as guide. But imposing British justice was like constructing a marble edifice, irrelevant and alien to people governed by their own laws and ways of doing things. Even so, his waiting room was full when he began hearing shauris—the petitions from the people—in the morning. He believed he was often used as a curiosity, as a test, or for an opinion, while the real, the binding decisions on the cases were taken elsewhere by tribal councils.

17 April, 1913

The powers of an ADC are greater than I at first suspected. I can give imprisonments up to 6 months, but beyond 1 month the sentence has to be approved by High Court. My Court entirely independent of the DC's …

Governor's Memoranda for PCs and DCs (1910)
(Native Policy, cont'd, page 7)

By upholding the authority of the Chiefs and Elders, I do not wish to imply that officers are to sit down and enforce blindly—possibly at the point of the bayonet—all orders issued by these men who, after all, are only savages. The main object of administering the people through their Chiefs is to prevent disintegration amongst the tribe …

THERE WAS A GOVERNMENT STATION in Voi and a temporary one in Taveta, between which his small dominion lay, and every quarter an ADC arrived from Voi to assist for a few days and to collect reports. The first one of these was a big, bluff man called Woodward. Corbin was lucky, Woodward told him over brandy, his area was so sparsely populated: "Mostly coastal people and foreigners." But even so: "Won't be long before a real test case comes along, old chap."

"Such as?"

"When a real hard one comes along, you don't know what to do—that is, you know what you have to do, but it doesn't feel right. It's a case you never forget. Welcome to the Colonial Service."

He wouldn't say what his own such case had been. But he had a word of advice: "Whenever you find things getting a bit too much for you, *go on safari.*" He emphasized the words. "And women … it's easier on safari. But don't bring them back. Concubinage is not tolerated any longer."

THERE WERE REGULAR FOOTBALL MATCHES in town, in which all the races participated. The post office was active; mail was collected and taken to Voi once a week. The *East African Herald* arrived regularly from Nairobi, and it was in one of its issues that Corbin learned of Captain Maynard's transfer out to Palestine. The settler community in Nairobi had picketed the Governor's residence in protest, and the paper carried a strongly worded editorial. On King's Birthday they had a march-past, the mukhi Jamali donated sodas, and that night the Indians held a function to which Corbin was invited.

As he surveyed the district he ruled over like a king—some of the tribesmen even confused him with his own monarch, King George—Frank Maynard would come to mind. A man who returned savagery for savagery, no longer needed in East Africa. Throughout the country, towns like Kikono were springing up, full of life, the whole land buzzing with a vitality it had not known for millennia, all due to European intervention. The likes of Maynard would be needed only if the imposed order broke down, a prospect that seemed remote.

11 May, 1913

Imagine waking up in the middle of the night to the sound of trees rustling, a hyena barking … and, of all things, a dissonant, whining hum. What could it be—some animal, a sick donkey braying, a lost calf—perhaps the stray dog Bwana Tim was wounded? Then gradually I realized what it was. What is it in human intonation that makes it identifiable? For that's what I could swear it was. People singing! I could not believe my ears. A faint sound of human singing, a chorus not in full control. Was I in some ridiculous dream? I sat up, pinched myself. The singing ceased after a while, but voices persisted intermittently. Something was going on. I walked to the window but desisted from opening it, if only because it would create its own racket. By this time the sounds had ceased altogether. It was eerie. I have never believed in ghosts, although in Mombasa I was told not to be too sceptical. Fortunately it was almost dawn, and soon the town was stirring. Upon inquiring later in the morning, I was told that the Indian Shamsis wake up at 4 A.M. to pray!

The administrative centre of Kikono consists of the government buildings, situated on the top of a low hill. My own "jumba" is a crooked wooden house with iron roof and no ceiling. The furniture has to be moved during rains, and the creaky verandah gives ample warning of any arrival. There are two bedrooms on one wing, facing back and front. In the rear of the house are the kitchen and a servant's hut. The office is an even more dilapidated affair. Beside it is the police station and post office. Out in front, in the compound, are a mbuyu tree and a large thorny bush, which overlook a sharp drop, itself covered by scrub. And beyond that is the rest of this little town, the brown mud-and-wattle huts that make up the business and residence section where the Indians and Swahilis live and run their dukas. The dispensary is in the rather lethal hands of the Indian Chagpar. A footpath runs down the hill on the west side, from my house, arrives in the town, and goes beyond to join the road to Voi.

Roughly half the Indians belong to the Shamsi sect of Islam and have a separate mosque. They are in touch with Voi, Mombasa, Nairobi, even Bombay and German East. Once or twice a year it seems they hold large feasts, and when they do not go to Voi for that purpose they collect in Kikono community members from the neighbouring towns and give themselves a regular jamboree. There air also Hindu, Punjabi, and Memon families, but quite often the distinction blurs.

Nowadays I mostly sleep through the pre-dawn Shamsi hum, but in the morning am awakened by the flapping wings of a flock of birds on the move and then the *cockorickoo* of a cock crowing somewhere.

THE SIMPLE QUIET OF A TOWN early in the morning—the gentle slap of the cool air, the sun just beginning to warm itself over the hilltops and trees. There is the very occasional clink of utensils—reticent, as if the woman frying vitumbua or tambi in some dark interior of a house is wary of shattering the peace—the yelp of the dog Bwana Tim, reputed to have been abandoned or lost by a European traveller, the angry protest or whine of a loose iron roof. Corbin would walk into his office next door and occupy himself for a while with the odd piece of correspondence or report, or even an unread newspaper. Then, with the sun a little higher up, he would go on a stroll through the town as it prepared to go about its business. "Jambo!" he would call out to someone.

"Jambo, bwana!" would come the reply. Sometimes he stopped at the little canteen for a cup of sweet black tea with ginger, which he liked but would not admit to Thomas, who looked after his cooking. The stall was owned by a man called Baruti, meaning "gunpowder," and the strong-flavoured tea was famed among travellers, who would gather there for refreshment and news.

He relished these early moments of the waking hours, without the bustle of activity, the irritating little petitions from the people that so often stumped government regulations and which would soon clutter up his day and take everything out of him.

3 July, 1913

... Indians came to petition for permanent status for the town. I told them the town plan would have to be approved by the Land Office, who were likely to recommend changes to the present plan. They were agreed in principle. Prepared memo. Man from Voi arriving 7th.

... Trying hard to get rupee balance right.... Thomas has dysentery. He has the annoying habit of singing "Once in Royal David's City" unceasingly.

THERE WERE NO EUROPEAN SETTLERS in the area, but the occasional travelling party, if it cared to stop, was welcomed, and indeed escorted into the village by the children and met with an askari. Once a family of Boers with two servants passed through on horseback and ox wagon, returning from German East, disappointed at their reception there by people they had taken for their kin (they left some German newspapers, which the ADC read with much interest); and weeks later a similar Boer family stopped for refreshments on their way into the German colony. At another time two Irishmen came away from a foray across the border with two ox wagons full of sisal bulbils in sacks, stolen from the thriving German plantations.

Kikono was situated close to where the seasonal Kito stream dipped southwards before meandering back north and away. To the east, in an area heavily wooded with shrubs and thorns, was the station of the MCA on a ridge that marked the beginning of the Taita hills. Somewhere else, Corbin was aware, was a French mission. The town of Taveta, which had grown because the CMS (Church Missionary Society) had set up there after being told to leave Moshi by the Germans, lay to the west, and in the distance along the road could be seen Kilimanjaro, Queen Victoria's present to the German Kaiser. In the south was shrubbery and the Taru desert, and the Pare Mountains were dimly visible directly in the southwest. It was a beautiful country. There were forests, lakes, and craters, and hills overhung with blue mist. And there were plenty of animals.

SOME TEN MILES AWAY FROM KIKONO, beyond a gauntlet of thorn and bush that had to be hacked through, on a crag a thousand feet high, stood the MCA station overlooking a vast territory. Its buildings of wood and iron stood out strikingly in the distance as one approached from the town. At its lonely, high perch it seemed to have the appearance of having fought off the bush forest and kept it at bay. The only way in, as you approached from Kikono, was to round the hill and come from behind.

On Sundays a handbell announced service in the mission; its peal ringing merrily through the countryside greeted Corbin as he climbed up the low rise on the beaten path. He was in the company of a curious, wonderstruck crowd of people, the more ragged of whom he had picked up on the way, the better dressed having descended the hill to escort him in. Behind him, as always, followed Thomas. This was their first visit to the MCA station.

SEND US, O ENGLAND, YOUR MEN said a wooden plaque hanging from the gate and decorated with a painted floral border. England had sent two women instead.

Miss Elliott and Mrs. Bailey, who had been waiting for him, welcomed Corbin anxiously and served him a drink of water. The place was truly an oasis, he observed. The compound was swept and tidy, and large trees provided shade. There were several modest buildings to one side, but the main building, where the two ladies had rooms, stood prominently apart. Immediately after he had drunk the water he was taken to where the service was to be held, under one of the trees.

A hundred or so converts, many in European-style attire, sat attentively on the ground. An equal number, perhaps more, of curious onlookers stood some distance away in the sun. Deacon Kizito conducted, leading with a sermon in English: "So he bringeth them into their desired heaven." He then spoke in Swahili with a peppering of Taita words. A boy in shorts and tucked-in shirt gave a five-minute discourse in Taita. A group of children sang, first in English and later in the local dialect. Finally Miss Elliott got up and announced the day's schedule of activities.

After the service Corbin was shown around the station—the hospital, the school and workshop, the staff hostel, the chapel. There were fruit and vegetable gardens. The Sunday school had thirty students, whom he left in the hands of Miss Elliott, as she recited Longfellow, to take a tour of the surrounding area with the deacon.

Corbin returned for lunch and tea with the missionary women. Thomas had been found useful in the kitchen and had even helped in the teaching that day. The deacon disappeared for some work.

Over tea they sat in the Mission house, on the verandah. Immediately below them was a drop of rock, bush, and trees. The countryside presented to their view was dull, languorous, and hazy in the afternoon heat. There were large stretches of thorny bush; mountains covered the horizon towards the west; a forest in the east looked black and impenetrable. Somewhere in the distance there was a play of lightning, a few quick strikes, and then came the muffled roll of thunder. For some moments they were preoccupied by the sight of a dusty trail—Masai youths herding cattle.

At length Miss Elliott stirred. "If there ever was an Eden ..." she said.

"What do you mean?" demanded her older companion severely.

"Surely Adam must have walked here in these very plains and hills, in this region of the earth ..."

"Before he was expelled to Europe?"

They had a curious relationship—the plain Miss Elliott, frail in mind and body, it seemed, though obviously not in faith, and the stern, protective Mrs. Bailey, who might have bounced bar brawlers in another life. She had served with her husband in West Africa, then, after his death there, she joined the floundering Mission of Christ in India, where she met Miss Elliott. The two decided Christianity could be served better in Africa.

They discussed the fact that the Mission had no following in Kikono. The women felt bitter about it, this town impregnable to their attentions, which nevertheless their Mission had had an unwitting hand in founding.

"The Indians are half-savages," Mrs. Bailey observed, beginning an explanation she had obviously thought out conclusively in detail.

"And therefore worse," said her companion. "You can do nothing with them."

"Gone too far the other way, she means. At least the African you can mould. But the Indian and the Mussulman are incorrigible in their worst habits and superstitions. They will always remain so."

"As Bishop Taylor said, 'The African yearns for our top hat and elastic-side boots, but the Indian will never let go his dhoti and will forever remain half-naked.'"

At this juncture his own Indian cook with the very Christian name Thomas arrived, in his parson's black, and Corbin got up to go.

14 August, 1913

Fortnum & Mason hamper arrived, all intact. (Thank you, Mother.) ... socks and darning needles—where *do* mine disappear?—cards from: Ken, Robbie ...

Ken: Do I want a post in Nyasaland? No—but, Oh for a day by the sea with a g&t! (Mombasa Club.)

I suppose it's all right for Thomas to take Sundays off for services at MCA.

Governor's Memoranda for PCs and DCs (1910)
(Promotion of Officers, page 20)

Junior Officers are required to pass an examination in Swahili and law, and only those that have passed will be eligible for promotion. But whilst proficiency in native languages, a sound knowledge of law and of the local ordinances and regulations, and skill in topography, will form important qualifications for promotion, the main tests will be the success of officers in their dealings with the general public.

3

"It has been a festival," wrote Alfred Corbin when it was over, "at the end of which a young man with the preposterous name of Pipa (meaning barrel) is in the lockup for creating a disturbance—and could very well be charged with spying, if I had a mind to do it. The Indians are sulking at this outcome—and my cook, for entirely different reasons, seems determined to poison me."

It had begun innocently enough.

"The King's representative is invited to our festival," the mukhi Jamali said. He had come with the invitation the week before, wearing a new blue-and-white embroidered cap, the kofia, perhaps in anticipation of the event. "Everywhere, they are invited and come," the mukhi added.

"Why, mukhi, I would be offended if you did not invite me," Corbin told him. "I would be delighted to attend."

And so he had gone.

EIGHT MEN DANCING round a tent pole, each with an eighteen-inch stick in his right hand, the left holding on to a long red or green ribbon which descended from the top of the pole. To the steady, seductive beat from the tabla and dhol, the intermittent screechy wail of the harmonium, and a rich Kathiawadi voice from the old country revelling in the happy occasion, the eight men weaved in and out past each other around the pole, over and over, in a movement as regular and intricate as the mechanism of a time-piece. And as they went swinging past each other they brought the middle of their sticks together in a sprightly click. The men wore loose white pyjamas and long shirts, coloured sashes round their waists, bands round their heads. Their shirttails went flying as they danced.

As the men danced past each other in ever smaller circles, their red and green ribbons wove a checkered sheath around the pole, until finally the eight limbs of the dance, the loose ends of the ribbons, were so shortened the men stood shoulder to shoulder, beating time with the sticks. Then the process reversed as the men spiralled outwards and the ribbons unwound.

At the back of the festival tent, called the mandap, Alfred Corbin stood beside the mukhi, in casual shirt and trousers and somewhat dazzled by the celebrations. The air was laden, a heady mix of strong perfumes and sweat, incense and condensed milk, and dust stamped through the mats after a long day. Boys raced about, babies wailed, old folk sat quietly in their corners, sherbet servers beseeched people to drink. And in all this chaos, the uninterrupted drumbeat in the background, the sharp, regular clicking of the dancers' sticks, which made him flinch, the dancers' dizzying motion, the weaving and unweaving of the checkered sheaths.

As he stood watching, a garba dance got under way with much excitement: a whirling circle of joyous, brightly clad women, nose studs glinting, bangles jingling. The garba enacted the first conversions of the community from Hinduism, several centuries ago in Gujarat, he was told. Corbin saw in it a flower opening and closing. The women, bending forward, clapping hands, approached the centre, then with a snap of fingers stepped back into the spinning circle. Corbin wondered if it was appropriate to stare and turned away his gaze.

A chair was produced for him and wearily he sat down and accepted a drink of sherbet. The men's dance had wound down, and the din had reduced somewhat, though there were shouts of approval as the garba grew faster, the women now performing with brass pots which they would release and catch again with their hands, clanking their rings upon them to the beat. Momentarily Corbin let his eyes close, held the cold sherbet glass to his forehead, felt the pleasant restful sensation.

When he opened his eyes again it was as if he had been transported, was in the midst of a vision. A striking young woman in white frock with a red pachedi around her shoulders was approaching, then receding, doing a rapid brass-pot dance with lithe movements of waist and hip and unconscious of the eyes upon her—envious, wondrous, angry—her own eyes large, black, and deep, on her lips an indifferent even arrogant smile. Her features were markedly distinct from the other women's, so that she seemed an outsider of some sort: tall and thin, fair, with long face, pronounced nose, full lips. The circle of women had broken, a few of the younger ones were dancing solo, and in between them danced this siren. The tabalchi-drummer beat faster and the agile dancers kept time, feet thumping, hips gyrating without inhibition, breath drawn sharply, faces glistening with sweat.

Embarrassed at what looked like exhibitionism for the sake of the white man, the mukhi turned towards Corbin, and the Englishman took his cue. Thanking the leaders, wishing them a good evening, he walked out of the tent and started up the path to his house, in the company of an askari, just as a group of boys came running into the tent breathing out kerosene-smelling flames from their mouths.

This was the first of three long nights of celebrations, which lasted till dawn, followed by a few hours of slumbrous stillness before the next day's festivities began anew. Many visitors were in town. There were processions with banners and ceremonial costumes. The police did a daily march-past, and there was neverending food for all and sundry. It was an occasion for kofias and kanzus, turbans, frocks, and pachedis. The ADC felt good that all this happened in his domain; under, so to speak, his benefaction.

... This I suppose is administration at its most rewarding, a vote of confidence and honour for the Government's representative.

EACH AFTERNOON OF THE FESTIVAL there arrived for this lord an offering of the day's food in a covered brass tray. The first offering produced an open altercation with his cook and personal servant.

"Heathen food, your eminence," said Thomas, shaking his head dismissively.

"Let's uncover it and see, shall we?" said Corbin indulgently.

The aromas were strong, and his askaris hovered nearby in case the mzungu rejected the offering. But the mzungu was not going to let it go without a try.

"All the same, sir, I will bring English food. Christian. I give this witchcraft to the police."

"Uncover it, man!"

And so, for three nights Corbin went to bed satiated on unfamiliar cooking he quite took to in the circumstances, relieved of the dreadful "English" cuisine usually provided by his cook. Long into the night came the beat of the dhol and drums, the screeching of a harmonium, bringing visions of whirling circles, the girl in white.

How would he replace Thomas? The man had become insufferable; from the deferential and unassuming small man Corbin had met in Mombasa, he had turned into an overprotective and domineering mother hen. His disapprovals were many and openly stated, especially concerning Corbin's relations with the "heathen" townsfolk.

Every Sunday stuffed into a black suit and wearing a black hat on top of his glistening hair, Thomas made his way with much ceremony to attend service at the Mission station, where he had been welcomed, his Indianness notwithstanding. Corbin himself only paid short formal visits, but on several occasions Thomas brought for his ungrateful master scones that he had evidently pocketed.

23 October

I feel sorry for poor Thomas ... but to forgo saffroned lamb "biryani" for a curried shepherd's pie and a kedgeree he calls trifle.... He has sulked mightily, exaggerating his attentions to increase my guilt all the more. Once he read in my presence a letter from home, whose details he refused to divulge, becoming resentful and aggressive at my questions, and I wondered if the missive was genuine at all. I recall how he insinuated himself into my patronage the first time we met. I did not question who he was, not very deeply that is, assuming Mombasa, like all large ports, to have all sorts of characters washing upon its shores whose backgrounds are not worth the trouble of inquiry. He has even punished me, I fear, with curried concoctions that have done my stomach no good at all.

27 October

We have made up, and I have dutifully swallowed Thomas's shepherd's pie, nothing less. And I have learned something about his life. He was born Hari, and was brought up, he told me, in a mission centre outside Bombay, and recalled two ladies not unlike the two stalwarts of the MCA, one of whom he spoke of rather fondly. He has left a wife and child there. He joined me in Mombasa, he says, at an impulse, when he thought he had been recognized by a priest who had known him in India. How much of the story is true I dare not conjecture. East is East ...

Yesterday, an astounding event from which only now I sit down to recover. The "happiness" had been over for two days, the last of the visitors were leaving. The local Indians dutifully went about their business. It was approaching noon, and I began drafting a reply to a query regarding our police contingent. (It seems Government House wants assurance of the preparedness of administrative centres for emergencies such as sudden attacks by the natives.) Suddenly there came shouts, sounds of scuffling and violent quarrelling outside. At first I only momentarily looked up. The askaris know their job (as I was in the process of saying in my memo). But something, the significance of which I was about to discover, made me get up and step out onto the verandah. What I saw was a brawl in progress outside the post office, involving none other than my servant, Thomas, an utterance from whom must have drawn me out. The sounds of the scuffle, with promise of general excitement and diversion, had travelled sufficiently far by now—the first spectators were already racing up the hill. I might have been amused, telling the askaris to get on with it, but this time I was irritated and walked down to the scene, barely beating the crowd to it.

Of the five men involved in the brawl, two were askaris barely holding on to a burly young Indian man, who stopped struggling at the sight of me. As if on cue, Thomas turned and saw me approach, which having done, he quite unnecessarily took hold of one of the Indian's ears and said rather ridiculously, "German spy, eminence."

"Enough," I said, and curtly asked the postmaster, who made up the fifth, why he wasn't at his job, and what this childish matata was about.

"Wasn't I on duty when this pig teased me?" he said.

"Mfalme!" roared the Indian at this provocation. "My lord, it was they who insulted me." He would have charged at someone had he not been under restraint by the askaris.

There followed an exchange, the foulness of which did not endear this Indian to my heart at all. He is called Pipa, I learned, and is a most surly sort. He has short-cropped hair on a large round head that gives him the appearance somewhat of a dolt. His clothes—shirt, trousers, and shoes—are quite respectable, so he appears to be a man of some means.

Pipa, it seemed, had come from German East for the celebrations. The morning after they ended he took to the post office a sack of mail, which he had brought with him from across the border. The postmaster showed annoyance, naturally, at this unusual quantity of mail. Thomas, hovering nearby, started scolding and abusing Pipa, who gave him a box on the ears.

I gave orders for Pipa to be put away in the lockup for the day, asked Thomas to go about his duties, and accompanied by two askaris proceeded to examine the mail in the office.

Letters by Indians of German East to kinfolk in Bombay and Porbandar and assorted villages in India—"Desh," as they call the home country—were understandable; as were letters to relations in Voi and Mombasa and Nairobi. They are, after all, subjects of the King, and their reliance on the British government for this most important service was touching. But most irregular were 3 letters from the Oberleutnant of Moshi Fort to Germans on our side. I opened all the letters. Most of them were in Gujarati or Swahili; a handful were in English and there was one in Greek. I allowed them to go with the regular mail. They were, of course, correctly stamped. I will send the German letters, appended with my translations, to Voi, though they seem harmless. One was for hand delivery to a Herr Lenz in

Mbuyuni, through which Pipa would pass on his way to Voi. He has to be watched, but I cannot hold him.

28 October, 7 A.M.

About the Pipa affair—

Last night the Shamsis had mosque (as usual). Considerably less singing, much discussion, the purport of which I had no doubt. I was resolved to be firm—the young man had to be taught a lesson. He had after all assaulted my servant—for whom … I have no great love but who after all is of my household. Later I heard a commotion outside, approaching up the hill, then coming to a halt not far off. The booted steps of the watchman outside on the verandah were reassuring. Suddenly the door was flung open. A young woman, head covered, walked in and fell at my feet. Behind her stood the helpless askari.

(Later)

"MHESHIMIWA," she said, "Great Sir," and looked at me with pleading eyes. (I was on my feet in surprise.)

She was the girl I had seen dancing at the celebrations. Even in everyday, simple attire she was striking in her looks. Her head-cover had fallen back and there was a wild look about her. She was speaking in Swahili and I could not wholly understand her, but I surmised that she was the betrothed of the lout Pipa whom I had locked up. She was at my feet yet had had the nerve to burst in past my askari, for which she had not even apologized. I was not seeking her apology though, and reassured her about her young man. She smiled a little, in thanks, and left. As I watched her from a window I observed a man come out from the shadows and follow her.

I stood reflecting on the inscrutability of the alien—how there must be matters of which one will never have an inkling—when there was a gentle knock on the door. Now the whole community picks up courage, I thought. I called out, and the mukhi walked in, fez in hand. I took a chair, and offered him one. "Bwana Corbin," he said.

He is a man of the world, his position involves travel. In spite of his humble and respectful approaches, he no doubt knows the place of an Assistant District Commissioner in the government's hierarchy. Powerless though the individual Indian is beside a European, as a community they have a voice that is heard. In Nairobi, as the *Herald* regularly reports, they are making a lot of noise; more than three-quarters of the country's business passes through their hands, in towns just as small as this one. And no less a personage than Mr. Churchill has supported their cause publicly. I reassured him, as I had the girl. The sergeant had been instructed to release the prisoner at ten o'clock. He thanked me. I offered him tea. My guardian angel Thomas showed displeasure, but hastened to the kitchen. The mukhi, having gone outside to pacify his community members, returned. Over tea I asked him in a friendly way if his community held themselves above government punishment even if they violated the law.

"Ah, Mr. Corbin.... But this was a small thing ..."

"Your man could be charged with spying," I said.

At this he was genuinely agitated "Mr. Corbin. He was given those letters. What could he have done? We are a subject people ..."

I laughed, and he joined me. I asked him what his people sought in this country, in the wilderness, so far from their own country and culture. "Peace and prosperity," he said. I repeated his words. "Yes, sir," he asserted, "with your protection. We seek but little. Already we have contributed to the Uganda Railway."

He did not remind me that he had an African wife, and children from her, of his commitment to Africa, or of the troubles in India from which his community was running. His discretion and reserve impressed me. In him his people have a good leader, I told him. The British government was pleased with his community, I said.

I asked him about the girl. Her name was Mariamu, he said. She lived with her mother and stepfather. She was his niece, moreover; her mother was his own sister Kulsa.

"Who is the stepfather?" I asked.

"Simba," he answered.

The word means "lion" and was obviously a nickname. I asked him who this "lion" was and he laughed. "Rashid the transporter," he said.

Apparently this man Rashid was a former railway coolie (therefore strictly speaking not one of the Shamsis) who like many others deserted his job when the man-eating lions at Tsavo seemed invincible, picking off the labourers at will. To the terrified Indians, their tormentors were not real lions at all but the spirits of those who had perished in the desert. How to explain, the mukhi said, when one minute a man is sitting next to you by a fire, inside a four-foot-high protective stockade, and the next minute you see his place empty and hear his screams in the distance? Or when a companion is snatched from the top of a tree where he's taken his bed, and lions are not supposed to climb?

"According to the coolies," the mukhi said, "the spirits of the desert were offended by the railway of the mzungu, and came to attack them as lions."

"Then this Rashid must be called Simba in jest," I offered.

The mukhi smiled assent. "Now he handles mules. That's what he knows. But he's a good provider ... and a very protective father. He's fond of the girl—perhaps too fond."

"Would he take to following the girl about?" I asked.

To which he responded, "Bwana Corbin is a keen observer."

"The girl is wild," the mukhi said. "She's inclined to go away by herself and the family is worried."

I wondered if it was she whom I had seen running in the distance the day I came here to take up my post. She had been coming from the direction of the river.

"And she is this young man Pipa's betrothed?" I asked.

"Yes, sir. He came to set the wedding date. He, too, has problems, but inshallah, God willing, they can give happiness to each other."

"And when is the wedding to take place?"

"In a few months, Bwana Corbin."

Pipa, meanwhile, will return to Moshi, where he has his shop and his mother.

THE INDIANS WERE GRATEFUL for the lenient treatment of the young man, and they showed their gratitude in abundance. Crates of tinned milk, a bottle of whisky, socks, underwear, soap, landed in Corbin's home. One result of the whole incident was his discovery of Thomas's practice of extorting favours from the businessmen using threats of influencing the ADC against them. After receiving a severe dressing down, Thomas fled.

It was some days later that Corbin found out that his servant had gone and joined the Mission station. Word got around that Bwana Corbin was looking for a new cook, and one day a plate of fresh chapatti arrived at his doorstep, which he ate with much relish. The askari told him it had been left by the girl Mariamu. The offering was repeated every Thursday, the eve of Juma, an auspicious day when orphans and beggars were fed.

Rohinton Mistry

Rohinton Mistry is the author of a collection of short stories, *Tales from Firozsha Baag* (1987), and three novels that were all shortlisted for The Booker Prize: *Such a Long Journey* (1991), *A Fine Balance* (1995), and *Family Matters* (2002). His fiction has won many awards, including The Giller Prize, the Commonwealth Writers' Prize Best Book Award, the Governor General's Literary Awards, the Canada-Australia Prize, the Los Angeles Times Book Prize for Fiction, and the Kiriyama Prize for Fiction.

In translation, his work has been published in more than twenty-five languages.

A Fine Balance

BY ROHINTON MISTRY

Winner 1995

≈

Prologue: 1975

The morning express bloated with passengers slowed to a crawl, then lurched forward suddenly, as though to resume full speed. The train's brief deception jolted its riders. The bulge of humans hanging out of the doorway distended perilously, like a soap bubble at its limit.

Inside the compartment, Maneck Kohlah held on to the overhead railing, propped up securely within the crush. He felt someone's elbow knock his textbooks from his hand. In the seats nearby, a thin young fellow was catapulted into the arms of the man opposite him. Maneck's textbooks fell upon them.

"Ow!" said the young fellow, as volume one slammed into his back.

Laughing, he and his uncle untangled themselves. Ishvar Darji, who had a disfigured left cheek, helped his nephew out of his lap and back onto the seat. "Everything all right, Om?"

"Apart from the dent in my back, everything is all right," said Omprakash Darji, picking up the two books covered in brown paper. He hefted them in his slender hands and looked around to find who had dropped them.

Maneck acknowledged ownership. The thought of his heavy textbooks thumping that frail spine made him shudder. He remembered the sparrow he had killed with a stone, years ago; afterwards, it had made him sick.

His apology was frantic. "Very sorry, the books slipped and—"

"Not to worry," said Ishvar. "Wasn't your fault." To his nephew he added, "Good thing it didn't happen in reverse, hahn? If I fell in your lap, my weight would crack your bones." They laughed again, Maneck too, to supplement his apology.

Ishvar Darji was not a stout man; it was the contrast with Omprakash's skinny limbs that gave rise to their little jokes about his size. The wisecracks originated sometimes with one and sometimes the other. When they had their evening meal, Ishvar would be sure to spoon out a larger portion onto his nephew's enamel plate; at a roadside dhaba, he would wait till Omprakash went for water, or to the latrine, then swiftly scoop some of his own food onto the other leaf.

If Omprakash protested, Ishvar would say, "What will they think in our village when we return? That I starved my nephew in the city and ate all the food myself? Eat, eat! Only way to save my honour is by fattening you!"

"Don't worry," Omprakash would tease back. "If your honour weighs even half as much as you, that will be ample."

Omprakash's physique, however, defied his uncle's efforts and stayed matchstick thin. Their fortunes, too, stubbornly retained a lean and hungry aspect, and a triumphal return to the village remained a distant dream.

The southbound express slowed again. With a pneumatic hiss, the bogies clanked to a halt. The train was between stations. Its air brakes continued to exhale wheezily for a few moments before dying out.

Omprakash looked through the window to determine where they had stopped. Rough shacks stood beyond the railroad fence, alongside a ditch running with raw sewage. Children were playing a game with sticks and stones. An excited puppy danced around them, trying to join in. Nearby, a shirtless man was milking a cow. They could have been anywhere.

The acrid smell of a dung-fire drifted towards the train. Just ahead, a crowd had gathered near the level-crossing. A few men jumped off the train and began walking down the tracks.

"Hope we reach in time," said Omprakash. "If someone gets there before us, we're finished for sure."

Maneck Kohlah asked if they had far to go. Ishvar named the station. "Oh, that's the same one I want," said Maneck, fingering his sparse moustache.

Hoping to spot a watch dial, Ishvar looked up into a thicket of wrists growing ceilingward. "Time, please?" he asked someone over his shoulder. The man shot his cuff stylishly and revealed his watch: a quarter to nine.

"Come on, yaar, move!" said Omprakash, slapping the seat between his thighs.

"Not as obedient as the bullocks in our village, is it?" said his uncle, and Maneck laughed. Ishvar added it was true—ever since he was a child, their village had never lost a bullock-cart race when there were competitions on festival days.

"Give the train a dose of opium and it will run like the bullocks," said Omprakash.

A combseller, twanging the plastic teeth of a large comb, pushed his way through the crowded compartment. People grumbled and snarled at him, resenting the bothersome presence.

"Oi!" said Omprakash to get his attention.

"Plastic hairband, unbreakable, plastic hairclip, flower shape, butterfly shape, colourful comb, unbreakable." The combseller recited in a half-hearted monotone, uncertain whether this was a real customer or just a joker passing the time. "Big comb and small comb, pink, orange, maroon, green, blue, yellow comb—unbreakable."

Omprakash gave them a test run through his hair before selecting a red specimen, pocket-sized. He dug into his trousers and extracted a coin. The combseller suffered hostile elbows and shoulders while searching for change. He used his shirtsleeve to wipe hair oil off the rejected combs, then returned them to his satchel, keeping in his hand the big dual-toothed one to resume his soft twanging through the compartment.

"What happened to the yellow comb you had?" asked Ishvar.

"Broke in two."

"How?"

"It was in my back pocket. I sat on it."

"That's the wrong place for a comb. It's meant for your head, Om, not your bottom." He always called his nephew Om, using Omprakash only when he was upset with him.

"If it was *your* bottom, the comb would have smashed into a hundred pieces," returned his nephew, and Ishvar laughed. His disfigured left cheek was no hindrance, standing firm like a mooring around which his smiles could safely ripple.

He chucked Omprakash under the chin. Most of the time their ages—forty-six and seventeen—were a misleading indicator of their actual relationship. "Smile, Om. Your angry mouth does not suit your hero hairstyle." He winked at Maneck to include him in the fun. "With a puff like that, lots of girls will be after you. But don't worry, Om, I'll select a nice wife for you. A woman big and strong, with flesh enough for two."

Omprakash grinned and administered a flourish to his hair with the new comb. The train still showed no sign of moving. The men who had wandered outside came back with news that yet another body had been found by the tracks, near the level-crossing. Maneck edged towards the door to listen. A nice, quick way to go, he thought, as long as the train had struck the person squarely.

"Maybe it has to do with the Emergency," said someone.

"What emergency?"

"Prime Minister made a speech on the radio early this morning. Something about country being threatened from inside."

"Sounds like one more government tamasha."

"Why does everybody have to choose the railway tracks only for dying?" grumbled another. "No consideration for people like us. Murder, suicide, Naxalite-terrorist killing, police-custody death—everything ends up delaying the trains. What is wrong with poison or tall buildings or knives?"

The long-anticipated rumble at last rippled through the compartments, and the train shivered down its long steel spine. Relief lit the passengers' faces. As the compartments trundled past the level-crossing, everyone craned to see the cause of their delay. Three uniformed policemen stood by the hastily covered corpse awaiting its journey to the morgue. Some passengers touched their foreheads or put their hands together and murmured, "Ram, Ram."

MANECK KOHLAH DESCENDED behind the uncle and nephew, and they exited the platform together. "Excuse me," he said, taking a letter from his pocket. "I am new in the city, can you tell me how to get to this address?"

"You are asking the wrong people," said Ishvar without reading it. "We are also new here."

But Omprakash glanced at the letter and said, "Look, it's the same name!"

Ishvar pulled a square of ragged paper out of his own pocket and compared it. His nephew was right, there it was: Dina Dalal, followed by the address.

Omprakash regarded Maneck with sudden hostility. "Why are you going to Dina Dalal? Are you a tailor?"

"Me, tailor? No, she is my mother's friend."

Ishvar tapped his nephew's shoulder. "See, simply you were panicking. Come on, let's find the building."

Maneck did not understand what they meant, till Ishvar explained outside the station. "You see, Om and I are tailors. Dina Dalal has work for two tailors. We are going to apply."

"And you thought I was running there to steal your job." Maneck smiled. "Don't worry, I am just a student. Dina Dalal and my mother used to be in school together. She's letting me stay with her for a few months, that's all."

They asked a paanwalla for directions, and walked down the street that was pointed out. Omprakash was still a little suspicious. "If you are staying with her for a few months, where is your trunk, your belongings? Only two books you have?"

"Today I'm just going to meet her. I will shift my things from the college hostel next month."

They passed a beggar slumped upon a small wooden platform fitted with castors, which raised him four inches off the ground. His fingers and thumbs were missing, and his legs were amputated almost to the buttocks. "O babu, ek paisa day-ray!" he sang, shaking a tin can between his bandaged palms. "O babu! Hai babu! Aray babu, ek paisa day-ray!"

"That's one of the worst I've seen since coming to the city," said Ishvar, and the others agreed. Omprakash paused to drop a coin in the tin.

They crossed the road, asking again for directions. "I've been living in this city for two months," said Maneck, "but it's so huge and confusing. I can recognize only some big streets. The little lanes all look the same."

"We have been here six months and still have the same problem. In the beginning we were completely lost. The first time, we couldn't even get on a train—two or three went by before we learned how to push."

Maneck said he hated it here, and could not wait to return to his home in the mountains, next year, when he finished college.

"We have also come for a short time only," said Ishvar. "To earn some money, then go back to our village. What is the use of such a big city? Noise and crowds, no place to live, water scarce, garbage everywhere. Terrible."

"Our village is far from here," said Omprakash. "Takes a whole day by train—morning till night—to reach it."

"And reach it, we will," said Ishvar. "Nothing is as fine as one's native place."

"My home is in the north," said Maneck. "Takes a day and night, plus another day, to get there. From the window of our house you can see snow-covered mountain peaks."

"A river runs near our village," said Ishvar. "You can see it shining, and hear it sing. It's a beautiful place."

They walked quietly for a while, occupied with home thoughts. Omprakash broke the silence by pointing out a watermelon-sherbet stand. "Wouldn't that be nice, on such a hot day."

The vendor stirred his ladle in the tub, tinkling chunks of ice afloat in a sea of dark red. "Let's have some," said Maneck. "It looks delicious."

"Not for us," said Ishvar quickly. "We had a big breakfast this morning," and Omprakash erased the longing from his face.

"Okay," said Maneck doubtfully, ordering one large glass. He studied the tailors who stood with eyes averted, not looking at the tempting tub or his frosted glass. He saw their tired faces, how poor their clothes were, the worn-out chappals.

He drank half and said, "I'm full. You want it?"

They shook their heads.

"It will go to waste."

"Okay, yaar, in that case," said Omprakash, and took the sherbet. He gulped some, then passed it to his uncle.

Ishvar drained the glass and returned it to the vendor. "That was so tasty," he said, beaming with pleasure. "It was very kind of you to share it with us, we really enjoyed it, thank you." His nephew gave him a disapproving look to tone it down.

How much gratitude for a little sherbet, thought Maneck, how starved they seemed for ordinary kindness.

THE VERANDAH DOOR had a brass nameplate: *Mr. & Mrs. Rustom K. Dalal*, the letters enriched by years of verdigris. Dina Dalal answered their ring and accepted the scrap of crumpled paper, recognizing her own handwriting.

"You are tailors?"

"Hahnji," said Ishvar, nodding vigorously. All three entered the verandah at her invitation and stood awkwardly.

The verandah, which used to be an open gallery, had been converted into an extra room when Dina Dalal's late husband was still a child—his parents had decided it would be a playroom to supplement the tiny flat. The portico was bricked and fitted with an iron-grilled window.

"But I need only two tailors," said Dina Dalal.

"Excuse me, I'm not a tailor. My name is Maneck Kohlah." He stepped forward from behind Ishvar and Omprakash.

"Oh, you are Maneck! Welcome! Sorry, I couldn't recognize you. It's been years since I last saw your mummy, and you I have never, ever seen."

She left the tailors on the verandah and took him inside, into the front room. "Can you wait here for a few minutes while I deal with those two?"

"Sure."

Maneck took in the shabby furnishings around him: the battered sofa, two chairs with fraying seats, a scratched teapoy, a dining table with a cracked and faded rexine tablecloth. She mustn't live here, he decided, this was probably a family business, a boarding house. The walls were badly in need of paint. He played with the discoloured plaster blotches, the way he did with clouds, imagining animals and landscapes. Dog shaking hands. Hawk diving sharply. Man with walking-stick climbing mountain.

On the verandah, Dina Dalal ran a hand over her black hair, as yet uninvaded by grey, and turned her attention to the tailors. At forty-two, her forehead was still smooth, and sixteen years spent fending for herself had not hardened the looks which, a long time ago, used to make her brother's friends vie to impress her.

She asked for names and tailoring experience. The tailors claimed to know everything about women's clothes. "We can even take measurements straight from the customer's body and make any fashion you like," said Ishvar confidently, doing all the talking while Omprakash nodded away.

"For this job, there will be no customers to measure," she explained. "The sewing will be straight from paper patterns. Each week you have to make two dozen, three dozen, whatever the company wants, in the same style."

"Child's play," said Ishvar. "But we'll do it."

"What about you?" she addressed Omprakash, whose look was disdainful. "You have not said a word."

"My nephew speaks only when he disagrees," said Ishvar. "His silence is a good sign."

She liked Ishvar's face, the type that put people at ease and encouraged conversation. But there was the other tight-lipped fellow, who frightened away the words. His chin was too small for his features, though when he smiled everything seemed in proportion.

She stated the terms of employment: they would have to bring their own sewing-machines; all sewing would be piecework. "The more dresses you make, the more you earn," she said, and Ishvar agreed that that was fair. Rates would be fixed according to the complexity of each pattern. The hours were from eight a.m. to six p.m.—less than that would not do, though they were welcome to work longer. And there would be no smoking or paan-chewing on the job.

"Paan we don't chew only," said Ishvar. "But sometimes we like to smoke a beedi."

"You will have to smoke it outside."

The conditions were acceptable. "What is the address of your shop?" asked Ishvar. "Where do we bring the sewing-machines?"

"Right here. When you come next week, I will show you where to put them, in the back room."

"Okayji, thank you, we will definitely come on Monday." They waved to Maneck as they left. "We will see you again soon, hanh."

"Sure," said Maneck, waving back. Noticing Dina Dalal's silent inquiry, he explained about their meeting on the train.

"You must be careful who you talk to," she said. "Never know what kind of crooks you might run into. This is not your little hamlet in the mountains."

"They seemed very nice."

"Hmm, yes," she said, reserving judgement. Then she apologized again for assuming he was a tailor. "I could not see you properly because you were standing behind them, my eyes are weak." How silly of me, she thought, mistaking this lovely boy for a bowlegged tailor. And so sturdy too. Must be the famous mountain air they talk about, the healthy food and water.

She peered a little closer, tilting her head to one side. "It has been over twenty years, but I can recognize your mummy in your face. You know Aban and I were in school together."

"Yes," he said, uncomfortable under her intense scrutiny. "Mummy told me in her letter. She also wanted to let you know I'll move in from next month, and she'll mail you the rent cheque."

"Yes, yes, that's all right," she said, dismissing his concern about the details and drifting again into the past. "Real little terrors we used to be in our school-days. And a third girl, Zenobia. When we three were together, it was trouble with a capital t, the teachers would say." The memory brought a wistful smile to her face. "Anyway, let me show you my house, and your room."

"You live here as well?"

"Where else?" As she led him through the dingy little flat, she asked what he was taking at college.

"Refrigeration and air-conditioning."

"I hope you will do something about this hot weather then, make my home more comfortable."

He smiled feebly, saddened by the place in which she resided. Not much better than the college hostel, he thought. And yet, he was looking forward to it. Anything would do, after what had happened there. He shuddered and tried to think of something else.

"This one will be your room."

"It's very nice. Thank you, Mrs. Dalal."

There was a cupboard in one corner with a scratched, misshapen suitcase on top. A small desk stood beside the cupboard. Here, as in the front room, the ceiling was dark and flaking, the walls discoloured, missing chunks of plaster in several places. Other stark patches, recently cemented, stood out like freshly healed wounds. Two single beds lay at right angles along the walls. He wondered if she would sleep in the same room.

"I will move one bed into the other room for myself."

He looked through the door beyond and glimpsed a room tinier and in worse condition, crowded by a cupboard (also with a suitcase on top), a rickety table, two chairs, and three rusting trunks stacked on a trestle.

"I am turning you out of your own room," mumbled Maneck, the surroundings depressing him rapidly.

"Don't be silly." Her tone was brisk. "I wanted a paying guest, and it is my great good luck to get a nice Parsi boy—the son of my schoolfriend."

"It's very kind of you, Mrs. Dalal."

"And that's another thing. You must call me Dina Aunty."

Maneck nodded.

"You can bring your things here any time. If you are not happy with the hostel, this room is ready—we don't have to wait for a special date next month."

"No, it's all right, but thank you, Mrs.—"

"Ahn, careful."

"I mean, Dina Aunty." They smiled.

WHEN MANECK LEFT HER FLAT, she began pacing the room, suddenly restless, as though about to embark on a long voyage. No need now to visit her brother and beg for next month's rent. She took a deep breath. Once again, her fragile independence was preserved.

Tomorrow she would bring home the first batch of sewing from Au Revoir Exports.

City by the Sea

Dina Dalal seldom indulged in looking back at her life with regret or bitterness, or questioning why things had turned out the way they had, cheating her of the bright future everyone had predicted for her when she was in school, when her name was still Dina Shroff. And if she did sink into one of these rare moods, she quickly swam out of it. What was the point of repeating the story over and over and over, she asked herself—it always ended the same way; whichever corridor she took, she wound up in the same room.

Dina's father had been a doctor, a GP with a modest practice who followed the Hippocratic oath somewhat more passionately than others of his profession. During the early years of Dr. Shroff's career, his devotion to his work was diagnosed, by peers, family members, and senior physicians, as typical of youthful zeal and vigour. "How refreshing, this enthusiasm of the young," they smiled, nodding sagely, confident that time would douse the fires of idealism with a healthy dose of cynicism and family responsibilities.

But marriage, and the arrival of a son, followed eleven years later by a daughter, changed nothing for Dr. Shroff. Time only sharpened the imbalance between his fervour to ease suffering and his desire to earn a comfortable income.

"How disappointing," said friends and relatives, shaking their heads. "Such high hopes we had for him. And he keeps slaving like a clerk, like a fanatic, refusing to enjoy life. Poor Mrs. Shroff. Never a vacation, never a party—no fun at all in her existence."

At fifty-one, when most GPs would have begun considering options like working half-time, hiring an inexpensive junior, or even selling the practice in favour of early retirement, Dr. Shroff had neither the bank balance nor the temperament to permit such indulgences. Instead, he volunteered to lead a campaign of medical graduates bound for districts in the interior. There, where typhoid and cholera, unchallenged by science or technology, were still reaping their routine harvest of villagers, Dr. Shroff would try to seize the deadly sickles or, at the very least, to blunt them.

But Mrs. Shroff undertook a different sort of campaign: to dissuade her husband from going into what she felt were the jaws of certain death. She attempted to coach Dina with words to sway her father. After all, Dina, at twelve, was Daddy's darling. Mrs. Shroff knew that her son, Nusswan, could be of no help in this enterprise. Enlisting him would have ruined any chance of changing her husband's mind.

The turning point in the father-and-son relationship had come seven years ago, on Nusswan's sixteenth birthday. Uncles and aunts had been invited to dinner, and someone said, "Well, Nusswan, you will soon be studying to become a doctor, just like your father."

"I don't want to be a doctor," Nusswan answered. "I'll be going into business—import and export."

Some of the uncles and aunts nodded approvingly. Others recoiled in mock horror, turning to Dr. Shroff. "Is this true? No father-son partnership?"

"Of course it's true," he said. "My children are free to do whatever they please."

But five-year-old Dina had seen the hurt on her father's face before he could hide it. She ran to him and clambered onto his lap. "Daddy, I want to be a doctor, just like you, when I grow up."

Everyone laughed and applauded, and said, Smart little girl, knows how to get what she wants. Later, they whispered that the son was obviously not made of the same solid stuff as the father—no ambition, wouldn't amount to much.

Dina had repeated her wish in the years to come, continuing to regard her father as some kind of god who gave people good health, who struggled against illness, and who, sometimes, succeeded in temporarily thwarting death. And Dr. Shroff was delighted with his bright child. On parents' night at the convent school, the principal and teachers always had the highest praise for her. She would succeed if she wanted to, Dr. Shroff knew it for certain.

Mrs. Shroff also knew, for certain, that her daughter was the one to recruit in the campaign against Dr. Shroff's foolish philanthropic plan of working in remote, Godforsaken villages. But Dina refused to cooperate; she did not approve of devious means to keep her beloved father home.

Then Mrs. Shroff resorted to other methods, using not money or his personal safety or his family to persuade him, for she knew these would fail hopelessly. Instead, she invoked his patients, claiming he was abandoning them, old and frail and helpless. "What will they do if you go so far away? They trust you and rely on you. How can you be so cruel? You have no idea how much you mean to them."

"No, that is not the point," said Dr. Shroff. He was familiar with the anfractuous arguments that her love for him could prompt her to wield. Patiently he explained there were GPs galore in the city who could take care of the assorted aches and pains—where he was going, the people had no one. He comforted her that it was only a temporary assignment, hugging and kissing her much more than was usual for him. "I promise to be back soon," he said. "Before you even grow used to my absence."

But Dr. Shroff could not keep his promise. Three weeks into the medical campaign he was dead, not from typhoid or cholera, but from a cobra's bite, far from the lifesaving reach of antivenins.

Mrs. Shroff received the news calmly. People said it was because she was a doctor's wife, more familiar with death than other mortals. They reasoned that Dr. Shroff must have often carried such tidings to her regarding his own patients, thus preparing her for the inevitable.

When she took brisk charge of the funeral arrangements, managing everything with superb efficiency, people wondered if there was not something a little abnormal about her behaviour. Between disbursing funds from her handbag for the various expenses, she accepted condolences, comforted grieving relatives, tended the oil lamp at the head of Dr. Shroff's bed, washed and ironed her white sari, and made sure there was a supply of incense and sandalwood in the house. She personally instructed the cook about the special vegetarian meal for the next day.

After the full four days of death ceremonies, Dina was still crying. Mrs. Shroff, who was busy tallying the prayer-bungalow charges from the Towers of Silence, said briskly, "Come, my daughter, be sensible now. Daddy would not like this." So Dina did her best to control herself.

Then Mrs. Shroff continued absentmindedly, writing out the cheque. "You could have stopped him if you wanted. He would have listened to you," she said.

Dina's sobs burst out with renewed intensity. In addition to the grief for her father, her tears now included anger towards her mother, even hatred. It would take her a few months to understand that there was no malice or accusation contained in what had been said, just a sad and simple statement of fact as seen by her mother.

Six months after Dr. Shroff's death, after being the pillar that everyone could lean on, Mrs. Shroff gradually began to crumble. Retreating from daily life, she took very little interest in the running of her household or in her own person.

It made little difference to Nusswan, who was twenty-three and busy planning his own future. But Dina, at twelve, could have done with a parent for a few more years. She missed her father dreadfully. Her mother's withdrawal made it much worse.

NUSSWAN SHROFF HAD EARNED his own living as a businessman for two years prior to his father's death. He was still single, living at home, saving his money while searching for a suitable flat and a suitable wife. With his father's passing and his mother's reclusion, he realized that the pursuit of a flat was unnecessary, and a wife, urgent.

He now assumed the role of head of the family, and legal guardian to Dina. All their relatives agreed this was as it should be. They praised his selfless decision, admitting they had been wrong about his capabilities. He also took over the family finances, promising that his mother and sister would want for nothing; he would look after them out of his own salary. But, even as he spoke, he knew there was no need for this. The money from the sale of Dr. Shroff's dispensary was sufficient.

Nusswan's first decision as head of the family was to cut back on the hired help. The cook, who came for half the day and prepared the two main meals, was kept on; Lily, the live-in servant, was let go. "We cannot continue in the same luxury as before," he declared. "I just can't afford the wages."

Mrs. Shroff expressed some doubt about the change. "Who will do the cleaning? My hands and feet don't work like before."

"Don't worry, Mamma, we will all share it. You can do easy things, like dusting the furniture. We can wash our own cups and saucers, surely. And Dina is a young girl, full of energy. It will be good for her, teach her how to look after a home."

"Yes, maybe you are right," said Mrs. Shroff, vaguely convinced of the need for money-saving measures.

But Dina knew there was more to it. The week before, while passing the kitchen on her way to the WC well past midnight, she had noticed her brother with the ayah: Lily sitting on one end of the kitchen table, her feet resting on the edge; Nusswan, his pyjamas around his ankles, stood between Lily's thighs, clasping her hips to him. Dina watched his bare buttocks with sleepy curiosity, then crept back to bed without using the toilet, her cheeks flushed. But she must have lingered a moment too long, for Nusswan had seen her.

Not a word was spoken about it. Lily departed (with a modest bonus, unbeknownst to Mrs. Shroff), tearfully declaring that she would never find as nice a family to work for ever again. Dina felt sorry for her, and also despised her.

Then the new household arrangement got under way. Everyone made an honest effort. The experiment in self-reliance seemed like fun. "It's a little like going camping," said Mrs. Shroff.

"That's the spirit," said Nusswan.

With the passing of days, Dina's chores began to increase. As a token of his participation, Nusswan continued to wash his cup, saucer, and breakfast plate before going to work. Beyond that, he did nothing.

One morning, after swallowing his last gulp of tea, he said, "I'm very late today, Dina. Please wash my things."

"I'm not your servant! Wash your own dirty plates!" Weeks of pent-up resentment came gushing. "You said we would each do our own work! All your stinking things you leave for me!"

"Listen to the little tigress," said Nusswan, amused.

"You mustn't speak like that to your big brother," chided Mrs. Shroff gently. "Remember, we must share and share alike."

"He's cheating! He doesn't do any work! I do everything!"

Nusswan hugged his mother: "Bye-bye, Mamma," and gave Dina a friendly pat on the shoulder to make up. She shrank from him. "The tigress is still angry," he said and left for the office.

Mrs. Shroff tried to soothe Dina, promising to discuss it later with Nusswan, maybe convince him to hire a part-time ayah, but her resolve melted within hours. Matters continued as before. As weeks went by, instead of restoring fairness in the household, she began turning into one of the chores on her daughter's ever-growing list.

Now Mrs. Shroff had to be told what to do. When food was placed before her, she ate it, though it did her little good, for she kept losing weight. She had to be reminded to bathe and change her clothes. If toothpaste was squeezed out and handed to her on the brush, she brushed her teeth. For Dina, the most unpleasant task was helping her mother wash her hair—it fell out in clumps on the bathroom floor, and more followed when she combed it for her.

Once every month, Mrs. Shroff attended her husband's prayers at the fire-temple. She said it gave her great comfort to hear the elderly Dustoor Framji's soothing tones supplicating for her husband's soul. Dina missed school to accompany her mother, worried about her wandering off somewhere.

Before commencing the ceremony, Dustoor Framji unctuously shook Mrs. Shroff's hand and gave Dina a prolonged hug of the sort he reserved for girls and young women. His reputation for squeezing and fondling had earned him the title of Dustoor Daab-Chaab, along with the hostility of his colleagues, who resented not so much his actions but his lack of subtlety, his refusal to disguise his embraces with fatherly or spiritual concern. They feared that one day he would go too far, drool over his victim or something, and disgrace the fire-temple.

Dina squirmed in his grasp as he patted her head, rubbed her neck, stroked her back and pressed himself against her. He had a very short beard, stubble that resembled flakes of grated coconut, and it scraped her cheeks and forehead. He released her just when she had summoned enough courage to tear her trapped body from his arms.

After the fire-temple, for the rest of the day at home Dina tried to make her mother talk, asking her advice about housework or recipes, and when that failed, about Daddy, and the days of their newlywed lives. Faced with her mother's dreamy silences, Dina felt helpless. Soon, her concern for her mother was tempered by the instinct of youth which held her back—she would surely receive her portion of grief and sorrow in due course, there was no need to take on the burden prematurely.

And Mrs. Shroff spoke in monosyllables or sighs, staring into Dina's face for answers. As for dusting the furniture, she could never proceed beyond wiping the picture frame containing her husband's graduation photograph. She spent most of her time gazing out the window.

Nusswan preferred to regard his mother's disintegration as a widow's appropriate renunciation, wherein she was sloughing off the dross of life to concentrate on spiritual matters. He focused his attention on the raising of Dina. The thought of the enormous responsibility resting on his shoulders worried him ceaselessly.

He had always perceived his father to be a strict disciplinarian; he had stood in awe of him, had even been a little frightened of him. If he was to fill his father's shoes, he would have to induce the same fear in others, he decided, and prayed regularly for courage and guidance in his task. He confided to the relatives—the uncles and aunts—that Dina's defiance, her stubbornness, was driving him crazy, and only the Almighty's help gave him the strength to go forward in his duty.

His sincerity touched them. They promised to pray for him too. "Don't worry, Nusswan, everything will be all right. We will light a lamp at the fire-temple."

Heartened by their support, Nusswan began taking Dina with him to the fire-temple once a week. There, he thrust a stick of sandalwood in her hand and whispered fiercely in her ear, "Now pray properly—ask Dadaji to make you a good girl, ask Him to make you obedient."

While she bowed before the sanctum, he travelled along the outer wall hung with pictures of various dustoors and high priests. He glided from display to display, stroking the garlands, hugging the frames, kissing the glass, and ending with the very tall picture of Zarathustra to which he glued his lips for a full minute. Then, from the vessel of ashes placed in the sanctum's doorway, he smeared a pinch on his forehead, another bit across the throat, and undid his top two shirt buttons to rub a fistful over his chest.

Like talcum powder, thought Dina, watching from the corner of her eye, from her bowed position, straining to keep from laughing. She did not raise her head till he had finished his antics.

"Did you pray properly?" he demanded when they were outside.

She nodded.

"Good. Now all the bad thoughts will leave your head, you will feel peace and quiet in your heart."

DINA WAS NO LONGER ALLOWED to spend time at her friends' houses during the holidays. "There is no need to," said Nusswan. "You see them every day in school." They could visit her after being granted his permission, but this was not much fun since he always hovered around.

Once, he overheard her in the next room with her friend Zenobia, making fun of his teeth. It only served to confirm his belief that the little devils needed monitoring. Zenobia was saying he looked like a horse.

"Yes, a horse with cheap dentures," added Dina.

"An elephant would be proud of that much ivory," continued Zenobia, raising the stakes.

They were helpless with laughter when he entered the room. He fixed each one with a black stare before turning away with menacing slowness, leaving behind silence and misery. Yes, it worked, he realized with surprise and triumph—fear worked.

Nusswan had always been sensitive about his bad teeth and, in his late teens, had tried to get them straightened. Dina, only six or seven then, had teased him mercilessly. But the orthodontic treatment was too painful, and he abandoned it, complaining that with a doctor for a father, it was surprising his condition had not been taken care of in childhood. As evidence of partiality, he would point to Dina's perfect mouth.

Distressed by his hurt, their mother had tried to explain. "It's all my fault, son, I didn't know that children's teeth should be massaged daily, gently pressed inward. The old nurse at Dina's birth taught me the trick, but it was too late for you."

Nusswan had never been convinced. And now, after Dina's friend left, she paid the price. He asked her to repeat what was said. She did, boldly.

"You have always had the habit of blurting whatever comes into your loose mouth. But you are no longer a child. Someone has to teach you respect." He sighed, "It is my duty, I suppose," and without warning he began slapping her. He stopped when a cut opened her lower lip.

"You pig!" she wept. "You want to make me look ugly like you!" Whereupon, he got a ruler and whacked her wherever he could, as she ran around trying to escape the blows.

For once, Mrs. Shroff noticed that something was wrong. "Why are you crying, my daughter?"

"That stupid Dracula! He hit me and made me bleed!"

"Tch-tch, my poor child." She hugged Dina and returned to her seat by the window.

Two days after this row, Nusswan tried to make peace by bringing Dina a collection of ribbons. "They will look lovely in your plaits," he said.

She went to her school satchel, got out her arts-and-crafts scissors, and snipped the ribbons into small pieces.

"Look, Mamma!" he said, almost in tears. "Look at your vindictive daughter! My hard-earned money I spend on her, and this is the thanks."

The ruler became Nusswan's instrument of choice in his quest for discipline. His clothes were the most frequent cause of Dina's punishment. After washing, ironing, and folding them, she had to stack four separate piles in his cupboard: white shirts, coloured shirts, white trousers, coloured trousers.

Sometimes she would strategically place a pinstriped shirt with the whites, or liberate a pair of pants with a hound's-tooth check among the white trousers. Despite the beatings, she never tired of provoking him.

"The way she behaves, I feel that Sataan himself has taken refuge in her heart," he said wearily to the relatives who asked for updates. "Maybe I should just pack her off to a boarding school."

"No, no, don't take that drastic step," they pleaded. "Boarding school has been the ruination of many Parsi girls. Rest assured, God will repay you for your patience and devotion. And Dina will also thank you when she is old enough to understand it's for her own good." They went away murmuring the man was a saint—every girl should be fortunate enough to have a brother like Nusswan.

His spirit restored by their encouragement, Nusswan persevered. He bought all of Dina's clothes, deciding what was appropriate for a young girl. The purchases were usually ill-fitting, for she was not allowed to be present while he shopped. "I don't want tiresome arguments in the shopkeeper's presence," he said. "You always embarrass me." When she needed new uniforms, he went to school with her on the day the tailors were coming, to supervise the measurements. He quizzed the tailors about rates and fabrics, trying to work out the principal's kickbacks. Dina dreaded this annual event, wondering what new mortification would be visited upon her before her classmates.

All her friends were now wearing their hair short, and she begged to be allowed the same privilege. "If you let me cut my hair, I'll swab the dining room every day instead of alternate days," she tried to bargain. "Or I can polish your shoes every night."

"No," said Nusswan. "Fourteen is too young for fancy hairstyles, plaits are good for you. Besides, I cannot afford to pay for the hairdresser." But he promptly added shoe-polishing to her list of chores.

A week after her final appeal, with the help of Zenobia in the school bathroom, Dina lopped off the plaits. Zenobia's ambition was to be a hairstylist, and she was overwhelmed by the good fortune that delivered her friend's head into her hands. "Let's cut off the whole jing-bang lot," she said. "Let's bob it really short."

"Are you crazy?" said Dina. "Nusswan will jump over the moon." So they settled for a pageboy, and Zenobia trimmed the hair to roughly an inch above the shoulders. It looked a bit ragged, but both girls were delighted with the results.

Dina hesitated about throwing the severed plaits in the dustbin. She put them in her satchel and raced home. Parading proudly about the house, she went repeatedly past the many mirrors to catch glimpses of her head from different angles. Then she visited her mother's room and waited—for her surprise, or delight, or something. But Mrs. Shroff noticed nothing.

"Do you like my new hairstyle, Mummy?" she asked at last.

Mrs. Shroff stared blankly for a moment. "Very pretty, my daughter, very pretty."

Nusswan got home late that evening. He greeted his mother, and said there had been so much work at the office. Then he saw Dina. He took a deep breath and put a hand to his forehead. Exhausted, he wished there was some way to deal with this without another fight. But her insolence, her defiance, could not go unpunished; or how would he look himself in the mirror?

"Please come here, Dina. Explain why you have disobeyed me."

She scratched her neck where tiny hair clippings were making her skin itch. "How did I disobey you?"

He slapped her. "Don't question me when I ask you something."

"You said you couldn't afford my haircut. This was free, I did it myself."

He slapped her again. "No back talk, I'm warning you." He got the ruler and struck her with it flat across the palms, then, because he deemed the offence extremely serious, with the edge over her knuckles. "This will teach you to look like a loose woman."

"Have you seen your hair in the mirror? You look like a clown," she said, refusing to be intimidated.

Nusswan's haircut, in his own opinion, was a statement of dignified elegance. He wore a centre parting, imposing order on either side of it with judicious applications of heavy pomade. Dina's taunt unleashed the fury of the disciplinarian. With lashes of the ruler across her calves and arms, he drove her to the bathroom, where he began tearing off her clothes.

"I don't want another word from you! Not a word! Today you have crossed the limit! Take a bath first, you polluted creature! Wash off those hair clippings before you spread them around the house and bring misfortune upon us!"

"Don't worry, your face will frighten away any misfortune." She was standing naked on the tiles now, but he did not leave. "I need hot water," she said.

He stepped back and flung a mugful of cold water at her from the bucket. Shivering, she stared defiantly at him, her nipples stiffening. He pinched one, hard, and she flinched. "Look at you with your little breasts starting to grow. You think you are a woman already. I should cut them right off, along with your wicked tongue."

He was eyeing her strangely, and she grew afraid. She understood that her sharp answers were enraging him, that it was vaguely linked to the way he was staring at the newfledged bloom of hair where her legs met. It would be safer to seem submissive, to douse his anger. She turned away and started to cry, her hands over her face.

Satisfied, he left. Her school satchel, lying on her bed, drew his attention. He opened it for a random inspection and found the plaits sitting on top. Dangling one between thumb and forefinger, he gritted his teeth before a smile slowly eased his angry features.

When Dina had finished her bath, he fetched a roll of black electrical tape and fastened the plaits to her hair. "You will wear them like this," he said. "Every day, even to school, till your hair has grown back."

She wished she had thrown the wretched things away in the school toilet. It felt like dead rats were hanging from her head.

Next morning, she secretly took the roll of tape to school. The plaits were pulled off before going to class. It was painful, with the black tape clutching hard. When school was over, she fixed them back with Zenobia's help. In this way she evaded Nusswan's punishment on weekdays.

But a few days later riots started in the city, in the wake of Partition and the British departure, and Dina was stuck at home with Nusswan. There were day-and-night curfews in every neighbourhood. Offices, businesses, colleges, schools, all stayed closed, and there was no respite from the detested plaits. He allowed her to remove them only while bathing, and supervised their reattachment immediately after.

Cooped up inside the flat, Nusswan lamented the country's calamity, grumbling endlessly. "Every day I sit at home, I lose money. These bloody uncultured savages don't deserve independence. If they must hack one another to death, I wish they would go somewhere else and do it quietly. In their villages, maybe. Without disturbing our lovely city by the sea."

When the curfew was lifted, Dina flew off to school, happy as an uncaged bird, eager for her eight hours of Nusswan-less existence. And he, too, was relieved to return to his office. On the first evening of normalcy in the city, he came home in a most cheerful mood. "The curfew is over, and your punishment is over. We can throw away your plaits now," he said, adding generously, "You know, short hair does suit you."

He opened his briefcase and took out a new hairband. "You can wear this now instead of electrical tape," he joked.

"Wear it yourself," she said, refusing to take it.

THREE YEARS AFTER HIS FATHER'S DEATH, Nusswan married. A few weeks later, his mother's withdrawal from life was complete. Where before she had responded obediently to instructions—get up, drink your tea, wash your hands, swallow your medicine—now there was only a wall of incomprehension.

The task of caring for her had outgrown Dina's ability. When the smell from Mrs. Shroff's room was past ignoring, Nusswan timidly broached the subject with his wife. He did not dare ask her directly to help, but hoped that her good nature might persuade her to volunteer. "Ruby, dear, Mamma is getting worse. She needs a lot of attention, all the time."

"Put her in a nursing home," said Ruby. "She'll be better off there."

He nodded placatingly, and did something less expensive and more human than shipping his mother to the old-age factory—as some unkind relatives would doubtless have put it—he hired a full-time nurse.

The nurse's assignment was short-lived; Mrs. Shroff died later that year, and people finally understood that a doctor's wife was no more immune to grief than other mortals. She died on the same day of the Shahenshahi calendar as her husband. Their prayers were performed consecutively at the same fire-temple by Dustoor Framji. By this time, Dina had learned how to evade the trap of his overfriendly hugs. When he approached, she held out a polite hand and took a step back, and another, and another. Short of pursuing her around the prayer-hall amid the large thuribles of flaming sandalwood, he could only smile foolishly and give up the chase.

After the first month's prayer ceremonies for Mrs. Shroff were completed, Nusswan decided there was no point in Dina's matriculating. Her last report card was quite wretched. She would have been kept back were it not for the principal who, loyal to the memory of Dr. Shroff, preferred to see the marks as a temporary aberration.

"Very decent of Miss Lamb to promote you," said Nusswan. "But the fact remains that your results are hopeless. I'm not going to waste money on school fees for another year."

"You make me clean and scrub all the time, I cannot study for even one hour a day! What do you expect?"

"Don't make excuses. A strong young girl, doing a little housework— what's that got to do with studying? Do you know how fortunate you are? There are thousands of poor children in the city, doing boot-polishing at railway stations, or collecting papers, bottles, plastic—plus going to school at night. And you are complaining? What's lacking in you is the desire for education. This is it, enough schooling for you."

Dina was not willing to concede without a struggle. She also hoped that Nusswan's wife would intervene on her behalf. But Ruby preferred to stay out of the quarrel, so next morning when she was sent to market with a shopping list, Dina ran to her grandfather's flat.

Grandfather lived with one of her uncles, in a room that smelled of stale balm. She held her breath and hugged him, then poured out her troubles in a torrent of words. "Please, Grandpa! Please tell him to stop treating me like this!"

Already started on the road to senility, he took a while to realize who Dina was exactly, and longer to understand what she wanted. His dentures were not in, making it difficult to decipher his speech. "Shall I get your teeth, Grandpa?" she offered.

"No, no, no!" He raised his hands and shook them vehemently. "No teeth. All crooked, and paining in the mouth. Bastard stupid dentist, useless fellow. My carpenter could make better teeth."

She repeated everything slowly, and at last he grasped the issue. "Matric? Who, you? Of course you must do your matric. Of course. Of course. You must matriculate. And then college. Yes, of course I will tell that shameless rascal to send you, I will order that Nauzer. No, Nevil—that Nusswan, yes, I will force him."

He dispatched a servant with a message for Nusswan to visit him as soon as possible. Nusswan could not refuse. He cared deeply about the family's opinion of him. After delaying for several days, citing too much work at the office, he went, taking Ruby along to have an ally by his side. She was instructed to ingratiate herself with the old man in any way possible.

Grandfather had misplaced more of his memory since Dina's visit. He remembered nothing of their conversation. He was wearing his teeth this time but had very little to say. With much prompting and reminiscing he appeared to recognize them. Then, ignoring Ruby altogether, he abruptly decided that Nusswan and Dina were man and wife. He refused to relinquish this belief, however much Dina coaxed and cajoled.

Ruby sat on the sofa holding the old man's hand. She asked if he would like her to massage his feet. Without waiting for an answer she grabbed the left one and began kneading it. The toenails were yellow, long overdue for a clipping.

Enraged, he tore his foot from her grasp. "Kya karta hai? Chalo, jao!"

Too startled at being addressed in Hindi, Ruby sat there gaping. Grandfather turned to Nusswan, "Doesn't she understand? What language does your ayah speak? Tell her to get off my sofa, wait in the kitchen."

Ruby rose in a huff and stood by the door. "Rude old man!" she hissed. "Just because my skin is a little dark!"

Nusswan said a gruff goodbye and followed his wife, stopping to turn and look triumphantly at Dina, who was trying to sort out the confusion. She stayed behind, hoping Grandpa would summon some hidden resource and come to her rescue. An hour later she too gave up, kissed his forehead, and left.

It was the last time she saw him alive. He died in his sleep the following month. At the funeral, Dina wondered how much longer Grandpa's toenails had grown under the white sheet that hid everything from view but his face.

FOR FOUR YEARS, Nusswan had been faithfully putting money aside for Dina's wedding expenses. A considerable sum had collected, and he planned to get her married in the near future. He was certain he would have no trouble finding a good husband—as he proudly said to himself, Dina had grown into a beautiful young woman, she deserved nothing less than the best. It would be a lavish celebration, befitting the sister of a successful businessman, and people would talk about it for a long time to come.

When she turned eighteen, he started inviting eligible bachelors to their home. She invariably found them repugnant; they were her brother's friends, and reminded her of Nusswan in all they said and did.

Nusswan was convinced that sooner or later there would be one she liked. He could no longer place restrictions on her comings and goings—she had outgrown those adolescent controls. So long as she did the housework and daily shopping according to Ruby's lists, relative calm prevailed in the house. Nowadays the quarrelling, if there was any, was between Ruby and Dina, as though Nusswan had delegated this function to his wife.

At the market Dina sometimes used her initiative and substituted cauliflower for cabbage; or she felt a sudden yearning for chickoos and bought them instead of oranges. Then Ruby promptly accused her of sabotaging the carefully planned meals: "Wicked, malicious woman, ruining my husband's dinner." She delivered the charge and the verdict in a matter-of-fact, mechanical manner, all part of her role as the dutiful wife.

But it was not always squabbles and bickering between them. More and more, the two women worked together amicably. Among the items that Ruby had brought to the house following her marriage was a small sewing-machine with a hand crank. She showed Dina how to use it, teaching her to make simple items like pillowcases, bedsheets, curtains.

When Ruby's first child was born, a son who was named Xerxes, Dina helped to look after him. She sewed baby clothes and knitted little caps and pullovers. For her nephew's first birthday she produced a pair of bootees. On that happy morning they garlanded Xerxes with roses and lilies, and made a large red teelo on his forehead.

"What a sweetie pie he is," said Dina, laughing with delight.

"And those bootees you made—just too cute!" said Ruby, giving her a huge hug.

But it was the rare day that passed entirely without argument. Once the chores were done, Dina preferred to spend as much time out of the house as possible. Her resources for her outings were limited to what she could squeeze from the shopping money. Her conscience was clear; she regarded it as part-payment for her drudgery, barely a fraction of what was owed her.

Ruby demanded an account down to the last paisa. "I want to see the bills and receipts. For every single item," she pounded her fist on the kitchen table, rattling the saucepan's lid.

"Since when do fishmongers and vegetable-women on the footpath give receipts?" fired back Dina, throwing at her the bills for shop purchases, along with the change kept ready after juggling undocumented prices. She left the kitchen while her sister-in-law searched the floor to retrieve and count the coins.

THE SAVINGS WERE SUFFICIENT to pay for bus fares. Dina went to parks, wandered in museums and markets, visited cinemas (just from the outside, to look at posters), and ventured timidly into public libraries. The heads bent over books made her feel out of place; everyone in there seemed so learned, and she hadn't even matriculated.

This impression was dispelled when she realized that the reading material in the hands of these grave individuals could range from something unpronounceable like *Areopagitica* by John Milton to *The Illustrated Weekly of India*. Eventually, the enormous old reading rooms, with their high ceilings, creaky floorboards and dark panelling, became her favourite sanctuary. The stately ceiling fans that hung from long poles swept the air with a comforting *whoosh*, and the deep leather chairs, musty smells, and rustle of turning pages were soothing. Best of all, people spoke in whispers. The only time Dina heard a shout was when the doorman scolded a beggar trying to sneak inside. Hours passed as she flipped through encyclopaedias, gazed into art books, and curiously opened dusty medical tomes, rounding off the visit by sitting for a few minutes with eyes closed in a dark corner of the old building, where time could stand still if one wanted it to.

The more modern libraries were equipped with music rooms. They also had fluorescent lights, Formica tables, air-conditioning, and brightly painted walls, and were always crowded. She found them cold and inhospitable, going there only if she wanted to listen to records. She knew very little about music—a few names like Brahms, Mozart, Schumann, and Bach, which her ears had picked up in childhood when her father would turn on the radio or put something on the gramophone, take her in his lap and say, "It makes you forget the troubles of this world, doesn't it?" and Dina would nod her head seriously.

In the library she selected records at random, trying to memorize the names of the ones she enjoyed so she could play them again another day. It was tricky, because the symphonies and concertos and sonatas were distinguished only by numbers that were preceded by letters like Op. and K. and BWV, and she did not know what any of it meant. If she was lucky she found something with a name that resonated richly in her memory; and when the familiar music filled her head, the past was conquered for a brief while, and she felt herself ache with the ecstasy of completion, as though a missing limb had been recovered.

She both desired and dreaded these intense musical experiences. The perfect felicity of the music room was always replaced by an unfocused anger when she returned to life with Nusswan and Ruby. The bitterest fights took place on days when she had visited the record collection.

Magazines and newspapers were far less complicated. Through reading the dailies, she discovered there were several cultural groups that sponsored concerts and recitals in the city. Many of these performances—usually the ones by local amateurs or obscure foreigners—were free. She started using her bus fares to go to these concerts, and found them a welcome variation on the library. The performers, too, were no doubt grateful for her presence at these meagrely attended evenings.

She lingered at the periphery of the crowd in the foyer, feeling like an imposter. Everyone else seemed to know so much about music, about the evening's performers, judging from the sophisticated way they held their programmes and pointed to items inside. She longed for the doors to open, for the dim lights within to disguise her shortcomings.

In the recital hall the music did not have the power to touch her the way it did during her solitary hours in the library. Here, the human comedy shared equal time with the music. And after a few recitals she began to recognize the regulars in the audience.

There was an old man who, at every concert, fell asleep at precisely four minutes into the first piece; latecomers skirted his row out of consideration, to avoid bumping his knees. At seven minutes, his spectacles began sliding down his nose. And at eleven minutes (if the piece was that long and he hadn't yet been wakened by applause), his dentures were protruding. He reminded Dina of Grandpa.

Two sisters, in their fifties, tall and lean with pointed chins, always sat in the first row and often clapped at the wrong moment, unnecessarily disturbing the old man's nap. Dina herself did not understand about sonatas and movements, but realized that a performance was not over just because there was a pause in the music. She took the lead from a goateed individual in round wire-rimmed glasses who wore a beret, looked like an expert, and always knew when to clap.

Then there was an amusing middle-aged fellow who wore the same brown suit at every concert, and was everyone's friend. He dashed around madly in the foyer, greeting people, his head bobbing wildly, assuring them what a splendid evening it was going to be. His ties were the subject of constant speculation. On some evenings they hung long, dominating his front, flapping over his crotch. At other times they barely reached his diaphragm. The knots ranged in size from microscopic to a bulky samosa. And he did not walk from one person to the next so much as prance, keeping his comments brief because, as he liked to explain, there were just a few minutes before the curtain went up, and still so many he had to greet.

Dina noticed in the lobby a young man who, like her, was engaged in observing from the edges the merry mingling of their fellow concertgoers. Since she usually arrived early, anxious to get away from home, she was there to see him sail up to the entrance on his bicycle, dismount cleanly, and wheel it in through the gates. The gateman allowed him this liberty in exchange for a tip. At the side of the building, he padlocked the bicycle, making sure to remove the briefcase from the rear carrier. He snapped the clips off his trousers and slipped them into the briefcase. Then he retired to his favourite corner of the lobby to study the programme and the public.

Sometimes their eyes met, and there was a recognition of their tacit conspiracy. The funny man in the brown suit left Dina alone but included him in his round of greetings. "Hello, Rustom! How are you?" he bellowed, and thus Dina learned the young man's name.

"Very well, thank you," said Rustom, looking over the shoulder of the brown suit at Dina watching amusedly.

"Tell me, what do you think of the pianist today? Is he capable of the depth required in the slow movement? Do you think that the largo—oh, excuse me, excuse me, I'll be back in a moment, soon as I say hello to Mr. Medhora over there," and he was off. Rustom smiled at Dina and shook his head in mock despair.

The bell rang and the auditorium doors opened. The two tall sisters hastened to the first row with synchronized hopping steps, unfolded the maroon-upholstered seats, and flopped down triumphantly, beaming at each other for once again winning their secret game of musical chairs. Dina took her usual centre aisle seat, roughly midway down the hall.

As the place began to fill, Rustom came up beside her. "Is this one free?" She nodded.

He sat down. "That Mr. Toddywalla is a real character, isn't he?"

"Oh, is that his name? Yes, he is very funny."

"Even if the recital is so-so, you can always rely on him for entertainment."

The lights dimmed, and the two performers appeared on stage to scattered applause. "By the way, I'm Rustom Dalal," he said, leaning closer and holding out his hand while the flute received the piano's silver A and offered its own golden one in return.

She whispered "Dina Shroff" without taking his hand, for in the dark she did not immediately notice it being held out. When she did, it was too late; he had begun to withdraw it.

During the interval Rustom asked if she would like coffee or a cold drink.

"No, thank you."

They watched the audience in the aisles, bound for the bathrooms and refreshments. He crossed his legs and said, "You know, I see you regularly at these concerts."

"Yes, I enjoy them very much."

"Do you play yourself? The piano, or—?"

"No, I don't."

"Oh. You have such lovely fingers, I was sure you played the piano."

"No, I don't," she repeated. Her cheeks felt a little hot, and she looked down at her fingers. "I don't know anything about music, I just enjoy listening to it."

"That's the best way, I think."

She wasn't sure what he meant, but nodded. "And what about you? Do you?"

"Like all good Parsi parents, mine made me take violin lessons when I was little," he laughed.

"You don't play it anymore?"

"Oh, once in a while. When I feel like torturing myself, I take it out of its case to make it screech and wail."

She smiled. "At least it must make your parents happy, to hear you play."

"No, they are dead. I live alone."

Her smile collapsed as she prepared to say she was sorry, but he quickly added, "Only the neighbours suffer when I play," and they laughed again.

They always sat together after that, and the following week she accepted a Mangola during the interval. While they were in the lobby, sipping from the chilled bottles, watching moisture beads embellish the glass, Mr. Toddywalla came up to them.

"So, Rustom, what did you think of the first half? In my opinion, a borderline performance. That flautist should do some breathing exercises before he ever thinks of a recital again." He lingered long enough to be introduced to Dina, which was why he had come in the first place. Then he was off, gambolling towards his next victims.

After the concert Rustom walked her to the bus stop, wheeling his bicycle. The departing audience had their eyes on them. To break the silence she asked, "Are you ever nervous about cycling in this traffic?"

He shook his head. "I've been doing it for years. It's second nature to me." He waited for her bus to arrive, then rode behind the red double-decker till their ways parted. He could not see her watching him from the upper deck. She followed his diminishing figure, her eyes sometimes losing him, then finding him under a streetlamp, travelling with him till he became a speck that only her imagination could claim was Rustom.

In a few weeks the concert regulars came to regard them as a couple. Their every move was viewed with concern and curiosity. Rustom and Dina were amused by the attention but preferred to dismiss it in the same category as Mr. Toddywalla's antics.

Once, on arriving, Rustom looked around to find Dina in the crowd. One of the first-row sisters immediately came up to his elbow and whispered coyly, "She is here, do not fear. She has just gone to the ladies' room."

It had been raining heavily, and Dina, soaked, was trying to tidy herself up in the ladies' but her tiny hanky was not equal to the task. The towel on the rod looked uninviting. She did the best she could, then went out, her hair still dripping.

"What happened?" asked Rustom.

"My umbrella was blown inside out. I couldn't get it straight quickly enough."

He offered her his large handkerchief. The significance of this proposal was not lost on the observers around them: would she or wouldn't she?

"No, thanks," she said, running her fingers through the wet hair. "It will soon be dry." The concertgoers held their breath.

"My hanky is clean, don't worry," he smiled. "Look, go in and dry yourself, I'll buy two hot coffees for us." When she still hesitated, he threatened to take off his shirt and towel her head with it in the lobby. Laughing, she accepted the handkerchief and returned to the ladies' room. The regulars sighed happily.

Inside, Dina rubbed her hair with the handkerchief. It had a nice smell to it, she thought. Not perfume, but a clean human smell. His smell. The same one she perceived sometimes while sitting next to him. She put it against her nose and breathed deeply, then folded it away, embarrassed.

It was still raining lightly when the concert ended. They walked to the bus stop. The drizzle hissed in the trees, as though the leaves were sizzling. Dina shivered.

"Are you cold?"

"Just a little."

"Hope you're not getting a fever. All that soaking. Listen, why don't you put on my raincoat, and I'll take your umbrella."

"Don't be silly, it's broken. Anyway, how can you ride your cycle with an umbrella?"

"Of course I can. I can ride it standing on my head if necessary." He insisted, and in the bus shelter they undertook the exchange. He helped her into the Duckback raincoat and his hand grazed her shoulder. His fingers felt warm to her cold skin. The sleeves were a bit long, otherwise it fit quite well. And nicely heated up by his body, she realized, as it slowly got the chill out of her.

They stood close together, watching the fine needles of rain slanting in the light of the streetlamp. Then they held hands for the first time, and it seemed the most natural thing to do. It was hard to let go when the bus came.

From now on, Rustom used his bicycle only to get to and from work. In the evenings he came by bus, so they could travel together and he could see her home.

Dina was happier meeting him without the bicycle. She felt he should give it up altogether, it was too dangerous in the city traffic.

Margaret Atwood

Margaret Atwood is the author of more than forty books—novels, short stories, poetry, literary criticism, social history, and books for children. Atwood's work is acclaimed internationally and has been published around the world. Her novels include *The Handmaid's Tale* and *Cat's Eye*—both shortlisted for The Booker Prize; *The Robber Bride*, winner of the Trillium Book Award and a finalist for the Governor General's Literary Awards; *Alias Grace*, winner of the prestigious Giller Prize in Canada and the Premio Mondello in Italy, nominated for The Booker Prize, the Orange Broadband Prize for Fiction, and the IMPAC Dublin Literary Award, and a finalist for the Governor General's Literary Awards; *The Blind Assassin*, winner of The Booker Prize and nominated for the IMPAC Dublin Literary Award; and *Oryx and Crake*, shortlisted for The Giller Prize, the Orange Prize, and the Man Booker Prize for Fiction and a finalist for the Governor General's Literary Awards. Her recent books of fiction are *The Penelopiad, The Tent,* and *Moral Disorder*. In 2007 she was a finalist for the Governor General's Literary Awards for *The Door,* her most recent book of poetry. She is the recipient of numerous honours, such as *The Sunday Times* Award for Literary Excellence in the U.K., the National Arts Club Medal of Honor for Literature in the United States, Le Chevalier dans l'Ordre des Arts et des Lettres in France, and, most recently, the Prince of Asturias Award of Letters in Spain. She has received honorary degrees from universities across Canada and internationally.

Margaret Atwood lives in Toronto with writer Graeme Gibson.

Alias Grace

BY MARGARET ATWOOD

Winner 1996

❧

PUSS IN THE CORNER

*She is a middle-sized woman, with a slight graceful figure. There
is an air of hopeless melancholy in her face which is very painful
to contemplate. Her complexion is fair, and must, before the
touch of hopeless sorrow paled it, have been very brilliant. Her
eyes are a bright blue, her hair auburn, and her face would be
rather handsome were it not for the long curved chin, which
gives, as it always does to most persons who have this facial
defect, a cunning, cruel expression.*
*Grace Marks glances at you with a sidelong, stealthy look; her
eye never meets yours, and after a furtive regard, it invariably
bends its gaze upon the ground. She looks like a person rather
above her humble station....*

SUSANNA MOODIE, *Life in the Clearings*, 1853

The captive raised her face; it was as soft and mild
As sculptured marble saint; or slumbering unweaned child;
It was so soft and mild, it was so sweet and fair,
Pain could not trace a line, or grief a shadow there!

The captive raised her hand and pressed it to her brow;
"I have been struck," she said, "and I am suffering now;

Yet these are little worth, your bolts and irons strong:
And, were they forged in steel, they could not hold me long."

EMILY BRONTË, "THE PRISONER," 1845

3.

1859

I am sitting on the purple velvet settee in the Governor's parlour, the Governor's wife's parlour; it has always been the Governor's wife's parlour although it is not always the same wife, as they change them around according to the politics. I have my hands folded in my lap the proper way although I have no gloves. The gloves I would wish to have would be smooth and white, and would fit without a wrinkle.

I am often in this parlour, clearing away the tea things and dusting the small tables and the long mirror with the frame of grapes and leaves around it, and the pianoforte; and the tall clock that came from Europe, with the orange-gold sun and the silver moon, that go in and out according to the time of day and the week of the month. I like the clock best of anything in the parlour, although it measures time and I have too much of that on my hands already.

But I have never sat down on the settee before, as it is for the guests. Mrs. Alderman Parkinson said a lady must never sit in a chair a gentleman has just vacated, though she would not say why; but Mary Whitney said, Because, you silly goose, it's still warm from his bum; which was a coarse thing to say. So I cannot sit here without thinking of the ladylike bums that have sat on this very settee, all delicate and white, like wobbly soft-boiled eggs.

The visitors wear afternoon dresses with rows of buttons up their fronts, and stiff wire crinolines beneath. It's a wonder they can sit down at all, and when they walk, nothing touches their legs under the billowing skirts, except their shifts and stockings. They are like swans, drifting along on unseen feet; or else like the jellyfish in the waters of the rocky harbour near our house, when I was little, before I ever made the long sad journey across the ocean. They were bell-shaped and ruffled, gracefully waving and lovely under the sea; but if they washed up on the beach and dried out in the sun there was nothing left of them. And that is what the ladies are like: mostly water.

There were no wire crinolines when I was first brought here. They were horsehair then, as the wire ones were not thought of. I have looked at them hanging in the wardrobes, when I go in to tidy and empty the slops. They are like birdcages; but what is being caged in? Legs, the legs of ladies; legs penned in so they cannot get out and go rubbing up against the gentlemen's trousers. The Governor's wife never says legs, although the newspapers said legs when they were talking about Nancy, with her dead legs sticking out from under the washtub.

IT ISN'T ONLY THE JELLYFISH LADIES THAT COME. On Tuesdays we have the Woman Question, and the emancipation of this or that, with reform-minded persons of both sexes; and on Thursdays the Spiritualist Circle, for tea and conversing with the dead, which is a comfort to the Governor's wife because of her departed infant son. But mainly it is the ladies. They sit sipping from the thin cups, and the Governor's wife rings a little china bell. She does not like being the Governor's wife, she would prefer the Governor to be the governor of something other than a prison. The Governor had good enough friends to get him made the Governor, but not for anything else.

So here she is, and she must make the most of her social position and accomplishments, and although an object of fear, like a spider, and of charity as well, I am also one of the accomplishments. I come into the room and curtsy and move about, mouth straight, head bent, and I pick up the cups or set them down, depending; and they stare without appearing to, out from under their bonnets.

The reason they want to see me is that I am a celebrated murderess. Or that is what has been written down. When I first saw it I was surprised, because they say Celebrated Singer and Celebrated Poetess and Celebrated Spiritualist and Celebrated Actress, but what is there to celebrate about murder? All the same, *Murderess* is a strong word to have attached to you. It has a smell to it, that word—musky and oppressive, like dead flowers in a vase. Sometimes at night I whisper it over to myself: *Murderess, Murderess*. It rustles, like a taffeta skirt across the floor.

Murderer is merely brutal. It's like a hammer, or a lump of metal. I would rather be a murderess than a murderer, if those are the only choices.

SOMETIMES WHEN I AM DUSTING the mirror with the grapes I look at myself in it, although I know it is vanity. In the afternoon light of the parlour my skin is a pale mauve, like a faded bruise, and my teeth are greenish. I think of all the things that have been written about me—that I am an inhuman female demon, that I am an innocent victim of a blackguard forced against my will and in danger of my own life, that I was too ignorant to know how to act and that to hang me would be judicial murder, that I am fond of animals, that I am very handsome with a brilliant complexion, that I have blue eyes, that I have green eyes, that I have auburn and also brown hair, that I am tall and also not above the average height, that I am well and decently dressed, that I robbed a dead woman to appear so, that I am brisk and smart about my work, that I am of a sullen disposition with a quarrelsome temper, that I have the appearance of a person rather above my humble station, that I am a good girl with a pliable nature and no harm is told of me, that I am cunning and devious, that I am soft in the head and little better than an idiot. And I wonder, how can I be all of these different things at once?

It was my own lawyer, Mr. Kenneth MacKenzie, Esq., who told them I was next door to an idiot. I was angry with him over that, but he said it was by far my best chance and I should not appear to be too intelligent. He said he would plead my case to the utmost of his ability, because whatever the truth of the matter I was little more than a child at the time, and he supposed it came down to free will and whether or not one held with it. He was a kind gentleman although I could not make head nor tail of much of what he said, but it must have been good pleading. The newspapers wrote that he performed heroically against overwhelming odds. Though I don't know why they called it pleading, as he was not pleading but trying to make all of the witnesses appear immoral or malicious, or else mistaken.

I wonder if he ever believed a word I said.

WHEN I HAVE GONE OUT OF THE ROOM with the tray, the ladies look at the Governor's wife's scrapbook. Oh imagine, I feel quite faint, they say, and You let that woman walk around loose in your house, you must have nerves of iron, my own would never stand it. Oh well one must get used to such things in our situation, we are virtually prisoners ourselves you know, although one must feel pity for these poor benighted creatures, and after all she was trained as a servant, and it's as well to keep them employed, she is a wonderful seamstress, quite deft and accomplished, she is a great help in that way especially with the girls' frocks, she has an eye for trimmings, and under happier circumstances she could have made an excellent milliner's assistant.

Although naturally she can be here only during the day, I would not have her in the house at night. You are aware that she has spent time in the Lunatic Asylum in Toronto, seven or eight years ago it was, and although she appears to be perfectly recovered you never know when they may get carried away again, sometimes she talks to herself and sings out loud in a most peculiar manner. One cannot take chances, the keepers conduct her back in the evenings and lock her up properly, otherwise I wouldn't be able to sleep a wink. Oh I don't blame you, there is only so far one can go in Christian charity, a leopard cannot change its spots and no one could say you have not done your duty and shown a proper feeling.

The Governor's wife's scrapbook is kept on the round table with the silk shawl covering it, branches like vines intertwined, with flowers and red fruit and blue birds, it is really one large tree and if you stare at it long enough the vines begin to twist as if a wind is blowing them. It was sent from India by her eldest daughter who is married to a missionary, which is not a thing I would care to do myself. You would be sure to die early, if not from the rioting natives as at Cawnpore with horrid outrages committed on the persons of respectable gentlewomen, and a mercy they were all slaughtered and put out of their misery, for only think of the shame; then from the malaria, which turns you entirely yellow, and you expire in raving fits; in any case before you could turn around, there you would be, buried under a palm tree in a foreign clime. I have seen pictures of them in the book of Eastern engravings the Governor's wife takes out when she wishes to shed a tear.

On the same round table is the stack of Godey's Ladies' Books with the fashions that come up from the States, and also the Keepsake Albums of the two younger daughters. Miss Lydia tells me I am a romantic figure; but then, the two of them are so young they hardly know what they are saying. Sometimes they pry and tease; they say, Grace, why don't you ever smile or laugh, we never see you smiling, and I say I suppose Miss I have gotten out of the way of it, my face won't bend in that direction any more. But if I laughed out loud I might not be able to stop; and also it would spoil their romantic notion of me. Romantic people are not supposed to laugh, I know that much from looking at the pictures.

The daughters put all kinds of things into their albums, little scraps of cloth from their dresses, little snippets of ribbon, pictures cut from magazines—the Ruins of Ancient Rome, the Picturesque Monasteries of the French Alps, Old London Bridge, Niagara Falls in summer and in winter, which is a thing I would like to see as all say it is very impressive, and portraits of Lady This and Lord That from England. And their friends write things in their graceful handwriting, *To Dearest Lydia from your Eternal Friend, Clara Richards; To Dearest Marianne In Memory of Our Splendid Picnic on the Shores of Bluest Lake Ontario.* And also poems:

> As round about the sturdy Oak
> Entwines the loving Ivy Vine,
> My Faith so true, I pledge to You,
> 'Twill evermore be none but Thine, Your Faithful Laura.

Or else:

> Although from you I far must roam,
> Do not be broken hearted,
> We two who in the Soul are One
> Are never truly parted. Your Lucy.

This young lady was shortly afterwards drowned in the Lake when her ship went down in a gale, and nothing was ever found but her box with her initials done in silver nails; it was still locked, so although damp, nothing spilt out, and Miss Lydia was given a scarf out of it as a keepsake.

> When I am dead and in my grave
> And all my bones are rotten,
> When this you see, remember me,
> Lest I should be forgotten.

That one is signed, *I will always be with you in Spirit, Your loving 'Nancy,' Hannah Edmonds,* and I must say the first time I saw that, it gave me a fright, although of course it was a different Nancy. Still, the rotten bones. They would be, by now. Her face was all black by the time they found her, there must have been a dreadful smell. It was so hot then, it was July, still she went off surprisingly soon, you'd think she would have kept longer in the dairy, it is usually cool down there. I am certainly glad I was not present, as it would have been very distressing.

I don't know why they are all so eager to be remembered. What good will it do them? There are some things that should be forgotten by everyone, and never spoken of again.

THE GOVERNOR'S WIFE'S SCRAPBOOK is quite different. Of course she is a grown woman and not a young girl, so although she is just as fond of remembering, what she wants to remember is not violets or a picnic. No Dearest and Love and Beauty, no Eternal Friends, none of those things for her; what it has instead is all the famous criminals in it—the ones that have been hanged, or else brought here to be penitent, because this is a Penitentiary and you are supposed to repent while in it, and you will do better if you say you have done so, whether you have anything to repent of or not.

The Governor's wife cuts these crimes out of the newspapers and pastes them in; she will even write away for old newspapers with crimes that were done before her time. It is her collection, she is a lady and they are all collecting things these days, and so she must collect something, and she does this instead of pulling up ferns or pressing flowers, and in any case she likes to horrify her acquaintances.

So I have read what they put in about me. She showed the scrapbook to me herself, I suppose she wanted to see what I would do; but I've learnt how to keep my face still, I made my eyes wide and flat, like an owl's in torchlight, and I said I had repented in bitter tears, and was now a changed person, and would she wish me to remove the tea things now; but I've looked in there since, many times, when I've been in the parlour by myself.

A lot of it is lies. They said in the newspaper that I was illiterate, but I could read some even then. I was taught early by my mother, before she got too tired for it, and I did my sampler with leftover thread, A is for Apple, B is for Bee; and also Mary Whitney used to read with me, at Mrs. Alderman Parkinson's, when we were doing the mending; and I've learnt a lot more since being here, as they teach you on purpose. They want you to be able to read the Bible, and also tracts, as religion and thrashing are the only remedies for a depraved nature and our immortal souls must be considered. It is shocking how many crimes the Bible contains. The Governor's wife should cut them all out and paste them into her scrapbook.

They did say some true things. They said I had a good character; and that was so, because nobody had ever taken advantage of me, although they tried. But they called James McDermott my paramour. They wrote it down, right in the newspaper. I think it is disgusting to write such things down.

That is what really interests them—the gentlemen and the ladies both. They don't care if I killed anyone, I could have cut dozens of throats, it's only what they admire in a soldier, they'd scarcely blink. No: was I really a paramour, is their chief concern, and they don't even know themselves whether they want the answer to be no or yes.

I'M NOT LOOKING AT THE SCRAPBOOK NOW, because they may come in at any moment. I sit with my rough hands folded, eyes down, staring at the flowers in the Turkey carpet. Or they are supposed to be flowers. They have petals the shape of the diamonds on a playing card; like the cards spread out on the table at Mr. Kinnear's, after the gentlemen had been playing the night before. Hard and angular. But red, a deep thick red. Thick strangled tongues.

It's not the ladies expected today, it's a doctor. He's writing a book; the Governor's wife likes to know people who are writing books, books with forward-looking aims, it shows that she is a liberal-minded person with advanced views, and science is making such progress, and what with modern inventions and the Crystal Palace and world knowledge assembled, who knows where we will all be in a hundred years.

Where there's a doctor it's always a bad sign. Even when they are not doing the killing themselves it means a death is close, and in that way they are like ravens or crows. But this doctor will not hurt me, the Governor's wife promised it. All he wants is to measure my head. He is measuring the heads of all the criminals in the Penitentiary, to see if he can tell from the bumps on their skulls what sort of criminals they are, whether they are pickpockets or swindlers or embezzlers or criminal lunatics or murderers, she did not say Like you, Grace. And then they could lock those people up before they had a chance to commit any crimes, and think how that would improve the world.

After James McDermott was hanged they made a plaster cast of his head. I read that in the scrapbook too. I suppose that's what they wanted it for— to improve the world.

Also his body was dissected. When I first read that I did not know what *dissected* was, but I found it out soon enough. It was done by the doctors. They cut him into pieces like a pig to be salted down, he might as well have been bacon as far as they were concerned. His body that I listened to breathing, and the heart beating, the knife slicing through it—I can't bear to think of it.

I wonder what they did with his shirt. Was it one of the four sold to him by Jeremiah the peddler? It should have been three, or else five, as odd numbers are luckier. Jeremiah always wished me luck, but he did not wish any to James McDermott.

I did not see the hanging. They hanged him in front of the jail in Toronto, and You should have been there Grace, say the keepers, it would have been a lesson to you. I've pictured it many times, poor James standing with his hands tied and his neck bare, while they put the hood over his head like a kitten to be drowned. At least he had a priest with him, he was not all alone. If it had not been for Grace Marks, he told them, none of it would have happened.

It was raining, and a huge crowd standing in the mud, some of them come from miles away. If my own death sentence had not been commuted at the last minute, they would have watched me hang with the same greedy pleasure. There were many women and ladies there; everyone wanted to stare, they wanted to breathe death in like fine perfume, and when I read of it I thought, If this is a lesson to me, what is it I am supposed to be learning?

I CAN HEAR THEIR FOOTSTEPS NOW, and I stand up quickly and brush my apron smooth. Then there's the voice of a strange man, This is most kind of you Ma'am, and the Governor's wife saying I am so happy to be of help, and he says again, Most kind.

Then he comes through the doorway, big stomach, black coat, tight waistcoat, silver buttons, precisely tied stock, I am only looking up as far as the chin, and he says This will not take long but I'd appreciate it Ma'am if you'd remain in the room, one must not only be virtuous, one must give the appearance of virtue. He laughs as if it is a joke, and I can hear in his voice that he is afraid of me. A woman like me is always a temptation, if possible to arrange it unobserved; as whatever we may say about it later, we will not be believed.

And then I see his hand, a hand like a glove, a glove stuffed with raw meat, his hand plunging into the open mouth of his leather bag. It comes out glinting, and I know I have seen a hand like that before; and then I lift my head and stare him straight in the eye, and my heart clenches and kicks out inside me, and then I begin to scream.

Because it's the same doctor, the same one, the very same black-coated doctor with his bagful of shining knives.

4.

I was brought round with a glass of cold water dashed in the face, but continued screaming, although the doctor was no longer in sight; so was restrained by two kitchen maids and the gardener's boy, who sat on my legs. The Governor's wife had sent for the Matron from the Penitentiary, who arrived with two of the keepers; and she gave me a brisk slap across the face, at which I stopped. It was not the same doctor in any case, it only looked like him. The same cold and greedy look, and the hate.

It's the only way with the hysterics, you may be sure Ma'am, said the Matron, we have had a great deal of experience with that kind of a fit, this one used to be prone to them but we never indulged her, we worked to correct it and we thought she had given it up, it might be her old trouble coming back, for despite what they said about it up there at Toronto she was a raving lunatic that time seven years ago, and you are lucky there was no scissors nor sharp things lying about.

Then the keepers half-dragged me back to the main prison building, and locked me into this room, until I was myself again is what they said, even though I told them I was better now that the doctor was no longer there with his knives. I said I had a fear of doctors, that was all; of being cut open by them, as some might have a fear of snakes; but they said, That's enough of your tricks Grace, you just wanted the attention, he was not going to cut you open, he had no knives at all, it was only a callipers you saw, to measure the heads with. You've given the Governor's wife a real fright now but it serves her right, she's been spoiling you too much for your own good, she's made quite a pet out of you hasn't she, our company is hardly good enough for you any more. Well so much the worse, you will have to endure it because now you will have a different sort of attention for a time. Until they have decided what is to be done with you.

THIS ROOM HAS ONLY A LITTLE WINDOW high up with bars on the inside, and a straw-filled mattress. There's a crust of bread on a tin plate, and a stone crock of water, and a wooden bucket with nothing in it which is there for a chamber pot. I was put in a room like this before they sent me away to the Asylum. I told them I wasn't mad, that I wasn't the one, but they wouldn't listen.

They wouldn't know mad when they saw it in any case, because a good portion of the women in the Asylum were no madder than the Queen of England. Many were sane enough when sober, as their madness came out of a bottle, which is a kind I knew very well. One of them was in there to get away from her husband, who beat her black and blue, he was the mad one but nobody would lock him up; and another said she went mad in the autumns, as she had no house and it was warm in the Asylum, and if she didn't do a fair job of running mad she would freeze to death; but then in the spring she would become sane again because it was good weather and she could go off and tramp in the woods and fish, and as she was part Red Indian she was handy at such things. I would like to do that myself if I knew how, and if not afraid of the bears.

But some were not pretending. One poor Irishwoman had all her family dead, half of them of starving in the great famine and the other half of the cholera on the boat coming over; and she would wander about calling their names. I am glad I left Ireland before that time, as the sufferings she told of were dreadful, and the corpses piled everywhere with none to bury them. Another woman had killed her child, and it followed her around everywhere, tugging at her skirt; and sometimes she would pick it up and hug and kiss it, and at other times she would shriek at it, and hit it away with her hands. I was afraid of that one.

Another was very religious, always praying and singing, and when she found out what they said I had done, she would plague me whenever she could. Down on your knees, she would say, Thou shalt not kill, but there is always God's grace for sinners, repent, repent while there is yet time or damnation awaits. She was just like a preacher in church, and once she tried to baptize me with soup, thin soup it was and with cabbage in it, and she poured a spoonful of it over my head. When I complained of it, the Matron gave me a dry look with her mouth all tight and straight across like a box lid, and she said, Well Grace perhaps you should listen to her, I have never heard of you doing any true repenting, much though your hard heart stands in need of it; and then I was suddenly very angry and I screamed, I did nothing, I did nothing! It was her, it was her fault!

Who do you mean, Grace, she said, compose yourself or it's the cold baths and the strait-waistcoat for you, and she gave the other matron a glance: There. What did I tell you. Mad as a snake.

The matrons at the Asylum were all fat and strong, with big thick arms and chins that went straight down into their necks and prim white collars, and their hair twisted up like faded rope. You have to be strong to be a matron there in case some madwoman jumps on your back and starts to tear out your hair, but none of it improved their tempers any. Sometimes they would provoke us, especially right before the visitors were to come. They wanted to show how dangerous we were, but also how well they could control us, as it made them appear more valuable and skilled.

So I stopped telling them anything. Not Dr. Bannerling, who would come into the room when I was tied up in the dark with mufflers on my hands, Keep still I am here to examine you, it is no use lying to me. Nor the other doctors who would visit there, Oh indeed, what a fascinating case, as if I was a two-headed calf. At last I stopped talking altogether, except very civilly when spoken to, Yes Ma'am No Ma'am, Yes and No Sir. And then I was sent back to the Penitentiary, after they had all met together in their black coats, Ahem, aha, in my opinion, and My respected colleague, Sir I beg to differ. Of course they could not admit for an instant that they had been mistaken when they first put me in.

People dressed in a certain kind of clothing are never wrong. Also they never fart. What Mary Whitney used to say was, If there's farting in a room where they are, you may be sure you done it yourself. And even if you never did, you better not say so or it's all Damn your insolence, and a boot in the backside and out on the street with you.

She often had a crude way of speaking. She said *You done* and not *You did*. No one had taught her otherwise. I used to speak that way as well, but I have learnt better manners in prison.

I SIT DOWN on the straw mattress. It makes a sound like shushing. Like water on the shore. I shift from side to side, to listen to it. I could close my eyes and think I'm by the sea, on a dry day without much wind. Outside the window far away there's someone chopping wood, the axe coming down, the unseen flash and then the dull sound, but how do I know it's even wood?

It's chilly in this room. I have no shawl, I hug my arms around myself because who else is there to do it? When I was younger I used to think that if I could hug myself tight enough I could make myself smaller, because there was never enough room for me, at home or anywhere, but if I was smaller then I would fit in.

My hair is coming out from under my cap. Red hair of an ogre. A wild beast, the newspaper said. A monster. When they come with my dinner I will put the slop bucket over my head and hide behind the door, and that will give them a fright. If they want a monster so badly they ought to be provided with one.

I never do such things, however. I only consider them. If I did them, they would be sure I had gone mad again. *Gone mad* is what they say, and sometimes *Run mad*, as if mad is a direction, like west; as if mad is a different house you could step into, or a separate country entirely. But when you go mad you don't go any other place, you stay where you are. And somebody else comes in.

I don't want to be left by myself in this room. The walls are too empty, there are no pictures on them nor curtains on the little high-up window, nothing to look at and so you look at the wall, and after you do that for a time, there are pictures on it after all, and red flowers growing.

I think I sleep.

IT'S MORNING NOW, but which one? The second or the third. There's fresh light outside the window, that's what woke me. I struggle upright, pinch myself and blink my eyes, and get up stiff-limbed from the rustling mattress. Then I sing a song, just to hear a voice and keep myself company:

Holy, holy, holy, Lord God Almighty,
Early in the morning our song shall rise to thee,
Holy, holy, holy, merciful and mighty,
God in three persons, Blessed Trinity.

They can hardly object if it's a hymn. A hymn to the morning. I have always been fond of sunrise.

Then I drink the last of the water; then I walk around the room; then I lift my petticoats and piss in the bucket. A few more hours and it will reek in here like a cesspool.

Sleeping in your clothes makes you tired. The clothes are crumpled, and also your body underneath them. I feel as if I've been rolled into a bundle and thrown on the floor.

I wish I had a clean apron.

Nobody comes. I'm being left to reflect on my sins and misdemeanours, and one does that best in solitude, or such is our expert and considered opinion, Grace, after long experience with these matters. In solitary confinement, and sometimes in the dark. There are prisons where they keep you in there for years, without a glimpse of a tree or horse or human face. Some say it refines the complexion.

I've been shut up alone before. Incorrigible, said Dr. Bannerling, a devious dissembler. Remain quiet, I am here to examine your cerebral configuration, and first I shall measure your heartbeat and respiration, but I knew what he was up to. Take your hand off my tit, you filthy bastard, Mary Whitney would have said, but all I could say was Oh no, oh no, and no way to twist and turn, not how they'd fixed me, trussed up to the chair with the sleeves crossed over in front and tied behind; so nothing to do but sink my teeth into his fingers, and then over we went, backwards onto the floor, yowling together like two cats in a sack. He tasted of raw sausages and damp woollen underclothes. He'd of been much better for a good scalding, and then put in the sun to bleach.

NO SUPPER LAST NIGHT or the night before that, nothing except the bread, not even a bit of cabbage; well that is to be expected. Starvation is calming to the nerves. Today it will be more bread and water, as meat is exciting to criminals and maniacs, they get the smell of it in their nostrils just like wolves and then you have only yourself to blame. But yesterday's water is all gone and I'm very thirsty, I am dying of thirst, my mouth tastes bruised, my tongue is swelling. That's what happens to castaways, I've read about them in legal trials, lost at sea and drinking each other's blood. They draw straws for it. Cannibal atrocities pasted into the scrapbook. I'm sure I would never do such a thing, however hungry.

Have they forgotten I'm in here? They'll have to bring more food, or at least more water, or else I will starve, I will shrivel, my skin will dry out, all yellow like old linen; I will turn into a skeleton, I will be found months, years, centuries from now, and they will say Who is this, she must have slipped our mind, Well sweep all those bones and rubbish into the corner, but save the buttons, no sense in having them go to waste, there's no help for it now.

Once you start feeling sorry for yourself they've got you where they want you. Then they send for the Chaplain.

Oh come to my arms, poor wandering soul. There is more joy in Heaven over the one lost lamb. Ease your troubled mind. Kneel at my feet. Wring your hands in anguish. Describe how conscience tortures you day and night, and how the eyes of your victims follow you around the room, burning like red-hot coals. Shed tears of remorse. Confess, confess. Let me forgive and pity. Let me get up a Petition for you. Tell me all.

And then what did he do? Oh shocking. And then what?

The left hand or the right?

How far up, exactly?

Show me where.

POSSIBLY I HEAR A WHISPERING. Now there's an eye, looking in at me through the slit cut in the door. I can't see it but I know it's there. Then a knocking.

And I think, Who could that be? The Matron? The Warden, come to give me a scolding? But it can't be any of them, because nobody here does you the courtesy of knocking, they look at you through the little slit and then they just walk in. Always knock first, said Mary Whitney. Then wait until they give you leave. You never know what they may be up to, and half of it's nothing they want you to see, they could have their fingers up their nose or some other place, as even a gentlewoman feels the need to scratch where it itches, and if you see a pair of heels sticking out from under the bed it's best to take no notice. They may be silk purses in the daytime, but they're all sows' ears at night.

Mary was a person of democratic views.

THE KNOCK AGAIN. As if I have a choice.

I push my hair back under my cap, and get up off the straw mattress and smooth down my dress and apron, and then I move as far back into the corner of the room as I can, and then I say, quite firmly because it's as well to keep hold of your dignity if at all possible,

Please come in.

5

The door opens and a man enters. He's a young man, my own age or a little older, which is young for a man although not for a woman, as at my age a woman is an old maid but a man is not an old bachelor until he's fifty, and even then there's still hope for the ladies, as Mary Whitney used to say. He's tall, with long legs and arms, but not what the Governor's daughters would call handsome; they incline to the languid ones in the magazines, very elegant and butter wouldn't melt in their mouths, with narrow feet in pointed boots. This man has a briskness about him which is not fashionable, and also rather large feet, although he is a gentleman, or next door to it. I don't think he is English, and so it is hard to tell.

His hair is brown, and wavy by nature—unruly it might be called, as if he can't make it lie flat by brushing. His coat is good, a good cut; but not new, as there are shiny patches on the elbows. He has a tartan vest, tartan has been popular ever since the Queen took up with Scotland and built a castle there, full of deer's heads or so they say; but now I see it isn't real tartan, only checked. Yellow and brown. He has a gold watch-chain, so although rumpled and untended, he is not poor.

He doesn't have the side-whiskers, as they have begun to wear them now; I don't much like them myself, give me a moustache or a beard, or else nothing at all. James McDermott and Mr. Kinnear were both clean-shaven, and Jamie Walsh too, not that he had anything much to shave; except that Mr. Kinnear had a moustache. When I used to empty his shaving basin in the mornings, I would take some of the wet soap—he used a good soap, from London—and I would rub it on my skin, on the skin of my wrists, and then I would have the smell of it with me all day, at least until it was time to scrub the floors.

The young man closes the door behind him. He doesn't lock it, but someone else locks it from the outside. We are locked into this room together.

Good morning, Grace, he says. I understand that you are afraid of doctors. I must tell you right away that I myself am a doctor. My name is Dr. Jordan, Dr. Simon Jordan.

I look at him quickly, then look down. I say, Is the other doctor coming back?

The one that frightened you? he says. No, he is not.

I say, Then I suppose you are here to measure my head.

I would not dream of it, he says, smiling; but still, he glances at my head with a measuring look. However I have my cap on, so there's nothing he can see. Now that he has spoken I think he must be an American. He has white teeth and is not missing any of them, at least at the front, and his face is quite long and bony. I like his smile, although it is higher on one side than the other, which gives him the air of joking.

I look at his hands. They are empty. There's nothing at all in them. No rings on his fingers. Do you have a bag with knives in it? I say. A leather satchel.

No, he says, I am not the usual kind of doctor. I do no cutting open. Are you afraid of me, Grace?

I can't say that I am afraid of him yet. It's too early to tell; too early to tell what he wants. No one comes to see me here unless they want something.

I would like him to say what kind of a doctor he is if he's not the usual kind, but instead he says, I am from Massachusetts. Or that is where I was born. I have travelled a good deal since then. I have been going to and fro in the earth, and walking up and down in it. And he looks at me, to see if I understand.

I know it is the Book of Job, before Job gets the boils and running sores, and the whirlwinds. It's what Satan says to God. He must mean that he has come to test me, although he's too late for that, as God has done a great deal of testing of me already, and you would think he would be tired of it by now.

But I don't say this. I look at him stupidly. I have a good stupid look which I have practised.

I say, Have you been to France? That is where all the fashions come from.

I see I have disappointed him. Yes, he says. And to England, and also to Italy, and to Germany and Switzerland as well.

It is very odd to be standing in a locked room in the Penitentiary, speaking with a strange man about France and Italy and Germany. A travelling man. He must be a wanderer, like Jeremiah the peddler. But Jeremiah travelled to earn his bread, and these other sorts of men are rich enough already. They go on voyages because they are curious. They amble around the world and stare at things, they sail across the ocean as if there's nothing to it at all, and if it goes ill with them in one place they simply pick up and move along to another.

But now it's my turn to say something. I say, I don't know how you manage, Sir, amongst all the foreigners, you never know what they are saying. When the poor things first come here they gabble away like geese, although the children can soon speak well enough.

This is true, as children of any kind are very quick to learn.

He smiles, and then he does a strange thing. He puts his left hand into his pocket and pulls out an apple. He walks over to me slowly, holding the apple out in front of him like someone holding out a bone to a dangerous dog, in order to win it over.

This is for you, he says.

I am so thirsty the apple looks to me like a big round drop of water, cool and red. I could drink it down in one gulp. I hesitate; but then I think, There's nothing bad in an apple, and so I take it. I haven't had an apple of my own for a long time. This apple must be from last autumn, kept in a barrel in the cellar, but it seems fresh enough.

I am not a dog, I say to him.

Most people would ask me what I mean by saying that, but he laughs. His laugh is just one breath, Hah, as if he's found a thing he has lost; and he says, No, Grace, I can see you are not a dog.

What is he thinking? I stand holding the apple in both hands. It feels precious, like a heavy treasure. I lift it up and smell it. It has such an odour of outdoors on it I want to cry.

Aren't you going to eat it, he says.

No, not yet, I say.

Why not, he says.

Because then it would be gone, I say.

The truth is I don't want him watching me while I eat. I don't want him to see my hunger. If you have a need and they find it out, they will use it against you. The best way is to stop from wanting anything.

He gives his one laugh. Can you tell me what it is, he says.

I look at him, then look away. An apple, I say. He must think I am simple; or else it's a trick of some sort; or else he is mad and that is why they locked the door—they've locked me into this room with a madman. But men who are dressed in clothes like his cannot be mad, especially the gold watch-chain—his relatives or else his keepers would have it off him in a trice if so.

He smiles his lopsided smile. What does Apple make you think of? he says.

I beg your pardon, Sir, I say. I do not understand you.

It must be a riddle. I think of Mary Whitney, and the apple peelings we threw over our shoulders that night, to see who we would marry. But I will not tell him that.

I think you understand well enough, he says.

My sampler, I say.

Now it is his turn to know nothing. Your what? he says.

My sampler that I stitched as a child, I say. A is for Apple, B is for Bee.

Oh yes, he says. But what else?

I give my stupid look. Apple pie, I say.

Ah, he says. Something you eat.

Well I should hope you would, Sir, I say. That's what an apple pie is for.

And is there any kind of apple you should not eat? he says.

A rotten one, I suppose, I say.

He's playing a guessing game, like Dr. Bannerling at the Asylum. There is always a right answer, which is right because it is the one they want, and you can tell by their faces whether you have guessed what it is; although with Dr. Bannerling all of the answers were wrong. Or perhaps he is a Doctor of Divinity; they are the other ones prone to this kind of questioning. I have had enough of them to last me for a long while.

The apple of the Tree of Knowledge, is what he means. Good and evil. Any child could guess it. But I will not oblige.

I go back to my stupid look. Are you a preacher? I say.

No, he says, I am not a preacher. I am a doctor who works not with bodies, but with minds. Diseases of the mind and brain, and the nerves.

I put my hands with the apple behind my back. I do not trust him at all. No, I say. I won't go back there. Not to the Asylum. Flesh and blood cannot stand it.

Don't be afraid, he says. You aren't mad, really, are you Grace?

No Sir I am not, I say.

Then there is no reason for you to go back to the Asylum, is there?

They don't listen to reason there, Sir, I say.

Well that is what I am here for, he says. I am here to listen to reason. But if I am to listen to you, you will have to talk to me.

I see what he's after. He is a collector. He thinks all he has to do is give me an apple, and then he can collect me. Perhaps he is from a newspaper.

Or else he is a travelling man, making a tour. They come in and they stare, and when they look at you, you feel as small as an ant, and they pick you up between finger and thumb and turn you around. And then they set you down and go away.

You won't believe me, Sir, I say. Anyway it's all been decided, the trial is long over and done with and what I say will not change anything. You should ask the lawyers and the judges, and the newspaper men, they seem to know my story better than I do myself. In any case I can't remember, I can remember other things but I have lost that part of my memory entirely. They must have told you that.

I would like to help you, Grace, he says.

That is how they get in through the door. Help is what they offer but gratitude is what they want, they roll around in it like cats in the catnip. He wishes to go home and say to himself, I stuck in my thumb and pulled out the plum, what a good boy am I. But I will not be anybody's plum. I say nothing.

If you will try to talk, he continues, I will try to listen. My interest is purely scientific. It is not only the murders that should concern us. He's using a kind voice, kind on the surface but with other desires hidden beneath it.

Perhaps I will tell you lies, I say.

He doesn't say, Grace what a wicked suggestion, you have a sinful imagination. He says, Perhaps you will. Perhaps you will tell lies without meaning to, and perhaps you will also tell them deliberately. Perhaps you are a liar.

I look at him. There are those who have said I am one, I say.

We will just have to take that chance, he says.

I look down at the floor. Will they take me back to the Asylum? I say. Or will they put me in solitary confinement, with nothing to eat but bread?

He says, I give you my word that as long as you continue to talk with me, and do not lose control of yourself and become violent, you shall remain as you were. I have the Governor's promise.

I look at him. I look away. I look at him again. I hold the apple in my two hands. He waits.

Finally I lift the apple up and press it to my forehead.

Mordecai Richler

Mordecai Richler (1931–2001) was and still is one of Canada's
foremost, most beloved novelists, a controversial and prolific
journalist, and an occasional scriptwriter. Born in Montreal, he left as
a young man to live in Paris and England, establishing himself as an
accomplished novelist with the publication of *The Apprenticeship of
Duddy Kravitz* (1959). He returned to live in Montreal in 1972.
During the course of his long career as a "scribbler" (as he called
himself), he wrote ten novels, several books of essays and non-fiction,
and the *Jacob Two-Two* children's books. He was widely published
internationally, and was the recipient of dozens of literary awards,
including two Governor General's Literary Awards, the
Commonwealth Writers' Prize, a Writers Guild of America Award, and
The Ruth and Sylvia Schwartz Children's Book Awards. He won The
Giller Prize in 1997 for his last novel, *Barney's Version,* which also
won The Stephen Leacock Memorial Medal for Humour. He was
made a Companion of the Order of Canada a few months before his
death on July 3, 2001.

Barney's Version

BY MORDECAI RICHLER

Winner 1997

✍

Clara

1950–1952

1

Terry's the spur. The splinter under my fingernail. To come clean, I'm starting on this shambles that is the true story of my wasted life (violating a solemn pledge, scribbling a first book at my advanced age), as a riposte to the scurrilous charges Terry McIver has made in his forthcoming autobiography: about me, my three wives, a.k.a. Barney Panofsky's troika, the nature of my friendship with Boogie, and, of course, the scandal I will carry to my grave like a humpback. Terry's sound of two hands clapping, *Of Time and Fevers*, will shortly be launched by The Group (sorry, the group), a government-subsidized small press, rooted in Toronto, that also publishes a monthly journal, *the good earth*, printed on recycled paper, you bet your life.

Terry McIver and I, both Montrealers born and bred, were in Paris together in the early fifties. Poor Terry was no more than tolerated by my bunch, a pride of impecunious, horny young writers awash in rejection slips, yet ostensibly confident that everything was possible—fame, adoring bimbos, and fortune lying in wait around the corner, just like that legendary Wrigley's shill of my boyhood. The shill, according to report, would surprise you on the street to reward you with a crisp new dollar bill, provided you had a Wrigley's chewing-gum wrapper in your pocket. Mr. Wrigley's big giver never caught up with me. But fame did find several of my bunch: the driven Leo Bishinsky; Cedric Richardson, albeit under another name; and, of course, Clara. Clara, who now enjoys posthumous fame as a feminist icon, beaten on the anvil of male-chauvinist insentience. My anvil, so they say.

I was an anomaly. No, an anomie. A natural-born entrepreneur. I hadn't won awards at McGill, like Terry, or been to Harvard or Columbia, like some of the others. I had barely squeezed through high school, having invested more time at the tables of the Mount Royal Billiards Academy than in classes, playing snooker with Duddy Kravitz. Couldn't write. Didn't paint. Had no artistic pretensions whatsoever, unless you count my fantasy of becoming a music-hall song-and-dance man, tipping my straw boater to the good folks in the balcony as I fluttered off stage in my taps, yielding to Peaches, Ann Corio,[1] Lili St. Cyr, or some other exotic dancer, who would bring her act to a drum-throbbing climax with a thrilling flash of bare tit, in days long before lap-dancers had become the norm in Montreal.

I was a voracious reader, but you would be mistaken if you took that as evidence of my quality. Or sensibility. At bottom, I am obliged to acknowledge, with a nod to Clara, the baseness of my soul. My ugly competitive nature. What got me started was not Tolstoy's *The Death of Ivan Ilyich*, or Conrad's *The Secret Agent*, but the old *Liberty* magazine, which prefaced each of its articles with a headnote saying how long it would take to read it: say, five minutes and thirty-five seconds. Setting my Mickey Mouse wristwatch on our kitchen table with the checkered oilcloth, I would zip through the piece in question in, say, four minutes and three seconds, and consider myself an intellectual. From *Liberty*, I graduated to a paperback John Marquand "Mr. Moto" novel, selling for twenty-five cents at the time in Jack and Moe's Barbershop, corner of Park Avenue and Laurier in the heart of Montreal's old working-class Jewish quarter, where I was raised. A neighbourhood that had elected the only Communist (Fred Rose) ever to serve as a member of Parliament, produced a couple of decent club fighters (Louis Alter, Maxie Berger), the obligatory number of doctors and dentists, a celebrated gambler–cum–casino owner, more cutthroat lawyers than needed, sundry school teachers and *shmata* millionaires, a few rabbis, and at least one suspected murderer.

Me.

---

[1] The correct spelling is Coreo.

I remember snow banks five feet high, winding outside staircases that had to be shovelled in the sub-zero cold, and, in days long before snow tires, the rattle of passing cars and trucks, their wheels encased in chains. Sheets frozen rock-hard on backyard clotheslines. In my bedroom, where the radiator sizzled and knocked through the night, I eventually stumbled on Hemingway, Fitzgerald, Joyce, Gertie and Alice, as well as our own Morley Callaghan. I came of age envying their expatriate adventures and, as a consequence, made a serious decision in 1950.

Ah, 1950. That was the last year Bill Durnan, five times winner of the Vézina Trophy, best goalie in the National Hockey League, would mind the nets for my beloved Montreal Canadiens. In 1950, *nos glorieux* could already deploy a formidable defence corps, its mainstay young Doug Harvey. The Punch Line was then only two thirds intact: in the absence of Hector "Toe" Blake, who retired in 1948, Maurice "The Rocket" Richard and Elmer Lach were skating on a line with Floyd "Busher" Curry. They finished second to bloody Detroit in the regular season and, to their everlasting shame, went down four games to one to the New York Rangers in the Stanley Cup semifinals. At least The Rocket enjoyed a decent year, finishing the regular season second in the individual scoring race with forty-three goals and twenty-two assists.[2]

Anyway, in 1950, at the age of twenty-two, I left the chorus girl I was living with in a basement flat on Tupper Street. I withdrew my modest stash from the City and District Savings Bank, money I had earned as a waiter at the old Normandy Roof (a job arranged by my father, Detective-Inspector Izzy Panofsky), and booked passage to Europe on the *Queen Elizabeth*,[3] sailing out of New York. In my innocence, I was determined to seek out and be enriched by the friendship of what I then thought of as the pure of heart, artists, "the unacknowledged legislators of the world." And those, those were the days when you could smooch with college girls with impunity. One, Two, Cha-Cha-Cha. "If I Knew You Were Coming I'd've Baked a Cake." Moonlit nights on deck, nice girls wore crinolines, cinch belts, ankle bracelets, and two-tone saddle shoes, and you could count on them not to

---

[2] Actually, Richard finished fourth in the scoring race. Ted Lindsay, of the Detroit Red Wings, won the title with twenty-three goals and fifty-five assists. Sid Abel came second, Gordie Howe third, and then Richard.

[3] It was the *Queen Mary*, which made its last voyage in 1967, encountering the *Queen Elizabeth* at sea at 12:10 a.m., on September 25, 1967.

sue you for sexual harassment forty years later, their suppressed memories of date-rape retrieved by lady psychoanalysts who shaved.

Not fame, but fortune eventually found me. That fortune, such as it is, had humble roots. To begin with, I was sponsored by a survivor of Auschwitz, Yossel Pinsky, who changed dollars for us at black-market rates in a curtained booth in a photography shop on the rue des Rosiers. One evening Yossel sat down at my table in The Old Navy, ordered a *café filtre*, dropped seven sugar cubes into his cup, and said, "I need somebody with a valid Canadian passport."

"To do what?"

"Make money. What else is left?" he asked, taking out a Swiss Army knife and beginning to clean his remaining fingernails. "But we should get to know each other a little better first. Have you eaten yet?"

"No."

"So let's go for dinner. Hey, I won't bite. Come, *boychick*."

And that's how, only a year later, Yossel serving as my guide, I became an exporter of French cheeses to an increasingly flush postwar Canada. Back home, Yossel arranged for me to run an agency for Vespas, those Italian motorized scooters that were once such a hot item. Over the years I also dealt profitably, with Yossel as my partner, in olive oil, just like the young Meyer Lansky; bolts of cloth spun on the islands of Lewis and Harris; scrap metal, bought and sold without my ever having seen any of it; antiquated DC-3s, some of them still being flown North of Sixty; and, after Yossel had moved to Israel, one step ahead of the gendarmes, ancient Egyptian artifacts, stolen from minor tombs in the Valley of the Kings. But I have my principles. I have never handled arms, drugs, or health foods.

Finally I became a sinner. In the late sixties, I began to produce Canadian-financed films that were never exhibited anywhere for more than an embarrassing week, but which eventually earned me, and on occasion my backers, hundreds of thousands of dollars through a tax loophole since closed. Then I started to churn out Canadian-content TV series sufficiently shlocky to be syndicated in the U.S. and, in the case of our boffo *McIver of the RCMP* series, which is big on bonking scenes in canoes and igloos, in the U.K., and other countries as well.

When it was required of me, I could rumba as a latter-day patriot, sheltering in the Great Cham's last refuge of the scoundrel. Whenever a government minister, a free-marketeer responding to American pressure, threatened to dump the law that insisted on (and bankrolled to a yummy degree) so much Canadian-manufactured pollution on our airwaves, I did a quick change in the hypocrite's phone booth, slipping into my Captain Canada mode, and appeared before the committee. "We are defining Canada to Canadians," I told them. "We are this country's memory, its soul, its hypostasis, the last defence against our being overwhelmed by the egregious cultural imperialists to the south of us."

I digress.

Back in our expatriate days, we roistering provincials, slap-happy to be in Paris, drunk on the beauty of our surroundings, were fearful of retiring to our Left Bank hotel rooms lest we wake up back home, retrieved by parents who would remind us of how much they had invested in our educations, and how it was time for us to put our shoulders to the wheel. In my case, no airmail letter from my father was complete without its built-in stinger:

"Yankel Schneider, remember him, he had a stammer? So what? He's become a chartered accountant and drives a Buick now."

Our loosy-goosy band included a couple of painters, so to speak, both of them New Yorkers. There was the loopy Clara and the scheming Leo Bishinsky, who managed his artistic rise better than Wellington did—you know, that battle in a town in Belgium.[4] He left a ball to go to it. Or interrupted a game of bowls. No, that was Drake.

A garage in Montparnasse served as Leo's atelier, and there he laboured on his huge triptychs, mixing his paints in buckets and applying them with a kitchen mop. On occasion he would swish his mop around, stand back ten feet, and let fly. Once, when I was there, the two of us sharing a toke, he thrust his mop at me. "Have a go," he said.

"Really?"

"Why not?"

Soon enough, I figured, Leo would get a shave and a haircut and join an advertising agency in New York.

I was dead wrong.

Go know that forty years later Leo's atrocities would be hanging in the Tate, the Guggenheim, MOMA, and The National Gallery in Washington, and that others would be sold for millions to junk-bond mavens and arbitrage gurus who were often outbid by Japanese collectors. Go anticipate

---

4 Waterloo, where the Duke of Wellington, and the Prussian field marshal Gebhard Leberecht von Blücher, defeated Napoleon on June 18, 1815.

that Leo's battered Renault *deux-chevaux*[5] would one day be succeeded, in a ten-car garage in Amagansett, by a Rolls-Royce Silver Cloud, a vintage Morgan, a Ferrari 250 *berlinetta*, and an Alfa Romeo, among other toys. Or that to mention his name today, in passing, I could be accused of name-dropping. Leo has appeared on the cover of *Vanity Fair* in Mephistophelian guise, replete with horns, magenta cape and tails, painting magic symbols on the nude body of a flavour-of-the-month starlet.

In the old days you could always tell who Leo was screwing, because, *tout court,* a white-bread-and-cashmere-twin-set young woman out of Nebraska, working for the Marshall Plan, would turn up at La Coupole and think nothing of picking her nose at the table. But today renowned fashion models flock to Leo's Long Island mansion, vying with one another to proffer pubic hairs that can be worked into his paintings along with bits of beach glass, bluefish skeletons, salami butts, and toenail clippings.

Back in 1951 my gang of neophyte artists flaunted their liberation from what they, *de haut en bas,* denigrated as the rat race, but the sour truth is, with the shining exception of Bernard "Boogie" Moscovitch, they were all contenders. Each one as fiercely competitive as any *Organization Man* or *Man in the Gray Flannel Suit,* if any of you out there are old enough to remember those long-forgotten best-sellers, modish for a season. Like Colin Wilson. Or the Hula Hoop. And they were driven by the need to succeed as much as any St. Urbain Street urchin back home who had bet his bundle on a new autumn line of *après-ski* wear. Fiction is what most of them were peddling. Making it new, as Ezra Pound had ordained before he was certified insane. Mind you, they didn't have to cart samples round to department store buyers, floating on "a smile and a shoeshine," as Clifford Odets[6] once put it. Instead, they shipped their merchandise off to magazine and book editors, enclosing a stamped, self-addressed envelope. Except for Boogie, my anointed one.

Alfred Kazin once wrote of Saul Bellow that, even when he was still young and unknown, he already had the aura about him of a man destined for greatness. I felt the same about Boogie, who was uncommonly generous at the time to other young writers, it being understood that he was superior to any of them.

---

[5] Actually, the 2CV was a Citroën. It was introduced at the Paris motor show in 1948, and taken out of production in 1990.

[6] Not Odets, but Arthur Miller in *Death of a Salesman*, p. 138. Viking Press Inc., New York, 1949.

In one of his manic moods Boogie would throw up lots of smoke, deflecting questions about his work by clowning. "Look at me," he once said, "I've got all the faults of Tolstoy, Dostoevsky, and Hemingway rolled into one. I will fuck just about any peasant girl who will have me. I'm an obsessive gambler. A drunk. Hey, just like Freddy D., I'm even an anti-Semite, but maybe that doesn't count in my case as I'm Jewish myself. So far, all that's lacking in the equation is my very own Yasnaya Polyana, a recognition of my prodigious talent, and money for tonight's dinner, unless you're inviting me? God bless you, Barney."

Five years older than I was, Boogie had scrambled up Omaha Beach on D-Day, and survived the Battle of the Bulge. He was in Paris on the GI Bill, which provided him with one hundred dollars monthly, a stipend supplemented by an allowance from home, which he usually invested, with sporadic luck, on the *chemin de fer* tables at the Aviation Club.

Well now, never mind the malicious gossip, most recently revived by the lying McIver, that will pursue me to the end of my days. The truth is, Boogie was the most cherished friend I ever had. I adored him. And over many a shared toke, or bottle of *vin ordinaire,* I was able to piece together something of his background. Boogie's grandfather Moishe Lev Moscovitch, born in Bialystok, sailed steerage to America from Hamburg, and rose by dint of hard work and parsimony from pushcart chicken peddler to sole proprietor of a kosher butcher shop on Rivington Street on the Lower East Side. His first-born son, Mendel, parlayed that butcher shop into Peerless Gourmet Packers, suppliers of K-rations to the U.S. Army during the Second World War. Peerless emerged afterward as purveyors of Virginia Plantation packaged ham, Olde English sausages, Mandarin spare ribs, and Granny's Gobblers (frozen, oven-ready turkeys) to supermarkets in New York State and New England. *En route,* Mendel, his name laundered to Matthew Morrow, acquired a fourteen-room apartment on Park Avenue, serviced by a maid, a cook, a butler-cum-chauffeur, and an English governess off the Old Kent Road for his first-born son, Boogie, who later had to take elocution lessons to get rid of his cockney accent. In lieu of a violin teacher and a Hebrew *melamed,* Boogie, who was counted on to infiltrate the family deep into the WASP hive, was sent to a military summer camp in Maine. "I was expected to learn how to ride, shoot, sail, play tennis, and turn the other cheek," he said. Registering for camp, Boogie, as instructed by his mother, filled out "atheist" under "Religious Denomination." The camp commander winked, crossed it out, and wrote "Jewish." Boogie endured the camp, and Andover, but dropped out of Harvard in his sophomore year, in 1941, and joined the army as a rifleman, reverting to the name Moscovitch.

Once, responding to persistent inquiries from an earnest Terry McIver, Boogie allowed that in the opening chapter of his discombobulating novel-in-progress, set in 1912, his protagonist disembarks from the *Titanic,* which has just completed its maiden voyage, docking safely in New York, only to be accosted by a reporter. "What was the trip like?" she asks.

"Boring."

Improvising, I'm sure, Boogie went on to say that, two years later, his protagonist, riding in a carriage with Archduke Francis Ferdinand of Austria–Hungary and his missus, drops his opera glasses as they bounce over a bump in the road. The archduke, big on *noblesse oblige,* stoops to retrieve them, thereby avoiding an assassination attempt by a Serb nutter. A couple of months later, however, the Germans invade Belgium all the same. Then, in 1917, Boogie's protagonist, shooting the breeze with Lenin in a Zurich café, asks for an explanation of surplus value, and Lenin, warming to the subject, lingers too long over his *millefeuille* and *café au lait,* and misses his train, the sealed car arriving in the Finland Station without him.

"Isn't that just like that fucking Ilyich?" says the leader of the delegation come to greet him on the platform. "Now what is to be done?"

"Maybe Leon would get up and say a few words?"

"A few words? Leon? We'll be standing here for hours."

Boogie told Terry he was fulfilling the artist's primary function—making order out of chaos.

"I should have known better than to ask you a serious question," said Terry, retreating from our café table.

In the ensuing silence, Boogie, by way of apology, turned to me and explained that he had inherited, from Heinrich Heine, *le droit de moribondage.*

Boogie could yank that sort of conversation-stopper out of the back pocket of his mind, propelling me to a library, educating me.

I loved Boogie and miss him something awful. I would give up my fortune (say half) to have that enigma, that six-foot-two scarecrow, lope through my door again, pulling on a Romeo y Julieta, his smile charged with ambiguity, demanding, "Have you read Thomas Bernhard yet?" or "What do you make of Chomsky?"

God knows he had his dark side, disappearing for weeks on end—some said to a *yeshiva* in Mea Shearim and others swore to a monastery in Tuscany—but nobody really knew where. Then one day he would appear—no, materialize—without explanation at one of the cafés we favoured, accompanied by a gorgeous Spanish duchess or an Italian contessa.

On his bad days Boogie wouldn't answer my knock on his hotel-room door or, if he did, would say no more than "Go away. Let me be," and I knew that he was lying on his bed, high on horse, or that he was seated at his table, compiling lists of the names of those young men who had fought alongside him and were already dead.

It was Boogie who introduced me to Goncharov, Huysmans, Céline, and Nathanael West. He was taking language lessons from a White Russian watchmaker whom he had befriended. "How can anybody go through life," he asked, "not being able to read Dostoevsky, Tolstoy, and Chekhov in the original?" Fluent in German and Hebrew, Boogie studied the Zohar, the holy book of the Cabbala, once a week with a rabbi in a synagogue on rue Notre-Dame-de-Lorette, an address that delighted him.

Then, years ago, I collected all eight of Boogie's cryptic short stories that had been published in *Merlin, Zero,* and *The Paris Review,* with the intention of bringing them out in a limited edition, each volume numbered, elegantly printed, no expense spared. The story of his that I've read again and again, for obvious reasons, is a variation on a far-from-original theme, but brilliantly realized, like everything he wrote. "Margolis" is about a man who walks out to buy a package of cigarettes and never returns to his wife and child, assuming a new identity elsewhere.

I wrote to Boogie's son in Santa Fe offering him an advance of ten thousand dollars, as well as a hundred free copies and all profits that might accrue from the enterprise. His response came in the form of a registered letter that expressed amazement that I, of all people, could even contemplate such a venture, and warning me that he would not hesitate to take legal action if I dared to do such a thing. So that was that.

Hold the phone. I'm stuck. I'm trying to remember the name of the author of *The Man in the Gray Flannel Suit.* Or was it *The Man in the Brooks Brothers Shirt?* No, that was written by the fibber. Lillian what's-her-name? Come on. I know it. Like the mayonnaise. Lillian Kraft? No. *Hellman. Lillian Hellman.* The name of the author of *The Man in the Gray Flannel Suit* doesn't matter. It's of no importance. But now that it's started I won't sleep tonight. These increasingly frequent bouts of memory loss are driving me crazy.

Last night, sailing off to sleep at last, I couldn't remember the name of the thing you use to strain spaghetti. Imagine that. I've used it thousands of times. I could visualize it. But I couldn't remember what the bloody thing was called. And I didn't want to get out of bed to search through cookbooks Miriam had left behind, because it would only remind me that it was my fault she was gone, and I would have to get out of bed at three o'clock anyway to piss. Not the swift bubbly torrent of my Left Bank days, nosirree. Now it was dribble, dribble, dribble, and no matter how hard I shook it, a belated trickle down my pyjama leg.

Lying in the dark, fulminating, I recited aloud the number I was to call if I had a heart attack.

"You have reached the Montreal General Hospital. If you have a touch-tone phone, and you know the extension you want, please press that number now. If not, press number seventeen for service in the language of *les maudits anglais,* or number twelve for service *en français,* the glorious language of our oppressed collectivity."

Twenty-one for emergency ambulance service.

"You have reached the emergency ambulance service. Please hold and an operator will come to your assistance as soon as our strip-poker game is over. Have a nice day."

While I waited, the automatic tape would play Mozart's *Requiem.*

I groped to make sure my digitalis pills, reading glasses, and dentures were within easy reach on the bedside table. I switched on a lamp briefly and scooped up my boxer shorts to check them out for skid marks, because if I died during the night I didn't want strangers to think I was dirty. Then I tried the usual gambit. Think of something else, something soothing, and the name of the spaghetti thingamabob will come to you unsummoned. So I imagined Terry McIver bleeding profusely in a shark-infested sea, feeling another tug at what's left of his legs just as a rescuing helicopter is attempting to winch him out of the water. Finally what remains of the lying, self-regarding author of *Of Time and Fevers,* a dripping torso, is raised above the surface, bobbing like bait in the churning waters, sharks lunging at it.

Next I made myself a scruffy fourteen-year-old again, and unhooked, for that first whoopee time, the filigreed bra of the teacher I shall call Mrs. Ogilvy, even as one of those nonsense songs was playing on the radio in her living room:

Mair-zy Doats and Do-zy Doats and lid-dle lam-zy div-ey
A kid-dle-y div-ey too, would-n't you?

To my astonishment, she didn't resist. Instead, terrifying me, she kicked off her shoes and began to wriggle out of her tartan skirt. "I don't know what's got into me," said the teacher who had awarded me an A+ for my essay on *A Tale of Two Cities*, which I had cribbed, paraphrasing here and there, from a book by Granville Hicks. "I'm robbing the cradle." Then, in my mind's eye, she spoiled everything, adding, with a certain classroom asperity, "But shouldn't we strain the spaghetti first?"

"Yeah. Sure. But using what thingamajig?"

"I fancy it *al dente*," she said.

And now, giving Mrs. Ogilvy a second chance, hoping for a better return this time, I travelled back through memory lane again and tumbled onto the sofa with her, incidentally hoping for at least a semi-demi-erection in my decrepit here and now.

"Oh, you're so impatient," she said. "Wait. Not yet. *En français, s'il vous plaît.*"

"What?"

"Oh, dear. Such manners. We mean 'I beg your pardon,' don't we? Now then, let's have 'not yet' in French, please."

"*Pas encore.*"

"Jolly good," she said, sliding open a side-table drawer. "Now I don't want you to think me a bossy boots, but please be a considerate lad and roll this on to your pretty little willy first."

"Yes, Mrs. Ogilvy."

"Give me your hand. Oh, have you ever seen such filthy fingernails? There. Like that! Gently does it. Oh yes, please. *Wait!*"

"What have I done wrong now?"

"I just thought you'd like to know it wasn't Lillian Hellman who wrote *The Man in the Brooks Brothers Shirt*. It was Mary McCarthy."

Damn damn damn. I got out of bed, slipped into the threadbare dressing-gown I couldn't part with because it was a gift from Miriam, and padded into the kitchen. Rummaging through drawers, I yanked out utensils and named them one-two-three: soup ladle, egg-timer, tongs, pie slicer, vegetable peeler, tea strainer, measuring cups, can opener, spatula ... and hanging on a wall hook, there it was, the thingamabob used to strain spaghetti, *but what was it called?*

I've survived scarlet fever, mumps, two muggings, crabs, the extraction of all my teeth, a hip-socket replacement, a murder charge, and three wives. The first one is dead and The Second Mrs. Panofsky, hearing my voice, would holler, even after all these years, "Murderer, what have you done with his body?" before slamming down the receiver. But Miriam would talk to me. She might even laugh at my dilemma. Oh, to have this apartment resonate with her laughter. Her scent. Her love. The trouble is, Blair would probably be the one to answer the phone, and I had already blotted my copybook with that pretentious bastard the last time I called. "I would like to speak to my wife," I said.

"She is no longer your wife, Barney, and you are obviously inebriated."

He would say "inebriated." "Of course I'm drunk. It's four o'clock in the morning."

"And Miriam's asleep."

"But it's you I wanted to talk to. I was cleaning out my desk drawers here and I found some stunning nude photographs of her when she was with me, and I was wondering if you would like to have them, if only to know what she looked like in her prime."

"You're disgusting," he said, hanging up.

True enough. But, all the same, I danced round the living room, doing my take on the great Ralph Brown's Shim Sham Shimmy, a tumbler of Cardhu in hand.

There are some people out there who take Blair to be a fine fellow. A scholar of distinction. Even my sons defend him. We appreciate how you feel, they say, but he is an intelligent and caring man, devoted to Miriam. Bullshit. A drudge on tenure, Blair came to Canada from Boston in the sixties, a draft-dodger, like Dan Quayle and Bill Clinton, and, consequently, a hero to his students. As for me, I'm dumbfounded that anybody would prefer Toronto to Saigon. Anyway, I've got his faculty group fax number and, thinking of how Boogie would have taken advantage of that, I sit down and wing one to Blair occasionally.

**Fax to Herr Doktor Blair Hopper né Hauptman
From Sexorama Novelties**

ACHTUNG
PRIVATE AND CONFIDENTIAL

Dear Herr Doktor Hopper,

Pursuant to your inquiry of January 26, we welcome your idea of introducing to Victoria College the old Ivy League practice of requiring selected coeds to pose naked for posture photographs, front, profile, and back. Your notion of introducing garter belts and other accessories is inspired. The project has, as you put it, great commercial potential. However, we will have to assess the actual photographs before we can take up your suggestion to market a new set of playing cards.

Sincerely,
DWAYNE CONNORS
Sexorama Novelties.

P.S. We acknowledge your return of our 1995 TOY BOYS calendar, but cannot send you a refund due to the many stains, and the fact that the August and September pages are stuck together.

Twelve forty-five a.m. Now I held the spaghetti thingamajig in my liver-spotted hand, wrinkled as a lizard's back, but I still couldn't put a name to it. Flinging it aside, I poured myself a couple of inches of Macallan, picked up the phone, and dialled my eldest son in London. "Hiya, Mike. This is your six a.m. wake-up call. Time for your morning jog."

"As a matter of fact, it's five forty-six here."

For breakfast my punctilious son would munch crunchy granola and yogurt, washed down with a glass of lemon water. People today.

"Are you okay?" he asked, and his concern just about brought tears to my eyes.

"In the pink. But I've got a problem. What do you call the thingee you strain spaghetti with?"

"Are you drunk?"

"*Certainly not.*"

"Didn't Dr. Herscovitch warn you that if you started up again it would kill you?"

"I swear on the heads of my grandchildren, I haven't had a drop in weeks. I no longer even order *coq au vin* in restaurants. Now will you answer my question, please?"

"I'm going to take the phone in the living room, hang up here, and then we can talk."

Mustn't wake Lady Health Fascist.

"Hi, I'm back. Do you mean a colander?"

"Of course I mean a colander. It was on the tip of my tongue. I was just going to say it."

"Are you taking your pills?"

"Sure I am. Have you heard from your mother lately?" I blurted out compulsively, having sworn I'd never ask about her again.

"She and Blair stopped over here for three days on October fourth, on their way to a conference in Glasgow."[7]

"I don't give a damn about her any more. You don't know what a pleasure it is not to be reprimanded because I forgot to lift the seat again. But, speaking as a disinterested observer, I think she deserved better."

"You mean you?"

"Tell Caroline," I said, lashing out, "that I read somewhere that lettuce bleeds when you chop it up and carrots suffer traumas when you pluck them out of the ground."

"Dad, I hate to think of you all alone in that big empty apartment."

"As it happens, I have what I think they now call 'a resource person,' or is it 'a sex worker,' staying with me tonight. What boors like me used to call 'a skirt'. Tell your mother. I don't mind."

"Why don't you fly over and haunt our house for a while?"

"Because in the London I remember best the obligatory first course in even the most stylish restaurant was grey-brown Windsor soup, or a grapefruit with a maraschino cherry sitting in the middle like a nipple, and most of the people I used to hang out with there are dead now, and about time too. Harrods has become a Eurotrash temple. Everywhere you turn in Knightsbridge there are rich Japs shooting movies of each other. The White Elephant is kaput, so is Isow's, and L'Étoile ain't what it used to be. I have no interest in who's banging Di or whether Charles is reincarnated as a tampon. The pubs are intolerable, what with those noisy slot-machines and pounding jungle music. And too many of our people there are something else. If they've been to Oxford or Cambridge, or earn more than a hundred thousand pounds a year, they are no longer Jewish, but 'of Jewish descent,' which is not quite the same thing."

I've never really been rooted in London, but I was once there in the fifties for three months, and another time in 1961 for a stay of two, missing the

---

[7] Actually, according to my diary, Blair and my mother stopped over on October 7th, and the conference was in Edinburgh.

Stanley Cup playoffs. Mind you, that was the year the heavily favoured Canadiens were eliminated in six games, in the semifinals, by the Chicago Black Hawks. I still wish I had caught the second game, in Chicago, which the Hawks won 2–1, after fifty-two minutes of overtime. That was the night referee Dalton McArthur, that officious bastard, penalized Dickie Moore, *in overtime,* for tripping, enabling Murray Balfour to pot the winning goal. An outraged Toe Blake, then our coach, charged onto the ice to bop McArthur one, and was fined $2,000. I had flown over to London in '61 to work on that co-production with Hymie Mintzbaum that led to such a nasty fight, resulting in our being estranged for years. Hymie, born and bred in the Bronx, is an Anglophile, but not me.

You simply can't trust the British. With Americans (or Canadians, for that matter) what you see is what you get. But settle into your seat on a 749 flying out of Heathrow next to an ostensibly boring old Englishman with wobbly chins, the acquired stammer, obviously something in the City, intent on his *Times* crossword puzzle, and don't you dare patronize him. Mr. Milquetoast, actually a judo black belt, was probably parachuted into the Dordogne in 1943, blew up a train or two, and survived the Gestapo cells by concentrating on what would become the definitive translation of *Gilgamesh* from the Sin-Leqi-Inninni; and now—his garment bag stuffed with his wife's most alluring cocktail dresses and lingerie—he is no doubt bound for the annual convention of cross-dressers in Saskatoon.

Once again Mike told me that I could have their garden flat. Private. With my own entrance. And how wonderfully dreadful it would be for his children, who had adored *Friday the 13th,* to get to know their grandfather. But I hate being a grandfather. It's indecent. In my mind's eye, I'm still twenty-five. Thirty-three max. Certainly not sixty-seven, reeking of decay and dashed hopes. My breath sour. My limbs in dire need of a lube job. And now that I've been blessed with a plastic hip-socket replacement, I'm no longer even biodegradable. Environmentalists will protest my burial.

On one of my recent annual visits to Mike and Caroline, I arrived laden with gifts for my grandchildren and Her Ladyship (as Saul, my second-born son, has dubbed her), my *pièce de résistance* reserved for Mike: a box of Cohibas, acquired for me in Cuba. It pained me to part with those cigars, but I hoped it would please Mike, with whom I had a difficult relationship, and it did delight him. Or so I thought. But a month later one of Mike's associates, Tony Haines, who also happened to be a cousin of Caroline's, was in Montreal on a business trip. He phoned to say he had a gift from

Mike, a side of smoked salmon from Fortnum's. I invited him to meet me for drinks at Dink's. Pulling out his cigar case, Tony offered me a Cohiba. "Oh, wonderful," I said. "Thank you."

"Don't thank me. They were a birthday gift from Mike and Caroline."

"Oh, really," I said, lumbered with another family grievance to nurse. Or cherish, according to Miriam. "Some people collect stamps, or bookmatch covers," she once said, "but with you, my darling, it's grievances."

On that visit Mike and Caroline settled me into an upstairs bedroom, everything mod, from Conran or The General Trading Company. A bouquet of freesias and a bottle of Perrier on my bedside table, but no ashtray. Opening the bedside-table drawer, searching for something I could use, I blundered on a pair of torn pantyhose. Sniffing them, I recognized the scent at once. Miriam's. She and Blair had shared this bed, contaminating it. Yanking back the sheets, I searched the mattress for tell-tale stains. Nothing. Har, har, har. Professor Limp Prick couldn't cut the mustard. Herr Doktor Hopper né Hauptman probably read aloud to her in bed instead. His deconstructionist *pensées* on Mark Twain's racism. Or Hemingway's homophobia. All the same, I retrieved a canister of pine spray from the bathroom and fumigated the mattress, and then remade the bed after a fashion before climbing back into it. Now the sheets were riding up on me, a maddening tangle. The room stank of pine scent. I opened a window wide. Freezing cold it was. An abandoned husband, I was obviously destined to perish of pneumonia in a bed once graced by Miriam's warmth. Her beauty. *Her treachery.* Well now, women of her age, suffering hot flushes and confusions, sometimes unaccountably begin to shoplift. If she were arrested, I would refuse to be a character witness. No, I would testify that she had always been light-fingered. Let her rot in the slammer. Miriam, Miriam, my heart's desire.

MIKE, BLESS HIM, is filthy rich, which he atones for by still wearing his hair in a ponytail and favouring blue jeans (Polo Ralph Lauren's, mind you), but, happily, no earrings. Or Nehru jackets any longer. Or Mao caps. He's a property baron. Owner of some choice houses in Highgate, Hampstead, Swiss Cottage, Islington, and Chelsea, which he accumulated before inflation hit, and converted into flats. He's also into some things offshore, which I'd rather not know about, and deals in commodity futures. He and Caroline live in modish Fulham, which I remember before the diy-trained yuppies invaded. They also own a dacha high in the hills of the

Alpes-Maritimes, not far from Vence, a vineyard running down its slopes. In three generations, from the *shtetl* to the makers of Château Panofsky. What can I say?

Mike is a partner in a restaurant for the smart set. It's in Pimlico, called The Table, the chef ruder than he is talented, which is *de rigueur* these days, isn't it? Too young to remember Pearl Harbor, or what happened to the Canadians taken prisoner at—at—you know, that impregnable outpost in the Far East. Not the one where the dawn comes up like thunder, no, but the place where the Sassoons struck it rich. Singapore? No. The place like the name of the gorilla in that film with Fay Wray. *Kong. Hong Kong.* And, look, I know that Wellington defeated Napoleon at Waterloo, and I remember who wrote *The Man in the Gray Flannel Suit*. Came to me unbidden. *The Man in the Gray Flannel Suit* was written by Frederic Wakeman[8] and the movie starred Clark Gable and Sydney Greenstreet.

Anyway, too young to remember Pearl Harbor, Mike invested heavily in the Japanese market in the early days and dumped everything at the propitious moment. He rode gold through the OPEC scare, whipping his stake past the finishing line, doubling it, and made another killing speculating in sterling in 1992. He had bet on Bill Gates before anybody had heard of E-mail.

Yes, my first-born son is a multimillionaire with both a social and a cultural conscience. He's a member of a trendy theatre board, a promoter of in-your-face plays wherein top people's leggy daughters feel free to pretend to shit on stage and RADA guys simulate bum-fucking with abandon. *Ars longa, vita brevis.* He's one of the more than two hundred backers of the monthly *Red Pepper* magazine ("feminist, antiracist, environmentalist, and internationalist"); and, not without a redeeming sense of humour, he has added my name to the subscription list. The most recent issue of *Red Pepper* includes a full-page ad, an appeal for donations by London Lighthouse, which features a photograph of a sickly young woman, her staring eyes rimmed with dark circles, looking into a hand-held mirror.

"SHE TOLD HER HUSBAND THAT SHE WAS HIV+. HE TOOK IT BADLY."

What was the poor bastard supposed to do? Take her to dinner at The Ivy to celebrate?

---

[8] *The Man in the Gray Flannel Suit* was written by Sloan Wilson (1955); and it was *The Hucksters*, by Frederic Wakeman, that was made into a movie starring Clark Gable, Deborah Kerr, and Sydney Greenstreet: MGM, 1947. Now also shown in a computer-coloured version.

In any event, as Mr. Bellow has already noted, more die of heartbreak. Or lung cancer, speaking as a prime candidate.

True, Mike shops for shiitake mushrooms, Japanese seaweed, Nishiki rice, and shiromiso soup at Harvey Nichols' Food Hall, but, emerging on Sloane Street, he always remembers to buy a copy of *The Big Issue* from the bum lurking there. He owns an art gallery in Fulham that has proven itself, as it were, having twice been charged with obscenity. He and Caroline make a point of buying works by as-yet-unknown painters and sculptors who are, in Mike's parlance, "on the cutting edge." My up-to-the-minute, state-of-the-art son is into gangsta rap, information highways (as distinct from libraries), "dissing," quality time, Internet, all things cool, and every other speech cliché peculiar to his generation. Mike has never read *The Iliad*, Gibbon, Stendhal, Swift, Dr. Johnson, George Eliot, or any other now-discredited Eurocentric bigot, but there isn't an overpraised "visible minority" new novelist or poet whose book he hasn't ordered from Hatchard's. I'll wager he never stood for an hour contemplating Velásquez's portrait of that royal family,[9] you know the one I mean, in the Prado, but invite him to a *vernissage* that promises a crucifix floating in piss or a harpoon sticking out of a woman's bleeding arsehole, and he's there with his chequebook. "Oh," I said, determined to keep our transatlantic phone call going, "I don't mean to pry, but I do hope you've spoken to your sister recently."

"Watch it. You're beginning to sound just like Mom."

"That's no answer."

"There's no point in phoning Kate. She's either just rushing out, or in the middle of a dinner party, and can't talk now."

"That doesn't sound like Kate."

"Come on, Dad. As far as you're concerned, she can do no wrong. She was always your favourite."

"That's not true," I lied.

"But Saul phoned yesterday to ask what I thought of his latest diatribe in that neo-fascist rag he writes for. Hell, it had only arrived in that morning's mail. He's incredible, really. It took him fifteen minutes to bring me up to date on his imaginary health problems and work difficulties, and then to denounce me as a champagne socialist and Caroline as a penny-pincher. Who's he living with these days, may I ask?"

---

[9] Las Meninas.

"Hey, I see the British are up in arms, because calves are being shipped to France, where they're confined to crates instead of being booked into the Crillon. Has Caroline joined the demos?"

"You can do better than that, Dad. But do come and see us soon," said Mike, his voice stiffening, and I guessed that Caroline had just floated into the room, glancing pointedly at her wristwatch, unaware that I was paying for the phone call.

"Sure," I said, hanging up, disgusted with myself.

Why couldn't I have told him how much I love him, and what pleasure he has given me over the years?

What if this were to be our last conversation?

"But death, you know," wrote Samuel Johnson to the Reverend Mr. Thomas Warton, "hears not supplications, nor pays any regard to the convenience of mortals."

And what if Miriam and I were never to be reconciled?

2

We have all read too much in literary journals about the unjustly neglected novelist, but seldom a word about the justly neglected, the scratch players, brandishing their little distinctions, à la Terry McIver. A translation into Icelandic, or an appearance at a Commonwealth arts festival in Auckland (featuring a few "writers of pallor," as the new nomenclature has it, as well as an affirmative-action mélange of Maori, Inuit, and Amerindian good spellers). But, after all these years as a flunk, my old friend and latter-day nemesis has acquired a small but vociferous following, CanLit apparatchiks to the fore. That scumbag is ubiquitous in Canada these days, pontificating on TV and radio, giving public readings everywhere.

It was through that self-promoting bastard's father, who is also traduced in *Of Time and Fevers*, that I met Terry in the first place. Mr. McIver, sole prop. of The Spartacus Bookshop on St. Catherine Street West, was the most admirable, if innocent, of men. A scrawny Scot, bred in the Gorbals, he was the illegitimate son of a laundry woman and a Clydeside welder who fell at the Somme. Mr. McIver would urge books on me by Howard Fast, Jack London, Émile Zola, Upton Sinclair, John Reed, Edgar Snow, and the Russian, you know, Lenin's laureate, what's-his-name? Anathema to

Solzhenitsyn. *Come on, Barney. You know it.* There was a splendid movie made in Russia about his memoirs of childhood. Hell, it's on the tip of my tongue. First name Max—no, Maxim—surname like a goyische pickle. Maxim Cornichon? Don't be ridiculous. Maxim Gherkin? Forget it. *Gorky. Maxim Gorky.*

Anyway, the bookshop had to be negotiated like a maze, towering stacks of second-hand books here, there, and everywhere, that could be sent tumbling if you didn't mind your elbows, as you followed Mr. McIver's slapping slippers into the back room. His sanctuary. Where he sat at his roll-top desk, elbows peeking out of his ancient, unravelling cardigan, conducting seminars on the evils of capitalism, serving students toast and strawberry jam and milky tea. If they couldn't afford the latest Algren or Graham Greene, or that first novel by that young American, Norman Mailer, he would lend them a brand-new copy, providing they promised to return it unsoiled. Students demonstrated their gratitude by pilfering books on their way out and selling them back to him the following week. One or two even dipped into his cash register, or stiffed him with a bad cheque for ten or twenty dollars, never turning up at the bookshop again. "So you're going to Paris," he said to me.

"Yes."

This, inevitably, led to a lecture on the Paris Commune. Doomed, like the Spartacist League in Berlin. "Would you mind taking a parcel to my son?" he asked.

"Of course not."

I went to pick it up at the McIvers' airless, overheated apartment that evening.

"A couple of shirts," said Mr. McIver. "A sweater Mrs. McIver knitted for him. Six tins of sockeye salmon. A carton of Player's Mild. Things like that. Terry wants to be a novelist, but ..."

"But?"

"But who doesn't?"

When he retreated to the kitchen to put on the tea kettle, Mrs. McIver handed me an envelope. "For Terence," she whispered.

I found McIver in a small hotel on the rue Jacob and, amazingly, we actually got off to a promising start. He flipped the parcel onto his unmade bed, but slit open the envelope immediately. "You know how she earned this money?" he asked, seething. "These forty-eight dollars?"

"I have no idea."

"Babysitting. Coaching backward kids in algebra or French grammar. Do you know anybody here, Barney?"

"I've been here for three days and you're the first person I've talked to."

"Meet me at the Mabillon at six and I'll introduce you to some people."

"I don't know where it is."

"Meet me downstairs, then. Hold on a minute. Does my father still run those ad hoc symposiums for students who laugh behind his back?"

"Some are fond of him."

"He's a fool. Eager for me to be a failure. Like him. See you later."

NATURALLY I WAS SENT an advance copy of *Of Time and Fevers*, compliments of the author. I've struggled through it twice now, marking the blatant lies and most offensive passages, and this morning I phoned my lawyer, Maître John Hughes-McNoughton. "Can I sue somebody for libel who has accused me, in print, of being a wife-abuser, an intellectual fraud, a purveyor of pap, a drunk with a penchant for violence, and probably a murderer as well?"

"Sounds like he got things just about right, I'd say."

No sooner did I hang up than Irv Nussbaum, United Jewish Appeal *capo di tutti capi,* phoned. "Seen this morning's *Gazette*? Terrific news. Big-time drug lawyer was shot dead in his Jaguar, outside his mansion on Sunnyside last night, and it's splashed all over the front page. He's Jewish, thank God. Name's Larry Bercovitch. Today's going to be a hummer. I'm sitting here going through my pledge cards."

Next, Mike rang with one of his hot stock-market tips. I don't know where my son gets his inside market information, but back in 1989 he tracked me down at the Beverly Wilshire Hotel. I was in Hollywood at the time for one of those television festivals, where they even have an award, rather than an electric chair in place, for the director of the "most brilliant" commercial. I had not come in quest of prizes but in search of markets for my rubbish. Mike said, "Buy *Time* shares."

"No 'hello.' No 'How are you, Daddy dear?'"

"Phone your broker as soon as I hang up."

"I can't even read that magazine any more. Why should I invest in it?"

"Will you please do as I say?"

I did, and bastard that I am, I was already anticipating the satisfaction I would squeeze out of dropping my bundle and blaming him for it. But a month later both Warner and Paramount pounced, the shares more than doubling in value.

I'm running ahead of myself. Filling my peddler's office that evening in Beverly Hills, I was obliged to take two functionally illiterate NBC-TV executives to dinner at La Scala; and mindful of Miriam's parting admonition, I was resolved to be civil. "You should send somebody else to L.A.," she had said, "because you're bound to end up having too much to drink and insulting everybody." And now, into my third Laphroaig, I espied Hymie Mintzbaum at another table with a bimbo young enough to be his granddaughter. Following that brawl in London, whenever Hymie and I ran into each other here or there over the years, at the international stations of the show-business Cross (Ma Maison, Elaine's, The Ivy, L'Ami Louis, et cetera, et cetera), we acknowledged each other's presence with no more than a nod. I would occasionally see him, accompanied by a fawning starlet wannabe, and pick up his gravelly voice drifting over tables in one restaurant or another. "As Hemingway once said to me ..." or "Marilyn was far more intelligent than most people realized, but Arthur wasn't right for her."

Once, in 1964, Hymie and I actually got to exchange words.

"So Miriam didn't take my advice," he said. "She finally married you."

"We happen to be very happy together."

"Does it ever start unhappily?"

And that night, twenty-five years later, there he was again. He nodded. I nodded. Hymie had obviously endured a face-lift since I had last seen him. He now dyed his hair black and wore a bomber jacket, designer jeans, and Adidas. As luck would have it, we all but collided in the men's room. "You damn fool," he said, "when we're dead it will be for a long time and it won't matter that the film we did in London was from Boogie's original story."

"It mattered to me."

"Because you were consumed with guilt?"

"After all these years, the way I look at it is Boogie was the one who betrayed me."

"That's not the way most people see it."

"He should have turned up at my trial."

"Rising from the grave?"

"Flying in from wherever."

"You're incorrigible."

"Am I?"

"Prick. You know what I'm doing now? A film-of-the-week for ABC-TV. But it's a very exciting script and could lead to big things. I'm with a Freudian analyst these days. We're working on a sensational script together and I'm fucking her, which is more than I ever got from any of the others."

Back at my table, one of the young executives, his smile reeking of condescension, said, "You know old Mintzbaum, do you?"

The other one, shaking his head, said, "For Christ's sake, don't encourage him to come to our table, or he'll start to pitch."

"Old Mintzbaum," I said, "was risking his life in the Eighth Army Air Force before you were born, you smug, insufferably boring little cretin. As for you, you cliché-mongering little shit," I added, turning to the other one, "I'll bet you pay a personal trainer to time your laps in your goddamn swimming-pool every morning. Neither of you is fit to shine old Mintzbaum's shoes. Fuck off, both of you."

NINETEEN EIGHTY-NINE THAT WAS. I'm jumping all over the place. I know, I know. But seated at my desk these endgame days, my bladder plugged by an enlarged prostate, my sciatica a frequent curse, wondering when I will be due for another hip socket, anticipating emphysema, pulling on a Montecristo Number Two, a bottle of Macallan by my side, I try to retrieve some sense out of my life, unscrambling it. Recalling those blissful days in Paris, in the early fifties, when we were young and crazy, I raise my glass to absent friends: Mason Hoffenberg, David Burnett, Alfred Chester, and Terry Southern, all dead now. I wonder whatever became of the girl who was never seen on the boulevard Saint-Germain without that chirping chimpanzee riding her shoulder. Did she go home to Houston and marry a dentist? Is she a grandmother now and an admirer of Newt? Or did she die of an overdose like the exquisite Marie-Claire, who could trace her lineage back to Roland?

I dunno. I just dunno. The past is a foreign country, they do things differently there, as E. M. Forster[1] once wrote. Anyway, those, those were the days. We had not so much arrived in the City of Light as escaped the constraints of our dim provincial origins, in my case the only country that declared Queen Victoria's birthday a national holiday. Our lives were unstructured. Totally. We ate when we were hungry and slept when we were tired, and screwed whoever was available whenever it was possible, surviving on three dollars a day. Except for the always elegantly dressed

---

[1] Actually, it was L. P. Hartley in *The Go-Between*, p. 1. Hamish Hamilton, London, 1953.

Cedric, a black American who was the beneficiary of a secret source of funds about which the rest of us speculated endlessly. Certainly it wasn't family money. Or the pathetic sums he earned for stories published in the *London Magazine* or *Kenyon Review*. And I dismissed as a canard the rumour rife among some other Left Bank black Americans that, in those days of crazed anti-communism, Cedric received a monthly stipend from the FBI, or CIA, to inform on their activities. Whatever, Cedric wasn't hunkered down in a cheap hotel room but ensconced in a comfortable apartment on the rue Bonaparte. His Yiddish, which he had acquired in Brighton Beach, where his father worked as an apartment-building janitor, was good enough for him to banter with Boogie, who addressed him as the *shayner* Reb Cedric, the *shvartzer gaon* of Brooklyn. Ostensibly without racial hang-ups, and fun to be with, he went along with Boogie's jest that he was actually a pushy Yemenite trying to pass as black because it made him irresistible to young white women who had come to Paris to be liberated, albeit on a monthly allowance from their uptight parents. He also responded with a mixture of warmth and deference whenever Boogie, our acknowledged master, praised his latest short story. But I suspected his pleasure was simulated. With hindsight, I fear that he and Boogie, constantly jousting, actually disliked each other.

Make no mistake. Cedric was truly talented, and so, inevitably, one day a New York publisher sent him a contract for his first novel, offering him a $2,500 advance against royalties. Cedric invited Leo, Boogie, Clara, and me to dinner at La Coupole to celebrate. And we did whoop it up, happy to be together, going through one bottle of wine after another. The publisher and his wife, said Cedric, would be in Paris the following week. "From his letter," said Cedric, "I gather he thinks I'm one dirt-poor spade, living in a garret, who will jump at his invitation to dinner."

This led us into jokes about whether Cedric could order chitlins at Lapérouse, or turn up barefoot for drinks at Les Deux Magots. And then I made my gaffe. Hoping to impress Boogie, who could usually be counted on for the invention of our most outlandish pranks, I suggested that Cedric invite his publisher and his wife to dinner at his apartment, where the four of us would pretend to be his hired help. Clara and I would cook, and Boogie and Leo, wearing white shirts and black bow-ties, would serve at table. "I love it," said Clara, clapping hands, but Boogie wouldn't have it.

"Why?" I asked.

"Because I fear our friend Cedric here would enjoy it too much."

An ill wind passed over our table. Cedric, feigning fatigue, called for the bill, and we dispersed separately into the night, each one troubled by his own dark thoughts. But, within days, the episode was forgotten. Once again we took to gathering in Cedric's apartment late at night, after the jazz clubs had closed, digging into his stash of hashish.

Those days not only Sidney Bechet, but also Charlie Parker and Miles Davis were playing in small *boîtes de nuit* which we frequented. Lazy spring afternoons we would pick up our mail and some gossip at Gaït Frogé's English Bookshop on the rue de Seine, or saunter over to the Père Lachaise cemetery to gawk at the graves of Oscar Wilde and Heinrich Heine, among other immortals. But dying, a blight common to earlier generations, did not enter into our scheme of things. It wasn't on our dance cards.

Each age gets the arts patrons it deserves. My bunch's benefactor was Maurice Girodias né Kahane, sole prop. of Olympia Press, publishers of the hot stuff in the Traveller's Companion Series. I can remember waiting for Boogie more than once on the corner of the rue Dauphine as he ventured into Girodias's office on the rue de Nesle, lugging last night's twenty-odd pages of porn, and, if he were lucky, coming away with maybe five thousand sustaining francs, an advance against a stroke-book to be delivered as soon as possible. Once, to his amusement, he collided with the vice squad, the men in trenchcoats from La Brigade Mondaine (The Worldly Brigade), who had barged in to seize copies of *Who Pushed Paulo, The Whip Angels, Helen and Desire,* and Count Palmiro Vicarion's *Book of Limericks*:

> When Titian was mixing rose madder,
> His model was poised on a ladder.
> "Your position," said Titian,
> "Inspires coition."
> So he nipped up the ladder and 'ad 'er.

On a whim, or just because a motorcycle ride was suddenly available, we would take off for a few days in Venice, or bum a ride to the *feria* in Valencia, where we could catch Litri and Aparicio and the young Dominguín in the Plaza de los Toros. One summer afternoon, in 1952, Boogie announced that we were going to Cannes to work as film extras, and that's how I first met Hymie Mintzbaum.

Hymie, built like a linebacker, big-featured, with black hair curly as a terrier's, brown eyes charged with appetite, big floppy ears, prominent nose misshapen, twice-broken, had served with the American Army Air Force 281st Bomber Group, based in Ridgewell, not far from Cambridge, in 1943; a twenty-nine-year-old major, pilot of a B-17. His gravelly voice mesmerizing, he told Boogie and me—the three of us seated on the terrace of the Colombe d'Or in St-Paul-de-Vence, that summer of '52, into our second bottle of Dom Perignon, every flute laced with Courvoisier xo, Hymie's treat—that his squadron's brief had been daylight precision bombing. He had been in on the second raid on the Schweinfurt ball-bearings factory in which the Eighth Air Force had lost 60 out of the 320 bombers that had set out from East Anglia. "Flying at twenty-five thousand feet, the temperature fifty below zero, even with heated flying suits," he said, "we had to worry about frostbite, never mind Goering's personal squadron of ME-109s and FW-190s, circling, waiting to pick off stragglers. Do either of you young geniuses," he asked, the designation "geniuses" delivered in italics, "happen to know the young woman seated in the shade there, second table to our left?"

Young geniuses. Boogie, that most perspicacious of men, couldn't handle liquor, it made him sloppy, so he didn't grasp that we were being patronized. Obviously Hymie, who was pushing forty at the time, felt threatened by the young. Clearly my manhood, if not Boogie's, was in question, as I had never been bloodied in combat. Neither was I old enough to have suffered sufficiently through the Great Depression. I hadn't cavorted in Paris in the good old days, immediately after its liberation, knocking back martinis with Papa Hemingway at the Ritz. I hadn't seen Joe Louis floor Max Schmeling in the first round and couldn't understand what that meant to a yid coming of age in the Bronx. Or caught Gypsy Rose Lee stripping at the World's Fair. Hymie suffered from that sour old man's delusion that anybody who had come after him was born too late. He was, in our parlance, a bit of a drag. "No," I said. "I have no idea who she is."

"Too bad," said Hymie.

Hymie, blacklisted at the time, was shooting a French *film noir* under a pseudonym in Monte Carlo, an Eddie Constantine flick, Boogie and I working as extras. He called for another Dom Perignon, instructed the waiter to leave the Courvoisier xo bottle on the table, and asked for olives, almonds, fresh figs, a plate of crevettes, some pâté with truffles, bread, butter, smoked salmon, and anything else you've got for nibbles there.

The sun, which had been warming us, began to sink behind the olive-green hills, seemingly setting them alight. A donkey-drawn wagon, led by a grizzly old geezer wearing a blue smock, passed clippity-clop below the terrace's stone retaining wall, and we caught the scent of its cargo of roses on the evening breeze. The roses were bound for the perfumeries in Grasse. Then a fat baker's boy puffed by our table, one of those huge wicker baskets of freshly baked baguettes strapped to his back, and we could smell that too. "If she's waiting for somebody," said Hymie, "he's shamefully late."

The woman with the gleaming hair seated alone two tables to our left appeared to be in her late twenties. Somebody's gift package. Her fine arms bare, her linen shift elegant, long bare legs crossed. She was sipping white wine and smoking a Gitanes, and when she caught us sneaking glances at her, she lowered her eyes, pouted, and reached for the book in her straw shoulder bag, *Bonjour tristesse*,[2] by Françoise Sagan, and began to read.

"Do you want me to invite her over to join us?" asked Boogie.

Hymie scratched his purply jaw. He made a face, wrinkling his forehead. "Naw. I think not. If she joined us, it could spoil everything. Gotta make a phone call. Back in a couple of minutes."

"He's beginning to bug me," I said to Boogie. "As soon as he gets back, I think we ought to split, man."

"No."

Hymie, back soon enough, began to drop names, a failing I cannot tolerate. Hollywood manna. John Huston, his buddy. Dorothy Parker, big trouble. The time he had worked on a screenplay with that stool-pigeon Clifford Odets. His two-day drunk with Bogie. Then he told us how his commanding officer had summoned all the air crews to a briefing in a Nissen hut before they took off on their first mission. "I don't want any of you girls faking mechanical trouble three hundred miles short of the target area, dropping your bombs on the nearest cow patch, and dashing for home. Gosh darn it. Holy smoke. You would be failing Rosie the Riveter, not to mention all those 4-F hymies raking it in on the black market stateside and fucking the girls you left behind. Better shit yourselves than try that story on me." Then he added, "Three months from now, two thirds of you will be dead. Any stupid questions?"

But Hymie survived, demobilized with some fifteen thousand dollars in the bank, most of it won at the poker table. He made straight for Paris, moving into the Ritz, he said, and not drawing a sober breath for six months. Then, down to his last three thousand dollars, he booked passage

---

2 It had to be some other book, as *Bonjour tristesse* wasn't published until 1954.

on the *Île de France,* and lit out for California. Starting as a third-assistant director, he bullied his way up the ladder, intimidating studio executives, who had served with honour in the War Bond drives on the home front, by wearing his flight jacket to dinner parties. Hymie churned out a *Blondie,* a couple of Tim Holt westerns, and one of Tom Conway's *The Falcon* series, before he was allowed to direct a comedy featuring Eddie Bracken and Betty what's-her-name? You know, like the stock-market brokers. Betty Merrill Lynch? No. Betty Lehman Brothers? Come off it. Betty like in those ads. When la-de-da speaks, everybody listens. *Hutton. Betty Hutton.* He was once nominated for an Academy Award, was three times divorced, and then the House Un-American Activities Committee caught up with him. "This sleaze-bag Anderson, my comrade," he said, "a five-hundred-dollar-a-week screenwriter, was sworn in by the committee and told them he used to come to my house in Benedict Canyon to collect weekly Party dues. How was I to know he was an FBI agent?"

Surveying our table, Hymie said, "There's something missing. *Garçon, apportez-nous des cigares, s'il vous plaît.*"

Then a Frenchman, obviously past it, well into his fifties, pranced onto the terrace. He was sporting a yachting cap, his navy-blue blazer with the brass buttons tossed over his shoulder like a cape: he had come to claim the young woman who sat two tables to our left. She rose to greet him, a butterfly disturbed, with a flutter of delight.

"*Comme tu es belle,*" he cooed.

"*Merci, chéri.*"

"*Je t'adore,*" he said, stroking her cheek with his hand. Then he called peremptorily for the waiter, *le roi le veut,* flashed a roll of francs bound with a gold clasp, and settled the bill. The two of them drifted toward our table, where she obliged him to stop, indicating the remnants of our feast with a dismissive wave of her hand, saying, "*Les Américains. Dégueulasse. Comme d'habitude.*"

"We don't like Ike," said the Frenchman, tittering.

"*Fiche-moi la paix,*" said Hymie.

"*Toi et ta fille,*" I said.

Stung, they moved on, arms around each other's waist, and strolled toward his Aston-Martin, the old man's hand caressing her bottom. He opened the car door for her, settled in behind the wheel, slipped on his racing driver's gloves, made an obscene gesture at us, and drove off.

"Let's get out of here," said Hymie.

Piling into Hymie's Citroën, we sped to Hauts-de-Cagnes, Hymie and Boogie belting out synagogue songs they remembered as we charged up the all-but-perpendicular hill to Jimmy's Bar on the crest, and that's when my mood began to curdle. Wintry is my soulseason. And that evening, perfect but for my fulminating presence, my heart was laden with envy. For Hymie's war experiences. His charm. His bankroll. For the effortless manner in which Boogie had been able to establish rapport with him, their joshing now often excluding me.

Years later, shortly after the murder charges against me had been dismissed, and Hymie was home again, now that the blacklist was a nightmare past, he insisted that I recuperate at the beach house he had rented for the summer in the Hamptons. "I know you don't want to see anyone, in your mood. But this is just what the doctor ordered. Peace and quiet. Sea. Sand. Pastrami. Divorcées on the make. Wait till you taste my kasha. And nobody will know anything about your troubles."

Peace and quiet. Hymie. I should have known better. The most generous of hosts, he furnished his beach house with wall-to-wall guests almost every night, most of them young and all of whom he set out to seduce. He would regale them with stories of the great and near-great he claimed to have known. Dashiell Hammett, a prince. Bette Davis, misunderstood. Peter Lorre, his kind of guy. Ditto Spence. Passing from guest to guest, he would illuminate them like a lamp-lighter. He would whisper into the ear of each young woman that she was the most gorgeous and intelligent on Long Island, and confide in each of the men that he was uniquely gifted. He wouldn't allow me to brood in a corner, but literally thrust me on one woman after another. "She's wildly attracted to you." Going on to introduce me, saying, "This is my old friend Barney Panofsky and he's dying to meet you. He doesn't look it, I know, but he just got away with the perfect crime. Tell her about it, kid."

I took Hymie aside. "I know you mean well, Hymie, but the truth is I'm committed to a woman in Toronto."

"Of course you are. You think I don't hear you coming on like a pimply teenager on the phone after I've gone to bed?"

"Are you listening in on the extension in your bedroom?"

"Look, kid, Miriam's there, and you're here. Enjoy."

"You don't understand."

"No, it's you who don't understand. When you get to be my age, what you regret is not the times you cheated a little, but the times you didn't."

"It's not going to be like that with us."

"I'll bet when you were a kid you clapped hands for Tinkerbell."

Early every morning, rain or shine, Hymie, who was then being treated by a Reichian analyst, would trot out to the dunes and let out primal screams sufficiently loud to drive any sharks lingering in the shallows back to sea. Then he would start on his morning jog, accumulating a gaggle of everybody else's children *en route*, proposing marriage to eleven-year-old girls and suggesting to nine-year-old boys that they stop somewhere for a beer, eventually leading them to the local candy store for treats. Back at the beach house, he would make both of us salami omelettes garnished with mounds of home fries. Then, immediately after breakfast, still hoarse from his dune therapy, Hymie, who was connected to the world outside by his phone, would put in a call to his agent: "What are you going to do for me today, you *cacker*?" Or he would get a producer on the line, cajoling, pleading, threatening, honking phlegm into his handkerchief, lighting one cigarette off another. "I've got it in me to direct the best American film since *Citizen Kane,* but I never hear from you. How come?"

I was often wakened in the early-morning hours by Hymie hollering into the phone at one or another of his former wives, apologizing for being late with an alimony payment, commiserating over an affair that had ended badly, or shouting at one of his sons, or his daughter in San Francisco. "What does she do?" I once asked him.

"Shop. Get pregnant. Marry, divorce. You've heard of serial killers? She's a serial bride."

Hymie's children were a constant heartache and an endless financial drain. The son in Boston, a Wiccan, and proprietor of an occult bookshop, was writing the definitive book on astrology. When not contemplating the heavens, he was given to writing bad cheques on Earth, which Hymie had to make good. His other son, a wandering rock musician, was in and out of expensive detox clinics, and had a weakness for hitting the road in stolen sports cars which he inevitably smashed up. He could phone from a lockup in Tulsa, or a hospital in Kansas City, or a lawyer's office in Denver, to say there had been a misunderstanding. "But you mustn't worry, Dad. I wasn't hurt."

Not yet a father myself, I deigned to lecture him. "If I ever have children," I said, "once they reach the age of twenty-one, they're on their own. There has to be a cut-off point."

"The grave," he said.

Hymie supported a *shlemiel* of a brother who was a Talmudic scholar, and his parents in Florida. Once, I found him weeping at the kitchen table at two a.m., surrounded by chequebooks, and scraps of paper on which he had made hurried calculations. "Anything I can do?" I asked.

"Yeah. Mind your own business. No, sit down. Do you realize that if I had a heart attack tomorrow, there would be twelve people out on the street, without a pot to piss in? Here. Read this." It was a letter from his brother. He had finally caught up with one of Hymie's movies on late-night television: prurient, obscene, meretricious, and an embarrassment to the family's good name. If he must make such trash, couldn't he use a pseudonym? "Do you know how much money he's in to me for, that *momzer*? I even pay his daughter's college fees."

I was not good company. Far from it. Waking in a sweat at three a.m., convinced I was still wasting away in that slammer in St-Jérôme, denied bail, a life sentence my most likely prospect. Or dreaming that I was being weighed again by that somnolent jury of pig farmers, snow-plough men, and garage mechanics. Or, unable to sleep, grieving for Boogie, wondering if the divers had messed up, and if, against all odds, he was still tangled in the weeds. Or if his bloated body had surfaced in my absence. But an hour later my concern would yield to rage. He was alive, that bastard. I knew it in my bones. Then why hadn't he shown up at my trial? Because he hadn't heard about it. He was on one of his retreats in an ashram in India. Or he was in a heroin-induced stupor in a hotel in San Francisco. Or he was in that Trappist monastery on Big Sur, trying to kick, studying his list of the names of the dead. Any day now I would get one of his cryptic postcards. Like the one that once came from Acre:

In those days there was no king in Israel, but every man did that which was right in his own eyes.
Judges, 17: 6.

The day after my release from prison, I had driven out to my cottage on the lake, jumped into my outboard, and covered every inch of the shoreline as well as the adjoining brooks. Detective-Sergeant O'Hearne had been waiting for me on my dock. "What are you doing here?" I'd demanded.

"Walking in the woods. You were born with a horseshoe up your ass, Mr. P."

Late one night Hymie and I sat on the deck, the two of us sipping cognac. "You were such a bundle of nerves when we first met," he said. "Sweating anger and resentment and aggression under that assumed hipster's carapace. But who would have guessed that one day you would get away with murder?"

"I didn't do it, Hymie."

"In France you would have got off with a slap on the wrist. *Crime passionnel* is what they call it. I swear I never thought you'd have the guts."

"You don't understand. He's still alive. Out there somewhere. Mexico. New Zealand. Macao. Who knows?"

"According to what I've read, afterwards there was never any money withdrawn from his bank account."

"Miriam found out that there were three break-ins into summer cottages on the lake in the days following his disappearance. That's how he probably found some clothes."

"Are you broke now?"

"My lawyer. Alimony. Neglected business affairs. Sure I'm broke now."

"We're going to write a screenplay together."

"Don't be ridiculous. I'm not a writer, Hymie."

"There's a hundred and fifty big ones in it for us, split two ways. Hey, wait a minute. I mean one third for you, two thirds for me. What do you say?"

Once we settled into work on the script, Hymie would rip scenes out of my typewriter and read them over the phone to a former mistress in Paris, a cousin in Brooklyn, his daughter, or his agent. "Now you listen to this, it's fabulous." If the reaction wasn't what he expected, he would counter, "It's only a first draft and I did tell Barney it wouldn't work. He's a novice, you know." His cleaning lady's opinion was solicited; he consulted his analyst, handed out pages to waitresses, and made revisions based on their criticisms. He could charge into my bedroom at four a.m. and shake me awake. "I just had a brilliant idea. Come." Slurping ice cream out of a bucket retrieved from the fridge, he would stride up and down in his boxer shorts, scratching his groin, and begin to dictate. "This is Academy Award stuff. Bulletproof." But the next morning, rereading what he had dictated, he would say, "Barney, this is a piece of shit. Now let's get serious today."

On bad days, dry days, he might suddenly sink to the sofa and say, "You know what I could do with now? A blow-job. Technically, you know, that's not being unfaithful. What am I worrying about? I'm not even married now." Then he would leap up, pluck his copy of *The Memoirs of Fanny Hill* or *The Story of O* from a bookshelf, and disappear into the bathroom. "We should do this at least once a day. It keeps the prostate in check. A doctor told me that."

Back at Jimmy's Bar, in 1952, we hit the road in Hymie's Peugeot[3] again, and the next thing I remember is one of those crowded, tiny, smoke-filled *bar-tabacs* with a zinc-topped counter in an alley off the market in Nice, and the three of us knocking back cognacs with the porters and truck drivers. We drank toasts to Maurice Thorez, Mao, Harry Bridges, and then to La Pasionaria and El Campesino, in honour of the two Catalan refugees in the company. And then, laden with gifts of tomatoes that still reeked of the vine, spring onions, and figs, we moved on to Juan les Pins, where we found a nightclub open. "'Tailgunner Joe,'" said Hymie, "my intrepid comrade-in-arms Senator Joseph McCarthy, that cockroach, actually never flew into battle ..."

Which was when a seemingly comatose Boogie suddenly shifted gears, going into overdrive. "When the witch-hunt is over," he said, "and everybody is embarrassed, as they were after the Palmer Raids, McCarthy may yet be appreciated with hindsight as the most effective film critic ever. Never mind Agee. The senator certainly cleaned out the stables."

Hymie would never have taken that from me, but, coming from Boogie, he decided to let it fly. It was amazing. Here was Hymie, an accomplished and reasonably affluent man, a successful film director, and there was Boogie, poor, unknown, a struggling writer, his publications limited to a couple of little magazines. But it was an intimidated Hymie who was determined to win Boogie's approval. Boogie had that effect on people. I wasn't the only one who needed his blessing.

"My problem," Boogie continued, "is that I have some respect for the Hollywood Ten as people, but not as writers of even the second rank. *Je m'excuse*. The third rank. Much as I abhor Evelyn Waugh's politics, I would rather read one of his novels any day than sit through any of their mawkish films again."

"You're such a kidder, Boogie," said a subdued Hymie.

"'The best lack all conviction,'" said Boogie, "'while the worst / Are full of passionate intensity.' So said Mr. Yeats."

"I'm willing to admit," said Hymie, "that our bunch, and I include myself in that lot, possibly invested so much integrity in our guilt-ridden

---

[3] Described as a Citroën on page 125.

politics we had little left for our work. I suppose you could argue that Franz Kafka didn't require a swimming-pool. Or that George Orwell never attended a script conference, but ..." And then, unwilling to tangle with Boogie, he unleashed his anger on me. "And I hope I will always be able to say the same for you, Barney, you condescending little prick."

"Hey, I'm not a writer. I'm merely hanging out. Come on, Boogie. Let's split."

"Leave my friend Boogie out of this. At least he speaks his mind. But I have my doubts about you."

"Me too," said Boogie.

"Go to hell, both of you," I said, leaping up from the table and quitting the nightclub.

Boogie caught up with me outside. "I expect you won't be satisfied until he punches you out."

"I can take him."

"How does Clara put up with your tantrums?"

"Who else would put up with Clara?"

That made him laugh. Me too. "Okay," he said, "let's get back in there, and you make nice, understand?"

"He bugs me."

"Everybody bugs you. You're one mean, crazy son of a bitch. Now if you can't be a *mensh*, you can at least pretend. Come on. Let's go."

Back at the table, Hymie rose to rock me in a bear hug. "I apologize. Humbly I do. And now we can all do with some fresh air."

Settling into the sand, on the beach in Cannes, we watched the sun rise over the wine-dark sea, eating our tomatoes, spring onions, and figs. Then we shed our shoes, rolled up our trouser bottoms, and waded in up to our knees. Boogie splashed me, I splashed him back, and within seconds the three of us were into a water fight, and in those days you didn't have to worry about turds or used condoms drifting in on the tide. Finally we repaired to a café on the Croisette for *oeufs sur le plat*, brioches, and *café au lait*. Boogie bit the end off a Romeo y Julieta, lit up, and said, "*Après tout, c'est un monde passable*," quoting only God knows who.[4]

Hymie stretched, yawned, and said, "Got to go to work now. We begin shooting at the casino in an hour. Let's meet for drinks at the Carlton at seven tonight and then I know of a place in Gulf-Juan where they make an

---

[4] Voltaire.

excellent bouillabaisse." He tossed us his hotel keys. "In case you guys want to wash up or snooze or read my mail. See you later."

Boogie and I strolled as far as the harbour to look at the yachts, and there was our French sugar daddy, sunning himself on his teak deck, out of the Mediterranean endlessly rocking, his squeeze nowhere in sight. He looked absolutely pathetic, wearing reading glasses, his sunken belly spilling over his bikini, as he perused *Le Figaro*. The stock-market pages, no doubt. Obligatory reading for those without an inner life. "*Salut, grand-père,*" I called out. "*Comment va ta concubine aujourd'hui?*"

"*Maricons,*" he hollered, shaking his fist at me.

"Are you going to let him get away with that?" asked Boogie. "Knock his teeth out. Beat the shit out of him. Anything to make you feel better."

"Okay," I said. "Okay."

"You're a fucking menace," he said, leading me away.

3

The script Hymie and I wrote on Long Island was never produced, but less than a year later, in 1961, he phoned me from London. "Come on over. We're going to write another picture together. I'm so excited about this project I've already written my Academy Award acceptance speech."

"Hymie, I've got a full plate over here. I spend every weekend in Toronto with Miriam, or she flies here and we go to a hockey game together. Why don't you get yourself a real writer this time?"

"I don't want a real writer. I want you, darling. It's from an original story I bought years ago."

"I can't leave here just like that."

"I've already booked you on a first-class flight leaving Toronto tomorrow."

"I'm in Montreal."

"What's the difference? It's all Canada, isn't it?"

Outside, it was fifteen degrees below zero, and another cleaning lady had quit on me. There were mouldy things sprouting in my fridge. My apartment stank of stale tobacco and sweaty old shirts and socks. In those days I usually started my morning with a pot of black coffee fortified with cognac, and a stale bagel I had to soak in water and heat up in an oven encrusted with grease. I was then already divorced from The Second Mrs. Panofsky. I was also a social pariah. Adjudged innocent by the court but condemned as a murderer, incredibly lucky to walk, by just about everybody else. I had taken to playing childish games. If the Canadiens won ten in a row, or if Beliveau scored a hat trick on Saturday night, there would be a postcard from Boogie on Monday morning, forgiving me my red-hot outburst, those harsh words I swear I didn't mean. I tracked down and wrote or phoned mutual friends in Paris and Chicago and Dublin and, you know, that artsy desert pueblo–cum–Hollywood *shtetl* in Arizona, favoured by short producers in cowboy boots, with those health-food restaurants where you can't smoke and everybody pops garlic and vitamin pills with their daily fibre. It's not far from where they made the atom bomb, or from where D. H. Lawrence lived with what's-her-name. Santa something.[1] But nobody had seen or heard from Boogie, and some resented my inquiries. "What are you trying to prove, you bastard?" I visited Boogie's old haunts in New York: The San Remo, The Lion's Head. "Moscovitch," said the bartender in The San Remo, "he was murdered somewhere in Canada, I thought."

"The hell he was."

At the time, I was also having my problems with Miriam, who would change everything for me: then, now, and forever. She was still vacillating. Moving to Montreal to marry me would mean giving up her job with CBC Radio. Furthermore, to her mind, I was a difficult man. I phoned her. "Go ahead," she said, "London will be good for you and I need some time alone."

"No, you don't."

"I can't think with you here."

"Why not?"

"You're devouring me."

"I want you to promise that if I'm in London for more than a month you'll fly over for a few days. It won't be a hardship."

She promised. So why not, I thought. The work wouldn't be rigorous. I needed the money desperately and all Hymie required was sympathetic company. Somebody to sit at the typewriter and guffaw at his one-liners, while he worked the phone, striding up and down, honking, chatting up bimbos, agents, producers, or his analyst: "I just remembered something significant."

---

[1] Santa Fe in New Mexico.

Hymie's film turned out to be one of his iffy patchwork-quilt projects, the financing stitched together by pre-selling distribution to individual territories: the U.K., France, Germany, and Italy. His once curly black hair had faded grey as ash, and he was now given to cracking his knuckles and picking at the fat of his palms with his thumbnails, rendering the flesh painfully raw. He had shed his Reichian analyst for a Jungian, whom he visited every morning. "She's incredible. A magus. You ought to see her yourself. Great tits."

Hymie now suffered from insomnia, chewed tranquillizers, and did the occasional line. He had been through an LSD session with the then-modish R. D. Laing. His problem was that nobody in Hollywood was in need of his services any more. His phone calls to most agents and studio executives in Beverly Hills went unanswered or were returned some days later by an underling, one of whom actually asked Hymie to spell his name. "Call me back, sonny," said Hymie, "when your voice has changed." But, as promised, we did whoop it up together in that suite Hymie had taken in the Dorchester, where he was encouraging the chambermaid to write poetry, and a waiter in the dining room to organize a staff union. We smoked Montecristos and sipped brandies and sodas while we worked, and called room service to send up smoked salmon and caviar and champagne for lunch. "You know something, Barney, we may never be able to check out of here, because I don't know if my backers can handle the bill." My long phone calls to Toronto, often twice daily, included. "Hey," Hymie would say, breaking off in the middle of acting out a scene, "you haven't spoken to your sweetiepoo in six hours. Maybe she's changed?"

Early one afternoon, maybe ten days into our collaboration, I phoned again and again, but no one answered. "She told me she'd be home tonight. I don't understand."

"We're supposed to be working here."

"She's a terrible driver. And they had freezing rain there this morning. What if she's been in an accident?"

"She's gone to a movie. Or dinner with friends. Now let's get some work done here."

It was five a.m., London time, before somebody picked up her phone. I recognized the voice at once. "McIver, you bastard, what in the hell are you doing there?"

"Who is this?"

"Barney Panofsky is who, and I want to speak to Miriam at once."

Laughter in the background. The clinking of glasses. Finally, she came to the phone. "My God, Barney, why are you still up at this hour?"

"You have no idea how worried I've been. You told me you'd be in tonight."

"It's Larry Keefer's birthday. We all went out to dinner and I invited everybody back here for a nightcap."

"I must have called ten times. Why haven't you called me?"

"Because I assumed you'd be asleep by now."

"How come McIver's there?"

"He's an old friend of Larry's."

"You're not to believe a word he says about me. He's a pathological liar."

"Barney, I've got a room full of guests here, and this is getting to be very embarrassing. Go to sleep. We'll talk tomorrow."

"But I—"

"Sorry," she said, her voice hardening. "I forgot. How could I? Chicago beat Detroit three–two tonight. Bobby Hull scored twice. So the series is tied now."

"That's not why I called. I don't care about that. It's you I—"

"Good night," she said, hanging up.

I considered waiting a couple of hours and then calling back, ostensibly to apologize but actually to make sure she was alone now. Fortunately, on reflection, I dismissed this as a bad idea. But I was in a rage, all the same. How that prick McIver must have enjoyed himself! "You mean he calls you from London for the hockey scores? Amazing."

FLUSH OR BROKE, Hymie lived like royalty. So just about every night we dined at The Caprice, The Mirabelle, or The White Elephant. Providing it was only the two of us, Hymie was the most engaging of companions, a born raconteur, charming beyond compare. But if there was a visiting Hollywood biggie at the next table, he was instantly transmogrified into a supplicant, who would tell one obviously irritated oaf how exciting it would be to work with him, and another that his last, unappreciated film was actually a production of genius. "And I'm not saying that just because you're here."

A couple of days before Miriam was due to fly into London at last, I made the mistake of trying to have a serious conversation with Hymie. "She's very sensitive, so I want you to make an effort not to be vulgar."

"Yes, Daddy."

"And your latest 'discovery,' that idiot Diana, is certainly not joining us for dinner while Miriam's here."

"Say we're in a restaurant, and I have to go and make weewee, do I put up my hand to ask permission?"

"And none of your prurient Hollywood gossip, please. It would bore the hell out of her."

I needn't have been apprehensive about Miriam meeting Hymie. She adored him at first sight, dinner at The White Elephant. He made her giggle harder than I ever had, that bastard. He got her to blush. And, to my amazement, she couldn't get enough of his salacious stories about Bette Davis, Bogie, or Orson. There I was, mooning over my loved one, my smile goofy in her presence, but definitely *de trop*.

"He told me you were intelligent," said Hymie, "but he never once mentioned that you were so beautiful."

"He probably hasn't noticed yet. It's not like I ever scored a hat trick or the winning goal in overtime."

"Why marry him when I'm still available?"

"Did he say I had agreed to marry him?"

"I didn't. I swear. I said I *hoped* that you would—"

"Why don't the two of us meet for lunch tomorrow, while I give him some typing to do?"

Lunch? They were gone for four hours, and when Miriam finally tottered into our hotel room, she was flushed and slurring her words, and had to lie down. I had booked us into The Caprice for dinner, but couldn't get her out of bed. "Take Hymie," she said, turning over and starting to snore again.

"What did you talk about for so long?" I asked Hymie later.

"This and that."

"You got her drunk."

"Eat up, *boychick*."

Once Miriam had flown back to Toronto, Hymie and I resumed our carousing. Hell for Hymie wasn't other people, as Camus had it,[2] but being without them. When I would quit our table at The White Elephant or The Mirabelle, pleading fatigue, he would move on to another table, uninvited but making himself welcome by dazzling the company with anecdotes

---

[2] Actually, it was Jean-Paul Sartre.

about bankable names. Or he would slide over to the bar, chatting up whatever woman was seated alone there. "Do you know who I am?"

One night it still chills me to remember, Ben Shahn turned up at The White Elephant with a group of admirers. Hymie, who owned one of Shahn's drawings, took that as licence to intrude upon his table. Pointing a finger at Shahn, he said, "Next time you see Cliff, I want you to tell him for me that he's a dirty rat."

Cliff, of course, was Odets, who had babbled to the House Un-American Activities Committee, naming names.

Silence settled like a shroud over the table. Shahn, unperturbed, raised his glasses to his forehead, peering quizzically at Hymie, and asked, "And who shall I say gave me the message?"

"Never mind," said Hymie, shrinking before my eyes. "Forget it." And retreating, he seemed momentarily befuddled, old, unsure of his bearings.

Finally, several months later, the day came when I sat with Hymie in a Beverly Hills screening room and watched the titles and credits of our film roll past. Startled, I read:

FROM AN ORIGINAL STORY BY BERNARD MOSCOVITCH.

"You bastard," I hollered, yanking Hymie out of his seat, shaking him, "why didn't you tell me it was from a story by Boogie?"

"Touchy touchy," he said, pinching my cheek.

"Now, as if I didn't have enough to handle, people will say I'm exploiting his work."

"Something bothers me. If he was such a good friend, and he's still alive, why didn't he show at your trial?"

In response, I reached back and managed to crunch Hymie's twice-broken nose for a third time, something I had longed to do ever since he had taken Miriam out for that four-hour lunch. He countered by pumping his knee into my groin. We carried on pounding each other, rolling over on the floor, and it took three men from the unit to untangle us, even as we went on cursing each other.

Alice Munro

Alice Munro grew up in Wingham, Ontario, and attended the
University of Western Ontario. She has published thirteen books—
Dance of the Happy Shades; *Lives of Girls and Women*; *Something
I've Been Meaning to Tell You*; *Who Do You Think You Are?*; *The
Moons of Jupiter*; *The Progress of Love*; *Friend of My Youth*; *Open
Secrets*; *Selected Stories*; *The Love of a Good Woman*; *Hateship,
Friendship, Courtship, Loveship, Marriage*; *Runaway*; and *The View
from Castle Rock*.

During her distinguished career she has received many awards and
prizes, including the WH Smith Award in the UK for the year's best
book, and, in the USA, the National Book Critics Circle Award, the
PEN/Malamud Award for Short Fiction, the Lannan Literary Award
for Fiction, and the National Arts Club Medal of Honor for
Literature. Her stories appear in magazines such as *The New Yorker*,
and she is in demand to visit many countries (such as Italy, in the
summer of 2008) to receive further honours, most of which she
modestly turns down.

In Canada, over her forty-year publishing career, she has won too
many prizes to list. They include three Governor General's Literary
Awards; several Libris Awards, given by the country's booksellers; the
Trillium Book Award; The CAA Jubilee Award for Short Stories; and
two Giller Prizes.

In 2005, she was included in *Time* magazine's list of the world's
one hundred most influential people, and she has been mentioned as a
potential winner of the Nobel Prize for Literature. She and her
husband divide their time between Clinton, Ontario, and Comox,
British Columbia.

The Love of a Good Woman

BY ALICE MUNRO

Winner 1998

⤲

The Children Stay

Thirty years ago, a family was spending a holiday together on the east coast of Vancouver Island. A young father and mother, their two small daughters, and an older couple, the husband's parents.

What perfect weather. Every morning, every morning it's like this, the first pure sunlight falling through the high branches, burning away the mist over the still water of Georgia Strait. The tide out, a great empty stretch of sand still damp but easy to walk on, like cement in its very last stage of drying. The tide is actually less far out; every morning, the pavilion of sand is shrinking, but it still seems ample enough. The changes in the tide are a matter of great interest to the grandfather, not so much to anyone else.

Pauline, the young mother, doesn't really like the beach as well as she likes the road that runs behind the cottages for a mile or so north till it stops at the bank of the little river that runs into the sea.

If it wasn't for the tide, it would be hard to remember that this is the sea. You look across the water to the mountains on the mainland, the ranges that are the western wall of the continent of North America. These humps and peaks coming clear now through the mist and glimpsed here and there through the trees, by Pauline as she pushes her daughter's stroller along the road, are also of interest to the grandfather. And to his son Brian, who is Pauline's husband. The two men are continually trying to decide which is what. Which of these shapes are actual continental mountains and which are improbable heights of the islands that ride in front of the shore? It's hard to sort things out when the array is so complicated and parts of it shift their distance in the day's changing light.

But there is a map, set up under glass, between the cottages and the beach. You can stand there looking at the map, then looking at what's in front of you, looking back at the map again, until you get things sorted out. The grandfather and Brian do this every day, usually getting into an argument—though you'd think there would not be much room for disagreement with the map right there. Brian chooses to see the map as inexact. But his father will not hear a word of criticism about any aspect of this place, which was his choice for the holiday. The map, like the accommodation and the weather, is perfect.

Brian's mother won't look at the map. She says it boggles her mind. The men laugh at her, they accept that her mind is boggled. Her husband believes that this is because she is a female. Brian believes that it's because she's his mother. Her concern is always about whether anybody is hungry yet, or thirsty, whether the children have their sun hats on and have been rubbed with protective lotion. And what is the strange bite on Caitlin's arm that doesn't look like the bite of a mosquito? She makes her husband wear a floppy cotton hat and thinks that Brian should wear one too—she reminds him of how sick he got from the sun, that summer they went to the Okanagan, when he was a child. Sometimes Brian says to her, "Oh, dry up, Mother." His tone is mostly affectionate, but his father may ask him if that's the way he thinks he can talk to his mother nowadays.

"She doesn't mind," says Brian.

"How do you know?" says his father.

"Oh for Pete's sake," says his mother.

PAULINE SLIDES OUT OF BED as soon as she's awake every morning, slides out of reach of Brian's long, sleepily searching arms and legs. What wakes her are the first squeaks and mutters of the baby, Mara, in the children's room, then the creak of the crib as Mara—sixteen months old now, getting to the end of babyhood—pulls herself up to stand hanging on to the railing. She continues her soft amiable talk as Pauline lifts her out—Caitlin, nearly five, shifting about but not waking, in her nearby bed—and as she is carried into the kitchen to be changed, on the floor. Then she is settled into her stroller, with a biscuit and a bottle of apple juice, while Pauline gets into her sundress and sandals, goes to the bathroom, combs out her hair—all as quickly and quietly as possible. They leave the cottage; they head past some other cottages for the bumpy unpaved road that is still mostly in deep morning shadow, the floor of a tunnel under fir and cedar trees.

The grandfather, also an early riser, sees them from the porch of his cottage, and Pauline sees him. But all that is necessary is a wave. He and Pauline never have much to say to each other (though sometimes there's an affinity they feel, in the midst of some long-drawn-out antics of Brian's or some apologetic but insistent fuss made by the grandmother; there's an awareness of not looking at each other, lest their look should reveal a bleakness that would discredit others).

On this holiday Pauline steals time to be by herself—being with Mara is still almost the same thing as being by herself. Early morning walks, the late-morning hour when she washes and hangs out the diapers. She could have had another hour or so in the afternoons, while Mara is napping. But Brian has fixed up a shelter on the beach, and he carries the playpen down every day, so that Mara can nap there and Pauline won't have to absent herself. He says his parents may be offended if she's always sneaking off. He agrees though that she does need some time to go over her lines for the play she's going to be in, back in Victoria, this September.

Pauline is not an actress. This is an amateur production, but she is not even an amateur actress. She didn't try out for the role, though it happened that she had already read the play. *Eurydice* by Jean Anouilh. But then, Pauline has read all sorts of things.

She was asked if she would like to be in this play by a man she met at a barbecue, in June. The people at the barbecue were mostly teachers and their wives or husbands—it was held at the house of the principal of the high school where Brian teaches. The woman who taught French was a widow—she had brought her grown son who was staying for the summer with her and working as a night clerk in a downtown hotel. She told everybody that he had got a job teaching at a college in western Washington State and would be going there in the fall.

Jeffrey Toom was his name. "Without the *B*," he said, as if the staleness of the joke wounded him. It was a different name from his mother's, because she had been widowed twice, and he was the son of her first husband. About the job he said, "No guarantee it'll last, it's a one-year appointment."

What was he going to teach?

"Dram-ah," he said, drawing the word out in a mocking way.

He spoke of his present job disparagingly, as well.

"It's a pretty sordid place," he said. "Maybe you heard—a hooker was killed there last winter. And then we get the usual losers checking in to OD or bump themselves off."

People did not quite know what to make of this way of talking and drifted away from him. Except for Pauline.

"I'm thinking about putting on a play," he said. "Would you like to be in it?" He asked her if she had ever heard of a play called *Eurydice*.

Pauline said, "You mean Anouilh's?" and he was unflatteringly surprised. He immediately said he didn't know if it would ever work out. "I just thought it might be interesting to see if you could do something different here in the land of Noël Coward."

Pauline did not remember when there had been a play by Noël Coward put on in Victoria, though she supposed there had been several. She said, "We saw *The Duchess of Malfi* last winter at the college. And the little theater did *A Resounding Tinkle*, but we didn't see it."

"Yeah. Well," he said, flushing. She had thought he was older than she was, at least as old as Brian (who was thirty, though people were apt to say he didn't act it), but as soon as he started talking to her, in this offhand, dismissive way, never quite meeting her eyes, she suspected that he was younger than he'd like to appear. Now with that flush she was sure of it.

As it turned out, he was a year younger than she was. Twenty-five.

She said that she couldn't be Eurydice; she couldn't act. But Brian came over to see what the conversation was about and said at once that she must try it.

"She just needs a kick in the behind," Brian said to Jeffrey. "She's like a little mule, it's hard to get her started. No, seriously, she's too self-effacing, I tell her that all the time. She's very smart. She's actually a lot smarter than I am."

At that Jeffrey did look directly into Pauline's eyes—impertinently and searchingly—and she was the one who was flushing.

He had chosen her immediately as his Eurydice because of the way she looked. But it was not because she was beautiful. "I'd never put a beautiful girl in that part," he said. "I don't know if I'd ever put a beautiful girl on stage in anything. It's too much. It's distracting."

So what did he mean about the way she looked? He said it was her hair, which was long and dark and rather bushy (not in style at that time), and her pale skin ("Stay out of the sun this summer") and most of all her eyebrows.

"I never liked them," said Pauline, not quite sincerely. Her eyebrows were level, dark, luxuriant. They dominated her face. Like her hair, they were not in style. But if she had really disliked them, wouldn't she have plucked them?

Jeffrey seemed not to have heard her. "They give you a sulky look and that's disturbing," he said. "Also your jaw's a little heavy and that's sort of Greek. It would be better in a movie where I could get you close up. The routine thing for Eurydice would be a girl who looked ethereal. I don't want ethereal."

As she walked Mara along the road, Pauline did work at the lines. There was a speech at the end that was giving her trouble. She bumped the stroller along and repeated to herself, "'You are terrible, you know, you are terrible like the angels. You think everybody's going forward, as brave and bright as you are—oh, don't look at me, please, darling, don't look at me—perhaps I'm not what you wish I was, but I'm here, and I'm warm, I'm kind, and I love you. I'll give you all the happiness I can. Don't look at me. Don't look. Let me live.'"

She had left something out. "'Perhaps I'm not what you wish I was, but you feel me here, don't you? I'm warm and I'm kind—'"

She had told Jeffrey that she thought the play was beautiful.

He said, "Really?" What she'd said didn't please or surprise him—he seemed to feel it was predictable, superfluous. He would never describe a play in that way. He spoke of it more as a hurdle to be got over. Also a challenge to be flung at various enemies. At the academic snots—as he called them—who had done *The Duchess of Malfi*. And at the social twits—as he called them—in the little theater. He saw himself as an outsider heaving his weight against these people, putting on his play—he called it his—in the teeth of their contempt and opposition. In the beginning Pauline thought that this must be all in his imagination and that it was more likely these people knew nothing about him. Then something would happen that could be, but might not be, a coincidence. Repairs had to be done on the church hall where the play was to be performed, making it unobtainable. There was an unexpected increase in the cost of printing advertising posters. She found herself seeing it his way. If you were going to be around him much, you almost had to see it his way—arguing was dangerous and exhausting.

"Sons of bitches," said Jeffrey between his teeth, but with some satisfaction. "I'm not surprised."

The rehearsals were held upstairs in an old building on Fisgard Street. Sunday afternoon was the only time that everybody could get there, though there were fragmentary rehearsals during the week. The retired harbor pilot who played Monsieur Henri was able to attend every rehearsal, and got to have an irritating familiarity with everybody else's lines. But the hairdresser—who had experience only with Gilbert and Sullivan but now found herself playing Eurydice's mother—could not leave her shop for long at any other time. The bus driver who played her lover had his daily employment as well, and so had the waiter who played Orphée (he was the only one of them who hoped to be a real actor). Pauline had to depend on sometimes undependable high-school babysitters—for the first six weeks of the summer Brian was busy teaching summer school—and Jeffrey himself had to be at his hotel job by eight o'clock in the evenings. But on Sunday afternoons they were all there. While other people swam at Thetis Lake, or thronged Beacon Hill Park to walk under the trees and feed the ducks, or drove far out of town to the Pacific beaches, Jeffrey and his crew labored in the dusty high-ceilinged room on Fisgard Street. The windows were rounded at the top as in some plain and dignified church, and propped open in the heat with whatever objects could be found—ledger books from the 1920s belonging to the hat shop that had once operated downstairs, or pieces of wood left over from the picture frames made by the artist whose canvases were now stacked against one wall and apparently abandoned. The glass was grimy, but outside the sunlight bounced off the sidewalks, the empty gravelled parking lots, the low stuccoed buildings, with what seemed a special Sunday brightness. Hardly anybody moved through these downtown streets. Nothing was open except the occasional hole-in-the-wall coffee shop or fly-specked convenience store.

Pauline was the one who went out at the break to get soft drinks and coffee. She was the one who had the least to say about the play and the way it was going—even though she was the only one who had read it before—because she alone had never done any acting. So it seemed proper for her to volunteer. She enjoyed her short walk in the empty streets—she felt as if she had become an urban person, someone detached and solitary, who lived in the glare of an important dream. Sometimes she thought of Brian at home, working in the garden and keeping an eye on the children. Or perhaps he had taken them to Dallas Road—she recalled a promise—to sail boats on the pond. That life seemed ragged and tedious compared to what went on in the rehearsal room—the hours of effort, the concentration, the sharp exchanges, the sweating and tension. Even the taste of the coffee, its scalding bitterness, and the fact that it was chosen by nearly everybody in preference to a fresher-tasting and maybe more healthful drink out of the cooler seemed satisfying to her. And she liked the look of the shop-windows. This was not one of the dolled-up streets near the harbor—it was a street of shoe- and bicycle-repair shops, discount linen and fabric stores, of clothes and furniture that had been so long in the windows that they looked secondhand even if they weren't. On some windows sheets of golden plastic as frail and crinkled as old cellophane were stretched inside the glass to protect the merchandise from the sun. All these enterprises had been left behind just for this one day, but they had a look of being fixed in time as much as cave paintings or relics under sand.

WHEN SHE SAID that she had to go away for the two-week holiday Jeffrey looked thunderstruck, as if he had never imagined that things like holidays could come into her life. Then he turned grim and slightly satirical, as if this was just another blow that he might have expected. Pauline explained that she would miss only the one Sunday—the one in the middle of the two weeks—because she and Brian were driving up the island on a Monday and coming back on a Sunday morning. She promised to get back in time for rehearsal. Privately she wondered how she would do this—it always took so much longer than you expected to pack up and get away. She wondered if she could possibly come back by herself, on the morning bus. That would probably be too much to ask for. She didn't mention it.

She couldn't ask him if it was only the play he was thinking about, only her absence from a rehearsal that caused the thundercloud. At the moment, it very likely was. When he spoke to her at rehearsals there was never any suggestion that he ever spoke to her in any other way. The only difference in his treatment of her was that perhaps he expected less of her, of her acting, than he did of the others. And that would be understandable to anybody. She was the only one chosen out of the blue, for the way she looked— the others had all shown up at the audition he had advertised on the signs put up in cafés and bookstores around town. From her he appeared to want an immobility or awkwardness that he didn't want from the rest of them. Perhaps it was because, in the latter part of the play, she was supposed to be a person who had already died.

Yet she thought they all knew, the rest of the cast all knew, what was going on, in spite of Jeffrey's offhand and abrupt and none too civil ways. They knew that after every one of them had straggled off home, he would walk across the room and bolt the staircase door. (At first Pauline had pretended to leave with the rest and had even got into her car and circled the block, but later such a trick had come to seem insulting, not just to herself and Jeffrey, but to the others who she was sure would never betray her, bound as they all were under the temporary but potent spell of the play.)

Jeffrey crossed the room and bolted the door. Every time, this was like a new decision, which he had to make. Until it was done, she wouldn't look at him. The sound of the bolt being pushed into place, the ominous or fatalistic sound of the metal hitting metal, gave her a localized shock of capitulation. But she didn't make a move, she waited for him to come back to her with the whole story of the afternoon's labor draining out of his face, the expression of matter-of-fact and customary disappointment cleared away, replaced by the live energy she always found surprising.

"SO. TELL US WHAT THIS PLAY of yours is about," Brian's father said. "Is it one of those ones where they take their clothes off on the stage?"

"Now don't tease her," said Brian's mother.

Brian and Pauline had put the children to bed and walked over to his parents' cottage for an evening drink. The sunset was behind them, behind the forests of Vancouver Island, but the mountains in front of them, all clear now and hard-cut against the sky, shone in its pink light. Some high inland mountains were capped with pink summer snow.

"Nobody takes their clothes off, Dad," said Brian in his booming schoolroom voice. "You know why? Because they haven't got any clothes on in the first place. It's the latest style. They're going to put on a bare-naked *Hamlet* next. Bare-naked *Romeo and Juliet*. Boy, that balcony scene where Romeo is climbing up the trellis and he gets stuck in the rosebushes—"

"Oh, Brian," said his mother.

"The story of Orpheus and Eurydice is that Eurydice died," Pauline said. "And Orpheus goes down to the underworld to try to get her back. And his wish is granted, but only if he promises not to look at her. Not to look back at her. She's walking behind him—"

"Twelve paces," said Brian. "As is only right."

"It's a Greek story, but it's set in modern times," said Pauline. "At least this version is. More or less modern. Orpheus is a musician travelling around with his father—they're both musicians—and Eurydice is an actress. This is in France."

"Translated?" Brian's father said.

"No," said Brian. "But don't worry, it's not in French. It was written in Transylvanian."

"It's so hard to make sense of anything," Brian's mother said with a worried laugh. "It's so hard, with Brian around."

"It's in English," Pauline said.

"And you're what's-her-name?"

She said, "I'm Eurydice."

"He get you back okay?"

"No," she said. "He looks back at me, and then I have to stay dead."

"Oh, an unhappy ending," Brian's mother said.

"You're so gorgeous?" said Brian's father skeptically. "He can't stop himself from looking back?"

"It's not that," said Pauline. But at this point she felt that something had been achieved by her father-in-law, he had done what he meant to do, which was the same thing that he nearly always meant to do, in any conversation she had with him. And that was to break through the structure of some explanation he had asked her for, and she had unwillingly but patiently given, and, with a seemingly negligent kick, knock it into rubble. He had been dangerous to her for a long time in this way, but he wasn't particularly so tonight.

But Brian did not know that. Brian was still figuring out how to come to her rescue.

"Pauline is gorgeous," Brian said.

"Yes indeed," said his mother.

"Maybe if she'd go to the hairdresser," his father said. But Pauline's long hair was such an old objection of his that it had become a family joke. Even Pauline laughed. She said, "I can't afford to till we get the veranda roof fixed." And Brian laughed boisterously, full of relief that she was able to take all this as a joke. It was what he had always told her to do.

"Just kid him back," he said. "It's the only way to handle him."

"Yeah, well, if you'd got yourselves a decent house," said his father. But this like Pauline's hair was such a familiar sore point that it couldn't rouse anybody. Brian and Pauline had bought a handsome house in bad repair on a street in Victoria where old mansions were being turned into ill-used apartment buildings. The house, the street, the messy old Garry oaks, the fact that no basement had been blasted out under the house, were all a horror to Brian's father. Brian usually agreed with him and tried to go him one further. If his father pointed at the house next door all crisscrossed with black fire escapes, and asked what kind of neighbors they had, Brian said, "Really poor people, Dad. Drug addicts." And when his father wanted to know how it was heated, he'd said, "Coal furnace. Hardly any of them left these days, you can get coal really cheap. Of course it's dirty and it kind of stinks."

So what his father said now about a decent house might be some kind of peace signal. Or could be taken so.

Brian was an only son. He was a math teacher. His father was a civil engineer and part owner of a contracting company. If he had hoped that he would have a son who was an engineer and might come into the company, there was never any mention of it. Pauline had asked Brian whether he thought the carping about their house and her hair and the books she read might be a cover for this larger disappointment, but Brian had said, "Nope. In our family we complain about just whatever we want to complain about. We ain't subtle, ma'am."

Pauline still wondered, when she heard his mother talking about how teachers ought to be the most honored people in the world and they did not get half the credit they deserved and that she didn't know how Brian managed it, day after day. Then his father might say, "That's right," or, "I sure wouldn't want to do it, I can tell you that. They couldn't pay me to do it."

"Don't worry Dad," Brian would say. "They wouldn't pay you much."

Brian in his everyday life was a much more dramatic person than Jeffrey. He dominated his classes by keeping up a parade of jokes and antics, extending the role that he had always played, Pauline believed, with his mother and father. He acted dumb, he bounced back from pretended humiliations, he traded insults. He was a bully in a good cause—a chivvying cheerful indestructible bully.

"Your boy has certainly made his mark with us," the principal said to Pauline. "He has not just survived, which is something in itself. He has made his mark."

Your boy.

Brian called his students boneheads. His tone was affectionate, fatalistic. He said that his father was the King of the Philistines, a pure and natural barbarian. And that his mother was a dishrag, good-natured and worn out. But however he dismissed such people, he could not be long without them. He took his students on camping trips. And he could not imagine a summer without this shared holiday. He was mortally afraid, every year, that Pauline would refuse to go along. Or that, having agreed to go, she was going to be miserable, take offense at something his father said, complain about how much time she had to spend with his mother, sulk because there was no way they could do anything by themselves. She might decide to spend all day in their own cottage, reading and pretending to have a sunburn.

All those things had happened, on previous holidays. But this year she was easing up. He told her he could see that, and he was grateful to her.

"I know it's an effort," he said. "It's different for me. They're my parents and I'm used to not taking them seriously."

Pauline came from a family that took things so seriously that her parents had got a divorce. Her mother was now dead. She had a distant, though cordial, relationship with her father and her two much older sisters. She said that they had nothing in common. She knew Brian could not understand how that could be a reason. She saw what comfort it gave him, this year, to see things going so well. She had thought it was laziness or cowardice that kept him from breaking the arrangement, but now she saw that it was something far more positive. He needed to have his wife and his parents and his children bound together like this, he needed to involve Pauline in his life with his parents and to bring his parents to some recognition of her—though the recognition, from his father, would always be muffled and contrary, and from his mother too profuse, too easily come by, to mean much. Also he wanted Pauline to be connected, he wanted the children to be connected, to his own childhood—he wanted these holidays to be linked to holidays of his childhood with their lucky or unlucky weather, car troubles or driving records, boating scares, bee stings, marathon Monopoly games, to all the things that he told his mother he was bored to death hearing about. He wanted pictures from this summer to be taken, and fitted into his mother's album, a continuation of all the other pictures that he groaned at the mention of.

The only time they could talk to each other was in bed, late at night. But they did talk then, more than was usual with them at home, where Brian was so tired that often he fell immediately asleep. And in ordinary daylight it was often hard to talk to him because of his jokes. She could see the joke brightening his eyes (his coloring was very like hers—dark hair and pale skin and gray eyes, but her eyes were cloudy and his were light, like clear water over stones). She could see it pulling at the corners of his mouth, as he foraged among your words to catch a pun or the start of a rhyme—anything that could take the conversation away, into absurdity. His whole body, tall and loosely joined together and still almost as skinny as a teenager's, twitched with comic propensity. Before she married him, Pauline had a friend named Gracie, a rather grumpy-looking girl, subversive about men. Brian had thought her a girl whose spirits needed a boost, and so he made even more than the usual effort. And Gracie said to Pauline, "How can you stand the nonstop show?"

"That's not the real Brian," Pauline had said. "He's different when we're alone." But looking back, she wondered how true that had ever been. Had she said it simply to defend her choice, as you did when you had made up your mind to get married?

So talking in the dark had something to do with the fact that she could not see his face. And that he knew she couldn't see his face.

But even with the window open on the unfamiliar darkness and stillness of the night, he teased a little. He had to speak of Jeffrey as Monsieur le Directeur, which made the play or the fact that it was a French play slightly ridiculous. Or perhaps it was Jeffrey himself, Jeffrey's seriousness about the play, that had to be called in question.

Pauline didn't care. It was such a pleasure and a relief to her to mention Jeffrey's name.

Most of the time she didn't mention him; she circled around that pleasure. She described all the others, instead. The hair-dresser and the harbor pilot and the waiter and the old man who claimed to have once acted on the radio. He played Orphée's father and gave Jeffrey the most trouble, because he had the stubbornest notions of his own, about acting.

The middle-aged impresario Monsieur Dulac was played by a twenty-four-year-old travel agent. And Mathias, who was Eurydice's former boyfriend, presumably around her own age, was played by the manager of a shoe store, who was married and a father of children.

Brian wanted to know why Monsieur le Directeur hadn't cast these two the other way round.

"That's the way he does things," Pauline said. "What he sees in us is something only he can see."

For instance, she said, the waiter was a clumsy Orphée.

"He's only nineteen, he's so shy Jeffrey has to keep at him. He tells him not to act like he's making love to his grandmother. He has to tell him what to do. *Keep your arms around her a little longer, stroke her here a little*. I don't know how it's going to work—I just have to trust Jeffrey, that he knows what he's doing."

"'Stroke her here a little'?" said Brian. "Maybe I should come around and keep an eye on these rehearsals."

When she had started to quote Jeffrey Pauline had felt a giving-way in her womb or the bottom of her stomach, a shock that had travelled oddly upwards and hit her vocal cords. She had to cover up this quaking by growling in a way that was supposed to be an imitation (though Jeffrey never growled or ranted or carried on in any theatrical way at all).

"But there's a point about him being so innocent," she said hurriedly. "Being not so physical. Being awkward." And she began to talk about Orphée in the play, not the waiter. Orphée has a problem with love or reality. Orphée will not put up with anything less than perfection. He wants a love that is outside of ordinary life. He wants a perfect Eurydice.

"Eurydice is more realistic. She's carried on with Mathias and with Monsieur Dulac. She's been around her mother and her mother's lover. She knows what people are like. But she loves Orphée. She loves him better in a way than he loves her. She loves him better because she's not such a fool. She loves him like a human person."

"But she's slept with those other guys," Brian said.

"Well with Mr. Dulac she had to, she couldn't get out of it. She didn't want to, but probably after a while she enjoyed it, because after a certain point she couldn't help enjoying it."

So Orphée is at fault, Pauline said decidedly. He looks at Eurydice on purpose, to kill her and get rid of her because she is not perfect. Because of him she has to die a second time.

Brian, on his back and with his eyes wide open (she knew that because of the tone of his voice) said, "But doesn't he die too?"

"Yes. He chooses to."

"So then they're together?"

"Yes. Like Romeo and Juliet. *Orphée is with Eurydice at last.* That's what Monsieur Henri says. That's the last line of the play. That's the end." Pauline rolled over onto her side and touched her cheek to Brian's shoulder—not to start anything but to emphasize what she said next. "It's a beautiful play in one way, but in another it's so silly. And it isn't really like *Romeo and Juliet* because it isn't bad luck or circumstances. It's on purpose. So they don't have to go on with life and get married and have kids and buy an old house and fix it up and—"

"And have affairs," said Brian. "After all, they're French."

Then he said, "Be like my parents."

Pauline laughed. "Do they have affairs? I can imagine."

"Oh sure," said Brian. "I meant their life."

"Logically I can see killing yourself so you won't turn into your parents," Brian said. "I just don't believe anybody would do it."

"Everybody has choices," Pauline said dreamily. "Her mother and his father are both despicable in a way, but Orphée and Eurydice don't have to be like them. They're not corrupt. Just because she's slept with those men doesn't mean she's corrupt. She wasn't in love then. She hadn't met Orphée. There's one speech where he tells her that everything she's done is sticking to her, and it's disgusting. Lies she's told him. The other men. It's all sticking to her forever. And then of course Monsieur Henri plays up to that. He tells Orphée that he'll be just as bad and that one day he'll walk down the street with Eurydice and he'll look like a man with a dog he's trying to lose."

To her surprise, Brian laughed.

"No," she said. "That's what's stupid. It's not inevitable. It's not inevitable at all."

They went on speculating, and comfortably arguing, in a way that was not usual, but not altogether unfamiliar to them. They had done this before, at long intervals in their married life—talked half the night about God or fear of death or how children should be educated or whether money was important. At last they admitted to being too tired to make sense any longer, and arranged themselves in a comradely position and went to sleep.

FINALLY A RAINY DAY. Brian and his parents were driving into Campbell River to get groceries, and gin, and to take Brian's father's car to a garage, to see about a problem that had developed on the drive up from Nanaimo. This was a very slight problem, but there was the matter of the new-car warranty's being in effect at present, so Brian's father wanted to get it seen to as soon as possible. Brian had to go along, with his car, just in case his father's car had to be left in the garage. Pauline said that she had to stay home because of Mara's nap.

She persuaded Caitlin to lie down too—allowing her to take her music box to bed with her if she played it very softly. Then Pauline spread the script on the kitchen table and drank coffee and went over the scene in which Orphée says that it's intolerable, at last, to stay in two skins, two envelopes with their own blood and oxygen sealed up in their solitude, and Eurydice tells him to be quiet.

"Don't talk. Don't think. Just let your hand wander, let it be happy on its own."

Your hand is my happiness, says Eurydice. Accept that. Accept your happiness.

Of course he says he cannot.

Caitlin called out frequently to ask what time it was. She turned up the sound of the music box. Pauline hurried to the bedroom door and hissed at her to turn it down, not to wake Mara.

"If you play it like that again I'll take it away from you. Okay?"

But Mara was already rustling around in her crib, and in the next few minutes there were sounds of soft, encouraging conversation from Caitlin, designed to get her sister wide awake. Also of the music being quickly turned up and then down. Then of Mara rattling the crib railing, pulling herself up, throwing her bottle out onto the floor, and starting the bird cries that would grow more and more desolate until they brought her mother.

"I didn't wake her," Caitlin said. "She was awake all by herself. It's not raining anymore. Can we go down to the beach?"

She was right. It wasn't raining. Pauline changed Mara, told Caitlin to get her bathing suit on and find her sand pail. She got into her own bathing suit and put her shorts over it, in case the rest of the family arrived home while she was down there. ("Dad doesn't like the way some women just go right out of their cottages in their bathing suits," Brian's mother had said to her. "I guess he and I just grew up in other times.") She picked up the script to take it along, then laid it down. She was afraid that she would get too absorbed in it and take her eyes off the children for a moment too long.

The thoughts that came to her, of Jeffrey, were not really thoughts at all—they were more like alterations in her body. This could happen when she was sitting on the beach (trying to stay in the half shade of a bush and so preserve her pallor, as Jeffrey had ordered) or when she was wringing out diapers or when she and Brian were visiting his parents. In the middle of Monopoly games, Scrabble games, card games. She went right on talking, listening, working, keeping track of the children, while some memory of her secret life disturbed her like a radiant explosion. Then a warm weight settled, reassurance filling up all her hollows. But it didn't last, this comfort leaked away, and she was like a miser whose windfall has vanished and who is convinced such luck can never strike again. Longing buckled her up and drove her to the discipline of counting days. Sometimes she even cut the days into fractions to figure out more exactly how much time had gone.

She thought of going into Campbell River, making some excuse, so that she could get to a phone booth and call him. The cottages had no phones—the only public phone was in the hall of the lodge. But she did not have the number of the hotel where Jeffrey worked. And besides that, she could never get away to Campbell River in the evening. She was afraid that if she called him at home in the daytime his mother the French teacher might answer. He said his mother hardly ever left the house in the summer. Just once, she had taken the ferry to Vancouver for the day. Jeffrey had phoned

Pauline to ask her to come over. Brian was teaching, and Caitlin was at her play group.

Pauline said, "I can't. I have Mara."

Jeffrey said, "Who? Oh. Sorry." Then "Couldn't you bring her along?"

She said no.

"Why not? Couldn't you bring some things for her to play with?"

No, said Pauline. "I couldn't," she said. "I just couldn't." It seemed too dangerous to her, to trundle her baby along on such a guilty expedition. To a house where cleaning fluids would not be bestowed on high shelves, and all pills and cough syrups and cigarettes and buttons put safely out of reach. And even if she escaped poisoning or choking, Mara might be storing up time bombs—memories of a strange house where she was strangely disregarded, of a closed door, noises on the other side of it.

"I just wanted you," Jeffrey said. "I just wanted you in my bed."

She said again, weakly, "No."

Those words of his kept coming back to her. *I wanted you in my bed.* A half-joking urgency in his voice but also a determination, a practicality, as if "in my bed" meant something more, the bed he spoke of taking on larger, less material dimensions.

Had she made a great mistake with that refusal? With that reminder of how fenced in she was, in what anybody would call her real life?

THE BEACH WAS NEARLY EMPTY—people had got used to its being a rainy day. The sand was too heavy for Caitlin to make a castle or dig an irrigation system—projects she would only undertake with her father, anyway, because she sensed that his interest in them was wholehearted, and Pauline's was not. She wandered a bit forlornly at the edge of the water. She probably missed the presence of other children, the nameless instant friends and occasional stone-throwing water-kicking enemies, the shrieking and splashing and falling about. A boy a little bigger than she was and apparently all by himself stood knee-deep in the water farther down the beach. If these two could get together it might be all right; the whole beach experience might be retrieved. Pauline couldn't tell whether Caitlin was now making little splashy runs into the water for his benefit or whether he was watching her with interest or scorn.

Mara didn't need company, at least for now. She stumbled towards the water, felt it touch her feet and changed her mind, stopped, looked around, and spotted Pauline. "Paw. Paw," she said, in happy recognition. "Paw" was what she said for "Pauline," instead of "Mother" or "Mommy." Looking around overbalanced her—she sat down half on the sand and half in the water, made a squawk of surprise that turned to an announcement, then by some determined ungraceful maneuvers that involved putting her weight on her hands, she rose to her feet, wavering and triumphant. She had been walking for half a year, but getting around on the sand was still a challenge. Now she came back towards Pauline, making some reasonable, casual remarks in her own language.

"Sand," said Pauline, holding up a clot of it. "Look. Mara. Sand."

Mara corrected her, calling it something else—it sounded like "whap." Her thick diaper under her plastic pants and her terry-cloth playsuit gave her a fat bottom, and that, along with her plump cheeks and shoulders and her sidelong important expression, made her look like a roguish matron.

Pauline became aware of someone calling her name. It had been called two or three times, but because the voice was unfamiliar she had not recognized it. She stood up and waved. It was the woman who worked in the store at the lodge. She was leaning over the balcony and calling, "Mrs. Keating. Mrs. Keating? Telephone, Mrs. Keating."

Pauline hoisted Mara onto her hip and summoned Caitlin. She and the little boy were aware of each other now—they were both picking up stones from the bottom and flinging them out into the water. At first she didn't hear Pauline, or pretended not to.

"Store," called Pauline. "Caitlin. Store." When she was sure Caitlin would follow—it was the word "store" that had done it, the reminder of the tiny store in the lodge where you could buy ice cream and candy and cigarettes and mixer—she began the trek across the sand and up the flight of wooden steps above the sand and the salal bushes. Halfway up she stopped, said, "Mara, you weigh a ton," and shifted the baby to her other hip. Caitlin banged a stick against the railing.

"Can I have a Fudgsicle? Mother? Can I?"

"We'll see."

"Can I please have a Fudgsicle?"

"Wait."

The public phone was beside a bulletin board on the other side of the main hall and across from the door to the dining room. A bingo game had been set up in there, because of the rain.

"Hope he's still hanging on," the woman who worked in the store called out. She was unseen now behind her counter.

Pauline, still holding Mara, picked up the dangling receiver and said breathlessly, "Hello?" She was expecting to hear Brian telling her about some delay in Campbell River or asking her what it was she had wanted him to get at the drugstore. It was just the one thing—calamine lotion—so he had not written it down.

"Pauline," said Jeffrey. "It's me."

Mara was bumping and scrambling against Pauline's side, anxious to get down. Caitlin came along the hall and went into the store, leaving wet sandy footprints. Pauline said, "Just a minute, just a minute." She let Mara slide down and hurried to close the door that led to the steps. She did not remember telling Jeffrey the name of this place, though she had told him roughly where it was. She heard the woman in the store speaking to Caitlin in a sharper voice than she would use to children whose parents were beside them.

"Did you forget to put your feet under the tap?"

"I'm here," said Jeffrey. "I didn't get along well without you. I didn't get along at all."

Mara made for the dining room, as if the male voice calling out "Under the N—" was a direct invitation to her.

"Here. Where?" said Pauline.

She read the signs that were tacked up on the bulletin board beside the phone.

NO PERSON UNDER FOURTEEN YEARS OF AGE NOT ACCOMPANIED BY ADULT ALLOWED IN BOATS OR CANOES.

FISHING DERBY.

BAKE AND CRAFT SALE, ST. BARTHOLOMEW'S CHURCH.

YOUR LIFE IS IN YOUR HANDS. PALMS AND CARDS READ. REASONABLE AND ACCURATE. CALL CLAIRE.

"In a motel. In Campbell River."

PAULINE KNEW WHERE SHE WAS before she opened her eyes. Nothing surprised her. She had slept but not deeply enough to let go of anything.

She had waited for Brian in the parking area of the lodge, with the children, and had asked him for the keys. She had told him in front of his parents that there was something else she needed, from Campbell River. He asked, What was it? And did she have any money?

"Just something," she said, so he would think that it was tampons or birth control supplies, that she didn't want to mention. "Sure."

"Okay but you'll have to put some gas in," he said.

Later she had to speak to him on the phone. Jeffrey said she had to do it.

"Because he won't take it from me. He'll think I kidnapped you or something. He won't believe it."

But the strangest thing of all the things that day was that Brian did seem, immediately, to believe it. Standing where she had stood not so long before, in the public hallway of the lodge—the bingo game over now but people going past, she could hear them, people on their way out of the dining room after dinner—he said, "Oh. Oh. Oh. Okay" in a voice that would have to be quickly controlled, but that seemed to draw on a supply of fatalism or foreknowledge that went far beyond that necessity.

As if he had known all along, all along, what could happen with her.

"Okay," he said. "What about the car?"

He said something else, something impossible, and hung up, and she came out of the phone booth beside some gas pumps in Campbell River.

"That was quick," Jeffrey said. "Easier than you expected."

Pauline said, "I don't know."

"He may have known it subconsciously. People do know."

She shook her head, to tell him not to say any more, and he said, "Sorry." They walked along the street not touching or talking.

THEY'D HAD TO GO OUT to find a phone booth because there was no phone in the motel room. Now in the early morning looking around at leisure—the first real leisure or freedom she'd had since she came into that room—Pauline saw that there wasn't much of anything in it. Just a junk dresser, the bed without a headboard, an armless upholstered chair, on the window a venetian blind with a broken slat and curtain of orange plastic that was supposed to look like net and that didn't have to be hemmed, just sliced off at the bottom. There was a noisy air conditioner—Jeffrey had turned it off in the night and left the door open on the chain, since the window was sealed. The door was shut now. He must have got up in the night and shut it.

This was all she had. Her connection with the cottage where Brian lay asleep or not asleep was broken, also her connection with the house that had been an expression of her life with Brian, of the way they wanted to live. She had no furniture anymore. She had cut herself off from all the large solid acquisitions like the washer and dryer and the oak table and the refinished wardrobe and the chandelier that was a copy of the one in a painting by Vermeer. And just as much from those things that were particularly hers—the pressed-glass tumblers that she had been collecting and the prayer rug which was of course not authentic, but beautiful. Especially from those things. Even her books, she might have lost. Even her clothes. The skirt and blouse and sandals she had put on for the trip to Campbell River might well be all she had now to her name. She would never go back to lay claim to anything. If Brian got in touch with her to ask what was to be done with things, she would tell him to do what he liked—throw everything into garbage bags and take it to the dump, if that was what he liked. (In fact she knew that he would probably pack up a trunk, which he did, sending on, scrupulously, not only her winter coat and boots but things like the waist cincher she had worn at her wedding and never since, with the prayer rug draped over the top of everything like a final statement of his generosity, either natural or calculated.)

She believed that she would never again care about what sort of rooms she lived in or what sort of clothes she put on. She would not be looking for that sort of help to give anybody an idea of who she was, what she was like. Not even to give herself an idea. What she had done would be enough, it would be the whole thing.

What she was doing would be what she had heard about and read about. It was what Anna Karenina had done and what Madame Bovary had wanted to do. It was what a teacher at Brian's school had done, with the school secretary. He had run off with her. That was what it was called. Running off with. Taking off with. It was spoken of disparagingly, humorously, enviously. It was adultery taken one step further. The people who did it had almost certainly been having an affair already, committing adultery for quite some time before they became desperate or courageous enough to take this step. Once in a long while a couple might claim their love was unconsummated and technically pure, but these people would be thought of—if anybody believed them—as being not only very serious and highminded but almost devastatingly foolhardy, almost in a class with those who took a chance and gave up everything to go and work in some poor and dangerous country.

The others, the adulterers, were seen as irresponsible, immature, selfish, or even cruel. Also lucky. They were lucky because the sex they had been having in parked cars or the long grass or in each other's sullied marriage beds or most likely in motels like this one must surely have been splendid. Otherwise they would never have got such a yearning for each other's company at all costs or such a faith that their shared future would be altogether better and different in kind from what they had in the past.

Different in kind. That was what Pauline must believe now—that there was this major difference in lives or in marriages or unions between people. That some of them had a necessity, a fatefulness, about them that others did not have. Of course she would have said the same thing a year ago. People did say that, they seemed to believe that, and to believe that their own cases were all of the first, the special kind, even when anybody could see that they were not and that these people did not know what they were talking about. Pauline would not have known what she was talking about.

IT WAS TOO WARM in the room. Jeffrey's body was too warm. Conviction and contentiousness seemed to radiate from it, even in sleep. His torso was thicker than Brian's; he was pudgier around the waist. More flesh on the bones, yet not so slack to the touch. Not so good-looking in general—she was sure most people would say that. And not so fastidious. Brian in bed smelled of nothing. Jeffrey's skin, every time she'd been with him, had had a baked-in, slightly oily or nutty smell. He didn't wash last night—but then, neither did she. There wasn't time. Did he even have a toothbrush with him? She didn't. But she had not known she was staying.

When she met Jeffrey here it was still in the back of her mind that she had to concoct some colossal lie to serve her when she got home. And she—they—had to hurry. When Jeffrey said to her that he had decided that they must stay together, that she would come with him to Washington State, that they would have to drop the play because things would be too difficult for them in Victoria, she had looked at him just in the blank way you'd look at somebody the moment that an earthquake started. She was ready to tell him all the reasons why this was not possible, she still thought she was going to tell him that, but her life was coming adrift in that moment. To go back would be like tying a sack over her head.

All she said was "Are you sure?"

He said, "Sure." He said sincerely, "I'll never leave you."

That did not seem the sort of thing that he would say. Then she realized he was quoting—maybe ironically—from the play. It was what Orphée says to Eurydice within a few moments of their first meeting in the station buffet.

So her life was falling forwards; she was becoming one of those people who ran away. A woman who shockingly and incomprehensibly gave everything up. For love, observers would say wryly. Meaning, for sex. None of this would happen if it wasn't for sex.

And yet what's the great difference there? It's not such a variable procedure, in spite of what you're told. Skins, motions, contact, results. Pauline isn't a woman from whom it's difficult to get results. Brian got them. Probably anybody would, who wasn't wildly inept or morally disgusting.

But nothing's the same, really. With Brian—especially with Brian, to whom she has dedicated a selfish sort of goodwill, with whom she's lived in married complicity—there can never be this stripping away, the inevitable flight, the feelings she doesn't have to strive for but only to give in to like breathing or dying. That she believes can only come when the skin is on Jeffrey, the motions made by Jeffrey, and the weight that bears down on her has Jeffrey's heart in it, also his habits, thoughts, peculiarities, his ambition and loneliness (that for all she knows may have mostly to do with his youth).

For all she knows. There's a lot she doesn't know. She hardly knows anything about what he likes to eat or what music he likes to listen to or what role his mother plays in his life (no doubt a mysterious but important one, like the role of Brian's parents). One thing she's pretty sure of—whatever preferences or prohibitions he has will be definite.

She slides out from under Jeffrey's hand and from under the top sheet which has a harsh smell of bleach, she slips down to the floor where the bedspread is lying and wraps herself quickly in that rag of greenish-yellow chenille. She doesn't want him to open his eyes and see her from behind and note the droop of her buttocks. He's seen her naked before, but generally in a more forgiving moment.

She rinses her mouth and washes herself, using the bar of soap that is about the size of two thin squares of chocolate and firm as stone. She's hard-used between the legs, swollen and stinking. Urinating takes an effort, and it seems she's constipated. Last night when they went out and got hamburgers she found she could not eat. Presumably she'll learn to do all these things again, they'll resume their natural importance in her life. At the moment it's as if she can't quite spare the attention.

She has some money in her purse. She has to go out and buy a toothbrush, toothpaste, deodorant, shampoo. Also vaginal jelly. Last night they used condoms the first two times but nothing the third time.

She didn't bring her watch and Jeffrey doesn't wear one. There's no clock in the room, of course. She thinks it's early—there's still an early look to the light in spite of the heat. The stores probably won't be open, but there'll be someplace where she can get coffee.

Jeffrey has turned onto his other side. She must have wakened him, just for a moment.

They'll have a bedroom. A kitchen, an address. He'll go to work. She'll go to the Laundromat. Maybe she'll go to work too. Selling things, waiting on tables, tutoring students. She knows French and Latin—do they teach French and Latin in American high schools? Can you get a job if you're not an American? Jeffrey isn't.

She leaves him the key. She'll have to wake him to get back in. There's nothing to write a note with, or on.

It is early. The motel is on the highway at the north end of town, beside the bridge. There's no traffic yet. She scuffs along under the cottonwood trees for quite a while before a vehicle of any kind rumbles over the bridge—though the traffic on it shook their bed regularly late into the night.

Something is coming now. A truck. But not just a truck—there's a large bleak fact coming at her. And it has not arrived out of nowhere—it's been waiting, cruelly nudging at her ever since she woke up, or even all night.

Caitlin and Mara.

Last night on the phone, after speaking in such a flat and controlled and almost agreeable voice—as if he prided himself on not being shocked, not objecting or pleading—Brian cracked open. He said with contempt and fury and no concern for whoever might hear him, "Well then—what about the kids?"

The receiver began to shake against Pauline's ear.

She said, "We'll talk—" but he did not seem to hear her.

"The children," he said, in this same shivering and vindictive voice. Changing the word "kids" to "children" was like slamming a board down on her—a heavy, formal, righteous threat.

"The children stay," Brian said. "Pauline. Did you hear me?"

"No," said Pauline. "Yes. I heard you but—"

"All right. You heard me. Remember. The children stay."

It was all he could do. To make her see what she was doing, what she was ending, and to punish her if she did so. Nobody would blame him. There might be finagling, there might be bargaining, there would certainly be humbling of herself, but there it was like a round cold stone in her gullet, like a cannonball. And it would remain there unless she changed her mind entirely. The children stay.

Their car—hers and Brian's—was still sitting in the motel parking lot. Brian would have to ask his father or his mother to drive him up here today to get it. She had the keys in her purse. There were spare keys—he would surely bring them. She unlocked the car door and threw her keys on the seat and locked the door on the inside and shut it.

Now she couldn't go back. She couldn't get into the car and drive back and say that she'd been insane. If she did that he would forgive her, but he'd never get over it and neither would she. They'd go on, though, as people did.

She walked out of the parking lot, she walked along the sidewalk, into town.

The weight of Mara on her hip, yesterday. The sight of Caitlin's footprints on the floor.

Paw. Paw.

She doesn't need the keys to get back to them, she doesn't need the car. She could beg a ride on the highway. Give in, give in, get back to them any way at all, how can she not do that?

A sack over her head.

A fluid choice, the choice of fantasy, is poured out on the ground and instantly hardens; it has taken its undeniable shape.

THIS IS ACUTE PAIN. It will become chronic. Chronic means that it will be permanent but perhaps not constant. It may also mean that you won't die of it. You won't get free of it, but you won't die of it. You won't feel it every minute, but you won't spend many days without it. And you'll learn some tricks to dull it or banish it, trying not to end up destroying what you incurred this pain to get. It isn't his fault. He's still an innocent or a savage, who doesn't know there's a pain so durable in the world. Say to yourself, You lose them anyway. They grow up. For a mother there's always waiting this private slightly ridiculous desolation. They'll forget this time, in one way or another they'll disown you. Or hang around till you don't know what to do about them, the way Brian has.

And still, what pain. To carry along and get used to until it's only the past she's grieving for and not any possible present.

HER CHILDREN HAVE GROWN UP. They don't hate her. For going away or staying away. They don't forgive her, either. Perhaps they wouldn't have forgiven her anyway, but it would have been for something different.

Caitlin remembers a little about the summer at the lodge, Mara nothing. One day Caitlin mentions it to Pauline, calling it "that place Grandma and Grandpa stayed at."

"The place we were at when you went away," she says. "Only we didn't know till later you went away with Orphée."

Pauline says, "It wasn't Orphée."

"It wasn't Orphée? Dad used to say it was. He'd say, 'And then your mother ran away with Orphée.'"

"Then he was joking," says Pauline.

"I always thought it was Orphée. It was somebody else then."

"It was somebody else connected with the play. That I lived with for a while."

"Not Orphée."

"No. Never him."

Bonnie Burnard

Bonnie Burnard's *Casino & Other Stories* was shortlisted for the inaugural Giller Prize and won the Saskatchewan Book of the Year Award. Her earlier story collection, *Women of Influence,* won the Commonwealth Writers' Prize Best First Book Award. Her first novel, *A Good House,* won The Giller Prize in 1999. She is the recipient of The Marian Engel Award, sponsored by The Writers' Trust of Canada. She lives in London, Ontario.

A Good House

BY BONNIE BURNARD

Winner 1999

∼

1955

Sylvia Chambers got sick the year her kids were all in high school. She was forty. Miracle drugs, said to be on the horizon, were not readily available and, although she spent several weeks in hospital, surgery was thought to lack promise in her particular case, was thought finally to be too high a price for her to pay. Rescue was not anticipated. She just began to feel a little strange in January, got quickly worse through the spring, and died in late July.

Bill didn't put a name to his wife's illness. He sat Patrick and Daphne and Paul down at the kitchen table and told them only that it was very serious. They heard their father's word, *serious,* and they knew the word was meant to warn them, but they didn't want warning. In these earliest months they put their faith in Doctor Cooper, who was old and lame and sure of himself, and in the strength of the prescriptions they picked up at the drugstore, and most of all in their mother's resolute nature. They expected her to get better.

At the end of February they took their parents' cherry bed apart as they were asked and brought it downstairs piece by piece and they helped their father move some of the living-room furniture into the front hall so the bed could be set up facing the picture window. Bill had told Sylvia that he was moving down with her. He could have borrowed a bed for the living room, could have kept the cherry bed upstairs for himself, but he'd decided he would not turn away from her at night, he would not leave her to go up the stairs alone. Barbaric, he thought, imagining himself on those stairs.

He knew what people around town believed, that Sylvia had married him because he was so obviously a reliable man, that she had simply made a sensible, level-headed choice. What people couldn't know was how good they had it here. How calm she could be, how capable, in spite of the fact that she was always open to nonsense. How with her sweat still sharp in his nostrils she could come down to breakfast looking so serene, so unaffected, right away able to become whatever the kids or the rest of the world required her to be. She moved so fast from the one kind of woman to the other. She'd told him once that it was kind of fun and, besides, didn't he realize, it was what a woman had to do. How else? she'd asked him. Against the odds, expecting almost nothing, he'd got it all. And now was going to lose it, was going to have to sit still and watch the step-by-step approach of his own loss.

The kids soon got used to having their mother in the living room and they got used to manoeuvring through the crowded hall to get up the stairs but each time they squeezed past the sofa or banged a shin on the sharp corner of the coffee table they were thinking, This won't last. This is just for now.

Patrick Chambers was older than Paul by four years and, finished with his growth spurts, had settled in at Bill's slightly less-than-average height. He would never reach his brother. He shared most of Daphne's facial features, although where her mouth was pretty his was simply firm and sharply defined. His eyes too were that bright, beautiful, Wedgwood blue, like Sylvia's, like Sylvia's father's. In addition to his size, he'd got broad, heavily muscled shoulders from Bill and dark, thick hair that he wore slicked back in a carefully groomed duck's ass, a D.A. When he compared himself to the other guys he decided it was safe enough to believe he was good-looking, the evidence seemed to be there in his school pictures, in the way some girls tensed up when he looked at them.

Daphne was Sylvia's height exactly and it was obvious that if her jaw had not been broken in such a peculiar way in that childhood fall, if the malformation of the healed jaw had not caused the alignment of her face to be noticeably and permanently askew, she would have been a ringer for her mother. She had the blue eyes and Sylvia's sturdy smile, the extremely pretty lips, the widow's peak under her bangs, the healthy swing to her long hair, the sophisticated, arched eyebrows that already required attention from Sylvia's tweezers.

Only Paul would not have been placed with the rest of the family in a crowd, his difference so obvious it was an occasional suppertime joke. Although the youngest, he had just recently and finally become taller than any of them and much taller than everyone else in grade nine, with most of his length in his hockey-strengthened legs. He wore his regularly clipped sandy-coloured hair in a no-nonsense brush cut, and down the sides of his nose and across his chin there was a ridge of acne which he did his best to ignore. He had just started to take Bill's straight razor down from the medicine cabinet and he would often come to the breakfast table temporarily patched with ripped-off bits of toilet paper, his blood seeping through and then quickly crusting up as he ate his cornflakes. His large eyes were an unusual grey-green, a colour previously unseen in any generation on either side, and the lashes that protected his large eyes were as long and thick and dark as a movie star's. Two of the girls in his grade-nine homeroom had already told him they would kill for those lashes.

If there was one trait the family shared, one thing that might have been locked in their genes and thus anticipated down the line, it was their extraordinarily beautiful, fine-boned hands. Bill's hands too, or maybe especially, even taking into account the fingers that had been blasted off in the North Atlantic.

Murray McFarlane, who was only an inch shorter than Paul but lanky and not so sure, not so deliberately physical in his movements, was in grade thirteen with Patrick and over the years since the summer of the circus he had gradually worked himself into the Chambers family. He had not disappeared after Daphne's fall, as another boy might have. He ate with them if he was around when a meal was put on the table, volunteered to help Patrick and Paul with seasonal chores like digging out after a big snowfall, taking the storms down, raking and burning the leaves at the edge of the creek in the fall. He exchanged with all of them modest and unusual Christmas presents: an abacus, a bubble-gum dispenser, a brass nameplate for the unused front door, which Bill promptly nailed to the back door.

In a nod to social convention, Patrick was sometimes invited to have dinner with Murray's family but these invitations were always date-specific and issued well in advance. Murray's parents were extremely devout Anglicans and quite a bit older, in their early sixties. Murray had been a last-chance baby. Both of his parents had been the only surviving offspring of very prosperous families and this misfortune allowed them many of the formalities and much of the ease of wealth. Mr. McFarlane's younger, bachelor brother Brady, whose boisterous good nature had been admired by some, had lived a short life ruled and eventually ended by the bottle and Mrs. McFarlane had lost a very young brother before the first war, to meningitis, and after the war a sister, her twin, to what the doctors thought must have been a cancer of the breast. Along with a double portion of prime, leased-out farmland, the McFarlanes owned a good third of the buildings on Front Street and the biggest feed mill in the county, which Murray's father continued to run, to keep himself occupied. They lived in Mrs. McFarlane's family home. It was one of the houses with a modest turret and a wide wraparound porch and Mrs. McFarlane sometimes entertained a few friends on her porch, with card tables set up for an afternoon of bridge or a summer luncheon.

Murray carried the loneliness common to his circumstances with no complaint. On a summer night he might take Daphne and maybe a couple of her girlfriends out to the lake to drive up and down the wide beach road in his father's dark blue hardtop Buick, cranking all the windows down to make the car feel like the convertible his father wouldn't buy. With no gears to shift and one hand light on the steering wheel, he would run his fingers back through his own severely trained D.A. and undo his shirt to his belt, exposing a narrow but nicely shaped chest. He always gave Daphne the front seat so she could control the radio and she'd find Bill Haley or Brenda Lee or Buddy Holly, turn them up full blast and sing her lungs out, sometimes hang out the window to sing her lungs out.

Tired of cruising, he'd stop the car on the beach to talk driver to driver to some other guy from school, the girls quiet when this happened, watching, listening, and then he'd pull away and swerve into the shallow waves, leaving long brief arcs of tire tracks behind them in the wet sand.

He studied with Daphne at the dining-room table, taught her how to write a convincing essay, challenged and praised her because he could see, anyone could see, that she was way above average. And he sat tight beside her at hockey games watching either Patrick's or Paul's team take on some other town. He didn't touch her or try to, didn't watch for a chance to shove her off balance or ruffle her hair or take one of her small expressive hands into his own. He had not yet outgrown his awkwardness, but he had a kind of skinny, lanky strength. One evening in the spring after Sylvia's illness had got a hold on her, after everyone understood her need to conserve what was left of her stamina, she called to Murray to say it was likely his turn to carry her out to the kitchen for supper. At her call, he hurried into the living room and scooped her from the bed easily, taking a firm grip on her back and her thin thighs so she would feel his confidence through her housecoat. He held her tight to his chest as he turned to get her through the door.

IN THE TIME BEFORE SYLVIA DIED the family often sat around after supper talking, their empty plates pushed toward the middle of the table to make room for their elbows or their folded arms. All her life Sylvia had been a better-than-average mimic. From the time she was a very young girl she had been able to cancel her own voice and bring someone else into the room, someone with an easily recognized cadence, an easily scoffed opinion. Although her face was thin now and her Wedgwood-blue eyes unnaturally large, she could still do a few people dead on, among them Katharine Hepburn and the town's shy young mayor and, with relish, her hopelessly cheerful sister-in-law, who had firmly established herself as the kids' least favourite aunt. All of the impersonations brought applause.

If Paul's height was mentioned, and it often was mentioned as one way to lighten the talk, Sylvia would say he must have been a foundling, a switch, brought to her hospital bed by mistake. She would describe some very tall mother somewhere puzzling over her short kid. But no one believed that this had actually happened because it was Paul and Paul alone who could do his mother's trick. Like a monster from a horror movie he could claw his hands, he could bend the top knuckles of his long fingers and keep the other knuckles locked straight. Paul and Sylvia often performed their trick together, smiling across the table at each other, pleased to be giving the others the creeps.

Two or three times in these months Sylvia called up some energy and tried to say what was actually on her mind. One night, with a deliberation only partially camouflaged by her casual approach, she said she was going to describe each one of them, their skills and their particular talents. She was going to explain why they'd been put on this earth.

After she said, "Patrick is quiet but steady. He can steady other people when they most need it. This has always been true and always will be," Patrick stood up from the table and bowed.

After she said, "Daphne has a mystery about her, something to remind people if they are capable of being reminded that things are not necessarily what they seem," Daphne got out of her chair to stand in the middle of the room and curtsy in all four directions, as if an attentive crowd surrounded them.

After she said, "Paul moves fast and thinks fast. And he is funny, and that is a wonderful and useful thing, never to be underestimated," Paul assumed the exaggerated modesty of a truly humble man, lowering his head solemnly, which made them snort with laughter because what Bill sometimes called his newfound cockiness had once or twice prompted a necessary reminder to Paul that his glorified status as the centre on the Bantam hockey team didn't automatically carry over.

Not finished, because under no circumstances would she have left him out of this, Sylvia turned to Murray. "Murray," she said, "is just good. Good as in, born that way." Believing he knew the truth about himself, Murray stayed right where he was, turned his face away, and shrugged his narrow shoulders.

Bill had been nodding yes while Sylvia spoke, as if they'd talked it over and decided together what was true. The kids knew full well that this kind of testimony was rare. Other kids whose mothers had not been moved down to the living room didn't get to hear themselves described so kindly. But in spite of their clowning they soaked it up, believed what their mother told them, took the words and stacked them away for future use against other words, a few of which they'd already heard.

Sometimes when supper was finished everyone would drift into the living room to surround Sylvia on the bed and talk. They would begin with shamelessly enhanced reports of recent events: somebody's drunk, raging brother-in-law evicted from a dance at the arena, a wedding already planned for July with the bridesmaids to be decked out in dark red velveteen, the highest stained-glass library window unaccountably broken on Thursday night, likely in the middle of the night by a book-hating cult, Daphne said.

From there they would move on to casual, recreational gossip, to conjecture and guesswork. When the momentum picked up they would home in on the oddest people, the misfits, or the ones they knew the least about, or the ones they didn't like. In full swing they encouraged and contradicted and interrupted and accused one another and lied as much as they had to, to keep it going. Sylvia still knew everyone they talked about, she hadn't been in bed long enough to forget how the world worked, and she egged them on and sometimes topped them with mildly nasty but apparently precise accounts from a distant past.

When she couldn't continue she would fade back into her stack of pillows and pronounce, "We are really, really despicable, every one of us," and Bill would respond with his own line, "We're not so bad we can't get worse." If Sylvia was very tired, the kids just squeezed her feet through the blankets as they made their way out of the living room.

Bill left Sylvia's daytime care to her mother because he still had to show up for work at the hardware store. And he still sat in the front booths of the Blue Moon with the other men who worked uptown, the wits, as they were called. The wits knew the situation with Sylvia Chambers and they tried to accommodate it, tried to group their working bodies around it. Normally they passed the time talking politics, casually confusing the facts and enlarging the issues to the point of hopelessness, repeating like slogans the words damnpoliticians and highertaxes. Some days, for a change of pace, they attacked rumoured advances in science or technology, their suspicions banked up by the always reliable tag team of half-baked information and rampant skepticism. But with Bill's situation as it was, they stalled, hesitated a half beat before they spoke, tempered their jumpy, mocking, scatter-gun talk with oblique half-phrased sentiments and couched clichés carefully aimed to miss the mark. They endured the occasional silence, asked short, gentle questions, not for any answer but for the gentleness itself.

This couldn't last. Worn down and fed up with gentleness and care, they conceived a plan.

The men knew that Sylvia had been moved down to the living room and that there was only the one bathroom in that house, so they decided that a group of dilettante carpenters would build her a downstairs bathroom. Archie Stutt was signed on and both grandfathers and the Anglican minister. Trevor Hanley, who had the Chev Olds dealership, said he'd come, said he was all warmed up because he'd just put the finishing touches to a shed out at the cottage last fall. And Archie said that he'd talk to the new guy at the Esso to see if he could be had.

Bill didn't put up any resistance. Although he'd pulled the old picket fence down on his own when he got home from overseas, he couldn't help with something like this because even now, more than ten years after he'd had to start relying exclusively on his left hand, it wasn't entirely trustworthy, not with precision work, not with heavy tools. And he wasn't in any position to leave his job at the hardware.

But he used his discount to pay for most of the materials and he borrowed a thirty-cup coffeemaker from the Presbyterian church. He made new coffee every morning and put it on a makeshift table in the kitchen near the back door because it was March and the ground was hard, the work was cold.

THE CONSTRUCTION STARTED from the outside. In the beginning the neighbourhood dogs congregated to bark their interest and this caused the yard squirrels to run straight up the hickories to hide in the winter branches. The squirrels returned when they saw there was nothing much to be feared and the men gave them names, engaged them in conversation. The new guy's language was rougher than what the older men were used to but they toned him down by declining to respond in kind, by taking the trouble to choose their own words. They were in the habit of controlling talk this way and they didn't think badly of him, they just assumed he'd been raised differently. Perhaps by wolves, the minister suggested early on.

Most of the men brought their own shovels and hammers and saws, their own tape measures. They dug through the thin snow into the earth, broke through the shallow frost with the mildest profanity and a bit of extra push from their steel-toed boots on the blades of their shovels. They hauled the lumber from the snowed-on pile in the driveway, built a frame for the foundation, and mixed cement in one of Archie's wheelbarrows. After it was poured, Archie fired up a propane heater under a makeshift tent, which was only an old stained tarp thrown over the lawn chairs, to help the cement set.

They framed three walls out square on the cold ground and pounded them together and after the walls were up Trevor Hanley made a sketch of a low-pitched roof that he said they would have to build with particular attention, making sure that the join to the house proper had integrity because if there was ever going to be a leak, that was where it would want to be.

The plumber came over to install the drain. He drilled holes through the old foundation wall and soldered extensions to the existing waterlines in the basement and when he said he had all the lines he'd need they built the subfloor, leaving him only a trap door, which he said was likely good enough. They covered the wall studs with plywood and tar paper and with siding that someone would paint white in the spring to match the rest of the house. The Anglican minister threw a half-dozen bundles of shingles onto the roof and climbed up after them.

Archie and a couple of the men on the town payroll dug a long trench from the new bathroom drain to the sewer line out on the street and laid a five-inch pipe to make the connection. Soon after the pipe was buried the wide snake of mounded dirt that would settle and sink by summer was covered by the last of the drifting snow.

The men moved inside, brought their tools and their noise and their blunt male talk into the kitchen. They used mallets to gouge a door-sized hole in the kitchen wall, trimmed the opening carefully with handsaws. The kids cleaned up, shovelled sawdust and chunks of plaster into boxes to be carried out to the garage and hauled away to the dump when someone had the time. Insulation was stuffed between the studs and covered with top-grade plywood and then a cupboard arrived and a mirror and a sink and a toilet. The plumber came back, and the electrician, bringing with him a small electric space-heater. A thick grey carpet was glued to the floor so it would be warm on Sylvia's bare feet in the middle of the night.

The grandfathers took off in one of Trevor's brand new '55 Chev pick-ups, a demonstrator, he called it, which meant it was the truck Trevor wanted to drive that year, and after cruising up and down the streets dis-cussing just who might have a loose door lying around they pulled into Bert Wynne's driveway and, sure enough, Bert had an oak door that he'd saved for just such a purpose up in the rafters of his shed. They offered him twenty dollars but he settled for ten, and after the door was home and hung on its frame with new, stronger hinges, Archie patched and smoothed the ragged plaster that surrounded it.

When the work was finished a dozen men pulled chairs around the kitchen table or leaned on the counter to share a forty-ounce bottle of Canadian Club, courtesy of Archie Stutt. They drank quietly, satisfied with themselves. There were no jokes and the few starts at gossip faded off from lack of worthwhile embellishment.

Sylvia's mother stripped the old kitchen wallpaper and burned it in the barrel down by the creek. She stayed with the paper as it burned, used the crowbar to push it down and down again into the fire. Waiting for the fire to do its work, she pulled her thick old cardigan tight and turned to watch the rush of the cold April creek on its way to the lake.

She repapered both the kitchen and the bathroom with a pattern very close in colour and design to what she'd stripped. It took her three days. She was helped by Margaret Kemp, who let herself off early from the hardware store.

The bathroom fixtures were pale sandy pink. Because she asked him to, Patrick drove Daphne down to Sarnia and over the Bluewater Bridge to Port Huron to buy two expensive sets of thick pink American towels and on the way home they stopped uptown at Clarke's for pink Kleenex and toilet paper, which was new on the market and very popular.

When the bathroom was absolutely finished, the men were invited back one evening for coffee and a slice of Sylvia's mother's specialty, double dark chocolate cake. Paul was the one picked to throw open the door on their work. Sylvia sat in a kitchen chair pretending she hadn't been watching and listening all along, hadn't already begun to use the toilet. She told them they'd done a tremendous job, said it would be so convenient for her, and, "Tell me, how can I ever thank you?"

TWO MONTHS AFTER its completion Sylvia was standing in the bathroom in the middle of the night, washing her sweaty face and neck, when she fell. She watched herself go down in the mirror. In the few seconds it took their father to get to her, the kids had time to make it only as far as the stairs where they could hear her loudly going after God a dozen different ways and then after their father, telling him in a cold middle-of-the-night voice that he would be doing them both a favour if he would just give up on pretending to understand.

"Give it the hell up," she said to him. "It doesn't help me."

And then they heard him helping her up to her feet, trying to soothe her with choked words and his own disciplined sobs.

Doctor Cooper dropped in twice a day every day after the night of the fall to give Sylvia shots in her hip, telling Bill privately that he should be warned that this drug might alter her nature a bit, there was no telling really, but it was the very best available for now.

Reverend Walker from the United Church came once a week, usually in the morning. On his first visit, after he had been served his coffee and muffin, he asked Sylvia's mother if she would leave them for a time and she did so reluctantly, closing the door behind her with perhaps a bit too much force. Bill told Sylvia he'd back Walker off if that was her wish but she said no, it was all right, he was only doing his job. She told no one what they talked about those once-a-week mornings.

Margaret Kemp began to come directly from work at the hardware to cook supper. She was an exceptionally tall, plain-faced, buxom woman in last year's low-heeled shoes who took care to camouflage the fullness of her figure with a slouch and close attention to dress patterns and pretty print blouses that she did not tuck into her narrow skirts. She wore just a touch of lipstick and it had never occurred to her to pluck her eyebrows. She would sometimes lick a finger to shape her brows but she would have been surprised to hear this.

Margaret dug right in. She scoured pots, scrubbed the kitchen floor on her hands and knees, stood Paul up on a kitchen chair to unscrew the ceiling light fixture so she could rinse the long-dead flies down the drain.

She could cook all right, but with no past experience judging appetites, she had a difficult time getting the quantities right. After a week of it she decided there was no such thing as too much, that whatever might be left over could be used up some other way, in a soup or a casserole or a stew. She decided better too much than too little and often she didn't have to decide anything at all because Bill's mother had sent a pot roast or someone from down the street had dropped off another ground-beef casserole.

She didn't sit down with them at the table. While Bill and the kids ate she went into the living room and found some nice music on the radio beside Sylvia's bed and then she brought basins of hot water and a wash-cloth and the softest of the towels, closing the door to the others and pulling the paisley drapes, turning back the sheet. When the bathing was finished she returned with a fresh basin and they washed Sylvia's hair, which had been cut short for the first time in her life and was now completely without sheen. There was always a jar of Noxema on the table beside the bed and Margaret rubbed it on Sylvia's back and arms and legs and feet, vigorously working the skin to try to keep the circulation going.

After Sylvia was clean, *refreshed* was the word she used, she chose one of the dozen nighties she'd been given since she'd been known to be sick and the two of them got it on her. Margaret changed the bedding religiously and quickly, helping Sylvia up and over to a chair, stripping the bed and making it new in no more than a minute. Without asking anyone's permission, she brought out the best quilts, after she'd found them carefully wrapped in the linen cupboard on one of her few trips upstairs.

She cooked separately for Sylvia, holding back a little on the salt and spices as Cooper had advised. She made good cream soup, mushroom or chicken or potato, served it in one of Sylvia's china soup plates. Sometimes she made salmon croquettes or Waldorf salad, enough for the two of them and no one else.

Sylvia appreciated all of this, particularly the bathing. She said that was almost the worst of it, not being able to keep herself fresh, and she refused to let her mother or Bill or Daphne bathe her. One late afternoon, while Margaret held a large hand mirror so she could comb her wet hair into place, Sylvia said to her, "Isn't life strange?"

Margaret held the mirror steady, tried to keep her own face hidden behind it. She had no way to guess what Sylvia was going to say. She had heard that some people spoke honestly when they believed they were dying, and sometimes to near strangers. She attempted to prepare herself, wondering how she could possibly be of any help to Sylvia when she herself had no faith, no magic, no way to believe in anything except the life that was right there in front of her. All she believed, all she'd ever been able to tell herself, was, You can't know what is going to happen to you and there usually isn't much choice when it does. Of course she could be strict with herself about this, that there was nothing whatsoever to be gained by crying or complaining or quitting, but how could she say such things to this pale woman in this bed? If there were other things you could say, they were not presenting themselves today.

But it wasn't about that, not at all. When Sylvia continued she said only, "We have known each other all this time and never really been friends until now."

Margaret put the mirror down on her lap and bravely reached to tuck a strand of hair behind Sylvia's ear. "Oh, well," she said. "Separate lives."

"But not now," Sylvia said. "Not any more."

Margaret nodded.

"I need you to help me with something," Sylvia said. "If you could."

"Yes," Margaret said, anticipating something practical now.

"Some time soon this is all going to get quickly worse," Sylvia said. "Like everyone else, I've been thinking about the kids." She stopped for a minute to measure her words. "I'd guess Patrick will go to anger, and Paul to tears. Daphne, I just don't know. Is there any way you could ...?"

"Yes," Margaret said, not because she understood what was expected of her but only because Sylvia believed it had to be a woman, otherwise she would not have asked. And here she was, a woman. "Yes," she said. "I will."

Margaret sometimes showed up with a few groceries and one time books from the library, some light history, a couple of dog-eared mysteries, but none of the books got read. Sylvia did ask for a good atlas, which Margaret drove into London to buy, and she spent some of her hours studying the changes in the world.

After a few weeks Margaret brought Daphne into her mother's bed and gave her the tray with the china soup plate and the silver spoon. She stood at the dusty picture window until the soup was half gone, asking Daphne questions about her schoolwork and her friends. She knew who Daphne's girlfriends were because she often saw them walking on the street together uptown, nudging shoulders as they talked, still a bit playful but serious too, newly careful with Daphne and with each other. You could see it in their posture, in their stern faces, the eyes that brazenly searched another's eyes with the promise of understanding. None of the girls came inside the house now, the farthest they could be coaxed was just inside the kitchen door, but this was easily recognized as one more clumsy, misplaced, well-meant gesture of respect.

As Daphne finished spooning the soup to her mother, Margaret asked herself how the boys would feel if she sent them out to the dusty windows with some newspapers and a bucket of vinegar water and then after the dishes were cleaned up she got her Harris tweed coat and her purse, said her goodnights, and let herself out the back door.

THE GRANDPARENTS usually dropped in after supper, after Margaret had left. They were sometimes accompanied by one of Sylvia's brothers and his wife or by her sister from out of town or by Bill's brother from Windsor with his cheerful wife and their young children. Kitchen chairs were carried in and placed haphazardly around the room, facing Sylvia. The nieces and nephews were allowed to sit briefly on the bed to embrace their aunt and then they sprawled out on the carpet to play secret little whispering games or snap or jumping jacks.

The adults tried to talk about things Sylvia might find interesting, Sandy Koufax and the Brooklyn Dodgers, Lassie, James Dean being killed like that, but everyone listened too politely, too attentively to the speaker, almost all of them were too unnaturally quick to laugh or offer agreement. Sylvia heard their words not as sentences deliberately formed to tell a person something but as dull, one-at-a-time thuds against the dull silence that had begun to wall her in. She heard the words as small, well-meant blows against a concrete bunker. Although she did not ever ask, Could they please just shut up and go home.

Occasionally they would forget themselves and talk just to each other, for which she was occasionally grateful. The most astute among them watched her closely as they talked, recognized for what they were the small, jerking movements of her hands, the slight ducking of her head as if to avoid something flying too low above her.

Daphne decided it would be nice to use the silver tray from the buffet to serve the cookies or squares the women always brought, and Bill's father, a heavy, large-boned man who spoke slowly and loudly, made a huge fuss over her as she circled the room with the tray, said she was coming along so nicely. Sylvia's father, thin and wiry and wheezing with emphysema, paid no heed to the conventions expected of him. He cried openly and said awful heartfelt things like "You were always the strongest," and "Half a life," and "Why can't I be taken instead," and always when he started the others took a deep, collective breath and prepared themselves to put an end to it.

The third or fourth time this happened Paul had to turn his suddenly streaming face to the living-room wall and, recognizing himself in his grandson, Sylvia's father left his armchair to go to Paul, making it worse. Patrick, who in just these few short months had learned to carry love as an unspeakable pressure inside himself, got up from his chair so fast he knocked it over. He took the stairs in five great leaps and slammed the bedroom door and after that night he wouldn't sit with them, would not even say hello when his grandfather came in the kitchen door.

Sylvia's mother remained stoic. A born coordinator, she discussed practical matters with Margaret to reassure herself that everything was well in hand. She took the laundry home with her because she had a new clothes dryer in her basement and she wrote the letters that had to be written to tell the news that had to be told, attempted to supervise the homework at the dining-room table. And privately but firmly she scolded Paul. "I can't abide this crying, Paul," she said. "Not now. And trust me, there will be plenty of time for it after."

One evening in the middle of a week when Sylvia appeared to have a resurgence of strength, she called Daphne to come into the living room alone. When the door was shut and Daphne was comfortable on the bed, Sylvia said she wanted to tell her how much she regretted that she wouldn't be around to help later, with her marriage and her babies. She lifted her hand when Daphne tried to speak, tried to say, Don't say that, Mom. Don't say that. Sylvia wanted badly to be frank, to be truthful. She wanted to say, Take your time when you think you're ready for a husband, don't just go by looks, make him talk, find out how he thinks. Or, Don't let your heart outshout your head. Or, Whatever happens to you, don't just settle. But she said what she had rehearsed.

"It seems to me that smart women look for comfort and loyalty when they're deciding on a husband and I think men want more or less the same thing. And it never hurts to have a bit of laughter thrown in." She didn't mention the long-ago break in Daphne's jaw, or her apprehension about men whose interest might be queered by the malformed face, who might, instinctively, turn away.

"Childbirth," she said, "isn't nearly as bad as some women will happily lead you to believe. A young body can be trusted." She put her hands on her own distended stomach. "There are specialized muscles in there with a job to do and one job only." She didn't say anything specific or descriptive about sex, except that Daphne shouldn't be afraid of it. "Sex is mostly just for comfort and fun," she said. "And meant to be."

Listening now with her eyes wide open and her hands covering her mouth, Daphne nodded and tried to lift her hands away. "I want three babies," she said. "I'm going to have three."

"Three is a very good number," Sylvia said. "Tell me what you'll call them."

"Girls will be Maggie or Jill or Paula," Daphne said. "Boys will be David or Daniel or Michael."

"Those are very fine names," Sylvia said. "I like those names a lot."

The next evening she called Patrick and Paul and Murray in and sat them down to tell them that they would soon have wives and children, which made them look down through their knees at their feet and shake their heads. Thinking about this talk all afternoon, she had known she would have to thread her way carefully between one son's rage and the other's anxious tears, and looking at them now she could see her boundaries announcing themselves in Patrick's clenched fists, in Paul's wet cheeks. What she wanted to say to them was, Take it slow, as slow as you can. And, Before you decide, have a good long look at the mother because a daughter usually turns out just the same or just the opposite. She wanted to say, Loud, silly girls often grow up to be loud, silly women, and sullen girls tend to stay sullen.

Instead, she told them, "Women expect strength from men, and gentleness and absolute loyalty. And a good ear." She said, "You will have to work hard if you expect to raise a family." Looking just at Patrick and Paul, meaning it as a joke, she said, "You might even have to think about giving up hockey." Then she took the deepest breath she could take. "Of course sex is fun," she said. "Likely, you have already discovered that. But you should try to get it into your heads that with just a little extra thought, a little extra time taken, it can be something altogether different, altogether more." She didn't make them sit there wondering if they had to say anything back to her about any of this. She shooed them out of the room like small boys told to stay away from the creek in the spring, hoping only that she hadn't lied to them.

Bill had offered to set up a small bed for himself in an empty corner of the living room in case his rolling around in his sleep disturbed Sylvia or gave her discomfort. As proof of his consideration, he borrowed a foldaway cot from the McKellars down the street and wheeled it into the dining room where it stood ready, sheets and all, but Sylvia told him no, she didn't want that, not yet. All these months they had continued to do what they could, when they could. Cooper had told them early on and pointedly to go ahead and take whatever pleasure was available to them.

Cooper told Bill now that Sylvia was on a very high dosage, which he was more than ready to up if he became convinced she needed it. He said that death comes in different ways to different people, more ways than an average layman could imagine, and that an easy death was still possible. He said there was no reason to anticipate extraordinary pain, not with the dosage he had her on.

Bill never did set up the cot. In the last week of July, Sylvia didn't want to eat anything and then she began to fall into an extremely deep sleep that could last the night and through the next day and overnight and halfway through the day again. Cooper said this was the blessing of her brain's own morphine, better than man-made.

When she came out of these sleeps she could speak only a few necessary words, could hardly take a drink, could only breathe and listen and watch. Bill stayed home and the kids got some time off from their summer jobs and someone stayed with her in the living room every minute, often two at a time. On the last of these sleeping days and nights Bill was with her and, exhausted beyond discipline, beyond even his time overseas, he crawled in and slept beside her. He woke from a dream of rolling fingers and knew without looking.

He took a few minutes for himself, stayed mute on his side of the bed, resisting full consciousness, making it wait. As was his sleepy habit, he reached to smooth her eyebrows, to try to smooth the lines from her forehead. Then he sat up, stood up in his pyjamas. He tidied her hair the best he could and straightened the pillow and then he made himself search beneath the quilts to find her hands, to bring them out over the quilts because she looked so strange lying there without her hands.

He manoeuvred through the hall and up the stairs to wake the kids, sitting for a few minutes on the top step to listen to the memory of Sylvia's voice telling him what to say to them when this day came, but by the time he reached the first warm bed he had nothing in him but silence. He couldn't help them when they opened their eyes.

When their first wretched grief, loud and clumsy beyond remembering, was almost spent, when the July sun, which was nothing more to him now than the blunt instrument, the mindless impulse of an emptied day, was fully risen, Bill went into the kitchen to phone Cooper and they all stayed in the living room until they heard the Cadillac pull into the driveway. Cooper brought fresh morning air in with him and turn by turn he put one warm arm around their shoulders, which quieted them and brought them back to their separate, independent selves, to the floating, airless absence that each of them had already begun to define as differently as they might have defined Sylvia's full life, given the chance. Then he asked that they go out to the kitchen.

Bill poured himself a glass of orange juice and sat down at the table, and because he couldn't bear the quiet now, because it was making him sick to his stomach and dizzy, he began to walk his kids step by step through their mother's funeral. He'd done nothing about it before, had been repulsed by the thought of anticipating it.

Paul and Daphne sat down with their father but Patrick opened the fridge door wide and slammed it shut, twice and hard. When he asked, "What the hell difference does it make what happens now?" Bill nodded yes and yes again, told him, "This is what we do."

After Bill finished outlining his plans for the funeral, Paul went outside to stand in the gravel driveway and Daphne went after him. The sun was over the garage now. It was promising to be a very hot day. They stood together for a few minutes and then she pulled on his arm to bring him back to the cool of the kitchen.

Cooper had called the undertaker and he must have called Margaret too because she was soon there, standing at the counter with her long back to them, opening a can of salmon, buttering a double row of bread. Bill went upstairs to get dressed and when he came back down he made the call to the grandparents.

Murray came in the kitchen door just after the undertaker. He sat down at the table and cried on his arms like a child, which caused Daphne to move across the room to stand close behind him.

Then Bill told the kids they might as well go and get dressed, so they went upstairs. After they had their clothes on, Daphne sat with Paul on his bed, her own tears mysteriously stopped by the racked renewal of his tears. Murray was slumped on the floor, leaning against the other bed with his back to Patrick, who was silent. They stayed that way until they heard Margaret come up the stairs to look through Sylvia's closet. Soon after she went back down they heard the unmistakable sound of the hearse on the gravel, backing carefully out of the driveway.

A WEEK AFTER Sylvia's funeral Margaret came through the kitchen door on a Sunday afternoon with a mostly roasted chicken. They had been given so many meals that week, scalloped potatoes and baked ham, meat loaves, baked beans, angel food cakes and butter tarts and fruit pies. A dozen empty casserole dishes, good sturdy ovenproof bowls taped with names to identify the owners, sat piled biggest to smallest on the counter. These were the dishes that moved around from one house to the next, following the need.

Margaret told Daphne as she opened the oven door that the chicken wanted only another quick half hour at three-fifty. She said she'd do up a few potatoes to go along with it and did Daphne think peas or corn or what? As they moved around the kitchen together, Margaret was careful to keep a respectful distance between them, careful not to touch Daphne even by accident. At the funeral and at the lunch in the church basement after the funeral she had noticed that Daphne pulled back slightly when anyone threatened to lay a hand on her. And people did try. People did assume you wanted it. She could sympathize with that, she knew what that felt like.

After they'd peeled the potatoes and got them started, she took off her apron, mixed a rye and water for herself and a rye and coke for Bill, and went into the living room to sit with him. They talked about nothing in particular for a few minutes and then she asked if maybe Patrick and Paul and Murray should take the bed back upstairs. Bill called the boys into the living room and asked them to do it, please, and he and Margaret watched them take the bed apart and carry it back up to their parents' bedroom, where they would reassemble it.

Margaret didn't mention Sylvia's side of the closet because Bill's mother had said that she and her friend Phyllis would attend to that. She'd said Phyllis had a sister in Toronto who was close to Sylvia's size.

Margaret had intended to stay just long enough to clean every inch of the emptied living room but when she was half finished Daphne led her to the table where a place had been set for her. After supper the boys returned the foldaway cot to the McKellars, and when Margaret was finished in the living room, they emptied the hall and put the furniture back where they thought it had always been.

IN SEPTEMBER, Patrick and Murray left for university. The previous spring, just before Patrick truly believed that his mother was going to die, when Murray and everyone else were sending in their applications, he had sent in his own, on the sly, consulting no one. His grade-thirteen year hadn't been his best, he knew that, but he didn't expect to fail anything either. They had written their exams, nine subjects for everyone, in the sweating heat of the June gym, and then they'd had to wait out the summer because the marking was not done by their own teachers but by anonymous markers in Toronto. In August when he got his results, and they were just high enough, he told Murray what he'd done. They had driven out to the lake. They were sitting in Murray's new hardtop Chev on the Casino hill with their transcripts open in their laps. Patrick said he must have been something less than human to be making plans for his future when his mother was dying.

Murray had got straight A's and this meant a substantial government scholarship to start him off. The next evening at his parents' dining-room table he directed the conversation in such a way that his mother was prompted to ask how Patrick Chambers had done and where was he planning to go?

A few days later Alex McFarlane came to Bill at the hardware store to say that he and Mrs. McFarlane would like to help Patrick out with some of the money they had put aside years ago for Murray. His little remaining hair was snow white and he had put on a suit to make his proposal. He said they had always regarded their university fund as money to be invested in the next generation, and now that Murray would be needing less of it, they didn't really want to waste it on anything else. He said they'd been south once for a winter holiday and hadn't found it all that appealing, the traffic, the humidity, the exorbitant cost of a hotel room. He said, "You've had a hard time here and I wish you would accept this as a gesture of our respect for Patrick and for you, and particularly, of course, for Sylvia."

Bill accepted the money on Patrick's behalf. Since Sylvia's death, one of the hardest questions he had been asking himself was how could he make sure the kids established themselves the way she would have wanted. That night when he sat Patrick down to tell him about Alex McFarlane's visit, he explained to him that such money didn't come freely. He said the onus would be on him some time later in his life to give over an equivalent amount to some other young person, someone whose potential was not matched by his circumstances. He said that was the way these things worked and that it was a private matter, not to be bandied about. He said Patrick might want to think about a small gift, a token of appreciation, likely something for Mrs. McFarlane. He said maybe Margaret could help with that.

After Patrick got his next paycheque from the feed mill, he went up to Margaret's apartment to tell her what his father had advised him to do and to hand her a twenty-dollar bill. The next day on her lunch hour she went over to Taylor's Fine China and found a lovely crystal rose bowl. She told Patrick she thought it would be appropriate because Mrs. McFarlane had a large garden and people said she was especially proud of her roses. She wrapped the bowl for him at the kitchen table in muted, all-occasion paper and when he asked her if he should get dressed up to take it over she told him, "No, you're fine as you are."

Even after getting the answer he wanted and borrowing Margaret's Pontiac to drive over to McFarlane's, Patrick wished he hadn't asked her for help. He had no idea how this consulting Margaret business had got started. Before their mother died they hardly even knew her and now she was supposed to be the one to ask. It wasn't that she was around too much, she only did what they wanted her to do and they appreciated it, it was that she was always ready to be around. Just sitting somewhere, ready.

Mrs. McFarlane came to the front door. She told Patrick that Mr. McFarlane had decided that morning to make a trip into Toronto, so he wasn't home. But because she knew what this was about, she invited him in and sat him down on the brocade sofa in her living room and brought him a bottle of Coke. She asked if maybe she should unwrap the present on her own. Patrick told her sure, why not.

She was very careful with the paper and the ribbon, and when she had the bowl unwrapped she held it in both hands up to the light coming in from the wide hall. She was very pleased. He had never seen a woman so pleased. "I saw this up there," she said, "and you know I almost bought it. Imagine." She set it carefully on the table in front of her. "I bet this is Margaret's doing," she said. "Your father has such a friend in Margaret."

The first week of September Patrick and Murray loaded up the hardtop Chev to make the move into London. Bill and Daphne and Paul followed in Bill's car, which was equally loaded. The university campus, thought to be one of the country's most beautiful, was spread with casual grace across fifty rolling acres at the edge of the city and set off from the city by high stone gates. The large sandstone college buildings with their bell towers, costly replications of British institutional architecture, had been distributed with precision, set carefully on the green hills like medieval jewels.

The boys soon found their separate residences and Bill and Daphne and Paul helped them carry their belongings up the stairs to their rooms. Both buildings were crawling with parents and boys hauling suitcases and boxes, the boys eager to be left on their own, the parents not very anxious to go. Some of the most reluctant parents had to be patiently shoved out of rooms and guided down the stairs to their cars.

Just before he started down, Bill turned to face Patrick. "This is an opportunity I myself didn't have," he said. "You be sure to make the best of it."

AT HOME, Daphne and Paul learned to cook. They could each do a good omelette and sausages and chops, although they never risked a roast and there were always potatoes, mashed or warmed-up mashed or fried, and pale green peas from a can or string beans or creamed corn. Paul, unaccountably, taught himself how to make pastry, went up to Clarke's for cans of cherry pie filling. They discovered him more than once rolling out pastry on Sylvia's marble board, his damp face smeared with flour.

The pages of Sylvia's cookbook, a large standard volume stuffed with all kinds of loose recipes in all manner of strange handwriting, were interspersed with a dozen black-and-white pictures of trim, energetic housewives. All of the housewives smiled big smiles and had short, tidy hair with crisp, crimped waves and narrow, belted waists and open-toed shoes and, flowing from their mouths, dialogue bubbles filled with handy household tips, their tried-and-true solutions for the persistent problem of small, unwanted visitors in the flour and the oatmeal, for mildew in basements, and for those noisy cupboard doors that can disturb a peaceful household.

Some of the book's pages were stained and many of the margins were filled with Sylvia's own handwriting, cryptic notes she'd made to herself. Often she had devised variations or substitutions. On some pages there was a check mark or a question mark, sometimes a warning to herself: Careful when doubling, or, Sounds better than it is, or, Everyone hated this, except Bill, who maybe just didn't want to say. On some pages a name had been written in the margin and firmly underlined.

Standing over the stove after school started that September, absent-mindedly stirring a soup that had been dropped off by her grandmother, Daphne leafed through the pages, looking for her own name. She eventually found it beside the recipe for Sea Foam Icing: Daphne, it said. Birthdays and other.

Margaret did not impose herself. She left them more or less alone to sort things out, calling only occasionally to ask if there was anything extra that needed to be done or to say that she was going over the border and did anyone need socks, underwear, khakis? The first time she was invited for a meal she hadn't prepared, she restrained herself, behaved as a guest would, graciously accepting Daphne's no when she asked if she could help with the dishes.

She didn't work with Bill at the hardware now. She had accepted an offer to cross the street to the pharmacy, where she was paid a substantially higher wage to keep a set of books that were not much more complicated than the hardware books. Bill told her he hated to see her go but he wasn't the guy in charge so he couldn't do anything about raising her pay.

As a going-away gift he gave her a pearl cluster brooch that he'd found nestled in cotton batting in a small blue box in Sylvia's dresser. When Margaret asked, he had to say he had no idea how Sylvia had come to have it.

Six weeks after the supper when she didn't wash the dishes, Bill and Margaret began to meet at the Blue Moon for their coffee breaks, sitting always in one of the smaller booths at the back. Sometimes they met for lunch, BLTs or soup of the day.

When it became clear to the wits that Bill had abandoned them, one of them told him in what passes in men for a whisper, "Just don't be too long about it. We can't guarantee your spot forever." It was the first joke anyone had directed at Bill in a long time. They all recognized a possibility when they saw one and they could see no purpose in his trying to continue on alone with those kids. None of them could have done it.

IN JANUARY, after one of Margaret's roast beef dinners, Bill asked everyone to stay around because he wanted to talk to them. Patrick and Murray were home for the weekend. Patrick had been coming home regularly, picking up every hour he could get at the feed mill. Supper had been conversational, lively. The boys were full of talk. Classes were indeed huge, professors were indeed weird, jocks thought they ruled the campus and were pretty much correct. No one bothered much with small-town boys.

Bill had not bought Margaret a diamond because she told him she would be happier with just the one ring, but the kids all knew what was coming and Bill knew they knew. He said the words he had decided to say, careful not to show any undue affection to Margaret, who sat across from him. He mentioned the word "mother" several times and, near the end of his very short speech, the words "make a life."

He understood that what he was about to do would be seen by some as too big a change too soon, or worse, just plain selfish, as if he was thinking mainly about himself. He had tried to prepare Margaret for a bit of resistance because he believed the kids were entitled to it, although he couldn't guess how their resistance might show itself. When they only nodded and tried to smile, each nod around the table an indication to him that they were ready to offer up the hardest gift they had ever been asked to give, before he'd even felt it coming he had made a private, lifelong promise to each of them, separately.

He had made his decision about Margaret in the late fall, the night he took her to the horse races in London, to thank her for all her time and trouble. It was the first time in twelve years that they had been absolutely alone together, with no expectation of interruption. On the way home, after she told him he was more than welcome, he reminded her of all the years they had worked side by side and then without flinching he asked what she would think about getting married.

Margaret smoothed her silky skirt over her long legs and then reached to touch his arm. She told him yes, she thought that would be the best idea.

If anyone had wanted to know, Margaret would have said that she felt honoured to be asked into Bill's life. There was that kind of formality around him now, maybe around any man in his position. But she would have said too that a man's love for a woman should get its start when the woman is young. She would have said that a man's love for a woman past thirty, say, was in fact love for the younger, remembered woman, the feeling strengthened maybe with time and familiarity, but really and always, if you could strip away the time and familiarity, you would see it was the younger, remembered woman who was loved, the basic woman. She would have said that she believed this was one of the main differences between men and women, because you could begin to love a man any time.

After they'd got back to town, Bill had parked his car on the street and gone up the stairs with Margaret to her apartment above the Hydro office. She stood very still while he lifted her sweater over her head and unzipped the long silky skirt. She was wondering as she stood very still how she could possibly begin all this with him, the actual touching, the actual movements of intimacy. She was forty-one years old. A good part of her experience with men had been gained when she was quite young and, more recently, before the possibility of Bill Chambers, while the lovemaking in her narrow bed had been by necessity discreet, perhaps because it had been discreet and limited in possibility and self-contained in its secrecy, it had been, compared to this, now, dreamlike. *Like a dream.* This *now* was meant to be the pleasurable evidence not of a true, prohibited, longed-for love but of Bill's plain desire that she should be with him in his life, through his life. She waited for her body to accept this difference. She relied on her instinct. Bill moved slowly, took them through it slowly. Her instinct told her to let him do this.

Once begun, it was not so difficult. The missing fingers were not missed and his skin under her tentative hands, under the surprisingly symmetrical islands of his dark body hair, was like warm crushed velvet, like something you might touch in the real, daylight world, a very fine, once-in-a-lifetime gift.

When their first moving together was done, curled into herself, holding herself, she told him that she could feel it in her fingertips. It had travelled like an undertow all the way through her. Gone everywhere.

Bill stretched out beside her in her narrow bed, sated and confused and quiet. He could not tell her, he would never be able to tell her how strange it was, the way Sylvia, a smaller woman, had seemed to fly apart when it happened for her, how he sometimes had to hold her tight to keep her in one piece and how other times he just pulled away to laugh and watch her fill the bed, watch her fly, and here she was, Margaret, a much larger, beautifully long-boned woman, making herself so small in his arms and in her own.

He had not tried to convince himself that he loved Margaret, not yet, but he did believe that a certain kind of marriage could be made from need and gratitude and amazement. He believed that Margaret's long-boned presence among them would keep the house safe, and familiar, and that in time, after some months or years, he would discover that he did love her. You could find love waiting for you. He believed that. And besides, he was not young. He did not wish to be young again.

Comforting her, stroking her arching neck and resting the back of his hand against the vein pulsing there, he began to construct a small sealed room to preserve and protect his life with Sylvia, to hold and protect all the past. There would be no end to what the room could contain and he would step inside at will, he would for the rest of his life remember everything, anything, any time he pleased. But he would never allow himself to speak to the things housed in that room because there could be no answer and he believed that such a silence would be the hardest thing his life could ever give him.

Michael Ondaatje

Michael Ondaatje is the author of five novels, a memoir, a non-fiction book on film, and eleven books of poetry. *The English Patient* received The Booker Prize; *Anil's Ghost* won the Irish Times International Fiction Prize, The Giller Prize, and the Prix Médicis. His latest novel, *Divisadero,* won the Governor General's Literary Awards. Born in Sri Lanka, Ondaatje came to Canada in 1962. He lives in Toronto.

Anil's Ghost

BY MICHAEL ONDAATJE

Winner 2000

❦

A nil had come out of her first class at Guy's Hospital in London with just one sentence in her exercise book: *The bone of choice would be the femur.*

She loved the way the lecturer had stated it, offhand, but with the air of a pompatus. As if this piece of information were the first rule needed before they could progress to greater principles. Forensic studies began with that one thighbone.

What surprised Anil as the teacher delineated the curriculum and the field of study was the quietness of the English classroom. In Colombo there was always a racket. Birds, lorries, fighting dogs, a kindergarten's lessons of rote, street salesmen—all their sounds entered through open windows. There was no chance of an ivory tower existing in the tropics. Anil wrote Dr. Endicott's sentence down and a few minutes later underlined it with her ballpoint in the hushed quiet. For the rest of the hour she just listened and watched the lecturer's mannerisms.

It was while studying at Guy's that Anil found herself in the smoke of one bad marriage. She was in her early twenties and was to hide this episode from everyone she met later in life. Even now she wouldn't replay it and consider the level of damage. She saw it more as some contemporary fable of warning.

He too was from Sri Lanka, and in retrospect she could see that she had begun loving him because of her loneliness. She could cook a curry with him. She could refer to a specific barber in Bambalapitiya, could whisper her desire for jaggery or jakfruit and be understood. That made a difference in the new, too brittle country. Perhaps she herself was too tense with uncertainty and shyness. She had expected to feel alien in England only for a few weeks. Uncles who had made the same journey a generation earlier had spoken romantically of their time abroad. They suggested that the right remark or gesture would open all doors. Her father's friend Dr. P. R. C. Peterson had told the story of being sent to school in England as an eleven-year-old. On the first day he was called a 'native' by a classmate. He stood up at once and announced to the teacher, 'I'm sorry to say this, sir, but Roxborough doesn't know who I am. He called me a "native." That's the wrong thing to do. *He* is the native and I'm the visitor to the country.'

But acceptance was harder than that. Having been a mild celebrity in Colombo because of her swimming, Anil was shy without the presence of her talent, and found it difficult to enter conversations. Later, when she developed her gift for forensic work, she knew one of the advantages was that her skill signalled her existence—like a neutral herald.

In her first month in London she'd been constantly confused by the geography around her. (What she kept noticing about Guy's Hospital was the number of doors!) She missed two classes in her first week, unable to find the lecture room. So for a while she began arriving early each morning and waited on the front steps for Dr. Endicott, following him through the swing doors, stairways, grey-and-pink corridors, to the unmarked classroom. (She once followed him and startled him and others in the men's bathroom.)

She seemed timid even to herself. She felt lost and emotional. She murmured to herself the way one of her spinster aunts did. She didn't eat much for a week and saved enough money to phone Colombo. Her father was out and her mother was unable to come to the phone. It was about one in the morning and she had woken her *ayah*, Lalitha. They talked for a few minutes, until they were both weeping, it felt, at the far ends of the world. A month later she fell within the spell of her future, and soon-to-be, and eventually ex-, husband.

It seemed to her he had turned up from Sri Lanka in bangles and on stilts. He too was a medical student. He was not shy. Within days of their meeting he focussed his wits entirely on Anil—a many-armed seducer and note writer and flower bringer and telephone-message leaver (he had quickly charmed her landlady). His organized passion surrounded her. She had the sense that he had never been lonely or alone before meeting her. He had panache in the way he could entice and choreograph the other medical students. He was funny. He had cigarettes. She saw how he mythologized their rugby positions and included such things in the fabric of their conversations until they were familiar touchstones—a trick that never left any of them at a loss for words. A team, a gang, that was in fact only two weeks deep. They each had an epithet. Lawrence who had thrown up once on the Underground, the siblings Sandra and Percy Lewis whose family scandals were acknowledged and forgiven, Jackman of the wide brows.

He and Anil were married quickly. She briefly suspected that for him it was another excuse for a party that would bond them all. He was a fervent lover, even with his public life to choreograph. He certainly opened up the geography of the bedroom, insisting on lovemaking in their nonsoundproof living room, on the wobbly sink in the shared bathroom down the hall, on the boundary line quite near the long-stop during a county cricket match. These private acts in an almost public sphere echoed his social nature. There seemed to be no difference for him between privacy and friendship with acquaintances. Later she would read that this was the central quality of a monster. Still, there was considerable pleasure on both their parts during this early period. Though she realized it was going to be crucial for her to come back to earth, to continue her academic studies.

When her father-in-law visited England he swept them up and took them out to dinner. The son was for once quiet, and the father attempted to persuade them to return to Colombo and have his grandchildren. He kept referring to himself as a philanthropist, which appeared to give him a belief that he was always on higher moral ground. As the dinner progressed she felt that every trick in the Colombo Seven social book was being used against her. He objected to her having a full-time career, keeping her own name, was annoyed at her talking back. When she described classroom autopsies during the trifle, the father had been outraged. 'Is there nothing you won't do?' And she had replied, 'I won't go to crap games with barons and earls.'

The next day the father lunched alone with his son, then flew back to Colombo.

At home the two of them fought now over everything. She was suspicious of his insights and understanding. He appeared to spend all his spare energy on empathy. When she wept, he would weep. She never trusted weepers after that. (Later, in the American Southwest, she would avoid those television shows with weeping cowboys and weeping priests.) During this time of claustrophobia and marital warfare, sex was the only mutual constant. She insisted on it as much as he. She assumed it gave the relationship some normality. Days of battle and fuck.

The disintegration of the relationship was so certain on her part that she would never replay any of their days together. She had been fooled by energy and charm; he had wept and burrowed under her intelligence until she felt she had none left. Venus, as Sarath would say, had been in her head, when it should have been the time of Jupiter.

She would return from the lab in the evenings and be met by his jealousy. At first this presented itself as sexual jealousy, then she saw it was an attempt to limit her research and studies. It was the first handcuff of marriage, and it almost buried her in their small flat in Ladbroke Grove. After she escaped him she would never say his name out loud. If she saw his handwriting on a letter she never opened it, fear and claustrophobia rising within her. In fact, the only reference to the era of her marriage she allowed into her life was Van Morrison's 'Slim Slow Slider' with its mention of Ladbroke Grove. Only the song survived. And only because it referred to separation.

> *Saw you early this morning*
> *With your brand-new boy and your Cadillac ...*

She would sing along hoping that he did not also join in with his sentimental heart, wherever he was.

> *You've gone for something,*
> *And I know you won't be back.*

Otherwise the whole marriage and divorce, the hello and good-bye, she treated as something illicit that deeply embarrassed her. She left him as soon as their term at Guy's Hospital was over, so he could not locate her. She had plotted her departure for the end of term to avoid the harassment he was fully capable of; he was one of those men with time on his hands. *Cease and desist!* she had scrawled formally on his last little whining billet-doux before mailing it back to him.

She emerged with no partner. Cloudless at last. She was unable to bear the free months before she could begin classes again, before she could draw her studies close to her, more intimately and seriously than she had imagined possible. When she did return she fell in love with working at night, and sometimes she couldn't bear to leave the lab, just rested her happily tired dark head on the table. There was no curfew or compromise with a lover anymore. She got home at midnight, was up at eight, every casebook and experiment and investigation alive in her head and reachable.

Eventually she heard he'd returned to Colombo. And with his departure there was no longer any need to remember favourite barbers and restaurants along the Galle Road. Her last conversation in Sinhala was the distressed chat she'd had with Lalitha that ended with her crying about missing egg *rulang* and curd with jaggery. She no longer spoke Sinhala to anyone. She turned fully to the place she found herself in, focussing on anatomical pathology and other branches of forensics, practically memorizing Spitz and Fisher. Later she won a scholarship to study in the United States, and in Oklahoma became caught up in the application of the forensic sciences to human rights. Two years later, in Arizona, she was studying the physical and chemical changes that occurred in bones not only during life but also after death and burial.

She was now alongside the language of science. The femur was the bone of choice.

David Adams Richards

Born in New Brunswick, David Adams Richards found his calling at the age of fourteen, after reading *Oliver Twist,* and embarked on a life of extraordinary purpose. He is the author of fourteen published novels and has received numerous awards and prizes throughout his career. Most notably, he is one of few writers in the history of the Governor General's Literary Awards to win in both the fiction (*Nights Below Station Street*) and non-fiction (*Lines on the Water*) categories. In addition to these two wins, he was nominated for *Road to the Stilt House* (in 1985), *For Those Who Hunt the Wounded Down* (in 1993), and *Mercy Among the Children* (in 2000). *Mercy Among the Children* was co-winner of The Giller Prize in 2000 and was shortlisted for the Trillium Book Award and the Thomas Head Raddall Atlantic Fiction Award. More recently, his novel *The Friends of Meager Fortune* won the Commonwealth Writers' Prize in 2007 and his novel *The Lost Highway* was nominated for the 2008 Scotiabank Giller Prize. Over the years, Richards has also won countless regional awards for his novels and was awarded the prestigious Canada–Australia Prize in 1992.

The New Brunswick region of the Miramichi has been at the heart of Richards's fiction throughout his career, although the characters and themes that populate his novels are universal. He has been compared to John Steinbeck, Thomas Hardy, and Dostoevsky for the way in which he is able to deal with eternal questions of ambition, love, honour, and betrayal. Many consider Richards to be one of Canada's greatest and most original living writers.

Mercy Among the Children

BY DAVID ADAMS RICHARDS

Winner 2000

❧

ONE

The small Catholic churches here are all the same, white clapboard drenched with snow or blistering under a northern sun, their interiors smelling of confessionals and pale statues of the Madonna. Our mother, Elly Henderson, took us to them all along our tract of road—thinking that solace would come.

In November the lights shone after seven o'clock on the stained-glass windows. The windows show the crucifixion or one of the saints praying. The hills where those saints lived and dropped their blood look soft, distant and blue; the roads wind like purple ribbons toward the Mount of Olives. It is all so different from *real* nature with its roaring waters over valleys of harsh timber where I tore an inch and a half of skin from my calves. Or Miramichi bogs of cedar and tamarack and the pungent smell of wet moosehide as the wounded moose still bellows in dark wood. I often wanted to enter the world of the stained glass—to find myself walking along the purple road, with the Mount of Olives behind me. I suppose because I wanted to be good, and my mother wanted goodness for me. I wanted too to escape the obligation I had toward my own destiny, my family, my sister and brother who were more real to me than a herd of saints.

My father's name was Sydney Henderson. He was born in a shack off Highway 11, a highway only Maritimers could know—a strip of asphalt through stunted trees and wild dead fields against the edge of a cold sky.

He did poorly in school but at church became the ward of Father Porier. He was given the job of washing Porier's car and cleaning his house. He was an altar boy who served mass every winter morning at seven. He did this for three years, from the age of eight to eleven.

Then one day there was a falling-out, an "incident," and Father Porier's Pontiac never again came down the lane to deliver him home, nor did Father ever again trudge off to the rectory to clean the priest's boots. Nor did he know that his own father would take the priest's side and beat him one Sunday in front of most of the parishioners on the church steps. This became Father's first disobedience, not against anything but the structure of things. I have come to learn, however, that this is not at all a common disobedience.

Back then, harsh physical labour seemed the only thing generations of Canadians like my grandfather considered work. So by thirteen my father wore boots and checked jackets, and quit school to work in the woods, in obligation to his father. He would spend days with little to comfort him. He was to need this strength, a strength of character, later on. He had big hands like a pulpcutter, wore thick glasses, and his hair was short, shaved up the side of his head like a zek in some Russian prison camp.

He worked crossing back and forth over that bleak highway every day; when the June sky was black with no-see-ums, or all winter when the horse dung froze as it hit the ground. He was allergic to horses, yet at five in the morning had to bring the old yellow mare to the front of the barn—a mare denied oats and better off dead.

My grandfather bought a television in 1962, and during the last few years of his life would stare at it all evening, asking Sydney questions about the world far away. The light of the television brought into that dark little house programs like *The Honeymooners*, *The Big Valley*, *Have Gun Will Travel*, and *The Untouchables;* and glowed beyond the silent window into the yard, a yard filled with desolate chips of wood.

My grandfather Roy Henderson would ask Dad why people would act in a movie if they knew they were going to be shot. He would not be completely convinced by my father's explanation about movie scripts and actors, and became more disheartened and dangerous the clearer the explanation was.

"But they die—I seen them."

"No they don't, Dad."

"Ha—lot you know, Syd—lot you know—I seen blood, and blood don't lie, boy—blood don't lie. And if ya think blood lies I'll smash yer mouth, what I'll do."

As a teen my father sat in this TV-lightened world; a shack in the heat of July watching flies orbit in the half dark. He hid there because his father tormented him in front of kids his own age.

I have learned that because of this torment, Father became a drunk by the age of fifteen.

People did not know (and what would it matter if they had known?) that by the time he was fifteen, my father had read and could quote Stendhal and Proust. But he was trapped in a world of his own father's fortune, and our own fortune became indelibly linked to it as well.

IN THE SUMMER OF 1964 my grandfather was asked by his employer, Leo Alphonse McVicer, to take two Americans fishing for salmon at the forks at Arron Brook. Roy did not want to go; first, because it was late in the year and the water low, and secondly, because if they did not get a fish he might be blamed. Still, he was obligated.

"Get them a fish," Leo said, rooting in the bowl of his pipe with a small knife and looking up with customary curtness. Roy nodded, as always, with customary willingness. He took the men this certain hot day in August to a stretch of the river at the mouth of the brook, where the fish were pooled. He took his boy, Sydney, with him, to help pole the canoe up river and make the men comfortable. Then in the heat of midday, he sent Sydney north in the canoe to scout other pools for fish while he spent his time rigging the lines and listening to the men as they spoke about places as diverse as Oregon and Honolulu, while being polite enough to have no opinion when they spoke of the quality of Leo McVicer's wood and his mill.

Sydney poled back down river later that afternoon, looking in the water, and saying the fish had gone far up but that four salmon rested here, taking the oxygen from the cool spring, lying aside the boulders at the upper edge of the rip.

These men were important. They had been instrumental in helping Leo McVicer and Leo wanted to amuse them the way Maritimers do—by pretending a rustic innocence under obligation to *real* human beings who have travelled from *real* places to be entertained.

So after three hours, Roy whispered to my father: "It would be better for Leo if they caught something—if they are here to help finance the new barker for his mill."

And with those words, and with his shirt covered in patches of sweat and dust, and with his neck wrinkled in red folds from a life under lash to sun and snow, with his blackened teeth crooked and broken, showing the smile not of a man but of a tobacco-plug-chewing child, and with all the fiery sinewy muscles of his long body, he set in motion the brutal rural destiny of our family. Asking one of the men to give him a rod, he tied a three-pronged jig hook to it, had Sydney pole above them and then drift silently down through the pool without pole in the water, to point out where the salmon were lying. He threw the jig where the pool joined the spring and jerked upwards. All of a sudden the line began to sing, and away ran the fifteen-pound salmon jigged in the belly. After twenty-five minutes he hauled the spent cock fish in, killed it, and hooked another. The Americans were laughing, patting Roy on his bony back, not knowing what Sydney and Roy and the wardens watching them knew—that this exercise was illegal. The wardens watching stepped out, confiscated the rods, and seized the men's brand-new Chevrolet truck.

Leo McVicer heard of this at seven o'clock, when he got back from the mill. He paced all night in quiet almost completive fury. My grandfather went back to work early that Monday, willing to explain. But Leo fired him on the spot, even though Roy had sought to please him. For that I was to learn was Leo McVicer. Never minding either that the great Leo McVicer had often poached salmon for New Brunswick cabinet members and the occasional senator from Maine who partied at his house. This of course my grandfather did not know. He was kept from knowledge of the decisions of his great friend, as he was kept out of the dark rooms of his gigantic house.

To be fired after years of faith and work broke him, and he sat, as my own father once said, "like some poor sad rustic angel confined to hell."

Still, there was a chance—if only one—to work his way back into the fold. That summer Leo's men were unsatisfied and twice threatened a wildcat walkout. Finally McVicer beat them to it, and locked the sawmill's gate.

For the next two weeks things existed at a simmer between Leo and his men. They milled about the yard like atoms bouncing off each other, collecting and separating, collecting again, in pools of dusty, loitering brown-shirted figures, caught up at times in wild gestures, at other times almost grief-strickenly subdued. And within these two states there was talk of sabotage and revenge. No trucks or wood moved on or off McVicer property, and they stood firm when a welders' supply truck tried to enter, howling to each other and holding it back with their bodies, knowing little in life except what bodies were for, to be bent and shoved and twisted and gone against. At the end, the welders' truck was defeated. With a jubilant shout from the men into the empty September heat, the driver turned back and a lone truck of herbicide was left unloaded in the yard.

Finally Roy Henderson asked my father's advice. What could he do to make things better for Leo, and regain his job?

There was one thing my father advised: "Go to the men." My father at fourteen stated, "Convince them to end their walkout." He added that Leo would be grateful—the contracts filled, the herbicide unloaded, and Roy would be considered instrumental in this.

Roy headed into the woods on a warm September afternoon, with the pungent smell of spruce trees waving in the last of the summer heat. Just before he arrived onsite three men cut the locks to the gate. They stormed the truck and rolled the hundred barrels of herbicide off it, busted the barrels open with axes, and dumped them all, along with forty barrels of pesticide from the warehouse, into the upper edges of Little Arron Brook. The new barker was sabotaged, a flare was lighted to engage the men in more hellery, and a fire raged.

All of this was documented by a local reporter. A picture was taken that day long ago. Unfortunately, standing on the hulking ruin of smouldering machinery, a half-crazed drunken smile on his face, was my grandfather. It made the front pages of the provincial papers. He had not exactly done what my father had advised him to. In fact he looked like a vigilante from the deep south stomping the ruins of innocence. It was how *they* wanted him to look.

I have this picture still. As faded as it might be, the image is strikingly familiar, savage and gleeful, as if in one moment of wilful revenge Roy had forgotten the reason for his journey that afternoon.

Grandfather told Dad that he had tried to stop, not start, the conflagration. But his picture, even faded to yellow in an old archival room, shows him a rather willing participant in the mayhem. As if his grin leering from a newspaper at me, a grandson he never knew, was his only moment of bright majesty, caught in the splendid orb of a flashbulb, which signalled our doom for the next thirty years.

All others there that day got away when the police arrived but grandfather, too drunk to run, fell from the machine he was prancing on, and crawled on his knees to the police car to sleep.

The fire burned eleven hundred acres of Leo McVicer's prime soft timber land; timber subcontracted to the large paper mill. After my grandfather's picture was published, this fire became known locally as the "Henderson horror."

"Roy is bad—his son is mad," the saying rose from the lips of everyone.

Meanwhile Roy Henderson, illiterate and frightened of people who weren't illiterate, had to go to court and pay a lawyer to defend him on both counts; that is, of poaching and the destruction of the barker. My father described Roy as he stood in court in a grey serge suit. He had lost his beloved television. He was confronted by a menacing prosecutor. He shook and cried. He was sentenced to three years. People teased him on the way out of court.

Sydney, at fourteen, would make him biscuits and hitchhike to Dorchester to visit. But Roy, who had never been in jail in his life, refused to eat.

"Tell Leo I will not eat unless he forgives me," he said, sniffing, and sitting with his hands on his knees. His hair was turning grey and grey hair stuck out of his ears; his eyes were as deep set, his brow as wide, as some rustic prophet. But Sydney knew he was no prophet. He gave Sydney this message, as the sunlight came in on his prison trousers:

"Tell him that my life is in his hands—and then see what he has to say. Tell him that the biscuits are hard now, and gettin' harder. Go on, fella—get goin'—"

My father left the prison, in his old red coat and torn gumboots, and ran all the way to Moncton—thirty-seven miles. He caught the train, went to Leo—not to the house, but to the office in McVicer's store that had served our community for years. The store was a monument to the class of people it served, where calendars of halter-topped blonde and blue-eyed girls shining Fords with Turtle Wax were hidden by Leo under the counter, and where diversified products were unknown but Humphrey work pants and boots, and corduroys for children, were sold, along with erasers and scribblers and pencils for school.

"I just lost me a hundred-thousand-dollar barker—and a million-dollar lot," Leo said, without looking at Dad but looking through some invoices of clothing that he believed he had not ordered. "Now I have to clean up the barrels that got into the brook," Leo said, flipping the pages. "Everyone—" flip, "the Sheppards—" flip, "the Pits—" flip, "the Poriers—" flip, flip, "and everyone else said it was yer dad—yer dad and no other dad—and what do you want me to do?"

"Go visit him so he'll eat."

"Go visit him and cheer him up so he'll eat a good breakfast—well, damn him."

My father went back to jail to see his dad. It was close to Christmas and snow had fallen and covered the cities and towns, the long raw southern New Brunswick hills were slick with ice.

My father pitied Roy yet could do nothing to rouse him. At first Roy did not believe that Leo, whom he had known since he was sixteen, wouldn't come to see him. He stood with his hands on the bars of the holding cell they had brought him to, looking out expectantly, like a child. He addressed his own child as if he was another species, a strange creature that one day had appeared in his little cabin, someone Roy himself never knew what to do with. And that is why often as not he addressed Sydney as "fella."

"Yer saying he won't come to see me, fella."

"That's what I'm saying, Dad. I'm saying that he won't come to see you."

"Let's just get this straight—not that he's busy and might come to see me some other time—or something like that there?"

"He won't come, Dad."

Roy's look was one of incomprehensible vacancy, as if from some far-away land he was listening to some strange music. Then his eyes caught his son's and became cognizant of what had been said, and perhaps also for the very first time who his son was, and what grace his son held. And realizing this he was shocked, and broken even more.

"Well I pity him then—for doin' that—is all I can say," Roy whispered. And he refused on principle—perhaps the only one he had left (and to prove, just once, grandeur to his son)—to eat.

A few weeks later, ill with pneumonia, Roy Henderson was taken to hospital on the Miramichi. He died there, and was buried in an old graveyard downriver, leaving my father alone.

I always said *I* would have done more. But my father felt he had done what he could. He never left his father alone. He walked 230 miles of road, appealing to McVicer to forgive. He fasted as his father did. He broke his fast only to take communion. He remained with his father to the end, even though it was a solitary vigil. But he would never seek revenge. Revenge, my father believed in his fertile brilliance, was anathema to justice.

After Roy's death Dad lived a primitive life, for what contact would he have with others? He would be teased whenever he went out to a dance; girls would string him along as a joke. He began to drink every day whatever he could find; to forget, as Sam Johnson has said, and I once found underlined in a book my father owned, "the pain of being a man."

The pain of being a man, or simply being cold or wet or tired. The old barn was long gone. His house was built of plywood and tarpaper. Its walls were insulated by cardboard boxes. It was fifteen by twelve and sixteen feet high—so it looked like a shoebox standing on end. That is something that I like to remember. Most of his life was lived principally here.

He lived three years alone hiding from people who might do something *for* him—I mean send him to foster care. But no one expressed any concern whatsoever on his behalf. Except for one man: Jay Beard, who lived in a trailer up on the main road and hired Dad to cut wood. At one time Dad got a job (as illegal as it must have been) planting dynamite to blow boulders at a construction site. He was not afraid and he was also nimble. He earned what was a good deal of money for him, and with it he bought both his mother's and father's graves their stones.

AT EIGHTEEN he was coming home from a long hot day in a lobster boat on the bay, where he worked helping bait traps. His skin was burned by the sun and saltwater and his hands were blistered by the rope and the traps. But that day he met Jay Beard, who was selling off many of his books, books Jay had inherited from his dead brother and had himself never read. Beard was actually looking for my father to sell these books to. My father bought three hundred paperbacks and old faded hardcovers, the whole lot for twenty dollars, and brought them home by wheelbarrow.

Then in early fall of that same year Sydney, who in reading these books had given up drink, went to Chatham to see a professor about the chance at a university education. The professor, David Scone, a man who had gone to the University of Toronto, disliked the Maritimes while believing he knew of its difficulties and great diversity. Looking at my father sitting in his old bib overalls and heavy woollen shirt proved what he felt. And he commented that it might be better for Dad to find a trade. This was not at all contradictory to Dr. Scone's sense of himself as a champion of people just like Father. In fact, being a champion of them meant, in his mind, he knew them well enough to judge them. And something he saw in my father displeased him.

"Yes, I know you have come here with your heart set on a lofty education—but look in another direction. A carpenter—how is that?—you seem like a man who would know angles." And then he whispered, as people do who want to show how lightly they take themselves, "It would not be as difficult for you as some things in here, philosophy and theology and all of that—"

Scone smiled, with a degree of naive self-infatuation seen only in those with an academic education, shook his head at the silliness of academia, while knowing that his tenure was secure and every thought he had ever had was manifested as safe by someone else before him. My father never had such a luxury. There was a time my father would have been beaten by his own father if it was known that he read. Knowing this, tell me the courage of Dr. David Scone.

My father said that being a carpenter might be nice and he liked carpentry but that he liked books more. Outside, the huge Irish Catholic church rested against the horizon, the sun gleaming from its vast windows and its cavernous opened doors; its steps swept clean, its roof reflecting the stains of sunlight, while on the faraway hills across the river the trees held the first sweet tinges of autumn.

"Well, then—you want to be a scholar, do you. So what books have you read, Sydney? Mystery—science fiction—Ray *Bradbury*—well, there's nothing wrong with that at all, is there?" He smiled. My father was about to answer. Dr. Scone was about to listen but he was called away by the head of the department, a rather rotund priest with thick downy cheeks and a bald spot on the top of his head. Father stood and nodded at Scone as he left. Then he walked home from Saint Michael's University and sat in his kitchen. He did not know how to go about qualifying for university. It had taken him five weeks to find the courage to do what he had done. Now he felt that the man had condescended to him. What surprised him was the fact that an educated man would *ever* do this. He had been innocent enough to assume that the educated had excised all prejudice from themselves and would never delight in injury to others—that is, he believed that they had easily attained the goal he himself was struggling toward. He did not know that this goal—which he considered the one truthful goal man should strive toward—was often not even considered a goal by others, educated or not.

He had by that evening discovered his gross miscalculation. He was angry and decided to write a letter, and sat down in the kitchen and started to write to this professor, in pencil on an old lined sheet. But when the words came he realized a crime had taken place. (This is how he later described it to my mother.) The crime was that he had set out in a letter to injure someone else. He was ashamed of himself for this and burned the letter in the stove, sank on his bed with his face to the wall.

Later I came to hate that he did not send it, but it was noble. And what was most noble about it was that it would never be known as such. Nor did that in itself alleviate his suffering over what the professor had said, or his memory of the professor's self-infatuated smile when he said it. That is, like most spoken injuries, Father had to sample it not only at the time it had taken place but for days and even weeks after, and again each time this well-known professor was interviewed in the paper about Maritime disparage or his life-long fight on behalf of First Nations rights. (Which became a lifelong fight at the same time it became a lifelong fight among his intellectual class, most of them ensconced in universities far away from any native man or woman.)

The fact that my father not only was a part of the demographic this professor was supposedly expert upon but had worked since he was a boy, and had his own ideas from years of violence and privation, made the sting ever sharper and fresher each time he heard Dr. David Scone lauded for his *utter decency* by our many gifted announcers on the CBC.

Yet by his honour—my father's honour—he could and did say nothing. Even when Dr. David Scone tried to influence my mother against him.

I know now it was because of an incident that happened when my father was a child of twelve. One day he and another boy were shovelling snow from the slanted church roof. The boy had robbed Dad's molasses sandwich and Dad pushed him. The boy fell fifty feet, and lay on his back, blood coming from his nose and snow wisping down over his face.

My father, perched high upon the roof next to the base of the steeple, was certain the boy had died. He did not believe in anything, had hated the priest after that certain incident, that falling-out I mentioned. But still he whispered that if the boy lived he would never raise his hand or his voice to another soul, that he would attend church every day. *Every damn day.* What is astounding is, as soon as he made this horrible pact, the boy stood up, wiped his face, laughed at him, and walked away. That boy was Connie Devlin.

I don't believe Devlin was ever hurt. I believe my father only thought he was. The bloody nose came when the boy fell, but was nothing to be upset over, and the boy liked the attention that happens when people think you are dead. I told my father this when I heard of his pact years later. I said, "Dad, you never touched the boy—so therefore God tricked you into this masochistic devotion. God has made you His slave because of your unnatural self-condemnation."

My father never answered; he just turned and walked away.

Connie Devlin was to plague Father all his life. And it was from that day forward my father's true life started. After that day, things happened *to* his life that showed, or proved to him at least, other forces.

What my father believed from the time his own father died was this: whatever pact you make with God, God *will* honour. You may not think He does, but then do you really know the pact you have actually made? Understand the pact you have made, and you will understand how God honours it.

TWO

My mother, Elly, was an orphan girl brought up by a distant relative, Gordon Brown, originally from Charlo.

My mom was reported to have had two siblings adopted by other families in other places. This fact, the fact that by her own family she was left in an orphanage, and then taken to the home of Gordon Brown, had a profound effect upon her. It made her solitary as a child, and nervous. She had many rituals to keep herself safe, because she felt anyone could come and take her away, and felt also that anyone had power to do what they wanted with her life. She therefore went to church every day, praying to God, and hoped for miracles in finding her siblings and her mom and dad, whom she never stopped looking for. She was considered odd by the people—even by her adopted parents and her stepbrother, Hanny Brown; pitied and looked upon with sadness as a very unclever girl. Worse for her social welfare, she saw miracles—in trees, in flowers, in insects in the field, especially butterflies, in cow's milk, in sugar, in clouds of rain, in dust, in snow, and in the thousands of sweet midnight stars.

"Why would there not be?" she once told my sister, Autumn Lynn.

But others of course tormented her continuously about this. No one considered her bright, and she left school at sixteen, her second year in grade eight, hoping for a life in the convent. Two years passed where my mother did chores for neighbours, babysat, and attended church. Then her friend Diedre Whyne—a girl who had a much more affluent family, who was sharp and gifted, had taken two years in one at school on two different occasions—took Mom under her wing, finding a job for her in Millbank, away from the prying eyes of the nuns at the Sisters of Charity. Thinking of the circumstances, who among us would have done differently?

In Millbank, still considering the convent, Mother met my father, when he was about nineteen or twenty. They met at the community picnic, where she was working the tables and he was helping hitch on.

To hitch on a load at a horsehaul—where a two-horse team proves its strength by hauling sleds with incredibly heavy loads—is extremely dangerous. Some men won't do it with their own teams because the horses are so hyped on tea they bolt as soon as they hear the clink of the hook being snapped to the sled. A man has to jump out of the way in a split second or be run over. However, my father earned extra money to buy more books, and if he was not oblivious to the danger, without conceit he was not concerned by it.

The last day of that particular long-forgotten horsehaul, the horses and even the horse owners now long dead, held in a large field near the main river, Sydney went to the huge canvas army tent for water. My mother was working the table just inside, which looked exactly the same as the outside except the grass blades were covered, and saw Father approaching. The old cook rushed to her side and forbade her to talk to him, for he was a danger to people.

This woman arranged a date for my mother with her nephew Mathew Pit, home from Ontario, where he had spent two months in the Don Jail. This date was arranged and Mathew picked Mother up that evening at her rooming house and drove to the sand pile, a kind of lovers' lane without the lane, near McVicer's sawmill.

He had asked his younger sister, earlier in the evening how he should behave, and how he should approach this great chance. Cynthia had smiled and in a moment of sisterly diplomacy that would be for years captured in his mind, and now years and years later in mine, said: "Give it to her."

Mathew parked, revved the engine, and, reaching over, put Mother's white bucket seat in the reclining position, so that she was no longer staring out the windshield but staring at the spotted ceiling. He opened a quart bottle of beer for her to drink, plunking it down between her legs. All about them the half-burned acres of land sat mute and secluded in midsummer and the old sawmill looked melancholy with its main building sunken and its huge gate rusted and locked. It reminded one of years of mind-numbing work, of cold and heat and a degree of futility seen in deserted overgrown places where life once flourished.

"McVicer has a million dollars and not one friend," Mathew said with country cynicism. "That's not how I'm going to turn out—here for a good time not a long time, I say—"

My mother said nothing, for McVicer had once visited her and had given her an apple, and an orange one Christmas day and a sock with a barley toy and nuts.

For twenty minutes or more not another word was spoken, and Mother's thoughts might have been as flat, her face may have been as uncommunicative as Joseph Conrad's Captain McWhirr, the hero of "Typhoon," who wrote to his parents, when a very young seaman, that his ship one Christmas day "fell in with some icebergs."

Certainly Mother must have felt that she had fallen in with some icebergs, and she was unresponsive, as he now and again reached over to keep the bottle between her legs upright.

Finally Mathew finished his own quart of beer; he did not hurry it, and supposed this is what my mother was eagerly waiting for him to do—finish. Then, with her still staring at the ceiling, and the quart bottle still plunked on an angle between her legs, he took off his shirt and showed her the two eagle tattoos on his biceps. Then he put his hands under her dress. Suddenly, after being dormant as a turnip for almost a half hour, she gave a screech.

"What the Jesus is wrong!" he said, as shocked at her screech as she herself was. "What did you think was going to happen here? For Christ sake—this is a date, ain't it?"

Mother got out of the car and walked back and forth in the evening drizzle as he followed her, snapping gum, with his hands in his pockets and a beer bottle dangling from his right hand, blackflies circling his broad blond head. Her arms were folded the way country girls do, her lips were pursed, as she walked back and forth trying to avoid him. Finally she went to a set of barrels and kneeled behind them.

"Please, Mr. Pit, thank you for the wonderful time but I would like to go home," she said.

He smashed his bottle in anger and upset the barrel she was hiding behind. "Get up outta that," he said as if hurrying a draft horse out of a cedar swamp. "This is the same stuff they use in Vietnam—to flush out the gooks."

"Yes—that is very nice thank you very much—Mr. Pit sir I would like to go home—"

"Go home now? We just got here!"

"Yes please Mr. Pit sir thank you very much." She kept her head down and her eyes closed as she spoke. She had been told not to sass her betters, never to think she was smart, and always to mind her manners. All of these recommendations from the Office of the Mother Superior, at the convent of the Sisters of Charity, she was trying hard to remember. She was told this more than others because she was a child without a father, and without a name. A few nuns as unclever as she had rapped her knuckles raw trying to make her remember the five points of obeisance to the Lord and to her betters, and told her she could not be a nun if she was a nuisance.

But she felt, and quite rightly, that Mathew was close to hitting her. If he had hit her, Mother would have only lowered her head and whispered that she was sorry. He yelled that she didn't understand what a good time meant, and she nodded and with head bowed walked behind him back to the car.

"I should leave you here," he said. "Bears and bugs to eat you—pussy and all. How would you like that?"

She did not know what he meant. She looked about her feet to see if there was a kitten.

"Please Mr. Pit I want to go home."

"You want me to drive you home?"

"Yes sir Mr. Pit."

"Give me a kiss and I'll drive you."

She turned and began to walk, head down, along the old derelict road toward the highway. He drove behind her, honking the horn.

"Yer some dumb to give up losin' yer cherry to a man like me—tell you that!" he said, his head out the window and his hand on the horn.

Finally, at the highway, she was persuaded to take a drive. She got into the back seat and sat like a child, her eyes closed, her lips recounting a decade of the beads.

Mathew phoned her six times in the next four days to ask her out again, telling her they would go to a different place. She was going to tell him she had mumps—but since she did not want to lie she told him that she "once" had mumps.

"It's that good-for-nothing Sydney Henderson," Mathew told her. "He has you braindead. He's almost like a devil the books I heard he reads and everythin' else!"

Her spurning made Mathew wretched. It was a wrong that went beyond all others. For how could Sydney Henderson—Sydney Henderson, the boy whose father tormented him in front of them, so everyone had howled in laughter, the boy Mathew had slapped at school trying to make cry (Sydney didn't)—have caught Elly's eye? How could God allow this to happen? Mathew did not know. He only knew he would break this spell.

By sudden inspiration Father was asked to a beach party by Cynthia, Mathew Pit's younger sister. She had been in trouble many times (once for biting a bride's ear), and already her face had a chameleon-like changeability seen in those who have studied social opportunity more than they have studied themselves—a beautiful face, no doubt, wanton at times, at times hilarious, but always resolute, fixed on purpose beyond her present state, which was rural poor.

For Mathew's sake Cynthia would break the attraction between Mother and Father. In the lazy heat of her upstairs room, beyond earshot of their mother, Mat lectured her on what she might do.

"I'm not going to do it with him—I won't go that far. He'll get a hand on it but nothin' else."

"I'm not asking you to do no more," Mathew said with a kind of anger he almost always felt. Then something else happened, again by afterthought. He had had on his person for a month, given to him by Danny Sheppard—for the purpose of giving it to Elly—a tab of blotter acid. He had forgotten about it. Now he gave Cynthia the tab, to spike my father's Coke. Cynthia took the blotter acid and put it in the back pocket of her tight terrycloth shorts, without comment. This was at ten past six on a Friday evening; their large old house, with its two gables, its front door facing the back yard, smelled of stale summer heat, peeled and poled wood, and fried cod, lingering from the kitchen up the dark, forbidding stairs.

My father drank a Coke at ten that evening. By this time Cynthia, bored with his conversation to her about Matthew Arnold (who wouldn't be at a beach party), had drifted away to one of the Sheppard boys—Danny. But Father in drinking this acid did not act out and become violent or paranoid as Mathew had hoped. Instead he walked all the way to Millbank and woke my mother by throwing pebbles at the window of Kay O'Brien's house next door.

"Sir, you have the wrong house," my mother said after watching him for ten minutes and deciding it must be her he was after. "You must throw your pebbles over here!"

"Why didn't you read my notes?" he said, throwing the last white pebble into her room.

My mother could barely read, and did not wish to tell him this, for the nuns had broken the skin of her knuckles many times with the rap of a pointer. Always, to her, letters had appeared backwards and upside down.

"I have no care for notes from big important people, and I think you are being some darn forward," she said hesitantly. "Besides, I am getting married."

"To who?" he asked, deflated.

"To Jesus Christ," she said.

"Maybe I can talk you out of it."

"Don't be improper."

"I see some angels near you."

"You are being funny at the Lord's expense," Mother said piously.

But to Father the vision was accurate. The night was drowned by soft and splendid moonlight, moonlight in every direction. It had formed a gliding path on the water from the east to his feet beneath him. It was as if he could walk on this moonbeam, see for miles, and not bother touching the ground. It was as if my mother was standing naked, with angels on her right and left shoulders.

"I walked up here because some force propelled me to—last night I never would have been so bold—I see you like this and I want to marry you."

"Go home, please—" she said. But she did not want him to go anywhere.

"Say you will marry me or I won't leave."

"Go home and I will think about it. You're Sydney Henderson, right?"

"I was when I started up here—"

"Go home—tomorrow you will know my answer."

The next day my mother, Elly, went to see my father, Sydney, in a dry, yellow hayfield near Arron Brook. He watched her walking toward him wearing a light cotton dress and a pair of sneakers. She walked up to him, all the while speaking to men he was haying with. Then stopping before him, she took his large face in her hands and kissed him to the great merriment and cheers of all the others. So I was told. It was here Dad saw my mom as a simple human being, good though she may be. He did not see the angels ever again. He saw her as beautiful—but simply a woman, whose breath when she kissed him smelled of the radish she had been eating.

Still they were seen together as two youngsters, without money or hope for a future, backward and living precariously with no indication that they could ever better themselves. Many people said they were grossly mis-matched. The Poriers, the Pits. McVicer himself. And McVicer had the Whynes invite Mom on a blueberry-picking excursion to Wisard Point. The Whynes were as prominent as the McVicers. Prof. David Scone was a friend of Diedre, and took an interest in Elly. Scone and Diedre were both very radical, and Elly was so shy she had a hard time looking at them directly. She also felt that there was a conspiratorial feel to the trip, to where Elly was positioned in the car, to who offered her water, to the questions asked her about Syd.

Dr. David Scone sat with her for a long time patting her hand with his but looking stern and irritated, as if some great weight was now upon his shoulders, some grave social duty (not realizing of course that it was the simple vulgarity of matchmaking). It was of course an age much like this age, when people conspired to look good more than be good. When they got to the blueberry field, Diedre picked beside her, and talked a long time about how David Scone held kind feelings for and was intent upon helping the poor of the Maritimes. He was Diedre's companion; platonic (it would seem). Professor Scone was most concerned with the plight of rural women, who had never been taken seriously. Now it was time that they were. (Dr. Scone seemed to have himself just discovered this, as if writers like Brontë or Hardy had not.) My mother said that would certainly be nice, to be taken seriously—especially in serious matters.

David Scone had black hair that curled over his ears. He was tall and thin, his arms were thin and weak looking. His black silky beard covered a milk white face. But Mom did not at all like the way he looked at her, which was with a steady haughty glance, as if everything she had ever done had been told to him by someone else.

I believe she recognized in Professor Scone the baffled pity and subtle condescension a man of education often has for others, and which others had held toward *her* all her life, a trait more mocking than considerate and known by the poor or the "disenfranchised" in a second. Also there may have been a certain hope involved. This could be sensed in the late-summer air and the wide expanse of trees where an old bear came out to gorge her-self on berries not far from them. That is, the new world had caught Mother up in its snare every bit as pernicious as the nun's pointer falling on her small white hands. Yes, they told her, she would have a great life without my father, but that she must be bold, inventive, and lie to get rid of him. To Diedre he was a physical monstrosity.

"God, whatever will you do?" Diedre had asked Mother that afternoon; and then she whispered: "David Scone is divorced and does like you very much, can't you tell? He also is a *professor!*—a professor showing interest in you—my dear—"

"I thought he was *your* boyfriend," Mother whispered back, trying to show interest out of politeness.

Diedre looked at her strangely and then smiled. "I do not have *boyfriends*, love."

"But I love Sydney," Mother said. There was a pause. Mother heard a grasshopper tick in the grass beside her bowl of blueberries, and stood and moved five paces away. Diedre followed and kneeled beside her once again. It was as if—and Mother sensed this—my father's feelings for her did not matter, that they believed Sydney had a calculating mind from which they would free her.

"Can Sydney after all his trouble learn about love?" Diedre whispered finally. My mother had been waiting for the shoe to drop. For all her young life, shoe dropping, reprimand coming, chores given were the things she knew about.

"If he had to learn it I would not seek it," Mother replied, still whispering, which showed in a truly elemental way that she would always match wits.

Within five minutes, a sharper, colder, and more longing wind came from the bay, and reminded one of autumn coming on.

"I will name one of my children Autumn," Mother said, "for the wind has informed me I will have a daughter." And again she stood and walked five paces. Again Deidre followed and plopped her bowl beside Mother's.

"So, Missy, did the wind inform you if that would be your fifteenth or sixteenth child?"

Late that evening, when she came back to her rooming house, a two-storey white building with a large enclosed veranda, and saw Sydney waiting for her on the steps, with battered boots on his feet, his hands bruised from work, his body aching from piling lumber at $1.65 an hour, she realized how much she did love him.

Diedre told my mother she could have a job in Fredericton far away from Sydney Henderson and my mother should count herself lucky. My mother did try to feel lucky, but could not. The road, the little leaves on the trees—all of this, the dusty quality of the clouds, all these *miracles* she would miss if she went away.

So that Sunday, three days after their blueberry-picking excursion and a day before she was supposed to go to Fredericton, Mom telephoned Diedre from her rooming house and said she could not possibly take this job.

"He's bullying you—he talked you out of it, hasn't he?" Diedre said. "Has he hit you or something?"

My mother whispered that this was not true, but she was crying so much the answer seemed a lie.

"I love you," Diedre said. "You will not ruin your life—I want to take care of you—but at times you are infuriatingly ungrateful. Think of *his* attitude toward you—and think of David Scone's attitude and how he cares so—"

"Does he care for all women, this Dr. David Scone from the university?"

"I can tell you all women," Diedre said excitedly.

"But then why did he fight with his ex-wife?" Elly whispered, tears running down her cheeks. "That is no way to honour someone. Sydney has not fought with me—and we believe the same things—"

"Don't be childish. David Scone's relations with his ex-wife is a private matter, and we are not discussing David Scone's attitudes but Sydney Henderson's attitudes toward you—"

"But," my mother whispered, "what are your attitudes toward Sydney?"

Diedre said that if Mother continued to speak like that she would just hang up on her and let her live with Sydney in a shack and see what would happen. So my mother, used to being bullied so that her fingers were arthritic by being rapped, said nothing else. Then Diedre, placated by my mother's silence, spoke:

"Just go over for a year—you will meet *real* people. I love you more than anyone does—but—let's just say this: Dr. David Scone knows something about this man—Sydney." Here she became short of breath, as people do when they wish to relay information that they fear might not be readily accepted. "Sydney went over to the office one day and tried to bully David into getting him enrolled. He did—with big plans about this and that. But David was not bullied and soon got rid of him! Take this job we have offered—it is your only chance! God—you're a child. Babies and diapers to that man—who as you know has been implicated in all kinds of things!"

My mother, staring at the dresser as Diedre spoke, saw the white stone Father had thrown into the room, and swayed by this, whispered, "Goodbye," hung up, and with a cardboard suitcase, and the white stone safely in her pocket, made her way to Dad's property.

Richard B. Wright

Richard B. Wright is the author of eleven novels, including *October, Adultery, Clara Callan,* and *The Age of Longing.* In 2001, *Clara Callan* won The Giller Prize, the Governor General's Literary Awards for Fiction, and the Trillium Book Award, and in 2002, the Canadian Booksellers Association Libris Award for Fiction Book of the Year and Author of the Year. *The Age of Longing* was shortlisted for both The Giller Prize and the Governor General's Literary Awards for Fiction in 1995. Wright's work has been published in Canada and internationally. He lives in St. Catharines, Ontario, with his wife, Phyllis.

Clara Callan

BY RICHARD B. WRIGHT

Winner 2001

⇌

1934

Saturday, November 3 (8:10 p.m.)

Nora left for New York City today. I think she is taking a terrible chance going all the way down there but, of course, she wouldn't listen. You can't tell Nora anything. You never could. Then came the last-minute jitters. Tears in that huge station among strangers and loudspeaker announcements.

"I'm going to miss you, Clara."

"Yes. Well, and I'll miss you too, Nora. Do be careful down there!"

"You think I'm making a mistake, don't you? I can see it in your face."

"We've talked about this many times, Nora. You know how I feel about all this."

"You must promise to write."

"Well, of course, I'll write."

The handkerchief, smelling faintly of violets, pressed to an eye. Father used to say that Nora's entire life was a performance. Perhaps she will make something of herself down there in the radio business, but it's just as likely she'll return after Christmas. And then what will she do? I'm sure they won't take her back at the store. It's a foolish time to be taking chances like this. A final wave and a gallant little smile. But she did look pretty and someone on the train will listen. Someone is probably listening at this very moment.

Prayed for solitude on my train home but it was not to be. Through the window I could see the trainman helping Mrs. Webb and Marion up the steps. Then came the sidelong glances of the whole and hale as Marion came down the aisle, holding onto the backs of the seats, swinging her bad foot outward and forward and then, by endeavour and the habit of years, dropping the heavy black boot to the floor. Settled finally into the seat opposite, followed by Mother Webb and her parcels. Routine prying from Mrs. W.

"Well now, Clara, and what brings you to the city? Aren't the stores crowded and Christmas still weeks off? I like to get my buying out of the way. Have you started the practices for the concert? Ida Atkins and I were talking about you the other day. Wouldn't it be nice, we said, if Clara Callan came out to our meetings. You should think about it, Clara. Get you out of the house for an evening. Marion enjoys it, don't you dear?"

Plenty more of this all the way to Uxbridge station when she finally dozed off, the large head drooping beneath the hat, the arms folded across the enormous chest. Marion said hello, but stayed behind her magazine (movie starlet on the cover). We quarrelled over something a week ago. I can't exactly remember what, but Marion has since refused to speak to me at any length and that is just as well.

On the train my gaze drifting across the bare grey fields in the rain. Thinking of Nora peering out another train window. And then I found myself looking down at Marion's orthopedic boot, remembering how I once stared at a miniature version of it in the schoolyard. Twenty-one Septembers ago! I was ten years old and going into Junior Third. Marion had been away all summer in Toronto and returned with the cumbersome shoe. In Mrs. Webb's imagination, Marion and I are conjoined by birth dates and therefore mystically united on this earth. We were born on the same day in the same year, only hours apart. Mrs. W. has never tired of telling how Dr. Grant hurried from our house in the early-morning hours to assist her delivery with the news that Mrs. Callan had just given birth to a fine daughter. And then came Marion, but her tiny foot "was not as God intended." And on that long-ago September morning in the schoolyard, Mrs. Webb brought Marion over to me and said, "Clara will look after you, dear. She will be your best friend. Why you were born on the same day!"

Marion looked bewildered. I remember that. And how she clung to my side! I could have screamed and, in fact, may have done. At the end of the day we fought over something and she had a crying spell under a tree on our front lawn. How she wailed and stamped that boot, which drew my eye as surely as the bulging goitre in old Miss Fowley's throat. Father saw some of this and afterwards scolded me. I think I went to bed without supper and I probably sulked for days. What an awful child I was! Yet Marion forgave me; she always forgives me. From time to time, this afternoon, I noticed her smiling at me over her magazine. Mr. Webb was at the station with his car, but I told him I preferred to walk. It had stopped raining by then. No offence was taken.

They are used to my ways. And so I walked home on this damp grey evening. Wet leaves underfoot and darkness seeping into the sky through the bare branches of the trees. Winter will soon be upon us. My neighbours already at their suppers behind lighted kitchen windows. Felt a little melancholy remembering other Saturday evenings when I would have our supper on the stove, waiting for the sound of Father's car in the driveway, bringing Nora up from the station. Certainly Nora would never have walked. Waiting in the kitchen for her breathless entrance. Another tale of some adventure in acting class or the charms of a new beau. Father already frowning at this commotion as he hung up his coat in the hallway. It's nearly seven months now, and I thought I was getting used to Father being gone, yet tonight as I walked along Church Street, I felt again the terrible finality of his absence.

Then I was very nearly knocked over by Clayton Tunney who came charging out of the darkness at the corner of Broad Street. It was startling, to say the least, and I was cross with him.

"Clayton," I said. "For goodness' sake, watch where you're going!"

"Sorry, Miss Callan. I was over at the Martins', listening to their radio with Donny, and now I'm late for supper and Ma's going to skin me alive."

And off he went again, that small nervous figure racing along Church Street. Poor Clayton! Always in a hurry and always late. Without fail, the last one into class after recess.

Tatham House
138 East 38th Street
New York
November 10, 1934

Dear Clara,

Well, I made it, and I am now at the above address. Tatham House is an apartment hotel for self-supporting women (I hope to become one soon).

It's very clean, well maintained and reasonably priced. It's also quite convenient. I stayed with Jack and Doris Halpern for a few days and then I found this place. The Halperns live "uptown" dozens of blocks away, but the subway can get you around the city so fast that you hardly notice distances. New York is not that hard to navigate once you get the hang of it. All the streets run east and west while the avenues go north and south and they are all numbered with a few exceptions like Park and Madison and Lexington. But brother, is it noisy! The taxi drivers are always honking their horns, and you really have to be careful crossing the street. Everyone seems to be in such a blasted hurry (I thought Toronto was bad). There are so many people out on the streets at all hours and I have to say, Clara, that I've never seen so many handsome men, though so many of them are swarthy. I guess they must be Italian or Greek or maybe Jewish. Awfully good-looking though. You also see a lot of coloured people down here.

Now about work! On Thursday, Jack took me to Benjamin, Hecker and Freed (an advertising agency) and introduced me to some people, including this writer Evelyn Dowling. How can I describe Evelyn? She reminds me of that song we used to sing when we were kids.

I'm a little teapot
Short and stout
Here is my handle
Here is my spout!

Remember that? She's only about five feet tall and nearly as wide and she has this big head of reddish hair. Wears beautifully cut tailored suits and expensive-looking shoes. She's not going to win any beauty contests, but she's very funny and obviously very successful. Smokes like the dickens. Just one Camel after another and her fingers are yellow with nicotine. Anyway, I did a voice test (several actually), and they liked what they heard, or at least that's what they told me. They haven't promised anything yet, but Jack thinks I am exactly what they are looking for with this new show that Evelyn is writing. Meantime, as I told Jack, I am in this big city and I have to pay bills for fairly important items like food and rent, but he said that he will find me some commercial work within the next week or so and I should be all right. Good Lord, I hope so! I have enough money to last about six weeks and after that I'll have to go on the dole or, what's more likely, they'll probably kick me out of their fair country. To tell you the truth though, I am pretty hopeful about all this. I had a very good feeling last Thursday when I was reading for these people. I just sensed that they liked what they heard, particularly Miss. D. So we shall see! Jack and Doris are picking me up in about an hour and we are going out to dinner. They've been just wonderful to me. So, all in all, I would say it's been a good first week and I'm not homesick yet, but *please* write.

Love, Nora

P.S. There's a hallway telephone on my floor and I can be reached at University 5-0040 in case of an emergency. I wish you would get a phone, but we've been through all that, haven't we? So I suppose you can use the Brydens' if you have to, but I wish you'd think about it again, Clara. Wouldn't it be nice if we could "talk" to one another once or twice a week? But what did Father used to say about saving your breath to cool your porridge?

Friday, November 16

This morning I awakened feeling put upon. Over the past few days the winds have blown the first storm of the winter through the village. In other years I welcomed the first snow because it covered November's greyness. Now the snow is just a nuisance that has to be shovelled away and I have been at it off and on since Wednesday morning. Then too I have been worrying about the last hundred dollars Wilkins owes me for Father's car. It was due on the first of the month, and all week I had made up my mind that he was going to take advantage and I would have to hire a lawyer and go through all that business to get the money. I am far too hasty in my judgement of others and probably too pessimistic about human nature. So now, look how benign a place this old world seems! An afternoon of brilliant sunlight (for November), and just as I got home from school, Mr. Wilkins came by with the hundred dollars, apologizing for the delay. God bless him! Now I must get Nora's share off to her; she sounds as though she could use it.

Dear Nora,

I'm glad that you have found a decent place to stay that isn't too dear. I hope you will be careful in that city. I know it would drive me to distraction just walking out the door into such crowds. How on earth do people earn their livings, and where, I wonder, does the food come from to feed so many mouths? There must be thousands out of work down there. We are surviving in the village, though over in Linden they are really up against it. The furniture factory has laid off nearly all the men and things are very flat with many families now on relief.

School is fine though Milton and I now have to do the work of three. Because we got on so well in the spring, I think the board just assumes that the school can be run by two people. They claim they haven't the money this year for another teacher, and that may be so, but I'm inclined to think that they are just being close about it. However there's nothing we can do. Milton is a pleasant fellow to work for, but he dithers a good deal and he lacks Father's authority as a principal. I suppose one can't be too hard on him, but I find he's not strict enough with some of the rougher children who could benefit from a good hiding now and then. I'm thinking in particular of the Kray brothers who are the bane of my existence these days.

Mr. Wilkins finally gave me the last payment for Father's car yesterday and the enclosed money order for fifty dollars is your share. I am sure you can put it to good use. To tell you the truth, I now regret selling the car. It has occurred to me more than once over the last little while that I might have kept it and learned how to drive. I just didn't think that way at the time of Father's death and maybe I was just in too much of a hurry to get everything settled. Speaking of getting settled, I have also dealt with the man from Linden Monuments who finally got around to seeing me the week before last. These people certainly take their time to conduct business; I've been after him since the summer. He wanted to sell me some folderol for the family headstone and showed me a catalogue which very nearly struck me dumb with amazement and horror: hundreds of dreadful little verses which attempt to reassure the living that the dead are not so badly off. Perhaps they aren't, but in any case I told him that plain words would have to do the job. And so alongside Mother's and Thomas's names and years will be Edward J. Callan, 1869–1934. I hope that's all right with you.

I think I have now mastered the furnace. It has been worrying me all fall, but Mr. Bryden has given me several lessons on how to start it and keep it going. There is a trick to all this. You have to be careful about allowing enough flame through the coals to burn off the gas, but you can't smother the flame or, of course, the darn thing will go out. I now appreciate the hours Father used to spend watching "this monster in the cellar." And in a way it is a "monster" that will have to be attended to and appeased every day of the blessed week from now until April. These days I am hurrying home at lunch to make sure that "he" is still breathing and satisfied, but I am also learning how to put enough coal in after breakfast ("building the fire," according to Mr. Bryden) so that it will last until I get home from school. I really had no idea what a chore it is just to keep warm. At the same time, there is an undeniable satisfaction in knowing how to do all this.

I was amused by your colourful description of Miss Dowling with her tobacco-stained fingers and tailored suits. You are certainly meeting some exotic creatures down there, aren't you?

I have noted the telephone number you gave me and passed it on to Mrs. Bryden who says hello and good luck. She will get in touch with you if I fall down the cellar stairs and brain myself some evening. And no, I am not going to rent a telephone. As you say, we've been through all that and I still maintain that, in my case, it's a waste of money. I doubt whether I would phone three people in a month and I see no reason why we can't keep in touch by letter. Do take care of yourself in that city, Nora.

Clara

P.S. Had our first winter storm this week but I am finally dug out!

Tatham House
138 East 38th Street
New York
November 25, 1934

Dear Clara,

Thanks for your letter, but please don't talk about falling down the cellar stairs. It gives me the willies when you say things like that. I know you are facing your first winter alone in that big house, but try not to be morbid, okay? Well, I've survived nearly a month down here and, to be honest, I'm really glad I made this move. New York is such a fascinating city and I've just been too busy to be homesick. People have been terrific to me. Americans are much more open in their ways than us. It sure doesn't take them long to get acquainted with you.

If you had been listening to the radio last Tuesday night to a program called "The Incredible Adventures of Mr. Wang" (if you get it up there), you would have heard my voice, though you might not have recognized me. I played a gangster's moll who is trapped in a warehouse surrounded by police and the inscrutable Mr. Wang, and my line was: "Let's get out of here. NOW!" That was supposed to be delivered in a "hard-boiled egg" kind of way according to the director. Mr. Wang is a detective along the lines of Charlie Chan or Fu Manchu. Do any of these names mean anything to you? Probably not. Anyway, it was fun to do, even if I only had that one immortal line. I know it's not *Uncle Vanya*, but it's a start.

I've also been doing some commercial work (thanks to Jack) for Italian Balm. The work is a little boring, but it pays well and, as Jack says, I'm getting all this experience. They seem to like my voice at the agency. Next week we start rehearsals for a show about a surgeon who performs all these life-saving operations. "Calling Dr. Donaldson." I am going to play the doctor's nurse, June Wilson, and I actually announce the show by saying through this microphone filter, "Calling Dr. Donaldson, Calling Dr. Donaldson." As if it were in a hospital ward. That will be an afternoon show. Evelyn is writing another serial about—get this—two sisters who live in a small town somewhere "in the heartland of America." The younger sister Effie is always getting into trouble (usually men) and the older sister Alice is the wise one who dispenses advice and gets her sister and others out of jams. Now guess which part they are grooming your kid sister for? Wrong! I am going to play the *older* sister, so there! It will be called "The House on Chestnut Street." According to Evelyn (and she should know), the big market in radio in the next few years is going to be in afternoon serial dramas for housewives. It makes sense when you think about it. Women are home all day washing and ironing and cleaning, and while they're doing all that, they can listen to programs about people who lead more interesting lives. It's the perfect escape when you're ironing your husband's shirt to listen to a woman falling in love with a handsome doctor or rich lawyer. There are a lot of food and cosmetic companies interested in this market so there should be plenty of sponsors out there.

The other thing that's happened is this. Jack and Doris took me to a party down in Greenwich Village the other night and I met this couple, Marty and Ida Hirsch. He's a playwright and he and Ida are producing this play. It's not Broadway or anything. In fact, I think it's fairly small potatoes, but they asked me if I would be interested in reading for a part. I had told them about my experience, limited though it was, with the Elliot Hall Players and my radio work up in Toronto. So they asked me and I said sure and next Wednesday I'm going to try out. I figure I have to get all the experience I can and this seems like a good opportunity. Marty asked me all about Canada and what the politics were like up there. He had this strange idea that we were still ruled by the King of England. I've discovered that Americans don't know a lot about some things. But Marty is a nice guy if a little opinionated, and I'm looking forward to joining this group. He told me I had a lot of moxie coming down here on my own from Canada. I've never heard that word before, have you?

Speaking of words, have you written any poems lately? It seems to me you were writing some in the spring just after Father passed away. How did they turn out?

Remember how you used to fill those scribblers with poems and then some Sunday morning, right out of the blue, start tearing the pages and burning them in the kitchen stove? The pipes would get so hot that Father would start grumbling about a chimney fire on the way. But he would never say a word to you about it, would he? Brother, if I'd done something like that, I would never have heard the end of it. I hope to goodness that if you're still feeding the stove with your poems, you're careful. Thanks a heap for the money and write again soon.

Love, Nora

Wednesday, November 28

Commotion in the classroom today. Started by the Krays. During the arithmetic lesson they began pushing and shoving and then they were on the floor at the back of the room punching and choking one another. I tried to separate them, but they wouldn't stop and I had to call Milton. I like to think I can manage these things, but the Krays incite a rage that I find so difficult to check it frightens me. At ten o'clock this morning, I could easily have smashed the yardstick across Manley Kray's face. Even looking at them provokes me: those brutal bullet-shaped heads, the grimy necks, the ringworm and smelly feet. At recess I sat listening to the measured strokes from Milton's office. He told me that he learned how to apply "the leather" from Father. "It was one of the first things he taught me, Clara. 'Even strokes, Milton,' he used to say. And you never apply them in anger. They have to see the justice in the exercise. You're just doing your job, not venting your frustration."

It's odd that Father never talked to me about strapping. Perhaps he didn't think I needed talking to. How wrong he was! I always have to be careful about my temper. Afterwards I stood by the window and watched the Krays walk out into the schoolyard. They were surrounded at once by the other boys who dislike the brothers but admire their defiance.

Mr. and Mrs. Cameron came by this evening with Willard Macfarlane. They were collecting winter clothes for the needy. Last Sunday I told them I had some things of Father's, including the new overcoat he bought on sale in Toronto last January and then refused to wear. He brought it home and, standing in it in front of the hallway mirror, decided that it was too grand. "I can't walk around in a coat like this when so many people are hard up," he said.

I told this story to Willard and the Camerons and they enjoyed it. "That sounds like Ed," said Willard holding up the coat. "But gosh Almighty, this is some coat. It's a dandy!" Since Father had bought it on sale, he couldn't return it and so the coat with its velvet collar hung all last winter in the hall closet. The Camerons told me that they are leaving at the end of the year. I shall miss them.

Saturday, December 1

I was out for a walk along the township roads this afternoon. A raw, windy end-of-the-year kind of day with the sky carrying snow somewhere. Approaching the village at nightfall (5:45), I passed Henry Hill who was too drunk to notice me although I wished him a good evening. Henry was singing a mischievous song about love and trying out a kind of jig in the middle of the road. And all this in Father's new overcoat! I am glad, however, that Henry will have a fine coat for the winter ahead. When I got home, I started this poem, the first in months.

In my father's overcoat
The drunken man performs a jig.
With arms flung wide
And overcoat unbuttoned to the wind
He dances in the street.
That sombre banker's coat
Now the glad rags
Of a foolish man.

It will perhaps go something like that.

Whitfield, Ontario
Sunday, December 2, 1934

Dear Nora,

According to the dictionary, *moxie* is American slang for courage, though a more precise synonym might be the old-fashioned word *pluck*. With the car business over now, the only thing I had left to do was clear out Father's dressers and closet. I should have done this ages ago, but I kept putting it off. Then last Sunday Mr. Cameron asked for donations of winter clothes for the needy, so I got busy and packed Father's things into boxes. On Wednesday evening the Camerons came by with Willard Macfarlane and took everything to the church hall. I thought that was the end of it, but then a strange thing happened. Well, strange to me at least. Late yesterday afternoon, just as I was coming home from a walk in the countryside, I saw a man in a long coat and he seemed to be shuffling about in the middle of the road, performing some kind of dance. As I drew nearer, I could see that it was Henry Hill. Drunk, of course. Then I noticed that he was wearing Father's new overcoat. Do you remember last January when he went down to Toronto and bought it? Saw it in a haberdasher's window on Yonge Street. It was a beautiful coat with a velvet collar, expensive as the dickens but marked down and Father thought it was a bargain. When he brought it home, however, he fussed about it. Said it was far too grand to wear around the village. "I look like a Toronto banker in it," he said. "People will think I'm putting on airs. It's a poor time to go about in a coat like this." He wanted to take it back, but it had been on sale. I told him it looked good on him and he shouldn't worry about what people might think, but of course he did, and I don't believe he wore that coat a half a dozen times all winter. And there it was on poor old Henry last night in the middle of Church Street! But then why not? Winter is coming on and Henry needs a coat like everyone else. Yet it was unsettling to see the old man lurching about in Father's new coat. Well, you've seen him in such a state! Watching him, I wondered if perhaps there was a poem somewhere in all that, though I'm beginning to doubt whether I have the talent or the discipline to write poetry. Still these doubts (hobgoblins who perch on my bedstead at night) don't keep me from trying. I experience this peculiar happiness while puzzling over the selection and arrangement of words on a page even if, in ordinary daylight, their lustre has mysteriously vanished and they seem only pale and worn. And, by the way, you were right. I did attempt some verses about Father's death, but they didn't work and they proved to be more useful in the stove, giving off, you might say, more heat than light.

On Friday evening I went with "the ladies of the village" to a performance of *The Merry Widow* at the Royal Alexandra. I don't know why I went; I don't really care for Lehar's pretty tunes and I felt a little misplaced travelling with a dozen older women and their husbands. Three carloads of us! Ida Atkins is after me to join the Missionary Society. "Dear Clara, it would be so good for you to get out. All alone in that big house now. And we do need some young blood." That's true, I suppose. Except for poor Marion, the "ladies" are all in their forties, fifties and onwards. Am I now at thirty-one perceived as a member of this group? I expect I am, though I can't help thinking that I'll grow old before my time if I join the M.S. The thought of setting aside Tuesday evening for the next thirty years is dispiriting, to say the least.

I shall miss you coming home on Saturday evenings this winter. I always listened for the sound of the train whistle and so did Father. I know that you used to get on one another's nerves, but he really did look forward to your coming home. The fact that you were often at one another's throats within fifteen minutes is not as important as the fact that he cared about you. After one of your arguments when you'd stay away for weeks, he would say, "I wonder how Nora is getting on." Of course he could never have admitted such feelings to you. It was not his way. I can well imagine how he would worry if he were still alive and with you now in New York City.

I'm very happy to learn that you are making your way in the radio business, Nora. Do be careful crossing the streets.

Clara

Dear Clara,

Thanks for your letter. Honestly, I can't see you with all those old ladies like Mrs. Atkins. I can picture Marion Webb, but she seemed "old" to me in high school and she's lame, poor thing. It's just too bad there aren't more people your age around the village, but I guess they're all married by now, aren't they? And here we are, both still on the shelf! Sometimes I'm glad to be on my own like this. I've always enjoyed going out to work and having my own money, but there are times when I think it would be nice to have a home and kids. The other day I saw this family. They were looking at Macy's windows which are all decorated for Christmas. The woman was about my age and pretty enough, but her husband!!! Was he a doll! He could easily have been in the movies. And they had these two cute young-sters, a boy and a girl. I have to admit I envied that woman. Oh well! Maybe Prince Charming is out there somewhere among these millions.

Do you remember me telling you about Marty and Ida Hirsch who run a theatre group? They asked me to read for a part in a play they've written, and a week ago I went down to this place on Houston Street. It's just a big hall on the third floor of this old factory, but they've made it into a kind of auditorium with a stage and a lot of chairs. There were about thirty people there and they call themselves the New World Players. They are planning to put on a series of one-act plays this winter on what they call social realism. They are nice enough people but very serious about politics. Before we started reading for the parts, there was a meeting and this guy gave a talk on how things are done in Russia. I didn't catch his name but he writes for a newspaper called *The Daily Worker.* He talked about capitalism and Communism and how there is no unemployment in Russia because the people there are looked after by the government.

Do you follow these things? History and civics were never my strong points in school. Anyway, I read for the part and I got it. I play this rich man's daughter-in-law. He owns a big factory where the workers are so poorly paid that they go on strike. His son has an argument with him because he thinks his father is being unfair and so he joins the strikers on the picket line and he's killed by a gang of thugs hired by the father to break the strike. I have a big speech over his dead body about exploiting the workers and so on. To me, the play is awfully preachy, but everyone else seems to think it's wonderful.

I'm keeping busy with the doctor show and more commercial work. The Wintergreen Toothpowder people really like me when I say, "Wintergreen makes your teeth shine, shine, shine!" There's a cute little tune that goes with that. You would hate it!! Evelyn is worried that my voice might become a little too familiar on the air so she's after me to be choosy about what I do. "Fair enough, Evelyn," I tell her, "but I have to eat and pay the rent." Evelyn lives in this swanky apartment overlooking Central Park (Jessica Dragonette lives in the same building, for goodness' sake), so E. tends to forget that poor working girls like me have got to earn a living. Jack and Doris have been terrific about inviting me to dinner, but I don't want to wear out my welcome. I don't think I could have survived without the Halperns.

What a fuss they made down here last week over that little French-Canadian doctor who delivered the quints! His mug was in all the papers and last Sunday night he gave a talk in Carnegie Hall. Carnegie Hall!!! They put him up at the Ritz-Carlton and practically gave him the keys to the city. Of course, when you tell people you're a Canadian, they think you lived in a cabin like Madame Dionne. Personally I think that having five kids at a time is too much like a dog having a litter of pups, but people down here just think it's the cutest thing and Doc Dafoe came across as a kindly old gent full of folksy wisdom. I'm beginning to sound like Evelyn. You should hear her go on about Shirley Temple.

I think I'll buy a radio with the money you sent, a nice little table model. It's funny. Here I am working in radio and I don't even own one. So I'll say goodbye for now and take care of yourself.

Love, Nora

P.S. Why would you write a poem about that dirty old Henry Hill and Father's overcoat? Aren't there nicer things to write about?

Whitfield, Ontario
Sunday, December 16, 1934

Dear Nora,

Just back from church and thought I'd drop you a line. Mr. Cameron introduced our new minister this morning and he delivered the sermon. All fire and brimstone! He sounds more like a Baptist preacher than a United Church man. His name is Jackson and he preached here for two or three Sundays in July. I didn't like him then and I don't like him now. Zealots just get my back up; I suppose I just don't like being reminded of my many spiritual imperfections every Sunday morning. Jackson would certainly not have been my choice, but many appear to like his old-fashioned evangelical style. His wife is a shy, pretty little woman and was sitting with the Atkins. I can see her being bullied by the likes of Ida Atkins and Cora Macfarlane.

After a mild spell, it's cold again up here and thank goodness I have mastered the art of keeping "the monster in the cellar" happy. I know now just how much to feed him and when to leave him alone to grumble away and digest his coals and keep me warm. That is our bargain: my labour for his heat. As I go about all this, I can't help thinking of those who are unable to afford a ton of good coal and who will have to make do this winter with green wood or lumberyard scraps. Many families are really up against it and I see it more and more every day now that the weather has turned around. This week a number of the children came to school wearing only light dresses and without coats or leggings. The Kray brothers are always half-dressed, though I suppose they would be in the best of times. Others are evidently without the means to clothe themselves. On Friday Clayton Tunney arrived, late as usual, in a pelting rain, wearing only a sweater and short pants. His hands were so chapped he could barely turn the pages of his reader. It's all very worrying and yesterday's *Herald* had a story about a man over in Linden who hanged himself in a railway shed last Sunday morning, leaving a wife and six children. Apparently he'd been laid off by the railway and couldn't bear the thought of going on relief. According to the paper, there was thirty-five cents in the house on the day he died. I keep wondering what was going through the poor fellow's mind as he fastened the rope around his neck and kicked away the bench. Or however he did it. They are taking up a collection for the family and I'm going to send a couple of dollars. I imagine there must be many such stories in that city of yours. I sometimes wonder if the politicians will ever sort out this problem of getting men back to work.

At least the Christmas concert can take people's minds off things, though I'm glad it's over for another year. On Saturday night as I played "Away in a Manger" for perhaps the hundredth time, I wondered if I would still be doing this in twenty years. In my mind's eye I could see a spare, dry woman of fifty-one in a black dress playing the piano while she watched the children of these children in bathrobes gathering by the doll in the crib. Behind the curtain on the stepladder, a spry sixty-year-old Alice Campbell was still throwing handfuls of confetti onto the sacred scene. I have always wondered about that "snow" in Palestine. It's startling, however, to realize that I've been playing for these concerts since I was sixteen. Do you remember when I took over from Mrs. Hamilton? You were in your entrance year and played one of the ghosts in a scene from *A Christmas Carol*. George Martin played Scrooge and forgot practically all his lines. This year his little boy Donald was one of the shepherds. Who says time isn't fleeting?

Last week I sent a little Christmas package, which I hope will reach you before the holiday. Please don't bother with anything for me. I'm sure that you are busy these days and of course money can't be all that plentiful. So nothing, please. I mean that, Nora.

All the best, Clara

P.S. Henry Hill and Father's overcoat are perfectly good subjects for a poem. The "niceness" of something, whatever that means, has nothing to do with it.

Monday, December 17 (1:30 a.m.)

Notes for a poem entitled *To a Thirty-Eight-Year-Old Father of Six Who Hanged Himself One Sunday Morning in a Railway Shed*.

It happened a week ago perhaps as I was walking to church, enjoying the freakishly mild weather. Your final Sunday felt almost like a late-September morning with its pale sunlit sky. There are things I would like to know. Were the children still sleeping when you closed the kitchen door a final time? Had you looked in on them before you left or is that just sentimental invention? When you think of it, who could bear to? Much better to walk away without a backward glance. But then perhaps you had not yet decided. When are such decisions made anyway? Are they thought through the night before or seized upon in some despairing moment? Your mind was unsettled after a sleepless night. You felt tired, a little dazed. There had been only minutes when you slept (or so it seemed). Between the hours of staring at the darkened shapes (the ceiling, the dresser, the chair, your wife's sleeping body), you lay half-listening to her troubled dream-words, the sighs and whispers born of worry and exhaustion. Perhaps before she slept you talked and the house with its tarpaper sides and cold hallways listened to the murmur of your long-married voices in a back bedroom.

"What are we going to do now Bert?"

"I don't know."

"You'll have to go down Monday morning and see the relief people."

You are about to say something but the baby stirs and whimpers, and your wife must get up and attend to the child. It's her job and you watch her bend across the crib or perhaps you don't. After all, you've seen her do it so many times over the years. Then bedsprings creak again as she settles in beside you.

"Did you hear what I said, Bert? You'll have to go down and talk to the relief people on Monday."

"I can't do that."

The words imprisoned in your head all day are now set free. The mere thought of dealing with those people can inflame your nerves.

"Well, you'll just have to, that's all. You know as well as I do, we're up against it."

But perhaps there were no words in bed the night before you died. Perhaps they had been said so many times before that your wife turned on her side and quickly fell asleep.

Now it is your last Sunday morning and she stands by the stove stirring the oatmeal. You watch her back and her bare feet in the mules. Your two oldest children are still sleeping but the other four are now at the table, tugging and pushing one another as children do awaiting breakfast. In his high chair the baby is excited and raps his spoon against the table. You see the corn syrup and the teapot and the milk bottle. When you opened the door, did your wife ask where you were going? Or were they used to you by now, accustomed to the ways of a quiet man who liked to be alone? "Daddy's going for his walk."

And so you went out into the Sunday morning streets, passing the churchgoers and the idlers leaning against the bank, leaving behind at last the houses and stores to cross the tracks behind the station. For a railway man, it wasn't hard to break the lock on that shed door. And what did you see in that place you chose for death? Pale sunlight through a cobwebbed window. Your entrance must have stirred the dust motes which settled finally on the shovels and the mattocks, on the iron wheel in the corner, and the overalls on the pegs against the wall, on the length of greasy rope and the girlie calendar. What were you thinking of as you looped the rope across the beam and made your knot? Hanging is a man's choice for death. A woman swallows Paris green, or steps in front of a freight train's yellow eye. What finally did you see, father of six? Were you looking at the floor or at the window with its patch of sky and cobweb? Or did you close your eyes before you kicked away that bench?

Tatham House
138 East 38th Street
New York
December 23, 1934

Dear Clara,

Your package arrived and, of course, I opened it. You know me! I could never wait until Christmas. The sweater is lovely and a perfect fit. Thanks so much. I've had so many compliments on it from the girls here. I've sent off a little something for you too, so there's no point in getting mad at me. I can buy my sister a Christmas present if I want to. But I certainly didn't get it in any swanky shop, believe me. It was just something I saw in the window of a store on Thirty-fourth Street, and as soon as I saw it, I thought, That's Clara! So Merry Christmas. I know it will be New Year's by the time you get it, but better late than never.

I went to Evelyn's last night for dinner. I felt kind of bad because earlier I'd arranged to go to the movies with a couple of girls here, but I wanted to see what kind of place Evelyn has. And you should see it! She lives in the San Remo Apartments on Central Park West. That's just about the ritziest part of town. Did I mention before that the radio singer Jessica Dragonette is in the same building? Evelyn has a Negro maid who served us drinks and dinner. Lamb chops and these wonderful little roasted potatoes and wine. Her apartment is filled with books and paintings and she has this enormous radio and phonograph machine. We listed to Gershwin and Porter show tunes and talked about "The House on Chestnut Street." Evelyn wanted to know all about Whitfield and what it was like growing up there. She was an only child and went to a fancy boarding school, so she was keen to find out what life was like in a small town. She wanted to know all about you and so naturally I told her that you are a schoolteacher who likes to write poetry and are obviously the brains in the family. I told her that we were raised by our father because Mother died when we were little kids. And I told her how I never really got along very well with Father, but that you seemed to know how to manage him. All kinds of family stuff. Evelyn would love to meet you and I think you'd like her. You're similar in many ways. Very critical of things in general. Oh, you'd have to learn how to tolerate her smoking and drinking, but I bet you'd find her terrifically interesting.

Well, this will be our first Christmas without Father and it feels kind of strange, doesn't it? I hope you don't find it too lonesome being there by yourself. The Halperns invited me to their place for dinner, which I thought was very considerate because being Jewish they don't celebrate Christmas. A few of the girls here who aren't going home for the holidays are having a little get-together on Christmas night and so maybe I'll look in on that too. The girls here are mostly my age or maybe a little younger. Most of them are secretaries and a few have pretty good jobs in some of the big department stores. One woman is a buyer for Gimbels and another woman named Frances is a nurse at Bellevue. That's a big psychiatric hospital and some of the stories she tells would make your hair stand on end.

When I look back at what I've written about my dinner with Evelyn in her swanky place, I can imagine you thinking, Well, there's Nora down in New York, living the life of Riley while thousands of people haven't got any jobs or money. I remember your story about that poor man in Linden. But I don't want you to think that I'm unfeeling. I see a lot of people on the streets down here who don't look too well off, but I don't know what I can do about it. I think Mr. Roosevelt is on the right track and things are picking up. I believe we have to look on the bright side if we want to get anywhere. I'll be thinking of you on Christmas Day, Clara. Hope you like your present.

Love, Nora

Monday, December 31

Letter from Nora who seems to be thriving in the great metropolis. Where does she get her ambition and enthusiasm? These characteristics are surely passed along through the blood. How did Yeats put it? "The fury and the mire of human veins." She can't have inherited any of this from Father who seemed content enough to spend his days in this village. Yet *seemed* is perhaps the correct verb, for how do I know how he really felt? Father was so closed-in about everything. As for Mother, I can't remember her doing anything but reading books and taking long walks.

Retirement party for the Camerons yesterday evening in the church hall. Ida Atkins in charge of the proceedings. It has not taken her long to boss around the new minister's wife. Helen Jackson is such a meek little thing. Confessed that she likes to read. Enjoys the novels of Lloyd C. Douglas and A. J. Cronin. Well, yes, I can see that but she also admits to an admiration for Emily Dickinson, which is a fine surprise. Husband standing apart with hands behind his back, rocking on his heels. Above all this female chatter. Ida Atkins's tiresome recruiting. "Now, Helen, you must help us to persuade Clara to get out of the house this winter. She has so much to offer our church. Her father passed away last spring. A wonderful man," etc., etc. Can she not detect my hostility, or am I simply too hypocritical and cowardly? I think I am a little.

A title for a poem came to me this afternoon. *Onset of Evening in Winter, 1934.* A painting in words. At dusk a woman is at the piano playing Mendelssohn's *Songs Without Words.* The oncoming night will be cold and so before she sat down to play she moved the bowl of African violets from the window ledge to the mantel. Now she looks out at the falling snow as she plays. What is she thinking of? The elusive nature of happiness. How it arrives unbidden, a brief thrilling moment, summoned perhaps by a smell, a line of verse, a melody. In the senses may be found our source of joy. How it alights upon the heart like a colourful and mysterious bird upon a winter branch. Now what on earth did I mean by all that? It was only a glimpse of what I was trying to get at, but it was all nonsense anyway. A woman at the piano looking out at falling snow! I blame Mendelssohn's lovely little tunes for turning me into such a wistful Sally. Decided it was time to throw some coal into the maw of the monster. That at least is honest labour, duly rewarded.

Austin Clarke

Austin Clarke is one of Canada's most accomplished and well-loved authors. Born in St. James, Barbados, Clarke came to Canada in 1955 to study at the University of Toronto. While pursuing a career in journalism, he began to write fiction, weaving his memories of a Barbadian childhood together with colonial and post-colonial themes as well as his personal experience of Canadian culture.

Clarke is the author of eleven novels and six short story collections, including *Choosing His Coffin: The Best Stories of Austin Clarke* (2004). Recurring subjects in Clarke's work explore black identity in North America, experiences of colonial and post-colonial culture, and varieties of immigrant life in Canada. His memoirs, *Growing Up Stupid Under the Union Jack* (1980) and *Love and Sweet Food: A Culinary Memoir* (1999), ably blend social commentary with warmly humorous reminiscences. *Growing Up Stupid* won the 1980 Casa de las Americas Literary Prize.

Clarke won the 1999 W.O. Mitchell Literary Prize, awarded each year to a Canadian writer who has produced an outstanding body of work and served as a mentor to other writers. *The Polished Hoe* (2002) won The Giller Prize (2002), the 16th annual Trillium Book Award, and the Commonwealth Writers' Prize for Best Book. It was also a finalist for the Hurston/Wright Legacy Award. His most recent novel, *More* (2008), was nominated for the 2008 Scotiabank Giller Prize. Clarke currently lives in Toronto.

The Polished Hoe

BY AUSTIN CLARKE

Winner 2002

≈

PART ONE

"**M**y name is Mary. People in this Village call me Mary-Mathilda. Or, Tilda, for short. To my mother I was Mary-girl. My names I am christen with are Mary Gertrude Mathilda, but I don't use Gertrude, because my maid has the same name. My surname that people 'bout-here uses, is either Paul, or Bellfeels, depending who you speak to ..."

"Everybody in Flagstaff Village knows you as Miss Bellfeels, ma'am," the Constable says. "And they respects you."

"Nevertheless, Bellfeels is not the name I want attach to this Statement that I giving you ..."

"I will write-down that, ma'am, as you tell it to me. But ..."

"This Sunday evening," she says, interrupting him, "a little earlier, round seven o'clock, I walked outta here, taking the track through the valley; past the two stables converted into a cottage; past the sheep pens and the goat pens, and fowl coops; and through the grove of fruit trees until I came to the Front-Road, walking between two fields of canes. In total darkness. But I knew the way, like the back of my two hands. Now, where we are in this Great House is the extremity of the Plantation Houses, meaning the furtherest away from the Main House, with six other houses, intervening. These consist of the house the Bookkeeper occupies; one for the Overseer, Mr. Lawrence Burkhart, who we call the Driver—that's the smallest house; one for the Assistant Manager, a Englishman, which is the third biggest after the Main House; and there is a lil hut for the watchman, Watchie; and then there is this Great House where we are. The Main House have three floors, to look over the entire estate of the Plantation, like a tower in a castle. To spy on everybody. Every-other house has two floors. Like this one. That would give you, in case you never been so close to this Plantation before, the lay of the land and of things; the division of work and of household."

"I sees this Plantation only from a distance, ma'am. I know it from a distance only," the Constable says.

"It was dark, and I couldn't see even my two hands outstretch in front of me. I took the way from here, right through the valley where the track cuts through it. I could make out the canes on both sides of me; and I could hear them shaking, as there was a steady wind the whole evening; the kind of wind that comes just before a heavy downpour of rain, like before a hurricane. They were 'arrows' shooting-out from the tops of canes. Crop-Season, as you well-know, is in full swing; and the Factory grinding canes, day and night. You could smell the crack-liquor, the fresh cane juice, strong-strong! What a sweet, but sickening smell cane juice is, when you smell it from near!

"Wilberforce, my son, who was home earlier, is my witness to the hour I left ...

"Have I told you about Wilberforce, yet? No? Pardon me. The memory is fading, Constable, the memory. The mind not sharp no more, and ... very often ... What was I telling you about?"

"You was talking about your son, Mr. Wilberforce, the doctor, ma'am."

"Yes! Wilberforce! My first-born. He isn't really the first of my thrildren I give birth to. He's the one outta the three who livedpast childbirth.

"Wilberforce, always with his head always inside a book, I keep telling him that with all that book-learning retain in his head, if he's not careful, he going burst his blasted brains!

"He, I gave birth to, in the year nineteen ... I told you that, didn't I?"

"You didn't tell me when Mr. Wilberforce born, ma'am."

"Nevertheless. Two more thrildren I had. A boy and a girl. I gave them the names I intended to christen them with, if they hadlive. William Henry. Two names I took from a English magazine. And Rachelle Sarah Prudence, the girl. Lovely English names I named my two dead thrildren with. One died eighteen months after the first one. The boy.

"My third-born, Wilberforce, became therefore my first-born. A mother's pride and joy.

"Wilberforce went to the best schools in this Island of Bimshire. Then overseas. He travel to countries like Italy, France, Austria and Europe; and when he return-back here to this Island, he start behaving more like a European than somebody born here. But, at least, he came back with his ambition fulfill. A Doctor. Of Tropical Medicines.

"Whereas, had the other two thrildren survive, I wanted them to followin the path of the Law. They would have made such lovely barsters-at-Law! You don't think so?"

"Yes, ma'am," the Constable says.

"My sweet boy-child, William Henry; and lovely Rachelle Sarah Prudence, the girl.

"Yes, Constable. Me. I, Mary-Mathilda ... I, Mary Gertrude Mathilda, although I don't use Gertrude, as I told you ..."

"Yes, ma'am."

"... left inside-here at seven o'clock this evening, and walked the four hundred and something yards from here to the Plantation Main House, and it take me fifteen minutes time to arrive there; and ..."

"Which night you mean, ma'am, when you left your residence of abode?"

"Which night I took the walk? Was it Saturday night, last night, or tonight Sunday night, is what you getting at?"

"I mean that, too, ma'am. But what I really getting at, is if the moon was shining when you leff your home and place of abode, on the night in question, walking to your destination? Or if you was walking in the rain. 'Cause with rain, I have to refer to footsteps. They bound to be footprints ..."

"If there are footsteps, those would be my prints in the ground, Constable. Bold and strong and deep-deep; deep-enough for water to collect in them. Deep-enough to match the temperriment I was in. I can tell you that my determination was strong.

"It was dark-dark, earlier tonight. But in that darkness, I was not hiding from anybody. Not from the Law; not from God; not from my conscience, as I walked in the valley of the shadow of darkness and of death. No. There was no moon. But I was not a thief, craving the darkness, and dodging from detection. Oh, no!

"A long time ago, before tonight, I decided to stop walking in darkness.

"With that temperriment and determination of mind, I firststarted, on a regular basis, to polish my hoe. And to pass a grinding-stone dip in cargrease, along the blade, since September the fifteenth last-gone; September, October, November just-pass, is three months; and every day for those months, night after night as God send, more than I can call-to-mind. And I have to laugh, why, all-of-a sudden, I went back to a hoe, I had-first-used when I was a girl, working in the cane fields, not quite eight years of age. The same hoe, weeding young canes, sweet potato slips, 'eight-weeks' yams, eddoes, all those ground provisions.

"This hoe that I used all those years, in the North Field, is the same hoe I used this Sunday night.

"If it wasn't so black outside, you could look through that window you sitting beside, and see the North Field I refer to, vast and green and thick with sugar cane, stretching for acres and acres, beyond the reach of your eyes, unmeasuring as the sea ...

"So, no, Constable. I was not seeking the shadows of night, even though the moon wasn't shining!

"I already stated to you that at seven o'clock, the hour in question, it was like a full moon was shining, by which I mean, as the saying in this Village goes, a full-moon alters the way men behave—and women, too!—turns them into lunatics, and—"

"Pardon me, ma'am. But on the telephone to the sub-station, in your perlimary Statement to Sargeant, Sargeant say that you say the night was dark, and no moon wasn't shining. Is so, Sargeant tell me to write down your Statement, in my notebook, using your exact words. So, I hope that I not stating now, in-front-'o-you, what you didn't state, nor intend to state, in your telephone Statement, ma'am?

"Sargeant send me to get your Statement offa you before he come himself. All we know is what you say when you call, that something happen, and you want Sargeant to come, and take your Statement, first-hand, from you. We don't know what happen and we don't yet know what is the circumstances. Sargeant would look after that. He say to say he have another important assignment. I am consequently here until Sargeant comes. But Sargeant coming ..."

"Soon, I hope."

"Sargeant soon will be here."

"... and so, what I mean by a bright night and the moon shining, is merely a comparison of my disposition towards darkness and light; something, as Wilberforce calls it, like the ironies of life. *Ironies*. He uses it all the time, and would say, 'Sitting down to eat food is full of ironies.' 'Life is full of ironies.' 'A full moon is full of ironies.' That is Wilberforce favourite word for it. *Ironies*.

"When there is a full moon, people behave strange. But tonight, with no moon at all, my behaviour was still strange, granted.

"Tonight, the thirteenth, a Sunday, in spite of no moon, the act that I committed, however the people in this Island wish to label it, is not a act, or behaviour of a woman ruled by a full moon; nor of a woman who chooses darkness over light, to move in, or to hide her act in.

"My footprints that you say might be evidence, was, in the darkness, strong footprints, if not stronger even than my temperriment itself. And my act went along with that. I was determined. And deliberate. Because I knew what my cause was. And I had a cause."

The lights dip from their brilliance; and for just one second, it is dark in the front-house, where they are; dark, as when, long ago, the wind would run through these same windows, and brush aside the flames from the mantles of the large acetylene lamps that have *Home Sweet Home* printed in white letters on their polished lampshades. Just for one moment, that moment that it takes for a mouse the same colour as the carpet to steal into a corner.

But wind cannot play those tricks with the electric lighting. The two bulbs hang low, just above their heads, from two long, ugly brown electrical wires, on which, during the day, and especially late at night, flies and other bugs make their homes, and their graves; and are stuck to death. The wind continues pushing itself through the windows, and brings on its breath the smell of flowers, poinsettia and lady-of-the-night and the strong smell of sugar-cane juice from the Factory. And the lingering intoxicating smell of burnt sugar canes; and the pungency of burnt cane trash, comes into the front-house with them ...

"From the time, way-way back, when Ma, my mother, out of need, sent me while I was still a lil girl, seven or eight, to the Plantation to work in the fields, from that time, I had a cause. And in particular from that day, when the midwife delivered Wilberforce, I have had a cause.

"And I am very sorry to have to talk this way to you, a Constable, sitting in my front-house, on a Sunday night, filling in for Sargeant, who promise me faithfully, to come later, and take my Statement.

"Incidentally, Sargeant and me, went-school together. Did you know that? He was always inquisitive. Always hunting-down answers. And lizards which he put in cigarette boxes, as coffins, to bury them. Now, we are from two different sides of the paling. But ..."

"How I should write-down your name, in its official status, ma'am?"

"My name is Mary-Mathilda. My full name is Mary Gertrude Mathilda. But I drop Gertrude because of my maid."

"The whole Village know your names and your surnames, ma'am. And they worships you."

"It began, this whole thing, many-many years ago, on a Sunday. A Sunday morning, close to midday, about ten-to-twelve o'clock. We were in the Church Yard of Sin-Davids Anglican Church. Near the graves and tombs and tombstones; where they buried Englishmen and sailors from Lord Horatio Nelson's fleet that went down in these waters.

"I remember that my shoes were burning my feet. And I had slip them off. To ease the pain. All through the sermon that the Vicar, Revern Dowd, was delivering from the pulpit, so high and powerful; above my head; high as the water tank in the Plantation Yard ... I couldn't follow one word that Vicar Dowd was talking, from so on high. His words were too big for me.

"Some words passed my ear, though. I remember that Revern Dowd had-take his sermon from One, Sin-Peter, three, seventeen. Whether I remember it on my own, or Ma had-remind me afterwards, Revern Dowd was saying how it is more better for a man to suffer for his well-doing, than for his evil-doing. I remember only those words, from that Sunday.

"It is better, if the will of God be so, that a man suffer for well-doing, than for evil-doing.

"Those were the words. I have walked with that text in my heart, since that Sunday. And if, right-now, you open my Bible there on that mahogany centre-table with the white crochet-cloth on it, you will see the text, mark by a palm-leaf cross from last Palm Sunday, One, Sin-Peter, three, seventeen ...

"It is better to suffer for well-doing, than ...

"I was a lil girl, then; no more than seven or eight; in such pain from my new shoes. My new shoes weren't purchase new, from Cave Shepherd & Sons, the Haberdasheries store down in Town. They was a pair that the youngest daughter of Mr. Bellfeels had grown outta. Hand-me-downs. Not through inheritance; but cast-aways. They were new to me, though. Mr. Bellfeels daughter, Miss Emonie, was the same size as me, in clothes and in height. But her shoes pinched like hell, because her feet were white feet; and very narrow.

"That Sunday morning was in the Easter season! It was Easter Even."

"If you don't mind me saying so, ma'am," the Constable says, "Easter is the time I like best outta the whole year o' going-church. Easter! Easter morning, with the singing of carols and psalms! *'O, all ye beasts of the sea!'*

'Praise Him, and glorify Him, forever!'

"And the sermon does be so sweet. But long. And then, after Easter, is Easter bank holiday! And flying kites! And holding goat-races!"

"The Collect that Sunday, the morning of Easter Even ... though I can't naturally call-to-mind the entire Collect, I remember this passage: '... *and that through the grave, and the gate of hell, we may pass to our joyful resurrection ...*'"

"What that mean, ma,am," the Constable says.

"*Resurrection,*" she says.

"*Amen!*" the Constable says.

"*We may pass to our joyful resurrection. Amen.*"

"For the carol-singing and the sermons, gimme Easter to Christmas, any Sunday morning, ma'am!"

"So, it was that on that same Sunday morning, Ma introduce me to this powerful man. Mr. Bellfeels. He wasn't Plantation manager then; just a field overseer. A driver, as we labourers called such men. Mr. Bellfeels the Driver.

"Ma was in the gang of women weeding in the North Field. In time, that same North Field was assign to me. And in time, because I was young and vigorous, I became the leader of the same gang of women.

"The sun was bright that Sunday morning of Easter Even. And it was in my face. So, I couldn't see his eyes. Mr. Bellfeels looked so tall, like the pulpit or the water tower, that I had to hold my head back, back, back, to look in his face. And still, I couldn't see his face, clear. This man who looked so tall, and me, a little girl, in pain from wearing his own daughter's shoes that was killing me.

"The sun was playing tricks in his face, too. So, neither of the two of we could see the other person too clear. But he could see my face, because he was looking down.

"Then, Mr. Bellfeels put his riding-crop under my chin, and raise my face to meet his face, using the riding-crop; and when his eyes and my eyes made four, he passed the riding-crop down my neck, right down the front of my dress, until it reach my waist. And then he move the riding-crop right back up again, as if he was drawing something on my body.

"And Ma, stanning-up beside me, with her two eyes looking down at the loose marl in the Church Yard, looking at the graves covered by slabs of marble, looking at the ground. Ma had her attention focused on something on the ground. My mother. Not on me, her own daughter.

"I could smell the rich, strong smell of the leather, just like the leather in the seats and upholstery of the Austin-Healey motor-car that Mr. Bellfeels own. Like the smell of new leather rising in my nose, when I stand in the shoemaker's galvanized shack, and watch him stitch-round the sole, with his awl, making a pair of boots. That smell. That smell of leather. And the feel of leather of the riding crop, passing over my dress, all over my body, as if it was his hand crawling over my body; and I was naked.

"That Sunday morning, in the bright shining sun, with Ma stanning-up there, voiceless, as if the riding-crop was Mr. Bellfeels finger clasped to her lips, clamped to her mouth to strike her dumb to keep her silence, to keep her peace. From that Sunday morning, the meaning of poverty was driven into my head. The sickening power of poverty. Like the smell of leather, disintegrating from animal skin into raw leather, curing in water; soaking in clean water that becomes mildew, before it is tanned and turn into leather, when it is nothing more than pure, dead, rotten, stinking skin. Froma animal.

"'So, this is lil Mary!' Mr. Bellfeels say.

"'Yes,' Ma told Mr. Bellfeels, 'This is my little Mary.'

"'Good,' Mr. Bellfeels say.

"And not a word more. And then, all of a sudden, the sun that had-went suddenly behind a cloud came out again, and was shining more brighter, and the light had-changed the same way, as in the story that we listened to in Sunday school from Bible Stories for Children. Like a miracle of light, this brightness ... and in this brightness cut short, there was this darkness; and in this blackness, Mr. Bellfeels disappeared.

"And me and Ma walked home. Not a word pass from Ma to me, in our entire journey from the Church Yard, passing the houses on the Plantation property, the Great House, the cottage made from two stables, passing the Pasture some distance from the Harlem Bar & Grill rum shop, cross-over Highgates Commons and Reservoir Lane, the crossroads that divide the Village from the Plantation, through the cane-brake, through the gully, through the other gullies growing Guinea grass and Khus-Khus grass; circumventing the North Field, and fields and lands of the Plantation ... it was the season for dunks. And we picked a few, and ate them while walking, as our journey consisted of a distance of some length, a mile, a mile and a half from Sin-Davids Anglican Church, to our house beside the road, but in the tenantry, on Plantation land.

"That Sunday, we had the usual food after Church. Me and Ma. Dry-peas and rice. The peas was prepared as doved-peas. The rice cooked with a lil salt beef boil-down-in-it, to add flavour.

"Yes, that Sunday afternoon, after we left the Church Yard and Mr. Bellfeels, we ate roast chicken, doved-peas, and some sweet potatoes that Ma had-stole from the very North Field, the Friday afternoon; one-or-two potatoes, hide-way in her crocus bag apron. We had to steal from the Plantation, to make-do.

"'*I borrow these offa the Plantation*,' she told me the Friday, smiling and happy. '*In other words, I steal them, Mary-girl!*'

"Constable, you don't know those days! Lucky you! Days of hardships. But days of great joy and spirit, nevertheless. The joy of a tough life. Cutting and contriving. If you didn't have it, you found a way to get it. Or a neighbour would come to your rescue.

"Or you steal it. All of us, regardless to position, place, complexion, the Ten Commandments, we-all exacted something from the Plantation. A head of eddoes pull-up outta the ground; you brek-off a piece of cane and suck it, to bring up the gas outta your stomach; pull-off a few red-tomatoes offa the vine in the Plantation kitchen garden; and hide them in a crocus bag.

"Every last man-jack, all of us, devout Christian-minded men and women attending Sin-Davids Anglican Church, three times a Sunday, going to Mothers Union every Wednesday night as God send, we all extracted our due from the Plantation.

"But we paid. We paid dear. With our lives. Every-last-one-of-us!

"Well, you shouldn't be a stranger to this history. You were bred and born right here, in this Village, in this Island of Bimshire. You see? Here I go, wandering-off again ..."

"I learning a lot o' history from you, ma'am. My mother and my gran-mother tell me some o' the history of here."

"You remember Clotelle, then? Clotelle who leff-back three nice lil girl-thrildren, when death grab her sudden, and unaware?

"Clotelle, who was always dress in black. From head to foot, mourning like a N'Eyetalian-'snora, as if mourning for a dead husband? Only thing, Clotelle never had one.

"But the Sunday morning, just before Matins, they found Clotelle henging from the tamarind tree in the Plantation Yard? And nobody didn't know how she got there? And it was Ma who Mr. Bellfeels ordered to cut down Clotelle, cause the Plantation-people was too ashamed and embarrass, and too scornful to touch a dead-body? And how, following after all the fuss that Clotelle mother made over the sudden death of her only child, they held the attopsy. And lo and behold, the attopsy disclose that Clotelle was five months' heavy, in the family-way! But it didn't take tummuch for the whole Village to know who the father was? And ..."

"I hear this from my gran-mother. They made a calypso on Clotelle."

"It climb to number one on the hit parade. It was a sweet calypso, too. It lasted one week ...

"Ma tell me she was sixteen when that sad tragedy happened to Clotelle. Ma tell me that she saw Clotelle laying down in the cane-brake, with her face washed in tears; and bleeding; and that it was later the same night, in all the rain, that Clotelle climbed up the tamarind tree; and how Clotelle had-use pieces of cloth that she rip-off from her own dress, with all the blood and all the man's semen staining it; and how Clotelle make a rope outta her own dress, and wrap-it-round the highest branch she could reach in the tamarind tree, and the rest you know. Yes. The rest you know. The *ironies* of history and of life, as Wilberforce like to say. Henging from the tamarind tree, in broad daylight the next day Sunday morning, they found Clotelle, just as Mr. Darnley Alexander Randall Bellfeels, and Mistress Bellfeels, and the two girl-thrildren, Miss Euralie and Miss Emonie, was stepping down the verandah of the Plantation Main House, to cross the gravel path, to get in the Austin-Healey motor-car, the chauffeur holding the door open for them to get in, to be driven to attend Matins at Sin-Davids Anglican Church, 'leven-o'clock-in-the-morning; butting and bounding the schoolhouse building where you went to Elementary School."

There is total deep silence. It seems as if the room descends also into darkness. Silence and darkness. And when the darkness rises, and the silence is broken, it is her voice humming the chorus of the calypso that remembers Clotelle's tragedy, that made the hit parade.

> "'Who full she up,
> And tie she up,
> Could cut she down.'

"Golbourne, now ..."

"I remember the whole song," the Constable says. "My gran-mother tell me that the tamarind tree in the Plantation Yard that Clotelle henged her-self from is a famous tree. One day, during slavery, my gran-mother say, they henged a slave, after they give him forty lashes, with a balata, for stealing a fowl; and they henged him from the same tamarind tree as Clotelle was henging from; and following ever-since from that day, all the tamarinds that this tamarind tree bear, have seeds the shape of a man's head. The head of the slave that they flogged and afterwards henged. Right here in Bimshire."

"You have a good memory. You are going to make a proper detective, following in the footsteps of Sargeant. Yes. Your gran knew the history of this Island backwards."

"Concerning the calypso, the part you just sang, that is the chorus ..."

"You have the memory of a barster-at-Law."

"I used to sing it!"

"Golbourne, now ... as I was saying, is a different story. Today, anybody who was to rest his two eyes on Golbourne, walking-'bout Flagstaff Village, with his goadies bulging through his pants, meaning his two enlarge testicles, the size of two breadfruits, wobbling-'bout inside his oversize pants, built specially by the tailor to commodate Golbourne's two things, anybody who see Golbourne in his present state would conclude that Golbourne born so. Not at all, Constable! Golbourne wasn't born with this disfiguration, looking like the Frenchman-fellow Wilberforce talks about, the man who used to ring the bells of Notre Dame Cathedral Church, somewhere in Paris-France. The Hunchback! Oh, no! Golbourne was a model of manhood. One of the most masculine men to ever walk this earth! Golbourne was such a man, in his prime, that I-myself ...

"But that night, twenty, twenty-something years ago, walking-cross the gap leading from the Plantation to the Village, holding hands with the nursemaid to the Plantation thrildren, walking her home, his bicycle in his next hand, Lord! Mr. Bellfeels two motor-car headlights picked them out, as he was returning from seeing a movie at the Empire Theatre. Those two high-beam lights picked Golbourne out before Golbourne could jump in the gutter to safety, and hide. That was the night-before. The Saturday. And Mr. Bellfeels lay-wait for Golbourne the following night, the Sunday, to see if he was going walk-home the nursemaid.

"That tragic night was a dark night. Mr. Bellfeels was in the canes of that section of the North Field, hiding. The canes were tall and green. And when Mr. Bellfeels stop beating Golbourne with his riding-crop, followed-up with kicks from his brown leather Wellingtons, in Golbourne's two groins, what you see today, in respect of the sameness in posture with the Hunchback of

Notre Dame, is the direct result of the venom in the beating administered by Mr. Bellfeels on Golbourne.

"Mr. Bellfeels, that avaricious man, had his hand buried inside Golbourne's pot. All this came out in the wash. Mr. Bellfeels had-wanted everything for himself. A man with such needs and wishes, my God!"

"My gran-mother tell me that Golbourne was the fastest body-line fast-bowler the Island o' Bimshire ever produce," says the Constable. "Appearing for the Flagstaff First Eleven Cricket Team, Golbourne, my gran-mother tell me, was more faster than Voss, the great Australian fast-bowler. Golbourne was like a freight train, with the new ball. Men uses to tremble when they had to face Golbourne, opening the bowling from the Plantation End, whiching is the north end, near the North Field. Men uses to wet their pants … I beg your pardon, ma'am … when the captain send them out to face Golbourne."

"Yes, opening from the North Field, with the new ball!"

"Golbourne tek eight wickets one Saturday. In the first innings. For fif-teen runs. Is still the record in the whole Wessindies. And before the first water-break, not to mention before lunch. In three overs, when a over was still eight balls per over!"

"But the worst was Pounce," Mary-Mathilda says. "Pounce never trouble a living-soul. Well-mannered? Would doff his cloth hat to the lit-tlest, most humble person; and likewise, to the most lofty. Saying, 'Good morning, my-lady,' to every woman. 'Good evening, sir!' to child and adult-man alike. But won't enter a church if yuh gave him a jimmy-john full of the strongest Mount Gay dark rum. But never a Sunday pass that you didn't see Pounce stanning-up at the same church window, *outside*; but in full view of the pulpit, for Passover, for Easter and for Christmas. And there Pounce would be; listening to every word that drop from the lips of Revern James, Pastor of the Church of the Nazarene, just down Reservoir Lane, by the West Field.

"Pounce came from a poor family, but decent. And it was only for a few sweet potatoes, and pulp-eddoes, you hear me, Constable? Not even a whole hole of potatoes, then. I counted them myself. Cause Mr. Bellfeels had the lack of decency to bring the *same* pulp-eddoes and sweet potatoes that he shoot Pounce for, injuring him with a gun loaded with course-salt, to Ma; and ask Ma to cook them in the pigeon-pea soup she was making for his dinner. That son-of-a-bitch! Pardon my French, Constable …"

"I didn't hear you use no bad-words, ma'am. My two ears close!"

"Ma was working inside the Plantation Main House, by this time, as nursemaid, following the consequences to Golbourne's former girlfriend, who died all of a sudden, one Monday night. From the pining and a broken heart, appears. There were three sweet potatoes and four pulp-eddoes Pounce tried to steal. I counted them myself. One, two, three. Three. And one, two, three, four. Four. They didn't even weigh much more than one pound! From the North Field. I was now leading a gang of slightly older women, weeding the sweet potato slips, of that North Field ...

"Constable, I am rambling again! I don't know what got-me-off on this topic, talking about the history of this place. But this Plantation touch all of we. All our lives was branded by this Plantation. You see it there, with its tall chimney belching smoke from the Factory grinding canes at this time of year, Crop-Season; and with the smell of cane-juice boiling; and the noise of the Factory itself, the machineries that is always brekking-down. And this sweet, sickening smell, a smell that sticks to your clothes, and to your mind, like the rawness and the scales from fish, from a piece of shark that many a evening I watched Ma scale in the kitchen of that same Plantation Main House, when she was promoted from being a field hand, to combination nursemaid; later, to Chief Maid. The position was nothing more than chief-cook-and-bottle-washer! I am talking now about the War-days, the First World War, Ma's days. Nevertheless, the times I am now talking about is World War Two, when it look as if a real World War was taking place right-here-in-Bimshire. We didn't have no concentration camps. The people living in this Village wasn't put behind no barbed wire, such as what Wilberforce tell me was the treatment of many, Jews and non-Jews, and people called Gypsies ... Constable, I always thought that a Gypsy was the name for a woman with a lovely voice! Those bad things happened in the outside-world; in Europe. But in this part of the universe, the Wessindies, nobody didn't torture nobody, nor squeeze nobody balls, by applying pliers, or lectricity to anybody testicles to pull the truth from outta him. Nobody down here suffer-so. Nor behave brutal-so. But, according to the *ironies* of life, as Wilberforce would say, it was the same suffering, historically speaking, between living on this Plantation and living-through the War in Europe. Much of a muchness. When you think of it. The same War. The same taking of prisoners. The same bloodshed. And the same not taking of no prisoners. So, in the eyes of Europe, we couldda been the same as Jews. It was war, and the *ironies* of war. It was *war*, Constable.

"Lord, I remember these things as if it was yesterday. The Friday evening before the Sunday in the Church Yard, when Mr. Bellfeels passed his riding-crop, as if it was his hand, all over my body ... round four or five the Friday evening ...

"A lorry had just crawl-over the hill, in low gear, right in front our house; and that lorry was packed to overflowing, with canes; so much so that the lorry driver had to slow down, and change from low gear into the jewel gear, to get over the hill, poor fellow. The weight of the canes, the age of the lorry, the smoke and the exhaust from the engine was almost burying Mr. Broomes the lorry driver; poor soul; and when he back-down, back into the jewel gear, in order to get over the crest of the hill, Mr. Broomes, poor fellow, was almost buried alive in all this smoke and exhaust; and then, this pullet. A Bardrock hen. The stupid fowl decide at this very same minute, whether she got blind by the smoke and the exhaust, or else was thinking that day had turn-into night, through the smoke from the old lorry engine, decided to cross the road; and *blam!* Mr. Broomes tried his best to slam-on the brakes—*Scrrrrrrreeeeenk!*—but too late. The pullet lay fluttering. Mr. Broomes, poor fellow, couldn't extricate himself from outta the cab of the lorry fast-enough; or in time to rescue the Bardrock; or, put it in the cab and carry it home to his wife; nor could he stop the lorry. It was still on the incline of the hill. And a minute later, the whole lorry of canes start backing-back, by itself, back down the hill; and as Mr. Broomes was occupied with the safety of the lorry, and the load of canes, he couldn't think about laying claim to the pullet; plus, all the feathers was now joining-in with the clouds of exhaust smoke. I was looking out the window seeing all this, when Ma in the kitchen, hearing the screeling of the brakes, and the racket from the fowl, start screaming.

"'*Take it! Take it!*' Ma say. '*Take it, before somebody-else! Quick, before anybody see you taking it!*'

"Ma had just come home, carrying her crocus bag apron full with sweet potatoes, in one hand, and her weekly wages, in the other.

"'*Quick, Mary-girl, before anybody see!*'

"Well, I tell you, Constable, that that Friday evening was the day I committed my first act of sin.

"But, I tell you also, that that Bardrock pullet was put in warm water with lil salt and lime juice, to draw it, Friday evening and all Saturday; and on the Sunday morning, into the iron buck-pot with some eschalots, fresh thyme, lard-oil and hot nigger-peppers. And it grace our table the next day,

Sunday, the same Sunday that after Church, I came face-to-face the first time, with Mr. Bellfeels.

"We had that chicken with doved-peas, as I told you. I am relating these foolish things to you, at a time like this, when I should be giving you a Statement of my deeds and misdeeds, in this stage of my life. But ..."

"Better late than never, ma'am," the Constable says.

"This is my history in confession, better late than never, which in your police work is a Statement. And I wonder, as I sit here this Sunday evening, why I am giving you this history of my personal life, and the history of this Island of Bimshire, altogether, wrap-up in one?"

"MA SERVED ME the part of that Bardrock hen that has the wishbone, and ..."

"Did you break-it-off, for luck?"

"'Wish,' Ma tell me, whilst she was sucking-out the two eyes from the chicken head. 'Wish, Mary-girl! Wish for the whirl. For the stars! You may be a poor, only-child of a poor, confuse mother ... but the wish you wish, can still be rich! And big! Wish big! God will bring your wish to fruitions, and make you a powerful woman, on this very Plantation. So, wish big, Mary-girl! Wish!'

"Ma's hand, slippery from holding the chicken head, slip-off the wish-bone, so the whole wishbone remain inside my fingers, whole. Was it my fate?

"Well, Constable, I carried that wishbone for years; hoeing in the North Field with it; tending elementary school with it, pin-to-my-dress; every-where. I would sit in Sunday School and run my hand over it, and dream as I followed the words in the Bible story of Daniel in the lions den; and the flight of the Israelites walking miles and miles over the hard, scorch earth, crossing the Arabian Desert ... is it the Arabian Desert, or the Sahara ... crossing the Sahara; and all those rock-stones and cracks in the ground and in their feet, just like how the ground here in Bimshire gets hard and dry when the sun come out following a downpour of rain. And I would catch myself in these daydreams and fantasies, far-far from that little Sunday School classroom, at the back of the church, travelling miles and miles away from this Island of Bimshire. Picturing myself in foreign countries, in Europe and in Germany—even during the War—in Rome-Italy, living like a N'Eyetalian countessa, dress in a white gown, a robe edged in silver and gold piping; and with goblets of wine, and bowls of grapes and olives, laid out before me; and I am reclining, as I see Eyetalian countessas nowadays, in some of the magazines my son subscribes to, recline.

"I had some fantastic daydreams and fantasies, in those days, Constable!

"And sometimes at night, sitting down here in this front-house studying my head; and listening to Wilberforce talk about his travels, the Danube, the river, so blue; crossing the Alps in a aeroplane coming from Rome-Italy, the place which made him think of 'The Ride of the Valkyries'; Austria and Vienna, where they can dance the waltz, and the polka in Poland, so nice; and throughout the whole night! Englund and even Scotland, after which I got my name, Mary, from one of their mad Queens. All those places I visited in my dreams and fantasies, while studying, while listening to my son, Wilberforce.

"However, I had visited those places in daydreams, even before I gave birth to Wilberforce!

"But I never visited Latin-Amurca. Nor any place in the Wessindies. And I wonder why?

"I won't tell you, since you are nothing but a boy, where exactly on my dress, on my person, I carried that wishbone! But I held on to it, as if I expected a full-grown Bardrock pullet to spring-up from that lil wishbone, and grace our dinner table, every Sunday after that first Sunday, for Ma and me, until I became a woman and could provide more better.

"And every day, in all that time, ten or maybe eleven years, I made a wish on that wishbone; a wish *never-ever* to forget Mr. Bellfeels; and how he moved the riding-crop over my entire body, as if he was taking off my clothes, and then taking off my skin. And every time my hand touch that wishbone I take a oath to myself to never to forget to give him back.

"Can I ask you a question, Constable, before I stray more farther? It's a personal question."

"You could axe me any question; or anything, ma'am. I hold it as a privilege if you cross-examine me."

"Before I ask. That bell. On the table, touch it for me. Let's see what Gertrude is up to. She's too quiet ... Thank you, Constable."

"I touch the bell."

"Thanks. The personal question. Do you attend Church?"

"You mean if I goes to Church? Or if I belongst to a particular 'nomination, or congregation? Well, the answer is part o' both. What I mean by that is this. I goes to Church, but on Eastersmainly. And then, Christmas, for the five o'clock service in the morning. Or if somebody that I know dead. Or pass away. Or, or if a friend o' mine is getting henged, meaning getting married, and ..."

"You know God, then, don't you, Constable?"

"I really and truly don't know, ma'am, if I know God. Or if God know me. I don't know God in the way I getting to know you, though, ma'am. I don't know if I should know God more better, or less better than I knowing you. We was never that close, meaning God and me.

"The only other thing I could say in regards to knowing God, is that I learned about God in elementary school. Every afternoon at Sin-Davids Elementary School for Boys, we had oral Scripture. That is where I went-school.

"You may not remember this, ma'am, but I uses to help you round the yard when I was a lil boy. 'Specially in the long vacation, June, July and August. I uses to sweep-up the yard with a coconut broom; feed the sheeps and the other stocks; wash-down the pigpens; and burn the trash and dry-leaves, in a' empty oil drum."

"And what is your name?"

"I name Bennett. Granville Chesterfield Bennett Browne. But they calls me Benn, ma'am. My proper name is Bennett."

"And you're a Constable in the Force!"

"Yes, ma'am."

"You have a nice name."

"My gran-mother give me these big-names."

"Years and years ago, Constable ... after Wilberforce finished at the same Sin-Davids, and start attending Harrison College ..."

"I went as far as Six Standard. And straight outta Six Standard, I join the Force."

"You did well, too! And your gran-mother gave you three nice names. Anglican?"

"Yes, ma'am."

"Confirmed?"

"Well, not exactly."

"It must be the police work. Oh, here Gertrude comes!"

"Evening, Mistress. Good evening, Constable."

"Good evening, ma'am," the Constable says.

"Constable, is there anything at all I can offer you? Cocoa-tea, or anything?"

"A cup o' cocoa-tea, please," the Constable says. "I don't normally drink cocoa-tea, but as I on duty, ma'am ..."

"Good! Cocoa, then. Bring the Constable a nice glass of milk, Gertrude. He could mix-in the cocoa on his own. I'll have my usual ..."

The Constable, who is about twenty-two years old, has a head shaven almost to its shining pate, as if it is purposely done this way to fit the policeman's peak cap, issued too small. He is handsome in his night uniform of black serge tunic and trousers; "for the occasion, boy; for the grave occasion," Sargeant had told him; and beside him, on the floor, he has rested his cap, that has a red band round the side. He is sitting up, in a straight-backed mahogany tub-chair; and is watching Gertrude with one eye; and with his other, Miss Mary-Mathilda Bellfeels—he calls her Miss Bellfeels, as she is known in the Village—to see if she is watching him watch Gertrude.

Gertrude is well-built, not fat, but with large breasts, round face, large brown eyes and a well-padded behind—a "big botsy," he calls it. Gertrude's skin is like velvet, black and smooth. She is five feet seven inches. The Constable sees her as a very appealing woman, for the first time, in this new light; but before tonight, and previously, on his own rounds, he would see her coming from Wednesday night prayer meetings, and revival meetings, particularly during Crop-Season; and in all these years, he never had eyes for her; never looked at her with lust. Because of the competition from other men, among them Manny who owns the Harlem Bar & Grill. So he went his way, and she hers. And then, on that Friday night, when the annual Harvest Festival of the Church of the Nazarene, where she was a Sister, ended, with the clapping and the shouting and the singing and the testifying and the sound of the joyful tambourines late in the humid, sweating air and in her spirit, Constable saw Gertrude holding Sargeant's hand, entering a field of canes.

He looks at her now, as she comes into this front-house, twice the size of the house in which he was born and still lives; facing him; the two of them thrown together in this Great House, with its shining floors, whose wood gives off the smell of freshly polished mahogany, and the smell of Hawes Furniture Polish; surrounding him with a smell of sweet sexual sweetness he imagines coming from her; and he lowers his eyes to watch her small, dainty feet, bare; uncovered; not dressed in washercongs, or even Indian slippers. They are greased with coconut oil. Yes. It is the coconut oil that he smells. Not the polished mahogany furniture, nor the Hawes Furniture Polish.

Gertrude moves silent as a cat, over the thick Persian carpets. He can see the sinews on the insteps of her feet; he can see how they change form when she walks; he sees the lighter colour of skin of her heels, from the rest of the rich black colour of her instep. Dots of red nail polish, the colour of blood, decorate eight toes. The nails of her little toes are too small to accommodate even one drop of this red blood.

The Constable can see also the outline of her panties, as she moves in front of the light from the bright bare, naked bulbs that reach two feet above the table on which the bell that he rang, *pling!*, stands. And he imagines her panties are pink, and plain and without an embroidered edge round the legs and waist; and he can see clear through to them, with the help of his imagination and the naked bulbs, to the thick hair between her legs, and better still, just as she holds her body over, without bending her knees, to open the doors of an ornate cupboard; and from it, take a large decanter of crystal cut glass.

The Constable thinks of panties, made of soft sea-island cotton, bought on time from the Indian merchants whom he sees coming through the Village on Sundays, just as food is being served in Village kitchens. The Constable closes his eyes and sees Gertrude naked in his newlust, as she pours a drink into a glass. The glass has a large belly. A round belly. Large and round, like the belly of the Vicar of the Anglican Church, the Reverend Mr. M. R. P. P. Dowd, M.TH. (Dunelmn)—Master of Theology; and the Constable makes a wish, and his wish is Gertrude's voice talking to him; and he smiles, for his wish has at last been granted; and she is telling him, "*Yes, come and take it*"; but it is not Gertrude's voice: it is Mary-Mathilda, the woman sitting beside him, whose voice he is hearing, who is saying, "Come and take it, your milk. Would you like something else, Constable?"

"The milk would do, ma'am."

"Constable's milk, and the brandy then, please," she says to Gertrude, who is still in the room; and to the Constable, "Are you sure you won't like something more strong than milk? In all my born days, I never met a police who drinks milk!"

"I loves milk, ma'am."

"Now, I am curious to know, Constable, if you ever had something you couldn't part with? A *taw-ee*. A nail. Piece of lead-pencil. A button. Anything. Like it was a, a kind of ... obsession you had. Like something religious. Wilberforce been telling me that the Catholics in Rome-Italy have obsessions like these. The Catholics we have in this Island, small in numbers, since we are basically English and Anglicans, and high-Anglicans to-boot, are like those Catholics in Rome-Italy. People with obsessions. I don't think that Anglicans have obsessions of such colour and nature, though. Do you? Wilberforce tells me that Catholics walk with a string of beads in their hand, or round their neck; and when they die, they insist, either in their Will, or in their last wishes, that that string of worrying beads, that is what they call them, worrying beads, be buried with them, in their coffin. Isn't that something? Mr. Bellfeels told me that the man who fathered him had his gold pocket watch and gold chain buried with him in his coffin, according to his last Will and Testament; and that just before the grave diggers pile-on the mould to bury the coffin, the undertaker jumpin the grave, saying that he forget to take off all the silver ornaments from offa the coffin; and he unscrewed the oval hole for viewing the corpse; and quickso, before the mourners could blink, *bram!*, the expensive gold pocket watch with matching gold chain was rip-outta the corpse hands, and almost was inside the undertaker paws before Mr. Bellfeels intervene.

"But when Mr. Bellfeels tell me that story, all I could do was laugh. *'I snap-on my right hand 'pon the fucker's wrist, and squeeze*, Mr. Bellfeels say he say, *and the fucker drop the watch in my left hand. With my right hand, I was choking the fucker. This is the same gold pocket watch you see me wearing all the time. My father watch.'*

"Mr. Bellfeels say that most Plantation-people want to carry their riches with them, to the grave. And they live just like that. Isn't that something?

"Poor people, on the other hand, leave-back their poorness for their offsprings to inherit. And their miseries. That is something!

"Well, that is the story about my wishbone. I lived with it, like I was a Catholic. And it lived with me, too. Carrying it all that time, from the age of eight, and for fifteen to twenty years, made it turn it into an ornament.

"But I need to get back to my Statement. I am sorry. I am sure that Sargeant did not send you here to listen to me wandering-off about wishbones and obsessions. You are here about the matter in question, and my preliminary Statement."

"But I enjoying listening to you talk about the history of the Island," the Constable says. "To-besides, we need to know the whole background to a person, for a Statement to be a statement worth its salt. Sargeant is coming. Sargeant pick me to proceed him, because he didn't want to come himself and upset you, by being the first to open the 'vestigation, and have to axe you questions that he have to axe you, because of his position. Sargeant say he can't cross the threshold of this Great House, just so, and precede to axe you questions. Sargeant tell me to tell you to-don't get worried. He not digging too deep into your business, as he and the majority o' Flagstaff people know the history of the Plantation. As aforemention, ma'am, Sargeant tell me to tell you so. Your son the doctor looks after Sargeant. We all know that. Been looking after Sargeant for years now, ma'am; and never-once charge Sargeant a copper-penny, for consultations, medicine, tablets nor proscriptions. Sargeant, as you know, have the pressure. High blood pressure. And your son is who save his life, by looking after Sargeant. Sargeant have the nerves, too. Tension and stresses from the job. We know how important you and your son is to the people of this Village. Sargeant say to tell you that he send his respects, under the circumstances."

"Under the circumstances."

"What is the real circumstances, though, ma'am? I have to put this in my report."

"Do you always drink milk when you are vestigating and taking Statements?"

"No, ma'am. I doesn't drink milk at all, but in your presence I would drink it."

"But you still like it."

"Suppose so. But I didn't get enough when I was small."

"Just milk?"

"Ulcers, too, ma'am. Occasionally, I takes something strong. Like at a wedding, or when Sargeant invite me at him, to hear the new piano that his daughter send-down from Amurca, two Christmases ago. From Brooklyn, I think, is where she lives."

"You play yourself?"

"Just a few chords. Tinklelling the ivories."

"Look at this Steinway. This Steinway is a gift, twenty-five years ago, when Wilberforce was five. Mr. Bellfeels wanted his son to have the same things in this Great House as his two daughters, Miss Euralie and Miss Emonie, had when they were growing up in the Plantation Main House.

"Wilberforce got the same as them.

"Gifts! Gifts is funny things, Constable. They could tie you to a person. And then you can't untie yourself, nor extricate your independence from that person. The knot round your neck is too tight. Gifts are unhealthy; but there are gifts. So, sometimes, you have to accept them with a smile, and a skin-teet, meaning you are far from sincere.

"There were always gifts, expensive gifts that really could not buy-me-off, even with the generousness buried inside the gifts themselves. Gifts were not enough.

"That old Steinway there, been standing like a dumb person, with no power of words. Mr. Steinway's tongue cut out. Ten-fifteen years, now.

"Wilberforce learned to play on it. And Miss Grimes smacked Wilberforce knuckles three evenings a week, learning his scales. Every four o'clock, Monday, Wednesdays and Friday, straight from Harrison College.

"One night, during this time, Mr. Bellfeels came over, and I offered him something to drink; and he took a Tennents Stout. That was his drink, when he was a more younger man. In later life, he switch to white rum. And that, plus a few more things, was what I couldn't stomach in him. Belching as he swallowing the Tennents. No class. A few coppers rackling-'bout inside his pockets, yes. But no class. The right complexion and colour of skin for living high-on-the-hog, in this Island, yes. But class? Not one bloody ounce. The man would break wind, pass gas in front of me, and his son—fart, then!—even carrying on this behaviour home, in front o' Miss Euralie and Miss Emonie. Mistress Bellfeels, his wife, in one of the few exchanges we ever had, told me such.

"I have seen Ma, whilst she was his maid, iron dozens of handkerchiefs, every Friday evening, rinsing-and-starching them on the Thursday; white cotton ones, with a light-blue border in all of them. And never-once Mr. Bellfeels used a handkerchief. Index finger gainst one nostril, and *phew!* Splat in the road, and watch the thick green stuff slide over a rock and disappear in the ground.

"I don't know how I managed to stomach his weight laying-down on top of me all those years; breeding me and having his wish; and me smelling him; and him giving-off a smell like fresh dirt, mould that I turned over with my hoe, at first planting, following a downpour of rain, when all the centipees and rats, cockroaches and insects on God's earth start crawling-out in full vision and sight, outta the North Field.

"And a man of his means! To live like that! And never think of dashing a dash of cologne, or some Florida Water over his face and under his two armpits ..."

She stops talking, as she dabs a handkerchief at her mouth; and then at her right eye; and then at her left eye. The Constable sits and wonders why women always wipe their lips first, when it is their eyes that express the emotion they no longer want to disclose.

Her body shakes a little. In his eyes, she is a woman past desire; a woman who wears her dress below the knee; a powerful, rich, "brown-skin" woman; a woman to fear. He remembers her screaming at him when he was her yard-boy, because he had not swept the garbage clean from the yard; that was years ago; and he can still hear her high-pitched voice that sent chills down his back. But each evening, when he was leaving, she placed a brown paper bag into his hand, told him, "Tell your mother I say how-d." The paper bag contained large and small tomatoes, cucumbers, red peppers, three eggs and leftover chicken legs for his mother; a brown sugar cake and a penny for himself.

He pulls himself together now; puts all thought of Gertrude, and thoughts of this rich, brown-skin woman's plight, out of his mind; and recaptures the dignity of being a Constable in the Constabulary of the Island of Bimshire Police Force.

He must not let this woman's personal appeal and her physical attractiveness affect his concentration.

He must not, under the circumstances, let her soften his duty to conclude his preliminary Statement; nor, considering the act in question, have her ruffle his thoughts on Gertrude.

He is once more a Constable in the Constabulary.

So, he straightens his shoulders and sits erect in the straight-backed tub-chair.

She does the same thing with her posture, in her chair, and smiles with him. She looks very beautiful to him, at this moment. Tempting as his grandmother told him she was, as a little girl. *"Many a man' heart skip a beat after that Tilda, before she even reach her teens. Any man would want to ravish Tilda's beauty and virginity. But she save everything for Bellfeels."*

"… And the nights Mr. Bellfeels came over, I remember how Wilberforce, then in Third Form, beginning to take Latin and Greek, the boy was so happy to hear his father play those lovely old tunes. In foxtrot time, mainly. And 'Ole Liza Jane.' 'Carry Me Back to Ole Virginny.' And the one that Wilberforce liked best, 'Banjo on My Knee.'

"You shouldda seen the three of us! Father. Mother. And child. And then, Wilberforce and me! Jumping-round on the carpets in this front-house! Skinning our teet, and imitating the rhythms of dancing like if we were Amurcan Negroes. Doing a jig.

"Years later, Wilberforce who had-spend time in France and Germany and Rome-Italy, was now at Oxford and the Imperial College, in Tropical Medicines, studying to be a doctor, learning about malarias and sleeping sickness, from-where he would write letters to me, usually once a week, though they didn't reach these shores till months later, sometimes, specially during the War; nevertheless, in two letters, in two consecutive weeks, flashing-back to those nights when Mr. Bellfeels play 'Ole Black Joe' on the Steinway, Wilberforce tell me in the two letters ... and these are his own words ... *'We carried on like slaves'*—Wilberforce exact words—*'like slaves on a plantation, we put on that pantomine to entertain that man, and were ignorant, and did not know the ironies in our behaviour.'*

"Wilberforce loves the dirt his father walk on. That much you must know. But, for me to see and to hear the chastisement in the tone of his words ...

"Since those letters arrive, this Steinway never had its lid lifted again after those words of reproach.

"It hurt my heart to know what betrayal of life we lived without knowing it! And had to live!

"Those evenings, Mr. Bellfeels would throw in a waltz; and a piece of the Classics, now and then. But he played 'Banjo on My Knee' every Saturday night. And 'Ole Black Joe.'

"Yes. Those Saturday nights were nights of Amurcan Negro songs, mainly. And even if I was in my vexatious moods, I still learn a lot from listening. Both in this Great House where he put me in, as the mother of his three thrildren, to live, even although only one of the thrildren survived past childbirth, and when I worked in the Main House. Yes, William Henry, named after two kings. Decease soon after birth. Rachelle Sarah Prudence, named after English ladies-in-waiting. Decease likewise, following birth. And Wilberforce. The living boy. Wilberforce Darnley Alexander Randall Bellfeels. W. D. A. R. Bellfeels, M.D., Doctor of Tropical Medicines, as Revern Dowd like to address him. Yes.

"I mothered Mr. Bellfeels outside-thrildren, and for that he put me in this Great House, and he gave them the name of Bellfeels, even to William Henry and Rachelle Sarah Prudence, before they dead.

"That is something in his favour, I suppose.

"Mr. Bellfeels never-even suggest I use his surname, to mean whatever the use of that name mean, in these circumstances. But I know what it could mean. I also know that behind my back, the Villagers call me Miss Bellfeels the Outside-woman. Gertrude told me. I forced it out of her. But praise God, he make my three thrildren, two dead and one still in the quick, legitimate and respectable citizens of Bimshire, bearing the name of Bellfeels. The name Bellfeels, for all the badness it conjure up, and mean to me personally; and the reputation it have in Flagstaff Village, is ... well ...

"On Sundays, when the sun cool-off a bit, you could find me in the Church Yard, looking down at the two slabs of white marble covering the graves of my two thrildren who passed-way."

William Henry Bellfeels, R.I.P. Rachelle Sarah Prudence, R.I.P.

"One Sunday evening, near seven o' clock, just before Evening-song-and-Service is to begin, I see the back of this man, in the Church Yard, bending down looking at the same two white marble slabs. Him. Mr. Bellfeels! Years ago that happened.

"Write-this-down in your black notebook, what I was saying, before I got sidetracked by talking about my three thrildren … Yes. Write-this-down …"

She looks up from her lap, and sees that the Constable's eyes are closed; and she stops talking for a moment, waiting to see if he will stir from his slumber; but his eyes remain closed; and his breathing is a bit loud; and she concludes with some resignation that he is asleep. The night is long. It moves at a slow pace. The night takes on the desultory pace of her words and of her recollections. Realizing he is fast asleep, she continues talking, nevertheless.

"Serving at Mr. Bellfeels table, my first elevation from out the fields, when I was a more younger woman, and was only bearing his weight on my belly, every Saturday night, regardless to whether I was having my menses, or not … Yes!

"That low-class bastard! Pardon my French, Constable, although you fast-asleep.

"Yes. I remember 'The Blue Danube.' And all those foxtrots he would play. People in those days used to dance so formal and lovely, wearing long dresses, with the men in long swizzle-tail coats, looking like undertakers and penguins. But the elegance! In those days! The *ironies* of elegance! And at the Crane Beach Hotel where the really rich, the really white people, went; or at the Marine Hotel down in Hastings District, where the lower-class Plantation-people who were really not white, went. The Marine Hotel was the class to which Mr. Bellfeels belong, by birthright. To the red-nigger Marine Hotel crowd, down in Hastings.

"But you should have seen the tribes of them dancing! Those were the days! I wish those days would come back, for the sake of my son Wilberforce, who is approaching the age for marrieding. Is time he find a woman to spend his life with. Yes. For Wilberforce sake, and for the sake of the art of dancing, I wish those days would return-back.

"In those days, the men of this Island *knew* how to dance! The Aquatic Club on Bay Street, down in Town, was another popular place. In those days, a person even with a complexion such as mine, 'a brown-skin bitch,' as I happen to know is what Gertrude calls me, not even a brown-skin bitch like me, could get-past that iron gate. Unless I was working there, as a servant. And at that, they had a entrance for servants, with a hand-painted sign, saying SERVANTS ONLY. Yes."

The Constable opens his eyes, looks around, convinces himself that he did not actually fall-off to sleep; and becomes alert, fiddling with his black notebook. She watches him; and smiles.

"Now, Wilberforce, being of a even more lighter complexion than me, don't have that trouble. You see what I mean? Yes. The Aquatic Club. The place where the best dancing was danced to the best music. The Percy Greene Orchestra, plus the Coa Alleyne Orchestra. Big bands, boy! Led by two black musicianers from right here in Bimshire. Two of the *best*! In the whole Wessindies! Nor only in Bimshire.

"Did you know that the Percy Greene Orchestra played once for Majesty? Yes.

"Yes! The King, George-the-Fiff, was in the Island once ... he wasn't really King then, he was the Prince o' Wales, to later become King ... and they held a dance, a Ball, what am I saying? A Ball. At the Aquatic Club. Proper; and decent, for His Majesty, George-the-Fiff. I know all this because Ma who—God rest her soul—was now promoted from weeding in the North Field, to a position within the kitchen staffs of the Plantation Main House, having a more higher status and position, as a consequence, but getting the same field-hand wage; and the Bookkeeper at the time, none other than Mr. Bellfeels, was appointed Chairman of the Royal Ball, by the Social Events Committee of the Marine Hotel, to be stage manager of the Ball held at the Aquatic Club, plus being in charge of making arrangements for transportation in private cars and hiring hired cars from Johnson's Stables; for making the banners and screamers, streamers; and buntings; for blowing up the red-white-and-blue balloons; for making-sure that the ball-room floor was waxed, and shining like dogs stones—as the saying goes—and slippery as ice; and just as treacherous; so that if a man step-off, and didn't hold his balance, like Harry-on-the-ice, moving his body in time to the rhythm of some of the slowest pieces of waltz-music that the Percy Greene Orchestra would play; if that man wasn't *good!* and didn't have perfect balance, nor a knowledge of waltzes, how to move his body in time to the rhythm, how to make his footwork move in and out to the intricate movements, he was in *bare* trouble! A man wasn't a man unless he could dance on that Aquatic Club floor, wax to a vexatious perfection! If he moved the *wrong* way, or turned too fast on that floor, wax like a sheet of ice, *brugguh-down!* Flat on his arse. In full view of the invited couples, and the eyes of the staffs looking-on through the glass hole in the swing-door leading to the kitchen.

"So, Mr. Bellfeels axe Ma to help-out that night, with the serving of the sangwiches and the eats and the drinks. Ma, and the other staffs of the Plantation, plus the servants of the rich white people; people like the two leading barsters-at-Law in the Island; the Solicitor- General; the doctors and business people; the Vicar, Revern Dowd; the manager-owner of Cave Shepherd & Sons, Haberdasheries down in Town, all of them-so contributed their personal staffs to the loyal service of the Royal Ball in honour and by Appointment to the King, George-the-Fiff. Ma and all of them were dressed in servant uniforms, black; with white aprons, white caps starch-and-ironed; and hard-hard-hard like deal board. Black stockings and black leather shoes. Yes!

"You shouldda seen Ma! Ma looked so beautiful. Like a queen! Pretty-pretty. Like a, like a movie-screen star. Like a young Mary Pickford!

"Yes. And, you should have seen the Bimshire ladies and gentlemen that night. It was like a fairyland, like Alice in Wonderland, like starlights burning on a Fiff of November, Guy Fawkes Day, as the King, George-the-Fiff, was in all his regalias and majesty and metals ... medals, weighing-down his shoulder blade, poor fellow, since, as he was in the flesh, such a diminnative small man to have to bear all those regalias and insignias pin to his chest, Ma say.

"And the King made a big-big point, that night. His Majesty dance with *all* the Bimshire ladies. Every last one. And not only the ones that were white, when they were presented to him, and wasn't ... and the King, poor fellow, who couldn't tell who-from-who, since they all looked white to him, traipsed the light-fantastic with every blasted one o' those whores! ... Ma tell me so.

"Ma tell me, also, something that hit me in the pit of my stomach. The strangest utterance. Ma tell me she wished she was *somebody-else* that night. To be able to take part in that Ball, dress in a long dress sweeping the floor, and dance with *her* King, George-the-Fiff; and take her rightful place in the Receiving Line of that gala; and she wished she was not who she was, a field hand, a harlot, a tool for a man who came into her house, small as it was, humble as it was, after the gala was over, and the Ball had come to its end with the playing of 'God Save the King,' and after the kitchen staffs had clean-up … And *robbed* her of her maiden. Yes!

"Took her virginity away from her.

"She had the right colour, as you can see from my own complexion, for him to want her. But not light-enough to warrant admission on her own oars, and cross the iron gates of the Aquatic Club, to attend the Ball for her king, His Majesty, George-the-Fiff! She had the looks, as you can see she handed down in me. She had everything. Except the accident of borning in the right bedroom. Ma. My mother. God rest her soul.

"There is a story-and-a-half I could tell you about the doings and the happenings in this small Island of Bimshire! Stories to make your head curl! Stories and skeletons bigger than the square-mile-area of this Island.

"It took Ma until she was on her deathbed before she could empty her heart and tell me. And seek her redemption before God called her to her judgment.

"Psalm 51, Constable, in the *Book of Psalms*.

"*Have mercy upon me, O God, according to thy lovingkindness.*

"Ma was reading this Psalm in the Bible, for days and days, just before she died. As a warning to me, she eventually confess. But he, Mr. Bellfeels, was already inside my system.

"She was sixteen the night it happened. When he *took* her.

"She went to her grave, at the ripe age of seventy-eight.

"Sixty-one, sixty-two years. Three-score-and-two, she carried that burden like I carried my wishbone, in secrecy, like a skeleton; speechless, and with no utterance. A stain on a white dress, in the wrong place, and that won't come out, regardless of the bleaching you put it through. A obsession, just like I walked with my wishbone. Not one iota passed her lips. Three-score-and-two years. A whole lifetime. Vouchsafe in the books of the Old Testament.

"Women of her generation knew how to carry burdens. And how to bury them. Inside their hearts. Concealed in their blood. They were strong women, then. Tough women. Women who gave birth in the fields today, and returned to raise their hoe and lift their load two afternoons later; within forty-eight hours. In the same fields. Yes."

She takes the fat-bellied crystal glass from the mahogany side table, and raises it to her lips. She makes no sound as she takes a sip. She places the snifter back onto the white doily in the middle of the rich, brown, shining table made by the Village joiner and cabinetmaker, from mahogany wood, in the shape of a heart. Three others, scattered through the large front-house, are in the shape of a spade, a diamond and a club. Each has the same white crocheted doily on it. One has her Bible.

"Ma lost the baby conceived in rape, the night His Majesty, *her* King, George-the-Fiff, danced in Bimshire. 'My God, the blood.' That is all Ma said. That is all she remember. It was my great-gran, Ma's gran-mother, with her knowledge of bushes and vines and leaves used for medicines; and cures; plus a lil touch of obeah and witchcraft, that saved Ma. Ma say that Gran brought this knowledge with her from Almina, in Africa. My great-gran. Yes.

"She had a name that sounded African. But I could never pronounce it, the right way. It sounded something like *Agne Beraku*; but in time, it went completely outta my mind, altogether. I do not know my great-gran's African name. Yes.

"I would see her, my great-gran-mother, just before she pass-away, bent almost in half; her face scenting the bushes; picking and picking; putting a leaf or a twig or a stem inside her mouth and chew on it, to test it; and then spitting it out; with her braided-up grey hair slipping out from underneat her white head-tie, and hanging low to the ground, searching-through worthless rocks and stones as if they were precious pearls and corals, picking a twig from this bush, a twig from the next; and putting all of them in her apron. Gran wore a apron, even when she was long-past-working in people kitchens. She spent most of her life in the kitchen at the Aquatic Club. It's a wonder to me, knowing what she must-have-went-through in them days, that she didn't put a lil twig from the wrong bush, or a stem of Poison Ivy, a lil-lil piece of the root, in the tureens of turtle soup those bastards liked her to cook for them! Yes.

"My great-gran. Her apron was like a badge of honour. In her apron, always white and starch-and-ironed, and pleated in straight lines from her waist down to below her two ankles, she would put those bushes—sersey bush, Christmas bush, miraculous bush, lignum-vitae bush, soursop leaves and leaves from the puh-paw trees, tamarind tree leaves and sugar-apple leaves ... I don't remember the other bushes! But I know that the sersey bush is what did the trick. Sersey bush that Gran boiled thick-thick until it came like tar; bitter and black; and that poor little girl, my ma, no more than seventeen, or sixteen, was made to drink that tar-tea every morning at five o'clock, until Mr. Bellfeels vim was worked out of her system. And at every six o'clock every evening, Gran put Ma in a bush bath, and soaked her until the sin, and the stain, and the mistake, came out in the form of blood. Yes!

"It take three days and three nights, with Ma's gran-mother sitting sleepless in a upright chair, for Ma to regain her salvation, and have release from the thing that Mr. Bellfeels sowed inside her, inside Ma.

"But blood was always in our lives. Blood, and more blood ... and that is why I did what I did."

M. G. Vassanji

M.G. Vassanji was born in Kenya and raised in Tanzania. He went to
university at MIT and took a doctorate in theoretical nuclear physics
at the University of Pennsylvania before coming to Canada in 1978.
While working as a research associate and lecturer at the University of
Toronto in the 1980s he began to dedicate himself seriously to a long-
standing passion: writing.

His first novel, *The Gunny Sack*, won a regional Commonwealth
Writers' Prize in 1990, and he was invited to be writer-in-residence at
the International Writing Program of the University of Iowa. In 1989
he quit his job and began researching *The Book of Secrets*, which won
the inaugural Giller Prize in 1994. That same year Vassanji was
awarded the Harbourfront Festival Prize in recognition of his
achievement in and contribution to the world of letters and was
chosen as one of twelve Canadians on the *Maclean's* Honour Roll.

Vassanji's other books include the acclaimed novels *No New Land*
(1991) and *Amriika* (1999) and the short story collections *Uhuru
Street* (1991) and *When She Was Queen* (2005). Vassanji became the
first writer to win The Giller Prize twice, in 2003, when his bestselling
novel *The In-Between World of Vikram Lall* garnered the award.

The Assassin's Song, Vassanji's most recent bestselling novel, was
shortlisted for the 2007 Scotiabank Giller Prize and the Governor
General's Literary Awards and was a finalist for the 2007 Rogers
Writers' Trust Fiction Prize and a *Globe and Mail* Best Book of 2007.
It was also shortlisted for the Crossword Prize in India. Vassanji lives
in Toronto with his wife and two sons.

The In-Between World of
Vikram Lall

BY M.G. VASSANJI

Winner 2003

≈

ONE.

Njoroge who was also called William loved my sister Deepa; I was infatuated with another whose name I cannot utter yet, whose brother was another William; we called him Bill. We had all become playmates recently. It was 1953, the coronation year of our new monarch who looked upon us from afar, a cold England of pastel, watery shades, and I was eight years old.

I call forth for you here my beginning, the world of my childhood, in that fateful year of our friendships. It was a world of innocence and play, under a guileless constant sun; as well, of barbarous cruelty and terror lurking in darkest night; a colonial world of repressive, undignified subjecthood, as also of seductive order and security—so that long afterwards we would be tempted to wonder if we did not hurry forth too fast straight into the morass that is now our malformed freedom.

Imagine an outdoor mall, the type we still call a shopping centre there, a plain stubby strip of shops on open land, with unpaved parking in front. It was accessible from a side road that left the highway, less than a mile away, at the railway station. Far out in the distance, the farthest that you could see through the haze over the flat yellow plains, rose the steep green slopes of the great Rift Valley, down which both the railway and the highway descended to reach us at the floor. Behind us lay most of the rest of Nakuru, the principal town of our province.

My family ran a provision store at this Valley Shopping Centre, which was ten minutes' walk from the Asian development where we lived. We sold Ovaltine and Milo and Waterbury's Compound and Horlicks—how they roll past memory's roadblocks, these trademarks of a childhood—and macaroni and marmalade, cheeses and olives, and other such items that the Europeans and the rich Indians who emulated them were used to. Beside us was a small bakery-café run by a Greek woman, Mrs. Arnauti, for the Europeans—as all the whites were called—who trundled down from their farms in their dust-draped vans and pickups to stop by for tea or coffee and colourful iced cakes and neat white sandwiches. Next to it was Alidina Greengrocers. On Saturday mornings, with the schools closed, my sister and I went down to the shop with our parents. Sun-drenched Saturdays is how I think of those days, what memory's trapped for me: days of play. Though it could get cold at times, and in the morning the ground might be covered in frost. At the other end of the mall from us, Lakshmi Sweets was always bustling at midmorning, Indian families having stopped over in their cars for bhajias, samosas, dhokras, bhel-puri, and tea, which they consumed noisily and with gusto. By comparison our end was sedate, orderly: a few vehicles parked, a few rickety white tables outside Arnauti's occupied by Europeans on a good day. My father and mother always ordered tea and snacks from Lakshmi, and my sister and I could go to Arnauti's, where we were allowed a corner table outside, though not our black friend Njoroge, who with quite a straight face, head in the air and hands in his pockets, would proudly wander off.

After hastily consuming sticky Swiss rolls and doughy cheese or spinach pies, Deepa and I ran out to play. There were two handcarts outside the shop for pulling loads, one of them had its handle broken and no one usually minded when we took it out to give each other rides. Deepa, who was seven, ran along beside Njoroge and me, and habitually, in domineering big-brother fashion, I refused her a place in our conveyance, became annoyed at her for running after us, a girl in her two long pigtails and Punjabi pyjama and long shirt. She cried, and every time she did that Njoroge would give her a ride, obligingly push the cart for her all around the parking lot, and I believed they had more fun together than he had with me. That was why I thought he was in love with my sister. Every time I said that, Mother would have a fit, but she never objected to our playing with our friend.

One morning just before noon a green Ford pickup drove up and parked outside our store; from it emerged a tall and slim white woman, with brown curls to her shoulders and trousers that seemed rather broad at the hips. She had a long and ruddy face with a pointed chin. She paused to scrutinize the shops in the mall and, I thought, stared severely for a moment at me and my companions, before bending to say something to the two children who were in the passenger seat. The door opened on the other side and out tumbled a boy of my age and a young girl who could have been six; from the back jumped out with some flair an African servant—well dressed in expensive hand-me-downs, as the more favoured servants of the Europeans usually were, much to the envy of other servants. This one sported a brown woollen vest and a tweed jacket. The woman escorted her two children to Arnauti's, where they sat at a table outside and in loud voices ordered from the waiter who had come running out to attend, and then she went over to my father's shop. Soon our own barefoot servant hurried out to hand the European woman's servant a bottle of Coke.

When she had finished her shopping, her servant was called and he carried her two cartons of purchases to the back of the pickup. Then Mrs. Bruce, as was her name, returned to Arnauti's patio and joined a table with two other women and a man. Her two children came out, where Njoroge, Deepa, and I, upon seeing them, now somewhat self-consciously continued our preoccupations with each other and our cart. The boy and girl stood quite still, outside the guardrail, staring at us.

Do you want a ride? I asked the boy suddenly.

Without a word he came and sat in the cart and we pushed him away at top speed with hoots and growls to simulate various engine sounds. When we stopped, after a distance, having gathered up a cloud of dust across the parking lot, the boy got out and dusted himself off as his sister whined, Now me, Willie, it's my turn now.

He paid her no attention but shook Njoroge's and my hands solemnly, saying, William—call me Bill, and pleased to meet you.

We shook hands wordlessly, then I pointed to my friend and said hesitantly: Njoroge.

That day Deepa and I stopped calling Njoroge by his English name. And I believe he also stopped using it for himself.

Now he in his turn pointed at me and said: Vic—Vikram.

Well then—jolly good, Bill said. Let's give those two girls a ride—

He wore shorts of grey wool, with a rather fine blue checked shirt. His hair, like that of his sister, was a light brown. And both wore black shoes and white socks. The girl was in red overalls, and two ribbons of a like colour tied her hair in clumps at the back. We drove the two girls with speed right up to the line of shops, as they hung on, clutching for dear life, screaming with joy.

The boy and girl came every alternate week like clockwork, and we awaited them with anticipation, for they represented something out of the ordinary and exotic, and Bill was always imaginative and original in his play and Njoroge and I learned much from him. Sometimes we were a Spitfire raining bullets on enemies, other times a racing car, or an Empire Airways plane, or the *Titanic* or the *QE2*, or the SS *Bombay*, the boat that regularly plied the ocean between Bombay and Mombasa.

They had rather refined accents, their language sharp and crystalline and musical, beside which ours seemed a crude approximation, for we had learned it in school and knew it to be the language of power and distinction but could never speak it their way. Their clothes were smart; their mannerisms so relaxed. But these barriers of class and prestige were not so inviolable or cruel at our level, and we did become friends. Mrs. Bruce would drop them off at our shop first thing before going off for her other chores on the main street, and return an hour or so later.

Njoroge and Deepa continued to have that closeness, their bond of protector and dependent; I deferred to Bill, because he was a little older, and also because he simply was a leader in our midst.

And the girl?—her name was Annie, and I came to think I was in love with her, and she with me. Ours was a natural pairing. We found each other like magnets, and we could watch the world together with laughter in our eyes.

And so when flight captain William Bruce went bangbanging in his Spitfire, shooting down Germans or Japs or Eyeties as he self-propelled with his feet, and went tumbling over, the handcart dragging him ignominiously in the dust like a fallen charioteer, who should catch my eye than Annie, wrinkling her nose a few times in an expression of bemusement and glee, which I returned with a wide grin, before we rushed to Bill's rescue and clucked appropriately at the grazed knees. And when the fisherman Njoroge, at Bill's instigation, took Deepa out in his boat, Bill serenading with a mock guitar, Annie had slipped her arm casually in mine and we stood behind watching. So many such moments I could recall, gentle as dewdrops, transient and illusory like sunbeams; charming as a butterfly's dance round a flower.

MUCH OF MY LIFE has been a recalling of her; my Annie. Each remembered moment, each fresh thought like a bead in a rosary. How old would she be now, I've asked myself countless times, and provided an answer. Now she would be in her early fifties. What would she look like, what would her life have been like, would we have kept up that friendship. Would she still sing. Who could have guessed her fate, that darling of a privileged family, that bundle brimming with life and future and charm? ... I go on and on.

My sister Deepa has always considered this proclivity of mine something of a sickness; Njoroge thought likewise, but showed some understanding of it. I do not deny the affliction. I never imposed it on those around me, I carried it like a private ache of no consequence to anyone but myself. Only lately have I admitted the obvious, that I let it deform me, freeze the essential core in me, so that for a large part of my adult life I remained detached from almost everything around me, explaining away this coldness as the result of a stoic, even mystical temperament.

She had freckles on her arms, and a few—exactly three, as I imagine it—on one side of her nose. And sometimes when she wore a dress her knickers might show, at which my sister would blink her eyelashes or look away in an almost unconscious response that I couldn't help noticing. She was a burden to Bill, who either ignored her pleas or paid extravagant attention to her. She brought her dolls over sometimes, when Deepa and she would disappear, before tiring eventually and emerging to play with us boys. Once the servant, Kihika, had to walk around with Annie's teddy bear in his hands so it could watch her play. This was evidently the aftermath of a recent tantrum. She, driven around in the cart by the rest of us, looking happily at my face, the tears now dry on hers; Kihika keeping pace, in his vest and tweeds, a tender smile on his face. It is a scene carved vividly in the brain, because it would return so often to tease and to torment.

ONE BRIGHT AFTERNOON Mrs. Bruce stayed away an unusually long time, and my parents wondered whether someone should be sent to look for her. Lunch hour was passing, Alidina Greengrocers and Arnauti's Café were already shuttered, Lakshmi Sweets was lifeless. Finally she arrived, two hours late, just when in a corner of the parking lot Bill, acting the part of a Special Branch inspector, toting a toy pistol he had brought along that morning, was administering a loyalty oath to the "uncovered" and "repenting" Mau Mau terrorist Njoroge, assisted by his faithful sergeant Vic and watched by an amused Kihika and the two girls. Bill's other, outstretched hand proffered a chocolate as prize for the renunciation.

I shall be loyal to the Queen of all of the British Empire, Njoroge was mumbling,... and the dominions ... I renounce the Mau Mau and the oath I have taken ... if I give help to the terrorists may I die ...

Mrs. Bruce had come out of the pickup and was walking toward us; suddenly she let out a terrifying shriek: Willie! Stop it at once! At once!

She had come to a trembling halt a few yards away; she uttered something inaudible and raised a hand to her forehead, closed her eyes. Kihika hurried over to steady her: Polé, mama, they got tired waiting, it's only a game. Ni muchezo.

She went with him to our shop, she sat down and accepted a glass of cold water. Tears were running down her face.

I am sorry, Mrs. Bruce, said Papa. We all know him and will pray for him in his sorrow ...

All of us children had gathered around in the shop and stood watching.

The cause of Mrs. Bruce's grief was a piece of news she had received during her visit to the shops downtown, news that my parents had also apparently received in the meantime. Just over an hour ago, Mr. Innes, the manager of the chemists Innes and McGeorge, upon returning home from work, had discovered his wife and daughter hacked to death by the Mau Mau.

That was the closest that the killings had come to us.

OUT IN THE DISTANCE, across the waters of Lake Ontario, the dim glow is the city of Rochester, I've been told, where Deepa now resides. The waves of this vast lake before us, under the midsummer night sky, produce a steady murmur, invoking for me the immensity of time and space, mocking the trivial rhythms of an ordinary human life and its perishable concerns. Yet that life is all we have and is perhaps more than we think it is, for we continue in each other, as the arrival of my young visitor reminds me.

One of the cats suddenly nuzzles strongly against my leg, then just as abruptly ceases, vanishing somewhere; I think it's the black one, Zambo, for whom this is the most but essential intimacy he'll allow.

Oh, he's gone, I mutter sheepishly, having reached out too late to stroke the cat.

There he goes, says Joseph, with a nod toward my back.

My young visitor has a surprisingly deep voice; his tall thin body with long black face rises like a silhouette before me in the dark. I'm still not sure why he agreed to come, what can he find here to interest and to keep him? He will start university in September, in Toronto. Meanwhile we are to be each other's soulmates, as per instructions from Deepa, who has sent him to me to cool off. He had become involved in student activism back home in Kenya, a tempting and hazardous preoccupation, so I understand Deepa's concern for him. You are his family there, Vic, said Deepa over the phone, drum some practical advice into him. Be his anchor when he needs you.

I'll try, sis, I replied. A young man like that wants to do his own bidding, he is not going to heed the cautionary advice of some middle-aged Asian man. Especially someone like me. I am the notoriously corrupt, the evil Vic Lall, remember?

Don't give yourself airs, she said. Besides, he'll do you good.

Which balances the equation, I surmise. Joseph has his instructions too. When he arrived yesterday, when I picked him up at the train station in Korrenburg, he was respectful but reserved. We have yet to break that reserve, behind which may hide all his suspicion and distrust of me. What does he know, think of me?

He has been away from home a month now, and from what I understand, he left just in time to escape the clutches of the police following a large riot. He must hide a lot of anger too, at his world.

I remember the day he was born, Joseph, twenty-three years ago, a tiny wrinkled baby in the arms of his mother Mary, not quite black but, surprisingly to me, brown. I had gone to visit his mother in hospital, with my own three-year-old son in tow. The two of us stood together in rapt admiration. The years of the Mau Mau disturbances were long over; what were once termed terrorists were now called freedom fighters, and in the seventies, in Nairobi, we had daring robberies to occupy our minds, and political assassinations. Once in a while a former freedom fighter would emerge from the forests, or publish a memoir, aided by a foreign scholar. The happy scene in the hospital room that afternoon, though, belied a painful reality, for the boy's father, my friend Njoroge, was not there.

That is the bond between us, Joseph and me, I realize, whatever else he may think about me. I knew his father.

TWO.

My father fussed over Mrs. Bruce, that afternoon of the attack on the Inneses, and was unwilling to let her go home alone, insisting that he call Mr. Bruce to take her away. She protested it was not necessary, evidently annoyed at the attention he pressed upon her, which he didn't seem to see, rather abjectly ingratiating himself further. I simply *cannot*, Mrs. Bruce, let you go. There are terrorists about, and a European lady alone on the road with her two children ... She had been seated on the stuffed chair across from his desk and given a glass of water; he himself had come around and stood before her, effectively blocking the aisle leading out from the store. Crates of tinned and bottled eatables stood piled waist-high on either side of him. Finally, after a few of my mother's veiled remarks and annoyed signals, Papa relented, and Mrs. Bruce walked away stiffly to her vehicle with her two children close beside her, Kihika following faithfully behind. When they had gone, Mother scolded Papa, Why do you have to be so craven in front of her, they don't care one cent for us. To which he said, Our children play with her children. Came the reply, So what, are they doing us a favour? Why didn't you offer to drive her home, then?

That last remark was unusually sarcastic; he looked at her, surprised, but didn't say a word.

Mother did not like Mrs. Bruce; she would look peevishly from behind the sanctuary of our shop window whenever the white woman came and dropped off her kids and servant and drove away to finish other business in town. But Mother was from India and not as intimidated by the angrez-log (as she called the Europeans) as Papa was; and her younger brother, our Mahesh Uncle, was an outspoken local radical whom, although he made her nervous by his ways, she also quite admired. Still, it did surprise me that my mother would feel so hostile toward the mother of our two European playmates.

WE HAVE BEEN AFRICANS for three generations, not counting my own children. Family legend has it that one of the rails on the railway line just outside the Nakuru station has engraved upon it my paternal grandfather's name, Anand Lal Peshawari, in Punjabi script—and many another rail of the line has inscribed upon it the name and birthplace of an Indian labourer. I don't know if such rails ever existed, with Punjabi signatures upon them, but myth is more powerful than factual evidence, and in its way surely far truer. We always believed in the story, in our home. Our particular rail, according to my dada, was the one laid just before the signal box, outside the station. He had used acid and a nib of steel wire to etch his name. There was many a time during a visit to the station when we would stare in the direction of that rail, if not directly at it, in that very significant knowledge central to our existence.

The railway running from Mombasa to Kampala, proud "Permanent Way" of the British and "Gateway to the African Jewel," was our claim to the land. Mile upon mile, rail next to thirty-foot rail, fishplate to follow fishplate, it had been laid by my grandfather and his fellow Punjabi labourers—Juma Molabux, Ungan Singh, Muzzafar Khan, Shyam Sunder Lal, Roshan, Tony—the cast of characters in his tales was endless and of biblical variety—recruited from an assortment of towns in northwest India and brought to an alien, beautiful, and wild country at the dawn of the twentieth century. Our people had sweated on it, had died on it: they had been carried away in their weary sleep or even wide awake by man-eating lions of magical ferocity and cunning, crushed under avalanches of blasted rock, speared and macheted as proxies of the whites by angry Kamba, Kikuyu, and Nandi warriors, infected with malaria, sleeping sickness, elephantiasis, cholera; bitten by jiggers, scorpions, snakes, and chameleons; and wounded in vicious fights with each other. They had taken the line strenuously and persistently six hundred miles from the Swahili coast, up through desert, bush, and grassland into the lush fertile highlands of the Kikuyu, then through forest down the Rift Valley and back up to a height of eight thousand feet, before bringing it to descend gently and finally to the great lake Victoria-Nyanza that was the heart of what became beloved Africa.

Anand Lal, my dada, stayed on in the new colony after his indentureship, picked Nakuru as the spot where he would live. A small thin man: rough chin and thin moustache, white lungi and loose shirt, and a fluffy white turban on the head. Thus he is captured, staring wondrously out of a photo, with three other Punjabi coolies and the legendary Colonel Patterson on a railway inspection trolley outside Machakos. It was 1897. I imagine him six years later, at the end of his second contract, seated atop a small pyramid of steel sleepers at the Nakuru railway yard, with a companion or two perhaps, chewing on a blade of grass or lunching on daal and rice from the canteen. The last key had been driven home on the railway, at Lake Victoria by an English lady, and he and a few others had been brought back here to complete work on the station. I see him contemplating the vast flat grassy plains of the Rift Valley, the pointed Mount Longonot, its sides grey with volcanic ash, rising up like the nipple on the breast of some reclining African god, the two escarpments in the distance, along whose steep slopes they had lain the railway in the direst of wet muddy conditions, the shimmering Lake Nakuru, its blue surface painted over by the white and pink of a million flamingos ... I see this turbaned young Indian who would be my dada saying to himself, This valley has a beauty to surpass even the god Shivji's Kashmir, and the cool weather in May is so akin to the winters of Peshawar ...

What makes a man leave the land of his birth, the home of those childhood memories that will haunt him till his deathbed? I received a warning telephone call late one morning, left home that night with my heart in my mouth; but for Indians abroad in Africa, it has been said that it was poverty at home that pushed them across the ocean. That may be true, but surely there's that wanderlust first, that itch in the sole, that hankering in the soul that puffs out the sails for a journey into the totally unknown?

For many years I did not know the exact circumstances that made my grandfather want to leave his home and cross the black water—as the exiling oceans were called in his homeland. Those circumstances had to do, as I came to find out, with a quarrel he had with his elder married brother soon after the death of their father, who had been the only shopkeeper and moneylender in his village. And so the prospect of going home, after his indentureship, even with a bit of money of his own now, must not have seemed so very compelling.

He found a job in Nakuru's railway machine shop, married a Punjabi girl living with her relations in Nairobi, received a decent dowry, and soon after opened a grocery store in Nakuru's only and burgeoning street at the time. The town had become a business centre for many of the sons and daughters of England's landed class who had come to settle and farm in the sunny and temperate clime of the Rift Valley.

DADAJI! DADAJI!—we would happily shout, Deepa and I and our several cousins, and scamper up to him for our candies, immediately after the Sunday family meal in my parents' home, when all the other adults had retired for their naps wherever they could. Seated on the armchair which was his siesta place, Dadaji would bring out a paper bag and hold it up and hand out to each of us, in turn, one choice sweet, always beginning with Deepa, the youngest, her mouth wide open like a puppy's. These presents were slight, compared with the chocolates we received from our parents, but the ritual was a delight; at times we felt that it was we who were the indulgent ones. Little could we even begin to imagine what his life had been like, what his thoughts were now. Sitting at his feet, we would often be treated to his stories. The lion stories were always the favourite, because they were scarier and so much more immediate and realistic than the Indian tales of Lakshman and Rama and Sita speaking with monkeys and devils in the enchanted forests of a distant land.

So we are sitting round a fire like this, he would say, drawing us into a circle, each of us representing a coolie friend, and he would place his large white handkerchief on the nearest child's head to represent a turban. Eh listen, you! So we are sitting round a fire like this, the six of us, Ungan Singh there, and there Birbal Singh, and Muzzafar and Chhotu and myself ... and Malik. Ungan, saying Aha!, plays his hand, thus, and we lean forward to look—a baadshah, a king of clubs. Wah! says Birbal, you had it all along, and Muzzaffar turns to Chhotu and says, Eh Lala Chhotu, if you had kept your ace! But there is no Chhotu! While we have been all admiring Ungan's king there in the middle like it was a bridegroom, Chhotu—the littlest coolie among us—has disappeared! And on the ground, leading to the bushes, is a trail left by his body—the poor fellow's feet—and a few, eka-do drops of blood. We start shouting and running about—here, there, here again, and the askaris and Nicholson Sahab arrive with their rifles ... Poor Chhotu, only his head was found—hanging from a tree branch, beside a baobab fruit! With his turban on!

Tell us more, tell us more, Dadaji!

But Dadaji was beginning to forget the details by the time we were around. Sometimes it was the skull that was found, beside a river, with Chhotu's turban beside it, all unwound. But of one thing he was certain, as he would sometimes say emphatically to our parents: those lions of Tsavo were the ghosts of dead men. Anyone eaten by a lion would himself come back to eat his fellows—otherwise, how did the lions time their attacks so perfectly?

It was a strange prospect, friends coming back to eat you. Then perhaps the lions didn't mean ill after all? Dadaji had no answer to that. Another thing he was certain about was that the lions all had hypnotizing powers.

For every mile of railway track laid, four Indians died, our radical Mahesh Uncle would remind us when he was around.

INDIA WAS ALWAYS FANTASYLAND to me. To this day, I have never visited my dada's birthplace. It was the place where that strange man with the narrow pointed face, bald head, and granny glasses, Gandhiji, had lived and died, and where the man with the white cap, Nehru, now ruled, and where the impossibly four-armed and pink-faced gods of my mother's statuettes and Lakshmi Sweets' annual calendar pictures had fought their battles and killed devils, and where Sir Edmund Hillary and Sherpa Tensing had that year conquered Everest. It was Vrndavan where the butter thief Nandlal Krishna presided, where Dadi was born and the goddess Dayamati had presided. My mother had a dresser on which she kept her statuettes of Rama and Durga and Hanuman and of course Ganesh, and at times of stress she went and stood in entreaty before them. Our daily preservation, especially in those nervous times, was due to their faithful intercession, she had no doubt about that. Even now, even here in this Canadian wilderness, I cannot help but say my namaskars, or salaams, to the icons I carry faithfully with me, not quite understanding what they mean to me. But I am convinced they represent some elemental force of nature, some qualities of it, like gravitation and the electric force and all other entities conjured up for us by scientists from our mundane existence. But I digress.

My father—proudly Kenyan, hopelessly (as I now think) colonial—went to India once, and brought back my mother.

He found everything in India dirty and poor, and for the most part he had a miserable time of it. Even to see the Taj Mahal you had to walk over gutters and push through a street fight, he would say. Beggars and touts everywhere; men standing around openly picking at their crotches. Even a taxi! he would exclaim. Even a taxi! You hail one, you want to feel posh and escape all the scum around you, you open the door and what happens? You step into a lump of fresh shit! It was one of his favourite stories, he would get graphic, and Deepa and I would roll with laughter. Mother would simply smile and say, There he goes again, with his taxi-shit story. It was 1944, the year he went, and the streets were in turmoil with strikes and demonstrations in aid of India's freedom. While walking along a street in

Peshawar once, Papa chanced to see a girl on a bicycle—evidently returning from college, her books clasped to the carrier behind her. She had one long pigtail almost down to her waist and she wore an embroidered cap. There was something in the face she made, when she had to halt and wait for a handcart full of smelly onion sacks to go past, that caught his fancy. It was like discovering a single, solitary rose blooming on the grimy sidewalk—he would go on, coming to the part designed to please my mother. Here were tongawallahs screaming at each other, the babagadi of half-rotten onions, an open kiosk selling tea and puris next to a gutter, everyone barefoot or in chappals and wearing dirty clothes, and this girl comes by on her cycle wearing a crisp pink and white shalwar-kameez, with glistening black hair, full pink cheeks, and flashing black eyes! Impulsively, he began humming a film song and followed the girl in a rickshaw until she reached home. The next day, waiting for her at the same place and time as he'd first seen her, he saw her and again followed her in a rickshaw. He then asked a boy, who had observed him staring after her as she went through the gates of her house, Tell me, what college does she attend? The boy gave a wink and told him, and so the following afternoon my father waited for the girl outside the college gates. Before he could muster the courage to speak to her, she said to him, Ay budhu, you oaf why do you follow me? You must be a stranger in these parts, don't you know my father is a police inspector? He'll have the pleasure of having both your legs broken for you. Nevertheless, she let him escort her home. She was enchanted by his foreign accent and awkwardly Indian ways. After a few days my father made an appointment with her father at police headquarters and did the unorthodox thing of proposing to marry his daughter Sheila.

Inspector Verma—my father would say, running forefinger and thumb above his lips to indicate his father-in-law's military moustache—did not speak a word for a full ten minutes, staring at a report in front of him, on his desk. His midmorning cup of tea came and he proceeded to drink it, he nibbled a Marie biscuit. My father had of course introduced himself in some detail. Finally Inspector Verma raised his head and eyed the brash young man who was by now utterly discomfited. He grilled him about his background, made sure my father realized that his antecedents in India amounted to nothing, being village banias at most, and that his father had demeaned himself further as a labourer. When Papa was completely deflated, Inspector Verma told him to send his relations with a formal proposal.

Inspector Verma was a widower, and also somewhat unusual; he worked for the British, and in his duties to maintain law and order he often had to arrest Congresswallahs agitating for independence, one of whom was his own son Mahesh, or send laathi charges against street demonstrators. Gandhi was in jail, there were sporadic riots between Hindus and Muslims. The civilizing order of the day, to the stern inspector, seemed to be on the wane, and the country was on the verge of falling apart. So he agreed to let his lovestruck daughter get away to a part of the world—be it in Africa— where the Empire still held firm, English values and manners still ruled the day.

My father returned to Kenya with my mother in late 1944. I was born the following year. In 1948, after the partition of India, in which Peshawar became part of Pakistan, my mother's kid brother Mahesh—one of the millions of refugees now—followed her to the colony. My father and his brothers called him "communist," because of his radical ideas, the term having a special ring to it in those days, meaning worthless intellectual ranter. My father actually tolerated him and could hold a conversation with him, but his brothers detested Mahesh Uncle. He was broad-shouldered and muscular, with a black untrimmed beard and wild glaring eyes behind his black-framed glasses. He was argumentative and sometimes ill-tempered, and he had a degree in English. And just to irk the settlers and the colonial Indians, on occasional days, such as India's national day, he paraded Nakuru's main streets in khadi, the pyjama and long shirt combination of homespun cotton that had been the symbol of Indian protest, the uniform of those who had fought for India's independence. It had the desired effect in this British colony, in the heart of white settlerdom, where they still believed in the fifties that the sun would never set on their empire.

MY MOTHER AND HER BROTHER had a very special closeness. Many times I came upon them sitting together on the sofa in silence, he having turned toward her, eyes lowered, his hands in his lap in respectful repose. A few times I saw her in that silent communion freely wiping tears from her eyes. She was very fair, her pink cheeks now fuller than when my father had first laid eyes on her, her hair still long and black and thick, her pride and (on washing days) her cross. They had lost their mother and been brought up by a taciturn, high-minded father unable to show his softer nature, especially to his son, and this had not been easy for them. With the independence and partition of India they had lost their homeland. That weighed heavily on all our family, but especially on those two, the freshest arrivals from there. By some perverse twist of fate, Peshawar, our ancestral home, had become an alien, hostile place; it was in Pakistan.

Mr. Innes, whose wife and daughter were slaughtered that Saturday, was a big, gruff, red-haired and -whiskered bully of a man, who always refused to serve Mahesh Uncle at Innes and McGeorge. Hey you, son of a coolie— he would bark briskly and harshly as soon as my uncle pushed through the glass doors. Out! Go back to cowland, Bengalee bastard! Undaunted by the insult, Mahesh Uncle would return on another day, always ostensibly intending to buy a tube of Colgate, which he could have bought for half the price from an Indian merchant, and which he didn't use anyway, patriot that he was, preferring the traditional charcoal concoction that went by the name of Monkey Brand. My Punjabi mother, though, was offended specifically by the description "Bengalee" applied to her brother: But you are not dark-skinned, how *dare* he call you a Bengali!

When our new friends the Bruce children entered our lives, Mahesh Uncle was no longer living with us. He had come as a teacher to the Indian school in Nakuru, but his indiscretions soon lost him the job. Finally Dadaji, through some contact, found him the post of manager of the Resham Singh Sawmills near Njoro, some twenty miles away.

AS MRS. BRUCE DROVE OFF from our parking lot that day of the Innes murders, she almost ran over Mahesh Uncle, who had to jump aside. He often came to spend weekends with us, a mill lorry dropping him off on Saturday and picking him up on Sunday. He had gone to our home and missed us, then walked up to the store. He too had heard of the gruesome incident.

They'll never learn, Mahesh Uncle said, looking in the direction of the pickup which had just barely avoided hitting him. Arrogant bastards, even as the forest fighters pick them off one by one ... and they say they don't understand why they are hated.

Must you now go and support those heinous murderers, my father muttered in irritation. Mahesh Uncle did not reply but looked away to meet my mother's smile of greeting.

THE DOG HAD BEEN HACKED on the head with a panga, though he was still breathing when found, lying on his side on the back stoop. The front door was unlocked but shut; the back door hung wide open. One servant had the day off, the other had disappeared. Laundry was hanging out for drying. The lunch awaiting Henry Innes when he came upon the scene of carnage was macaroni casserole, with fruit and custard for dessert. Mrs. Innes, forty years old, was discovered in the sitting room where she had died from her wounds, one of them a blow to the neck. She was Kenya-born, and her husband had come to the country some ten years earlier. Their eleven-year-old girl, Maggie, was in her shorts when the attack occurred; she had run up to her bedroom in terror, where she was followed and met her end.

For the remainder of that day, right into the late evening when in Nakuru's residential areas doors were fastened and alarms checked, the talk at home and over the phone and with neighbours was about nothing else but the Innes murders. The following day's Sunday papers brought all the details and important opinions. There was a boxed message from the Governor of Kenya, Sir Evelyn Baring, on the front page and a quote from Mrs. Innes's father in England. There were calls for the Governor to resign for not being firm on terrorists. Special Branch officers were photographed in the wooded area outside the Innes house. Clara Innes, it was reported, had been an indefatigable community worker, a tireless dogsbody at the RSPCA and the annual flower show.

The Mau Mau are devils, I said, echoing my mother. Her term was "daityas" from mythology. Krishna had slain many daityas, even as a child. Rama had slain the ten-headed Ravana, and Mau Mau were like that wily daitya, changing shapes at will in the forest, impossible to defeat.

Njoroge and I were sitting in the backyard, having finished with our toy spear, bow and arrow, and gun. All were gifts, made for us from wood and string by Njoroge's grandfather Mwangi. We always took strict turns on who was to be Indian and who cowboy, who cop and who robber. We never played Mau Mau and Special Branch. It was one of those times when, after involved play and play-acting, we sat beside each other and felt close. Perhaps our play provoked questions about our lives that we then felt the need to share but simply couldn't. I do recall that his being different, in features, in status, was not far from my consciousness. I was also aware that he was more from Africa than I was. He was African, I was Asian. His black skin was matte, his woolly hair impossibly alien. I was smaller, with pointed elvish ears, my skin annoyingly "medium," as I described it then, neither one (white) nor the other (black).

Yes, said Njoroge, in response to my observation, they are brave devils. Brave, sure, brave—I said, not to be outdone in bravado—a daylight attack too, and the Europeans carry guns!

It was close to the time of our Sunday family lunch at home, and all my uncles, aunties, and cousins had already gathered, with our dada and dadi. Smells of hot ghee and spices filled the air in the backyards, ginger and garlic and chicken from one house, saffron and onion from another, fresh phulki chappatis and daal from yet another. Lilting melodies and sad lyrics from Saigal, Hemant Kumar, and Talat filled the air, courtesy of KBC's Hindustani service on the shortwave. One song, a favourite among kids, went,

> *O darling little children, what do you hold in your fists? In our fists* (sing the beggar children in chorus) *we hold our fates!*

Soon the songs would give way to the one o'clock news delivered in depressingly funereal tones. Whatever the news, it always sounded tragic. African music played in some of the servant houses. In one song, in Swahili, the singer lamented being sent to Bulawayo to the diamond mines.

Deepa came running out from our house and hurriedly sat down beside us, on her haunches.

Mrs. Innes was brave, wasn't she? Deepa must have heard a snatch of our conversation, probably from the French window above our heads.

She died, Njoroge said.

I don't want to die, Deepa said. I don't want to be a hundred.

In her mind, at that time, to die meant to reach exactly a hundred years.

Njoroge's grandfather Mwangi called him from their flat, a neighbour's servant quarter, and our friend stood up to go. Deepa took a few steps to follow him, then stopped. He turned, smiled, and waved briefly.

OUT IN THE DISTANCE, on the spit of land needling the giant lake, Joseph's gone fishing with two young friends he has found, a girl of ten and a boy of eight from the neighbourhood. If he catches anything large enough he'll bring it back for the barbecue. Sometimes he shows off to his young friends a few deft moves of soccer, and other kids from the few houses nearby come scampering down to join in the play. It is the boy who reminds me of Annie—the innocence with which he runs his hand up and down Joseph's arm, for instance, to feel the black skin, is so reminiscent of my friend from long ago. It has occurred to me—how can it not?—that my picture of my past could well have, like the stories of my grandfather, acquired the patina of nostalgia, become idealized. But then, I have to convince myself, perhaps a greater and conscious discipline and the practice of writing mitigate that danger. I do carry my album of photos with me and my acquired newspaper cuttings and other assorted material, and there is always Deepa to check facts with. Still, what can ultimately withstand the cruel treachery of time, even as one tries to undermine it?

Joseph too has an obsession with the past, that of his people, the Kikuyu. Many peoples in East Africa resisted the European colonization, but they had early on been subdued by the superiority of rifles against arrows and spears. It was the Kikuyu, at least a large section of the tribe, who organized a systematic guerrilla war that struck large terror among the settlers. And it was the Kikuyu who paid the harsh price of British countermeasures and settler rage.

We may need their methods, Joseph says to me once, with a sparkle in his eyes and all the earnestness of his age, speaking of the Mau Mau. Even these days, right now, my people are being oppressed, they are being driven from their homes and butchered. But we will fight back—with guns, not machetes!

He is referring to the recent occurrences of ethnic violence back home, in which the victims have been the Kikuyu of the Nakuru region, whose ancestors were immigrants from across the Aberdares. The youth of his people, he assures me, are now ready to take on their enemies. But the government, as I well know, itself implicated in condoning the ethnic violence, has always been nervous and vigilant about new breeds of militants inspired by those heroes of the past.

Violence and civil war lead nowhere, Joseph, I tell him. Nobody wins. We all lose.

I don't think I sound convincing. We exchange looks, and turn away from each other to face the lake lying still in the dark.

Alice Munro

Alice Munro grew up in Wingham, Ontario, and attended the University of Western Ontario. She has published thirteen books—*Dance of the Happy Shades*; *Lives of Girls and Women*; *Something I've Been Meaning to Tell You*; *Who Do You Think You Are?*; *The Moons of Jupiter*; *The Progress of Love*; *Friend of My Youth*; *Open Secrets*; *Selected Stories*; *The Love of a Good Woman*; *Hateship, Friendship, Courtship, Loveship, Marriage*; *Runaway*; and *The View from Castle Rock*.

During her distinguished career she has received many awards and prizes, including the WH Smith Award in the UK for the year's best book, and, in the USA, the National Book Critics Circle Award, the PEN/Malamud Award for Short Fiction, the Lannan Literary Award for Fiction, and the National Arts Club Medal of Honor for Literature. Her stories appear in magazines such as *The New Yorker*, and she is in demand to visit many countries (such as Italy, in the summer of 2008) to receive further honours, most of which she modestly turns down.

In Canada, over her forty-year publishing career, she has won too many prizes to list. They include three Governor General's Literary Awards; several Libris Awards, given by the country's booksellers; the Trillium Book Award; The CAA Jubilee Award for Short Stories; and two Giller Prizes.

In 2005, she was included in *Time* magazine's list of the world's one hundred most influential people, and she has been mentioned as a potential winner of the Nobel Prize for Literature. She and her husband divide their time between Clinton, Ontario, and Comox, British Columbia.

Runaway

BY ALICE MUNRO

Winner 2004

❧

SILENCE

On the short ferry ride from Buckley Bay to Denman Island, Juliet got out of her car and stood at the front of the boat, in the summer breeze. A woman standing there recognized her, and they began to talk. It is not unusual for people to take a second look at Juliet and wonder where they've seen her before, and, sometimes, to remember. She appears regularly on the Provincial Television channel, interviewing people who are leading singular or notable lives, and deftly directing panel discussions, on a program called *Issues of the Day*. Her hair is cut short now, as short as possible, and has taken on a very dark auburn color, matching the frames of her glasses. She often wears black pants—as she does today—and an ivory silk shirt, and sometimes a black jacket. She is what her mother would have called a striking-looking woman.

"Forgive me. People must be always bothering you."

"It's okay," Juliet says. "Except when I've just been to the dentist or something."

The woman is about Juliet's age. Long black hair streaked with gray, no makeup, long denim skirt. She lives on Denman, so Juliet asks her what she knows about the Spiritual Balance Centre.

"Because my daughter is there," Juliet says. "She's been on a retreat there or taking a course, I don't know what they call it. For six months. This is the first time I've got to see her, in six months."

"There are a couple of places like that," the woman says. "They sort of come and go. I don't mean there's anything suspect about them. Just that they're generally off in the woods, you know, and don't have much to do with the community. Well, what would be the point of a retreat if they did?"

She says that Juliet must be looking forward to seeing her daughter again, and Juliet says yes, very much.

"I'm spoiled," she says. "She's twenty years old, my daughter—she'll be twenty-one this month, actually—and we haven't been apart much."

The woman says that she has a son of twenty and a daughter of eighteen and another of fifteen, and there are days when she'd *pay* them to go on a retreat, singly or all together.

Juliet laughs. "Well. I've only the one. Of course, I won't guarantee that I won't be all for shipping her back, given a few weeks."

This is the kind of fond but exasperated mother-talk she finds it easy to slip into (Juliet is an expert at reassuring responses), but the truth is that Penelope has scarcely ever given her cause for complaint, and if she wanted to be totally honest, at this point she would say that one day without some contact with her daughter is hard to bear, let alone six months. Penelope has worked at Banff, as a summer chambermaid, and she has gone on bus trips to Mexico, a hitchhiking trip to Newfoundland. But she has always lived with Juliet, and there has never been a six-month break.

She gives me delight, Juliet could have said. *Not that she is one of those song-and-dance purveyors of sunshine and cheer and looking-on-the-bright-side. I hope I've brought her up better than that. She has grace and compassion and she is as wise as if she'd been on this earth for eighty years. Her nature is reflective, not all over the map like mine. Somewhat reticent, like her father's. She is also angelically pretty, she's like my mother, blond like my mother but not so frail. Strong and noble. Molded, I should say, like a caryatid. And contrary to popular notions I am not even faintly jealous. All this time without her—and with no word from her, because Spiritual Balance does not allow letters or phone calls—all this time I've been in a sort of desert, and when her message came I was like an old patch of cracked earth getting a full drink of rain.*

Hope to see you Sunday afternoon. It's time.

Time to go home, was what Juliet hoped this meant, but of course she would leave that up to Penelope.

PENELOPE HAD DRAWN a rudimentary map, and Juliet shortly found herself parked in front of an old church—that is, a church building seventy-five or eighty years old, covered with stucco, not as old or anything like as impressive as churches usually were in the part of Canada where Juliet had grown up. Behind it was a more recent building, with a slanting roof and windows all across its front, also a simple stage and some seating benches and what looked like a volleyball court with a sagging net. Everything was shabby, and the once-cleared patch of land was being reclaimed by juniper and poplars.

A couple of people—she could not tell whether men or women—were doing some carpentry work on the stage, and others sat on the benches in separate small groups. All wore ordinary clothes, not yellow robes or anything of that sort. For a few minutes no notice was taken of Juliet's car. Then one of the people on the benches rose and walked unhurriedly towards her. A short, middle-aged man wearing glasses.

She got out of the car and greeted him and asked for Penelope. He did not speak—perhaps there was a rule of silence—but nodded and turned away and went into the church. From which there shortly appeared, not Penelope, but a heavy, slow-moving woman with white hair, wearing jeans and a baggy sweater.

"What an honor to meet you," she said. "Do come inside. I've asked Donny to make us some tea."

She had a broad fresh face, a smile both roguish and tender, and what Juliet supposed must be called twinkling eyes. "My name is Joan," she said. Juliet had been expecting an assumed name like Serenity, or something with an Eastern flavor, nothing so plain and familiar as Joan. Later, of course, she thought of Pope Joan.

"I've got the right place, have I? I'm a stranger on Denman," she said disarmingly. "You know I've come to see Penelope?"

"Of course. Penelope." Joan prolonged the name, with a certain tone of celebration.

The inside of the church was darkened with purple cloth hung over the high windows. The pews and other church furnishings had been removed, and plain white curtains had been strung up to form private cubicles, as in a hospital ward. The cubicle into which Juliet was directed had, however, no bed, just a small table and a couple of plastic chairs, and some open shelves piled untidily with loose papers.

"I'm afraid we're still in the process of getting things fixed up in here," Joan said. "Juliet. May I call you Juliet?"

"Yes, of course."

"I'm not used to talking to a celebrity." Joan held her hands together in a prayer pose beneath her chin. "I don't know whether to be informal or not."

"I'm not much of a celebrity."

"Oh, you are. Now don't say things like that. And I'll just get it off my chest right away, how I admire you for the work you do. It's a beam in the darkness. The only television worth watching."

"Thank you," said Juliet. "I had a note from Penelope—"

"I know. But I'm sorry to have to tell you, Juliet, I'm very sorry and I don't want you to be too disappointed—Penelope is not here."

The woman says those words—*Penelope is not here*—as lightly as possible. You would think that Penelope's absence could be turned into a matter for amused contemplation, even for their mutual delight.

Juliet has to take a deep breath. For a moment she cannot speak. Dread pours through her. Foreknowledge. Then she pulls herself back to reasonable consideration of this fact. She fishes around in her bag.

"She said she hoped—"

"I know. I know," says Joan. "She did intend to be here, but the fact was, she could not—"

"Where is she? Where did she go?"

"I cannot tell you that."

"You mean you can't or you won't?"

"I can't. I don't know. But I can tell you one thing that may put your mind at rest. Wherever she has gone, whatever she has decided, it will be the right thing for her. It will be the *right* thing for her spirituality and her growth."

Juliet decides to let this pass. She gags on the word *spirituality*, which seems to take in—as she often says—everything from prayer wheels to High Mass. She never expected that Penelope, with her intelligence, would be mixed up in anything like this.

"I just thought I should know," she says, "in case she wanted me to send on any of her things."

"Her possessions?" Joan seems unable to suppress a wide smile, though she modifies it at once with an expression of tenderness. "Penelope is not very concerned right now about her *possessions*."

Sometimes Juliet has felt, in the middle of an interview, that the person she faces has reserves of hostility that were not apparent before the cameras started rolling. A person whom Juliet has underestimated, whom she has thought rather stupid, may have strength of that sort. Playful but deadly hostility. The thing then is never to show that you are taken aback, never to display any hint of hostility in return.

"What I mean by growth is our inward growth, of course," Joan says.

"I understand," says Juliet, looking her in the eye.

"Penelope has had such a wonderful opportunity in her life to meet interesting people—goodness, she hasn't needed to meet interesting people, she's *grown up* with an interesting person, you're her *mother*—but you know, sometimes there's a dimension that is missing, grown-up children feel that they've *missed out* on something—"

"Oh yes," says Juliet. "I know that grown-up children can have all sorts of complaints."

Joan has decided to come down hard.

"The spiritual dimension—I have to say this—was it not altogether lacking in Penelope's life? I take it she did not grow up in a faith-based home."

"Religion was not a banned subject. We could talk about it."

"But perhaps it was the way you talked about it. Your intellectual way? If you know what I mean. You are so clever," she adds, kindly.

"So you say."

Juliet is aware that any control of the interview, and of herself, is faltering, and may be lost.

"Not so *I* say, Juliet. So *Penelope* says. Penelope is a dear fine girl, but she has come to us here in great hunger. Hunger for the things that were not available to her in her home. There you were, with your wonderful busy successful life—but Juliet, I must tell you that your daughter has known loneliness. She has known unhappiness."

"Don't most people feel that, one time or another? Loneliness and unhappiness?"

"It's not for me to say. Oh, Juliet. You are a woman of marvellous insights. I've often watched you on television and I've thought, how does she get right to the heart of things like that, and all the time being so nice and polite to people? I never thought I'd be sitting talking to you face-to-face. And what's more, that I'd be in a position to *help* you—"

"I think that maybe you're mistaken about that."

"You feel hurt. It's natural that you should feel hurt."

"It's also my own business."

"Ah well. Perhaps she'll get in touch with you. After all."

PENELOPE DID GET IN TOUCH with Juliet, a couple of weeks later. A birthday card arrived on her own—Penelope's—birthday, the 19th of June.

Her twenty-first birthday. It was the sort of card you send to an acquaintance whose tastes you cannot guess. Not a crude jokey card or a truly witty card or a sentimental card. On the front of it was a small bouquet of pansies tied by a thin purple ribbon whose tail spelled out the words *Happy Birthday*. These words were repeated inside, with the words *Wishing you a very* added in gold letters above them.

And there was no signature. Juliet thought at first that someone had sent this card to Penelope, and forgotten to sign it, and that she, Juliet, had opened it by mistake. Someone who had Penelope's name and the date of her birth on file. Her dentist, maybe, or her driving teacher. But when she checked the writing on the envelope she saw that there had been no mistake—there was her own name, indeed, written in Penelope's own handwriting.

Postmarks gave you no clue anymore. They all said *Canada Post*. Juliet had some idea that there were ways of telling at least which province a letter came from, but for that you would have to consult the Post Office, go there with the letter and very likely be called upon to prove your case, your right to the information. And somebody would be sure to recognize her.

SHE WENT TO SEE her old friend Christa, who had lived in Whale Bay when she herself lived there, even before Penelope was born. Christa was in Kitsilano, in an assisted-living facility. She had multiple sclerosis. Her room was on the ground floor, with a small private patio, and Juliet sat with her there, looking out at a sunny bit of lawn, and the wisteria all in bloom along the fence that concealed the garbage bins.

Juliet told Christa the whole story of the trip to Denman Island. She had told nobody else, and had hoped perhaps not to have to tell anybody. Every day when she was on her way home from work she had wondered if perhaps Penelope would be waiting in the apartment. Or at least that there would be a letter. And then there had been—that unkind card—and she had torn it open with her hands shaking.

"It means something," Christa said. "It lets you know she's okay. Something will follow. It will. Be patient."

Juliet talked bitterly for a while about Mother Shipton. That was what she finally decided to call her, having toyed with and become dissatisfied with Pope Joan. What bloody chicanery, she said. What creepiness, nastiness, behind the second-rate, sweetly religious facade. It was impossible to imagine Penelope's having been taken in by her.

Christa suggested that perhaps Penelope had visited the place because she had considered writing something about it. Some sort of investigative journalism. Fieldwork. The personal angle—the long-winded personal stuff that was so popular nowadays.

Investigating for six months? said Juliet. Penelope could have figured out Mother Shipton in ten minutes.

"It's weird," admitted Christa.

"You don't know more than you're letting on, do you?" said Juliet. "I hate to even ask that. I feel so at sea. I feel stupid. That woman intended me to feel stupid, of course. Like the character who blurts out something in a play and everybody turns away because they all know something she doesn't know—"

"They don't do that kind of play anymore," Christa said. "Now nobody knows anything. No—Penelope didn't take me into her confidence any more than she did you. Why should she? She'd know I'd end up telling you."

Juliet was quiet for a moment, then she muttered sulkily, "There have been things you didn't tell me."

"Oh, for God's sake," said Christa, but without any animosity. "Not that again."

"Not that again," Juliet agreed. "I'm in a lousy mood, that's all."

"Just hold on. One of the trials of parenthood. She hasn't given you many, after all. In a year this will all be ancient history."

Juliet didn't tell her that in the end she had not been able to walk away with dignity. She had turned and cried out beseechingly, furiously.

"What did she tell you?"

And Mother Shipton was standing there watching her, as if she had expected this. A fat pitying smile had stretched her closed lips as she shook her head.

DURING THE NEXT YEAR Juliet would get phone calls, now and then, from people who had been friendly with Penelope. Her reply to their inquiries was always the same. Penelope had decided to take a year off. She was travelling. Her travelling agenda was by no means fixed, and Juliet had no way of contacting her, nor any address she could supply.

She did not hear from anybody who had been a close friend. This might mean that people who had been close to Penelope knew quite well where she was. Or it might be that they too were off on trips to foreign countries, had found jobs in other provinces, were embarked on new lives, too crowded or chancy at present to allow them to wonder about old friends.

(Old friends, at that stage in life, meaning somebody you had not seen for half a year.)

Whenever she came in, the first thing Juliet did was to look for the light flashing on her answering machine—the very thing she used to avoid, thinking there would be someone pestering her about her public utterances. She tried various silly tricks, to do with how many steps she took to the phone, how she picked it up, how she breathed. *Let it be her.*

Nothing worked. After a while the world seemed emptied of the people Penelope had known, the boyfriends she had dropped and the ones who had dropped her, the girls she had gossiped with and probably confided in. She had gone to a private girls' boarding school—Torrance House—rather than to a public high school, and this meant that most of her longtime friends—even those who were still her friends at college—had come from places out of town. Some from Alaska or Prince George or Peru.

There was no message at Christmas. But in June, another card, very much in the style of the first, not a word written inside. Juliet had a drink of wine before she opened it, then threw it away at once. She had spurts of weeping, once in a while of uncontrollable shaking, but she came out of these in quick fits of fury, walking around the house and slapping one fist into her palm. The fury was directed at Mother Shipton, but the image of that woman had faded, and finally Juliet had to recognize that she was really only a convenience.

All pictures of Penelope were banished to her bedroom, with sheaves of drawings and crayonings she had done before they left Whale Bay, her books, and the European one-cup coffee–maker with the plunger that she had bought as a present for Juliet with the first money she had made in her summer job at McDonald's. Also such whimsical gifts for the apartment as a tiny plastic fan to stick on the refrigerator, a wind-up toy tractor, a curtain of glass beads to hang in the bathroom window. The door of that bedroom was shut and in time could be passed without disturbance.

JULIET GAVE A GREAT DEAL OF THOUGHT to getting out of this apartment, giving herself the benefit of new surroundings. But she said to Christa that she could not do that, because that was the address Penelope had, and mail could be forwarded for only three months, so there would be no place then where her daughter could find her.

"She could always get to you at work," said Christa.

"Who knows how long I'll be there?" Juliet said. "She's probably in some commune where they're not allowed to communicate. With some guru who sleeps with all the women and sends them out to beg on the streets. If I'd sent her to Sunday school and taught her to say her prayers this probably wouldn't have happened. I should have. I should have. It would have been like an inoculation. I neglected her *spirituality*. Mother Shipton said so."

WHEN PENELOPE WAS BARELY THIRTEEN YEARS OLD, she had gone away on a camping trip to the Kootenay Mountains of British Columbia, with a friend from Torrance House, and the friend's family. Juliet was in favor of this. Penelope had been at Torrance House for only one year (accepted on favorable financial terms because of her mother's once having taught there), and it pleased Juliet that she had already made so firm a friend and been accepted readily by the friend's family. Also that she was going camping—something that regular children did and that Juliet, as a child, had never had the chance to do. Not that she would have wanted to, being already buried in books—but she welcomed signs that Penelope was turning out to be a more normal sort of girl than she herself had been.

Eric was apprehensive about the whole idea. He thought Penelope was too young. He didn't like her going on a holiday with people he knew so little about. And now that she went to boarding school they saw too little of her as it was—so why should that time be shortened?

Juliet had another reason—she simply wanted Penelope out of the way for the first couple of weeks of the summer holidays, because the air was not clear between herself and Eric. She wanted things resolved, and they were not resolved. She did not want to have to pretend that all was well, for the sake of the child.

Eric, on the other hand, would have liked nothing better than to see their trouble smoothed over, hidden out of the way. To Eric's way of thinking, civility would restore good feeling, the semblance of love would be enough to get by on until love itself might be rediscovered. And if there was never anything more than a semblance—well, that would have to do. Eric could manage with that.

Indeed he could, thought Juliet, despondently.

Having Penelope at home, a reason for them to behave well—for Juliet to behave well, since she was the one, in his opinion, who stirred up all the rancor—that would suit Eric very well.

So Juliet told him, and created a new source of bitterness and blame, because he missed Penelope badly.

The reason for their quarrel was an old and ordinary one. In the spring, through some trivial disclosure—and the frankness or possibly the malice of their longtime neighbor Ailo, who had a certain loyalty to Eric's dead wife and some reservations about Juliet—Juliet had discovered that Eric had slept with Christa. Christa had been for a long time her close friend, but she had been, before that, Eric's girlfriend, his *mistress* (though nobody said that anymore). He had given her up when he asked Juliet to live with him. She had known all about Christa then and she could not reasonably object to what had happened in the time before she and Eric were together. She did not. What she did object to—what she claimed had broken her heart—had happened after that. (But still a long time ago, said Eric.) It had happened when Penelope was a year old, and Juliet had taken her back to Ontario. When Juliet had gone home to visit her parents. To visit—as she always pointed out now—to visit her dying mother. When she was away, and loving and missing Eric with every shred of her being (she now believed this), Eric had simply returned to his old habits.

At first he confessed to once (drunk), but with further prodding, and some drinking in the here-and-now, he said that possibly it had been more often.

Possibly? He could not remember? So many times he could not remember?

He could remember.

CHRISTA CAME TO SEE JULIET, to assure her that it had been nothing serious. (This was Eric's refrain, as well.) Juliet told her to go away and never come back. Christa decided that now would be a good time to go to see her brother in California.

Juliet's outrage at Christa was actually something of a formality. She did understand that a few rolls in the hay with an old girlfriend (Eric's disastrous description, his ill-judged attempt to minimize things) were nowhere near as threatening as a hot embrace with some woman newly met. Also, her outrage at Eric was so fierce and irrepressible as to leave little room for blame of anybody else.

Her contentions were that he did not love her, had never loved her, had mocked her, with Christa, behind her back. He had made her a laughingstock in front of people like Ailo (who had always hated her). That he had treated her with contempt, he regarded the love she felt (or had felt) for him with contempt, he had lived a lie with her. Sex meant nothing to him, or at any rate it did not mean what it meant (had meant) to her, he would have it off with whoever was handy.

Only the last of these contentions had the least germ of truth in it, and in her quieter states she knew that. But even that little truth was enough to pull everything down around her. It shouldn't do that, but it did. And Eric was not able—in all honesty he was not able—to see why that should be so. He was not surprised that she should object, make a fuss, even weep (though a woman like Christa would never have done that), but that she should really be damaged, that she should consider herself bereft of all that had sustained her—and for something that had happened *twelve years ago*—this he could not understand.

Sometimes he believed that she was shamming, making the most of it, and at other times he was full of real grief, that he had made her suffer. Their grief aroused them, and they made love magnificently. And each time he thought that would be the end of it, their miseries were over. Each time he was mistaken.

In bed, Juliet laughed and told him about Pepys and Mrs. Pepys, inflamed with passion under similar circumstances. (Since more or less giving up on her classical studies, she was reading widely, and nowadays everything she read seemed to have to do with adultery.) Never so often and never so hot, Pepys had said, though he recorded as well that his wife had also thought of murdering him in his sleep. Juliet laughed about this, but half an hour later, when he came to say good-bye before going out in the boat to check his prawn traps, she showed a stony face and gave him a kiss of resignation, as if he'd been going to meet a woman out in the middle of the bay and under a rainy sky.

THERE WAS MORE THAN RAIN. The water was hardly choppy when Eric went out, but later in the afternoon a wind came up suddenly, from the southeast, and tore up the waters of Desolation Sound and Malaspina Strait. It continued almost till dark—which did not really close down until around eleven o'clock in this last week of June. By then a sailboat from Campbell River was missing, with three adults and two children aboard. Also two fish boats—one with two men aboard and the other with only one man—Eric.

The next morning was calm and sunny—the mountains, the waters, the shores, all sleek and sparkling.

It was possible, of course, that none of these people were lost, that they had found shelter and spent the night in any of the multitude of little bays. That was more likely to be true of the fishermen than of the family in the sailboat, who were not local people but vacationers from Seattle. Boats went out at once, that morning, to search the mainland and island shores and the water.

The drowned children were found first, in their life jackets, and by the end of the day the bodies of their parents were located as well. A grandfather who had accompanied them was not found until the day after. The bodies of the men who had been fishing together never showed up, though the remnants of their boat washed up near Refuge Cove.

Eric's body was recovered on the third day. Juliet was not allowed to see it. Something had got at him, it was said (meaning some animal), after the body was washed ashore.

It was perhaps because of this—because there was no question of viewing the body and no need for an undertaker—that the idea caught hold amongst Eric's old friends and fellow fishermen of burning Eric on the beach. Juliet did not object to this. A death certificate had to be made out, so the doctor who came to Whale Bay once a week was telephoned at his office in Powell River, and he gave Ailo, who was his weekly assistant and a registered nurse, the authority to do this.

There was plenty of driftwood around, plenty of the sea-salted bark which makes a superior fire. In a couple of hours all was ready. News had spread— somehow, even at such short notice, women began arriving with food. It was Ailo who took charge—her Scandinavian blood, her upright carriage and flowing white hair, seeming to fit her naturally for the role of Widow of the Sea. Children ran about on the logs, and were shooed away from the growing pyre, the shrouded, surprisingly meager bundle that was Eric. A coffee urn was supplied to this half-pagan ceremony by the women from one of the churches, and cartons of beer, bottles of drink of all sorts, were left discreetly, for the time being, in the trunks of cars and cabs of trucks.

The question arose of who would speak, and who would light the pyre. They asked Juliet, would she do it? And Juliet—brittle and busy, handing out mugs of coffee—said that they had it wrong, as the widow she was supposed to throw herself into the flames. She actually laughed as she said this, and those who had asked her backed off, afraid that she was getting hysterical. The man who had partnered Eric most often in the boat agreed to do the lighting, but said he was no speaker. It occurred to some that he would not have been a good choice anyway, since his wife was an Evangelical Anglican, and he might have felt obliged to say things which would have distressed Eric if he had been able to hear them. Then Ailo's husband offered—he was a little man disfigured by a fire on a boat, years ago, a grumbling socialist and atheist, and in his talk he rather lost track of Eric, except to claim him as a Brother in the Battle. He went on at surprising length, and this was ascribed, afterwards, to the suppressed life he led under the rule of Ailo. There might have been some restlessness in the crowd before his recital of grievances got stopped, some feeling that the event was turning out to be not so splendid, or solemn, or heartrending, as might have been expected. But when the fire began to burn this feeling vanished, and there was great concentration, even, or especially, among the children, until the moment when one of the men cried, "Get the kids out of here." This was when the flames had reached the body, bringing the realization, coming rather late, that consumption of fat, of heart and kidneys and liver, might produce explosive or sizzling noises disconcerting to hear. So a good many of the children were hauled away by their mothers—some willingly, some to their own dismay. So the final act of the fire became a mostly male ceremony, and slightly scandalous, even if not, in this case, illegal.

Juliet stayed, wide-eyed, rocking on her haunches, face pressed against the heat. She was not quite there. She thought of whoever it was— Trelawny?—snatching Shelley's heart out of the flames. The heart, with its long history of significance. Strange to think how even at that time, not so long ago, one fleshly organ should be thought so precious, the site of courage and love. It was just flesh, burning. Nothing connected with Eric.

PENELOPE KNEW NOTHING of what was going on. There was a short item in the Vancouver paper—not about the burning on the beach, of course, just about the drowning—but no newspapers or radio reports reached her, deep in the Kootenay Mountains. When she got back to Vancouver she phoned home, from her friend Heather's house. Christa answered—she had got back too late for the ceremony, but was staying with Juliet, and helping as she could. Christa said that Juliet was not there—it was a lie—and asked to speak to Heather's mother. She explained what had happened, and said that she was driving Juliet to Vancouver, they would leave at once, and Juliet would tell Penelope herself when they got there.

Christa dropped Juliet at the house where Penelope was, and Juliet went inside alone. Heather's mother left her in the sunroom, where Penelope was waiting. Penelope received the news with an expression of fright, then—when Juliet rather formally put her arms around her—of something like embarrassment. Perhaps in Heather's house, in the white and green and orange sunroom, with Heather's brothers shooting baskets in the backyard, news so dire could hardly penetrate. The burning was not mentioned—in this house and neighborhood it would surely have seemed uncivilized, grotesque. In this house, also, Juliet's manner was sprightly beyond anything intended—her behavior close to that of *a good sport*.

Heather's mother entered after a tiny knock—with glasses of iced tea. Penelope gulped hers down and went to join Heather, who had been lurking in the hall.

Heather's mother then had a talk with Juliet. She apologized for intruding with practical matters but said that time was short. She and Heather's father were driving east in a few days' time to see relatives. They would be gone for a month, and had planned to take Heather with them. (The boys were going to camp.) But now Heather had decided she did not want to go, she had begged to stay here in the house, with Penelope. A fourteen-year-old and a thirteen-year-old could not really be left alone, and it had occurred to her that Juliet might like some time away, a respite, after what she had been through. After her loss and tragedy.

So Juliet shortly found herself living in a different world, in a large spotless house brightly and thoughtfully decorated, with what are called conveniences—but to her were luxuries—on every hand. This on a curving street lined with similar houses, behind trimmed bushes and showy flower beds. Even the weather, for that month, was flawless—warm, breezy, bright. Heather and Penelope went swimming, played badminton in the backyard, went to the movies, baked cookies, gorged, dieted, worked on their tans, filled the house with music whose lyrics seemed to Juliet sappy and irritating, sometimes invited girlfriends over, did not exactly invite boys but held long, taunting, aimless conversations with some who passed the house or had collected next door. By chance, Juliet heard Penelope say to one of the visiting girls, "Well, I hardly knew him, really."

She was speaking about her father.

How strange.

She had never been afraid to go out in the boat, as Juliet was, when there was a chop on the water. She had pestered him to be taken and was often successful. When following after Eric, in her businesslike orange life jacket, carrying what gear she could manage, she always wore an expression of particular seriousness and dedication. She took note of the setting of the traps and became skilful, quick, and ruthless at the deheading and bagging of the catch. At a certain stage of her childhood—say from eight to eleven—she had always said that she was going to go out fishing when she grew up, and Eric had told her there were girls doing that nowadays. Juliet had thought it was possible, since Penelope was bright but not bookish, and exuberantly physical, and brave. But Eric, out of Penelope's hearing, said that he hoped the idea would wear off, he wouldn't wish the life on anybody. He always spoke this way, about the hardship and uncertainty of the work he had chosen, but took pride, so Juliet thought, in those very things.

And now he was dismissed. By Penelope, who had recently painted her toenails purple and was sporting a false tattoo on her midriff. He who had filled her life. She dismissed him.

But Juliet felt as if she was doing the same. Of course, she was busy looking for a job and a place to live. She had already put the house in Whale Bay up for sale—she could not imagine remaining there. She had sold the truck and given away Eric's tools, and such traps as had been recovered, and the dinghy. Eric's grown son from Saskatchewan had come and taken the dog.

She had applied for a job in the reference department of the university library, and a job in the public library, and she had a feeling she would get one or the other. She looked at apartments in the Kitsilano or Dunbar or Point Grey areas. The cleanness, tidiness, and manageability of city life kept surprising her. This was how people lived where the man's work did not take place out of doors, and where various operations connected with it did not end up indoors. And where the weather might be a factor in your mood but never in your life, where such dire matters as the changing habits and availability of prawns and salmon were merely interesting, or not remarked upon at all. The life she had been leading at Whale Bay, such a short time ago, seemed haphazard, cluttered, exhausting, by comparison. And she herself was cleansed of the moods of the last months—she was brisk and competent, and better-looking.

Eric should see her now.

She thought about Eric in this way all the time. It was not that she failed to realize that Eric was dead—that did not happen for a moment. But nevertheless she kept constantly referring to him, in her mind, as if he was still the person to whom her existence mattered more than it could to anyone else. As if he was still the person in whose eyes she hoped to shine. Also the person to whom she presented arguments, information, surprises. This was such a habit with her, and took place so automatically, that the fact of his death did not seem to interfere with it.

Nor was their last quarrel entirely resolved. She held him to account, still, for his betrayal. When she flaunted herself a little now, it was against that.

The storm, the recovery of the body, the burning on the beach—that was all like a pageant she had been compelled to watch and compelled to believe in, which still had nothing to do with Eric and herself.

SHE GOT THE JOB in the reference library, she found a two-bedroom apartment that she could just afford, Penelope went back to Torrance House as a day student. Their affairs at Whale Bay were wound up, their life there finished. Even Christa was moving out, coming to Vancouver in the spring.

On a day before that, a day in February, Juliet stood in the shelter at the campus bus stop when her afternoon's work was over. The day's rain had stopped, there was a band of clear sky in the west, red where the sun had gone down, out over the Strait of Georgia. This sign of the lengthening days, the promise of the change of season, had an effect on her that was unexpected and crushing.

She realized that Eric was dead.

As if all this time, while she was in Vancouver, he had been waiting somewhere, waiting to see if she would resume her life with him. As if being with him was an option that had stayed open. Her life since she came here had still been lived against a backdrop of Eric, without her ever quite understanding that Eric did not exist. Nothing of him existed. The memory of him in the daily and ordinary world was in retreat.

So this is grief. She feels as if a sack of cement has been poured into her and quickly hardened. She can barely move. Getting onto the bus, getting off the bus, walking half a block to her building (why is she living here?), is like climbing a cliff. And now she must hide this from Penelope.

At the supper table she began to shake, but could not loosen her fingers to drop the knife and fork. Penelope came around the table and pried her hands open. She said, "It's Dad, isn't it?"

Juliet afterwards told a few people—such as Christa—that these seemed the most utterly absolving, the most tender words, that anybody had ever said to her.

Penelope ran her cool hands up and down the insides of Juliet's arms. She phoned the library the next day to say that her mother was sick, and she took care of her for a couple of days, staying home from school until Juliet recovered. Or until, at least, the worst was over.

During those days Juliet told Penelope everything. Christa, the fight, the burning on the beach (which she had so far managed, almost miraculously, to conceal from her). Everything.

"I shouldn't burden you with all this."

Penelope said, "Yeah, well, maybe not." But added staunchly, "I forgive you. I guess I'm not a baby."

Juliet went back into the world. The sort of fit she had had in the bus stop recurred, but never so powerfully.

Through her research work in the library, she met some people from the Provincial Television channel, and took a job they offered. She had worked there for about a year when she began to do interviews. All the indiscriminate reading she'd done for years (and that Ailo had so disapproved of, in the days at Whale Bay), all the bits and pieces of information she'd picked up, her random appetite and quick assimilation, were now to come in handy. And she cultivated a self-deprecating, faintly teasing manner that usually seemed to go over well. On camera, few things fazed her. Though in fact she would go home and march back and forth, letting out whimpers or curses as she recalled some perceived glitch or fluster or, worse still, a mispronunciation.

AFTER FIVE YEARS the birthday cards stopped coming.

"It doesn't mean anything," Christa said. "All they were for was to tell you she's alive somewhere. Now she figures you've got the message. She trusts you not to send some tracker after her. That's all."

"Did I put too much on her?"

"Oh, Jul."

"I don't mean just with Eric dying. Other men, later. I let her see too much misery. My stupid misery."

For Juliet had had two affairs during the years that Penelope was between fourteen and twenty-one, and during both of these she had managed to fall hectically in love, though she was ashamed afterwards. One of the men was much older than she, and solidly married. The other was a good deal younger, and was alarmed by her ready emotions. Later she wondered at these herself. She really had cared nothing for him, she said.

"I wouldn't think you did," said Christa, who was tired. "I don't know."

"Oh Christ. I was such a fool. I don't get like that about men anymore. Do I?"

Christa did not mention that this might be because of a lack of candidates.

"No, Jul. No."

"Actually I didn't do anything so terrible," Juliet said then, brightening up. "Why do I keep lamenting that it's my fault? She's a conundrum, that's all. I need to face that.

"A conundrum and a cold fish," she said, in a parody of resolution.

"No," said Christa.

"No," said Juliet. "No—that's not true."

After the second June had passed without any word, Juliet decided to move. For the first five years, she told Christa, she had waited for June, wondering what might come. The way things were now, she had to wonder every day. And be disappointed every day.

She moved to a high-rise building in the West End. She meant to throw away the contents of Penelope's room, but in the end she stuffed it all into garbage bags and carried it with her. She had only one bedroom now but there was storage space in the basement.

She took up jogging in Stanley Park. Now she seldom mentioned Penelope, even to Christa. She had a boyfriend—that was what you called them now—who had never heard anything about her daughter.

Christa grew thinner and moodier. Quite suddenly, one January, she died.

YOU DON'T GO ON FOREVER, appearing on television. However agreeable the viewers have found your face, there comes a time when they'd prefer somebody different. Juliet was offered other jobs—researching, writing voice-over for nature shows—but she refused them cheerfully, describing herself as in need of a total change. She went back to Classical Studies—an even smaller department than it used to be—she meant to resume writing her thesis for her Ph.D. She moved out of the high-rise apartment and into a bachelor flat, to save money.

Her boyfriend had got a teaching job in China.

Her flat was in the basement of a house, but the sliding doors at the back opened out at ground level. And there she had a little brick-paved patio, a trellis with sweet peas and clematis, herbs and flowers in pots. For the first time in her life, and in a very small way, she was a gardener, as her father had been.

Sometimes people said to her—in stores, or on the campus bus—"Excuse me, but your face is so familiar," or, "Aren't you the lady that used to be on television?" But after a year or so this passed. She spent a lot of time sitting and reading, drinking coffee at sidewalk tables, and nobody noticed her. She let her hair grow out. During the years that it had been dyed red it had lost the vigor of its natural brown—it was a silvery brown now, fine and wavy. She was reminded of her mother, Sara. Sara's soft, fair, flyaway hair, going gray and then white.

She did not have room to have people to dinner anymore, and she had lost interest in recipes. She ate meals that were nourishing enough, but monotonous. Without exactly meaning to, she lost contact with most of her friends.

It was no wonder. She lived now a life as different as possible from the life of the public, vivacious, concerned, endlessly well-informed woman that she had been. She lived amongst books, reading through most of her waking hours and being compelled to deepen, to alter, whatever premise she had started with. She often missed the world news for a week at a time.

She had given up on her thesis and become interested in some writers referred to as the Greek novelists, whose work came rather late in the history of Greek literature (starting in the first century b.c.e., as she had now learned to call it, and continuing into the early Middle Ages). Aristeides, Longus, Heliodorus, Achilles Tatius. Much of their work is lost or fragmentary and is also reported to be indecent. But there is a romance written by Heliodorus, and called the *Aethiopica* (originally in a private library, retrieved at the siege of Buda), that has been known in Europe since it was printed at Basle in 1534.

In this story the queen of Ethiopia gives birth to a white baby, and is afraid she will be accused of adultery. So she gives the child—a daughter—into the care of the gymnosophists—that is, the naked philosophers, who are hermits and mystics. The girl, who is called Charicleia, is finally taken to Delphi, where she becomes one of the priestesses of Artemis. There she meets a noble Thessalian named Theagenes, who falls in love with her and, with the help of a clever Egyptian, carries her off. The Ethiopian queen, as it turns out, has never ceased to long for her daughter and has hired this very Egyptian to search for her. Mischance and adventures continue until all the main characters meet at Meroe, and Charicleia is rescued—again— just as she is about to be sacrificed by her own father.

Interesting themes were thick as flies here, and the tale had a natural continuing fascination for Juliet. Particularly the part about the gymnosophists. She tried to find out as much as she could about these people, who were usually referred to as Hindu philosophers. Was India, in this case, presumed to be adjacent to Ethiopia? No—Heliodorus came late enough to know his geography better than that. The gymnosophists would be wanderers, far spread, attracting and repelling those they lived amongst with their ironclad devotion to purity of life and thought, their contempt for possessions, even for clothing and food. A beautiful maiden reared amongst them might well be left with some perverse hankering for a bare, ecstatic life.

Juliet had made a new friend named Larry. He taught Greek, and he had let Juliet store the garbage bags in the basement of his house. He liked to imagine how they might make the *Aethiopica* into a musical. Juliet collaborated in this fantasy, even to making up the marvellously silly songs and the preposterous stage effects. But she was secretly drawn to devising a different ending, one that would involve renunciation, and a backward search, in which the girl would be sure to meet fakes and charlatans, impostors, shabby imitations of what she was really looking for. Which was reconciliation, at last, with the erring, repentant, essentially greathearted queen of Ethiopia.

JULIET WAS ALMOST CERTAIN that she had seen Mother Shipton here in Vancouver. She had taken some clothes that she would never wear again (her wardrobe had grown increasingly utilitarian) to a Salvation Army Thrift Store, and as she set the bag down in the receiving room she saw a fat old woman in a muumuu fixing tags onto trousers. The woman was chatting with the other workers. She had the air of a supervisor, a cheerful but vigilant overseer—or perhaps the air of a woman who would assume that role whether she had any official superiority or not.

If she was in fact Mother Shipton, she had come down in the world. But not by very much. For if she was Mother Shipton, would she not have reserves of buoyancy and self-approbation, such as to make real downfall impossible?

Reserves of advice, pernicious advice, as well.

She has come to us here in great hunger.

JULIET HAD TOLD LARRY about Penelope. She had to have one person who knew. "Should I have talked to her about a noble life?" she said.

"Sacrifice? Opening your life to the needs of strangers? I never thought of it. I must have acted as if it would have been good enough if she turned out like me. Would that sicken her?"

LARRY WAS NOT A MAN who wanted anything from Juliet but her friendship and good humor. He was what used to be called an old-fashioned bachelor, asexual as far as she could tell (but probably she could not tell far enough), squeamish about any personal revelations, endlessly entertaining.

Two other men had appeared who wanted her as a partner. One of them she had met when he sat down at her sidewalk table. He was a recent widower. She liked him, but his loneliness was so raw and his pursuit of her so desperate that she became alarmed.

The other man was Christa's brother, whom she had met several times during Christa's life. His company suited her—in many ways he was like Christa. His marriage had ended long ago, he was not desperate—she knew, from Christa, that there had been women ready to marry him whom he had avoided. But he was too rational, his choice of her verged on being cold-blooded, there was something humiliating about it.

But why humiliating? It was not as if she loved him.

It was while she was still seeing Christa's brother—his name was Gary Lamb—that she ran into Heather, on a downtown street in Vancouver. Juliet and Gary had just come out of a theater where they had seen an early-evening movie, and they were talking about where to go for dinner. It was a warm night in summer, the light still not gone from the sky.

A woman detached herself from a group on the sidewalk. She came straight at Juliet. A thin woman, perhaps in her late thirties. Fashionable, with taffy streaks in her dark hair.

"Mrs. Porteous. Mrs. Porteous."

Juliet knew the voice, though she would never have known the face. Heather.

"This is incredible," Heather said. "I'm here for three days and I'm leaving tomorrow. My husband's at a conference. I was thinking that I don't know anybody here anymore and then I turn around and see you."

Juliet asked her where she was living now and she said Connecticut.

"And just about three weeks ago I was visiting Josh—you remember my brother Josh?—I was visiting my brother Josh and his family in Edmonton and I ran into Penelope. Just like this, on the street. No—actually it was in the mall, that humongous mall they have. She had a couple of her kids with her, she'd brought them down to get uniforms for that school they go to. The boys. We were both flabbergasted. I didn't know her right away but she recognized me. She'd flown down, of course. From that place way up north. But she says it's quite civilized, really. And she said you were still living here. But I'm with these people—they're my husband's friends—and I really haven't had time to ring you up—"

Juliet made some gesture to say that of course there would not be time and she had not expected to be rung up.

She asked how many children Heather had.

"Three. They're all monsters. I hope they grow up in a hurry. But my life's a picnic compared with Penelope's. *Five.*"

"Yes."

"I have to run now, we're going to see a movie. I don't even know anything about it, I don't even like French movies. But it was altogether great meeting you like this. My mother and dad moved to White Rock. They used to see you all the time on TV. They used to brag to their friends that you'd lived in our house. They say you're not on anymore, did you get sick of it?"

"Something like that."

"I'm coming, I'm coming." She hugged and kissed Juliet, the way everybody did now, and ran to join her companions.

SO. PENELOPE DID NOT LIVE in Edmonton—she had *come down* to Edmonton. Flown down. That meant she must live in Whitehorse or in Yellowknife. Where else was there that she could describe as *quite civilized*? Maybe she was being ironical, mocking Heather a bit, when she said that.

She had five children and two at least were boys. They were being outfitted with school uniforms. That meant a private school. That meant money.

Heather had not known her at first. Did that mean she had aged? That she was out of shape after five pregnancies, that she had not *taken care of herself*? As Heather had. As Juliet had, to a certain extent. That she was one of those women to whom the whole idea of such a struggle seemed ridiculous, a confession of insecurity? Or just something she had no time for—far outside of her consideration.

Juliet had thought of Penelope being involved with transcendentalists, of her having become a mystic, spending her life in contemplation. Or else— rather the opposite but still radically simple and spartan—earning her living in a rough and risky way, fishing, perhaps with a husband, perhaps also with some husky little children, in the cold waters of the Inside Passage off the British Columbia coast.

Not at all. She was living the life of a prosperous, practical matron. Married to a doctor, maybe, or to one of those civil servants managing the northern parts of the country during the time when their control is being gradually, cautiously, but with some fanfare, relinquished to the native people. If she ever met Penelope again they might laugh about how wrong Juliet had been. When they told about their separate meetings with Heather, how weird that was, they would laugh.

No. No. The fact was surely that she had already laughed too much around Penelope. Too many things had been jokes. Just as too many things—personal things, loves that were maybe just gratification—had been tragedies. She had been lacking in motherly inhibitions and propriety and self-control.

Penelope had said that she, Juliet, was still living in Vancouver. She had not told Heather anything about the breach. Surely not. If she had been told, Heather would not have spoken so easily.

How did Penelope know that she was still here, unless she checked in the phone directory? And if she did, what did that mean?

Nothing. Don't make it mean anything.

She walked to the curb to join Gary, who had tactfully moved away from the scene of the reunion.

Whitehorse, Yellowknife. It was painful indeed to know the names of those places—places she could fly to. Places where she could loiter in the streets, devise plans for catching glimpses.

But she was not so mad. She must not be so mad.

At dinner, she thought that the news she had just absorbed put her into a better situation for marrying Gary, or living with him—whatever it was he wanted. There was nothing to worry about, or hold herself in wait for, concerning Penelope. Penelope was not a phantom, she was safe, as far as anybody is safe, and she was probably as happy as anybody is happy. She had detached herself from Juliet and very likely from the memory of Juliet, and Juliet could not do better than to detach herself in turn.

But she had told Heather that Juliet was living in Vancouver. Did she say *Juliet?* Or *Mother. My mother.*

Juliet told Gary that Heather was the child of old friends. She had never spoken to him about Penelope, and he had never given any sign of knowing about Penelope's existence. It was possible that Christa had told him, and he had remained silent out of a consideration that it was none of his business. Or that Christa had told him, and he had forgotten. Or that Christa had never mentioned anything about Penelope, not even her name.

If Juliet lived with him the fact of Penelope would never surface, Penelope would not exist.

Nor did Penelope exist. The Penelope Juliet sought was gone. The woman Heather had spotted in Edmonton, the mother who had brought her sons to Edmonton to get their school uniforms, who had changed in face and body so that Heather did not recognize her, was nobody Juliet knew.

Does Juliet believe this?

If Gary saw that she was agitated he pretended not to notice. But it was probably on this evening that they both understood they would never be together. If it had been possible for them to be together she might have said to him, *My daughter went away without telling me good-bye and in fact she probably did not know then that she was going. She did not know it was for good. Then gradually, I believe, it dawned on her how much she wanted to stay away. It is just a way that she has found to manage her life.*

It's maybe the explaining to me that she can't face. Or has not time for, really. You know, we always have the idea that there is this reason or that reason and we keep trying to find out reasons. And I could tell you plenty about what I've done wrong. But I think the reason may be something not so easily dug out. Something like purity in her nature. Yes. Some fineness and strictness and purity, some rock-hard honesty in her. My father used to say of someone he disliked, that he had no use for that person. Couldn't those words mean simply what they say? Penelope does not have a use for me.

Maybe she can't stand me. It's possible.

JULIET HAS FRIENDS. Not so many now—but friends. Larry continues to visit, and to make jokes. She keeps on with her studies. The word *studies* does not seem to describe very well what she does—*investigations* would be better.

And being short of money, she works some hours a week at the coffee place where she used to spend so much time at the sidewalk tables. She finds this work a good balance for her involvement with the old Greeks— so much so that she believes she wouldn't quit even if she could afford to.

She keeps on hoping for a word from Penelope, but not in any strenuous way. She hopes as people who know better hope for undeserved blessings, spontaneous remissions, things of that sort.

David Bergen

David Bergen's novel *The Time in Between* won the 2005 Scotiabank Giller Prize, The McNally Robinson Book of the Year Award, and the Margaret Laurence Award for Fiction. It was also named a Kiriyama Prize Notable Book and longlisted for the International IMPAC Dublin Literary Award. Bergen is also the author of a collection of short fiction, *Sitting Opposite My Brother,* a finalist for The Manitoba Book of the Year Award, and the novels *A Year of Lesser,* winner of The McNally Robinson Book of the Year Award and a *New York Times* Notable Book, *See the Child,* and *The Case of Lena S.,* winner of The Carol Shields Winnipeg Book Award and a finalist for the Governor General's Literary Awards. His latest novel is *The Retreat,* which was nominated for the 2008 Scotiabank Giller Prize.

David Bergen lives in Winnipeg.

The Time in Between

BY DAVID BERGEN

Winner 2005

Ⓐ

In the evening Charles took a cyclo up to Thanh Thuy Street and stopped at a painted green gate and looked in on a garden where a dog slept. He called hello. The lights in the house were on and the door was open and inside the first room Charles saw a couch and a coffee table and a cup of tea that was still steaming. He waited and eventually a woman appeared. He called out again, and she looked into the darkness, holding her hand up as a visor. She was dressed in jeans and a button-down white shirt. She wore cloth slippers. She walked toward Charles and said, "I do not speak English." She opened the gate and said, "Come in, please." Charles stepped inside and said, "I'm looking for Hoang Vu, the artist."

The woman bowed slightly and left him standing in the courtyard. The dog lifted its head and blinked.

A young girl entered the room, stopped, and stared. She was wearing shorts and a big T-shirt and her hair was in braids.

"Hello," Charles said.

The girl said hello. Her pronunciation was exact. She asked, "Are you rich?" and then laughed and backed out of the room as Hoang Vu appeared. He was wearing a white shirt and black polyester pants and socks with broad stripes of white and baby blue. The elastic was gone on the socks and they had drooped at his heels.

"You have come," Vu said. "Good, good." He motioned at the couch and told Charles to sit. He sat across from him, lit a cigarette, and said that he had many friends in many places, in London, in Montevideo, in Paris, but it was always nice to meet someone new, and that was why, that afternoon with Thanh, he had asked Charles to visit. He stood and excused himself and left the room, and in a moment he returned with two glasses and a bottle of whiskey, which was a third full. He poured generously, handed

Charles a glass, and said, "To new friends." They touched glasses and drank. Vu finished his and poured himself another. "I know a little about you," he said. "Tell me more."

Charles talked about his life back on the mountain and about his three children, and then he said that almost thirty years ago he had fought in Vietnam and now he was coming back for a visit. He said the country surprised him. He didn't really know what he had expected.

"This is the case, isn't it?" Vu said. "We set sail in a particular direction, certain of the route, and then find ourselves loose." He paused and tilted his head. "Or adrift. That is more correct. Yes."

Charles said that it was, and he complimented Vu on his English.

Vu dismissed this. "As I said, I have foreign friends, and with these friends I must speak English. How many people from Uruguay know Vietnamese? You see." He drank and then leaned forward, elbows on his knees, and said that it was to his benefit to meet people who came from another place, because that could only add to his artistic vision. "Imagine sitting in a room by yourself with nothing to look at, no one to talk to. I need other people. I need images. I need the solid world. I am asked sometimes why I don't move to another country where there is more freedom, and my answer is that I cannot be an artist elsewhere. How would I remain faithful? From which place would I tell my story? Finally, of course, the artist is alone, like Dang Tho, the writer we talked of the other day. I feel great envy and great pity for him. He has succeeded in angering the authorities, but he is also separate. This is what happens, isn't it? A man has a vision which is not political, but others make it so, and so the vision is made smaller because some person of little consequence decides that the man with the vision is too big, too proud."

Vu stopped. "I am talking too much," he said. He drank quickly and then said, "Dang Tho's answer to all the attention around the novel was to turn away. He did not write another book. And of course, though the war did not kill him, the time after the war probably will. He is a man bathed in a sad blue light."

He stood and left the room once again, coming back a few minutes later with a plate of satay pork garnished with mint and wrapped in rice paper. Vu began talking about his time after the war, about returning to Hanoi and the difficulty of life. He said that his niece—he lived with his sister and her daughter—had been born a long time after the war, good for her, and with fortune she would never have to suffer. He had run out of cigarettes and he called for the girl. She left and returned some time later, handed him a pack of Raves, and moved sideways out of the room, her bare feet brushing the tile. Vu poured more whiskey for them both, lit a Rave, and closed his eyes. He said, "I love everything. Art. Books. Women. There is an Indian writer, Tagore, a poet. I love him. I love languages. French. André Gide. Sinhalese, German, Arabic." He paused.

"You speak Arabic?" Charles asked.

"Maybe. A good poet is Nguyen Du. 'In another three hundred years, Will anyone weep, remembering my Fate?' Or Tan Da, he wrote about getting drunk. Do you like poetry?" He was looking at Charles. Then, before Charles could answer, Vu was off on several more lines, from *Hamlet* this time, and then back to a Vietnamese poet, Nguyen Khuyen, and he recited in a soft voice, and though Charles did not understand the words or their deeper meaning, he felt that he had arrived at some unlikely place.

Vu got slowly drunk. His conversation began to meander. He quoted both Kahlil Gibran and Ernest Hemingway. He said, "I read *The Prophet* years ago when I was in school. How do you say his name, Kawleel Zibrun? Like that. And Hemingway, you know that one about the fish where the old man comes back with nothing? That's it. You fly over things, you must, and you arrive on the other side with nothing. You ask me, do I believe? I love the tiniest flower, that rock, that tree, the indigo moon. I am not a Communist. I can believe. But that's a big question. Everyone's question."

They drank and when the whiskey was gone Vu wandered into another room and came back with a bottle of brandy and poured a little into their glasses. He raised his glass, studied it, and then he ducked his long face and drank quickly.

At two in the morning Charles shook Vu's hand by the green gate. The moon was full and the streets were bright. Vu offered Charles his bicycle, even began to set off to find it, but Charles stopped him, saying he would walk up to one of the busier streets until he found a taxi.

He did not know when he lost his way but he supposed it might have been just after he turned off Thanh Thuy Street. He had come down a small lane that he did not recognize and he had arrived at a beach. He did not know this particular beach. It was different from the one at My Khe; debris floated on the water. He walked and he was aware of his own breathing and the roiling of his stomach. He passed shuttered shops and he wandered through small streets and crossed large thoroughfares. Always, he looked for the bright neon sign of the Binh Duong Hotel, but he never saw it.

He walked by an old man sitting in a metal chair by a child's swing. Charles tried to talk to the man, but he was sleeping. On a dead-end street, near a cluster of buildings that turned out to be a carpet factory, he was set on by a man brandishing a long knife. The man talked to him quickly and moved the knife in short thrusts through the air. Charles backed up until he was at the gate. He took out his cigarettes and offered the man the pack. The man put the knife in the waistband of his shorts, took the pack, and lit a cigarette, all the time watching Charles. The man made a motion with his free hand, a curling of his fingers. The knife was still tucked away. Charles was drunk. If he had not been drunk he would have swung at the man, who was small and thin. His shorts were dirty and his T-shirt was torn. Charles stepped forward and in a single motion the man pulled out the knife once more and swung at Charles's waist. The knife slit his shirt. Charles looked down. Put his hand to his waist and felt something wet. "Fuck," he said and he looked at the man, who clicked his teeth and circled Charles and passed the knife by his face. In the darkness the man was a black ghost, and it came to Charles, in the haze of his drunkenness, that he was going to die. The man crouched and muttered some words that were foreign and fluttered about in the air. There was the knife in one hand and the cigarette in the other and as the man shuffled clockwise he drew on the cigarette and then exhaled at Charles. Charles thought of the money in his wallet. He reached for it and the man cried out and lunged forward. Charles swivelled and watched the knife slide past his rib cage. The man stumbled and fell. Charles knew then that he should kick the man in the chest and in the head, but instead he stood there, offering his wallet. The man rose and was going to reach for the wallet when from the courtyard of the carpet factory there came a whistling sound, a shout, and the rattling of a gate, and the man fled.

It was the night guard of the factory who beckoned. "You, come," he said, and he led Charles through a small metal gate and into the showroom. He made Charles sit on a rolled-up silk rug. He returned with a glass of water and handed it to Charles. "Okay?" he asked.

Charles looked at his stomach. The knife had barely scratched his abdomen, leaving the slightest trace of blood. He nodded and thanked the guard. A single light shone down on the spot where he sat. The night guard was an old man with bowed legs. He carried a magazine and a cup of tea. Keys hung from his belt. He spoke quickly and then left and returned some time later and directed Charles out to the taxi he had found. Charles offered the guard money, but he moved his hands back and forth and said, "Happy, okay?" and he closed the taxi door. Riding home through the quiet streets, Charles saw the moon and the clouds around the moon. His chest hurt. He could not remember if his attacker had hit him in the chest. He didn't think so, but he could not remember.

In his room, he showered and then lay on his bed in shorts and waited for a sleep that would not come. He recalled the attack as something that had happened quickly and with little warning. He had been more curious than alarmed, as if he were a spectator at the scene of his own execution, and he wondered at what point indifference had set in. He saw Vu's long face, the dark high cheekbones, heard the soughing of his voice.

And then he sat up, as if from a dream, though he had not been asleep. Thoughts had been dipping like swallows in and out of his head. He had discovered a kind of narrative but the story had turned out badly. He put it down to a brief sleep that had produced a nightmare in which his attacker, just before sticking him with the knife, had whispered in his ear, "What we have on our hands is always enough."

He was shaking. His mouth was dry. He got up and drank some water. The manner of his own death was an important one. To be killed by a wastrel and a drunk in the dirty streets of Danang was not what he had imagined. The man had been missing two front teeth, and contrary to the dream, he did not speak English, neither was he any sort of a philosopher.

Charles sat in a chair and watched the sun rise. It came quickly, red turning to orange and then yellow and finally white. He recalled mornings like this on the mountain when the children were younger, mornings when he sat and waited for their voices or the padding of their feet, and always it was Ada who came to him first, settling into his lap, the smell of sleep on her breath, her bare arms around his neck. "Daddy," she said, and nothing more. She didn't need more. Sitting there, her head pressed against his neck, was enough.

ON THE WEEKEND he took the train up to Hue. From his window seat he saw the occasional aqueduct and the cliffs falling away into the fog below and then the ocean breaking through that fog.

In Hue it was cold and windy and raining. He found a small room for ten dollars a night and then walked the streets close to the Perfume River. As arranged, he met Jack and Elaine for dinner. They ate noodles and tiny whole fish fried in garlic. Jack drank Festi, Elaine and Charles ordered beer. The restaurant was cold; rain drove against the shuttered windows. Elaine said that the car ride up had been beautiful. She described the hairpin turns and the colour of the ocean far below. Charles watched her as she talked. At her neck was a silver necklace and as she talked she fingered the necklace and sometimes it seemed that her hand wanted to reach across the table, but it didn't. Jack seemed distracted. He looked out the open doorway or he watched other customers and, once, he struck up a conversation with the owner of the restaurant, a tall man wearing a beret. Later, Charles complimented Jack on how well he spoke Vietnamese.

"How do you know?" Jack asked, and grinned.

"Don't listen to him," Elaine said. "Jack always says that a good ear helps you hear the tones. Jack thinks he is a singer."

"And you?" Charles asked Elaine.

"She doesn't want to speak the language," Jack said. "Anything that smells of this country, she throws away or deliberately ignores."

Elaine moved her food around on the plate with a fork. "I enjoyed this fish," she said. "I like being here, right now." Her head lifted. "Jack likes to show off, to use his halting Vietnamese, which is really quite elementary. And he thinks that talking to a restaurant owner who wears a beret, that this somehow raises our estimation of Jack Gouds. May I?" She reached for Charles's cigarettes. Took out one and lit it. Her hand was shaking.

Jack watched her. He said, "When did you pick that up?"

Elaine exhaled. "Oh, long long ago. Before we met. Millions of years ago, in fact."

Jack said to Charles, "She's impossible."

Charles took a cigarette for himself and shrugged. Beyond the open door he saw the rain and a cyclo driver curled up under his canopy.

Elaine said, "Charles and I are going to see the Citadel tomorrow. Aren't we."

Charles said that that would be fine.

Jack nodded and said, "Good, good," and then explained that both tourists and locals were pillaging the grounds of the Citadel, prying up ceramic tiles that had been laid a thousand years earlier. It was a shame, he said.

Elaine said, "We are not the kind of people who plunder. Are we, Charles?"

Charles, trying to save Elaine, said that he knew nothing about the history of the Citadel. He said that history was not his strength, but still he liked walking through castles and museums.

"Well," Elaine said happily, "that's exactly what we'll do." And she told Charles they should meet there at noon. It was easy to find, in the middle of town.

On parting, Jack seemed to want to repair the evening. He held an umbrella above Elaine's head and said that he had been bad company. He was sorry. Charles waved the apology away. In the driving rain, he was aware of Elaine studying him, and then her mouth moved and she said, "See you tomorrow."

He rode back to the hotel by cyclo. His feet and hands were cold, his head felt light, and he saw the images that passed as if they were happening elsewhere and at another time: a man leaning over a pool table; a child crying beside a chicken; a woman sleeping inside her jewellery shop; a boy being beaten with a stick by two other boys while several people looked on and laughed; a basket of bread; a man and a fridge on a bicycle.

That night he sat at a small desk and opened Dang Tho's novel to the blank pages at the back where he had written the few lines in Hanoi and the date, October 4. Now, he wrote Elaine Gouds's name. And then he wrote, "In Hue. It is raining. The room is damp and chilly. Ate fish the size of pencils. She is sharper than him by far. Than I am, as well."

AT THE CITADEL the next day, Charles walked past small iron cannons and foundering sculptures, on down the walkway between two shallow pools, and came upon Elaine sitting in an alcove full of sunshine. He said her name and she looked at him and said that the sun's heat was making her sleepy. They sat and looked out at the grounds. Several French tourists took photographs of their group by the entrance to the Midday Gate. Elaine said that she had thought of Charles all night. "I couldn't sleep. The room was cold. I imagined a day of looting." She laughed. Closed her eyes. Her hair was pulled back in a short ponytail. The marble spiral of her ear. Her eyes opened, caught him looking. He shifted, aware of the sun on his knees.

"Sixteen years I've been married to Jack," she said. "We met in college. He wrote for the paper, I was on the debating team. We moved around a lot at first and finally bought a house in a suburb outside of Kansas City. And then about a year ago Jack started to get restless and to talk about going overseas, doing something different with our lives. We went back and forth, with him really pushing and me resisting. I loved my life. I had started up a small catering business with a friend and I didn't want to walk away. And then Jack suggested Vietnam and I said, Okay." She paused and whispered *okay* again. She removed the cap from a bottle of water and drank. Then she said, "I was thinking about you being here so many years ago. How old were you?"

Charles hesitated, then said, "Eighteen."

Elaine considered this. "I was ten when I first heard about it. I remember things. Or maybe I think I remember. The television reports. The images. That little girl running down the road screaming. The helicopters lifting off of roofs." She touched his arm.

"I saw that photo," Charles said. "The one of you with your horse."

"Albany. I was older there."

"Did you know Jack already?"

She nodded. "I did."

"You had a good life."

"You mean spoiled."

He said he didn't mean that. He said that there were times when he wished his own children could have had more.

She asked him then about his children and he gave her the bare facts of his life. Sara, the mountain, the twins, Ada. He said that he had just talked with Ada the week before and that hearing her voice from such a great distance had carved out a space inside him. "Maybe it was her worry for me. I don't know." He paused and then said, "We used to go duck hunting together. She didn't like to shoot very much but she always said if she was going to eat the duck, she might as well kill it. Not a hypocrite, that one."

"You're lucky," Elaine said. "I can't get anything out of Jane. Sometimes she'll talk to her father. Never to me. I think she's afraid that she *is* me. Or will be me. And she loves Jack. I remember my own father, waiting for him to come home from work. The smell of him, something like ink, the feel of his suit jacket, the way it hung like a real person across the back of the chair. Sometimes I would wear one of his jackets around the house." Elaine folded her hands and slipped her feet out of her sandals. "I don't eat duck," she said.

The heat of the sun had pushed Charles down into himself and her words floated about, here and there, landing, slipping away, returning. He thought she might be waiting for him to jump so that she could catch him.

She said that she and Jack would be taking the children down south to Dalat for a two-week holiday. They'd planned this a while ago. Then she said, "You get to go home soon."

He shrugged and said he had no immediate plans. He had a three-month visa.

"So, two more months," she said. Her voice was brighter. She stood and pulled him upward and hooked an arm into his as they walked through the grounds.

Charles said that he didn't know much history and he would be hard pressed to explain why the Citadel existed. Elaine said that if Jack were present he would give a running commentary on wars fought and each emperor's most important lover and the succession of rulers. She said that she preferred it with Charles; she liked the absence of noise. "Jack likes to trample on other people's space."

They walked along the gravel lanes into the grassy areas and up onto a plateaulike structure that used to be a courtyard. It was a peaceful place in a state of disrepair. Further on, they found an old man working in the sun, refashioning clay carvings of swords and cannons. They stood and watched him work. A young girl sat beside him drawing in the mud with her finger.

Elaine asked Charles why he was sad. What secrets did he have?

He was quiet for a while and then said that his secrets, if he had any, were small and unimportant. "I don't know that I am any sadder than other people. Than you, for instance."

"I'm not sad," she said. "I refuse to be. I think you are mistaking sadness for longing. I was imagining your caboose. How romantic it must be." Then, before he could respond, she said that she had had enough of Hue and she thought she might return to Danang before Jack. By train. "We could travel together," she said. "If you like."

Charles turned, looked at her for a moment, and said that she should do what she wanted.

"You know what I want," she said.

"Come with me, then," he said, and he was immediately sorry. He felt he had nothing to offer her.

"That's better." She took his hand and held it.

ON THE TRAIN, coming down through the pass from Hue, Charles said that when he had first arrived in Vietnam he'd come down by train through Hue and on to Danang, and so he'd taken this leg of the trip before. He remembered a young girl on the train, with two birds and her grandmother. The girl had chattered. The birds were noisy. The grandmother was affectionate and seemed happy. Charles said that at that point everything felt normal and good and he'd been quite hopeful. He hadn't known what would happen.

Elaine looked at him. "What I like best is figuring you out."

Charles said, "The first time I saw you I thought that you were beautiful but I also thought that you were very self-centred."

She said she was. "Always have been, in some ways."

"And that you loved your children more than you loved him."

"You saw that?"

"I did."

She said, "I imagine standing at the edge of a rift, and far below there is a deep gorge. You are at one edge, I am at the other and attempting to cross a narrow and treacherous bridge." Elaine seemed pleased by this image. She sat up and asked, "How far am I on the bridge? Near the middle or just at the beginning?"

They were seated across from a girl who wore tight white corduroy pants. She had a round face with a jag of red lipstick, and an older man, with a thin moustache, was talking to her as if he had hopes of something more than conversation. The girl's hair was long and dark and Charles was reminded of his daughter Ada.

Charles took one of Elaine's hands and held it. Her knuckles, the sharpness against his palm. He said, "What you want, I can't give you."

She turned quickly and said, "A few nights with Charles Boatman. That's all I want. I don't expect anything else."

"You know that's not what you want."

Elaine stood and said she was going for a cigarette. She slipped by Charles, stepped out into the aisle, and walked toward the end of the car. The girl in the facing seat was watching. She probably didn't understand English, but she was watching and Charles was aware of her curiosity, of how she feigned sleep and shifted in her seat.

Charles rose and joined Elaine, who was standing by the open door of the car. The greenery rushed by and fell toward the ocean. Elaine turned to Charles and began to finger the buttons on his blazer. Then she dropped her cigarette on the floor and ground it out with the toe of her shoe. She put her head against his chest. "Oh," she said. Then she lifted her chin and kissed him on the mouth, tentatively at first, then deeply. Charles kissed her back. After, she stood hugging herself and said, "I'm shivering." Far below them the water was green and azure and white and then blue. "Come," he said and guided her back to their seats, and they sat and after a while she leaned her head against his shoulder and fell asleep. He wanted to wake her, but he didn't. The girl across from them was still watching.

IT WAS MIDAFTERNOON when they arrived in Danang. The station was cool and wet. A family of six was gathered near the last car, all dressed in formal wear. Elaine held Charles's arm as they walked out onto the platform. She said that she wanted to see him. He could come by for dinner that night.

He felt the pressure of her hand and he lifted his head to look past her and he said, "I'm not sure."

She did not respond, simply hailed a taxi and then pressed her cheek against his and said, "Charles." Then she got into the taxi and was gone.

He took a cyclo to the hotel. He could still feel where her hand had touched him. Later, in his room, he lay in his underwear on the bed. He watched the ceiling fan slowly turn and recalled her expression on the train as she pushed her head against his chest and said, "Oh." After she had kissed him and drawn away, he had seen the wet inside of her lower lip and her perfectly straight teeth and the flash of one silver filling. He fell into a light sleep and woke to the ring of the phone and the clear image of himself as a dentist bending toward her and extracting a flawed tooth. Above him the fan still turned. The phone rang and rang. And then stopped.

Much later, he sat up. Poured himself whiskey and drank. Then he dressed and went down the stairs and out into the street and walked toward the harbour. He followed Bach Dang Street till it curved with the waterfront and then he turned and walked back, stopping at a restaurant that extended out over the water where he had a beer and watched the lights of the boats in the harbour, the ferries passing by.

After he had paid he left the restaurant and followed the walkway, the water on his left now. A strong wind was blowing and bits of garbage blew across his path. For a moment he paused at the edge of the harbour to light a cigarette, and as his hands cupped the match he saw the corpse of a dog, hugely distended, moving back and forth with the waves. Footsteps behind him. He turned as three men in suits passed by. Charles stepped back. He heard the men's sudden laughter and the wind and the clicking of the palm trees. The bloated moon. A hole had opened up before him.

In his room, with trembling hands, he took out a small pipe and a package of tinfoil, crumbled bits of hashish into the pipe, and lit it and drew. He lay on the bed and ascended with the twisting smoke, up, past the swirling fan, beyond the ceiling and into a night sky hurled through with celestial beings that blinked and disappeared and then blinked again.

THE FOLLOWING MORNING the hotel clerk handed Charles an envelope. Charles folded it into his pocket and went across the street to the café and ordered a coffee. Then he took out the envelope and opened it. It was from Elaine. She'd written, "Charles. Last night during that fierce wind a lamp standard was knocked down just outside our house and a loose wire danced across the pavement. It was all chaos and pandemonium. And the largest moon ever. Over there. Don't be so sure that you know what is at stake here. I can look after myself. You know where I am. Elaine."

Charles laid the note on the table. Her handwriting was lovely, black looping threads like the strands at the back of her neck when she pulled her hair up. All chaos and pandemonium. He wondered if she was aware of her own perfection. Such ease with herself and the spaces she moved through, the effortlessness of language, the expectation that she should get what she wanted. This frightened him. Outside, on the street, a boy walked by carrying his shoeshine case and Charles thought of Hanoi, of sitting by Hoan Kiem Lake and of having his shoes shined, while above him in a blue sky a balloon had lifted into the air. The night before he had had a vivid dream in which a man who he thought looked like Dang Tho was standing and staring across a river. If Charles was in the dream at all, it had been as an observer, but he had woken shaking, his mouth dry. He put the note back into his pocket and left the café and found himself at the airline office, where he bought an open ticket for Hanoi.

The next day he rented a motorcycle and rode up past Monkey Mountain and walked down to the empty beach that curved between two points of rock. In a grove of small pines, he sat on his jacket and watched the fishermen out at sea. Several times over the next week, he returned to that same beach. Once, a young soldier approached him and said, in broken English, that he must pay. Charles said that he did not understand. The boy was carrying a machine gun and he shifted it and stared out toward the sea and then turned back to Charles and repeated that payment was needed to sit on the beach. "One thousand dong," the soldier said. Charles considered this and shook his head. The soldier moved a black boot through the sand and then turned away to walk up the beach.

That afternoon, returning to his hotel, Charles saw Elaine step through the lobby doors and out onto the street. Her back was to him and she walked purposefully, a black bag swinging from her left hand. She turned the corner and disappeared. In the hotel the desk clerk handed him a piece of yellow paper, folded once. He climbed the stairs to his room. Inside, he sat down and unfolded the paper. She wrote, "I came by and, again, you were gone. Where are you, Charles? Why are you doing this? We are old enough to follow our feelings and I sense that you have certain feelings. I have no patience for games, if that is what you intend." She said that they would be leaving for Dalat the following morning. "This is childish," she wrote.

He put the note down and then picked it up and reread it. Then he took a piece of blank paper and responded. He said that his fifth-grade teacher, Miss Everly, had looping handwriting just like hers. And in the early afternoons, during quiet reading, when the sun poured through the venetian blinds, dust motes floated around Miss Everly's head. He said that only recently had he become aware of the mercilessness of time, of its cruel push. "I'm sorry, Elaine," he wrote. And then he signed his name.

He put the note into an envelope and wrote her name on the outside. Then he went down to the lobby and asked the desk clerk to deliver the envelope to Mrs. Gouds and he described the house and the street it was on. He gave the clerk a sum of money and asked, "Do you understand?" The clerk said that he understood. He knew the house, and he knew the American family that lived there. The letter was safe.

Charles spent the next days wandering the city. Once, he found himself in her neighbourhood and he went by her house. The windows were shuttered and the front door was padlocked. One evening in a small restaurant at the north end of the city Thanh walked in and sat with him and drank iced coffee. The night was humid. Moths banged against the glass of the lanterns that hung above the tables.

"You have been absent," Thanh said.

Charles said that he had been walking, and then sleeping, and then walking some more. "I saw Dang Tho in a dream," he said. "He was melancholy. He was standing and looking across a deep river. There was no view of the other side." He shrugged and said that it was, in the end, just a dream.

"Yes, but dreams can warn us," Thanh said. "Or indicate something." He looked at Charles and said, "You are sad."

"You sound like Elaine Gouds," Charles said. "She says the same thing."

Thanh offered him a ride back to the hotel but Charles said he would walk. He was slightly drunk, but this time he did not lose his way. On a corner close to the hotel a prostitute in magenta tights and a blue skirt teetered toward him and called out, "How many days?" Then she said, "You have hunger?" and she pointed at her legs. She was close to him and he saw her dark eyes, the light powder on her cheeks and forehead, the strap of her silver purse against her wrist. In the distance, leaning against the wall of the hotel, a boy was smoking and watching. Charles led the girl back to the hotel. He was aware, as they walked, of the boy following them. They passed through the lobby, where the night clerk, lying on the vinyl couch by the fish tank, raised his head and observed Charles and the girl and then put his head back down.

They climbed the stairs to the room. Inside, he turned on a lamp and the girl sat on a chair and crossed her legs. He took out the package of tinfoil and prepared his pipe. Lit it and inhaled. After he had released the smoke he asked her if she liked to smoke. She smiled and got up and began to lift her top. "No, no," he said, and he went to her and took her arm and led her to the bed, where they sat, side by side, and shared the pipe. She did not seem to be a novice; she held the smoke and exhaled carefully. He saw that her fingernails were dirty.

When they'd finished the pipe, Charles stood and went over to the desk and laid it down beside the lamp. He turned and said that he was glad to be with her. Her skirt was short and she wore a black tank top with small rhinestones sewn along the edges. He told her his name, Charles, but she had a hard time pronouncing it. She tried, giggled, and tried again. Her voice was high-pitched. She uncrossed her legs and said the word *want* as if she were trying to capture Charles. He went over to her, touched her face and her hair, undressed her, and then undressed himself. They lay on their backs beside each other for the longest time. Their hips and arms touched. The fan above them seemed to turn slower and slower. At some point she lifted a bare arm and pointed at the ceiling, and his eye followed the line of her forearm and beyond to her index finger.

He rolled onto his side and studied her. Her breasts were small, almost nonexistent. He lifted himself onto an elbow and traced her collarbone with a finger. Her eyes were wide open and showed no emotion. Then, he put on his pants and stood by the open window, smoking a cigarette. She went to the bathroom and returned and slipped back into her clothes, and when she was ready to leave, he handed her one hundred dollars.

She was surprised and perhaps even a little frightened by this, but she put it into her purse. When she left he stood by the open window and waited. It took a long time, but finally he heard the sound of her heels on the sidewalk below, and then nothing.

HIS DREAMS IN THOSE LAST DAYS were dark. In order to escape he fell back on drink and hashish. He found that the drug helped him float and the dreams that came to him then were softer and more fluid. He tried not to sleep, exhausted himself, and ended up on his bed in the late afternoon, waking to the sound of nightlife and the flashing of the hotel sign, disoriented, his mouth dry. He would walk then. Up and down the streets of Danang. He became familiar with the landmarks, the different shops, and came to know certain restaurant owners. Bartenders welcomed him as a regular. He tried not to think of who he was, of his children, of his past, of Elaine, or of anything else that might press some sort of anguish upon him. He grew to appreciate White Horse cigarettes. He became fond of a certain Vietnamese whiskey. He knew where he was going.

One night, at a small restaurant on Bach Dang Street, Charles ordered an iced coffee and smoked the last of his cigarettes as he sat and watched the fishing boats enter the harbour. He spoke to no one except the waiter, an older man who occupied his own table in the far corner and drank something dark and viscous from a small glass. When he finally rose and paid the bill, it was near midnight. A solitary cyclo was waiting on the sidewalk. He waved the driver away and walked up toward his hotel. The evening was warm and there was still some bicycle traffic and the occasional taxi. Otherwise it was quiet.

Close to the hotel he passed three prostitutes, who called out to him. One he recognized from the previous week. Her face was powdered white and the magenta tights she wore now seemed excessive. She called out his name, "Chawz," and began to follow him, but he shook his head and passed on. She said something hard in Vietnamese and laughed and the other two women laughed as well.

He climbed five flights of stairs to the room. Inside, he turned on a lamp and sat on a chair, took out a glass, and poured whiskey and then drank. Then he went over to the small desk and opened a drawer and took out his pipe and prepared and lit it. His hand was trembling. He steadied it and focused on the small glow of the pipe. He went to the window and looked down at the three women on the corner. A motorcycle pulled up and idled, and when it left it took along the girl who had mocked Charles.

He put out the pipe and lay down on the bed and watched the ceiling fan turn. He closed his eyes and slipped in and out of sleep. From a great distance he heard rain and voices and then rain again and the banging of the shutter in the wind. He saw his children lined up, their faces pressed together, clamouring for his attention. He saw all the women he had known. He saw Elaine. She was standing under her awning, and she was telling him to step carefully. He began to speak and then he woke to the backfire of a motorcycle in the street. He sat up and saw the dark sky beyond the window.

It was very late. The wind had pushed the rain through the open window. He closed the window, and some time later he went to the desk, wiped it off with a towel, and began a letter. He addressed it to his children. He told them about himself. He told them what they had never known. He apologized, and then he folded the letter, placed it in an envelope, and put the envelope into a pouch inside his suitcase.

It was the middle of the night when he left his hotel and walked out onto the street. He was carrying a tote bag and in the bag were a rope and a ten-pound cinder block, which he had found at a construction site a few days earlier. The streets were empty and the rain and wind had let up. He walked up toward Bach Dang and finally found a driver sleeping in his cyclo. He woke the man and told him, "My Khe."

The ride to the ocean was quiet, though roosters crowed and occasionally the soft echo of voices carried over onto the street. A ship sounded its horn and Charles heard the creak of the pedals on the cyclo and the deep breathing of his driver. He saw his own hands and considered them for a while and thought about how easily one could choose this path.

From the cyclo now he saw the outline of Monkey Mountain. He dismounted on the beach road, paid his driver a good amount, and then walked toward the shore. A dog appeared out of the darkness and stood before him, growling. Its rear end was furless and as the animal circled Charles could see it favoured a hind leg; a reprobate creature that saw an equal in Charles. Charles picked up a stick and swung out, hitting the dog across the snout. It howled and backed away, its rear furrowing the sand. "Get lost, you piece of shit," Charles said, and the dog tilted its head, as if the language it heard was unexpected. Charles continued toward the water. He intended to take a basket boat out past the breaking waves. There were numerous boats along the beach and he chose one close to the shore. It was heavier than he had imagined and he had to rest as he dragged it toward the water. More than once he went down on his knees and had to catch his breath. When he did this, the dog slid in closer and Charles threw things— sand, rocks, shells, empty cans—to keep the mongrel back. Even when the boat was in the water the dog sat near the shoreline and lifted its head and howled, as if aware of what was to pass.

Pulling the boat out into deeper water, Charles had difficulty fighting the surf. The waves kept pushing him back toward land. When the water became too deep, he hoisted himself up into the boat and landed heavily against the cinder block in the tote bag. He sucked air through his teeth from the pain. The boat rolled with the ocean. He took a paddle and worked his way past the breakers, out toward the open sea. He struggled for a long time and when he finally paused and looked back, the lights of the houses at My Khe were distant and foggy. The dog, both sight and sound, had disappeared.

He put the paddle down and looked at his bag. What he did next he did with speed and clarity. He opened the bag and took out the rope and the block. He tied the rope to the block, fitting it through one of the small openings, and he fastened it with a taut line hitch. Then he took the other end of the ten-foot rope and looped it around his left ankle. This too he tied with a hitch. Finally, he stood, picked up the block, and threw himself and the block overboard. The water was warm but even so he felt a quick shock and he sucked in air. He thought, briefly, of his children and he pitied them.

When the rope uncoiled to its full length, he was pulled down. He did not panic but sank with the weight of the cinder block. If he had wanted he could have loosened the rope and swum to the surface, but he didn't. As he felt the pressure build on his ears and temples he released the air in his lungs and swallowed the ocean water. His last sensations were a burning in his chest and things brushing either side of his face. These were his arms lifting past his head and reaching toward the surface as if to grasp at the last of the bubbles that floated upward and broke into the night air.

The block hit the ocean floor first. Then Charles's heels touched and his legs buckled slowly and he came to rest on his back. A school of blowfish circled above him and moved on. Within a few hours a cuttlefish had found him and slid past his mouth and ears and finally settled in beneath a raised shoulder. The following day, a tiger shark would stray from its group and nose the man's leg, finally settling on the right foot, working the teeth through the canvas shoe into the flesh. But the man's eyes would go first, nibbled at by the smaller animals on the ocean floor, until a blue swimming crab would appear and pry free first the right eye and then the left. Sea horses would study the holes, and then slide away.

On the surface, the basket boat would disappear, carried by the tides toward the shore. A Russian oil tanker would anchor above the corpse for several days. The stern anchor would land beside Charles Boatman and catch the rope and drag his body along for several hundred feet. For over a month the currents would toss the body until, finally, Charles Boatman would be delivered up onto the land from which he had come.

Vincent Lam

Vincent Lam was born in London, Ontario, to parents from the expatriate Chinese community of Vietnam. He grew up in Ottawa, where he was raised on his father's stories and the works of C.S. Lewis and Roald Dahl. Throughout his youth, he nurtured two ambitions, to write and to practise medicine. He managed to fulfill both, enrolling in medical school at the University of Toronto, all the while working on his writing.

While crafting his debut collection of short stories, *Bloodletting & Miraculous Cures*, Lam worked in the emergency room at Toronto East General Hospital and helped fight the 2003 SARS outbreak. "An emergency physician is often in the centre of a storm of tensions and drama," he says. "We work in a world that is both medical and personal, where the stakes are high and events are unpredictable. As a doctor, I respond to the world around me, and act within that world. As a writer, I do something fresh and new on the page."

Lam's depiction of four medical students who become doctors in *Bloodletting & Miraculous Cures* was so unique and accomplished that the collection won the 2006 Scotiabank Giller Prize—Canada's most prestigious literary award. He is the youngest writer, and the only first-time author, to win it. Shaftesbury Films is developing *Bloodletting & Miraculous Cures* into a TV drama series for The Movie Network.

Lam is currently working on a first novel, *Cholon, Near Forgotten*, and continues to work as an emergency physician in Toronto.

Bloodletting & Miraculous Cures

BY VINCENT LAM

Winner 2006

❧

CONTACT TRACING

—
—
—

November 16, 2002 (from the files of the World Health Organization)
First known case of atypical pneumonia occurs in Foshan City,
Guangdong Province, China, but is not identified until much later.

February 10, 2003 (from the files of the World Health Organization)
The WHO Beijing office receives an email message describing a "strange
contagious disease" that has "already left more than one hundred people
dead" in Guangdong Province in the space of one week. The message fur-
ther describes "a 'panic' attitude, where people are emptying pharmaceu-
tical stocks of any medicine they think may protect them."

DR. FITZGERALD STILL HAD HIS WATCH, so on the second day of his
admission he timed it. Through the glass, he could see when someone was
coming, and it took them a little while to get in to him. Anyone who needed
to come into Fitzgerald's respiratory isolation room had to don a second
N95 mask over the one that was already pressing a red welt into their face,

a clear face shield, a second hairnet, a first pair of gloves, then an isolation gown over the one they were already wearing, then a second pair of gloves, then a second layer of shoe covers. Then they would wave to Fitzgerald to make sure that he was wearing his mask securely before coming in. But this preparation time didn't count. Fitzgerald timed the minutes of human contact starting when the person entered the room, and ending when the person left. Usually, it was one of the nurses. Dr. Zenkie saw him once each day.

They addressed him as Dr. Fitzgerald even though he had become a patient. When he was alone in the room, he didn't want them to call him doctor, because it somehow implied that he should be partly floating above this illness and yet have some control over it. These were the obligations attached to the word, which he had no energy or ability to live up to. Each time he saw a nurse begin her ritual preparations to enter the isolation room, he decided that he would ask her to not call him doctor. However, once she entered and addressed him in this way, he could not ask her to call him anything else. With someone else in the room, he became scared to give up his title, this dark-cloaked word. Suddenly, this label which felt taunting and futile when he was alone became, with someone else present, his best and last and only piece of clothing which, despite its flaws, could hardly be discarded—except for this he was now naked, stuck in this isolation room that was always humming with its dedicated ventilation fans. What would he be if not a doctor? His self before becoming a physician seemed like a half-remembered, dreamed version of himself, a persona that was impossible to resume in his present life. Although he longed to shed the medical shell when he was alone, it was frightening to try to remember how to be anything else in the presence of others.

They took his vitals, and checked his intravenous line. The fever clawed at his skin and he gripped the armrests of the chair to control the shaking while the nurse took his blood pressure. The nurses brought the food as well, so the attendants wouldn't be exposed. Then they left. Seven minutes, was what he timed each day. Seven minutes of human contact in twenty-four hours. Between these minutes, Fitz kept the television on. The same clips played again and again, and encouraged time to evaporate. Each day, the numbers on the television mounted. One hundred and sixty-seven cases worldwide. Eight in Toronto. Thousands quarantined, and now the horrible, fascinating spectacle of new cases blooming, spreading, the numbers bursting bright on maps like dandelions on a mowed lawn after the rain.

March 15, 2003 *(from the files of the World Health Organization)*

"This syndrome, SARS, is now a worldwide health threat," said Dr. Gro Harlem Brundtland, Director-General of the World Health Organization. "The world needs to work together to find its cause, cure the sick, and stop its spread."

(Initial consultation note of Dr. R. Zenkie, FRCPC, dated March 15, 2003—excerpted from chart with permission of Toronto South General Hospital)

ID: Dr. Fitzgerald, 29 years old
OCC: Flight evacuation physician
CC: Cough, fever
Dear Dr. Chen,

Thank you for this consultation. Dr. Fitzgerald is a previously healthy young man who saw you in the emergency department on March 10 with four days of fever, progressively worsening dry cough, diffuse myalgias, and occasional rigours. I agree with your impression at that time that the chest X-ray appeared typical of an atypical pneumonia. You prescribed a course of azithromycin and advised Dr. Fitzgerald to rest at home. In the following days, Dr. Fitzgerald became progressively more short of breath and noted his own tachypnea at rest.

It has since become apparent that a patient whom Dr. Fitzgerald transported from Shenzhen, China, to Vancouver, Canada, has died of pneumonia and DIC at the Oceanside Community Hospital and that Dr. Fitzgerald likely contracted his illness, which we suspect to be SARS, from this patient. Dr. Fitzgerald was seen again in the emergency department on March 14 by yourself, and then by myself at your request. Isolation and respiratory precautions were implemented.

Initial physical examination revealed a muscular young man with a good oxygen saturation of 95 percent on 4 litres nasal prongs, however with an O$_2$Sat of 88 percent on room air. Mild tachypnea, fine inspiratory crackles noted throughout all lung fields, with mild indrawing and accessory muscle use. Chest X-ray reveals diffuse patchy densities and air bronchograms suggestive of widespread consolidation.

We have admitted Dr. Fitzgerald into a negative pressure isolation room. He has developed a coarse tremor. We have continued the azithromycin, have added ceftriaxone, acyclovir, ribavirin, as well as a pulse course of solumedrol. This broad regimen will be continued until there are any developments concerning the appropriate treatment of SARS. Dr. Fitzgerald's clinical condition has worsened, and today he requires 10 litres of O_2 by face mask in order to maintain an O_2Sat of 91 percent. He is somewhat anxious. Having said that, he is a robust young man who will hopefully improve, although his thoughts have become rather morbid. His coarse and bothersome tremor is not in keeping with the SARS picture that other centres are reporting. There are no focal deficits. Tracing and quarantine of Dr. Fitzgerald's contacts is being undertaken by the Department of Public Health. Several of his contacts have already been hospitalized.

Thank you for involving me in this timely and interesting case. I will continue to copy you on the chart notes, although you will likely not receive these reports until you have completed your own quarantine period.

Yours truly, Dr. R. Zenkie, FRCPC

Consultant in Infectious Diseases, Toronto South General Hospital

WHEN FITZGERALD WAS ADMITTED, Chen was quarantined as an unprotected contact. Fitz asked Zenkie about his flight crew. All quarantined, afebrile, except Niki, who had been in the cabin with him and the patient who was now Canada's first SARS fatality. Niki was admitted at Holy Mercy, and requiring an FiO_2 of a hundred percent. It had been a routine patient transfer—Shenzhen to Vancouver. Pneumonia and sepsis. Now the patient was dead, which was also not outside routine, but what was new was that they were sick, they had made others sick, and the whole world was now holding its breath while learning this new word, SARS.

Dr. Zenkie puzzled over Fitzgerald's tremor. This was not part of what most centres were reporting, but of course no one could say what to expect. Fitzgerald knew this shakiness. When he had gotten the fever and cough, he had figured he would blur away the time with some single malt. Probably a viral pneumonia, he and Chen had figured, but best to start the azithro just in case.

For the most part, he had kept the alcohol just below the surface—a quick shot in the back of the plane, one or maybe two with a meal, a glass of comfort before sleeping in the hotel rooms that looked the same all over the world. It was always there, but he told himself that he was disciplined about it. He paced and timed himself to the next one, and figured that as a flight doc he passed the effects off as being dazed from the time change and sleep deprivation. That and breath mints. Niki must know, of course, but Fitzgerald believed that when the tight spot came in a flight, he was up for it and sharp.

Apart from the rationed nips, the binges called him like old friends who were impossible to outgrow, who wanted to visit him on his days off. He would sink down through the first four or five that made him feel right, then swim into the next few rounds where there was a peaceful warm slowness, and then the weight of it would pull him to the bottom of the bottle where it was just one after another, automatic as if the drinking itself would be enough. Enough for what? Enough.

This time, though, the breathing bothered him. When he drank to the point where he usually felt soft and floating, instead the numb edges were fringed with a panic. One night he dreamed that he was in the Lear jet with Ming. She was the patient, but she opened her duffle bag to reveal a newborn child. The baby was blue, floppy, and she threw it at Fitzgerald. It was a girl, mottled and cold, limbs draped down from the naked torso which he cradled. He said, "You're the baby doctor." Ming said, "I just deliver them. The rest is your game." Then she went to the front of the plane to chat with the pilots. Fitzgerald began mouth-to-mouth and chest compressions. On the infant, the mouth-to-mouth was little breaths puffing out a single birthday candle, the CPR was a tap-tap-tapping on the chest, as if using a manual typewriter. Tap tap. Firm. Not too hard or fast—lest the spindly metal arms with the letters on their tips become jammed. The plane dropped—a weightless moment—air pocket? Turbulence? Then a hiss, and the oxygen masks dangled from the ceiling. Fitzgerald tried to hold a mask to his face and deliver rescue breaths to the limp baby. Breathe the mask, puff the baby, but he couldn't keep it up. Too much switching, fumbling, he needed both hands to hold the baby, but one hand to grab the mask and one hand for compression. He was faint, vision clouded. Ming and the pilots chatted casually, their masks strapped to their faces. Fitz would have to stop breathing for the baby, just suck on a mask himself. At this point, when he had decided to abandon the child but had not yet given up the baby to hold his face to the mask, Fitzgerald woke—shaking, gasping. Drank from the bottle next to his bed.

It was perhaps because he was drunk that he waited a couple more days to return to hospital. By March 14, the sparks of plague headlined news broadcasts. Public Health phoned, left messages. Fitzgerald listened to all eleven urgent voice mails that exhorted him to check his temperature, to call Public Health, to report to hospital if he had a fever or any respiratory symptoms. A man in an isolation mask came to the apartment building, and on the short-circuit monitor Fitzgerald watched him stand in the lobby, buzz Fitzgerald's apartment, pull on latex gloves. Fitzgerald didn't answer. He was drowning in lung fluids and tried to flush this away with alcohol, but even when the alcohol began to recede his lungs were still filling from illness, so he returned to the hospital. Chen was on duty, again.

And now the withdrawal. Of course, Fitzgerald had his own diazepam stash at home for the shakes, but he hadn't brought them with him to hospital. It didn't hurt anyone, he told himself, and he only "treated himself to a session" when he had some time off, and then weaned himself to that "cool place" before he was scheduled to fly again. Now he wished he had brought a bottle, never mind diazepam.

(Initial consultation note of Dr. R. Zenkie, FRCPC, dated March 18, 2003—excerpted from chart with permission of Toronto South General Hospital)

ID: Dr. Chen, 31 years old

OCC: Emergency physician

CC: Shortness of breath, fever

Dear Dr. Chen,

Thank you for this consultation. As you know, you developed a fever and some mild shortness of breath on March 17, which was the third day of your quarantine after contact with a probable SARS patient, Dr. Fitzgerald. You alerted me and, after we discussed the matter on the phone, you presented to the hospital (travelling appropriately with an N95 mask in a private vehicle) and were admitted directly into a respiratory isolation room. At present, I note that you have only mild shortness of breath not requiring supplementary oxygen. Your X-ray findings demonstrate diffuse infiltrates consistent with an early case of SARS. You are otherwise healthy. Ceftriaxone, azithromycin, acyclovir, ribavirin, and solumedrol have been initiated. Since we agreed that no other physician should be exposed by becoming involved in your care, I will address you in the consultation notes.

Contact tracing is being carried out by the Department of Public Health. Thank you for another interesting consultation, although I regret that you have now come under my care. As per your request I will ensure that your wife, Dr. Ming, who is currently under quarantine, receives copies of the medical record.

Yours truly, Dr. R. Zenkie, FRCPC

Consultant in Infectious Diseases, Toronto South General Hospital

AT QUARTER TO MIDNIGHT, Dr. Chen was admitted to the respiratory isolation room adjacent to Dr. Fitzgerald's. These rooms were fishbowls, walled with glass and humming with the fans that created a negative pressure environment, sucked the air out to be filtered. Each of the rooms had a television and a phone. From inside the room, the occupant could see nurses and doctors passing in the hallway, appearing and disappearing with the casual nerve of those who had not been imprisoned. There were curtains that could be drawn on the inside, but the cardiac and saturation monitors that trailed wires from Chen and Fitzgerald's bodies were always watching them, a peephole even with the curtains drawn. Fitzgerald wrote the extension number of his phone on a piece of paper and held it up to the glass. Chen called him.

"Sorry," said Fitz. "I gave you this SARS thing."

Chen said, "It's an infection. It's not you."

"Did you give it to anyone?" Fitzgerald knew that Ming and Chen had married a year ago, that they were now Mr. and Mrs. Chen, although she still used Dr. Ming. "You still single, or what?"

"My wife's in quarantine. Afebrile, though. She's been on call a lot this week so we haven't seen each other much. Maybe for the best ... considering."

"Right."

"It's late," said Chen. He looked up at the curtains.

"Sure. Hey, what's your phone extension? We can catch up."

Fitzgerald realized that there was a time when he would have simultaneously wanted Ming to have contracted this illness and yet given anything for her to be healthy. Now this was all far away, dull and subject to illumination by the impartial swinging spotlight of infectious illness. He was glad that Chen was here, a familiar face.

THE NEXT MORNING, Fitz turned up his oxygen to fifteen litres per minute. He watched TV. SARS was now in Canada, Germany, Taiwan, China, Thailand, Hong Kong, Vietnam, and Singapore. The numbers seemed to grow by multiplication instead of addition. The cloud of humidified oxygen that blew into his face left him breathless, and through the glass he saw Chen talking on the phone. He talked for a long time. Hung up. Looked like a man who was adapting to being a fish in a tank. Seven minutes, Fitz thought. The windows of this ward looked over the back of the hospital where there was now a tent, and a line of hospital staff waiting to be screened for entry. As if the hospital was worth lining up for. The nurse who brought lunch (forty-five seconds) was one he had not met before, Dolores. Her eyes were red. She told Fitz that this was no longer a regular ward, that it was the new SARS unit, to which nurses had been assigned by lottery.

EARLIER THAT DAY, Dolores had sat down in the cafeteria for the second SARS Strategic Meeting among a masked, garish army of yellow and blue isolation gowns. None of the Toronto South General nurses knew that there would be a lottery. The creation of a dedicated SARS unit was explained by the administrator who wore a grey dress and a mask. It would be simple. All of the ward nurses had to be entered in the lottery. If someone didn't want to be in the draw, there was a sheet of paper they could sign, said the administrator. If you signed this paper, you were out of the lottery but you also forfeited recognition of your seniority. Seniority was what nurses built over a career, what entitled them to a better choice of shifts, to the first pick of holidays, to be the last one laid off in a spasm of restructuring, what made a nurse somebody. A masked union rep sat next to the administrator, nothing else for her to say. If you signed the paper, you had to leave the room. You weren't fired, but would possibly be reassigned, depending on what was required after the results of the lottery.

Some who had recently graduated from nursing school got up quickly, signed the paper, and were gone. They didn't have much seniority, and some had small children. One nurse stood and asked if they could exercise their retirement instead of signing the paper. The union rep looked like she was about to answer, but then turned to the administrator instead. The two of them murmured mask to mask. The union rep stood and said, "This situation does not annul any previously determined benefits."

The union rep and the administrator conferred, and produced another sheet of paper for nurses who wanted to exercise their retirement. Another small number stood one by one to sign. They looked at their colleagues, but because of the masks could not tell whether the glances were farewell smiles, gazes of consolation, or eyes met as a warning. Most of the nurses who signed the second sheet of paper had been at the hospital since before many of the younger nurses were born. One had actually delivered one of the junior nurses because the doctor couldn't get there in time.

Dolores kept her seat. Her divorce settlement had only just been completed. There were the three kids, the second mortgage, and the twelve years of seniority which were too many to throw away. In one box were everyone's names. In another box were yellow and red tags. One by one, the union rep drew a name, the administrator drew a tag, stapled the name to the tag. The red tags meant the SARS unit. Dolores's name was drawn, and then out came a red tag.

Afterwards, those with yellow tags tried to suppress the relief and laughter of a near miss, embarrassed at their good fortune while standing amid those who held red tags. Those who had been selected for the SARS unit only met the eyes of others who held the same colour tag. Some cried openly, or left the room to do so. One woman with a yellow tag offered it to her friend who had a red one, and who was just back from her honeymoon, but the trade was refused. Grief and trauma counsellors were available in the next room, said the union rep over the murmur. No one offered Dolores a trade. Management left the room once the lottery was completed.

March 18, 2003 (from the files of the World Health Organization)
Data indicate that the overwhelming majority of cases occur in health care workers, their family members, and others having close face-to-face contact with patients ...

AFTER LUNCH, and the noontime vitals and IV replacements (two minutes, fifteen seconds), Fitzgerald called Chen. Through the glass, they could see each other's monitors. Chen had been on the phone all morning with Ming and his family members. Fitzgerald had been flipping between news channels. They compared and discussed their vital signs, which were all abnormal. Chen said, "You remember Sri's funeral?"

"Sure. Everyone was there—even though it was the day before the royal college exams."

"Ming and I were talking about it. One day he felt a little itchy, thought his eyes looked a bit yellow. Did you know he had me order the labs? Dead within a year. It was astounding."

"Pancreatic cancer," said Fitz. "Nasty."

"Did you know that Sri once made eggs Benedict for a patient?"

"Eggs Benedict?" "You know, poached eggs with that lemony sauce."

"Must have been a good cook."

"We were juniors, and Sri had this patient, Mr. Olaf. Cannonball lesions all over his lungs, brain mets, all his family dead in Sweden. He had written a will on lined paper, that his clothes and books should go to his landlady. Olaf had no visitors, and I remember Sri saying how sad it was that he was all alone. He was always smiling, though, reading his Swedish Bible, and the chaplain came every day. So one day we're rounding, and Mr. Olaf has this look … as if he's figured out some amazing thing. You can tell he's just bursting to tell us what he's thought of, and right in the middle of our rounds he picks up and says, 'Doctors, excuse me, sirs, but may it be possible to kindly arrange for me to partake in some eggs Benedict? Perhaps with bacon?'

"The staff guy was Arnold. He writes an order in the chart: EGGS BENE-DICT. Later that day, we're in a family conference and Sri gets paged. He goes off, comes back, says that the nurses are upset at the order, saying it's an inappropriate order to put in a medical chart, yada yada yada, and who do the doctors think the nurses are, anyhow, personal chefs? Later, Sri calls the kitchen himself and asks them if they make eggs Benedict. He finds a cook who says he can make it, but that he doesn't think he's allowed to deviate from the regular menu. Sri calls again. He finds some other guy who says he'd be happy to make anything, but he doesn't know the Benedict variety of eggs. Meanwhile, the nurse has decided to make it into an *issue*. You know how it is, once an *issue* is created. The nurse asks the dietitian to consult, because of course Olaf has high blood pressure and high choles-terol. The dietitian doesn't know what this is all about, but she writes dietary recommendations in the chart—a low-salt, low-fat diet. Arnold sees this, so he just writes: LOW-SALT, LOW-FAT DIET AS PER DIETITIAN. Next day, Mr. Olaf is eating his low-salt, low-fat porridge and tea with no sugar or milk for breakfast while we're rounding. Doesn't say a word until the end of the rounds, when he shyly says, 'Excuse me, doctors, sirs, I apologize humbly for my lavish request of the eggs Benedict. But would it be possible to restore the regular food?' You should have seen him, poking that hard porridge.

"Arnold writes DAT on the chart. Later, Sri is paged while we're in a seminar. He goes off, comes back, says another nurse is peeved about these contradictory orders. First, eggs Benedict, then low-salt low-fat, then DAT. Sri cancels all the previous orders and writes DAT—DIET AS TOLERATED again. The next morning, I see he's got some little containers with him. I ask him what they are, and he says it's his lunch. But later, when we're rounding, there's Mr. Olaf with a great big spread of eggs Benedict and bacon and home fries, digging in like he's found a preview of heaven. All the time while we're rounding, he's smiling and nodding at Sri, grinning like a madman."

"Sri was a good guy," said Fitzgerald. "I barely recognized him at the viewing—that open casket thing they do."

"Lost a lot of weight. I hadn't seen him since he got sick. So fast, eight months. At least a few times I saw Sri with his little stack of containers, then Olaf died a week later. One day, I think he had waffles."

Fitzgerald said, "Isn't it amazing how weight loss changes the face? Especially when the body is supine. Changes the way everything sits."

"Gravity shapes everything," said Chen. "First, I couldn't believe that he was gone. Then, I couldn't believe that I couldn't believe it. After all, how many dead people have we seen? How many have we watched die?"

Fitz coughed, and it took him like a shaking fist, forced him to put down the phone until he was able to stop and wipe the perspiration from his face. He picked it up again and said, "You want to order something?"

"What, fancy eggs?"

"I'd like a seared tuna steak with wasabi mashed potatoes and vintage port."

"Pan-fried crabs," said Chen, "with lots of scallions and garlic."

"Scallops. Big, fat Nova Scotia scallops browned in butter with asparagus, wild rice, and a bottle of Gewurztraminer."

March 19, 2003 (from the files of the World Health Organization)
Brother-in-law of Guangdong doctor dies in a Hong Kong hospital.

BOTH OF THEM WATCHED TV ALL DAY. Switched between the stations. Mostly stayed on the news, the SARS clips over and over again: mask shortages, enforced quarantines, panic spreading like flight trajectories between cities. Later that night, after dinner, Fitz called Chen. Through the glass, Chen saw Fitzgerald hold the phone, a spasm of coughing, his hands shaking like the tailpipe on a cold car. Chen said, "This shakiness business of yours. I know you have a few from time to time."

"What?"

"Booze. Are you withdrawing?"

"I guess."

"Get some diazepam."

"No way. Zenkie's writing it up. 'Tremor: A Novel Aspect of the SARS Syndrome.' You want to take away his paper?"

"What if you seize?"

"Fuck it. I'd rather be famous. The Zenkie-Fitzgerald Tremor—an atypical manifestation of SARS. I'm going to be a co-author."

"You better tell Zenkie, and get some diazepam."

"Right, I'll tell him and in forty seconds the whole hospital will know."

Chen was about to say that it didn't matter, because after the night when Fitz had arrived for a shift with the sweet smell on his breath, his speech slurred, and was asked to leave and stop seeing patients, it didn't make a difference whether people knew he was withdrawing. But Chen didn't say it, because maybe Fitz didn't know how much people had talked in that indelible way. Fitz had resigned from the hospital the next day, signed on with the flight company. Chen said, "Instead, you'll seize and die."

"Who said death was so bad?"

"Did someone say that?"

Fitz had a coughing fit, and then, "When did we forget what it meant to die?"

"Probably at night."

"Yeah, it would have been late."

"One night ... I was very tired," said Chen. "There was this hysterical family. You know the kind—they stare at you when you sit down to write a chart, they grab you to tell you that they read something on the Internet. Their mother was going to die. It had taken me a long time to convince them that there was no other way. Every half-hour I would get paged, and the nurse would say, 'They want to speak to you again.' Don't you hate that? When it's not even a particular problem, but they just want to speak to you? Finally I told them that Mom wasn't going to die tonight, that they should save their strength for the next day."

"And as soon as they left, she died."

"Of course."

"Always the way."

"It was three o'clock. I had been running back and forth from emerg and it had finally quietened down. I told the nurse that she didn't need to check on the woman until the morning. We both knew."

"You didn't call the family."

"I just couldn't. I was exhausted. I called when I woke up, and filled out the death certificate as if she had just passed away. By the time they got to the hospital and started their wailing and carrying on, I was out the door."

"That's not so bad. They needed the sleep. Imagine if they came in at three o'clock? The whole floor would be awake, and then you'd be fucked."

"Later, I felt like maybe I should have called. But I just felt that way kind of theoretically. I didn't really care."

"You took care of the patient, right?" said Fitz. "The rest is your own business. What's your temp today?"

"Thirty-nine." Neither of them wanted to take too much antipyretic. Both of their livers were already reeling from the cocktail of drugs.

"I'm forty," said Fitz. Even through the glass, Chen could see the sweat-glaze on Fitz's skin, and a slight collapse of facial features. "One morning, I was post-call. I went to that park in Kensington, you know the corner stand where they make fresh chocolate croissants and serve latte out the window? Yeah. Those mornings when the weather is so fresh, and you're kind of stoned but awake, on those days sometimes I wouldn't sleep, I would take the ferry to Centre Island. Wander around. Watch the moms and kids on the toy train."

Fitzgerald didn't mention the rum he put in his postcall latte. Not a lot, just enough to soothe. He said, "That was my plan. I had my nice big latte, my warm croissant, and the sun was just up. This woman is walking across the park. She goes up to this picnic table where this guy looks like he's asleep, slumped over. I don't know why she does this, but she tries to wake him up. He doesn't wake up. She shakes him. He's just lying there, and I'm drinking my latte thinking either he's dead, or he's a heroin addict. I decide that he's probably not dead because he's too floppy, unless he just died, so he's probably a junkie. People gather around while this woman slaps the guy and shouts at him. I laugh because she tries to move him and obviously she's never moved anyone before—his head just flops back and goes *bonk* when she drags him onto the ground. On the dirt, mind you, it's nice and soft. I zip up my jacket, because otherwise you can see my scrub top. This woman freaks out. She starts to scream, 'Call 911, call 911,' and all these people look at her like maybe this is performance art? Finally, someone takes out a cellphone and calls.

"I imagined what would happen if I went over there. He would be fine, just a junkie on junk, but I'd be standing there all doctor-like and therefore unable to escape. Or, maybe he would be dead. Then I'd start CPR, although if he was dead all that time it wouldn't matter, but if I was playing Mr. Doctor then I'd have to do something to make it look good, I'd have to do mouth-to-mouth and he would vomit in my mouth, and then whether he was okay or dead, by the time the ambulance guys came, either some home-less guy would have stolen my croissant and latte or it would be cold."

"But then ..." prompted Chen, and he saw from Fitzgerald's slump that the funny ending and heroic anecdote that these types of stories usually concluded with would not come.

Fitzgerald said, "So the woman starts CPR. She hasn't even checked for a pulse, and in fact I think I can see him breathing, so she would totally fail an ACLS course. Anyhow, she's doing it like squirrel CPR. *Boop boop boop* on his chest. Must have seen it on TV. She's got the two-hand thing going, elbows locked, but she's barely touching the guy. I figured that if he was actually alive, her CPR wasn't going to hurt him much, and if he was dead, none of this would matter. Then the ambulance came. I had to watch, because I was convinced that he was breathing, just to see whether I was right. Sure, they tubed him. I heard him sucking on the tube, and they weren't pumping him. See? I knew he had vital signs."

"Sometimes you can tell from a distance," said Chen.

"Sure," said Fitzgerald. A coughing fit. He wondered if he would have told the story if the ambulance crew had started CPR, if in fact the guy had died. No. He knew that he would have just kept it to himself. As it was, Chen was the first person he had told.

"Did you go to Centre Island?"

"Yeah, but that whole incident soured my day."

"It's cute out on the Island, isn't it? All the rides, and the kids in the swan boats, driving those little cars."

"I like it out there," said Fitzgerald. Fitzgerald thought of a ferry trip to the Island with Ming before she met Chen, and was surprised that he could remember this without bitterness, without needing to know whether Chen knew that Ming and Fitzgerald had once spent a sunny afternoon on Centre Island. He felt good, that it was mostly a pleasant memory of a woman whom he now hardly knew, and of himself as a person remembered. A slight pang, of course, but after an unusual length of sobriety he was able to see that this was mostly a pang for his present aloneness, and that there was no truth to representing it otherwise. "Listen, if I go down the drain, and I think I will, I don't want to be tubed or resuscitated or anything. It's not worth it."

(Portion of progress note of Dr. R. Zenkie, FRCPC, dated March 20, 2003—excerpted from chart with permission of Toronto South General Hospital)

... and as his clinical situation continues to worsen, Dr. Fitzgerald has indicated his wish to not be resuscitated should he deteriorate to the point that he requires intubation. He has told me that should this occur, he would not want to expose other staff to the SARS *infection by performing such a high-risk procedure, since he judges that in this instance his chances of survival would be slim. I am inclined to wonder whether Dr. Fitzgerald may be suffering from an acute situational depression, and therefore may not be competent to make this decision. At this point, I am refraining from writing a DNR order, because of my doubts about the state of Dr. Fitzgerald's mental health.*

Yours truly, Dr. R. Zenkie, FRCPC

Consultant in Infectious Diseases, Toronto South General Hospital

(NB: Also on March 20, Dr. Zenkie ordered diazepam 10 mg by mouth every one hour as needed by Dr. Fitzgerald to treat persistent tremor. No other explanation of this order is noted in the chart.)

DOLORES EXPLAINED to the daycare director that she, herself, had no fever, no respiratory symptoms, that she was screened daily at the hospital and checked her own temperature at home at least twice. Certainly, her children were perfectly healthy. She had had no unprotected contact, she said, and could not be considered to be a suspect or probable case. The daycare director said that it wasn't that she had any problem with the situation. No, it was just that the parents of the other children felt ... uncomfortable. Dolores asked why those parents didn't just keep their kids at home, then. Well, that would be unfair to them, said the daycare woman, and it wasn't that she was forbidding Dolores's kids from coming, it was just that maybe they should ... think about things a bit. Already, Dolores's children had told her that the other kids wouldn't play with them, had been told not to by their parents.

Dolores found a babysitter who could provide both daycare for the little ones and after-school care for Dolores's older daughter. Dolores told her that she worked in the sanitation industry, and explained to the kids that they shouldn't tell anyone that Mommy was a nurse. Why not? her daughter asked. Because people are silly, Dolores said. For how long do we keep it secret? her son asked. Dolores said that she wasn't sure how long it would be. It might be a while.

ON MARCH 21, Chen saw that Fitzgerald sucked on his oxygen with all the heaving muscles in his chest, that he ate ice from a cup next to him. Chen called Fitzgerald and asked how he was doing. Great, replied Fitzgerald.

"Hey, you remember that guy, that old German internist, the one who did his residency in India? He would talk that crazy German-accented Hindi to all the Indian patients. They loved him. What was his name, Glug-something? Gland?"

"Gerstein."

"Were you there when he convinced that woman she needed a spinal tap?"

"Remind me."

"The one-in-a-hundred thing ..."

"Oh, of course," said Fitzgerald. Both he and Chen began to laugh. Dr. Gerstein had been their attending when they were consulted about a patient with a headache. Her story raised suspicions of a subarachnoid hemorrhage, and the CT scan was negative. Dr. Gerstein explained to the woman, in the German-accented Hindi-influenced English he had learned in Bombay, that even though the CT scan was negative, there was a one percent chance that it could be wrong, and a lumbar puncture was necessary in order to be certain.

"One percent," she said. "I'm scared of needles."

"A subarachnoid could kill you," Dr. Gerstein said.

"But one percent. That's one in a hundred. You would put a needle into my spinal cord for one in a hundred?"

"Actually, into the spinal canal. We would avoid the cord."

"Maybe I'll take my chances," the woman said. "One percent isn't bad."

At that, Dr. Gerstein made for the door, leaving Dr. Chen and Dr. Fitzgerald standing at the woman's bedside. They did not know whether to follow him. They knew that this woman needed the lumbar puncture, and that sometimes Gerstein would abandon difficult tasks, such as convincing a patient of the wisdom of medical guidance, to his house staff. At the door, Gerstein turned, widened his stance. He made his hands into a pistol and raised them, pointed the two-fingered barrel straight at the woman.

He said, "I just picked up one of a hundred Mauser pistols that were sitting here outside the room. One of them is loaded, and I don't know which one. Regardless, the gun is trained on your forehead. I'll leave it up to you. Would you like me to pull the trigger?"

The woman's eyes were fixed on the muzzle of Gerstein's fingertips.

"The safety is off, shall I pull the trigger?"

Chen and Fitzgerald's chests thumped in sudden fear. Gerstein stood absolutely still, stared down his gun barrel until he smiled—not ironically, not exactly kindly, but mostly with sadness at the reality of decision making.

Fifteen minutes later, clear cerebrospinal fluid trickled into the needle embedded between that woman's fourth and fifth lumbar vertebrae.

"Like a gunslinger in a western," said Chen. "High noon at the spinal tap corral." Both he and Fitz were laughing.

Fitz said, "You think we'll die?"

"Maybe." The laughter continued.

"Me, more likely. I'm on a hundred percent." He knew that Chen was only on four litres of oxygen per minute. "It's not so bad," said Fitzgerald. "If we die with only a few hundred others, we'll be SARS martyrs. If thousands get it but they find a cure and our deaths help, then it's worthwhile. If this thing just goes wild and the whole world dies by the millions, then we'll miss the worst of it. See? Can't lose." By the time he had finished saying this, they were both sober.

"When I try to remember, I can't recall when I learned about death," said Chen. "How it's ordinary, but like a sudden hole in the world. I learned it, then I forgot, or maybe I just began to ignore it. Ming and I were talking about kids. Maybe next year."

"I'm a fuckup anyhow. Better for me to croak. You stick around." The mention of Ming made Fitzgerald angry and sick with himself, his drinking, his aloneness. He told himself resolutely that losing her hadn't influenced the shape of his life, but when he drank he did not believe this. When the bottle sank him below the comfort zone, Ming was one of the if-only-it-had-been-another-way things that became vivid. Fitzgerald decided from Chen's comfortable manner with him that Ming had never mentioned Fitzgerald, and only once at a departmental party had they all been in the same room. He and Chen had never been very close, but when you do months of "team medicine" together, you end up acting like buddies out of necessity. Now, being in respiratory isolation together, calling each other on the phone, it was like those times.

"Not what I meant," said Chen.

"That's the way it is. I told Zenkie to write a DO NOT RESUSCITATE on my chart."

"You're being crazy."

"Of course not. It's just common sense. Look, everyone who gets tubed dies. While they're getting tubed, the resuscitation team catches it. Then some of the people who tubed the guy who died get so sick that they need to be tubed. And so on. They should cut us off from everyone, like a leper colony."

"This is early, a new disease. There're intubated people who haven't died yet."

"Come on. You think we ever beat outbreaks? They run their course, they burn themselves out. It's just a question of how many people get burnt up in the process. Spanish flu, forty million dead, more than the First World War."

"Something like that."

(Transcript of Dr. R. Zenkie, FRCPC, dictated March 22, 2003—never transcribed because of deviations from standard dictation format—recovered from electronic transcription system with permission of Toronto South General Hospital)

ID: I am Dr. Ronald Zenkie, infectious disease consultant and avid nature photographer

CC: Fever, shortness of breath, heightened awareness of societal paranoia

(nervous laugh)

To whom it may concern,

(pause for coughing fit)

I am taking the unusual step of dictating my own admission note. Today, I woke with chills and myalgias. My temperature, measured orally, was 39. Over the day, I have become progressively more short of breath, and have developed a cough.

I think I have a cold, just a regular cold, but these days you never know.

(pause for coughing fit)

Erase last sentence, please.

It is probable that I am suffering from a relatively innocent upper respiratory tract infection. However, it must be noted that I may be perceived as being at high risk for contraction of SARS, and thus it is appropriate that I mandate my own admission to the SARS unit in the interests of public safety.

How about that, huh? Down with the ship.

(prolonged bout of laughter and coughing)

Shit. Erase last sentence and expletive, please.

I have discussed my clinical responsibilities, which will be assumed by Dr. Waterman, who will act as the interim attending staff on the SARS unit.
Yours truly, Dr. R. Zenkie, FRCPC
Consultant in Infectious Diseases, Toronto South General Hospital

(Addendum to SARS Bulletin 14, issued on March 25.)
To All Staff,
We are sad to inform you that after a short illness, Dr. R. Zenkie has suc-cumbed to SARS. Our condolences to his family, and thanks for his twenty-six years of service to the Toronto South General Hospital. Staff members who have been in contact with Dr. R. Zenkie have been contacted person-ally, but are reminded that they are now on work quarantine. All such staff should leave their homes only to go to work, using a private vehicle such as a personal car or a taxi. Masks must be worn between home and hospital at all times. At home, all such staff are reminded to sleep in separate rooms from their spouses, to sit at a minimum distance of 1 metre (3 feet) from family members during meals, and preferably to eat in a separate room. There should be no physical contact with children or other family members. All staff on work quarantine should shower at work, or shower in a sepa-rate area of the home from their family members, because of the possible aerosolization of SARS infectious material within showers. Body tempera-ture should be measured a minimum of twice per day, and any oral temper-ature greater than 38 must be reported immediately. Dr. Zenkie is survived by his wife, Amita, who is admitted in our SARS unit and asks that dona-tions be made to UNICEF in lieu of flowers or gifts. The memorial service for Dr. Zenkie is indefinitely postponed, and we would remind staff that all gatherings of hospital staff outside of the hospital are forbidden.
Yours truly,
SARS Action Management Team

THE MORNING RUSH. The line behind the hospital trailed out of the tent and into the parking lot. There was an April drizzle but people did not huddle close to each other's umbrellas. Those with umbrellas stood their ground, and those with bare heads stood at a more than socially polite dis-tance from each other, and gradually became wet. Arriving for the day shift. Dolores eyed the boxes of masks to see whether the blue ones, which were the least constrictive, were available. There were no blue masks. Only the white, itchy ones.

She saw that some people produced blue masks from their pockets and bags. They had hoarded the comfortable masks, she realized. Dolores had not done so, but decided that the next time she saw a box of the blue masks she would slip five or six of them into her purse. If it rained tomorrow, she thought, then she should bring an umbrella. Or maybe not. If she brought one, someone might try to stand too close to her.

Ahead, people filed past the dispensers of antiseptic handwash, squirted the bottles, and rubbed their hands and forearms. They gathered up their daily bundle of isolation gowns and scrubs, stood one by one in front of the masked screeners so that body temperatures could be measured with the ear probe, and to answer the same screening questions asked the day before. Dolores saw that one man had his temperature taken a second time. He shook his head. Then a third. He protested. A fourth. A look of resignation. A screener pushed a second mask at him and led him out the side flap of the tent, to somewhere else. Dolores saw that there were security people at each corner of the tent. They did not move, but they, like Dolores, watched this happen. What was the difference between being led away and being taken away? None, she decided, when a security guard stood at each corner of the tent, when everyone had instructions to follow.

Dolores began to feel warm. The line murmured, looked down, continued to move forward and present their ears for temperature measurement. Yes, she definitely felt warm. It was 7:20, and she should already be getting a signover report from the night shift, but she definitely felt a heat. Then she coughed. A cough. One, and was there another? It did not seem so, but her body temperature was intense, her heart beating. She was not yet inside the tent. She was still in the portion of the line that stood in the drizzle, that was still connected to the outside world of wind and water, a world that did not exist inside the hospital. Suddenly, Dolores wondered who would pick up the kids from the sitter and bring them home if she couldn't? Their father now lived three time zones away, her closest family was two time zones distant. What would happen if she got to the front of the line and had a temperature? They couldn't live with the babysitter. They would end up in a foster home until she got better. 7:23. Or what if she didn't get better?

No one noticed, Dolores thought, as she ducked out of the line, as she made for her car. She did not look back to see whether anyone followed her with their eyes. Now, she had missed report. All the way home she felt hotter and hotter, more and more inflamed. A fit of coughing at a red light, but maybe she had just swallowed wrong? Told herself to drive carefully. She slammed the car door, rushed into the house in her wet shoes, made for the bathroom, and only once the digital thermometer was in her mouth did she think, *But if I have a temperature, then I don't want to be in contact with my kids.*

The metal wand under her tongue, she remembered with a panic the report she had read that speculated that SARS infectious material might remain contagious even for days outside of the body. What was she doing? What was she thinking? She was in the process of contaminating her children's home. Whereas all this time she had been thinking only of the problem of picking up her children from the babysitter and bringing them home, now she wanted more than anything to keep them away from this place—this place that she was now transforming into a cesspool of disease. She felt a tickle, a scratchiness, needed to cough, needed to hold the thermometer under her tongue.

Beeeep.

36.6. Afebrile. No fever.

Dolores sat on the toilet, drank a glass of water. The cough seemed to be gone. She took her temperature again, and wrote it down on a scrap of paper from her purse. And again, shoes still dripping onto the bathroom mat. Wrote down the second temperature. Did it five times, all of the temperatures perfectly normal. The cough was gone. She averaged the five temperatures. The average was 36.5. Normal.

The phone rang. It was the nurse in charge of the SARS unit. Dolores had been seen ducking out of the line.

"No, no," she said, "not a fever. Just dizziness. I get this sometimes, these horrible episodes of dizziness. Usually lasts a few days.

"No, not a fever.

"No, don't send public health, no, it would be a waste.

"Definitely not.

"I checked five times.

"Yes.

"Yes.

"I know exactly what it is, so book me off the schedule for at least three days."

(Transcript of an evening news clip of April 3, 2003—reproduced with permission of CBC Television)

Today, an unusual occurrence at the Toronto South General Hospital SARS Unit: This morning, alarms indicated a breach in the SARS respiratory isolation rooms. What is known as a Code Orange alert was activated, placing the facility in Disaster Response mode. After several minutes, the Code Orange was deactivated. Hospital officials assure us that there was no external breach, and that no unprotected hospital staff were placed at risk. Initially, hospital officials refused to explain the incident, but with speculation heightening throughout the day, a statement has been released. It seems that a SARS patient, Dr. Fitzgerald, became unable to breathe and collapsed within an isolation room. As the SARS medical team donned their protective gear in order to enter the room and administer treatment to Dr. Fitzgerald, the SARS patient in the room adjacent to his, Dr. Chen, broke through the glass partition between their rooms with an intravenous pole, in order to initiate emergency treatment for Dr. Fitzgerald. The Code Orange alarm was activated by this glass being broken but, once again, hospital officials insist that no unprotected staff were exposed. Dr. Fitzgerald is reported to be in critical condition. Dr. Chen is reported to have cut his arm on broken glass, but is otherwise stable. The hospital declined to comment on their assessment of Dr. Chen's actions, which they described as being "outside standard protocol." Dr. Chen was reached briefly by phone, and stated, "In a critical situation, it takes too long to put on the SARS gear, and people die in the delay, but I've already got SARS, so I don't need the protection."

Extreme measures at urgent times.

Meanwhile, on the world front, the number of cases has exceeded two thousand. Chinese authorities have announced three hundred and sixty-one new SARS cases and nine new deaths. In Hong Kong, there is strong evidence that the disease has spread beyond its initial focus within hospitals, with secondary and tertiary cases almost certainly occurring in the community at large.

Elizabeth Hay

Elizabeth Hay is the author of three highly acclaimed, bestselling novels: *A Student of Weather*, *Garbo Laughs*, and, most recently, *Late Nights on Air*, winner of the 2007 Scotiabank Giller Prize.

She is also the author of two story collections, *Small Change* and *Crossing the Snow Line*, and two books of creative non-fiction, *The Only Snow in Havana* and *Captivity Tales: Canadians in New York*. In 2002 she received The Marian Engel Award for her body of literary work.

Hay was born in Owen Sound, Ontario. She worked for CBC Radio in Yellowknife, Winnipeg, and Toronto, lived in Mexico for a time, and for several years called Manhattan her home. Elizabeth Hay lives in Ottawa.

Late Nights on Air

BY ELIZABETH HAY

Winner 2007

～

On the Barrens something happened to their sense of time. They were living every second of bad weather in a land that was barely out of the ice age, a place no different from how it had been a hundred years or a thousand years ago. They were seeing what Hornby and Samuel Hearne had seen, what aboriginal hunters had seen when they hunted here, far back. And so seconds ticked forwards and years swept backwards, and they got used to thinking of time passing in tiny increments and huge leaps.

Ralph would say that the long wait for the wind to die down—another two days of being wind-bound and ice-bound—made him think of Agamemnon waiting to set sail from Aulis. The north winds kept blowing day after day until they sacrificed Iphigenia, poor girl; then the winds fell away, the thousand ships set sail for Troy, and one thing led to another, until Aeneas fled his burning city and fetched up on the shores of Carthage, "where he broke poor Dido's heart," said Ralph, throwing Harry a sympathetic look.

With tender timing Eleanor and Gwen then compared the bruises on their legs, rolling up their pants and exposing shins that looked as if they had been beaten with sticks, but it was the ice they'd fallen against and battled through. The bruises filled Harry's mind with memories of his life with Dido. She'd been like a stray, a waif that he'd found by the shore and brought home. During those six weeks, she'd never talked very much. Never really confided in him. The black eye had been her fault, she'd said. And the bruise he saw on her arm happened from banging into a cupboard. He had to suppose that when she was with him she was just resting, recovering, biding her time until she was ready to leave.

FINALLY, AT ONE IN THE MORNING, the sky began to clear. They could make out four or five ptarmigans in the meadow beyond the willows. Through binoculars they studied the male, its red markings above the eyes, its plumage a mottled brown until it flew up, and then its wings flashed white.

"What does ptarmigan taste like, I wonder," murmured Gwen.

"Ptough," said Ralph.

Eleanor remarked that seeing ptarmigans on Ptarmigan Lake was rather like seeing Harry on Harry Lake.

"You mean I washed myself in Harry?" cried Gwen.

"How lovely," said Harry.

IT WAS NOON of the next day. They were almost out of Ptarmigan Lake, having broken free of their snow-locked, weather-bound state by throwing caution to the winds. In the morning they'd hauled their canoes with ropes across the middle of the frozen lake, making several miles of progress. Gwen managed to tape the sound by hanging her tape recorder around her neck and holding the microphone between her teeth; Harry snapped a picture for what he called broadcasting posterity.

They skirted the blackest ice, the last stretch so rotten his feet did a little dance as he sped across. And then they were in open water. July 7.

In the early afternoon, a line of light blue appeared at the lower edge of the sky and in the distance something moved. A palomino boulder was swimming slowly across the lake. They paddled towards it and saw their first caribou, large and handsome, like a heavily built deer with a rack of dark antlers.

By evening the sky was clear. The light luminous and rich. Not brilliant as in the Mediterranean (where Harry once removed a splinter from a woman's finger on the streets of Sète in light that acted like a magnifying glass). Gentler. Almost autumnal. The hills didn't have light on them, they were in light, the way something is in water.

To Harry it seemed the Barrens relaxed. *One day something relaxed inside and I saw things in a new way.* The words came from an old book about an old botanist, and he felt the truth of them as they left behind frozen lakes and entered a land of flowing rivers. On July 8 they were on the Hanbury River, skimming along with the current, running two rapids and making three portages and completing a total of twenty-three miles. A grand day. That night they reached Sifton Lake and it too was melted, the next night they took advantage of an evening with almost no wind to keep paddling, hour after hour, in the pure golden light.

At midnight they beached their canoes and were about to make camp on an invitingly grassy bank when they saw, just across a small cove, something move.

They slipped back into their canoes and paddled closer. The grizzly was smaller than they'd imagined and very curious. It came to the water's edge, then waded into the water, climbing atop a rock several feet from shore. From there it stood watching them for fifteen minutes, brownish-blond, face like a wide dish, close-set eyes. At a distance of fifty yards, or less, they took pictures in the evening light. Then the bear turned around, waded back to shore, and ambled up onto a grass-covered knoll, where it lay down and went to sleep. They had no firearms, having failed to take Teresa's advice, and Harry suspected they'd been far too trusting, but the charmed evening had emboldened them. Even so, they paddled a full hour before they set up camp.

Several days after that, on July 13, a muskox in the afternoon. The bizarre beast appeared suddenly after miles of nothing. Dark massive head, down-curved horns, a fur coat like a chocolate-brown kilt, except along the uppermost part of the animal's back where it was lighter in colour as if faded by the sun. In the 1920s, said Ralph, after the decimation of the buffalo, muskox furs were in such demand for carriage robes that only protective legislation, inspired in no small part by John Hornby's observations and recommendations, saved them from being wiped off the face of the earth. This fellow stood on the riverbank with the blue sky behind him and sparse leafiness around his feet. After a few minutes he lumbered off into the distance, Ralph in careful pursuit with his camera, Eleanor calling after him to be careful: *Ralph!*

The next day, a group of three muskoxen. The animals thundered off and the humans inherited their flies. At supper mosquitoes plunged into the soup, kamikaze pilots in love with soggy death. Harry's emptied bowl had a dozen dead mosquitoes in the bottom. Eleanor took the bowl, turned it three times, and read the mosquitoes like tea leaves.

"I see a boy stung by bees," she said to Harry. "Six bee stings. No seven."

"Not a girl stripping off her clothes?" cracked Gwen, handing her own bowl to gypsy Eleanor, who turned it three times and said she saw a sudden change of course followed by a wedding.

Ralph instructed Eleanor to see money in his mosquito-leaves, huge sacks of it, mountains of it. But Eleanor saw, instead, a great expanse of water and suggested to Ralph that he might be going overseas.

By now Gwen's hair was sun-streaked and her face ruddy. "'As brown in hue as hazel nuts and sweeter than the kernels,'" remarked Harry, addressing her with a gleam in his eye.

She blushed and raised her hands, which were too dried and cracked to close. "They feel like baseball mitts," she said.

Harry surprised her by taking one of her hands in his. "I have just the thing."

From his pack he produced a tin of udder balm for chapped and swollen teats, then proceeded to work the ointment into her skin, especially her split fingertips. "What about your feet? Take off your boots," he said.

"What is the smoothest part of Gwen?" He reached for her bare foot, only to exclaim, "Not the heel!" His eyes widened. "You could do permanent damage with this heel."

Gwen's heels had never been so in the limelight, her rough, raspy heels. Harry would see them again when her tent blew down and she was out flying around in the middle of the night in bare legs and white heels and nightie, trying to re-stake and prop it up, while Eleanor held it down from inside. From his tent door Harry shouted at her to lay it flat and bring their sleeping bags in here, and Gwen shouted something back that he couldn't make out, for in the wind their voices tore like fabric.

Gwen later admitted she had seriously underestimated the importance of good shelter by bringing "that shitty tent," which sagged like a soft berry picked by the weather and manhandled between its fingers.

That night they lay across the floor of Harry's tent like four slumbering sardines.

Where the Darrell River met the Hanbury River, they passed into the Thelon Game Sanctuary. It wasn't a definite shape but a continuation of what they'd seen, yet it took on the shape in Harry's mind of a garden, a garden in the wilderness. Now there were scattered trees again, more and more trees. On a single day, July 15, they portaged around Macdonald Falls, Dickson Canyon, and Ford Falls, about three and a quarter miles in all. Between the first and second carry, they walked back along the edge of Dickson Canyon and saw rough-legged hawks above, and churning water below, as well as three large pools to one side fed by the rapids, each pool feeding the one below, deep green water in which grayling swam. On a hill Harry noticed muskox hair caught in the willows and low trees, the soft wool called *qiviut*, so Eleanor informed him when she came alongside. She picked tufts of it off the twigs and slipped them into her pocket, reminded of poor Absalom caught by his beautiful hair in the branches of the biblical oak, and of Lorna holding that tuft of hair in her dead hand, and of the first Dido whose spirit wouldn't leave her dying body, Virgil said, until Iris descended and cut off a tress of her hair.

When finally they came to a halt that day, Harry soaked his head and feet and sore knee in the Hanbury River. They were on a beautiful sand dune—white sand beyond their tents, white snow above the sand. Fox and caribou tracks in evidence. And Gwen washing her hair.

"Always washing your hair," Harry said to her.

"Always watching me wash my hair," she said back.

She got him to stand behind her and wave away the flies and he felt like a painter with "Woman Shampooing Hair" on his easel.

"Your face is thinner," he told her when she turned around, her head wrapped in a towel. "You've developed cheekbones."

Eleanor looked up and watched the two of them for a long moment. The out-of-doors as beautician, she thought. Tanning Gwen's skin, lightening her hair, lengthening it (hair grows three times as fast in the summer she'd learned from Lorna Dargabble, as do toenails). Gwen's shirt was bone-coloured, bleached by the long light. And now the animals were appearing and the story was coming to an end, the story her father was reading to her when he died, since that would have been what happened: the ostracized, runaway girl would have been helped by the animals in the forest, and then some admirer would have come along, perhaps a secret admirer who had always appreciated her without knowing he was in love. And wouldn't the girl be looking the wrong way at the time, since isn't it the hardest lesson in the world, learning to appreciate people if you've never felt appreciated?

THEY WERE FINDING THINGS, one after the other. A black thread hanging from a low willow. A weathered orange pip on a rock. A lantern base of heavy glass, and some fox traps left behind at the foot of a portage. A hand-made sled runner, or so it appeared to Ralph, who pronounced it made in

Captain Back's time. The 1830s. In the absence of trees that shed their leaves in autumn, objects could sit in the open for decades, centuries.

One night Harry caught a sizable grayling, a fish that was dull-brown in the water but vivid out of its element—in its death throes it went through a troubled array of colours from purply blue-black on its body to brilliant red spots on its large dorsal fin. Harry knelt to clean and fillet the pretty fish. He cut across the backbone, but left the tail in place in order to have something to hold on to when he skinned it. The carcass he threw into the river, having first shown Gwen what the fish had been eating: smaller fish, partially digested, the colour and consistency of grey glue. Gwen had her cassette recorder over her shoulder and she taped the sounds of scraping, eviscerating, slicing, rinsing.

This was the night, July 17, Eleanor elected not to go to bed at all in order to experience the brief middle-of-the-night twilight with its profusion of violet clouds directly overhead and its yellow gleam in the northern sky. Dressed in wool pants, wool jacket, gloves, with bug repellant smeared on her face and neck, she lay on her back on the warm, mattressy tundra whose thick growth held on to the day's heat. Tweedy smells rose from the soft tangle straight into her nostrils. The colours and textures at eye level, the russets, browns, blacks, reds, formed an embrace so gently erotic she dozed off with a smile on her lips, only to come awake when a ptarmigan whirred by, or a snowy owl flew down and sat on a big stone twenty feet away, or loons cried in the distance. The loon's long call seemed to her like a statement of the hour, a horizontal sound that tapered off into the horizon, while its laughter was vertical, high, flashy, rippling. The Barrens themselves were horizontal, but vertical, too, she thought. A vertical world of air: a country of clouds, an abundance of wind.

"You were the only sleepers," she said in the morning. "Everything else was awake."

The air, she claimed, was ten degrees warmer in among the plants than a foot above, and several degrees warmer still inside the actual blossoms. Ralph, wanting proof, knelt beside her and felt the warm air swell up from the heated plants, the tundra less a riot of colour, he said, to her everlasting delight, than a peaceful demonstration. She thought of the cool air that blows over your skin when you meet someone. Then with some few you feel warmer, as it was warmer by these vivid ten degrees close to Ralph, and close to the arctic ground, to the tussocks of moss and low cushion plants and ground-hugging berries and spreading mats of grasses and flowers and such.

Together they examined the tiny complete world at their fingertips. Over the last few weeks she'd identified flowers like yellow arnica, white-petalled arctic dryad with its look of wild roses, yellow and violet oxytrope and wild sweet pea, pressing them into her pocket-sized notebook and making sketches and lists: of the chickweeds or starworts with their little white star-like flowers, the violet and yellow louseworts rising up out of the moss, the pink arctic fireweed, yellow arctic poppy, twiggy Labrador tea with its neat, round clusters of white flowers and narrow rolled-under leaves, the butter-cups, milk-vetch, white and purple saxifrage, the small, white bells of the arctic heather, the red-violet clusters of Lapland rosebay like miniature rho-dodendrons, the dwarf pink azalea.

When she and Ralph stood up, their eyes took in the full extent of the boundless northern wastes. Every foot of evenly rising plains and worn-away hills was as detailed as the small bit they were standing on.

A long-tailed jaeger flew overhead, its tail like a dark, slender, beautiful paintbrush. Sometimes, said Ralph, the canny suitor, he felt life ripple through him, connecting him to every other living thing, and his own exis-tence was the least of it and the most of it. Yes, she said.

They came down off the tundra as if hand in hand, and joined Harry and Gwen at the water's edge. The river and the landscape it ran through stretched in immensity on either side—what vastness they had dropped in to visit—yet in each other's company, this fellowship of four souls, they felt light-headedly secure.

THE NEXT EVENING Eleanor came upon Harry sitting by himself on a knoll not far from the campsite, smoking a cigarette. She sat beside him and without looking at her he reached over and took her hand. The tundra rolled away into the distance, the undulating barren hills, the immense light.

"I want to know something," he said to her. "When Dido phoned you, did she even mention my name?"

Eleanor didn't answer for a moment. "Do you mean, did she say she wanted to see you or talk to you? No, Harry. She didn't."

Harry nodded. With a bitterness he wished he could rise above, he said, "I can't figure out what she sees in Eddy."

Eleanor reflected. "Maybe he makes her feel good about being bad."

Harry let out a short laugh.

"There's Gwen," said Eleanor.

They saw her heading off on her own, walking towards a ridge of land a short distance away. Her head was down. Her tape recorder was around her neck and she steadied it with one hand. She waved flies away with the other.

"What will become of her, do you think?" asked Eleanor.

"Eddy's going to ruin her life."

"I meant Gwen."

"Ah," said Harry.

Gwen had shortened the shoulder strap on her cassette recorder and hung it low enough on her chest to see the levels on the VU meter; easier to walk this way too. She looked down, alert to sounds, but otherwise lost in what Harry would have called a brown study; she was thinking about his soft, swollen ear and about his other appendages, wondering about them idly, not so idly, as the look of the scruffy heath imprinted itself on her eyes.

At the sound of loons, she automatically pressed record and stood listening to birds that mated for life, their beautiful mad laughter. What held her eye, however, was the look of her hand on the microphone. So weathered and chapped compared to the silver-metallic stem she was holding carefully, no rings on her fingers to click against the metal and transfer to the dark spool of tape, her equipment solid and unchanging and Japanese, her veins purply under the roughened, reddish-brown skin. She saw her hand on a doorknob, pushing open a bedroom door, and the phrase "inquiry without walls" came into her head, the Barrens like Berger's commission: you learned a great deal, more than you wanted to know sometimes, more than you knew what to do with. Could there be a more primitive, naked, intimate sound than the heavy breathing, the solitary moan and whimper she'd heard from inside Harry's tent an hour ago? The physical side of life, which stretched in utter loneliness and tenderness all around her.

A wolf, white, old, mangy, arthritic, slowly stretched and yawned on the riverbank as they paddled by. A harbinger, had they but known. By now it was July 20 and they were on the wide, smooth, east-flowing Thelon River, seven days from the end.

Ralph spotted shapes moving in the distance. Gwen thought they must be geese, they were used to geese running along the shore. They drew closer and the scales fell from their eyes. A group of fifteen caribou were crossing the river ahead of them, antlers like high heels rising from their heads.

They paddled to the south side of the river, as did Harry and Eleanor, and waited with thumping hearts for the caribou to come towards them along the shore, but the animals clambered out of the water and went the other way. Then another smaller group swam across the river and they too went up the sloping bank through low willows and spruce, then up over the rocky ridge and out of sight.

They had lunch on the rise of land above the river and realized they were on the edge of a large herd. Caribou in the hundreds were all around them, in the distance and moving slowly, or not moving at all, blending in like boulders on the open tundra of grass and heath and rounded hills. What they'd been hoping for was finally happening.

La foule. The word came unbidden to Ralph from accounts of the great migrations of the past. It was like witnessing the arrival of a myth: the caribou emerged from the land and belonged to it, tentative, purposeful, graceful, shy, their colours buff, brown, grey, pale, Gwen's colours when she first arrived at the station. What they were seeing was the mass arrival of something beautifully recessive and fleeting. They could have missed it just as easily, a few hours one way or the other.

Ralph nestled against the lip of a low hill and looked through long grass at the large herd on the other side. Eleanor was close to him. Not far away was Gwen, her cassette recorder around her neck, her microphone in her hand, when a cow and calf came thundering right up to them, unaware of their presence, then ran off a bit, then came closer again. Soon several caribou were eating willow leaves just twenty feet below them. Gwen taped the sounds of their soft lips pulling off small leaves, the quiet sounds of chewing. A male reached around and scratched his back leg with his antlers. Dark, velvet, bone.

Black antlers above the greenery, the willows, the water. The look of heavy mascara around their eyes. The ripples of movement that occurred when one animal started and the rest followed. They were like camels in the sand dunes, beautiful on the blond hills, moving and gathering, arranging themselves in small, elegant groups around the willows, like a series of almost still-lifes.

Harry called softly. A group of ten was coming down the shore towards their canoes. The others followed him and stood very still under the high-pitched hum of clouds of gnats, watching intently and with enormous excitement. Gwen taped the sound of hooves splashing at the water's edge. Loud, their coming and going, yet subdued, and soon over. The large numbers that gathered on their side of the river all afternoon were spooked about seven in the evening. Having filed down to the water and along it, maybe five hundred, seven hundred animals, they suddenly drew back up over the bank and over the hill and out of sight across the tundra.

"I think we're in a thin place," Ralph murmured, remembering his father's passion for the Celts. "Where seen and unseen meet."

That being the very definition of this ancient caribou crossing, where the river narrowed and offered passage to the other side. The animals were every bit as sensitive as the witnesses at the Berger Inquiry had claimed, and this wasn't even their most skittish time. The calving and post-calving had occurred farther north, and now, less urgently, they were engaged in the long return to the timberline.

So quiet, whispered Eleanor. So easily not seen, and then so easily lost. She and Ralph stood together watching straggling cows with their calves, and solitary calves. On the opposite shore a bull and a calf entered the water and began to swim across, a twosome. But halfway, the calf dropped out of sight and didn't resurface, no matter how long they kept looking.

THEY WERE ALONE AGAIN "in the land of feast and famine." Nothing for so long, and then abundance, and then nothing again, but a nothing haunted by the previous abundance.

That night, thumbing backwards through Whalley's book, Ralph came upon Edgar, raw-boned and white in his photograph. Parted hair and ears sticking out. Then Hornby's emaciated face after one of his starving winters near Fort Reliance. The sunken, glittering eyes. The amiable smile. The head of hair still dark and thick. In 1925, the year before his last journey, Hornby was travelling with James Critchell-Bullock, an ex-army officer turned traveller-photographer-collector. After a squalid winter near Artillery Lake, holed up in a collapsing cave dug into the side of a sand esker, they were making their miserable way to Hudson Bay. On the evening of July 23, they sighted "a large group of caribou moving south-west on the south shore: about two thousand animals, mostly females, 'moving all over the hills making a tremendous noise calling to one another … a beautiful sight on the sand hills with the gold of the sunshine reflected on the water.'" Another sixty miles and the two men came to the sharp double bend in the river that took Hornby's fancy and sealed his fate, for on the north side rose a fine stand of white spruce that inspired thoughts of building a house and overwintering.

Ralph set down the book, understanding an aspect of Hornby for the first time: he had been seduced by the idea of a well-built home instead of a filthy cave or soggy tent or crummy tarp. The tiny, extraordinarily tough, self-destructive Englishman had actually been seeking a wild kind of comfort.

In himself something similar was going on. He felt a growing desire to be attached, not to a place but to a person. For years he'd made a habit of keeping his options open, of not letting himself be pinned down, an approach to life that seemed almost juvenile to him now. They'd come such a long distance already, he and Eleanor and the others. They were two-thirds of the way there, two-thirds of the way home, and he felt more sure of his next step than he'd ever felt about anything. Eleanor wasn't even forty and he was sixty-one, but on the last night of their trip he would ask her to marry him.

THE NEXT DAY they paddled on. The air was calm. The mosquitoes ferocious, almost as plentiful as the caribou hair in the bushes and at the water's edge, white, brittle, hollow hairs and some finer fluff, a floating mattress of hair. The shore, formerly flat and hard, was churned up by hooves.

Clumps of Labrador tea among the rocks. A few terns overhead. Ashes from their small tea fire blown about by a sudden gust of wind. And the need to make twenty-two, twenty-three miles a day if they were to reach Beverly Lake on time.

And again they were among the caribou. Thousands of them were crossing the river that afternoon. In their canoes they drifted with the current while the caribou circled around them and continued swimming to shore, then climbed the bank, their dark antlers magnificent amidst the greenery in this paradise of leafiness and sky. Clumps of trees thickened into woods on the hills, hair covered the water, the shore, the grass. Grunting, so many of them now, like pigs rooting, mud and grass churned up. A heavy manure smell in the air. And Gwen recording.

More and more came, the hillside emptied and filled again. Caribou filed across the horizon on a high ridge, then down the steep slope to the water, a line of strolling players with the sky behind them and a wolf invariably bringing up the rear. The effect was joyous and spellbinding and sobering. Over supper Eleanor said she felt like giving thanks for Judge Berger, who would see to it that these vanishing herds were protected.

"The government must rue the day they appointed him," chuckled Ralph.

"He's a special man," Eleanor said, fingering the medallion's chain around her neck. "I can't imagine anyone else in the part."

No one disagreed. For five minutes.

Then Gwen wondered aloud if he wasn't too gullible. He gave the impression of believing every word every native witness said, but weren't they as human as anyone else, as capable of self-interest and poetical exaggeration? She wondered if the bond they felt with the land and the animals was as genuine now as in the past, before they had high-powered rifles and snowmobiles.

Harry said she had a point, but insisting on purity wasn't fair. The natives felt a connection to the land, he said, that was almost incomprehensible to us. He said he had the sense of miraculous brakes being applied. He was betting on Berger, betting he would manage to delay for a considerable time the onslaught of development. "And if that's possible, what isn't?"

THE NEXT AFTERNOON they were looking at John Hornby's grave in the sun. Three simple, weathered, wooden crosses shored up by rocks piled at the base of each one. EC. JH. HA. The ruined cabin just to the left, its bottom logs still in place, but the roof fallen in, and the walls. Some caribou antlers inside the cabin and more just outside the door. It was July 22.

They had come 350 miles, from old Fort Reliance to this beautiful spot, an open bank rising up steeply on the north side of the river to the famous stand of spruce. Late afternoon, the warm sun shining, and after an hour of looking and taking photographs, they decided to stay for the night. Gwen wandered around the little makeshift cemetery, the remains of the cabin, and then she headed off on her own, her brown canvas tape recorder bag over her shoulder.

Harry was making supper. He was saying to Eleanor that young Edgar's fate reminded him of what happened to the Eskimo girl in the Thierry Mallet story. The last one left alive carries on.

He'd borrowed Ralph's copy of Whalley's biography and read the final pages that described Edgar letting the fire in the stove die out. Edgar placed his companions' papers and his own diary in the cool ashes, then lay down on his bunk and pulled the blankets up and over his head. Whalley imagined the sounds he might have heard, perhaps "the faint sound of ptarmigan feeding outside," and the effect of the silence, "like wings folding about him."

What Harry admired so much was Whalley's restraint in telling the story. Whalley was like Berger in that way. He didn't pick on people. He didn't ridicule Hornby for his mistakes, or excoriate him. He could have so easily. A journalist would have.

He added another stick to the fire and saw Ralph coming up from the river, but he didn't see Gwen. And then he heard her.

GWEN HAD CLIMBED the wooded slope that rose gently behind the cabin, looking for signs of Hornby and finding them in the axe cuts in old stumps that she'd read about. She had her eyes down to negotiate the branch-littered ground, the thick ground cover. A little farther and she thought she might get a fine view of the river below. In the northwest corner of this fringe of trees between cabin and open Barrens, she expected to find the windbreak of stones Hornby had erected from which they watched for caribou. In her mind she was with Hornby and Edgar and Harold Adlard as they made the same ascent, alone or together, early on when they were healthy and strong, and then later when they were desperate. Once, they saw thirty caribou in the distance and thought salvation was at hand, but the animals disappeared before they could get close to them. She turned to look south towards the river, but the twisted, slow-growing trees, some of them at least four hundred years old, still blocked the view. She turned back and saw something blondish-brown out of the corner of her eye. Fifty feet away? They aren't huge animals. They don't have to be huge. It lifted its nose and sniffed.

Experts say to avoid eye contact. To back away quietly. Not to turn and run.

Gwen's scream coincided with her seeing a set of small, black, gleaming eyes. She turned and ran.

It was like going full tilt down a flight of stairs covered in books. She felt her feet go out from under her even as she tumbled forward, and instinctively she grabbed at the nearest tree and slowed her descent at the expense of her arm. Her right shoulder wrenched out of its socket. Then she was lying in a small heap, the pain so intense she couldn't make a sound.

Her head slid forward to rest on the ground and she bit down on the dead branch that offered itself, aware in a flickering part of her brain of an age when biting down on wood offered the only consolation in moments of physical agony. Her shoulder wasn't there, nauseatingly not there, but her heart was bouncing her off the ground. She heard the bear behind her, then beside her. She heard its heavy breathing. She felt it nose her left leg and she bit harder into the wood. It nosed her leg a second time and she closed her eyes, lay completely still, apart from her thumping, cartoonish heart. She smelled the animal. Heard the saliva bubbling in its mouth. Kept as quiet as she always had at the dining-room table when a wave of fury would darken her father's face. She braced herself for more pain, and heard the bear moving, and realized it was moving away.

When they found her, she was coming slowly towards them like a shell-shocked survivor of the trenches or the highway. She saw them and sank to her knees.

Harry was beside her.

"Shoulder," she managed.

She felt his hands on her shoulder, and with a slight, subtle adjustment her arm was amazingly back in place.

"I thought you were proposing," he would say later, bringing a weak smile to her face.

He helped her to her feet and she breathed out, "We're not camping here."

The next morning, before the others were up, Harry went down to the water. They had paddled two hours beyond Hornby Point (he and Eleanor taking more of the load in their canoe so that Ralph could paddle alone as Gwen rested her shoulder, to say nothing of her mind) and they'd camped on a steep bank on the opposite side of the river, to be extra sure. Harry hadn't slept much, thinking about Gwen and the grizzly, wondering if they were travelling under a lucky star or if their luck had run out. He would never forget the sight of her coming down the slope. She looked damaged, lopsided, wrong. They had to brush twigs and leaves off her cheeks and forehead, but the imprint remained for hours.

They'd talked at length about how long it lasted, her encounter with the bear. Not as long as she thought, he was sure of that; a second with a grizzly is an eternity by any measure. He'd heard her terrifying scream, they all had, and they'd come charging up the hill and through the trees, but she hadn't heard them. They were downwind for one thing. In Gwen's mind there was only the noise of the bear's breathing, a kind of huffing, a moist huffing, and the powerful reek of animal, and the memory of small, cold eyes. It nosed her leg "like a teacher tapping your shoulder in the hall," she said, and she'd tapped Harry's shoulder to demonstrate, not hard: sending a chill down his spine. *Detention, young man.*

Now, as he came down to the water, he saw a tiny calf, its side ripped open, resting under a tree. It struggled to its feet upon seeing him and ran desperately into the water, then tottered back to shore, then back into the water and back to shore, where it collapsed, "all tuckered out," he would tell the others at breakfast. Using the biggest stick he could find, he put the little chap out of its misery with three hard blows. Then he reached for his knife. It took him a long time to dress the meat; he was reminded as he worked of his grandfather, of all the furriers and trappers and woodsmen who constituted a dwindling breed of their own. Often they were the most soft-hearted of men, and it had to do with being on the land so much, something the anti-trappers would never understand. That night they had caribou veal and it was certainly his most delicious and most poignant culinary dish.

Eleanor told them about her father speaking very fondly of a dinner he'd had at the Waldorf Hotel in New York. Green turtle soup, double breast of grey partridge, and strawberry mousse. This meal was just as memorable, "but I wonder if I'll talk about it quite so much."

"Gwen?" Harry offered her seconds.

She was hungry, as hungry as someone who's just escaped the firing squad, and she held out her plate. She'd done everything wrong, she knew, fleeing when she should have stood her ground, turning herself into prey. Yet here she was, still alive. The world around her tingled with life.

Gwen saw admiration in Harry's eyes, and in Ralph's and Eleanor's too, and she basked in it. But when they told her how brave she was, she shook her head. "You should hear me when I get a paper cut."

Later, she would say the bear's eyes were like Eddy's, small and mean. Harry would turn his hand into a microphone, "Now tell us how you *really* feel." And Gwen would smile, until he dropped his microphone-hand back into his lap. Then suddenly she remembered the shoulder bag containing her tape recorder and tapes. Back there, back where she'd fallen. Back being pawed by the grizzly bear. Thus occurred their first irretrievable loss.

Gwen sat disconsolate on a flat stone and the trip ran like a reel through her mind, erasing itself as it went along. The tinkling ice on Charlton Bay, the songbirds on Pike's Portage, the sounds of paddling, straining, cursing, of crackling fires and roaring rapids and wriggling fish, of mosquitoes being slapped and long tent zippers being opened and more rapidly shut, of gargantuan snores, of footsteps among the ankle-turning stones and the whish-y tread of boots on tundra. Of Ee-zay saying pee-nuts ba-ta. Of ice-hauling accompanied by the tap of her teeth on the microphone. Most prized of all, the tapes of the Barren-ground caribou, their clicking hooves and strenuous swimming and muted eating, since who had ever recorded them before?

Harry's efforts were good-hearted, if clumsy. He suggested she could recreate what she'd lost, using sound effects and words. Gwen let out a despairing groan, but he was patient. He told her what mattered more than sound effects was the effect of sound. He liked remembering car tires going through puddles and over melting snow on the street outside school, blue jays in the woods, squirrels high in the trees—sounds that evoked the soft days when winter was turning to spring and long summer holidays were around the corner. We had a bell in the Town Hall, he said. Tom Finnegan rang it every day at noon and at five in the afternoon. If it rang hard and successively, it meant fire. Train whistles were wonderful too, and dogs barking in the distance. And the radio. I always loved the sound of the radio. "What's the first sound you remember?" She shook her head. "Come on, Lippy." And she gave in and laughed a little.

"Maybe it was the rain," she said.

"And what about the first thing you heard on the radio?"

"'Blue Suede Shoes.' I was four years old."

That set Harry off. His first piece on air was a movie review he recorded in a bedroom closet because he couldn't stand his roommate hearing him read the script. A month later he was hosting a program, and two years afterwards he was working in Toronto. "That's how quickly fortunes can turn," he said, thinking as much of what had come after as what had gone before.

This was the evening they saw a strangely beautiful group of caribou emerge from the water and slowly approach, their pattern governed by hunger and available food—by the arrangement of leaves on willows fifty feet away. No matter how they moved around the low trees, reaching up or down or forward or around, the animals seemed exquisitely placed, as if by an Old Master.

Their little group of four was also being reconfigured. In the mornings Ralph took Eleanor a cup of tea, unzipping the door of the tent she shared with Gwen, and singing snatches of songs to her when she arrived at the campfire. One evening he reached for her hand and they moved in three-four time across the widest dance floor in the world.

There were summers in Gwen's childhood when her father's favourite brother came to visit from the States, and the anticipation of his arrival, that keen pleasure, was like this one of watching Ralph and Eleanor together. To witness the two brothers greet each other, to gauge the level of their affection, to watch her sociable uncle take pleasure in her unsociable dad and her dad take pleasure in her uncle—all this was high, ardent drama. She wanted to see every moment of mutual delight and there was never quite enough to satisfy her. Did her uncle know—did he have any idea—how much her father loved him?

Something blossoms in an unlikely place. An oasis of trees miles above the treeline. An arctic river warmer than any other water they'd come upon. The four of them bathed in the waters of the Thelon, wading out into it, almost swimming. On shore they towelled themselves dry and dressed, and there was no feeling to equal the splendour of warm clothes on river-cold skin.

The next morning Ralph said to Eleanor within Gwen's hearing, "I was dreaming about you last night."

"What was I up to?"

"You were pointing with your finger at very specific places on your body that you wanted me to kiss, and I obliged you with pleasure."

THEN NO SOONER had all of this closeness come about than it dispersed. That night Eleanor asked Harry what he was going to do with himself next, and he surprised them by saying he wanted to leave Canada behind for a while, not radio but Canada; his friend Max Berns knew people at Broadcasting House in London; he might well move to England.

In thinking it through over the past weeks, turning this way and that in his thoughts, he'd reminded himself of caribou at the river's edge. They retreated once, twice, three times. He'd never known before that migration wasn't one unbroken forward movement; it was sideways, backwards, forwards, a passage enlivened with indecision in the face of real and imagined danger. They came to the river, they shied away. He wasn't like Eleanor, he thought. He felt attuned not to the God within but to the uncertainty within. His connection was with the poor, dumb animals.

Eleanor had her own surprise. She'd been thinking about opening up a bookstore just down the street from the post office in Yellowknife, and she'd almost convinced Ralph to be her partner. Ralph grinned. "She wants my pretty coins," he said.

And once again Gwen's favourite uncle was back in the States and the first day of school was looming.

2008 FINALISTS

Joseph Boyden

Joseph Boyden's first novel, *Three Day Road*, was selected for The Today Show Book Club; won the Rogers Writers' Trust Fiction Prize, the CBA Fiction Book of the Year, the Amazon.ca/Books in Canada First Novel Award, and the McNally Robinson Aboriginal Book of the Year Award; and was shortlisted for the Governor General's Award for Fiction. His second novel is *Through Black Spruce*. Boyden divides his time between Northern Ontario and Louisiana.

Through Black Spruce

BY JOSEPH BOYDEN

Finalist 2008

❧

1

Gill Nets

When there was no Pepsi left for my rye whisky, nieces, there was always ginger ale. No ginger ale? Then I had river water. River water's light like something between those two. And brown Moose River water's cold. Cold like living between two colours. Like living in this town. When the whisky was Crown Royal, then brown Moose River water was a fine, fine mix.

You know I was a bush pilot. The best. But the best have to crash. And I've crashed a plane, me. Three times. I need to explain this all to you. I was a young man when I crashed the first time. The world was wide open. I was scared of nothing. Just before Helen and I had our oldest boy. The first time I crashed I was drunk, but that wasn't the reason I crashed. I used to fly a bush plane better with a few drinks in me. I actually believe my eyesight improved with whisky goggles on. But sight had nothing to do with my first crash. Wait. It had everything to do with it. Snowstorm. Zero visibility. As snow blinded my takeoff from the slick runway, I got the go-ahead with a warning from the Moosonee flight tower: harder snow coming.

An hour later and I'd made it a hundred miles north of Moose River on my way to pick up trappers not wanting but needing to come in from their lines. A rush to find them with night coming. I had a feeling where they'd be. Me, I was a natural in a plane. But in snow? One minute I'm humming along, the next, my fuel line's gummed and I'm skidding and banging against a frozen creek. The crazy thing? Had I come in a few feet to the left or right, blind like I did, I would have wrapped my plane around black spruce lining the banks. Head a mush on the steering. Broken legs burning on a red-hot motor. The grandparents sometimes watch out. *Chi meegwetch, omoshomimawak!*

My plane wasn't too damaged, but this was a crash nonetheless. And I emerged from the first true brush with *it*. The long darkness. No need to speak its name out loud.

Soon as I forced the door open, the snow, it stopped falling. Like that. Like in a movie. And when the cloud cover left on a winter afternoon a hundred plus miles north of Moosonee in January, the cold came, presented itself in such a forceful way that I had two choices.

The first was to assume that the cold was a living thing that chased me and wanted to suck the life from me. I could get angry at it, desperate for some sense of fairness in the world, and then begin to panic.

Or my second option was to make up my mind that the cold, that nature, was just an unfortunate clash of weather systems. If I made my mind up this second way, that the physical world no longer held vengeance and evil just beyond the black shadow of spruce, then I'd try and make do with what I had. And when I realized what an idiot I was for ending up here all alone without the proper gear—just a jean jacket with a sweater under it and running shoes on my feet—I'd get angry, desperate for some sense of fairness in the world, and begin to panic.

Me, I preferred the first option, that Mother Nature was one angry slut. She'd try and kill you first chance she got. You'd screwed with her for so long that she was happy to eliminate you. But more than that, the first option allowed me to get angry right away, to blame some other force for all my troubles. The panic came much quicker this way, but it was going to come anyways, right?

And so me, I climbed out of my cockpit and onto the wing on that frigid afternoon in my jean jacket and running shoes, walked along the wing, fearful of the bush and the cold and a shitty death all around me. I decided to make my way to the bank to collect some firewood and jumped onto the frozen creek.

I sank to my chest in that snow, and immediately realized I was a drunken fool. The shock of fast-flowing ice water made my breath seize, tugging at my legs, pulling at my unlaced running shoes so that the last thing my feet felt was those shoes tumbling away with the current.

By the time I flopped back onto the wing, my stomach to my feet had so little feeling that I had to pull my way back to the cockpit with wet fingers, tearing the skin from them when they froze to the aluminum. My breath came in hitches. When I tried my radio, and my wife finally picked it up, she couldn't understand me. She thought I was a kid fooling around on his father's CB and hung up on me.

Like I said, panic came quick. I could waste more time and the last of my energy calling back, hoping to get Helen to understand it was me and that I needed help now, but how to tell her exactly where I was? They might be able to find me tomorrow in daylight, but not now with the night closing in. And so I did what I knew I had to do. I crawled out of the cockpit again, onto my other wing, and threw myself off it, hoping not to find more water under the snow.

I hit hard ice this time, and it knocked the little breath left out of me. My jeans and jacket were already frozen worse than a straitjacket, and the shivers came so bad my teeth felt like they were about to shatter. I knew my Zippo was in my coat pocket but probably wet to uselessness.

Push bad thoughts away. One thing at a time. First things first. I crawled quick as I could, trying to stand and walk, and I frankensteined my way to the trees and began snapping dry twigs from a dead spruce.

After I made a pile, I reached into my chest pocket, breaking the ice from the material that felt hard as iron now. My fingers had lost all feel. I reached for my cigarettes, struggled to pull one from my pack, and clinked open the lighter. I'd decided that if the lighter worked, I'd enjoy a cigarette as I started a fire. If the lighter didn't work, I'd freeze to death and searchers would find me with an unlit smoke in my mouth, looking cool as the Marlboro Man. On the fifteenth thumb roll I got the lighter going. I was saved for the first time. I reached for my flask in my ass pocket and struggled to open it. Within five minutes I had a fire going. Within fifteen I'd siphoned fuel from my tank and had one of the greatest fires of my life burning, so hot I had to stand away from it, slowly rotating my body like a sausage.

The darkness of a James Bay night in January is something you two girls know well. Annie, you're old enough to remember your grandfather. Suzanne, I don't know. I hope so. Your *moshum*, he liked nothing more than taking you girls out, bundled up like mummies, to look at the stars and especially the northern lights that flickered over the bay. He'd tell you two that they danced just for you, showed you how to rub your fists together to make them burn brighter. Do you remember?

My first crash ended good. My old friend Chief Joe flew out to me the next morning, found me by the smoky fire I'd kept burning all night. We got my plane unstuck and had a couple of good drinks and he gave me a spare pair of boots. Then Joe went to find those trappers and I got my gas lines unfrozen and flew home to Helen.

Joe quit flying soon after that. He was ready for something else. Me, I kept going. I had no other choice. A wife who wanted children, the idea of a family to feed coming to us like a good sunrise on the horizon. I made my choices. I was young still, young enough to believe you can put out your gill net and pull in options like fish.

The snow's deep here, nieces. I'm tired, but I have to keep walking. I'm so tired, but I've got to get up or I'll freeze to death. Talking to you, it keeps me warm.

2

Dumb

They keep him on the top floor, the critical one. I can smell the raw scent of him. It lingers just under the soap of the birdbath his nurse Eva gave him earlier. I'm close to his ear, close enough to see a few grey hairs sprouting from it. "Can you hear me?" I'm gone eight months, then home for a day, only to have this happen. "Eva tells me to talk to you. I feel stupid, but I'll try for a few minutes before Mum comes back. She can't catch me, though." She'd take it as a sign of me weakening, of finally becoming a good Catholic girl like she's always wanted.

I stand up, see white outside the window, a long view of the river and three feet of snow, the spruce like a wrought iron fence in black rows against the white. So cold out today. The sky is blue and high. No clouds to hold any heat.

Dr. Lam wanted to fly him down to Kingston but was concerned he wouldn't make the journey. He'll die down there. I watch as snowmobiles cut along the river, following the trail from Moosonee. Their exhaust hangs white in the air. February. The deadest month. The machine that helps him breathe sounds like the even breath of some mechanical sleeping child. A machine hooked up to his arm beeps every second or so. I think it is the machine that tells the staff that his heart still beats.

I hear the pad of footsteps entering the room and I turn, expecting my mother, black hair eight months ago mostly white now so that when I first saw her nothing made sense. But it's Eva, so large in her blue scrubs, all chubby brown face. I always thought nurses wore white uniforms and silly-looking hats. But in this hospital they dress like mechanics. I guess that's what they are.

Eva checks his vitals and jots them down on his clipboard. She turns him on his side and places pillows behind to prop him up. She told me it is to prevent bedsores. A month now he's been here and all they can tell me is he remains in a stable but deeply catatonic state. The chances are slim that he'll ever wake again. The injuries to his head were massive, and he shouldn't be alive right now. But is he really alive, lying there? I want to ask Eva as she rubs his legs.

"Come help me, Annie," she says. "Do the same to his arms. Keep the circulation going. It's vital."

"Ever weird," I say, standing on the other side of the bed, holding his arm in my hands, kneading it.

"What is?"

"Touching him. My whole life I can't ever remember touching him at all."

"Get over it." Eva breathes heavily as she works. She huffs and puffs. I've known her all my life and she's always been fat. Bigger than fat. She is my apple-faced, beluga-sized best friend. "Have you been talking to him?" she asks.

I shrug. "That's even more weird," I say. "It's like talking to a dead person."

"You better apologize, you," Eva says. "You will upset him with talk like that."

When Eva moves on to the next room I sit back down and stare into his face. He looks half the size as when I left last year. The doctors had to shave his long black hair shot with grey. And he looks older now than his fifty-five years. He has so many faded scars on his head, white zigzags against salt-and-pepper fuzz. I can picture him waking up and grinning, his two missing front teeth making him look like a little boy. Mum says he lost all the weight when he went out in the bush on his traplines last summer and autumn. I knew something was very wrong when she said he went out to trap in summer. What was he hunting? A tan?

As if I've beckoned her, my mum appears, sitting down in the chair beside me. She passes me a Styrofoam box. "Eat," she says. "You've gotten as skinny as him, Annie."

"I'm not hungry," I say.

"They need to check on him," Mum says, rubbing his head like he's a gosling.

"Eva was just here, Mum. Trust her. She knows what she's doing."

"My show's on," she says, picking up the remote.

I've got to get out of here. The woman drives me mad with her talk shows and the cheap psychology she gleans from them. She's even nuttier now that my sister hasn't come home. Suzanne has been gone two years. Everyone in this place, even my mum, believes she is dead. But I hold out and hope.

IT'S SO COLD OUTSIDE, the battery on my snowmobile drained again. I yank on the starter cord until my arm feels like it's going to rip off my body. I flip the choke a couple of times once more, crank the throttle, and on the next pull it rattles to life. Pulling my moosehide hat tight over my ears, I roll out onto the river, the wind so cold my eyes water and the tears freeze on my cheeks. Goddamn it's hard to be back here.

A couple of people coming over on their machines from the Moosonee side flip waves to me, but I pretend I don't see them. I need a new ski-doo. I've stuffed enough money away from my adventures in New York to get one. Maybe a Polaris. Maybe a Bombardier to keep it Canadian. The trail leads off Moose Factory and onto the river. Moosonee squats on the other side's bank, its church steeple fingering the sky. The houses run their wood stoves so hard that the smoke hangs white and thick just above, not wanting to dissipate.

I steer right and away from town down the river to the bay. A fifteen-mile trip to my camp. My family's old goose camp. When I get there, I know I'll stare out at the frozen white of James Bay stretching off to Hudson Bay, just as I've been doing every day since I came back, and truly know I'm living on the edge of the world.

The tide's coming up, pushing slush along the river's banks. I stay closer to the middle. It's so wide here I have a dozen snowmobile trails to choose from. As kids, Suzanne and I would try to swim across but tired before crossing a fraction of it.

I think my cabin's on fire when I approach, smoke pouring out of the open windows and door, but then I see Gordon sitting dejected in his parka outside on a snowbank. When I stomp inside, I find the wood stove's flue shut tight. I flip it open and watch the smoke in the stove turn to fire again. Coughing, I grab the pen and paper from the kitchen table, march outside, and hand it to him. "What the hell were you thinking, shutting the flue?" I ask. The poor bastard's hands are almost blue in the cold. "And why aren't you wearing any mitts?" I sit down on the snowbank, peel my mitts off, and shove them at him.

His writing is close to indecipherable, his hand shakes so bad. *You told me to shut if house got too hot.*

"I told you to shut the *damper* when it got too hot," I say, "not the flue." I'm not angry at him anymore, something more like stunned aggravation in my voice. The poor bastard. I help pull his lanky frame out of the snow by yanking him up by the parka. I lead him inside to the smoky warmth.

ALTHOUGH I HAD PLANNED TO, I don't go back to the hospital the next day. Northern Store is paying big for marten hides this year, so I decided to run a trapline to teach my city Indian, Gordon, a little bit about the bush. We could have taken my snowmobile, but I have him out on snowshoes today, and he's getting better, remembering to drag his heels and point the toes of the snowshoes up when he walks. The exercise is wicked, having to push through the deep drifts, the world frozen solid but us working so hard that we have to be careful not to sweat. We cut along a creek, checking boxes nailed five feet up the good spruce, baited with pieces of goose, a snare wire to grip the marten's furry neck when it sticks its hungry head in. I've got over a dozen traps along this stretch. All of them are empty. Maybe we'll have to try a new place.

Gordon and I could have moved into my mum's when I came back here, dragging him with me, but I knew that setup would all fall apart in a few days. She hates that I'm so far from town, living like a savage on the edge of the bush. She worries a seizure will come while I'm driving my ski-doo and I'll fall off and die. I've lived with these fits my whole life. Still, she worries. I considered renting a place in Moosonee but figured I had a perfectly good camp, and besides, I can't stand all the stares I get in town now that all of this has come down.

I sit in the snow by the frozen creek and light a cigarette. No way I'm going to come back home just to gain weight and get all depressed. The sky is a high blue, and it's so cold today, the world is silent. I offer Gordon a smoke. He takes one. He's not much of a smoker, him, but I've learned he likes one once in a while.

"So, Gordo," I say, looking at his thin face, the sparse whiskers around his mouth frosted white. "What do you make of northern living?"

He nods his head all seriously. Some days I wish he could speak, but there's something nice about having a friend who never talks back, who's always forced to listen.

"Would you rather be on the streets of Toronto, or do you like it better here right now?"

He shrugs, and then points with his mittened hand at the ground he sits on.

"I'm torn," I say. "Maybe we'll head back to NYC after spring goose hunt. I'm going to keep in shape, get more work."

He nods.

I know what the cold will do to my skin, dry it out and wrinkle it so I look twice my age after one winter. I'm moisturizing three or four times a day now, won't let it happen. Jesus, listen to me. My uncle Will, he'd get a kick out of me now. His tomboy niece is really just a sissy girl.

"Let's go, Gordo," I say, pulling myself up. "More traps to check. Not much light left."

3

For You

Moosonee. End of the road. End of the tracks. I can sense it just beyond the trees, nieces. It's not so far away through the heavy snow. That place, it can be a sad, greedy town. You fall into your group of friends, and that's that. Friends for life, minus the times you are enemies. Not too many people around here to choose from for friends, or for enemies. So choose right. In this place, your people will die for you. Unless they're mad at you. If you are on the outs with a friend, all bets are off. You don't exist.

I'm down to my last couple of friends and have been for years. Maybe it's like anywhere, but we're some vengeful bunch. I blame it on the Cree being a clan-based people. Each clan has its own best interests in mind. And whenever you have your own best interests in mind, someone gets left out and gets angry.

I need, though, to back up a little, me. For you, Suzanne. For you, Annie. I am the one who watched out for you from a distance since your earliest years when your father left your mother to do whatever he went to do. I am the first to say I was not perfect at this job. But I worried for the both of you.

In my waking world, I was not worthwhile. I hadn't been for years. Booze will do that to a man. But booze is not the root of the problem. Just a condition. When you lose something, something that was your whole world, two choices present themselves. Dig through the ash and burnt timber, through the bits of ruined clothing and blackened shards of dinner plates and waterlogged photo albums that was the sum of your life, and find something inside you that makes you want to go on. Or you allow that black pit that is born in the bottom of your belly to smoulder, and spend your days trying to dampen it with rye.

I am a keeper of certain secrets, just as your mother, Lisette, is the keeper of her own. Me, I don't know where this comes from. The Mushkegowuk people love nothing more than to chatter like sparrows over coffee in the morning, over beer at night. There's something unifying, something freeing about rolling around in the dirty laundry of your neighbours, picking it up and pointing out the stains, sniffing it almost gleefully for the scent of grief.

I need to share a secret with you. Just one right now. But it's the one that hurts the most. Your grandfather, Annie, he wanted your ability for visions but only gained it partially. He didn't want or care for what you have, Suzanne, your beauty, your charisma. But I wanted the gifts that both of you girls possess. Wanted them full on. I fancied myself a chief in an earlier life, a man of the people, leading them through troubled times, photographed like Sitting Bull, my profile stern in its wisdom. But I didn't get your gifts. Or maybe I did, only just a little. Not enough.

Months before I watched you, Annie, leave with your friend Eva to go to Toronto, something happened that maybe pushed us all over the edge. Suzanne, you'd been gone from home over a year at that point. Many moons, eh? Too many. Where'd you go? Call you mother. She worries.

I need to tell you both about that night. Me, I like drinking at my own kitchen table, having friends come over. We can smoke in the house and drink as much as we want. I rarely drank anywhere else. Me, I'd become a homebody over the years when I wasn't out in the bush. I'd even watch TV once in a while when I got bored. History Channel. Bravo. Discovery Channel. One show called *Crime Scene Investigation*. Good stuff. But one night, Joe invited me over, so I went. Joe, we call him Chief, Chief Joe Wabano, although he's never officially held the title. He's got the big belly of a chief and the paycheque from driving tugs up the bay to the isolated communities. And when he gets drunk, he likes to let people know exactly what he's thinking.

I must have been bored that night. My truck wouldn't start so I walked the few miles into town to see Joe. Cold spring evening, and I remember how good it felt to walk, buzzed already from a few lonely drinks at home, the stars up above winking at me. A car passed me as I made it to the bridge by Taska's, and as it slowed I saw it was Marius driving, two big white friends stuffed in with him. Suzanne, you and Gus were missing at that point, had dropped off the face of the world, it seemed. The Netmakers were blaming us, and we blamed them. But I didn't think twice about all that at the time.

Me and Joe and his woman, we phoned Gregor, the white schoolteacher and famous pervert, to join us when we got into our drinks pretty good. But it was a weeknight, and he had to teach the next morning. Too bad. Gregor would have driven me home if he'd showed up. I remember feeling restless at Joe's, like I knew a snowstorm was coming and I was unprepared. You've got that gift, Annie, but much stronger than me, a gift that pops up in our family once in a while. It comes with your seizures, the ability to see into the future, and maybe, if you develop it, to heal. But you're going to have to work on it, and it's not like you can enrol at Northern College to learn what you need. Me, I pity your road. It's lonely. Few people will ever appreciate your gift.

I stayed as long as it took to drink a handful of rye and gingers before I told Joe I was tired out. When I saw he was tired, too, I told him walking home would be good for me. I walked Ferguson Road along the Moose River, the water flashing its nicest bits in the moonlight to my left, the black water pushing itself down into James Bay. I cut across the bridge again and onto Sesame Street, nicknamed for all the kids that live and play on it summer and winter.

I thought I felt the grandfathers in my step that night, the town behind me now, the scent of the dump up ahead on the gravel road. A crisp night that whispered of summer. The flash of headlights somewhere far down the road to my back made me want to step into the bush. I knew, nieces, but I didn't listen to my gut. I kept walking. The car gunned it behind me, then slowed when I saw my own shadow on the gravel ahead. It passed, then turned and came back so that its lights blinded me. Three men climbed out, the car idling. They stepped into the headlights. Three big men.

"*Wachay* there, Will." I recognized Marius's voice. My stomach dropped out from me. "Something I've been meaning to ask you," he said. I could tell by the voice that he'd had more to drink than me. "Where'd that little bitch niece of yours disappear to with my brother?"

"Don't you call her that," I said. I felt sparks behind my eyes. Marius walked toward me and I clenched my fists. I knew what was coming, nieces, but I didn't know at the time why it was coming. I'd done nothing to him. He got up close enough to me I could smell his leather jacket. He looked back to his friends as if to say something and then used the momentum of turning back to swing his fist into my face, white light filling my eyes as his knuckles squashed my nose. I fell backwards like a tree.

I lay on my back, the gravel sharp beneath my head, the sky above me like it was full of northern lights, and watched as the two white guys with him stared down at me. I could tell even by their silhouettes that they were ugly like only white guys who've been raised like dogs can be. They began to kick me, and I remember the sound of my ribs cracking, of my head being shocked so that I worried I'd die.

Those Mohawk down south claim that a warrior doesn't cry out when he's tortured then slow-roasted over a fire. I'm no Mohawk, me. I screamed with each kick, my head splitting open, the blood choking down the back of my throat until my cries became gags. When his friends were done, through my eyes swelling shut I saw Marius bend down. He straddled me, sat on me with his full weight and leaned to my ear, whispered with his stinking breath, "I can kill you any time I want. And I will, one day soon." I felt his breath on my earlobe.

I don't know how long I lay there. Something, someone maybe, told me that I eventually had to surface if I was going to live, and believe it or not, it was a tough decision to make. For me, my life's been hard, and sometimes I'm so tired out from losing the things I love that it feels easier to just give up and slip away.

A voice I knew, the voice of my father, talked to me, and in my head I saw him squatting beside me in the black, on his haunches, his one real leg bent under him, his wooden prosthesis straight out in front like one of those fancy Russian dancers.

"It's not you that you live for," he said to me in Cree. "It can't be. It's the others." Not very specific, but I knew who he was talking about.

"What do I got to give to anyone?" I asked. I could tell he was looking down at me, staring at my wounds. He didn't answer my question.

When he got up to go, I did too. I did the same as he did, floating away from the ground and becoming a night mist that dissolved into the black sky.

But this is not how I entered into the dream world, nieces. I just got a taste of it then. I didn't enter the dream world for many more months. After the beating, I remember emerging from my hibernation slow, blinking my eyes to the light of bright sun through a window beside me, the whoosh and hiss of some machine standing guard by my bed. I remember not smelling so good, me. Something like rot. The beep of another machine when I closed my eyes to the light. My head thumped. I dreamed I was a sturgeon on river's bottom pushing up stones with my nose for crayfish. I remember being prodded by doctors, and I remember slipping back down to the bottom of that warm river.

When I was a boy, I used to sleep in a long, white room in Moose Factory, the same island that holds the hospital. My school used to be the biggest building on the island before they built the hospital. It was white-washed and scrubbed clean with wood soap and the greasy sweat of Indian kids. The boys, we slept in one long room upstairs above the dining hall. The girls, they slept in a room beside us above the laundry room and kitchen. Me, I dreamed of slipping into the girls' dormitory in the middle of the night and learning how to make babies. All the boys did. Some of my friends claimed they managed to learn this way, but me, I don't buy it. I did learn how to French kiss during recess once, though, with a skinny girl named Dorothy.

I healed over time. We all do. Your mother, she came to visit me in the hospital after the beating. She would bring a book with her and try to read it to me so that I was forced to pretend sleep. She's a good woman, your mother, but she's been weakened by Oprah.

When I went home, my two remaining friends in the waking world, Chief Joe and Gregor, they came to visit more regular than usual. As spring progressed, we got into some drinking on my porch while looking out over the river for beluga whales. Gregor, he came to Moosonee twenty years ago to teach at the high school for a year and never left. Gregor, he's not exactly white. He's as dark as me and came from a country in eastern Europe or something. Eastern something, I can't remember. All I know is the place has changed its name so often I don't know it. But he keeps his accent, especially when he's drunk. He sounds kind of like Dracula, which can be funny. Funny and creepy sometimes. You get used to anything, though, after a few years.

I remember how Gregor and Joe sat with me on my porch like I was some new celebrity. Spring is the time when the belugas come this far up, the dozen miles or so from the bay, to make babies and gorge on whitefish. Gregor spotted a beluga, ghost white in the dark river about a hundred yards out. I'd been watching it swim, back and forth, for a while. If I was an Inuit, I'd be getting in my boat and going to get dinner. But I've tried beluga. Too fatty. Not a good taste at all. Like lantern oil. Give me KFC any day.

"Look now, boys. Vales!" Gregor said, standing and pointing out, rubbing his thighs. On numerous occasions, Gregor had almost lost his teaching job due to inappropriate behaviour, especially with his female students, like asking to hold their hands so he could check the fingernails for dirt or touching their hair when they answered a question right. He says these are European behaviours. He's what Lisette calls lecherous. But he's a funny one, him. "My god," he said. "Beautiful vales." He stared sad at the beluga as another spouted and appeared close to it. Joe took another beer from the case by his foot.

"Look at us," I said. "Three fat guys on a porch. Does our life need to be this way?" And that's when I made the mistake of sharing with them that my beating made me realize I needed a big change in my life. I needed to get in shape. I was going to start jogging.

"You're reacting to the violence perpetrated against you," Chief Joe said, just like a real chief, using words he wasn't too sure of. "You try running, your heart will explode and you will die. I don't want you to die. What you need now is another drink and some serious counselling."

4

Learning to Talk

Eva's working the early shift at the hospital, so I'm up before the sun, pulling on my winter gear. I've stuffed the stove with wood and turned the damper down. "I'll be back before you need to put more wood in," I say to Gordon, "so don't mess with it today, okay?" He lies with his eyes open on his bunk across the room. I don't know if he ever sleeps. "If you're bored, you can chop wood. Just don't cut your damn foot off."

At the hospital, I stop in the cafeteria for a coffee, look at the exhausted faces of the night-shift workers. This is one depressing place.

Up on the top floor, I sit beside his bed and sip on my coffee, flip through a magazine. I look at him, his face calm, mouth turned down. He twitches once in a while, and this always startles me. I keep expecting to look at him and find him staring back. He lies here in this room hovering close to death because of me. Even if this is only partly true, he is here because of me.

My mother typically arrives mid-morning, so I plan to briefly cross paths with her out of respect, then get a few more supplies at Northern Store before heading back. I think I'll begin a new trapline today. Eva barges in, after I've already closed my magazine. I heard her heavy breathing while she was still halfway down the hall. There are a couple of girls I know in ads in that magazine, and the feeling that I'm missing out washes over me.

"Morning, Annie." She reaches to me and touches my hair.

"Any news on him?" I ask, pointing with my lips.

"Same old, same old, sis." Eva busies herself once more taking vitals. "I'm worried his muscles are atrophying. You should do the exercises on his legs and arms I showed you."

I nod.

"I noticed that bony ass of his is beginning to bruise. I'm going to shift him again."

I watch her do this, help where I can. His body is warm. Although he doesn't much look it, he's still alive. "Maybe I should read to him, or something," I say.

"That would be a start. But wouldn't it be more interesting for him if you talked of some of your adventures? Of our adventures, even?"

I shrug.

When I'm back alone with him, I hold his hand. My heart's not in it. "Can you hear me? Do you want me to read a magazine article to you?" I feel foolish. "Well, if you're not going to respond, then I won't say anything at all." I look at my watch. A little after eight. At least two hours to kill before Mum gets here. I stand and pace. The seconds tick by with the beep of his monitor. This will drive me crazy.

"What do you want me to say?" I stop and look at him. "I've apologized a hundred times." Suzanne's the one who should be here. "I bet you believe she's still alive," I say to him. "Nobody else around here does but you and me, I bet." I am the only one who holds out hope. I worry I hold on only because I am so angry with my sister. He's here in that bed, and I'm forced to be standing here, because of her. Maybe all this is partly my fault, but she's the real one to blame.

Two hours still. Would anybody really know, really care, if I just left? I sit down beside him and pick up the magazine again, flip through it once more and stare at the fashion ads. A close-up of a white girl with porcelain skin, holding a jar of face cream to her cheek. A handsome man and a longhaired woman ballroom dancing across another page. I drop the magazine. "Should I try to explain how we ended up here?" I ask. His mouth twitches. "Should I at least tell you my side of the story?" His hand sits limp on the white sheet. "I won't get up and leave you. I'll just do it. I'll tell you a story."

I think of what I can possibly say to him that he doesn't already know. But I can hear Eva's voice telling me that isn't the point. The point is that there's comfort in a familiar voice. Medical journals sometimes discuss this.

"I don't know where Suzanne is," I tell him. "But I know where she's been. I saw those places myself." Where to begin? Begin with my sister, I guess. "Listen carefully, you, and I'll tell you what I know."

I lean close to his ear so that if anyone outside were to walk by they wouldn't hear me. I'll share this story with him but no one else.

Where do I start? My mother's Christian friends, the real Bible-spankers, they say Suzanne's dead, that she couldn't handle the pressure of success. She won't be back to this world because she's in Jesus' bosom now. Their saying that didn't surprise me. Those ones, they're the doom-and-gloom club. It's the old men, the true Indians, the ones who smile at me sadly and turn away in the Northern Store, who know something of the truth.

I think Suzanne's troubles, they started with boys. Don't they always? I tried to convince myself growing up that boys were gross and worthless.

Snotty little things. But I was a tomboy. When I was a kid I secretly wished I'd been born a boy.

Everyone knew, though, that the boys couldn't resist Suzanne. But you want to know something? They couldn't resist me, either, especially when I hit those shitty years of puberty. Maybe it's my father's height. Maybe it's my mother's Cree cheekbones. The boys have liked me since adolescence, and when I didn't giggle and run and come right back again like a puppy, like the other girls, the names started and the teasing grew.

The air's so dry in here. I take his hand in mine. It feels soft as tissue paper. The gesture doesn't feel natural, but I force myself to hold it and not let go.

I glance at my watch. Fifteen minutes have passed. I've barely noticed. My hand begins sweating in his dry palm. Hey, you know what? Maybe there *is* something I can tell you that you wouldn't know about me.

No way I could defend myself from the horny little bastards, the Johnny Cheechoos and Earl Blueboys and Mike Sutherlands who waited for me after school, crouching behind the walls of the Northern Store, ready to follow me and ask me if I'd kiss them, and when I was a little older, if I'd blow them.

Marius Netmaker, he once had something for me even if he was six years older and had a pitted face from chicken pox, a big belly from eating too well too often. But he was strong and unpredictable. A bull moose. You weren't the only one to learn that.

Here's something I can tell you. When I was fifteen, Marius approached me one day when the snows had left and the sun made small flowers bloom along the road. School was done for the day. I stood by the fence separating the schoolyard from the dirt road, ready to run to my freighter canoe and the freedom of the river. The blackflies had just started coming out. I stood by myself, but close enough to Suzanne and a couple of her girlfriends to hear their talk about boys. Marius had picked some of the flowers from the roadside and walked up and tried to hand them to me, not able to look me in the eye. Suzanne and her girlfriends watched all this like ospreys. Marius mumbled a few words that I couldn't make out.

I was horrified that a twenty-year-old, one with a bad complexion and the habit of getting drunk on bootleg rye and beating people up, was doing this to me. "Speak up, Marius," I said loud enough for the girls to hear. "Time is money." Suzanne and her friends giggled, as only thirteen-year-olds can. He looked at me then, and his eyes flashed for just a second. He mumbled something more and I glanced over to Suzanne and her friends, gave them the *what's going on?* look, then muttered to Marius, "You bore me," before turning away and leaving him standing there with the tiny purple flowers in his big sweaty hand. As I walked away, I heard the girls laughing. I felt the guilt. I regretted hurting him unnecessarily, not knowing then the grudges he could hold.

Now I can't help but wonder if this was what started the whole war going. I doubt it. I think our two families have hated each other for a long, long time.

I stop talking, let go of his hand. I've been rubbing it with my own, and I'm worried it might irritate him. This is stupid. Look at me. I've already turned this story into one about me. Maybe I'm more to blame for all of this than I want to admit. There's no denying our two families hate each other. My family is a family of trappers and hunters who like the quiet of our place. Marius's family started as bootleggers, sneaking whisky and vodka onto the dry reserves north of us by snowmobile in winter. They built false bottoms on the wood sleighs they pulled behind their ski-doos, filling those bottoms with bottles and water, placing a floorboard over their stash and letting it all freeze overnight before hitting the rough trails. They bragged about never breaking a bottle.

In the last few years, the Netmakers discovered that cocaine and crystal meth were easier to smuggle up, and they are responsible for the white powder falling across James Bay reserves and covering many of the younger ones in its embrace. They are the importers to Moosonee and to other isolated communities around us. They are the connection to the Goofs, the silliest name for a motorcycle gang I ever heard. How are you supposed to be scared of that? The Goofs are a puppet gang of the Hells Angels. That's what the cops say, anyways. When I think of these puppet Goofs, I picture sock monkeys on Harleys, their button eyes angry, their blood-red sock-heel mouths clenching cigarettes and sneering. But I watch the damage they do to our people here. A clenched fist is stuffed into the heads of these puppets.

Still, the Nishnabe-Aski, the band police on the reserves, can't do anything about it. But my family knows. The Netmakers know. Everyone in Moosonee, in Moose Factory, in Kashechewan and Fort Albany and Attawapiskat and Peawanuck knows the deal. And it's this knowing, this choosing of sides, that has helped spawn the hatred. This hatred crept into our two very different households like the flu at night, infecting all of us as we slept with sweating angry dreams of killing the other, of turning this place where we live into our own vision of it.

Somehow the youngest Netmaker, Gus, had avoided his family's business, but I'd seen how tempted he was by the easy money and the dread that people felt for his kin. I saw it because I used to date him.

The same view of spruce against snow greets me from the hospital window. I watch snowmobiles come up the bank from the river. I see people talking outside below me, breath hanging above their heads like cartoon thought bubbles. Maybe I'll go down to the cafeteria and grab another coffee. Mum's going to be here soon. I go back to his bed and gently take one of his legs in my hands, bend and straighten it to keep the muscles and tendons from freezing up. Mum's coming, and I suddenly realize I have more to say to him. Funny how that works, eh? I'm hoping she'll be late today. I'll tell him something else quick, some of which I'm sure he already knows, that we all know.

Suzanne left my mother and me on Christmas morning two years ago and climbed on the back of Gus's ski-doo. I remember a light snow fell that must have tickled her face. She and Gus, they drove across the frozen river, through the black spruce and into the wilderness. They were heading south with the plan of selling the ski-doo once they reached the little town that has a Greyhound station. They planned on taking that bus all the way to Toronto. But almost two hundred miles of frozen bush separated Moosonee from the town with the bus station. And don't forget. I knew Gus's ski-doo all too well. I was the one who used to ride on the back of it with him. It was a piece of shit.

Suzanne. Such a Cree beauty. You know. The pride of our nation soon as she became a teen and didn't go the way of so many other girls around here. Funny, I never thought of her as exceptionally pretty. I'd seen her enough times in the morning those last couple of months, hungover and sad, long black hair a nest of greasy straw. I was her older sister, after all, older by two years. Sometimes, that felt like a lifetime.

She never thought of herself as beautiful either. She was always surprised when the subject came up, as it did so often, different men trying their moves on her at dances, dropping by our house in the hopes of glimpsing her. But there are only so many men in this place. And Gus Netmaker was the clear winner. He was the artist, drew eagles and bears and painted them in the colours of the northern lights. I'd brought him home first. A friend, I told him, told everyone. Not a boyfriend. He wore his hair cut spiky short and had a silver ring in his left ear. The girls said he looked like Johnny Depp.

I let Gus go into Suzanne's arms, encouraged it even, and ignored the sting. I was made for other things. Mum, though, she recognized before anyone else did what damage would follow.

I can hear Mum now, talking to Eva outside the door in the hallway. I touch my hand to his face, just lightly, wanting to see what it feels like. He looks so skinny, so skinny and old now. What's happened to him, to all of us, this last year?

5

Talking Gun

There's a dirt road you know well, nieces, that runs past my house, goes past the dump and the healing lodge, the place the town sends Indians when they don't need a hospital but more a place to dry out or get away from abusive husbands. The dirt road, it's a two-mile stretch beside the Moose River to town. If I go left out of my house instead of right, the road becomes a snowmobile trail that, if you follow it long enough, will eventually get you to Cochrane nearly two hundred miles south of here. I'm an early riser, me. Even if I'm up drinking till midnight, I'll still wake at five, wide awake and with cloudy eyes, staring out at the dawn.

And so I tried jogging early in the morning when I knew Marius would still be asleep, and I realized I wanted my two friends with me because I no longer wanted to be out of my house alone. I had finally learned fear. Marius had taught me the kind of fear that threatened to make me a shut-in.

I began running most every morning, shuffling in my old boots down the dusty road. I'd walk down my drive when the sun rose, trying to stop myself from looking for Marius but doing it anyways. I was getting crank calls a lot of nights since my return home. Nothing on the other end but steady, deep breathing.

Each morning I'd take my first few steps and force my legs to do more than a walk, the pain shooting up my spine and into the back of my head. But I kept the legs moving, moving at a pace they hadn't in years, my breath short after a hundred yards, promising myself I'd cut down on the smoking.

I'd try to imagine something chasing me, a polar bear or even an angry marten. Crows screamed at me from the telephone poles.

Most days, I hoped to make it past the dump to the lodge and back. A mile each way. The healing lodge is the halfway point to town. I kept myself going on the vision of one day being able to run into town, running around it for everyone to see me, then turning and making my way back home in a dust cloud, running so fast they'd think I could fly.

I once tried to get Joe out with me. "I thought about it," Joe said. "But my truck's running fine, so I don't see the point."

Your mother thought I was crazy, too. Too many days I lay on my couch with a seized-up back or pulled leg muscles. "What are you thinking, Will?" she'd ask between chapters of whatever inspirational book she'd be reading to me. "You're too old for this kind of nonsense. Did you shake something loose when you hit your head?"

I'd tell her the world was a different place now, a far more dangerous place. I only spoke in generalities.

I avoided heading into town in the couple of months after my beating. I didn't want to have to explain the discoloured bags under my eyes, my new fear. But eventually the desire to drink came back. And it came full on. I lasted as long as I could, lasted until my emergency stash of rye under the kitchen sink ran dry.

The first day I walked back into the world of other people, straight to the LCBO for a bottle, all was good. But on the walk home, I was followed by Marius's car, driving slow. I didn't come out of my house after that for a long time.

I noticed something, nieces, in those days after my beating when I drank alone. With no one to talk with much, I began talking to myself. That, by itself, isn't so crazy. But then, with too much rye in me, things started talking back. My sofa called me a fat ass when I sat on it. When I'd lean in to drink from the tap, it told me to get a glass. The secret in my closet began to beckon me. Drinking alone isn't a good practice for anybody. It leads to lonely melodrama. I remember calling Chief Joe one afternoon when it was bad, but he didn't pick up. I tried Gregor, but he didn't answer, either. Must have still been at school. He somehow talked them into letting him coach the girls' volleyball.

I sat on my porch and stared at the river, glass of whisky in my hand. I remember humming to myself, and the tune took on a life of its own. I called it Mosquito Song. The bastards were bad that afternoon and early evening, finally awake from their long winter sleep, all of them starved for my blood. Do mosquitoes get drunk on the blood of a drunk man? I hope so.

Joe called back that night. "Come on over, Joe," I said. "I'm drunk."

"Not tonight. I got my granddaughter with me. We're playing dolls."

I hung up.

I don't get angry much, me. You know that, nieces. I don't know what set it off, then I thought of Marius and of me being scared and you, my missing niece, Suzanne, and this is what I think caused it. I called Joe back.

"Bad connection," I said. "I'm gonna go jog again tomorrow. You should come, you."

"We'll see how my truck's running."

I heard a child's laughter in the background. It made me sad. "It'll be good for you."

"You shouldn't be drinking alone," Joe said.

"Yeah, me, I'm gonna run tomorrow. Maybe I'll see you." We hung up, and I stood to pour another drink, stumbling a little to the kitchen. Headlights swam along the road, and I turned off the kitchen light quick and stared out. A pickup truck. It slowed a little by my house, then pushed by.

Suzanne, I thought more of you then, tried to remember how long ago you'd left with Marius's brother, Gus. Christmas. Not this last, but past. Twelve months, plus the handful of the new year. Seventeen months I counted out. There was a magazine around the house somewhere with pictures of you in it. Those were near a year old. You looked pretty, like a pretty anybody girl that anyone sees in those magazines. Except your eyes. Sad eyes. My father's eyes. They made you look different than the others in those magazines.

Your mother has other magazines with you in them. Lots, so many that I was impressed, and amazed at how busy you must have been. You are famous, my niece. But you have disappeared with your boyfriend, Gus, and this makes you more famous, especially around here.

One magazine has pictures of you naked, covering yourself with your arms and hands in all the right places, and I was embarrassed to look at them, wondering what kind of clothes or jewellery or perfume my niece was supposed to be selling with not a stitch on. I tried to make sure those pictures didn't fall into the hands of Gregor. But of course they did.

Lisette was scared and proud to show them to me. "Can you believe this is Suzanne?" she asked, looking into my eyes. "This magazine is the most famous of them all, and look, it's your niece." I watched my sister's thin fingers trace your outline.

Suzanne, when you left for the south and became famous, you kept in touch with your mother, but not with Annie. My two nieces had some kind of fight. Many fights. But that's nothing new. One jealous of the other for her looks, the other for her visions. And when your mother didn't hear from you, Suzanne, that last Christmas, she got worried, told me her mother's instincts were telling her something bad. Your mum called your agent in Toronto when your cell phone only switched to messages and then, after a time, went dead. Imagine that. I know someone with a cell phone. You really are famous.

The agent said he didn't know a thing. Lisette even contacted the Netmakers to see if they'd heard from Gus. And then the Netmakers took this as a chance to begin calling your mother and saying you were trash—just look at those pictures in those magazines!—and look how you had led Gus away from them and probably to some sick fate. And that in turn left me to wonder why Marius wanted to kill me.

Marius. I remember him when he was just another kid playing on the dirt road. And now he was a biker with a wispy goatee who sold drugs to the new kids playing in the dirt. No. He's above that now. He brings in the drugs and recruits kids to sell the drugs to other kids. Cocaine. Hash. Crack. Something called ecstasy. What's that? I must admit the name is appealing. Your mother was the one who told me all this. Gregor and Joe filled in some juicier bits. Your mother knows everything despite never being the one to gossip. She just sits and watches and takes it all in like an Arctic owl. Me, I wouldn't do drugs. I always stuck with the rye. You always know what you're gonna get.

The night that I talked to Joe and my furniture and kitchen appliances, that night when I finally went to bed, on my back, head spinning, that is the night that what I keep wrapped up in a blanket in my closet came to life. It had wanted to before. But I'd always ignored it, was always drunk enough to pass out and forget it tried to talk to me. But this night was different. It had to be my new fear.

The floor lifted and fell like I was on a James Bay gale. I drifted and rolled and drifted and rolled. No smart Indian would be caught dead out on the bay in the weather of spring or autumn. Winds come up fast and churn the shallow waters into monster waves that have taken many lives. I lost some good friends, me, many years ago in autumn. Out goose hunting, a family in three freighter canoes. Wind came up with the snow squalls, and the shallow bay made some big waves fast. Nine of eleven in that family dead. Six of them kids.

Bad water on James Bay. What can you do? No use to a Cree unless it's winter and he can snowmobile across it. That's what I say. Me, I stick to the rivers. Everything you need there between the two banks. Fish. Geese. Water. Of course water. All you need is some fishing line and a gun. A gun. Never think of guns in bed in this state.

I kept it wrapped up in a blanket in that closet, the blanket muffling its annoying talk that I couldn't ignore. This one, she's old. A real collector's item. My father's rifle from the war. That rifle, it did a lot of bad things. My father didn't tell me much of this. The gun did. It's a real chatterbox once it gets going.

Son of Xavier, the gun whispered. *Son of Xavier,* it said. *Come here and unwrap me. You're strangling me in this blanket. Please.* I tried hard to ignore it, nieces. *Son of Xavier,* it said. *Unwrap me. I have a story for you. A story to tell you.*

6

Just a Week

There's something I love about being on the river before dawn breaks, the world still asleep as I follow the frozen spine of the Moose on my snowmobile. Despite a restless night filled with dreams of the cabin burning down because Gordon stuffed the wood stove too full till it glowed red, the push of the wind—this morning the thermometer outside the window read minus 40 Celsius—makes me feel as awake as I've felt in years. Ever cold! The kind of cold that can kill you if you make one stupid mistake is invigorating, to say the least. I'd love to see one of those fashion models I ran with not so long ago be able to do this. I'd love to see Violet or Soleil crank up her own snow machine or chop a cord of wood or set a marten trap. Why did I summon the faces of those two women? This simple whispering of their names makes my teeth clench.

Again last night, as I squirmed and flopped around in my bunk, the idea of climbing into Gordon's bed and asking him to hold me washed over me and pushed sleep even further away. He and I were on that romantic track not so long ago, especially when I'd just brought him up here. But the violence that exploded so soon after our arrival pushed all semblance of normalcy away, those events an earthquake that toppled our houses to the ground. I'm thinking now, though, that letting another human get close to me might not be the worst thing. We'll see.

I would never have imagined anything sexual with him when I first met him. But he cleans up well. I've put a few pounds on his lanky frame and reintroduced into his world the importance of bathing. He's a good-looking guy, him. Striking. And in the city he proved to be more than physically capable. He's my protector.

I slow down to go over a pressure crack in the ice, and when I give my snowmobile gas it lurches before catching. The belt's wearing out. I'm going to have to replace it.

I stomp the snow from my boots when I get inside the hospital vestibule, the hot, dry air making my throat tickle. I get a coffee in the cafeteria and head up to the top floor. Again today the desire to just head right back outside and drive away tugs at me, but I have to be a good niece and put my time in, maybe find it inside myself to pray to whoever's up there that my uncle will miraculously find consciousness again.

When I walk into his room, the curtain is drawn around his bed, and I'm overwhelmed with the understanding he has died. A sound comes out of my throat and my legs weaken. I promise I will come every day. Please. But then I hear humming and recognize the voice. I drop my coat and my snow pants onto a chair and collapse onto the one next to it. Eva's big head appears from behind the curtain. I think of a walrus emerging from an ice hole. I can be so horrible even when I don't mean to be.

"Just cleaning him up," she says. "Wanna help?"

"Think I'll pass," I say. "That's why you get paid the big bucks."

"Another monster bingo at the arena this weekend," she says. I can hear the splash of water, the squeezing of it from the sponge. "Wanna come with me?"

"*Mona,*" I say. "No. You're the one who's lucky with that."

"Well maybe Gordon will want to get out, get into town. You ever think of that?"

When Eva's finished, she pulls back the curtain, the squeal of the tracks making me grit my teeth. "Clean as a whistle," she says, squeezing herself into a chair across the room. I look at the long, thin form of my uncle under the sheet. "I switch to night shift in a few days, so you probably won't be seeing much of me for a while."

Something in that news makes me horribly sad, afraid even. I want Eva here when I'm here. She's the only one I trust, who I can talk to. "Are visitors allowed at night?"

"Nope."

When I'm alone with him I get up and begin my pacing. "So, what do you want me to talk about today?" I look over at him. "Don't be shy. Tell me." As usual, I have a couple of hours to burn before Mum arrives. "Maybe I'll sneak you out of here this weekend, Uncle," I say. "I'll steal a wheelchair and push you over to the monster bingo. You might enjoy that."

Monster bingo. Eva won big, what, ten months ago. It feels like a lifetime ago. It was her idea to bring me on a vacation down to Toronto with some of the winnings. I'd never left this place before, not really. Maybe I'll talk to you about that, Uncle. After all, that's where it all started, really, didn't it? Eva having a hard time with her man and thinking a trip to a real city, a place far south where we'd never been, might be a good idea. Some idea.

I sit by his bed and look at his face. I take his hand in mine. The action still feels weird. You can tell he's busted his nose a couple of times. Ever crazy, my uncle. He's one of the great northern bush pilots. Everyone in this town has a different wild story about flying with him. It's hard to picture it now, but the story is he was something of a lady's man in his youth. He's had a hard life, though, lost everything more than once. I look behind me to make sure no one's at the door, then turn back and lean closer to him and begin telling him the story of Eva and her monster bingo.

I'd just gotten back from my camp, had a wicked case of food poisoning from an old tin of ravioli, which was the only food I had left. I'd failed to kill any geese all that week of hunting. You would have been ashamed of me, Uncle, not even able to call in one flock to my blind. I crawled back home in my freighter canoe, barfing out of both orifices every half mile. So awful. Worst of all, it wasn't till I'd gotten back to Mum's house in Moosonee that I remembered in my sick daze I'd left the door to my camp wide open to the animals and the elements. No way to begin a long journey, is it? Even if I didn't know at the time I was about to begin one.

I remember waking up to my mother's brown face the morning after I got home, the corners of her eyes etched in thin creases, more worry lines than smile lines. Her face looked taut, I remember, tired, but still beautiful. She has the intense stare of your father, Uncle, my grandpa Xavier. I smile at her, and this must surprise her. She cocks her head, looking confused before smiling back. Flash of white teeth. "You must be feeling better," she says. "I can't even think of the last time you smiled at me. Just like a little girl." She reaches out to touch my cheek. It is my turn to pull back.

"I don't feel that good, Mum." I feel bad for doing this as I watch her smile fade a bit. But this is a game we've always played. I'll give her some empathy and next she'll be asking me to come to Sunday mass with her.

"Eva's here to visit."

"Make her some tea, Mum. I need the washroom." I climb out of bed when she leaves, my legs unsure as I make my way to the bathroom.

I consider a shower but don't want to keep Eva waiting, am startled by Suzanne's face staring back at me from the mirror, water dripping off the sharp cheekbones. But no, this face is heavier around the mouth, eyes that don't sparkle like Suzanne's. I've lost weight in these last days, am dehydrated. I peel off my T-shirt and can see the line of ribs below the weight of my breasts, my ribs something I've not seen on myself for a long time. I leave the dieting and the picky eating to my sister. Running down the dusty streets of Moosonee in sneakers, running to nowhere, running from something, I leave that to Suzanne.

In the kitchen, Eva sits heavy in a chair, my mother across from her and holding the baby, Hugh. Baby Hughie, I call him, fat and complacent as his mother, staring at my mum like an Indian Buddha, allowing her to coo into his face. The only time that boy makes a fuss is when he's hungry, and he likes to let the world know it, screeching till he's red faced, not shutting up until Eva plugs him onto her huge tit and his cries turn to sucking. I want to like this baby, but he makes it really hard.

"Ever tired looking!" Eva says when I sit down at the table with them. My mother stands and with practised comfort swings Hugh onto her hip, heads for the counter and pours me a tea. I watch her take two slices of white bread from the bag and slip them into the toaster. Today I will accept her care.

"I'll never get used to you going out in the bush alone," my mother says, handing me the hot mug.

"I keep telling Annie that the more time she spends out there, the weirder she gets," Eva adds. They laugh.

My mother places a plate of toast in front of me. "You should be able to keep this down. You need to put something in your belly." I hand Eva a piece and bite into mine. I am hungry. I finish the toast before I realize I have. I watch as my mother puts two more slices in the toaster.

Eva keeps smiling at me. She knows something I don't. She jiggles her leg like she has to go to the bathroom.

"What's got you so excited?" I ask her. "Junior offer you his hand in marriage or something?"

"Ever!" Eva says. "Just because he's my baby's daddy doesn't mean I want to marry him." Everyone on both sides of the river knows better.

"What's up, then?" I ask.

"Do you really want to know?" Eva asks. I nod. My mother, intent for the news, comes to the table, Hugh still on her hip. She hands me a second plate of toast and sits. "You know how I had a good feeling about the bingo last weekend? Guess who won."

"Get out!" I say. "You did? How much?"

"A lot," Eva says. "A game of telephone pole." Then in a whisper, looking at me, eyes lit up: "Fourteen thousand dollars!"

"Get out!" I say again. "No way. Fourteen grand?" The gnaw in my belly isn't from the ravioli.

"Way," Eva says.

My mother claps her hands, jiggling Baby Hughie. "So much money, Eva! What are you going to do with it all?"

"Me and Junior are going to leave Hugh with Junior's *kookum* and go down to Toronto for a vacation."

The gnaw in my stomach grows stronger. "You can go on ten vacations with that kind of cash," I say. Not that I'd go, but why wouldn't she invite me somewhere? As if she knows what I'm thinking, Eva says she'll take me shopping at the Northern Store. I'm happy she won something, but really, she already pulls in great money as a nurse. I barely get by trapping and guiding. I'm still forced to live with Mum when I'm not at my camp.

To try and make some kind of connection with Hughie, I offer to carry him down the long dirt road that takes us to Sesame Street and then to downtown. Downtown! Ever funny. A dusty street that runs from the train station to the boat docks, the Northern Store and KFC attached, a chip stand that's open only in summer, the bank, Taska's Store and Arctic Arts. About it.

The boy is heavy, just lies in my arms watching the world from lidded eyes in fat little cheeks. He falls asleep to the rhythm of my walk. Wish I had a *tikanagan* to carry him on my back.

"What else you going to do with that money?" I ask as we turn onto Sesame Street, quiet now with the kids mostly in school.

"I don't know, me. Haven't thought too much about it." Eva huffs from the walking. "Save most of it, I guess."

"Ever boring. Spend it. You'll win more." The day is warming up, the remaining snow trickling in small rivers from the washboard road and down to the river.

We stop at the bridge over the creek and stare down at the black water pouring into the Moose. Stolen bicycles dumped here last year stick up from the surface. I look down at Hugh still sleeping in my arms, get the urge to pull a Michael Jackson and dangle him over the current so that Eva flips out. I can be mean. He's so fat I'd probably drop him. My arms and lower back ache.

"What you smiling at?" Eva asks.

"Nothing."

We walk down to the main road, make a left toward the train station at Taska's. We head to the big water tower by the station, the top of it painted with an osprey and Cree syllabics by one of the Etherington boys a long time ago. Paint job holding up still. Impressive. Kids playing hooky congregate in front of what used to be a pool hall but is now a Pentecostal church, along with the usual suspects, the old rubbies. Remi Martin, Porkchop, Stinky Andy. They wave hello and try to call us over to get spare change. "Not too shabby for a *Nishnabe,*" Porkchop shouts at me. I smile and keep walking. I pass Hugh back to Eva when he wakes up, whining.

"I'm going to have to nurse him," Eva says, making a squishy face at her boy.

"Let's go sit at the KFC."

The Northern Store, our shrine to civilization way up here in Indian Country, provides us with overpriced groceries, wilting fruits and vegetables that cost a whole cheque, clothes and bicycles and boots and televisions and stereos all lit up by bright fake lighting. In back you can still bring in your pelts and sell them for prices that have plummeted over the last years. We'll go in later.

Now we walk into the restaurant attached to it. Kentucky Fried Duck. The Bucket of Sickness. *Anishnabe* soul food. My god, the people around here love it. Today the stink of grease makes my stomach turn. "Ever smell good!" Eva says, sitting with me and coyly lifting her shirt and plugging Hugh on. The kid at the counter, Steve, watches, his pocked face entranced.

"They going to make us buy anything?" I ask.

"Grab me a lunch pack and a Diet Pepsi just in case," Eva says. "And get yourself something, skinny. My treat." I do as ordered, deciding that the only thing I'll be able to keep down is a Pepsi and a coleslaw.

With Eva and Hugh fuelled up, we go to the Northern Store, walk up and down the bright aisles, neither of us really wanting to buy anything. But what else is there to do on a weekday morning? Mostly *kookums* and *moshums* hobbling along, pushing carts in front of them. In their lives, they've gone from living on the land in teepees and *askihkans*, hunting, trapping, trading in order to survive, to living in clapboard houses and pushing squeaky grocery carts up and down aisles filled with overpriced and unhealthy food. The changes they've seen over the course of decades must make their heads spin. Diabetes and obesity and cancer plague our community, in communities all across the north, if you believe APTN, the Indian TV channel. Experts seem puzzled. *Gaaah!* That's what you'd say, Uncle.

Carrying a few bags of groceries and some new baby clothes for the boy, I walk Eva down to the water-taxi docks. We chat with a few of the old ones who sit patient in the sterns of their freighters for a fare over to Moose Factory. It's still early enough in the year that they haven't gotten rid of the wooden cabins on their boats that keep customers protected from the wind. I help Eva into one, and the water taxi tips dangerously with her weight. The grandpa who's driving leans to the far side to balance it.

"We'll talk soon," I say. "Call me before you leave for Toronto. I'm going to head back out to the bay in a couple of days to finish up work."

Eva nods and smiles, cradling Hugh in her lap, back to sleep already. "I'll call," she says.

And so this is the way my world once went, Uncle, me always ready to pack up and head into the bush, trying to leave this place that is home, trying to make my way up or down the river, in whichever direction seemed the best one to take me. This was my life.

My legs cramp from leaning to him, and so I let go of his hand and stand up to do some more pacing. Mum's going to be arriving soon and I'll have to finish today's story quick. Instead of sitting again, I lean over my uncle. He looks pretty tough with this new buzz cut. The hair must be soft as a baby chicken's, but when I touch it, it is as wiry as steel wool. "Tough old nut," I say. I lean closer to finish what I've started.

I got ready to head back out to my camp again, a new bag of flour and salt and fresh tins of Klik packed into my boat. But then Eva calls. She's crying. "I caught Junior looking at the internet porn again," she sobs.

"Caught him with his pants down around his ankles and his little chub in his hand." I don't say anything. "On top of it, he left the computer on last night, and I looked. He's been on a chat line and posted a picture of himself that is like from ten years ago when he was skinny and you should see who he's talking to and what he's saying." Eva breaks down more, and I wait. "I told him our trip to Toronto is off." She's so strong when she's a nurse, but the girl is lost when it comes to men.

"You can always come stay with me, Eva," I say. I look out the window and down to the shore where my boat waits.

"Screw him," she says. "I'm still going down to Toronto. I already booked off time at work. I want you to come with me." Her voice is a sniffle now. "Let's go down together, Annie. I'll leave Hugh with my mum. She agreed already. We'll have a girls' week and go find a Chippendales." I laugh at this, and she laughs, too.

"Can you imagine me in a place like Toronto?" I ask. "I'd be dead in two days."

"Please," Eva begs.

"I can't, Eva. But someone will go with you. Come up to my camp with me instead. It'll be good for you."

"I'm going to Toronto. I want you to come with me."

I want to tell her I need to take care of my camp, that the door was left open, that I badly need to do a sweat so the geese will come back to me.

"I can't. I'm sorry."

When she's calmed enough, we get off the phone, and I kiss my mother goodbye and head down to the shore. I climb into my freighter and pull the cord on my outboard. It roars to life. I sit and let it idle. I lean over to untie the rope, but my hand stops. I just stare at it, shaking a little. I must still be sick from the food poisoning. My hand reaches back and turns the motor off. I step out of my boat and head back up the bank, into my house. I pick up the phone and dial Eva's number. "I'll come with you," I tell her. I tell her, Uncle, that I'll go just for a week.

Anthony De Sa

Anthony De Sa grew up in Toronto's Portuguese community. His short fiction has been published in several North American literary magazines. He attended The Humber School for Writers and now heads the English department and directs the creative writing program at a high school for the arts. *Barnacle Love* is De Sa's first book, and he is currently at work on a novel. He lives in Toronto with his wife and three sons.

Barnacle Love

BY ANTHONY DE SA

Finalist 2008

⁓

Of God and Cod

There is nothing he can do. He is lifted high into the air by the swells
that roll, break, and crash upon themselves. His dory is smashed, the
flotsam scattered: pieces of white jagged wood afloat, tangled in knotted
rope, nothing much to grab hold of before the ocean lifts him higher, only
to drop him into its turbulent waters, catching him in the current. Again, he
pierces the surface, the biting cold filling his gasping lungs as he coughs and
sputters. It is the moment he needs. He reaches into his sweater and draws
out the crucifix, which glistens in the moon's light. He twirls it between
puckered fingers, places it in his mouth—between his clicking teeth. He
feels its weight and shape cushioned on his tongue, closes his blue lips and
allows himself to let go, to sink beneath the foaming surface into the dark
molasses sea.

Big Lips. Are you here?

THE PORTUGUESE CALL IT *SAUDADE*: a longing for something so indefi-
nite as to be indefinable. Love affairs, miseries of life, the way things were,
people already dead, those who left and the ocean that tossed them on the
shores of a different land—all things born of the soul that can only be felt.

Manuel Antonio Rebelo was a product of this passion. He grew up with
the tales of his father, a man who held two things most sacred, God and
cod—*bacalhau*—and not always in that order. His father's words formed
vivid pictures of grizzled brave fishermen and whale hunters who left their
families for months to fish the great waters off Terra Nova, the new land.
Visions of mothers shrouded in black, of confused wives—the pregnant

ones feeling alone, the others glad for the respite from pregnancy—spun in his mind. And then there were the scoured children, waving in their Sunday finery. The small boys bound in worn but neatly pressed blazers and creased shorts. The little girls scattered like popcorn in their outgrown Communion dresses as they watched their fathers' ascents onto magnificent ships. In his dreams Manuel saw the men with their torn and calloused hands, faces worn, dark and toughened by the salted mist. As a child he would sit by the cliffs for hours, dangling his bare feet over the side of the hundred-foot drop to the shore, kicking the rock with his pink heels, placing his hands over his eyes to shield the sunlight, already yearning for the fading figures of the White Fleet.

"One day I'll disappear," he'd say aloud.

He could make out the faint shadow of a large fish that circled just under the skinned surface of the water.

"Did you hear that, Big Lips?" he shouted.

As if in response, the large grouper seemed to stop. Manuel could see the fish's fins fanning against the mottled blue and green of the ocean's rocky shallows. He had once befriended one of these gentle giants. The villagers believed that these fish could live for up to one hundred years. This was in part due to the story of Eduarda Ramos, one of the village midwives, who insisted she had reclaimed her wedding band from the belly of a large grouper her son had caught—fifty-three years after she had lost the ring while cleaning some fish by the shore.

As the large fish swam away and disappeared into the ocean's darker depths, Manuel couldn't help but wonder if the fish he had named was still alive. If the fish he had just seen was Big Lips.

Manuel's yearning became a palpable ache. The Azores held nothing for him. The tiny island of São Miguel was suffocating, lost as it was in the middle of the Atlantic. Early in life he knew the world his mother had formed for him was too small, too predictable. He was the oldest boy. But it wasn't for this reason alone that Manuel carried the burden of his mother's dreams. He bore a close resemblance to his father: the liquid steel colour of his eyes, his thick stubborn mound of blond hair, and the round angelic features of his face. The blunt noses, darker skin, and almost black, shrimp-like eyes that adorned his siblings had been borrowed from his mother's side. Manuel thought they were all pretty and he loved them, but he also knew that in his mother's mind they held no promise.

"You are your father's son. He lives in you," she'd sigh. "You possess his greatness." Manuel felt her breasts pressed flat against his back, her sharp chin digging into his head. "I can smell it in your breath's sweetness."

Maria had plucked Manuel out of her brood and he became the chosen one. Her ambitions for her son were firm rather than clear: Manuel would become a man of importance, learned and respected in the village and beyond. He would have the advantage of private tutors, which meant his siblings would need to keep the bottoms of their shoes stuffed with corn husks to clog the holes and keep their feet dry. Manuel was often ashamed of himself as he walked up Rua Nova with his brothers and sisters, his polished shoes shining like the blue-black of a mussel. He would be taught a rigorous catechism by the village priest, Padre Carlos. The teachings of God would make him fair and virtuous.

"It's all for you, *filho*," she'd say, often in front of her other children as they went about, cowering, in their daily chores. It was only because they loved Manuel and never once blamed him for anything they were denied that he began to resent his mother's cruelty.

His ten-year-old brother Jose came home one day with a sick calf that he walked through the front door and into their narrow dark hallway. Everyone smiled and watched as the brother who loved animals above anything else tugged at the sickly calf, urged it out the back door toward a patch of tall grass. But the pastoral calm was interrupted by the sharp crack of dry wood. Manuel saw his young brother fall to the packed-earth floor like a ball of dough. His cheek lay pressed against the floor, he was afraid to lift his head. He licked the blood that trickled from the corner of his mouth. Manuel looked to his mother, who held the splintered end of the broom over her shoulder. She picked the boy up by the scruff of his collar and he dangled from her clenched fist.

"You get this filthy beast out of here. This is our home, not a barn," her voice shook.

Jose turned the nervous animal around and, still in a daze, directed the reluctant calf back out the front door. Albina and the others continued their work. Maria Theresa da Conceição Rebelo sat back down on the chair and poured the beans into the sagging lap of her apron. Manuel picked up the splintered broom. Looking straight at his mother, he flung the broken handle across the kitchen. The stoneware bowls that had been carefully set on the barnboard table smashed. He heard the drawn breaths of his sisters. His mother stood and the beans sprung from her apron across the floor. She cocked her trembling hand over her shoulder. He stood still for what seemed like an eternity, challenging her with his unblinking glare. She lowered her arm as he stormed after his brother.

He was twelve then. Manuel vowed that somehow he would make it all better. Freedom would provide opportunities for his siblings. But first, he would have to save himself.

Now, at the age of twenty, Manuel maintained an indifference to Maria's ambitions. Every spring he would venture to the same spot and perch himself on the overhang. He would look out to the sea, feel the warming winds against his pale smooth skin. His still-boyish cowlick pressed against his forehead. He'd carefully roll each of his socks into a ball, stuff them into his new leather shoes, to kick his now yellowed heels against the cliff wall with a vigour that had only intensified during the months he had spent in the mildewed Banco Micaelense, counting out *escudos* with a vacant smile, throwing open all windows to breathe in the sea, hearing Amalia's despair on the radio, her riveting outbursts of emotion. He knew it was time to tell his mother.

"*MÃE*, I'M GOING AWAY FOR A WHILE," he said.

She continued to hang the laundry on the line, the stubborn stains facing the house, the cleaner sides billowing toward the neighbours. She held wooden clothespins in her mouth—sometimes three at a time—securely between her crowded teeth.

"*Mãe*, look at me," he urged. "I need to go. I need to be part of a bigger world. I need to know if there's room out there for me."

Her job was only interrupted for a fraction of a second. Manuel realized she had been waiting for this. Only yesterday she had walked into the bank, and he had noticed a disguised sadness in her step as she approached him in his white shirt and tie; she had pressed the shirt that morning and was pleased that the crease in his cuff had held. She continued hanging the clothes as if she hadn't heard. But Manuel could sense her anger, the disappointment in allowing herself to believe it was possible for her children to want for themselves the same things she did. Maria Theresa da Conceição Rebelo stopped. Manuel looked away for a moment to catch the silhouettes of his brothers and sisters behind the muslin curtains of the house. Albina was twenty-two and the oldest child. Her hands rested on their young brothers, Mariano and Jose. They were eighteen, only ten months apart. Candida was fifteen and sat on the sill with her back leaning against the drapes. He had expected them to be there, listening from inside their shared bedrooms. He chose to move his blurred vision back toward his mother. His eyes travelled up to her hair, to the wisps that looped up, barely held by her hair comb. *When did her hair turn grey?* he thought.

"*Mãe—*"

"You look like your father."

She walked toward the house wiping her hands on a torn apron, kicking with her bare feet the feeding hens that got in her way. As she reached the door, she bent down and scooped one of the hens up and under her freckled arm. Turning to face her son, she stroked the chicken's head with her free hand before her swollen, red fingers closed around its thin neck and tugged; just one quick yank before the bird's head fell, still jerking.

"Your supper will be ready soon," and she slammed the door.

THEY HAD NOT SPOKEN. The night before he left, his mother had locked herself in her room. He found a package, brown folded paper tied neatly with trussing string, outside her bedroom door. He knew she wouldn't come out. It had been too painful the first time, fifteen years back, when she had wrapped some cheese, bread, *chouriço*, and a few loose sheets of paper and bundled them all together with an embroidered dishtowel before she embraced her husband Antonio for the last time.

Manuel untied the knots, their whorls flicking against the parcel. He stood in front of her door, hoping she'd hear the rustling of paper. He was mindful of refolding the paper and rolling the string into a ball—his mother could use it again. In the parcel, Manuel found a yellowed fisherman's sweater smelling of ocean, and in a tiny envelope made of tin wrap, his father's gold crucifix and chain. They were the only things that she had left of her husband; his body had been buried at sea. There were no words written on the paper or in the folds. He checked. He tried knocking, then stopped after three soft raps and put his lips to the door, touching the grain.

"*Adeus, Mãe,*" he whispered.

He couldn't recall exactly what his father looked like, only his blue-grey eyes and warm smile. But he did remember sitting on his father's knee and looking for the gleaming crucifix buried in his father's chest hair. This was the same chain that he now placed around his neck. He swung the sweater under his arm and tossed his duffle bag over his shoulder, his fingers whitened by the strain. Later, tucked in his socks or wrapped in his under-wear, Manuel would discover the gifts secretly offered, for fear of their mother's disapproval, by his siblings: Albina's embroidered *M* handker-chief, the copper whistle Jose used to herd cattle, and Mariano's pocket knife. Also in his bag, pressed between his cotton undershirts, was a black-and-white photograph of Candida, lips pursed like a Hollywood actress caught in a hazy cloud of smoke. Manuel walked down the silent corridor and out the front door.

HE ARRIVED IN THE COBBLED SQUARE of Ponte Delgada before day-break. The rigged ships waited, tethered to the docks; their white sails reflected the morning moon but barely rippled in the early breeze behind the makeshift altar. The altar had been constructed on the docks and bore the symbol of an intertwined cross and anchor. The sails would form the backdrop for the traditional farewell mass. Soon the square would be filled with crowds pushing their way up to the front, wanting to be touched by the priest, blessed by his hand.

Manuel once understood that desire and need. He had reached out as a young boy when faced with the loss of his father. But his trust had been betrayed and his want silenced. He hadn't thought of Padre Carlos for a while. Some things were best pushed far back into the dark places of the mind. But the impending voyage, his mother's inability to understand his decision, had awakened the loneliness he had felt as a boy.

"Those who serve me, serve God," Padre Carlos had whispered.

He could still feel the priest's hot breath behind his ear.

"It's between us and God. Do you understand?"

He shook his head, trying to drive away the fear and anger he still held for the priest his mother had entrusted with her young son.

He opened his eyes to the early sky, ribbons of gold and pink, and the sounds of families trickling in to claim the coveted spots closest to the altar. The altar boys were busy preparing for mass, and the pesky vendors with their bloated and teetering carts encircled the square, droning, "*Pequeno almoço! ... Pão torrado, queijo! ... Pequeno almoço!*" Manuel responded to the stabs of the man's nasal voice announcing breakfast by fumbling in his pocket for some *escudos*.

"AND AS THESE BRAVE MEN leave for the cold and foggy seas, we pray for them—for their work and sacrifice." The priest paused for effect, then the homily continued toward its crescendo.

"And we stay behind: mothers, wives, children. We remain! … And with us remains the promise that only God can return them safely to us." He lowered his head.

Manuel looked around. *Maybe they came*, he allowed himself to hope. He stopped himself by swinging his duffle hard over his back.

He would be one of fifty-three men on board. Together, they would spend days thrown against the ship's hull, stomachs churning with only the veined whites of their eyes exposed to the bitter spring cold. He was the first to walk past the embracing dusters, the wailing women and the oblivious children. He boarded the *Argus*, made his way down into her belly to begin the 1954 *campanha*. Unlike the other men on board who ventured and risked their lives for God, country, and family, Manuel knew that he would risk his life for a new beginning. He didn't look back.

THE POUNDING OF THE SEA was relentless. During the long days, the men talked of the foreign trawlers that hauled in thousands of pounds of cod while no man's life was endangered.

"But we are Portuguese … we need to protect the traditions of the fisherman." Manuel heard these words. His eyes caught the streaks of orange embers coming from their cigarettes, their bodies dark and unseen as their hands gesticulated in circles or slashes only to stop and glow with every inhalation. "One man, one boat, one line dropped to the depths of the ocean," another man in the huddle finished the sentiment. Manuel had remained silent for days. When he wasn't retching into a tin pail from the constant motion or covering his nose and mouth with his sweater to filter the dank odours that wafted beneath the deck, he listened and learned: heard the men call him *Boneco*—doll, because of his big blue eyes and round face.

Once off the Grand Banks, each man was assigned his own wooden dory that dangled precariously off the side of the mother ship. These fourteen-foot vessels would be their homes through the long days of fishing. The thrashing cod were the only guests invited on board. At four o'clock in the morning the men were lowered into the black ocean, to push off immediately from the vessel—once one hit water, a wave could be fatal, crashing the dory into the side of the *Argus*, destroying the craft and killing the man. For some of these old dorymen it was their fortieth voyage. Francisco Battista Rego was the oldest. Inscrutable, at sixty-two he had visited the Grand Banks forty-three times, so often in fact he said that he had forgotten what a summer in his native Terceira was like. The seas called out to him, and for months he left his wife and children. For six months of the year—from May to October—these men were his family, a family he had come to know more intimately than his own.

One night, as the men slept up against each other so as to keep warm, Francisco *Golfinho*, the dolphin, snuggled up to Manuel *Boneco*.

"I'll watch over you," Golfinho whispered.

He reached over and grabbed Manuel's hand, pulled him closer.

"Don't panic, show no fear—the panicked are dead."

Manuel could see the man's stubby fingers, made rounder by his missing fingernails, encase his own smallish hand—as a father's would his son's. He thought of his own father and was comforted by Francisco's protective words that came when Manuel felt loneliest, most vulnerable. Other men had busied themselves with writing letters to wives, mothers, children, or brothers—someone back home who needed to know they were alive and well. He could not write home, not with the way things had been left. Only shattered images remained. But the act of writing soothed him, so Manuel began to write letters also. They all began with "Dear Big Lips ..." Then, in the cool pink of daybreak, he'd move up on deck and let shredded pieces of paper slip from his fingers like confetti.

He was physically drained. Here they all were, hand-lining for cod from their dory boats all day, only to return to the ship at sundown to begin splitting, gutting, and salting the day's catch. It was the brandy, the songs, and the old yarns repeated by tired, dizzy men that kept them alive. And every morning they would once again prepare to descend into the sea, push off from the *Argus* and venture far through the thick fog to drop their lines two or three hundred feet into the abyss.

Manuel awaited the promise that the tedious months in their berths would be broken occasionally by a visit to St. John's, when the ship would make a scheduled call to replenish supplies, make repairs to sails or engines, and provide shore leave. Other times there was a need to land injured men or just to seek some shelter from the storms that tore across the sheet of black water and tossed the White Fleet like toy boats. He had heard of how the fishermen became a prominent part of Newfoundland life. They visited the Fishermen's Centre and window-shopped along Water and Duckworth streets with the bits of money they had to spend. They remembered their families back home, buying souvenirs: toys, stockings, perfume, toothpaste. At the post office, the men sent mail home or picked up parcels they had ordered the year before from the Eaton's catalogue.

One Saturday morning, word spread along the crowded bunks that the fleet would finally call into St. John's before returning home. Manuel could scarcely contain his excitement. A blend of joy and confusion tumbled among the men. Some howled with pleasure as they mockingly groped each other like passionate lovers, or practised their English out loud: broken words and phrases like *how much?* or *you look beautiful today.* Many went looking for comforts, a clean girl, and certain houses were glad to provide them.

Manuel had dressed carefully and made his way to the deck. He held on to the smooth railing, leaned his torso over the open sea as if to breathe in churning air. Some of the men ran naked on the upper deck, drew up cold sea water and doused themselves, rubbed their goose-pimpled limbs and their stubbled necks with amber bars of glycerin soap. Manuel closed his eyes and then opened them again to catch the rhythmic beacon atop the outline of a distant shore. It was *Cabo de Espera*, the "cape of waiting," as the Portuguese had named it. He had waited so long and it was only now that it had become so palpable. Manuel smiled.

Many of the veteran fishermen seemed amused by the frenetic energy that consumed the younger men. Manuel couldn't help but think they were recalling a time when they would have been swept into the madness. Now, they appeared content to save their money and make a bit more by sitting on the piers, mending sails or repairing the long lines of hooks as they smoked and drank Portuguese wine. Many of the residents bought things from the fishermen, indulgences like cigarettes and wine. Some men had even developed relationships with families in St. John's.

Before coming up on deck Manuel had allowed himself to feel a moment of guilt for abandoning his mother's dream. He had carefully made his bed, the way he had been taught. He was afraid, and yet he knew it was the only way in which he could construct a future, for him and for them.

The *Argus*'s hull kissed the pier's concrete side. Manuel scanned the enormous wharves, looked up toward the city of St. John's as the ship's horn blew and a group of pigeons lighted and flew across his view like a net cast against the open sea.

He stepped onto the gangway and slowly descended. The morning sun bathed the regular facades of the port buildings, with their pitched roofs and masonry walls, that stood along the road. With every step his eyes caught the white or yellow gabled trim, the paved roads and flash of glass. Angular shadows that splayed across sidewalks. He looked up to the teetering city built in tiers, splattered with green, vermilion, and white clap-board houses. It was so different from the whitewashed world he came from, and the moment his feet touched solid ground he knew that this place was his promised land.

It wasn't difficult to find his way around. Manuel simply followed the throngs of fishermen as he dodged the cars and trucks that sputtered past on both sides of the narrow road. His first stop was at the Arcade store, where a pile of white shoes greeted him. He was told that the locals called these Portuguese sneakers, something even the poorest of fishermen could afford. Manuel was stunned by the sheer amounts of clothing and food; shelves stocked all the way to the edge, some things piled two or three high. The weight on these shelves made their centres sag close to the worn wooden floors. He didn't know where to begin.

"Can I help you?"

Manuel turned to meet an attractive woman with a slight overbite that made her upper lip look full when her mouth was closed. She was slightly older than Manuel, twenty-five or so, he thought. She did not look at him, simply looked down, held her thin fingers clasped in front of her, and swung her body from side to side.

"Thank you," Manuel managed to say.

He crouched to look up into her eyes. His inquisitive gesture made her smile. Her eyebrows were thin and pencilled. Her mossy green eyes were set wide apart, made wider by the way her hair was pulled into a ponytail.

"Is that the size you want?" she asked, pointing at the shoes he held tucked under his arm.

"*Irmão. Irmão.*"

"Mary!" she called out. She then lowered her voice when she saw him twitch. "Mary, he's talkin' in Portuguese. Don't know what I'm saying," she added.

"Brother. For my brother," came out of his mouth, as if in answer.

"That's better," she said. "Now what size is your brother? What size, though?"

He looked down at her gold name tag: *Linda*. He pointed to her name and mouthed the word in a nervous stutter. When she smiled he continued, "Is mean beautiful in Portuguese." Her face flushed red and her head tilted to the side.

"Anything else I can help you with?"

Linda had wrapped the gifts he had purchased in their own separate packets: shoes for his brothers and slips and stockings for his sisters—he smiled to himself remembering the embarrassing gestures made to Linda in his attempt to describe what he wanted. For his mother he had found a tortoiseshell hair comb, encrusted with small crystals along its scalloped edge. He knew that she would think it was too dear for her to wear, but he wanted her to have something nice. Manuel had insisted that Linda clearly write the names of his siblings on their respective packets. He couldn't help but notice her relief when he used the word *sister* as she scrawled Albina and Candida on the stiff brown parchment. Everything needed to be wrapped well, for the packets would be sent home by mail. Linda directed him to the post office.

Once relieved of his parcels, Manuel was guided by a couple of other Portuguese fishermen to where Mateus lived, a man known to provide the comforts of home to seafaring men. He did not enter the home located just below the towering gloom of the Basilica of St. John the Baptist. He had been avoiding the church ever since he landed. Manuel simply stood outside Mateus's house and bathed in the familiar sounds of the accordion and trill voices of amateur *fadistas*. He knew that here he would find wine and food but most importantly, he knew inside was the man who had lived in St. John's since he was a boy. The man had left Portugal hidden in the dory of the ship, in search of his father. The man would help Manuel.

MANUEL SPENT THE REST OF HIS DAY weaving in and out of shops, dizzied by the display of things to buy: coffee, sugar, and vegetables he had never seen. He saw women smoking casually as they moved along the hills that undulated upward to the church. There were men in suits and hats who walked along with purpose and importance. They angled their shoulders so as not to hit the narrow bay windows that jutted every so often into the crowded sidewalks. Other men lumbered along the roads in coveralls or thigh-high rubber boots, pushing carts or lugging crates over their shoulders. Manuel saw a Chinese man sorting through vegetables and felt compelled to follow him up a narrow series of steps, past a war statue, up to yet another layer of the city to be explored. Manuel looked up at a large sign with a panda bear sipping from a bowl. He opened the door and heard the tinkling of chimes. Manuel twirled the noodles on his fork—he wasn't quite sure what the sticks that lay next to his plate were for—and forced the swirling mounds of sweetly covered noodles and scotched lengths of squid into his mouth.

After his meal he continued to walk through the streets of the city. He didn't worry about getting lost. From almost any point in St. John's he could look out toward the Narrows and into the sea. He could then let his eyes work their way back to the wharf, where he could see the White Fleet's forest of masts and sails. He could see the long lengths of rope and chain that held the ships firmly against the dock. Some ropes had been covered in long underwear and plaid flannel shirts that flapped in the warm air. He could see the decks of the ships covered with the dory sails, allowed to dry in the waning summer sun.

Tired, Manuel found a spot in a park at the top of the hill. He sat under the shade of a tree, surrounded by the magnificent homes where all the rich, fine men lived, he assumed.

Manuel recognized a few of the Portuguese fishermen playing soccer in their bare feet. Some young boys played with them. Soon there were people gathering to sit on benches or sprawl on checked blankets. They watched the game played in the meadow near the bandstand as the dark-skinned Portuguese players dazzled everyone with their footwork. The grunting only drew louder claps at the friendly sportsmanship. Manuel took off his shoes and socks in the comfort of sounds and sights familiar but new. He flicked the cool blades of grass between his toes. A sailor began playing his accordion—some lilting Portuguese waltzes—under the roof of the band-stand. With the music dancing in his head, Manuel turned and looked out to the sparkling, still water in the harbour. *Life in this new land is determined by being so close to the ocean*, he thought. It was as if the cliff he had dangled his feet from all his life was the same rock and mineral that formed along the shores of this land. The drift may have occurred millions of years before but there was sameness, an intimate sense of belonging that closed the chasm of ocean between here and his home—between all things left behind and his future.

Manuel's eyes had grown heavy and he had fallen asleep. His eyes opened slightly at the sound of the first gust of foghorns blowing. Manuel drew his knees close to his chest and wrapped his arms around his legs. The park now lay empty in front of him. He could see sails crawling up the masts and the men filing in thin lines like ants, winding their way down the streets toward the docks.

The time spent on land had been short. The men boarded the ship wearily, their minds drunk with stories just waiting to be told. There were only a few days left before the *Argus* and other ships would turn their noses home, and underneath the layer of fatigue were the fired spirits of men who knew they would be with their real families soon. But the promise of the new land would not be erased from Manuel's mind. He closed his eyes in the warm knowledge he would stay.

The foghorns blared again.

The wind had picked up in the dusk and Manuel reached for his father's sweater, which he had knotted around his waist. He pulled it over his head. With a desperate hope, he thrust his hand up under his sweater and patted his chest. His mind's veil lifted and he pictured his father's gold crucifix in its foil packet pressed under the centre of his mattress. There was no hesitation as he clambered down the steep hills toward the wharf. There were times when he thought he would stumble down the sloping streets, that his burning thighs wouldn't be able to stop the momentum building with every leap. He sprung onto the ramp, pushed himself through the thick clumps of returning men. Manuel's boots clanged against the iron mesh gangway, the metallic sound reverberating in his panicked head. He reached the mouth of the doorway, threw himself down its gullet in a single bound, felt the walls like a blind man, pupils ill-adjusted to the gloom as he charged into an open room strewn with narrow rows of rotting bunks. He flipped over his mattress and grabbed at the tinfoil envelope. He unfolded the flaps and drew out the twirling cross.

The foghorns blew again, deep and long.

Manuel leapt up the stairs in a fluid motion, the necklace now secured beneath his father's sweater. As he came up on deck, Manuel's eyes met Francisco Golfinho's clean-shaven face and tender stare. Manuel looked over Francisco's shoulder to the city of St. John's. He pushed up against Francisco, tried to wedge himself between some men who sang in a drunken stupor at what had been the gangway's opening. The ropes and chains had been drawn and the ship had pushed away from the dock. He looked down at the widening gap of black water. He looked toward the colours all muted and hazy in the early moon's light. Francisco Golfinho leaned in and placed his hand on Manuel's shoulder. Manuel could smell the traces of aftershave and bacon fat mingling on Francisco's skin.

"Look at it," Manuel whispered. His eyes scanned the skyline. "It's like I want to ... touch it, hold on to it."

"It's time to find our way back home." Francisco slapped Manuel's shoulder twice. Manuel thought of his mother. Over the months her face had softened in his mind. He thought of all the ways in which his siblings had suffered so much, had loved him unconditionally because they believed in their mother's fiction.

Francisco Golfinho moved his hand to the small of Manuel's back and Manuel reluctantly turned from the city. They were both caught by a mob of revelling men and Manuel staggered, then fell onto the ship's deck, where he choked on his disappointment, swallowed the snot in the back of his throat and wept.

IT WOULD BE THE FINAL DAY OF FISHING before returning home. Manuel pushed off from the *Argus*, as he had done so many times before. But on this day he set the oars into the oarlocks and rowed out into the ocean's vastness with a renewed sense of vitality; he had seen a part of the world that seemed boundless and felt he must be part of it. With these thoughts swimming in his mind he drifted for hours in the dense fog. He could hear the voices of the other men singing as they fished, but no vision could pierce the wall of white mist. He tried to row in a certain direction but then realized there was no direction, no bearing.

The long days passed. Alone on his dory, Manuel gnawed at the bluish-white flesh of the cod he'd caught. Taste had abandoned him now and all that remained was his fear. During the day the sun pounded his head as he lay rocking on the dory's bottom. To cool his mind, Manuel remembered himself as a boy, diving into the waters every morning, burlap sac and a forged trident in hand. He would make his way to what he called the clam stone, a large rock formed by lava that flowed toward the shore, only to bubble into a solid black form millions of years ago. He would step onto its hollowed smoothness worn by sand, sea, and time. Manuel would pick at all the bounty trapped at low tide—*God's gift*. There was always the initial stab when he dove into the ocean. But then his eyes would adjust to the wonderful world of the green waters. He loved the feeling of his hair being free, individual strands swarming around his head. The sense of control: holding his breath till his lungs burned, kicking his way to the sun-drenched surface before taking in another deep breath and going under again. He would spear only what was necessary, only what they could eat that day. But before he left he would always mangle one of the smaller fish he had caught and make his way to the rocky bottom, dive down along the drop wall and gently offer his hand and wiggle the bait, hoping the large black grouper would appear again. It never did.

It was a cold night when Manuel lay down flat on the bottom of the dory, made the sign of the cross and looked up at the stars. He thought of the dream he had sacrificed and all the things he would never know. And then he prayed. The dory rocked, lifted and twirled, a mere twig caught by the force and power of the ocean. The storm was building and Manuel knew that it was only a matter of time.

FRIGHTENED BY THE IMPENETRABLE DARK, he breaks the surface, gasps and coughs up the crucifix. Salt water splashes against his face, forces his lips open, gushing in like an uninvited guest as he chokes on bile.

Don't panic—the panicked are dead.

His perfectly round face remains above water, then disappears under a small rolling wave, only to bob and break the surface again. Suddenly, there is nothing but ocean and a promising sky full of fading stars. The ocean has been lulled. The worst has passed. Manuel tilts his head back, ears submerged just under the waterline. He tries kicking his numb legs to propel himself into a back float—if only for a short while more. His burning arms and wrists circle in vain. He looks up at the sky, urging the sun to arrive and warm him. His heavy worn leather shoes were the first things to sink into the ocean's muddy depths. His wool pants followed, his childhood fishing belt sinking with them. But the fisherman's sweater, its pounds of soaked cabling, cannot be allowed to go, not just yet. He moves with the dancing waves. Only, he does not lead.

"Manuel," he hears a familiar voice call in singsong.

He recognizes the voice he has not heard in years.

"Big Lips, is that you?" Manuel says.

He sees the large grouper burst out of the water, its olive and grey shimmering body twisting over him in an arc. He thinks he sees the fish grinning at him with those balloon lips before its black-blotched shape plunges into the water without a splash.

"Big Lips. Come back!"

He waits, but hears only the lapping of water breaking under his chin. The sea invites him down once again. His arms no longer push through the water, his legs abandon him. Manuel Antonio Rebelo looks up at the new sun as he fills his lungs with air and slips once again under the surface, this time with eyes shut.

As he drops, he sees his father's smile, his mother's expression of betrayal, his abandoned brothers and sisters, and the women and children he will never know. He breathes out his last pocket of air, bubbles rising from him to pop on the surface. Manuel feels a tightening in his chest and arms, an inability to move and direct his weight. But instead of going down, his frame is tilting and twirling under the water's current. He feels himself dragged across and up, up toward the surface light. There is a gash of cold air before he feels the thud of his numb weight hitting a boat's wooden floor.

He adjusts his sight to see the face of a leathery man: toothless smile, uneven stubble, and half-soaked cigarette dangling from the corner of his mouth, cantilevered on his lip.

"Hmmm," is all the man grunts.

Manuel lies trembling on a nest of jumbled net. He grabs hold of the boat's edge, retching onto the wooden floor. There is a sense that he is not quite saved. He is thankful to lie curled, wound tightly in a ball as woollen blankets are draped over him. Every so often he squints at the back of a plaid woollen jacket, green rubber boots, and a man's piston arms, elbows pointing back, bringing the oars up with his hairy knuckles. Again and again. He falls in and out of an exhausted sleep.

"What do they call you, b'y, now?" the man asks.

"Manuel."

He had taken a few lessons in basic English before setting sail and had picked up more from the men on board the *Argus*. He learned everyday words—*house, girl, boy, food*—and phrases: "What is your name?" which required the proper response, "*My name is Manuel.*" But, the leathery man did not offer his name in return.

Manuel can only think of fresh water, food, and warmth. He can hear the mumbled questions this man is asking, but right now he is too spent to respond. All Manuel can do is think of home, his mother, the men of the *Argus*, and the news that will greet them all. Suddenly, a new, distant voice pierces his thoughts.

"Dad! Dad! Did you catch anything?" the echo travels.

Manuel struggles to lean up on his elbow and looks over the rim of the tiny boat for the first time. His eyes can only distinguish a girl's slight figure and the glint of sun radiating from her. She stands atop a glossy bed of kelp and runs her hands through her light brown hair, adjusts some strands behind her ears and tugs the hem of her flower-print skirt over her rubber boots. Manuel squints at a glare that flashes off her leg. The bottom of the boat scuffs onto land, tilts slightly to one side, then stops.

"Pepsi, my love. Your father caught you a big one."

He roars with laughter as he hauls the wet twine, heaves the bow of the boat further up and carves into the pebbled shore.

"Been out to sea too long, but he's home now." He looks over his shoulder, then adjusts his voice to a whisper.

Manuel looks at his daughter; he can see she is absorbed by her father's "catch."

"He's some mother's boy, understand. We gotta take good care of him."

As her father busies himself with unloading the dory, the girl traces Manuel's lips with her index finger. Manuel struggles to keep his eyes open. He sees her clasping her hands together as if in prayer. She raises her chin to the sky exposing her long white neck. Manuel doses his eyes. As his mind retreats into a deep sleep he thinks he hears her mumble, "Thank you, Lord."

REASON TO BLAME

Manuel's eyelids flutter when she lifts his head to give him water. It dribbles from the corners of his mouth, trickles down his chin and neck. Pepsi smiles when this happens, scrunches up her shoulders and giggles. She takes care of Manuel. When she thinks he's asleep she combs his hair, lightly outlines his eyebrows, and then moves down the bridge of his nose with her finger. Manuel senses her excitement in daring to hover her lips over his as he lies in his makeshift cot with his eyes closed. He grumbles something and snorts a bit. Pepsi thinks he is going to wake up, and moves quickly to the foot of his cot to slip her father's best socks onto Manuel's feet. She smiles. Her face is small, her hair is straight and divided by a long line of white scalp; each half falls down her face, hiding the corners of her eyes. She reaches into a bowl and unravels a steaming towel, which she drapes over his face. "Shhh. Close your eyes," she whispers. Manuel sinks back into the pillow. The heat of the towel makes his skin tingle, scalds as it surges up his nostrils and then lulls him momentarily. When she removes the cooling towel Manuel smiles. She pretends she does not notice. He sees her eyes darting quickly to the task at hand as she stretches his skin taut with her thumb and forefinger, then carefully shaves in the direction of his growth. Manuel's eyes move down her slender neck, down to her small breasts hidden beneath her sweater, then up again. Hers is not the sun-stained neck of a Portuguese girl. Manuel's knotted throat burns as the tears pool in his eyes.

"Shhh. It'll be all right. Pepsi's here, now. Shhh," she whispers in a singsong.

Caro Mãe,

I hope this letter reaches you. I'm alive! Weak, but saved. I've made it to my terra nova, lost for drowned but saved by a fisherman—a good man, Andrew. You always said that God's real messenger was the fisherman; well, he's mine and he's delivered me, taken me into his home.

When I left, there was so much that remained unsaid. Father's crucifix hangs from my neck still, lies close to my heart.

I feel certain about what it is I need to say, what it is you need to hear.

I always knew I didn't want to stay. I think you knew that also. I knew that if I stayed in our town, on our stifling island, I'd be consumed by what it was you hoped and dreamed for me. Please understand, *Mãe*. Don't be disappointed. I want to leave a mark on this world, *Mãe*, and I know it's what you've always wanted also. I need you to believe there is a place for me here, a tomorrow. I'm certain of it and always have been.

Your loving son,
Manuel

"YOU ... UGLY GIRL!" he roars as he stumbles in.

Manuel hears him from the main room. He tilts his head back to see Pepsi getting out of her bed. She has begun to leave her door open at night. Manuel sees her struggle as she jackknifes her body, pivots, then swings from under the covers her pink stump that ends just below the knee. Her good leg dangles over the edge of the bed. She squints his way; it's dark and her eyes haven't adjusted well enough to know if he's seen her. She reaches for her wooden leg, the one she has outgrown, that rests on the floor next to her chamber pot. Her hands blur as they weave the leather straps and secure the metal brace to her thigh—the moulded cup meets the hardened flesh where her leg should be. He's not sure how he feels about it—she is not whole. But, when she brushes by him he is caught in her smell of cotton sheets and the peppered sweetness of cinnamon. There is intrigue in her difference—something fragile that needs his tending. Manuel wants to hold her, touch her.

Pepsi meets her father at the front door. He loses his balance and tries to grab on to the wall. It's not enough. She's there to direct the running fall toward his bedroom, where he flops onto his bed. Manuel tries to get up and help but then falls back against his pillow. She struggles with Andrew's coat and kneads him like dough, gaining momentum to flip him over onto his back. Manuel can smell him from where he is: beer, stale piss, the spice of tobacco in damp wool, the flakes of a fish pie always evident on his stubbly chin and cardigan. Pepsi looks back again to see if Manuel is awake. He moves up to rest on his forearm. He wants to help her. She waves him off and hauls her father's boots from his feet and then threadbare socks before hoisting his legs up onto the mattress and pulling the covers under his chin. Manuel has made it to Andrew's room, leaning against the door frame.

"Thank the Lord you won't be runnin' away like your mother." Andrew cups her face with his hand and brushes her lips with his sausage-like thumb. Unnoticed by him, she spits his fingers away.

"You're my ... my sweet ugly girl. And a wooden leg to boot."

He smiles when he whispers these words, breathes out his judgment. His body now relaxes, his weight moulding itself to the mattress as he sinks into a drunken sleep, mouth wide open.

She comes out of his room. "Go to sleep, Manuel. I'll take care of things."

Manuel moves back to the cot, urged by her hand on the small of his back. She turns on the tap. The gush of water splatters against the cement basin. She finds the empty Javex bottle hidden in the cabinet under the sink, and grabs a wooden spatula. She moves past Manuel into her father's room. She kneels before his sleeping lump, pulls back the covers and undoes his zipper. She looks away and with the spatula fishes for his penis, and expertly aims it into the neck of the jug. A good couple of taps on the hollow plastic jug wakes him just enough to hear the running water. It's all that's needed—the hot, cloudy pee trickles, then gurgles into the bottle.

Caro Mãe,

Every day I get stronger. Andrew and his daughter, Pepsi, are taking good care of me. They ask for nothing. I want to help, to show them my gratitude. There are so many stories to tell ... of the big ship, its men, how I was swallowed by the sea, of St. John's and its streets and people ... I hope you have received my gifts that I mailed to you while in St. John's. I pray that you got my first letter before the black news that must have greeted you from the commander of the fleet.

You were visited fifteen years ago with news of our dear father's death; the idea that you and all my brothers and sisters would hear those same words fall from the mouth of an unknown man, pains me. But I am alive, *Mãe*, and this must give you some comfort.

Please don't see this decision I have made as a rejection of the promise you saw in me. I will work hard to show you that it still burns inside me, brighter than ever.

Every time I breathe in the brackish mist, it reminds me of home. The new land is far, and even though it smells just like home, I find that now I can breathe. I don't know why I want you to know this other than a month has passed and the November winds here are building, getting colder and forceful, and I have yet to hear a word from you.

Please don't be angry with me. You have my brothers and sisters to look after. Love them as I do.

Your son,
Manuel

"PLUCKED OUTTA the water, my boy."

The days are punctuated by Andrew's repeated boast. He puffs himself up like he's caught a prize fish and they're going to take his picture for the local newspaper. Manuel cannot help but smile with gratitude at his outbursts.

Manuel is feeling strong enough to help Andrew skin the animals that he has hunted and trapped: rabbits, deer, and an ugly animal Andrew calls moose. Manuel has made the job easier by driving some large rusty hooks into the trunk of an old tree out back. He shows Andrew, mostly with exaggerated gestures, how to tie the legs of the dead animal together with rope, loop the rope through the eyehook and then the pulley to drag and hoist the carcass against the tree. The animal's body stretches and drapes toward the ground and Manuel's sharp knife cuts into its flesh, thinly separating the hide from that milky blue membrane that encases the meat. Every so often, Manuel cannot help but gaze at the naked cabin through the curtain of steam that rises from the animal. The oxblood paint flakes along its planked sides. Two small windows jut out slightly in the front and the black narrow door sits crooked on its hinges. The wind has ravaged the bleak little house that sits on the grassy hill. But all Manuel can think of is the warmth and comfort within those walls and sagging roof. On a few occasions, he has caught Pepsi looking out the window. She always turns away in time. It's all play and it makes him want her more.

Earlier, that morning, Manuel had been roused from his sleep by Pepsi's excited giggles. "Wake up, Manuel. Come see." Somewhat groggy, Manuel lumbered half-naked to the front door and stepped outside. Snowflakes, large and generous, fell languidly from the sky in silence. They fell on Manuel's hair and lashes, his bare shoulders and feet, where they disappeared into the heat of his skin. Manuel raised his hands, tried to catch the flakes between his fingers. Bewildered, he turned toward the house. Pepsi squatted in the doorway, held her robe's sleeve in her mouth. Manuel had twirled like a boy, raised his head to the snow's newness, opened his mouth and flicked his tongue.

"You better watch yourself, young lady," Andrew says as he and Manuel return to the house. Pepsi continues to stare out the window as if she has not heard him.

"That man's not for you. A good strong man needs a good woman to make him a life, you hear?"

Manuel has grown quite used to them talking about him as if he doesn't understand a word. Truth be told, he doesn't understand *many* of the words, but he is clear about the passion behind these foreign sounds.

"I prayed for him, though. He's for me. He's the answer," her whisper fades.

There are times when Manuel notices the fear in Andrew's eyes. At other times, he's embarrassed by Andrew's mocking.

"You stupid girl ... there is no answer. Look at you." He shakes his head as he walks out the front door.

Before she can react, Manuel moves toward the sink to rinse his blood-stained hands. Duty washes over her; she confidently grabs his hands and scrubs them. She doesn't look at him. Manuel allows her to scour his hands with a brush. They begin to burn in their rawness but he doesn't draw them back. It helps to let her father's words wash away with the blood and grime; they swirl in the basin and lose themselves in the drain. Her neck begins to relax; she turns to face him and her mouth smiles but her eyes betray her. Manuel lets her clean under his nails. He buries his nose in her hair, breathes in and moves into her warmth. She nudges his head a bit and her shoulders drop. Manuel can hear her exhale. He doesn't care about her crooked leg.

Caro Mãe,

I still have not heard from you. Your refusal to send me a letter only adds to the heaviness that weighs in my heart. It has taken hold of my mind.

I am growing fond of this girl. Pepsi. She is sixteen but already a woman of work, just like the girls back home. I know you'd like her, *Mãe*, the same way you liked Silvia before she left to go to school in the city. But, there is something about this girl, Pepsi; she makes all of my plans for this new land seem right, even real. I'm capable of taking hold of my dreams and moving on with my new life.

You used to say that the young don't know what they want. I am not so fragile as to believe that anymore. I'm a man, not a boy. The worth of things in life comes with risk. You taught me that. There is no doubt in my mind that my decision was the right one. Please have faith in me; you always have.

Send something soon, *Mãe*. Let me know if you are all well. My strength is with me, now.

Your son,
Manuel

MANUEL HAS ASKED PEPSI to mail the letters he's written, all addressed to São Miguel, Açores. Pepsi asks who Maria Theresa da Conceição Rebelo is. She looks relieved when Manuel tells her. He wonders what his mother must be thinking now—if she even knows; it's been weeks, has she received word yet that her son has met his father's same fate—lost at sea? Or, could his letters have reached her first, saving her from this torment. Or after, with news of a resurrection? He is eager for a response.

"Fishermen need to live by the sea, don't they, Manuel?"

"Yes, Andrew," Manuel nods.

Andrew begins to dress in layers of coats and then tops off his head with a hat, the fur-lined flaps framing his ruddy face. He is off to check his traps. His padded frame can barely fit through the narrow door. As he hunkers down to go out he turns to look at Manuel, who is writing a letter, and then quickly moves to look at his daughter, who lifts a heavy roasting pan out of the oven in a billow of steam and brushes her wet bangs away from her face with her forearm. He grunts as he moves out the door like a lumbering bear.

"My father told me we have to keep quiet about this or they'll send you to some farm in Ontario, Manuel ... to work."

"Is okay, Pepsi. Shhh. I no say nothing." Manuel picks at her loose hair and tucks some strands behind her ears.

"I don't want anyone to know, Manuel." They both sit on Manuel's cot. "No one."

"I don't know why she left. I thought it was me, or more her disappointment in giving birth to me? It was all too much for her, I suppose. Growing up I wanted to know—I wanted a reason to blame. Do you understand, my darling?"

Manuel didn't ask the question about her mother, although he had often wondered. She had been seven when her mother left her, them. Her father never made much sense when he tried to explain. But in his lame drunken attempts, deep down Pepsi knew *he* was the reason.

"*This barren heath*—that's what she called this place; it's too far from Brigus to be called anything. But this was the place where she gave birth to me, alone. And as the years passed I began to notice the sadness in her eyes. Maybe she wanted a reason to blame too."

Pepsi fixes her eyes on the front doorknob and talks. She looks up at Manuel to see if he is listening.

"I guess I'll never know."

"You father no say why?"

"Ah, whatever Father tried to do to reassure my mother was never enough, though. A child can see things, you know, Manuel."

"Is hard for lose a mother. But memories you have, no? This make you strong. It make *me* strong."

She smiles at Manuel's much-improved conversation. She is tired and flushed but happy to keep going.

She tells Manuel of her yearly birthday trip to St. John's where, if need be, she would get fitted for a new leg and brace. She swings her head from side to side with each memory: the smells of her mother's cooking, the hours her mother spent teaching her to read, the little dog her mother had left behind who ran after a blowing leaf then disappeared over the cliff. Pepsi rushed to the edge and saw his body smashed and crooked against the shore rocks.

"All I have left of my mother is this strand of almost-pink pearls she bought for me at a place called Kresge's, in Toronto—that's what the box said. She sent them to me on my tenth birthday along with a note: *Dear Pepsi, Please don't be angry. I just couldn't any longer. I needed to breathe.*" She rolls her fingertips along the necklace.

Manuel wants to kiss her.

"It wasn't even signed and it was all she ever sent me. I don't even know what my mother's signature looks like, but I'm certain her *L* for Lucille is looped both on the top and bottom, big loops." She draws the letter with its curlicues in the air like a child.

Caro Mãe,

You have not written. I know you are angry but I need to know that you understand.

Pepsi has no mother. Life hasn't been easy for her but she's strong. She's what I've always wanted.

Mãe, remember when Jose brought that calf home, the one we had to tear from its mother's belly? He brought that calf through the front door … you yelled at him, struck him. He nursed it back; he slept in that barn for weeks, fed it milk in a bottle until it was strong and ready. You thought he was afraid to come back. But you were wrong, *Mãe.* He stayed in that barn because there was purpose for him, something to care for. It made him strong. It made me strong.

It's not your fault. I don't write this to hurt you—you are my mother and I love you. But I needed a purpose too.

I know you are disappointed in these words but I am not angry or bitter. The life you gave me was a gift but it is mine and I must cherish it. Please understand.

Manuel

"I NO THINK I GO, Andrew."

Pepsi trips against the bench as she clears the table. They both look at Manuel.

"Well ... guess you should rest up a while longer." Andrew speaks to Manuel but follows Pepsi, tries to lock his eyes with hers.

Pepsi goes into her room and busies herself with folding the laundry, not looking as her father leaves the house. She turns to see Manuel scanning her body, moving down to her legs, where his eyes stop. He knows she is uncomfortable with his stare but he can't seem to tear himself away. Manuel's glare is snapped by Andrew's shadow as it moves across her window. It will be a long walk to Brigus, via crooked roads and barren fields of rock toward his weekly night in town. Pepsi moves to shut her bedroom door.

"Pepsi?"

Manuel loves the way her name sounds. He rests his forehead against her door. She hasn't shut it in weeks. He waits a little longer before calling out again, and taps at the door.

"Pepsi?"

"Come in," and as quickly as the words roll off her tongue, Manuel opens the door and can see that she is nervous. She is fidgeting with the pleats of her skirt. She sits now at the edge of her bed looking out. At night, Manuel has caught her sitting in the same spot, rubbing oil of wintergreen—its familiar fresh scent was used to massage Manuel's joints—around her hardened stump, preparing it for the next day's pounding and grinding. Now, she just sits there, back straight, silently looking out the window. She moves the blanket over her leg. Manuel moves behind her small frame and runs a hand along her hair and down her neck. She catches his hand with her cheek and traps it there. Manuel sits beside her and moves his free hand under the blanket. She is tense but when she kisses his knuckles that rest in the crook of her neck, Manuel takes it as a sign, an invitation. His hand moves along her wooden leg then touches her brace— a tangle of warm wood and cold metal. Her back tenses. He doesn't flinch.

His other hand dislodges from her neck and shoulder and he cups her smallish face, forces her pleading eyes to meet his. Manuel drags the back of his hand down over the raised grain of the wooden shin. He kisses her papery eyelids. His hand flips over and his fingertips continue up her leg, traversing the stainless steel bridgework, up, up toward her inner thigh. She looks at him, her silence invites him further. He moves his hand down again and wedges a finger between the wooden leg and her worn stump. He nestles it there and feels a strange exhilaration. She pulls at her skirt, tries to cover her shame.

"Shhh … Manuel no hurt Pepsi."

She closes her eyes and feels his fingers on her brace, as if he made it flesh.

Caro Mãe,

I will continue to write in the hope that these letters will somehow make their way into your heart. You've never felt anything like it. In one day there can be a downpour of rain, blustering snow, and sunshine. The snow is quite nice but it's so cold. Andrew says it gets so cold your pee can freeze.

I'm sure you're preparing for Christmas, *Mãe.* I miss the smell of pine crushed beneath our feet, sweet masa, and the smell of our home in the damp night. I hope my siblings are all well. I can still picture them in my mind but I'm certain so much has changed. Please tell them I miss them.

Laughter is returning to this house. It lives in this country, I know. A house needs laughter.

I hope that when Albina reads these letters to you that you are not angry. Please write or let Jose or Candida write something … I long to hear from someone.

Albina, write something. Please let me know how all my news and thoughts are being received. She need not know.

Merry Christmas.
Manuel

HE DOESN'T WANT to think back. Although his heart aches for the familiar, he needs to look forward. There is a merciless rattle in his brain: It was fate that tossed him into the sea, alone and lost; It was fate that hooked him onto the line of a fisherman; It must then be fate that made Manuel turn up to that dove-grey sky that always visits after a storm—look up at the heavens only to find Pepsi. He will not tempt that fate. She has been good to him, nursed him and loved him. Manuel owes it to her to love her back.

"Pepsi!" Andrew's voice stabs through Manuel's thoughts. "Where are my pants?" he shouts from his room.

"They were reekin' of screech, soiled to the grain. So I washed them."

Pepsi has found a new confidence and strength. Andrew storms in from his room. Pepsi's eyes do not leave her father's. She will not let him win. He can't say anything for the longest time. Pepsi hums as she trusses the bird.

"That's what it's about, Manuel. Mark my words. You give them everything they could ever ask for only to have them walk on you like the dirt they think you are."

"Dad, I didn't—"

"Don't you 'Dad' me. Respect!" he sputters. "It's all I've ever asked of you in this house. Respect!" He struggles to put on his coat, then goes out and slams the door.

Manuel moves recklessly behind her, kisses her neck.

"Tell me, Pepsi—tell about that day." It is his favourite story. It is filled with everything he wants in life: beginning with sacrifice and ending with hope and promise. Manuel digs his hands under the neckline of her dress, holds the weight of her breasts.

"Well," she begins, welcoming the distraction, "that day ..." Pepsi turns and smiles before continuing. "That day, I was coming home from St. John's where I stupidly thought I could sell my pearls. I thought I could get enough money to get my hair done at a salon and maybe buy a pretty dress. A girl likes a pretty dress, Manuel. That lady at the pawnshop sat there in her stool behind the counter looking at her large black and white television. She saw me from the corner of her eye and pretended not to notice. I laid my pearls gently on top of the glass display. She bit one of the pearls with her greying teeth and showed me its plastic core, dropped the string of pearls back on the counter, *clickety-click*, all the while looking up at her television, and resumed tapping her fingers on the counter to our pet Juliette—a girl with a beautiful voice and perky smile. You'd like her, Manuel ..."

Manuel rubs her hardening nipple between his thumb and forefinger. She is comfortable with the way his calloused hands move across her body. When she turns her face to kiss him, she no longer looks awkward, afraid.

"Manuel, let me finish the story."

He knows she doesn't want him to stop and he knows the end of the story; the lady had made a mistake. The pearls were real. Her mother gave them to her. How she prayed during the bus ride home, prayed to all the saints in heaven. *Please, Jesus, give me a new leg—flesh and bone ...* How she imagined her leg growing, a ticklish tingling, and then, her final prayer: *Dear Lord, please give me a man—a family to take care of.*

"That very next morning, like every other morning, I went down to the shore to meet my father. When I saw him rowing in toward the shallows, his boat cutting through the foam, I saw that he'd brought me a gift richer than a new leg or real pearls—he'd brought me you." She breathes out her last words, then playfully whips his face with the damp tea towel.

Caro Mãe,

I'm writing this on the eve of Christmas. It is now two full months and I must beg your forgiveness. Is this why you have not written? Or is it because I have made it clear I have no plans of returning? Before I left I told you that our small island held nothing for me. I still believe this to be true. What is it, *Mãe*? Tell me.

I find myself exhausted by the pace at which the images of life back home run across my mind: growing up as a boy, patches of green fields and beds of calla lily, Gilberto—our toothless dog, my brown-eyed siblings, your hard-working hands against your black dress and veil. And then in a wave I think of my pressed cotton shirts and new leather shoes with their tight shoelaces, windows that would not open, houses too narrow. I gulp for air but there is nothing but chalk and dust. But these are my images, my burdens. Believe me when I say I do not blame you, *Mãe*.

My thoughts are with you all this Christmas.

Manuel

THE DAY BEGINS filled with the joy and promise that only Christmas can bring. Pepsi has gotten up early to get everything done: the chicken is stuffed, the dough is pounded into plump balls and allowed to rise in the kitchen's heat. Manuel imagines he is in his own little house, not Andrew's. Children are playing around the tinselled tree, a girl and a boy. They're trying to peek at their presents. Manuel is looking through the window outside. Pepsi is cooking up a wonderful meal, stuffing and roast potatoes with *chouriço*, and she's making his favourite cod dish to remind him of home. Manuel walks in, twirls his daughter then throws the boy high into the air and catches the giggling copy of himself securely in his arms ...

"Manuel, Father didn't come home last night. Do you know where he got to?"

"I go look for him, Pepsi. You no worry."

Manuel circles the fields, then runs to the cliffs to see if there is any unfortunate evidence. For hours he looks along the coast, down toward the foamy cove, then scans the landscape. He does not want to go back empty handed. He returns only to hear some muffled shouts coming from inside the shed. Andrew is curled around an empty jug. He looks up and shields his eyes from the white sky. He then smiles at Manuel. It has been a while since Andrew has smiled at Manuel in that way. It feels good.

Manuel drapes Andrew over his shoulder like the animals he drags to the tree. Andrew is much larger than Manuel, big and heavy. Manuel manages to drop him into his chair. Pepsi slams a lid onto the counter. Andrew struggles but cannot pull himself up to the table.

"Everything is cold," she says. The candles have burned down to nothing.

"*Feliz Natal*, Andrew." Manuel smiles.

Pepsi decides not to ruin the day further. "Dad, will you cut the bird now?" she asks.

"Why don't you ask the man of the house?" he slurs.

His words are filled with bitterness. Manuel pretends they have not hurt him. Pepsi is about to say something until her father breaks in: "I have a gift for you, Manuel."

Manuel looks to Pepsi, who twists her hair into tight ringlets.

"Dad, please don't embarrass me." She struggles to get up. "Please don't do this to me."

"Shush!" He pounds the table with his knotted fist. Pepsi tries to push herself away but Andrew pins her small hand firmly against the tabletop. She lowers herself back onto her chair and sits hunched over. Her eyes dart across the room then up to the wooden beams before she drops her chin against her breastbone. "This is still my house, though, and I want to say something."

He narrows his eyes at Manuel as if daring him to a challenge.

"Manuel. We have taken you in and treated you like family."

Manuel lowers his head, ready for his censure.

"You well know no man could'uv done more for you. It's time you made plans, I'd say."

With these words he lifts himself from his chair and half stumbles toward the Christmas tree. He falls to the floor, where he clumsily searches for a gift. He crawls back to the table with a smug grin. The present he clutches is wrapped in the brown paper used to wrap meat at the butcher's. There are smeared traces of blood on the parchment. He flings the packet across the table as he pulls himself up and takes his seat.

"Thank you, Andrew." Manuel is unsure of the offering. "I bless by you ... and Pepsi. Thank you."

Manuel begins to work his fingers around the package. He glances up, expecting to meet Pepsi's gaze. He's confused by the way she stares at his hands unravelling the string, flipping the gift over before lifting the centre fold. Her eyes look at nothing else. In a split second his letters slip from his hands and fan themselves on the table.

The room begins to spin. Manuel glimpses the smirk on Andrew's face, the tree, the perfectly browned chicken sitting in the middle of the set table, gleaming plates and flickering candles. The images swarm in his head. Bile rises from his stomach, sharp and sour. Then he sees Pepsi getting up and tripping over her lifeless leg. She cannot look at him. She falls down and drags herself the rest of the way across the floor. She reaches her threshold, pushes the door open with her shoulder and is swallowed by the dark mouth of her room. Manuel sits still and numb. The door closes. He hears the click of the lock and the din of his own silence over her father's simmering laughter.

Marina Endicott

Marina Endicott was born in Golden, British Columbia, and grew up in Nova Scotia and Toronto. She worked as an actor and director before moving to London, England, where she began to write fiction. Since returning to Canada in 1984, she has worked as dramaturge at the Saskatchewan Playwrights Centre and associate dramaturge at the Banff Playwrights Colony. She now teaches creative writing at the University of Alberta.

Endicott's first novel, *Open Arms,* was nominated for the Amazon/Books in Canada First Novel Award in 2002 and serialized on CBC Radio's *Between the Covers.* Her stories have been featured in *Coming Attractions* and were shortlisted for both the Journey Prize and the Western Magazine Awards. She's had three plays produced, and her long poem, *The Policeman's Wife, some letters,* was shortlisted for the CBC Literary Awards in 2006. She is currently at work on a novel about the Belle Auroras, a sister-trio vaudeville act touring the Canadian prairies in 1909, as well as series of young adult novels called *Time in Hand.*

Good to a Fault

BY MARINA ENDICOTT

Finalist 2008

⌘

1. Left turn

Thinking about herself and the state of her soul, Clara Purdy drove to the bank one hot Friday in July. The other car came from nowhere, speeding through on the yellow, going so fast it was almost safely past when Clara's car caught it. She was pushing on the brake, a ballet move, graceful—pulling back on the wheel with both arms as she rose, her foot standing on the brake—and then a terrible crash, a painful extended rending sound, when the metals met. The sound kept on longer than you'd expect, Clara thought, having time to think as the cars scraped sides and changed each other's direction, as the metal ripped open and bent and assumed new shapes.

They stopped. The motion stopped. Then the people from the other car came spilling out. The doors opened and like milk boiling over on the stove, bursting to the boil, they all frothed out onto the pavement. It seemed they came out the windows, but it was only the doors.

An old woman was last, prying herself out stiffly. Her lap was covered with redness, roses growing there and swelling downwards, and she began to screech on one note. The man, the driver, was already shouting. The line of curses streaming out of his mouth hung visible in the heavy air. Their car was the colour of butterscotch pudding, burnt pudding crusted on it in rust. The whole driver's side had crumpled inward, like pudding-skin when it is disturbed.

Clara's ears were not working properly. There was a vacuum around her where no sound could ring. She could see all the mouths moving. She swallowed to clear her ears, but pressure was not the problem. What had she done? All of this.

The membrane of silence burst. There was the noise—Clara felt it hit. Her body vibrated like a tuning fork. She kept her mouth shut. She put her hands up to her lips and held them closed with her fingers.

The man was flailing his arms in big circles, his head jutted forward to threaten her. 'What kind of a driver are you?" he was yelling, for the benefit of everyone nearby. "My fucking *kids* can drive better than that! My *kids*!"

The little girl sitting on the pavement looked almost happy, as if her pinched face had relaxed now that some dangerous thing had actually happened. Clara sat down beside her. Strange to be sitting down right on the street, she thought. The road was warm. Cars whipped by, their wheels huge from this low down.

The man strode over, almost prancing. "You fucking *hit* us! What were you doing?"

"I'm sorry," Clara said.

It was out, the whole thing was her fault. In the case of a disputed left-hand turn, the turning party is always at fault. The man's face was blotched with red stuff. His hair was dusty. He might be thirty, or forty. She should be getting his insurance information, giving him hers.

She got up, trembling knees making her slow. The women kept wailing. The younger one, a baby clutched to her breast, came rushing at Clara—to strike her, Clara thought, flinching away.

"My baby! You could of killed us!" The woman's shirt flapped open, Clara saw her pale breast, there in the middle of the street. And then her eyes, glaring dark in her shocked face. Shreds of skin stuck to her shirt. Whose—the baby's? He lolled in her arms, maybe unconscious, his blue sleeper stained with matter, redness. Clara reached out to touch the poor little creature's forehead, but the mother leaped back, crying, "Get away! Get away from us!"

The old woman was stupidly plucking her bloody skirt away from her body, bits of flesh falling. Wherever Clara turned there were more. A boy, bleeding, holding his head. His clothes were dirty, he must have been knocked out onto the road. Where was the other one? Clara caught at the girl's shirt and hauled her back from the other lane of traffic.

"Get your hands off her," the mother shouted. "What are you trying to do now?" There was no way to speak, to tell what she had meant. She had been driving to the bank on her lunch hour. The bank would be going on without her—how tenderly she longed for the line-up, and herself standing there, safe.

The younger child sat down on the road, feeling his head. He seemed to be poking into his skull, his finger buried in blood. Clara was afraid that this was hell, that she had died when the cars hit; that maybe there was no such thing as death, that she would be living this way from now on, in hell. Then the police came, and there was a siren winding closer, so the ambulance was coming.

Clara knelt down on the black street beside the boy and took his hand, pulling it gently away from his scalp. "I think you've got a cut there," she whispered. "Give me your hand. Let the doctors look at it, you don't want to make it worse."

He stared up at her, eyes flickering over her face, trying to read her like a book, it seemed.

"They'll be here to help us in a minute," she said. "I'm sorry, I'm so sorry."

A PARAMEDIC, CLEAN AND YOUNG, leaned in the window to say they were taking the grandmother away, and the nursing mother. The police officer nodded, signalling something, so that the paramedic grunted and stood upright. He banged once on the door to say goodbye. Another ambulance arrived. The children and the man were packed into it. In the cramped back seat of the police cruiser, Clara was left to the last. The paramedics insisted that she go too, although she said she was all right. The second tow-truck was there already taking her car.

They bundled her up onto the bench in the back, and she sat down on the edge.

"What will they do with the Dart?" the girl asked. "All our stuff is in it."

"We were living in our car," the man said, accusing Clara.

The paramedic asked him to be quiet, so he could check his pulse, or to stop the quarrel. They were all silent, after that.

IT WAS CHERRY JUICE on the grandmother. Mrs. Pell, she was called. She'd been eating a big bag of Okanagan cherries. There was a little blood, from the children, but most of the frightening mess was juice and pulp. The baby was all right. The little boy, Trevor, had a bandage on his head, but it was only a scalp wound, no concussion; instead of using stitches they had glued it shut with blue space-age glue. The girl's scraped arm had been cleaned. The father was fine.

But the mother was not well. She had a fever, and there were clusters of tiny bruises. Not from the accident. The emergency nurse stared at them, touching with her fingers.

The father roamed the halls. The mother was put into a room, the baby lying beside her on the narrow hospital bed. The children sat silent beside their mother. Not knowing what else to do, Clara arranged for the TV to be connected, whenever the technician next came round.

CLARA PURDY HAD BEEN DRIFTING for some time in a state of mild despair, forty-three and nothing to show for it. Her racing heart woke her from dreams at three each morning to fling the covers away, angry with herself for this sadness, this terror. Six billion people were worse off. She had all the money she needed, no burdens—she was nothing, a comfortable speck in the universe. She felt smothered, or buried alive, or already dead.

Her mother had died two years before, leaving her the plain bungalow in a quiet area of town. Whether she wanted it or not. There she lived, like someone's widow, all alone. She worked in insurance, at the same firm for—it would be twenty years next winter. The time seemed too gauzy to bear the weight of twenty years.

Clara imagined that people saw her as pleasant enough, intelligent, kind. A bit stuck-up, she got that from her mother. But sad, that she'd never had children; never gotten over her short, stupid marriage; never travelled or gone back to school and made something of herself.

Her self was an abandoned sampler, half the letters unstitched, the picture in the middle still vague. Looking after elderly parents had made her elderly. The eight months of her stillborn marriage might have been her whole life. She had returned home to care for her father as he died, and then stayed for her mother's long illness, and nothing had pried her out again. She was too reserved, maybe; she'd made a mess of her few brief attachments since the divorce.

Instead of the heavy work of being with people, she gardened, read books on spirituality, and kept the house trim. She missed her beautiful, exasperating mother. When she was sad, she bought expensive clothes, or went to a movie by herself—two movies in a row sometimes. Anyway, she had no excuse for sadness. A grown woman doesn't pine away because her difficult mother died, because her father had died long before—or because she'd trickled her life away on an old tragedy that now seemed overblown.

She went to the Anglican church, to the early service, Book of Common Prayer first and third Sundays. Not *in the church* the way her mother had been, managing and holding court. Clara was not on the coffee list, and did not read the lesson: she was shy in a certain way, not to make an issue of it, and did not find it easy to speak in public loudly enough to be heard, even with that high-tech tiny microphone on the long black stalk. She did the flowers when her turn came round in the rotation, but after church, and in the dark when she awoke at 3 a.m., she thought continually about how useless she was in the world.

One Saturday a twisted woman stood in line ahead of her at the grocery store. Old but undaunted, this woman had complicated aluminum crutches and a large backpack. All business. The clerk helped load her grocery bags into the backpack, and eased it up onto her back—they must have done this before. Driving home, Clara saw the old woman moving along, spiderly with her crutches and pack. Clara slowed down, wanting to offer her a lift, but she had seemed very proud in the grocery store. It would be miserable to be rebuffed. Clara let her foot fall more firmly on the accelerator. The radio was spouting some story about a mother who had drowned her two children in the bathtub. The neighbour, on the radio, was saying she had heard the children crying, and that at the time she'd been grateful when the crying had stopped, but now she wished she'd—Clara snapped it off.

The world was full of people struggling along with heavy suitcases, poor men dawdling in doorways until they could get their eyes to focus on the sidewalk, children with bloody noses darting past on skateboards—it was laughable, when you began to watch for who needed help. She saw an elderly gentleman fall painfully to his knees, getting off a bus, and that time she almost made herself take action; but a boy got there before her. He helped the old man up and dusted off his trousers, shaking his head at the state of the streets. A native boy skinny and bruised, fit for care himself.

There was some barrier between Clara and the world that she couldn't budge. Sometimes she thought she would have to go and work in Calcutta with the Sisters of Charity. Everything was wrong with the world—she could not keep on doing nothing.

IN EMERGENCY, Clara was the last to be examined and let go. She phoned her office to say she wouldn't be back that afternoon, then bought magazines and puzzle books and went upstairs to 3C, the multi-purpose ward where the mother had been put. The whole family was huddled around her on the bed closest to the door. Old Mrs. Pell was sitting on the orange leatherette chair. It would recline, Clara knew from the months her father had spent in hospital, but the grandmother was sitting up, staring at the door. She must have seen Clara, but she said nothing, didn't even blink her turtle eyes.

The husband turned his head from where he sat on the bed, then stood abruptly, dislodging the baby from its comfort and startling the older children.

"You've got a nerve coming up here," he said, sullen rather than aggressive. Clara understood: she should have brought more than magazines. There was a machine in the elevator alcove. But when Clara returned with five cans of juice, only the mother was left in the room.

"They went outside for a smoke," she said.

"The children too?"

"Well, what was he supposed to do with them? I've got my hands full here."

The baby lay still beside her, mouth open, in a calm stupor. Two empty formula bottles on the bed table. Clara added the cans of juice, shifting them around to make room.

"It wasn't your fault," the mother said. Lying there pale and skinny, she said that. But it wasn't true. Clara was an insurance adjuster, and knew about fault.

"My name is Clara," she said, as if that was the correct thing to do, introduce yourself to the person you've put in hospital.

"Lorraine Gage."

"Purdy, sorry. I'm Clara Purdy."

"My husband is Clayton. And the kids are Darlene and Trevor," Lorraine said formally. "And this is Pearce."

"What a nice name, Pearce. Have they—do they know what's—" *Wrong* seemed like the wrong word to use. She sat in the orange chair, so Lorraine didn't have to crane her neck uncomfortably. "What's going on with you?"

"They're doing tests. They took some blood already. They'll be back to get me pretty soon, some scan or other. It won't hurt."

"No, that's good."

"There's something—I haven't been too good for a while. The crash just made me notice."

The baby stirred. Lorraine folded her arm more gently around him where she had been tightening her hold. "All right, it's all right," she said to him, softer than Clara had yet heard her. "This is one good baby," Lorraine said. "My others were good too, but this one! So easy! Hardly know he's there except he holds your hand. Look."

She lifted a corner of the sheet, showing the baby's fist wrapped around her thumb. Tiny, even fingers, tiny fingernails.

"Even in his sleep," Clara said, shaking her head as if it was a miracle. Anything was a miracle, any moment of ordinary time just then.

The husband stuck his head around the corner. "Found the TV," he said. "Lounge down the hall."

"Okay," Lorraine said. "I know where you're at."

"Yeah. Button up your overcoat," he said, to Clara's surprise. He let go of the door handle and disappeared.

Lorraine smiled. Her teeth were jumbled and not in good shape, the two eye teeth sharply jabbing over the others, but the smile warmed her face.

"You belong to me," she said, and it took Clara a minute to realize that she was filling in the line of the song, not telling Clara that her life was no longer her own.

WHILE THEIR DAD WAS BUYING CIGARETTES, not paying attention to them, Darlene tugged Trevor's hand and pulled him into the stairwell. Flights of grimy metal steps wheeled endlessly upward and downward, making her dizzy. But they were going to get in trouble if they were always hanging around in the lounge by themselves. If they stayed out of sight they would not be kicked out, they could stay close to their mom.

"You be Peter and I'll be Penny," she said. "If anybody asks us."

This was 3. They climbed up to 7, and then up the single longer flight to a dead end, with one door. That probably led to the roof.

Quiet up there. The stairs were not too dirty. Somebody had tossed a brown paper bag with a banana skin and a whole apple in it. Darlene washed the apple carefully with spit and polished it on her T-shirt. Trevor's legs were shaking. Darlene pushed up against him, anchoring him to the cool concrete wall so he could calm down. She and Trevor ate the apple, bite for bite, and sat without talking.

LORRAINE AND CLARA WERE STILL ALONE, reading magazines, when an orderly arrived. There was some small inconvenience getting Lorraine onto the gurney. Clara helped by holding the baby's head away from the belt. He had downy hair, and a pale red birthmark almost faded at his nape. His neck was small. The skin was smooth there; her fingers traced the mark.

"You come too," Lorraine said.

The attendant seemed to think that was normal. Clara hesitated, but someone would have to hold the baby during the test, and the grandmother had vanished. They wheeled along corridors and into a different elevator, down a few floors, more halls. The orderly left them parked outside an unmarked door and went inside. He came out, and left.

There was a considerable wait.

"Jesus, I could use a cigarette," Lorraine said, her voice distorted from lying flat.

"I'm afraid you—" Clara stopped, hearing herself sounding like her mother, sweetly domineering.

"Well, I know that! They don't let you smoke in hospitals, I know that. I don't let them smoke around the baby anyways. It's no good for them, second-hand smoke."

"Smokers in my office building have to go around the back now. There's a dirty overhang where they leave the trash, and you'll see six or seven people huddled under there in a snowstorm."

"Got to have their smokes, though."

"I smoked myself," Clara said. "Then my father had cancer, and it was easier to quit."

Smoke seemed to be winding around them in vapourish tendrils. The possibility of a long drag, breath you could see. Proof of life. Clara had not wanted a cigarette so badly for years. She could feel her fingers falling into place as if they held one.

"I don't smoke much any more," Lorraine said. "Late at night I'll have one of Clayton's."

"Well, if I could do that, one or two a day, I'd still be smoking," Clara said.

"Yeah, lots of people can't."

They fell into silence.

A few minutes later the baby woke. He did not cry, but he moved restlessly, his mouth pursing and his fist searching. He gnawed on his curled fingers till they were wet, until Clara asked if she should run and find another bottle.

"Don't go," Lorraine said. "I can nurse him, it's okay." Her eyes stayed on Clara, rather than straying to the baby. She knew where he was.

"I'll stay," Clara said to reassure her.

The door finally opened, and a technician in a lead apron came out to steer the gurney through. She gave Clara the baby to hold and said it would be a few minutes.

Clara stood there in the hall, suddenly alone. No nurses, no station. She began to walk back and forth along the windowed hallway near the closed door, jiggling the baby slightly up and down. He liked up and down better than side to side, she found. She found it astonishing that the baby did not cry or find her frightening or frustrating. He seemed to have forgotten his hunger. His fist closed around her fingers and he brought her hand close to his mouth and then stared, transfixed, at the size or shape or texture of her skin. The smell, she thought. Probably mostly soap. Different from his mother, at any rate.

At the end of the hall a low windowsill looked like a good place to sit. She let him stare, first at the glass, and then, his focus visibly altering, out at the courtyard garden below. He held on to her blouse with one hand, his perfect miniature fingers clutching the silk into even gathers.

No one came down the hall, no one disturbed them. Far in the distance, Clara could hear machinery rumbling and whirring. She could imagine the scan moving over Lorraine, and Lorraine trying to lie still, trying not to be afraid. Pearce put one hand on the glass, looking at the empty garden.

DARLENE LEFT TREVOR SLEEPING ON THE STAIRS and went down alone. At each landing shiny linoleum halls ran away in every direction. Picking a floor, she wandered quietly along. Every room she passed held people in flimsy gowns coughing or lying suspiciously still. On TV when they knew people were dead a blue light flashed on and off. *Code Blue.*

She was mostly invisible, but one nurse at a desk asked her, "Are you lost?"

"No," Darlene said, not quite stopping. "My dad is having an operation to his heart, I'm just waiting to see how it turns out."

The nurse looked at her. "What's your name?"

"Melody Fairchild," Darlene said. "I'll go back and wait with my mom. She's pretty upset. I was looking for a place to get juice for my baby brother."

The nurse rolled her chair backwards to the little fridge for a couple of boxes of apple juice and handed them over the counter, then added a pack of cookies from her drawer. A bell rang somewhere so she stopped paying attention to Darlene. Maybe it was a blue light going off.

The lobby? She could check the payphones for quarters and look in the shop. But she should go back for Trevor. She found the stairwell and ran up all those spiralling, echoing metal steps. But the landing was empty, he was gone. Or this was the wrong set of stairs.

A DOCTOR—too young and pretty to be real—arrived to talk to Lorraine. The husband had come back from the lounge with the little boy trailing cautiously after him, wanting to see Lorraine, but when the doctor entered the husband edged toward the door, an awkward beetle trying to scuttle away without being seen.

"Why don't I take the children downstairs for some supper?" Clara asked Lorraine. It was after six.

Lorraine said, "Clay?"

"I'll give the baby to Mom," the husband said, taking him, and out he went.

They couldn't all leave her, Clara thought, but the doctor must have been used to avoidance. "We just have a few questions," she said, making it mild. "Dr. Porteous will come by too, in a few minutes. He's the consultant."

Lorraine's eyes were slightly too wide open, the whites of her eyes showing. But to the little boy she said calmly enough, "Go get some supper with Clara, that's a great idea. You'll be fine with her."

The little girl hung at the door, a shadow. She glared at the boy like he'd done something wrong.

Clara did not try to take their hands. She went to the door and let them follow. In the elevator she said, as if she knew what to do with children, "Darlene, can you push the one marked *L*? Trevor can push the button on the way back up."

In the cafeteria line-up the little girl snaked out her hand to Clara's wrist. Without volition, Clara's hand pulled back. The girl's eyes rose sidelong, diamond-edged, to check what she was thinking.

"Where did you get this?" she asked, almost accusing. It was a bracelet, six or seven strands of beads in different colours, pretty.

"I got it—oh, in some store, I can't remember which," Clara said, forcing herself not to turn away, not to be cruel.

"In the Saan store, I bet," the girl said, triumphant. "I saw it there!"

Clara wanted to give it to her, but couldn't find a way to do it that would make up for having pulled her hand back. Suddenly everything made her so tired! She must have a vitamin deficiency. Or it was the trauma. She never shopped at Saan. *Shoddy goods*—her mother's voice rang in her ears.

"Yes," she said. "I think it was Saan."

The children ate their French fries. She had to go back to the counter three times for ketchup: twice for Trevor and once, separately, for Darlene. Trevor put mustard on his, too, but he had already filled his pockets with mustard packs himself.

"It's a pity to waste those chicken nuggets," Clara said.

"Oh, we won't *waste* them!" Trevor said, his voice squeakier than she'd expected.

"We'll take them up for Dad and Gran," Darlene said, patient with her rich ignorance.

Clara jumped up and went back for roast chicken dinners for the husband and the grandmother. The children loved the stainless steel hats meant to keep the dinners warm. They begged to carry one plate each, so she let them. Trevor dropped his right in front of the elevators.

"Better than dropping it *in* the elevator," Clara said, pleased with how calmly she took it. They told the morose kitchen helper about the spill, and got another dinner.

Upstairs, Lorraine was alone in the room. The lights were out, except a small bulb over the sink. Red from the sun's low angle streamed in the window.

Clara said, "Trevor, will you carry it very carefully?" He nodded, glad to be given a second chance. "Take these down to the lounge to your father and your grandmother, then." Darlene walked behind Trevor so he would not be distracted.

Lorraine was lying on her side in a fresh hospital gown, with the bed lowered.

"The doctor came in," she told Clara. Forgetting that Clara had been there, or maybe having no other way to begin telling it. "They think, they're pretty sure, I've got cancer."

She had the fortitude to say it right out like that, no hesitation. What kind, was all Clara could think to ask. "I'm sorry," she said, instead.

"It's not your fault," Lorraine said, and almost laughed.

It was the second time she'd said that to Clara.

DOWN IN THE LOBBY the booth selling stuffed animals was closing for the evening. A little cat caught Clara's eye, with a beaded collar like her bracelet, for Darlene, and a small mottled-green pterodactyl for Trevor. She didn't have the gall to go back up and disturb the family again, so she shoved the toys into the bottom of her bag.

At home, Clara called Evie, the office manager. Easier to deal with Evie than Barrett, the Regional Director, whose petty vanity required constant coddling. "I'm sorry to bother you in the evening like this, but I'm going to be away for a few more days," she said.

"Are you hurt? Is it worse than you thought?" Evie asked, relishing catastrophe.

"It's not—I'm fine, but—" Rather than explain the whole thing, and have Evie talking it over with Mat and the others, Clara said, "I am a little shaken up. I think I'll need a few days. The Curloe inspection was put off till the nineteenth anyway, and otherwise ..."

"Oh, no, you stay home. You get some good rest. You're no good to us if you're a nervous wreck, are you? What a thing to happen. How are the other people?"

"Oh, they're fine, they're fine, no one was badly hurt."

"But it could have been. A baby, too, you said?"

Had she said that? Why go into any detail at all? Because she had been buzzing from the accident still, frantic with dreadful possibilities, words spilling over.

"Evie, I've got to go, I'm going to lie down now."

She lay in bed wakeful, the accident replaying in her mind. She said her prayers, naming each of them, and prayed that Lorraine's cancer would be healed, as far as she could reach to God, knowing that it would be no use.

2. In clover

Early Saturday morning, Clara gave up on sleep and went back to the hospital. The husband and the children and Mrs. Pell must have slept in the visitors' lounge. Clara had brought a box of muffins, and juice for the children. Underneath a stack of magazines she'd packed some puzzle books and an old etch-a-sketch from the hall closet, which Trevor was happy to see.

The children were grubby. Clara offered to wash their faces, but Clayton declined. In a huff with her, or in some permanent state of huff he lived in.

He took Trevor off to the men's room. Darlene went by herself to the women's. Ten minutes later Clara found her there, sitting on the sink counter with her legs folded under her, ferociously reading a home decorating magazine. Clara backed out—but then, remembering the toys in her purse, pushed the bathroom door open again, and set the little white cat on the counter beside Darlene.

"This cat reminded me of you," she said, shy about giving a present.

Darlene looked at it but did not touch it.

"I thought you might like the bead collar," Clara said. So Darlene wouldn't have to speak, she held out the other toy, Trevor's. "And will you give this one to Trevor?"

Darlene unfolded her stick-thin legs. She put the magazine down, carefully away from the splashes by the sink. "It's a pterodactyl," she said. "I'll tell him what it is." She got down, sliding the cat along the counter, and took the pterodactyl. Clara held the door open for her, and Darlene ran down to the lounge, her bare feet making no noise, the hospital already home.

Lorraine's bed was rumpled and she looked ugly and uncomfortable. A nurse was settling an older woman back into the bed to the left of the door. Lorraine strained herself upwards, trying to get into a half-sitting position.

"Some kind of lymphoma is what they think," she said.

Clara nodded.

"It's weird to say it out loud," Lorraine said.

"I know."

"It's a shock. They tried to tell me about it last night, they sent in an older doctor in the evening. The little bruises, those are petechiae. I just thought they looked kind of pretty, like a brooch of moles."

They were pretty. Little constellations, a sweet dark splatter of paint on Lorraine's arm, another patch on her leg just above the knee. Now they seemed hostile as snake bites.

"I hadn't heard of them before," Clara said.

"Me neither. Or I'd have known to go get looked at." Lorraine moved fretfully in the bed, tugged at her pillow "These are lumps of dough. I wish I had my little pillow out of the car."

They were silent.

"I've got this fever," Lorraine said, after a moment. "They left me a bunch of pamphlets. *Your Cancer and You.*" The stack of papers sat, radioactive, on the night table.

"You look a little flushed," Clara said, hating the sound of her own voice so falsely, unspontaneously cheerful.

"They want me to stay in till they can get it down. There's—a bunch of more tests to do, there's—" Lorraine stopped talking.

The woman in the other bed moaned behind the curtain. Then she was silent too.

"Ovarian," Lorraine whispered. "She had a rough night."

Clara's head was aching badly She couldn't seem to stop hearing her own words, and Lorraine's too, repeated in her mind during the silences. Fever, *fever*, fever, *more tests*, more, a little flushed, *a little flushed.*

"I think they'll probably let us stay here—them, I mean—one more night, but it isn't too good for the kids, in the lounge. I want them to go. There's some kind of a—some accommodation, Clayton's getting the details, if there's room."

Clara murmured something, one of those noises which encourage further conversation without committing the speaker to an exact opinion.

"They shouldn't of seen any of this."

No. Clara could see the dark circles under Trevor's eyes. Even the baby Pearce seemed lethargic, less comfortable and safe than right after the accident. Lorraine's distress infected them all, she thought. And nothing to do all day but wander from the TV lounge to the room.

"It's hard on everyone," she said. Innocuous enough, but the husband, coming in, took exception to it anyway.

"Hard on you?" he sneered. "Hard to sit and watch the results of what you did?"

Lorraine pushed him with her pale hand. "Quit it, Clay" she said. "She didn't give it to me."

"This whole thing," he began, and then petered out, his face pulling down in the chin. He had a sharp face, almost good-looking, with smooth beige skin. His chin was as small and rounded as a girl's, and he could look defeated in an instant. It must make him seem vulnerable, Clara thought, trying to make out what Lorraine had seen in him. He was not big, but had a springy build with muscles stretched over his bones. He looked strong but unhealthy, surly and eager at the same instant. A dog who's been badly treated, and has gone vicious, but wants you to fuss over him anyway.

The minutes stretched by in a silence that Lorraine seemed to want.

He sat quietly enough on the end of her bed, but couldn't settle. He shifted and re-crossed his legs every few seconds, until Clara found her own legs tensing, watching him. His eyes darted too quickly checking Lorraine, checking the clock, the window, Clara—to see what mischief she was making?—back to his own hands, flexing and fisting on whichever pant leg was uppermost at the time. He didn't wear a wedding ring, Clara noticed, but many men did not. Lorraine had one, and an engagement ring, nestled close together as they were made to do. People's Jewellers, Clara thought, before she could stop herself. Or Wal-Mart.

But just when she had dismissed their marriage and their whole lives this way, Clayton leaned forward on the bed and grasped Lorraine's hand. He bent his mouth to her curled fingers, and then bent his head farther forward, over her sheeted lap, and said, "No."

Lorraine brought her other hand to curve over his head through his dirty hair. She said it too. "No, I know. It can't be."

Clara got up without making a sound, and left the room.

THE LANDING AT THE TOP OF THE STAIRWELL was cold, the second evening. She should go steal Trevor a blanket from an empty bed, Darlene thought. It was probably warmer out on the roof. The big metal door had one of those release bars. She leaned on the bar, feeling it give. If she pushed it all the way down the alarm might go off. There was no sign, though.

She pushed it anyway. No sound. The heavy door swung open. She nudged Trevor with her toe and took his little springy fingers, and they stepped out into the evening darkness, and the warmth. Tarry black gel oozing up through the pebble coat of the wide expanse of roof. The wall all around was too low, be careful!

Darlene got Trevor to hold her wrist while she leaned over to see cars and people like ants, toy ambulances going into the garage door down there. If she fell, someone would scoop her up and put her in bed next to her mom, her legs strung up to the ceiling in white casts.

She was going to throw up. She twisted up and backwards and grabbed Trevor's arm, almost yanking them both over, *whoo!* But not quite.

They were okay. They sat there. The soft black tar smelled good. And it was warmer out in the air.

ON SUNDAY MORNING, after a second sleepless night, Clara found herself in tears during the Hosanna. She hated crying in church and had stayed away for months after her mother's death. But here she was again, eyes raised up to the wooden rafters of the roof. No heaven visible up there. Some water spilled over, before she got angry enough to stop.

After coffee hour, not knowing what else to do, Clara stayed to talk to the priest, Paul Tippett. His own life seemed to be a shambles; she didn't know how he could help, sitting in his poky office with a cup of weak coffee in front of him. Clara held hers on her lap.

"What is the worst of it?" he asked her, when she had explained about the accident. His large-boned, unworldly face was kind.

"The worst? Oh!" Clara had to look away, her eyes half-filling again.

"Take your time," he said, his gentle expression undisturbed. He must be used to tears, of course; but not from her, she'd hardly spoken to him before now.

He listened.

"I see what they need," she finally said, "but I am unwilling to help." But that was not it, she was not unwilling—she was somehow stupidly ashamed of wanting to help.

It was probably part of his training not to speak, to let people go on.

"The mother, Lorraine, is very ill. From before the accident, nobody knew about it. It's cancer, lymphoma. Advanced. Her family has nowhere to go. They were living in their car, and the two older children are—and the baby ten months old, too young to be without his mother—how will they cope with a baby in a shelter? The grandmother, I suppose, because the father is not a—but she's not—"

Clara stopped babbling.

She had worked in shelters, serving supper, making beds, setting up the cardboard dividers that shut each person off from the next, two feet away. It was not possible for her to send them to a shelter. During the Hosanna, in the high cascading descant, she'd known what she had to do. If any of this was true, if there was God. She had wanted useful work; this was it. And if there was no God, then even more, she had to do it.

"I don't want them in my house," she said. But maybe she did.

"No one could plausibly expect you to take them in," the priest said. "There are agencies …"

"It's not what's plausible, it's what I ought to do."

"You've visited them," he commended her. "Many would not think to do as much."

Many would not think to do as much, she thought, almost laughing. What a convoluted construction. A life in the pulpit. Except there was no pulpit in their church, he just stepped forward, with his tiny chest-hung microphone waiting to catch every word as it dripped from his lips. She stood up, needing to move, and put her coffee cup down on his overflowing desk.

"Visiting the hospital is—nothing! My life does not seem very worthwhile," she said. "Or even real." And that just sounded stupid and self-involved.

He looked thoughtful. Or was honest enough not to argue with her assessment.

With a sudden welling of defeat, Clara left.

The priest shifted her cup to a more stable spot, and rubbed his thumb along his smooth desk-drawer ledge. Her dress, deep indigo or iris purple, seemed to stay hovering in the room, filled his eyes still.

Clara Purdy: single, childless of course, took care with her appearance; fortyish, and not in good spirits for some time since her mother's death. He'd never had to deal with the mother. English, some cousin of an earl's, wasn't she? A piece of work, by all accounts. (*"They fuck you up, your mum and dad."*) Her funeral had been his first duty at St. Anne's, the week he and Lisanne had arrived. In parish archive photos the mother was aloof, fine-boned, with a 30s filmstar glamour even in old age. Clara must take after her father. Odd to think of a middle-aged woman chiefly as a daughter. Pleasant enough, quiet, careful. Insurance, at Gilman-Stott—but then the contradiction of that flower-petal colour. Lisanne admired her clothes, or envied them, depending on the mood of the day. Almost-Easter, true violet, perfect purple. Porphyry, periphery, preface ... He drew back from the precipice.

Carnelian, or more than red—true coral for Lisanne, who would be waiting for him at home, fretful muscles sharp behind her black-wire eyebrows. The hospital chaplain was away all summer in England, locum at a parish in the Lake District. Maybe Lisanne would have liked that. Cerulean. Paul wondered how he could bear another hospital visit.

He took both cups and emptied them in the meeting hall sink. All the other cups had been bleached and dried and put away. He rinsed these last two and stacked them in the cupboard damp—rebellion.

CLARA WALKED THROUGH HER THREE-BEDROOM BUNGALOW, working out where to put everyone. The grandmother in the guest room, the baby with her, in a wicker laundry basket padded and lined with a flannel sheet. The father: the pull-out couch in the small bedroom that had been her own father's den. The grandmother couldn't sleep on that thing. Nowhere left to put the children but her own bed. She cleared the soul-help books off the bedside table and piled them in the garage; she pulled off the linen cover and replaced it with a striped one, made up the other beds, and found towels for everyone, as if they were guests.

She looked around at her light, orderly house. Then she went back to the hospital to pick up the family. What was left of them.

TREVOR WAS NOT IN THE LOUNGE, but Darlene knew where to find him. She ran up all the stairs and let herself out onto the roof. Where was he? There, around the side of the little hut. She ran across the melty roof floor, pebbles oozing sideways under her feet.

"Look," Trevor said when she caught him. "This door's open."

He slid his fingers into the crack and pulled it open. Black inside there, and a glimmer of light. A bare bulb on the wall inside. They stepped through onto a metal cage floor, suspended over darkness. A chain ran across, blocking steep metal stairs.

Then they heard a grinding noise. "Down there," she said. "It's the elevators."

Their eyes adjusted to see that they were right on top of the elevators, a huge hole, with metal cables going down, down, seven floors. One elevator was coming up. Trevor craned out to watch, holding on with one hand and leaning out under the railing.

"Don't!" Darlene said. "It will come up and cut your head off."

"No," he said. "It has to stop down there."

It cranked and cranked and cranked, until with a sigh and a jerk it stopped.

In the silence, Darlene said, "We're going to the woman's house."

"Mom too?"

"Of course not." She did not say, "Stupid."

THE FATHER CAME INTO THE KITCHEN while Clara was making a bedtime snack for the children. They were safe, sitting in front of the television in the den, blankly watching *The Jungle Book* with Mrs. Pell the grandmother.

"I'm going to need some cash," he said, hovering between threat and casual assumption.

"No," she said. Easy enough to open her wallet, give him a twenty. No.

"Can't get by on nothing, we got nothing left now."

"No cash." She looked up at the calendar. It was still Sunday. She'd sat in church today, deciding to do this, or realizing that it was not a decision.

"Tomorrow I'll get you an appointment at Manpower, we'll find you some temporary work."

"Fine!" His hands went flinging palm-up in submission, as if she'd won some fight. "Fine help you are."

He left, shouldering past her closer than he needed to, but she stood still. She was a little frightened, but only for a moment, because she was doing the right thing. She was surprised at herself, and again thought that she was doing the right thing—but maybe a foolish thing.

Listening in the den, Darlene ran her fingernails along the carpet. Her mom had clipped them when they cleaned up before they left her at the hospital, and the skin on Darlene's fingertips was frayed-up, nervous. She was having a hard time seeing with her eyes but her fingers were working overtime. She closed her eyes and combed along the carpet, and listened to the evil snake sssinging: *Trust in me, just in me, Sleep safe and sound, Knowing I am around ...*

WHILE THE BATHWATER RAN, Clara pulled off Trevor's shirt and shorts. His ribs were sharp under his bluish skin, but he did not look malnourished. A sore on the left side, probably a mosquito bite he'd scratched. She popped him in.

"Hot! Hot!" His little body squirmed away from the water, almost levitating.

She grabbed him out again, with a rush of fear in her throat, and put her hand into the water to check—she was sure she had checked—yes, it was only warm.

"It's not hot," she said. "Put your foot in first, and see. It's warm."

He tried his foot, obediently and said *hmm*. He brought the other foot in, and stood there letting the water get used to him. Then he squatted, his pointy bottom submerged, but kept his arms wrapped around his large-boned knees.

"How old are you?" she asked. She imagined six or seven.

"I'm five!" he told her. He was big. Or her ideas of size were wrong.

"Sing," he ordered. She wanted to comfort him—he was only five. As she lathered up the soap she started off on a winding minor tune, the sad pig song her own mother had sung for her.

> Betty Pringle, she had a pig.
> Not too little, not very big.
> While he lived, he lived in clover
> Now he's dead, and that's all over.

Clara held each hand in turn and washed his thin arms, trying not to tickle him. With his free hand he crowned his kneecaps with bubbles.

> Billy Pringle lay down and cried.
> Betty Pringle lay down and died.
> That's the end of one, two, three:
> Billy, Betty, poor piggy.

"Like my mom," she heard a voice behind her say. It was Darlene standing in the bathroom doorway. Her long eyes sharp as diamonds again, her arms trembling.

"Like my mom, laid down and died."

"She's not dead yet," Clara said, rattled. Stupid thing to say! Her hands were soapy. "She's ill, Darlene, but Jesus will look after her. Jesus died for us, you know." Oh, how had that come out of her mouth?

"Like the pig," said Trevor in the bathtub.

IT WASN'T UNTIL TEN O'CLOCK THAT NIGHT, when the children had finally gone to sleep, that Clara realized she had not left a place for herself. She got a blanket and a pillow and lay on the sofa in the living room. She startled awake all night at every noise, then lay planning and thinking what to do: how much vacation time she had left, what files she needed to clear up at work, what to feed them all. The grandmother went to the bathroom many, many times. At least the baby didn't cry. The father got up and ate noisily about 2 a.m. But she could deal with him, and the children needed help. About dawn, she fell into a deep sleep.

THE CHILDREN WERE STARING AT HER, in broad daylight.

"My dad's gone," Darlene said.

"He took your stuff," Trevor told her sadly.

Her nightgown was awry. She pulled it straight and rolled off the couch, wrapped in the afghan, and went to check. He had taken her mother's old car, which she had been using since the accident. The stereo from the den, the silver clock from her dresser. The silver teapot, but not the Spode cups and saucers, which were worth far more. Nothing she couldn't spare. A loaf of bread and some ham. The money from her wallet, but not the credit cards.

"He'll be back when that runs out," Mrs. Pell said, coming to join the party. She hadn't spoken since coming to Clara's house—Clara couldn't remember ever having heard her deep voice, rasping like a plumber's snake scraping the side of the pipe.

Darlene stood beside Clara looking out the front door at the empty driveway. Trevor held on to Darlene's T-shirt at the back.

"Will we have to go to the shelter now?" he asked her.

"No," Darlene answered.

She looked up at Clara.

The baby started to wail in the bedroom, and Mrs. Pell showed no signs of going to attend to him. Clara was thinking what to do.

She could report Clayton, they'd probably catch him quickly. But what would she report—a missing person or a car thief? She could choose to say she'd lent him the car, she could get him to come back.

Instead she went into the bedroom and picked up the little baby, the new one, the morning dew. The baby quieted immediately holding her hand, his other arm clinging to Clara's neck, his body conforming to hers, his head warm against Clara's face.

Mine, she thought.

3. Spilt milk

When Clara got to Lorraine's room in the afternoon, after picking up a loaner car at the garage, Lorraine was too tired to talk. The tests had worn her out, or just the discovery of her illness. Clara put the flowers in a vase the freckly nurse found for her, and left a box of shortbread cookies from her neighbour Mrs. Zenko on the window ledge.

Clara didn't know whether to tell Lorraine that Clayton was gone. It would upset her, but it was hardly Clara's secret to keep, and she dreaded Lorraine finding out somehow and blaming her—or shrieking at her again. Lorraine's face screaming, her finger pointing, Pearce at her bare breast on the street: these images returned to Clara's mind too often already. She prickled with guilt for not telling her, but Lorraine didn't even ask about him. Perhaps he had told her he was going, had said he *wouldn't stay in that house*, some bluster like that. Clara sat in the straight blue chair, not the orange recliner, and talked about the children, how they were settling in. She asked if Lorraine was able to express (proud of herself for pulling that unfamiliar word from memory), and if she should bring Pearce in later.

"No, keep on with the formula. I can't nurse him now, all this stuff they're putting in me. It was about time to stop him anyways, he's nine months old. He'll be a year, September 10th. But it was such a pleasure, why stop? Easier, too, when we were moving around all the time. Didn't have to clean bottles or buy those plastic baggies ..."

Lorraine's voice threaded out, as if she'd gone to sleep on the thought of travelling, safe in their seashell car, her whole family close around her and her baby at her breast.

Clara watched her for a while, until she was sure she was either asleep or tired of company. She went home, stopping on the way to get fried chicken for supper, which was a great hit and made her believe she might almost be able to manage them.

ON TUESDAY MORNING Darlene waited until Clara had been gone ten minutes before she got up from the living room and went down the hall. Gran was watching TV, propped back on one elbow with her old potato feet on the table, in the little bedroom where their dad had slept that one night. Darlene could imagine him going around the house, the look on his face, walking past Clara out in the living room, finding the car keys in her handbag. She did not want to have to tell her mom about him being gone. In Gran's room Pearce lay sleeping in the basket, with a bottle drooling out of his mouth. Gran had dumped her stuff out onto the floor, as usual. It smelled like her in there: old teeth and hair.

Darlene had already gone through the desk in the living room: bills all tidy and a cheque-book: $5,230 in the balance place, that was a *lot*. She had put it back carefully at the same angle.

No reason she shouldn't go in Clara's room. It was hers and Trevor's for now; maybe she felt like a nap. Their pyjamas were folded on the bed. The other furniture all matched, but it was all old. The chair by the window was covered with faded cloth. There were dents in the carpet where other chairs or dressers must have been before. Green walls, like her mother's sweater that Darwin gave her. Darlene loved the smell in there—like flowers, and maybe a long time ago someone had smoked a cigarette. It was lucky that she and Trevor got to sleep in here. For now. In the night-table drawers she found almost nothing: a nail-clipper and file and some flat blood-coloured cough drops. She tasted one, but it was disgusting. She spat it out, dried it off and put it back in the package: The dresser held a hundred sweaters, it looked like, smelling of clean wool and perfume. She was tempted to pull one out and rub her face in it, but she did not think she could fold it back properly, and then Clara would know.

Where was anything good? Darlene didn't even know what she was looking for. Not candy or money, they wouldn't be in here. The closet: she dragged the armchair over and pulled boxes off the top shelf. Old cream-coloured satin shoes, with a sway-backed heel and a button. They couldn't have ever fitted Clara, they were about her own size. She put them on, liking the ladylike arch in her foot, but didn't dare button the stiff strap, or take a step in them.

In a yellow box she found government stuff and old browned photo-copies, little pictures with wavy edges of guys in uniform. A bunch of letters tied up in string might be good, but Darlene was too chicken to open the string. If she couldn't get it tied right it would be like that time in Espanola.

In another yellow box, a marriage license for Clara Purdy and Dominic Raskin, 1982. Why wasn't she Clara Raskin, then? Some photos, a few letters, all jumbled together.

There was a noise in the front hall—Clara coming back?

Darlene had half-scrambled the yellow box back to the top shelf when she realized it was her grandmother banging the screen door, going out for a smoke. She could hear her yelling to Trevor, "You put the channel back when I get back!" and Trevor saying yes, yes.

She put the box on the shelf anyway. Another time, when she knew how long she'd have. She fluffed the clothes to make them look ordinary, fitted the chair back into its dents in the carpet by the window, and scuffed her sock feet over the drag-lines made by the chair. Trevor was shrieking in the living room. Gran yelled at him to shut up, and then Pearce was crying. She could do the bathroom any time—but there was still the kitchen.

THE NURSE MUST HAVE JUST BEEN IN. Lorraine sat propped up, flipping channels, the sheets tucked tight around her. She looked sick, and Clara said so.

"It's the fever," Lorraine said. "They can't get it to stay down. Is Trevor okay?"

"He's happy outside. He likes the old birch tree that my father planted when I was born."

"A tree planted when you were born? How big is it?"

"It's not *that* big, I'm only forty-three."

"I didn't mean that," Lorraine said, coming close to a laugh. It seemed to hurt her chest. "How about Darlene?"

"She can tell me what they're used to, now—" Now that Clayton was gone. Clara steered away from that. "She's very good with Pearce, too. If he cries she can calm him better than any of us."

"He crying a lot?"

"Oh no, I didn't mean—Just when once in a while he makes a murmur."

"Because he's a good baby, he doesn't cry."

"He's a perfect baby. You must be missing him."

Lorraine began to sob. Clara sat watching, in an agony of guilt. After a moment, though, Lorraine stopped. As if crying took more energy than she was prepared to expend. "Spilt milk," she said. "They took that other lady out—the ovarian one. She went in for surgery, but when they opened her up they couldn't do anything. They sewed her back up and sent her home to Wilkie."

Difficult to respond to that.

"That's the bad part," Lorraine said. She patted the bed restlessly and fumbled with the small flowered pillow that Clara had remembered to bring in for her.

"Can I fix it?" Clara slid her arm under Lorraine's neck, lifting her head gently. In one quick motion Clara slipped the flowered pillow out, shook it into softness again, and smoothed it into a double fold to fit nicely beneath Lorraine's ear.

"You're good at that."

"I had practice with pillows, looking after my mother for many years while she was ill."

They sat together in silence for a while but Lorraine was still restless. "We were on our way to Fort McMurray. Clayton's got a job lined up there. His cousin has an RV dealership, used, and now that so many people can't find any place to live up there, there's lots of people buying. Clayton was going to help Kenny fix up trailers, there was one on the lot that we could use while we figured our where to live. It would have been okay for a while, until we found something better."

"Lots of work up in Fort McMurray, they say."

"He can do a lot of things you wouldn't expect," Lorraine said. "He's a good cabinet-maker. He upholsters furniture, too, and that's hard work. That's what his cousin wanted him for, to reupholster the trailer fittings. He'd surprise you, how good he is."

Maybe he'd gone on without them, Clara thought.

Lorraine stopped talking, and twisted her head from side to side. "My neck hurts."

"Do you want me to see if they can give you something?"

"I don't want to take anything. I'm already taking stuff. I don't know."

Clara thought the fever was increasing. "It's hard," Lorraine said.

"Yes," Clara said. Not knowing what else to say.

ON THE VERY TOP SHELF of the last kitchen cupboard Darlene found a brown envelope taped down on a glass pedestal thing. Tons of money in it. It added up to seven hundred and something, counting pretty quick, one ear open for Clara coming back from the store. But it was no good to her, it was strange pink money from England. The car! She jumped down from the counter. Too far, so the balls of her feet hurt, but she didn't get caught.

Finding the house in surprising disarray, Clara tidied the living room and the TV room, and the hall, and the back steps—Trevor had made a fort there with blankets and pillows—before making lunch. Mrs. Pell went to her bedroom and shut the door, and they all left her alone. Clara gave Pearce a bottle. He stared into her eyes thoughtfully while he drank, his fingers splayed against her chest.

When he fell asleep she did three loads of laundry. She remembered to phone and extend the insurance on her mother's car, thinking she might be liable if Clayton got into another accident. She made cookies and started a list of necessities on the door of the fridge: formula, diapers, chicken soup from an envelope. They did not like canned. She wrote down everything the children asked for. It seemed like they were all in cotton wool, or that same smothering membrane which had been bothering Clara herself lately.

After supper Clara walked them to the park in the darkening evening. The children played on the flat merry-go-round, Trevor standing in the middle and Darlene running it around and around, faster and faster, until she could jump up too and they went spinning on and on through the indigo night air.

Clara stood a little distance away from their orbit, letting Pearce rest against her chest, feeling the weight and the balance of his body against hers. It wasn't so hard, being with children.

4. Counting money

AT TEN THAT NIGHT Clara went back through the hospital to Lorraine's silent room. The window was a dark rectangle in the white wall. She turned off the overhead fluorescent light, left on the small yellow bulb over the sink, and pulled the alcove curtain partway across so it wouldn't glare in Lorraine's eyes. Now they could see the lights of the city across the river, the pretty bridges, the night sky. Deep shadowy blue, not black, even so late.

"I'm worried about the kids," Lorraine said. Easier to talk in the darkness. "I'm worried about Clayton too, but not as much. He can take care of himself, more or less."

Now would be the time to mention Clayton's departure.

But Lorraine said, "I'm afraid."

All Clara could think of was, "Don't be." An unforgivable, asinine thing to say. She did not want to remember her father dying, or the horrors her mother went through. "I'm sorry. Of course you are afraid. I guess I mean, don't let superstition trap you into pretending to be positive all the time. There is no jinxing, and being blindly optimistic doesn't help."

"What does help then?"

"I pray, but it does not always—" She could think of no word but *suffice*, which would sound pompous. "It's hard to know what to pray for."

Lorraine snorted, and flapped her hands onto the sheet. "I know what to pray for! That my, this, *thing* will go away. That I will have my kids back with me. That everything will go on the way it was the day before we came to Saskatoon, when I was worrying about how to find work and a place to live, not how to *live*."

It was not a tirade, but a considered statement.

"I had enough worry before. I'm not going to worry now. I'm not going to pray either. I'm going to be patient and wait for this to happen." She corrected herself. "Wait for this to go away."

There were blue marks under her eyes, and her skin was puffy. The steroids, affecting her already. If her fever could be brought down they were assessing her for chemo in the morning, Clara knew, and then would come a bad time. For a moment she was glad she had been with her mother during that long struggle, so she knew a little about it, to be able to help Lorraine.

"Is there anything you like to read? Magazines? *People*? Or something more serious while you've got some quiet time?"

"Some of each," Lorraine said. Her pointy smile was very tired.

One more thing, though. "I don't know what to do about Darlene. She wants to see you, of course. Should I put her off, or bring her in?"

"Don't bring Trevor, not right now. But you could bring Darlene. I need her to get some stuff from the car, now that I think of it. Good thing you said."

Clara had forgotten their car, in the impound lot. "They gave us the knapsacks, that first day ... I've got the children's things."

"Yeah, but I got some stuff hidden in there, in the Dart. We were living in there for the last couple weeks. You know how it is. You have to keep your stuff somewhere."

From her tone Clara supposed it was money or even drugs. But she would not be a good judge. Maybe papers, that kind of treasure. "I'll bring Darlene tomorrow. I meant to ask if there is anyone that I should call for you. I'm not sure if Clayton has had a chance to do that."

"Nice way of putting it," Lorraine said. "No, there's no one. No one that I know where they are, anyways."

This time Clara stopped herself from saying she was sorry She decided again not to get into Clayton's absence. "You look like you could sleep," she said. "I'll bring books tomorrow."

"Yeah," Lorraine said. "I'll catch up on that summer reading I've been meaning to get to. Don't bring Pearce. That would be hard on him."

"All right," Clara said. "I'll keep him at home. He's good, he's doing well."

"Thank you." Lorraine closed her eyes and turned her head away from Clara before she opened them again. The window looked out on all the lights across the river, a million glinting sparks.

WALKING DOWN THE HALL, thinking ahead to breakfast for the children, Clara did not see Paul Tippett until he took her arm, right beside her. She jumped, and he apologized, both of them speaking in whispers because it seemed so late. The hospital was closing down around them, patients being put into storage for the night.

"How is your family?" he asked,

"The mother, Lorraine, is not doing very well," Clara said. It felt disloyal, to say it out loud. Superstition. She was as bad as anyone.

Paul Tippett looked sad, the clear lines of his face blurred. She was sorry, because she liked him, as far as she knew him. He seemed crippled by diffidence, but always kind.

"Will you do something for me?" she asked. "Will you visit her?" She could see him pull away involuntarily, like she had pulled away from Darlene's snatching hand. "Tomorrow, I mean, or—not, as a parishioner, to comfort her—but I've got her children, and her husband's gone—oh, but don't tell her that. Just to ease her mind, that I'm not a monster, because she has no choice, she has to put them somewhere, and I'm the only—" Clara stopped. She was making a fool of herself.

He stared at her, in the lowered light of the night hall. "The husband has gone?"

"Yes," she said, not mentioning the car, or the teapot, or his weak threat. "But he might come back."

Paul thought Clara Purdy had experienced a radical change since he'd last seen her. She seemed charged with energy. *The force that through the green fuse drives the flower*. It was involvement that put you into time, perhaps. He shook his head, astonished at the brightness of her face, then saw that she thought he was refusing her request.

"No, no—I will," he said quickly. "I will visit her. Sorry, I was thinking of something else. I'll tell her how fortunate her family is, to be with you."

He couldn't remember her house. A bungalow. "You have enough room for all of them, do you? What's her last name?"

"Gage. Lorraine Gage—in this ward."

He wrote it in his little calendar book and gave her a quick apologetic smile, for his reluctance. She could not help smiling back. She did like him. Too bad about Mrs. Tippett, that cold fish.

LORRAINE LAY IN BED COUNTING MONEY. Seventy-seven dollars in the glove compartment. Lucky sevens. Three twenties, a ten, a five, the $2 bill saved for years. Whore's money, Clayton would call that. Not loose, for anyone to find (meaning Clayton, of course), but stuck between the back two pages of the map book. They were not going to get to Newfoundland or Labrador. $189 left in the bank, but she thought Clayton probably had her bank card, and he knew her PIN. A hundred dollars—one $100 bill— hidden, taped inside a box of tampons in the cardboard box in the trunk. He would not have found that, but the worry was that someone might throw out the box.

She could hardly stand to think about money. What would Clayton do? He had $300 and some left on the Husky Gas card before it maxed out. But no car, so gas wasn't going to do him much good. They could eat, though, at Husky station restaurants. If he decided to take the kids on to Fort McMurray, which she wondered if he was planning on doing, since he was obviously not at Clara's any more.

$189, $300, how long would that last?

At a certain point every time in all this figuring, Lorraine would feel her neck stiffen and swell from tension, and she'd fling the whole thing out of her mind.

She lay still, mostly. Moving made her feel weird, and whatever drugs she was pumped full of seemed to make it easier to be still. If things were ordinary, she'd be in the car, Pearce nestled in her elbow, worrying about money and thinking ahead to what work she could get in Fort McMurray. Worrying about who would look after the kids while she waitressed or cleaned houses again; about gas and how much a bunch of bananas and some fig newtons had taken out of the purse. She moved her feet under the pale green sheet and stared with torn-open eyes around the room. Here she was.

The moon made bars of yellow light that gradually drifted across the room. She could tell she must have slept when she saw the moonlight far- ther advanced on her sheets, on the end of the bed, on the wall. The moon rose in the east and set in the west, just like the sun. Sometimes with the sun. She'd sat nursing Pearce in the car while the others ate outside in the sun at a Taco Bell, last week. His mouth pulling, pulling, his eyes staring at her in a trance of happiness, and the white moon visible in the blue day sky.

She could not die on them. $77, $189, $100. It took her a few minutes to work it out in her foggy head. $366. Well, that was a lucky number. She liked threes and sixes. Clayton couldn't feed them all on that for long. He'd have to go to the food bank. Mom Pell had money somewhere, but she wouldn't give it up for food, at least not for the kids. Lorraine let herself hate Mom Pell for the cherries she'd insisted on buying, that huge six-dollar bag of BC cherries that had probably caused the whole thing, anyways. Making Clayton drive too fast to make up for stopping. Bits of red pulp clinging to everything after the crash, like your own body and brains turned inside out, like one of the children had been badly hurt. Lorraine's chest ached, the breasts and the inside too, wanting to have Pearce and the others there with her. She was filled with panicky rage just thinking about Clay and Mom Pell, but the children were so sweet. Except there was no money.

$77, $189, $100. How long did it take for welfare to kick in last time? But they weren't residents of Saskatchewan, they'd get sent back to Winnipeg on the bus. They couldn't leave her, though, and she was entitled to health care anywhere in Canada, they were always saying.

They needed $1200. Six for an apartment, another six for the damage deposit. First and last months' tent. Who knew how long it would take for Clayton to get paid, no matter how fast he found a job. There was no way. They'd be in housing, if there was room. Or a shelter. Clayton would not be good at looking after the kids on his own in a shelter, and Mom Pell was worse than useless. She would have to talk to the kids. They'd need some kind of—the thought of a weapon for them: a nail file, a pin—

Lorraine sat up and vomited neatly into a green plastic kidney basin. She lay back down. It might all be a dream. The moon had floated off, leaving the room dark and deserted. In a while, she slept.

Rawi Hage

Rawi Hage was born in Beirut, Lebanon, and lived through nine years of the Lebanese civil war during the 1970s. He immigrated to Canada in 1992.

He is a writer, a visual artist, and a curator. His writings have appeared in *Fuse Magazine, Mizna, Jouvert, The Toronto Review, Montreal Serai*, and *Al Jadid*. His visual works have been shown in galleries and museums around the world, including the Canadian Museum of Civilization and the Musée de la civilisation in Quebec City.

Hage's first book, *De Niro's Game*, was a finalist for The Scotiabank Giller Prize and the Governor General's Literary Award, and won numerous awards, including the International IMPAC Dublin Literary Award. Hage lives in Montreal.

Cockroach

BY RAWI HAGE

Finalist 2008

⁓

I am in love with Shohreh. But I don't trust my emotions anymore. I've neither lived with a woman nor properly courted one. And I've often wondered about my need to seduce and possess every female of the species that comes my way.

When I see a woman, I feel my teeth getting thinner, longer, pointed. My back hunches and my forehead sprouts two antennae that sway in the air, flagging a need for attention. I want to crawl under the feet of the women I meet and admire from below their upright posture, their delicate ankles. I also feel repulsed—not embarrassed, but repulsed—by slimy feelings of cunning and need. It is a bizarre mix of emotions and instinct that comes over me, compelling me to approach these women like a hunchback in the presence of schoolgirls.

Perhaps it's time to see my therapist again, because lately this feeling has been weighing on me. Although that same urge has started to act upon me in the shrink's presence. Recently, when I saw her laughing with one of her co-workers, I realized that she is also a woman, and when she asked me to re-enact my urges, I put my hand on her knee while she was sitting across from me. She changed the subject and, calmly, with a compassionate face, brushed my hand away, pushed her seat back, and said: Okay, let's talk about your suicide.

Last week I confessed to her that I used to be more courageous, more carefree, and even, one might add, more violent. But here in this northern land no one gives you an excuse to hit, rob, or shoot, or even to shout from across the balcony, to curse your neighbours' mothers and threaten their kids.

When I said that to the therapist, she told me that I have a lot of hidden anger. So when she left the room for a moment, I opened her purse and stole her lipstick, and when she returned I continued my tale of growing up somewhere else. She would interrupt me with questions such as: And how do you feel about that? Tell me more. She mostly listened and took notes, and it wasn't in a fancy room with a massive cherrywood and leather couch either (or with a globe of an ancient admiral's map, for that matter). No, we sat across from each other in a small office, in a public health clinic, only a tiny round table between us.

I am not sure why I told her all about my relations with women. I had tried many times to tell her that my suicide attempt was only my way of trying to escape the permanence of the sun. With frankness, and using my limited psychological knowledge and powers of articulation, I tried to explain to her that I had attempted suicide out of a kind of curiosity, or maybe as a challenge to nature, to the cosmos itself, to the recurring light. I felt oppressed by it all. The question of existence consumed me.

The therapist annoyed me with her laconic behaviour. She brought on a feeling of violence within me that I hadn't experienced since I left my homeland. She did not understand. For her, everything was about my relations with women, but for me, everything was about defying the oppressive power in the world that I can neither participate in nor control. And the question that I hated most—and it came up when she was frustrated with me for not talking enough—was when she leaned over the table and said, without expression: What do you expect from our meeting?

I burst out: I am forced to be here by the court! I prefer not to be here, but when I was spotted hanging from a rope around a tree branch, some jogger in spandex ran over and called the park police. Two of those mounted police came galloping to the rescue on the backs of their magnificent horses. All I noticed at the time was the horses. I thought the horses could be the answer to my technical problem. I mean, if I rode on the back of one of those beasts, I could reach a higher, sturdier branch, secure the rope to it, and let the horse run free from underneath me. Instead I was handcuffed and taken for, as they put it, assessment.

Tell me about your childhood, the shrink asked me.

In my youth I was an insect.

What kind of insect? she asked.

A cockroach, I said.

Why?

Because my sister made me one.

What did your sister do?

Come, my sister said to me. Let's play. And she lifted her skirt, laid the back of my head between her legs, raised her heels in the air, and swayed her legs over me slowly. Look, open your eyes, she said, and she touched me. This is your face, those are your teeth, and my legs are your long, long whiskers. We laughed, and crawled below the sheets, and nibbled on each other's faces. Let's block the light, she said. Let's seal that quilt to the bed, tight, so there won't be any light. Let's play underground.

Interesting, the therapist said. I think we could explore more of these stories. Next week?

Next week, I said, and rose up on my heels and walked past the clinic's walls and down the stairs and out into the cold, bright city.

WHEN I GOT HOME, I saw that my sink was filled with dishes, a hybrid collection of neon-coloured dollar-store cups mixed with flower-patterned plates, stacked beneath a large spaghetti pot, all unwashed. Before I could reach for my deadly slipper, the cockroaches that lived with me squeezed themselves down the drain and ran for their lives.

I was hungry. And I had little money left. So it was time to find the Iranian musician by the name of Reza who owed me forty dollars. I was determined to collect and I was losing my patience with that bastard. I was even contemplating breaking his santour if he did not pay me back soon. He hung out in the Artista Café, the one at the corner. It is open twenty-four hours a day, and for twenty-four hours it collects smoke pumped out by the lungs of fresh immigrants lingering on plastic chairs, elbows drilling the round tables, hands flagging their complaints, tobacco-stained fingers summoning the waiters, their matches, like Indian signals, ablaze under hairy noses, and their stupefied faces exhaling cigarette fumes with the intensity of Spanish bulls on a last charge towards a dancing red cloth.

I ran downstairs to look for the bastard at the café, and god behold! Two Jehovah's Witness ladies flashed their Caribbean smiles and obstructed my flight with towering feathery straw hats that pasted a coconut shade onto the gritty steps of the crumbling building where I live. Are you interested in the world? they asked me. And before I had a chance to reply, one of the ladies, the one in the long quilted coat, slapped me with an apocalyptic prophecy: Are you aware of the hole in the ozone above us?

Ozone? I asked.

Yes, ozone. It is the atmospheric layer that protects us from the burning rays of the sun. There is a hole in it as we speak, and it is expanding, and soon we shall all fry. Only the cockroaches shall survive to rule the earth. But do not despair, young man, because you will redeem yourself today if you buy this magazine—I happen to have a few copies in my hand here— and attend Bible gatherings at our Kingdom Hall. And afterwards, my handsome fellow, you can go down to the basement and listen to the leader (with a cookie and a Styrofoam cup in hand) and he will tell you that transfusions (be they administered through a syringe, a medical doctor, or perverted sex) are a mortal sin. Then and only then will you have a chance. Repent! the woman shouted as she opened the Bible to a marked page. She read, The words of the Lord my son: *Therefore will I also deal in fury: mine eye shall not spare, neither will I pity: and though they cry in mine ears with loud voice, yet will I not hear them.* Buy this magazine (the word of the Lord included), my son. Read it and repent!

How much? I asked, as I liberated my pocket from the sinful weight of a few round coins sealed with idolatrous images of ducks, geese, bears, and magisterial heads. They were all I had.

Give me those coins and pray, because then, and only then, you will have the chance to be beamed up by Jesus our saviour, and while you are ascending towards the heavens, you can take a peek down at those neighbours of yours who just slammed their door in our faces. You can watch them fry like dumplings in a wok, and I assure you that our Lord will be indifferent to their plight, their sufferings, their loud cries of agony and regret and pain—yes, pain! And may God save us from such harrowing pain.

I kissed the Jehovah's Witness ladies' hands. I asked them to have mercy on me in that sizzling day to come. Dying from fire is a terrible thing. If I had to choose, I would certainly want something less painful, quicker, maybe even more poetic—like hanging from a willow tree or taking a bullet in the head or falling into a senseless eternal slumber accompanied by the aroma of a leaky gas stove.

I left the ladies and ran down to the Artista Café on St-Laurent, still hoping to find Reza in a circle of smoke and welfare recipients and coffee breath. As my feet trudged the wet ground and I felt the shivery cold, I cursed my luck. I cursed the plane that had brought me to this harsh terrain. I peered down the street and hesitantly walked east, avoiding every patch of slush and trying to ignore the sounds of friction as car wheels split the snow, sounds that bounced into my ears, constant reminders of the falling flakes that gather and accumulate quietly, diligently, claiming every car windshield, every hat, every garbage can, every eyelid, every roof and mountain. And how about those menacing armies of heavy boots, my friend, encasing people's feet, and the silenced ears, plugged with wool and headbands, and the floating coats passing by in ghostly shapes, hiding faces, pursed lips, austere hands? Goddamn it! Not even a nod in this cold place, not even a timid wave, not a smile from below red, sniffing, blowing noses. All these buried heads above necks strangled in synthetic scarves. It made me nervous, and I asked myself, Where am I? And what am I doing here? How did I end up trapped in a constantly shivering carcass, walking in a frozen city with wet cotton falling on me all the time? And on top of it all, I am hungry, impoverished, and have no one, no one ... Fucking ice, one slip of the mind and you might end up immersing your foot in one of those treacherous cold pools that wait for your steps with the patience of sailors' wives, with the mockery of swamp monsters. You can curse all you wish, but still you have to endure freezing toes, and the squelch of wet socks, and the slime of midwives' hands, and fathoms of coats that pass you on the streets and open and close, fluttering and bloated like sails blown towards a promised land.

I am doomed!

When I entered the café, I peeled myself out from under layers of hats, gloves, and scarves, liberated myself from zippers and buttons, and endured the painful tearing Velcro that hissed like a prehistoric reptile, that split and separated like people's lives, like exiles falling into cracks that give birth and lead to death under digging shovels that sound just like the friction of car wheels wedging snow around my mortal parts.

I spotted Professor Youssef sitting alone at his usual table. That lazy, pretentious, Algerian pseudo-French intellectual always dresses up in gabardine suits with the same thin tie that had its glory in the seventies. He hides behind his sixties-era eyeglasses and emulates French thinkers by smoking his pipe in dimly lit spots. He sits all day in that café and talks about *révolution et littérature.*

I asked the professor if he had seen Reza, the Iranian musician, but he did not respond. He just gave me his arrogant smile.

I knew it, I knew it! The professor wants to shower me with his existentialist questions. The bastard plays Socrates every chance he gets. He has always treated the rest of us like Athenian pupils lounging on the steps of the agora, and he never answers a question. He imagines he is a pseudo-socialist Berber journalist, but he is nothing but a latent clergyman, always answering a question with another question.

Is it a yes or a no? *C'est urgent*, I shrilled at him, intending to interrupt his epistemological plot.

Non! J'ai pas vu ton ami. The professor pasted on his sardonic smile again, puffed his pipe, and changed the position of his legs. He leaned his body into the back of the chair and looked at me with an intellectual's air of dismissal, as if I were a peasant, unworthy of the myopic thickness of his glasses. He does not trust me. He smells me through his pipe's brume. I know he suspects me of stealing his last tobacco bag, which I did. But he cannot prove it. Now whenever I approach him, he acts as if he is repositioning himself in his chair in order to say something valuable and profound, but I can see him through his pipe's smog, gathering his belongings closer to his body, hugging his bag like a refugee on a crowded boat.

I turned away from the professor, thinking that I would like to choke Reza, the Middle Eastern hunchback, with the strings of his own musical instrument. He owed me, and I was in need. He always managed to extract money from me, one way or another. He either gave me long monologues about Persia and the greatness of its history, or he re-enacted the tears of his mother, whom he will never see again before she dies because, as he claims, he is an unfortunate exile. But I know that all Reza cares about is numbing his lips and face. He is always sniffing, and if it's not because of a cold, it is because of an allergy, and if it is not because of allergy, it is because of a natural impulse to powder his nose with "the white Colombian," as he puts it. But there was nothing I could do now except dress again in my armour against the cold and go back to my room and wait for Reza to call.

At home I lay in bed, reached for my smokes, and then for no reason became alarmed, or maybe melancholic. This feeling was not paranoia, as the therapist wrote in her stupid notes (notes that I had managed to steal); it was just my need again to hide from the sun and not see anyone. It was the necessity I felt to strip the world from everything around me and exist underneath it all, without objects, people, light, or sound. It was my need to unfold an eternal blanket that would cover everything, seal the sky and my window, and turn the world into an insect's play.

Mary Swan

Mary Swan is the winner of the 2001 O. Henry Award for short fiction and is the author of the collection *The Deep and Other Stories*. Her work has appeared in several Canadian literary publications, including *The Malahat Review* and *Best Canadian Stories,* as well as in American publications such as *Harper's*. She lives with her husband and daughter near Toronto.

The Boys in the Trees

BY MARY SWAN

Finalist 2008

⥈

WEDNESDAY'S CHILD—1888

Three people love me in this world, and that should be enough. One is my mother, and I will never leave her. One is my sister, who is the best of us, the hope of us. Like in the garden. The last is my father, who takes care of us, but doesn't always see.

There are families in church with children like steps on a stair, and babies, and grandmothers in black bonnets. And there are people who have no one at all. No one could love the tattered woman who mumbles outside Malley's tavern, and Mr. Envers used to set down his mug of tea and tell my mother it was a terrible thing to outlive everyone, to be all alone. When we first came to this town Rachel had to write an essay for Miss Alice, about her family. Parents and grandparents, where they came from, what they did. There was a silence at the dinner table and then my father said, *That's no one's business; no one has any right to ask that.* Rachel said that she had to, that it was an essay, and he gave her a look that he didn't often give, and was silent for the rest of the meal. Later, in the kitchen, my mother told about her own parents, and what she knew of theirs. A ship our great-grandfather had owned, and how he was lost. A curved sword someone had brought back from war. She said it was all true but her voice sounded like a story, like the stories she used to tell when she pulled the covers up over us, smoothed them with her hand.

They came in the evening, in the dark. A brisk knocking at the door. I was at the foot of the stair; my father, in his shirtsleeves, opened it, letting in a whisper of dying leaves along with a rush of cold, sharp-scented air.

Wednesdays at eleven o'clock I go across the road to Dr. Robinson, and I see the week like a hill now, sloping up to a peak and then sliding down again. At first it was like waves building and crashing over my head. People on the street, the dark hallway, the unfamiliar room and the questions. He asked my mother things, asked me things, that were so private I didn't even have words for them. But now I know what things look like, behind the gleaming door. Dr. Robinson examines my tongue, touches my face with his clean fingers, pulling down the skin beneath my eyes. Holds my wrist and counts without seeming to count. He told my mother that she didn't always need to come with me, that he could send for her if need be, just across the road. The first time I went alone she watched me from the front porch, and each time I looked back she waved her hand. When I returned she was still there, sitting on the outside chair. She smoothed my hair back and gave me her sad smile and I told her it was fine, that the laughing girl had been there for a little while.

He stepped out onto the front porch, closed the door, and I couldn't hear a thing they were saying. Only Rachel's happy voice from the kitchen, where she was helping my mother. I couldn't hear the words they were saying but it was so strange, this knock in the dark, my father stepping out in his shirtsleeves, that I didn't continue up. I sank down onto the third stair and waited, smoothing my skirts over my knees.

They were there as long as I can remember, there in the room where mist trailed by the window, in the darker, noisier room. The jumping boy and the laughing girl. Not every moment, not every day, but enough to be without surprise. Sometimes I talked to them but they never answered, and I don't know that they even saw me. The way I saw them was hard to explain, something like a thought that ravels away when you try to catch hold of it. Sometimes words came into my head and I spoke them was out loud; once my mother said, *Who are you talking to, Lily? Are you talking to someone?* When I said, *The jumping boy,* she dropped the plate she was holding; it smashed with a terrible sound and bits lay jagged on the floor. Her voice when she spoke so slow and careful, but with something humming beneath. She asked, and I told her how the boy jumped straight in the air, so high, his light hair flopping. How the girl sometimes had smudges where she'd touched her cheek with her fingers. I was still in the bed and though my mother's voice was slow and soft, it frightened me a little, something did.

Just the two of us there; maybe I was very young, Rachel not yet born. I wanted to tell her about the children and yet I didn't, and I worked my finger in the hole in the brown blanket, making it bigger, but my mother didn't tell me to stop. I had never questioned, never thought before that maybe they were only mine. The jumping boy, the laughing smudgy-cheeked girl, and sometimes the other who was just a streak of color at the edge of my looking.

My mother asked me questions, in the soft voice that soothed, with the hum beneath that frightened. What did they look like, what were they doing, were they happy or sad. When I asked, she said they were children she knew once. And when I asked where they were now, she just said, *Gone.* And then she did a strange thing. She walked toward the bed, the broken shards crunched beneath her feet, and with all her clothes on, even her shoes, she crawled under the bedclothes and put her arms about me, and we both fell asleep again, even though it was already day.

There was someone else, but only Constable Street came in with my father when the door opened, the tip of his nose red. Miss, he said with a nod, but my father walked by as if he didn't even see me, fetched his coat. His face wiped clean of everything, smooth as stone.

The graves in the churchyard are marked by straight standing stones, and although the church is not old, there are so many. Mothers and fathers and children, whole families, sometimes, buried together. Rachel and her friends play a game, hold their breath when they walk by on the way to the gaping doors of the church. When I fainted there on the steps it was just like the other times, the buzzing getting louder, muffling the voices around me. The yellow mesh becoming denser and denser before my eyes until it closed in completely, blotted everything out. My mother felt the tug on her arm as I started to slide down but she wasn't strong enough, and when I opened my eyes I screamed at all the faces, bending over me. Dr. Robinson put his fingers on my wrist and asked if this had happened before, and I heard Rachel say that it happened almost every day, but I forgave her. That is how I came to sit on a chair in his office the first time, the scratch of his pen and everyone seizing on the word that he gave me, as if it said everything, as if it could hold every part of me, each dark part. Now I sit in that chair every Wednesday and things are checked, and then we talk. I've told him about the pebbles I carry in my mouth, but not about the other things.

My mother came from the kitchen, wiping her hands, and the constable nodded to her too, looked down at his shuffling feet. He said there was just a little matter to clear up, and my father said nothing at all, as the front door closed behind them.

I was born in Halifax, where the ship first docked; my mother says there was no money to go any farther. She says there was one tiny room, that we lived there for years, maybe three, maybe four, but I don't remember. Only swirls of mist and the sound of gulls, and maybe a game that we played, my mother sitting with her face in her hands. My father worked in an office on the docks, but he had to leave. We sailed up the river to Montreal, and those same gulls wheeled around our boat.

When Rachel asked, my mother said it was nothing. Some confusion, some little problem at the business, perhaps, and Rachel went lightly up to bed. I wondered why two constables would walk across town in the dark, for nothing.

In the evenings Rachel does her lessons at the kitchen table, and when she's finished she sometimes draws pictures of houses, of trees, on pieces of paper my mother saves for her. My father brought home a blotter, tucked under his coat, for the surface of the table is uneven, scarred and gouged by people we've never known. Rachel has made up stories about them, the families who walked through the rooms that are now ours, who ate their meals here, sat in these chairs. One family she calls the Whippets; they have two wild boys named Joshua and David. The deepest gouge on the table was made by David Whippet, with a pocketknife he was given for his birthday, and he was sent to his room for twenty-one days. Now when something is broken or spilled, my father says, *Which Whippet did that?*

I wonder about the families, the real families, and where they've gone. Marks of their anger, their errors, the only things we have to know them by. Walking toward the mouth of the church we have to pass the standing stones and I think how they may die before me, my father and my mother. Rachel must have her own life, tend our memories but nothing else. Mrs. Toller went to bed with a bottle of laudanum; I heard my father tell my mother. And a man named Meyer was found hanging in a barn. When I open my eyes in the morning there's always a moment when I wonder if it's a good thing.

My mother and I sat in the little front room that was filled, like the whole house, with things other people had left behind. The worn spot on the arm of the settee where she sat sewing, the spot rubbed bare by a stranger's hand. The needle flashed as she raised it, pulling the thread tight. She jabbed her finger and crumpled the white shirt to the floor. Then bent to pick it up again, smoothed it on her lap.

Dr. Robinson counted my pulse, checked my heart, looked in my eyes, my mouth. He asked questions, so many questions. When I slept, what I ate, about my monthlies. All these my mother answered. Then he said that I had a condition, that there was a name for it. The name was *chlorosis*, and he wrote it down on a thick piece of creamy paper. The scratch of the pen drowned out by a raised voice from beyond the door, a woman's voice, chiding a servant. Sound of something that might have been a slap. He looked up at that but said nothing. Passed the paper to my mother and leaned back in his chair, hands on the edge of the desk. Loose threads, a button missing on his vest.

He told my mother that he'd been reading about this green sickness lately, that it was not uncommon in girls my age, that there were things that could be done. I meant to listen, but found I hadn't. Realized, when he stood up, that I'd been staring, just staring at the dangling stray threads, the place where a button belonged.

And is it better or worse, to know that there's a name? Things I felt long before I knew the words for them. Things change when you put a name to them, but they don't disappear. Just change.

My father seemed pleased with the word, asked each day if I'd walked, if I'd rested, if I'd taken the Blaud's pills. He said if it was to be meat every day then I should have it, and my family sat around me with their pale plates, potatoes and cabbage, a slice of bread. My mother knew how hard it was; meat, if I must eat it, I like burned black, hard like a stone in my mouth, bitter like the taste of Rachel's charcoal stick. A bit of chicken I could bear, not easily, but I could bear it, but the bloody taste of beef was an agony, though I cut the pieces as small as I could, made motions with my jaw and tried to swallow them straight down. They sat at the table day after day, my plate half full while theirs were wiped clean. Telling their bits of news over my bowed head as if there was nothing else they needed to do, nowhere else to be. The three people who love me in this world.

We sat and listened to the ticking of someone else's clock, to the wind picking up outside. My mother said she didn't know what was wrong. She told me instead about the look of my father's boots when they first met, a story I thought I'd heard before. I stood and pushed aside the curtain a little; there was a high, cold moon and I could see the fallen leaves skittering away in the dark.

My mother's hands are always red and sore and with all the cleaning and washing when we came to the new house they got worse, her fingers covered in raw spots where the swollen skin had cracked and split. Some days I had to do her buttons. Before she went to sleep she smeared her hands with a thick grease, and then she had to lie on her back with her arms straight, palms up outside the covers. Once my father came home with a little pot of cream he'd bought at Mr. Marl's pharmacy and he sat across from her in the kitchen, working it in, kneading from her wrist to the tip of her fingers, stroking her palm, pressing her knuckles.

Her sore hands made my father angry. He said we should hire a servant; he said she shouldn't have to do so much, with only me to help, but she just said, *Oh, William.* Money was still owed to someone for something; I'd heard them talking about that behind their closed door. And even I knew that if Rachel's only dresses were mine made over, if we had to use the tea leaves twice, and sometimes twice again, then there was no money to hire a servant. But my father said soon there would be, said this was a town where he could climb higher and higher. Already in charge of the Sunday school, and there'd been talk of him joining a club. He said that we should go out more, make calls; he said that was how things worked here, how connections were made. And my mother said she would, but just now there was so much to do.

It was strange to hear my father talk that way. In the cities we had lived in people on the same stair knew us a little but mostly, as he used to say, we could keep ourselves to ourselves. In Toronto each time the fat woman came with her basket he brushed by her in the doorway, even when she asked him to stay. Leaving my mother to thank her for the things she brought, to answer the questions, all the questions. The fat woman wanted to know all our business, writing in her little book. She spoke kind words but her lips had a way of folding, her eyes looking everywhere. She told my mother about other families she visited, where the husband was ill or paralyzed, or just gone. She said that my mother was lucky, that her man was perfectly healthy, that there must be something he could do. Buildings to be built, streetcar tracks to be laid. As if it were all his fault. Still, she was the one who read Mr. Marl's advertisement, who learned that his bookkeeper had recently died. My father polished his boots and walked to the station; he was gone two days and when he came back he brought a posy of white flowers for my mother, a piece of beef, wrapped in greased paper. He said all our troubles were over.

Behind me, my mother said, Your father loves us. *Said,* It will be fine, go up to bed. *I thought then of safe places, how they had come to be this little white house, the yard with its high board fence. Dr. Robinson's office when the door is closed and maybe, just maybe, the streets I know in this town. How suddenly they were all shriveling back down to a dot, to the room where my mother sat, to the space on the cushion beside her. How she was sending me away.*

Something happened in Halifax, something happened in Montreal, and maybe in England before. My father knows; my mother may. In Toronto he lost his job, though at first he didn't say. One morning he forgot to take his bread and my mother fretted, saying she knew he wouldn't spend money for something from a stall, and she took it to the factory for him. We went early to bed that night while they spoke in the other room, and Rachel whispered that she'd already known, that she'd seen him one day when she took a different way home from school, sitting on a bench, staring down at his hands. Terrible days came after.

The children were everywhere in my room; they were chanting a rhyme and although I could hear every word I couldn't catch hold of any of them, just the echo they left in the air. The darting child left trails of color, made me dizzy, and for the first time in months I reached under my mattress for the bone-handled knife, rolled down my stocking.

Rachel recites the kings and wars of England, she knows *amo amas amat,* and all the capitals of Europe. Perhaps if I'd gone to school. My mother saying no to my father, in a hard voice. Saying, *You **know** why.* She taught me to read from the Bible, her own mother's name written inside in faint, spiked letters, and from the newspaper when we had one. That was easier, the letters larger, the words more familiar. But not as beautiful as the

Bible, as the words in the Bible. When my mother read from the Bible I felt as if I were in a green field, with sun on my face, or sitting by a stream, hearing water over smooth stones. Though I hadn't done either of those things. It wasn't like in church, not like hearing Reverend Toller; he read different parts. Darkness and screaming, the plagues of Egypt, the sufferings of Job. Reverend Toller's Bible was filled with terrible tests. Abraham on the mountain with his knife raised, and Isaac bound tight, looking into his eyes.

My father said it wasn't enough to be able to read, to write my name. In Toronto, before the men took our furniture, Mr. Envers used to come, already unwinding his long, greasy scarf when my mother opened the door. He was no taller than she was, his hair stuck flat to his head and his beard stained yellow, tumbling down his front. The little bundle of books, tied with a bit of rope. One of the books had maps and he opened it to the middle and touched the page, his fingers yellowed like his beard, the nails almost as long as my father's. *This is England*, he said, *where you are from, the Atlantic Ocean your parents crossed. This is Halifax, where you were born, and Montreal. Toronto, where we sit now.*

And all the words brought pictures, a forest and a vast stretch of ruffled water, gulls wheeling and dancing, a cobbled street slick with rain. I couldn't see how that happened, as if the pictures were somehow folded into a dot on a page, like a bud that's waiting, that looks like nothing until it opens. There was something I almost understood then, understood in the same way I see the leaping boy, from the corner of my eye. There was something I almost had, but Mr. Envers didn't notice. Instead he picked up Rachel's ball from the floor and said, *This is the Earth, the North Pole and the South. This is England, here, and Canada, America. And this round Earth spins and spins, so quickly we cannot feel it.* Then my mind slid away, for that I couldn't grasp at all.

Mr. Envers came through the winter and the spring and his voice was hoarse, not much above a whisper, and sometimes he coughed until tears ran down his cheeks. Then my mother would make him a cup of tea if she had any leaves, and he would tell her about boys he had taught, now doctors and lawyers and one in the government. How they'd never forgotten him. The lessons got shorter and shorter, the time with the cup longer. Once he asked my mother if I was good with a needle.

Then Rachel called out and I went to her, across the dark hall. She was sitting up in bed, and in the bit of moonlight that slipped through the top of her window her hair was a sooty tangle, her eyes deep in her face. What was the noise? she said. A bang, a loud bang, it woke me. Hush, *I said,* there was no noise, no noise; it must have been a dream. *She sank back down onto her thin pillow and I sat on the edge of the bed beside her, held her hand until it slipped away from mine.*

This is the first real house we've lived in, all the rooms just ours. The kitchen and the three bedrooms. The front room with its heavy brown furniture, the privy in the back. When my father brought us to it, helped my mother down from the wagon that had carried us from the station, she clasped her hands together, rested her chin on them like someone praying, and smiled and smiled. Not her sad smile, but a different one. Inside my father wound the clock on the wall, and when it started to tick he put a hand on her shoulder and said that this was our real beginning. She took his hand and lifted it to her lips, and Rachel ran upstairs and down, through the front door and out the back, and came in again, saying, *There's a yard, is it ours? And a little tree right in the middle.*

The yard is ours, with a fence along one side, and along the back where the laneway runs. On the other side a mass of bushes, covered with red berries at the end of summer. A tree that's not much taller than Rachel, and a little shed that my father said was for chickens. He came home one day with three in a wicker basket, and a small rooster with a drooping comb that Rachel named Simon Peter.

The chickens were for me, my father said, for me to take care of. I never said, but I didn't like anything about them. The greedy way they went after the food I scattered, and they pecked at me, at each other, and squawked and chased Simon Peter away when he came too close. Some days there were no eggs at all and my father went back to the market, thinking he'd been cheated. He came home with another rooster, a big, strutting fellow he called Lord Bray, and the hens didn't peck at him, didn't flap him away, they all lay down for him. Simon Peter was for the pot but Rachel cried and pleaded and we kept him too, until one morning I found him in a little ruffled heap by the canes, Lord Bray with blood on his beak. Simon Peter's feathers swirled all around the back step where my mother and I plucked him, and we tried to gather them all up again. When asked, my mother said that he had flown away over the high fence, and I could tell that it pained her, watching Rachel lift the fork to her mouth.

My room was empty and silent now but still I couldn't settle, and when I heard the front door I took my shawl and sat at the top of the stair. I heard my father say, Nothing to fret about, *and he said that Mr. Lett had posted bail, that it was so late because they had to wait for the Odd Fellows meeting to finish. He asked my mother for a cup of tea, and as they moved to the kitchen my father said that he had to appear in court at noon, that it was a misunderstanding, that it would all be fine. Then the scrape of the stove being stirred, the rattle of the kettle, covered their voices. Only once, my mother saying,* What will become of us? *Saying,* I can't bear it, *to start again.*

My mother thought we should grow our own vegetables, now that we had a yard, and my father turned over a square of earth, held up his own red hands at the end of the day and said he'd been too long in an office. He made a low fence around our garden, to keep the chickens out, and we planted potatoes and carrots, a few sweet peas. When the work was done Rachel made a sign for each row, and we all stood together in our own yard. The light was thick and golden, the sun moving down; we looked back to the house that was all ours, the brown door and the step where my mother and I sometimes sat, and that moment went on and on.

We checked every day, watched the green shoots push through the soil, more and more of them, and when we thought it was time my mother and I went out with a bowl to pull some carrots for our dinner. But the carrots we pulled were tiny, stunted things, some just a tangle of roots; my mother pulled more and more, all the same, and she put her hand to her cheek, leaving a muddy print, saying, *What did I do? What did I do wrong?*

The green-eyed woman who looked after Mr. Cowan next door was hanging out clothes; she must have heard us for she pushed through the bushes and came to look. *Didn't you thin them at all?* she said, and she told my mother that she should have pulled the seedlings, many of them, told her that was the only way the others could grow straight and strong. *Have you never grown a carrot before?* she said, and my mother said no, that she'd never had a bit of earth before. Her cheeks red, as if she'd said a shameful thing. *Never mind,* the woman said. *You can try again next year; next year you'll know.* And she said that Mr. Allen had a few nice carrots left to sell, that no one would have to know. But my mother said that wouldn't be honest, and the woman gave a little shrug, a smile. All we'd gathered just made one small serving on my father's plate, but he said they were the best he'd ever tasted.

I must have fallen asleep, leaning at the top of the stair, for the next thing I knew was my father's hand on my shoulder, his voice whispering, Go back to bed now Lilian, go to sleep now. *I heard him close the door of their room, heard his cufflinks chink in the little china dish, heard the creak of the bed as he sat on it. But I don't know that anyone really slept in our house that night. Only Rachel, deep in her dreams. There were footsteps and creakings and murmurings, and if they stopped there were other sounds that dragged me back. A dog barking somewhere close, a tree moaning. The clock ticked louder than it ever did in the day, as if it was ticking right inside my head.*

Days I stay in bed Rachel often sits with me, not asking me to talk but just keeping me company, telling me things. Jokes and stories, what she learned at school, things she thought about. Like the days we used to share a bed, when she was two and I was seven, how she curled up against me, how she chattered and patted my face until one of us slept. Not long ago, sitting on the edge of my bed, her face hard to make out in the rain-colored room, she told me that Miss Alice had read a poem by Mr. Tennyson, that all the girls had tears in their eyes. And then she said wasn't it a strange thing to cry? The way it sneaks up, the way you know it's coming but you can hardly ever stop it. The way your throat goes thick, something happens in your stomach. I didn't say, but I realized that's the way I feel. Almost all of the time.

My father's eyes were red-rimmed and the ends of his trousers dark with damp; he said he'd woken early and been out walking. My mother's cheek scored as if she'd slept on something harsh instead of her own clean pillow. We blinked at each other around the kitchen table as if we'd just come out of some dark cave, as if we couldn't bear the morning light. Even Rachel eating quietly, looking a question that she didn't ask.

One Sunday after church my father said, *Let's walk a little; it's such a beautiful day.* He held out his arm to my mother, and after a moment she took it. We were always near the last to leave, not liking the crush at the door, so the footbridge was empty when my father led us there. And it was a beautiful day, patches of snow still on the ground, especially beneath the trees at the edge of the river, but the sun was high and the air was soft, our coats unbuttoned. Rachel skipped ahead, her long hair lifting and floating, until my mother called her back, her voice a little sharp. Perhaps because she had to speak loudly to be heard over the tumbling water. It had been a sudden thaw, the river running high and fast, and already two boys had been lost. We didn't know them, we hardly knew anyone, but my mother wept for them all the same.

There came a point, near the middle of the bridge, when my heart began to race. The way the boards moved, just a little, beneath our feet, and I wasn't sure that I could carry on. But the way back was just as far; my feet slowed and I could no longer hear the rushing river, my heart thumping and thumping in my ears, in every part of my body. My parents walking slowly ahead, and Rachel just ahead of them, and I felt so strange that I wondered if I was dying, wondered if this was what it was like, if this was the moment when it was done. But I wasn't ready, and I had always believed I would be ready. It was a mistake and I had to move, before they were lost to me.

I looked at the back of the houses on the far side of the river, the secret side of the houses, and some of them had boats, had rowboats upside down near the water's edge, and I thought, *An upside-down boat will not hold anyone.* But with that thought came a sound like far-off laughter, and I found I was thinking of a woman in a long white dress, leaning back on faded cushions while someone rowed one of those boats. The blue one, maybe, that was almost the color of the sky. Rowing along the green river on a warm summer's day, with a parasol, perhaps, to shade her from the sun. Trailing her fingers in the water, and I knew how the water would feel, warm and silky. The trees along the riverbank were bare but I saw how they would be, in summer, in full dark leaf. And all the weeping willows, their branches curving down to make a sheltered place there on the riverbank, a place where a person could sit and be content. My heart slowed down and I could hear the churgling river again, as I looked at the place where I would sit, in summer, and watch a boat glide by with the tiniest splash of oars. I saw my father and Rachel walking hand in hand, almost at the other side, saw my mother had missed me, had turned and started back for me, and my feet moved again; I made my feet move.

On the far side the steps were splintered and worn but they were solid enough, and ahead of us, to the left, was the back of a yellow brick cottage, with a small sign in one window saying *Fine Photography*. My father said, *That's what we should do; we should have our photograph taken. What do you say, Naomi?* And Rachel said, *Can we do it now, right now?* Tugging at his hand, but he wasn't looking at her. He said my mother's name again, said, *To mark our new life. What do you say,* but all she said was that no one would be there on the Sabbath. He knocked at the little back door anyway, went round to the front, just a step from the narrow street, and finally the front door opened and there was a man with his hair all ruffled, his suspenders hanging looped at his sides. After he had closed the door again, my father said he would come back another day and arrange it all.

He was strange that day, my father, in such high spirits. He led us up a narrow, winding street that climbed the hill, as if he knew exactly where he wanted us to go. Though there were not so many houses as on our side of the river, they grew larger and larger as we reached the top of the climb. Enormous houses of red or yellow brick, of stone, some with turrets, with colored glass in the windows, with long verandas looking down on the river, looking down on the rest of the town. We came to a place with iron gates standing open, and he led us a little way up the curved drive. Another house with many chimneys, a glassed room built out on one side that had colored streaks, maybe birds, flitting behind the windows. *Mr. Marl's house,* my father said. *We shall have a house like that one day.* My mother said, *Oh, William,* but Rachel took it up, saying, *Really? Will we really?* My father said, *Of course we will,* and he stooped a little to put an arm around her shoulders, pointing out the windows, the rooms, asking her to choose which one would be hers. *We must go,* my mother said, plucking at his cuff. *What if someone comes and finds us?* My father said, *What if they do?* But he turned away all the same.

My father pushed back his chair, said he had no appetite, and he caught my mother's hand as she reached to take his plate and held it for a moment. Then he left the kitchen and we heard his footsteps going back and forth, back and forth, in the room above our heads. After I had watched Rachel cross the road to school he came down with his hat in his hands, said he had errands to do in town. My mother asked if he would get a few nails to fix the loose board on the chicken coop, but he said he would do it another day.

Dr. Robinson counts my heartbeats, looks in my mouth and my eyes. Once he tried the electric box; he gave me his own white handkerchief and said it was a shame that it had upset me. Said that he knew it would help, that we would try again, but not for a month or two. When I went home I still had the handkerchief crumpled in my hand; I washed it and pressed it and put it under my pillow so I wouldn't forget to take it back.

After the checking Dr. Robinson sits behind his desk, all his buttons sewn on. I sit in the chair and listen to him talk and it doesn't take so long now, for me to be able to stop staring at the toes of my shoes. He talks about how the treatment is working, how I am progressing, and it may be true, although there are always things I don't tell him. He asks how my mother likes the town, says that his own wife came from the city, as he did, that she found it difficult, at first. He talks about his son, Rachel's friend, how there are things a mother doesn't understand, things about being a boy. Sometimes when I raise my eyes he's not even looking at me, and sometimes he calls me someone else's name, but I never say. I know what it's like to have someone bring you back, even if it's done in the gentlest way.

Dr. Robinson reminds me of some nice type of dog, I don't know why. Maybe his brown eyes, the way his mustache droops over the corners of his mouth. The type of dog that would follow you everywhere, that would sleep on the end of your bed and only ask you to be kind to it. The type of dog that would always try to protect you, even when it couldn't. My mother had a dog like that once, in England. Its name was Blackie, and one day it ran into the road and was crushed by a brewer's cart. She never wanted another.

Dr. Robinson talks, and sometimes he stops and I can't even hear him breathing. I watch until he blinks his eyes, puts his hands on the desk, asks if I have any questions. One day I heard myself ask if it's true, that every life has a purpose. I didn't mean to ask it, I felt my face flush, I didn't know where to look, but he answered as if there was nothing strange in it, nothing strange in my speaking. He said he believes that's true, though a purpose can be many things. He told me about a promise he had to make once, to do no harm. Then he asked if I'd been thinking about that, asked what I think my purpose is. *Like the garden*, I said, and he waited for me to say more but I couldn't go on, my mind a jumble.

There was a bite in the air and the chickens pecked the ground around my feet, even though I'd scattered the grain in a wide circle. I was very tired, but I thought how it was Tuesday, and almost the top of the week. When I went back inside my mother was humming, heating up the stove and saying maybe she'd bake a cake later, if she had enough flour, saying we all needed something to cheer us up a little.

When my father polished his boots and came on the train without us, a man he met told him that Mr. Marl owns half the town. That may not be true, but his name is everywhere in Emden. On the big factory, the office block on the square, on the pharmacy and the jeweler's shop. In the newspaper. My father says Mr. Marl also started with nothing, says that is proof that anything is possible here, says this is our new beginning. He goes into the world each day, in a shirt we keep white and mended, in the boots he polishes himself. He returns from the world to the house, and the house is different when he does, when he is there. Just different. There are things he doesn't know, because we don't tell him, or because he doesn't see.

In the evenings my father sits in the armchair, the one with the stain no amount of scrubbing can remove, and while my mother sews he reads the paper out loud and the clock of our new life ticks and ticks. He reads the whole paper, even the deaths and marriages, and sometimes he will stop and say, *Another one gone, Lil, but plenty left for you. John Dawes, from church,* he said once. *Now there's a fine young man. Or Alec Lyon, steady and hardworking, and he'll inherit the mill.* As if all I had to do was decide, as if I would ever have a life like that, a normal life. He says things like that, and yet he was happy with the word, Dr. Robinson's word, and if he was happy with the word, that must mean he thought something needed to be explained. Maybe he sees more than he thinks, or more than he lets himself say. I know that my father loves me, but I don't know if he knows anything about me. I don't think he's ever held my hand in the street; I don't remember ever walking with him, just the two of us, alone.

When my father came back he had bought the nails after all and the sound of the hammer blows echoed, the chickens running in mad circles to the farthest corner of the yard. When he came in he rolled his shirtsleeves down and walked around the downstairs rooms, touching things but not picking them up, not even really looking at them. My mother asked would I wash some windows and I pumped the bucket as full as I could carry, gathered the rags. But my father stopped me at the foot of the stair, said he needed a piece of music for the Sunday school, a piece by Bach that Miss Alice had, and would I go and fetch it now. I didn't say, but I wondered why he needed it then, with my hair wrapped up, my sleeves already rolled.

I wondered why Rachel couldn't bring it, why he couldn't ask Rachel when she came home at noontime. He held the door open and watched me on my way, the first time he'd been still all morning. On the porch chair there was a package, wrapped in brown paper and tied with string. A small package, strangely shaped, like a lumpy letter L, and I wondered why he hadn't brought it inside.

Rachel was born late, not like me, and my mother said that was why she had such a mass of dark hair. She sometimes meets my father after his work, and they walk through the town together. She can recite the kings and wars of England, all their dates, and she draws the trees arching over the river, draws our white house, draws Mr. Allen's store on the corner, with its square sign, with its baskets of pears in front. She holds out her hand under the table and takes my meat, sits on the end of my bed when I'm too weary to rise. I watch her from the upstairs window when she goes to school; there's a point where she disappears, the angle of Mr. Allen's store, and I feel my heart thump until I see her again, stepping up to Miss Alice's front door. Every day the same.

Rachel is twelve now and women's things will happen to her, but it won't be like me. One night in my bed the leaping boy put his mouth to my ear and whispered, *Beware.* And I sat straight up and realized that he had been gone, they had all been gone, and I had no idea how long. I thought of my mother, the waiting in her shoulders, and that's why I minded. The only thing I have to give her.

Rachel's friends told her that Will Toller has a crooked arm because his mother was frightened by a snake when she was carrying him, and she asked my mother if that was true. My mother looked even sadder, and she told Rachel that a mother and the child she carries are one flesh, that things can't help but be passed on.

Once outside the house I forgot my tiredness, forgot the strange, long night. The trees were standing still, red and orange against a clear blue sky, and though the air was cool on my cheeks, the sun was bright. Outside his store Mr. Allen was polishing apples on a little table and I thought of a pie my mother could make, thought of how one of those red apples would taste if I picked it up and bit into it. I thought that later I might take my walk by the river, instead of around and around the yard, and that thought carried me across the road to raise the knocker on the faded blue door, and I didn't even worry that it might be Mrs. Barnes who opened it, that I might have to look at her baffled gray eyes, repeat my sentence again and again.

Reverend Toller said there was evil about, in the shape of people who said they could talk to the dead. People who said that the dead appeared and rapped and spoke through them. Reverend Toller said that a woman in this very congregation had held such a gathering, invited such a person into her home. I wondered if my mother would have gone, if she'd known.

My mother's hands are cracked and sore and her hip aches, especially in rainy weather. She tells my father that she will make calls, join committees, but not just yet. I wonder that he doesn't know, what she can and cannot do. She goes to the shops in town, and if she will have a lot to carry, I go with her. People know her name, talk to her about the weather or the latest news. She smiles her sad smile and answers them, agrees about the sun or the clouds, *tsks* at the sad fate of Mrs. Toller. She is different in the shops, not completely, but a little. In her black dress, in her bonnet.

Our real life is in the house; it is only in the house that she hums sometimes, or sings a bit of one of my father's songs, or a hymn from church. In a house with five rooms there is always something to do, but sometimes she cuts a slice from a loaf that's just baked and we sit on the back step and tilt our faces to the sun. We are as close as thought, and even if she doesn't know the details of all my secrets, she knows their shape. Days I stay in bed I hear her footsteps moving through the house, climbing the stairs, and she strokes my forehead and whispers that she will take care of me always. We were one flesh, when she carried me.

My mother never asks about the children but there is a waiting in her shoulders, the way she bows her head, that eases when I tell her things. Sometimes, in an evil way, I fold my lips and say nothing; I don't know why. But not often. I watch her bend to the stove, watch her straighten up and rub at her sore hip, and everything lightens when I start to speak. She sinks into the chair across from me, the towel still in her hand, her eyes on my face. So many years we have done this, my hair growing longer, my mother's turning gray, but the children always the same.

It was Miss Alice who opened the door, as neat and gentle as always, and she had me come in while she searched out the music. The hallway was dark after the blue day but I saw a flicker of white, maybe the laughing girl flitting in and out of rooms. Through an open doorway on my left side I saw the pupils at the long school table, heads bent over their work. I saw Rachel's bent head, the parting I had made in her hair that morning, and then she looked up and smiled at me, we smiled at each other.

Years ago my mother told Mr. Envers that I was very good with a needle, and some days that is true. Other days my mind is a jumble and even her voice comes to me from far away. After the terrible days in Toronto my father brought my mother a posy of white flowers, and she put them in the mug with the picture of the woman in a boat and set them on the windowsill. On each stem there were small green buds, and day by day they changed. Lighter strips showing, growing wider, the green folds pushing apart so slowly. Two were like that, maybe three, though the others stayed tightly closed. We had to leave before I could see them completely open, but I suppose it might not have happened at all. The first flowers turning brown and limp around the edge of their petals. We took the mug but left the posy lying in a little puddle on the sill.

The package was gone from the outside chair and when I opened the door the house was silent, no sound of my mother's humming, not even the ticking clock. She had been mixing her cake when I left and there was a smell in the air, as if it had burned in the stove, and I wondered how I could have been gone so long. I started down the hall to find her, but my father called me from the top of the stair. I had the music in my hand, black notes dancing, and I held it out but he kept his hands behind his back, asked me to bring it up to him. The third stair cracked, like it always did, as I climbed toward my father. He stood very still, his hands behind his back, and I thought of the game he used to play with Rachel, wondered if it was finally my turn to guess which hand held the surprise.

S & W 32 D.A. 3½ INCH BARREL
New Model. Nickeled and Rubber stock. 5 Shot.
Weighs 13 oz., of elegant design and finest workmanship
   throughout.
Extra plating and Engraved handle, gives very fine
   "grip." $8.00

DIRECTIONS FOR USE. *Half cock the arm;* raise the barrel catch to its full
   height and tip the barrel forward as far as it will go. Place the
   charges in the chambers and return the barrel to its place, being sure
   to have the barrel catch down, when the arm is ready for use.

While Carrying the Pistol Fully Charged, allow the hammer to rest in the
   safety catch. After the first discharge, allow the hammer to rest on
   the *exploded cartridge* until the next discharge, and so on until all
   are fired. Do not let your thumb slip off the hammer.

Credits